Here is what some of the girls who have read Kate Petty's brilliant 'Girls Like You' books have said:

Some of the best books I have read . . . I got addicted [to the 'Girls Like You' books].
Jasmin

I thought they were great! I've even got my mates on to them now!
Hannah

I've never read anything so good.
Jenna

[*Alex*] is a great read for any girls who love both tennis and boys!
Heather

It's just what you need when you're stressed after school.
Lucinda

. . . every chance we get we are reading one of [the 'Girls Like You'] books (I'm starting to think our form teacher is getting seriously sick of us reading all the time!)
Emma

When I was reading them, I felt like I was there, watching everything happen. [The 'Girls Like You'] books are soooo cool!
Kate

I love them so much I can never put them down.
Sophie

Also by Kate Petty

Summer Cool
Makeover

For younger readers

The Nightspinners

KATE PETTY

Summer Cool

Dolphin Paperbacks

With thanks to Anna Rosen

First published in Great Britain in 2005
by Dolphin paperbacks
an imprint of Orion Children's Books
a division of the Orion Publishing Group Ltd
Orion House
5 Upper St Martin's Lane
London WC2H 9EA

A catalogue record for this book is available
from the British Library

Typeset at The Spartan Press Ltd,
Lymington, Hants

Printed and bound in Great Britain by
Clays Ltd, St Ives plc

ISBN 1 84255 501 4

www.orionbooks.co.uk

Summer Cool

Holly

ONE

I had to ring my friend Josie straight away when I got home from Barbados. She was never in, of course. I left loads of messages for her, ordering her to call me back just as soon as she could. The summer holidays were half over and I was desperate for us to do what Maddy and *her* friends had done, before it was too late.

I decided to ask the other two, Alex and Zoe, over for the night anyway. I'd almost given up on Josie when she eventually rang me back.

'Hey Holly – it'th Jothie!' She sounded most peculiar.

'Josie?'

'The thame. Don't laugh, Holly. I'm in agony. I've just got a brathe.'

'A what?'

'A *brathe*!'

'Bad luck. Does all your food get stuck in it?'

'I don't know,' she wailed. 'I've only had it for two dayth, and it thtill hurtth.'

'So how do you manage to play the clarinet?' Josie had already spent ten days this holiday tooting her little heart out on a music course.

'I don't. Thatth why I had to wait until the muthic courthe wath out of the way. I won't be able to play again for a year. Anyway – why were you so botthy about me ringing you? I'm not tho thure I want to hear about your amathingly ecthotic time in Barbadoth now.'

'You don't have any choice. But listen, this is why I've been trying to get hold of you. When I was in Barbados I

3

met this girl called Maddy, and she knows Hannah Gross from your music course, and they did this cool thing where they all agreed to have a holiday romance and meet up afterwards to report. No cheating. I wanted to catch you before you went to Cornwall so we can do the same. Come over tomorrow night? The others are. We can plan it then.'

'Romanthe? With thith thing in my mouth? You mutht be joking! But I'll come anyway. I do want to hear about Barbadoth really. And the entire cricket team.'

(I'd better explain. The holiday in Barbados was with my dad and the under-16s cricket team from the school where he teaches. Mum went as nurse and us daughters went free. Absolutely a one-off, you understand – we don't usually go further than Wales.)

Josie's speech was vastly improved by the time they all came over. I think she was doing it a bit for effect before, but she said the brace was much less painful. Not pleasant. Glad I don't have to have one. She arrived before Zoe and Alex to help me organise the pizzas – she said it was the first time she'd felt like eating anything. I think she'd even lost weight, and she was fairly thin to start off with. Josie's got long, fairish hair and blue eyes – and a brace. She's always had sticking-out teeth, but I think she'll be really pretty once they're straightened out.

I was allowed to have the front room for the sleepover. My bedroom's a box room over the front door and barely big enough for me, let alone four of us! I used to share bunk beds with my younger sister, Abby. She still has the bunks and the big room to go with them but I was allowed to decorate my little room exactly as I wanted – fake fur cushion covers, fairy lights from IKEA and all my own posters. It's fab. My parents say we'll never be able to afford a mansion, but I love our house and I wouldn't want to move, even if it was to somewhere bigger.

Alex lives in our road. She's got loads of brothers. They're all energetic and sporty, and so's her dad, but her mum's a bit of a doormat. Probably has to be, running around after that lot. Alex used to be a complete tomboy – it took her for ever to get round to wearing a bra – but though she's tall and skinny with short hair and freckles she's looking more like a girl these days. She's got a wicked sense of humour too. Everybody laughs a lot when Alex is around. She's one of those people who can remember jokes and do impressions. She turned up in her 'sweats' as she calls them, from playing tennis. 'Like the metal, Josie,' she said. 'Gives a whole new meaning to the "flashing smile".' So, of course, Josie flashed her metal smile. Alex handed over a Tesco bag with four cans of shandy. She'd somehow persuaded her dad to buy it for us. She's got him wrapped round her little finger.

Between us we hauled down mattresses and campbeds and duvets and sleeping bags. My little sister seems to spend half the holidays away at sleepovers, so we could have had her room, but there isn't a TV or video in there. Anyway, it was cool transforming the front room. Basically we just made a big nest in front of the TV and cleared a space on the coffee table for food and drink.

Zoe turned up just as we'd finished getting the room ready. Alex, Josie and me have been together since the infants, and we were a threesome for ages. Zoe moved in a bit later. Alex knew her already because the twins are friends with Zoe's younger brother – you know how it is. The four of us are pretty close these days, especially in the holidays (not least because Josie's parents took her away from our school after the first year). But this summer I'd been in Barbados, Zoe had been to Italy and Josie had been on the music course, so there was a whole load of catching up to do.

See Zoe and you'd assume she was a model or a pop star – she's that gorgeous. In fact she can't sing to save her life (she is brilliant at acting though). But underneath that fabulously beautiful exterior is a keen, keen brain. She took up debating last term and she's brilliant at that too. Demolishes the opposition – usually male, usually making the assumption that she's an airhead – with a few well chosen incisive comments. Makes your hair stand on end. Honestly, she even makes 'This House believes bloodsports should be abolished' – or whatever – exciting!

We've got our priorities right, so we concentrated on eating our pizzas before talking, but once we'd got started the others made me tell them about Barbados and the girl I'd met there – Maddy. And, of course, the boy I'd met there, too – Jonty Hayter.

'So you've already had one romance!' said Zoe. 'That's not fair! Are you expecting to have another one?'

'*I* thertainly won't,' said Josie, 'me and my metal mouth.'

'I don't think I do romance, do I?' said Alex.

'Shut up! Shut up! *Shut up*!' I yelled. 'You mean lot. I'm not going to talk about it until later, when you're prepared to hear me out. OK? Now, be quiet. Watch the video.' I pointed the remote at the TV and all noise subsided as the opening credits for *Titanic* rolled.

In fact we didn't discuss the romance plan again until *Titanic* was over and we'd all cried buckets and were snuggled up in our makeshift beds. Josie had snitched more than her fair share of duvet and Alex was mucking about and making more jokes than usual at my expense so I thought it was time for a bit of control here. (It's not my fault I'm a teacher's daughter.)

'OK!' I shouted. 'Now I'm going to tell you my plan, whether you like it or not.'

'I like it already!' said Alex in a 'Goodness Gracious Me' voice, while Josie took the opportunity to haul the duvet over to her side again. I chose to ignore them both.

'These four girls, right? – Maddy, Hannah – from Josie's music course, and two others, all had a sleepover at the beginning of the holidays. *Where* they agreed to have holiday romances and report back on them at the end of the holidays. Well, I know for a fact that Maddy had a romance—'

'Ha! So did Hannah,' said Josie, 'eventually, but I didn't know it wath to order. And it nearly didn't happen . . .'

'Well, having to report back obviously focused the brain,' I carried on. '*Anyway* . . . I met Jonty and he was brilliant and I'm madly in love with him—'

'I'm glad for you, Holly,' said Alex – her American agony-aunt voice this time.

'*Anyway* – ' I said again, 'I'm going to stay with his family for a week. What I haven't told you is that the Hayters are, like, *mega*-rich. They're blue-blooded aristos who go back to the Domesday Book with a vast estate in Warwickshire and a house in Chelsea and they go huntin' and shootin' and have balls and stuff – and Mum is worried that we'll find we don't have anything in common.'

'She might have a point there,' said Zoe, popping her eyes and suppressing a smile.

'Maybe she does, but I think love should *triumph* over our differences, don't you? Jonty's so cute – he doesn't care that I'm not rich!'

'Of course not,' said Alex. 'He just loves you for your

raven tresses, your shining eyes, your bushy tail and your adorable personality.'

'Wow. A ball,' said Josie wistfully. 'Lucky you.'

'Thank you. Exactly.' I wished they'd all shut up and listen. 'So, that's *my* holiday romance, and I'll tell you all how I got on the last weekend before term starts – and we all go into year ten. My God – soon we'll all be *fifteen*! Maddy's fifteen next month.'

'So am I,' said Zoe. 'OK. My problem is, I don't plan to do anything much for the next couple of weeks. I didn't exactly find romance in Tuscany with my family – mind you, everyone there was English or American, and *white*!' she said with a laugh. 'Even after three weeks! Except for me and my brother. And Mum of course. Back to the point, girl – so what chance do I have back here? I might just go on this Community Theatre thing with Tark. We'll see. No promises. But I'll *try*, Holly, I'll *try*!'

Alex was still laughing. 'Tennis tournament – county number. Fit young men by the score, but interested in *me*? I think not. The women maybe.' We looked at her quizzically. She shrank. 'Tennis, you know!'

'Phew,' said Josie. 'I thought maybe there was something you weren't telling us!'

'Maybe there is,' said Alex. 'But romance I will seek. With a fit young man. And I will report back, on love games, lost balls and every other corny tennis pun you can think of. Happy?'

I considered. 'I suppose it doesn't *have* to be with a member of the opposite sex . . .' I said cautiously.

'Whatever!' said Josie. 'Anyway, you can all hear about my holiday now, because mine is actually quite exciting.'

'Oh good,' said Alex. Zoe gave me a quick sympathetic smile.

'The music course was boring,' said Josie. 'The boys were pathetic. Well, Hannah's one was OK. And there were one or two others, I suppose.'

'But none of them fancied you. Carry on,' said Alex.

'I couldn't care less,' said Josie, slightly wounded, 'because we're off to our cottage in Cornwall as usual, and there are squillions—'

'Thkwillionth?' said Alex.

'A great number – ' said Josie carefully, '– of gorgeous guys down there. And there is one I have had my eye on for some time now and I shall force him to lock braces with me before the holiday is over and report back.'

'Does he wear a brace too?' I asked. It seemed unlikely.

'He might do,' said Josie. 'And if he doesn't, I might have to look for someone who does. OK? Have I passed?'

'Excellent!' Zoe clapped. 'I think we've done very well, don't you Holly? And now I want to watch something really bad on TV and drink alcohol – if it's all the same with you guys.'

Two

'I can't find him anywhere.' Dad was peering through his reading glasses at the small print of *Burke's Peerage*. 'Perhaps he's an impostor.'

'I doubt it,' said Mum, switching off the TV. 'Here, let me look. My eyesight's better for the wee type.' (Needless to say, Mum's Scottish.)

'No,' said Dad. 'I can see all right. There are Hayters listed here, but none called Brian and none in Warwickshire.'

'Tell you what,' said Mum. 'It's probably the reverse.

They're probably posher. I bet they're double-barrelled. Are you sure they're not double-barrelled dear?' She turned to me.

'Don't think so.' I was beginning to get fed up with their sudden interest in Jonty's family. They said it was because they weren't just going to let me go off and stay with him without checking them out, but they were sniggering a bit too much and I didn't like it.

Abby piped up from where she was reading in the corner with the cat on her lap. 'Jonty's real name is Jonathan James Rye Clermont-Hayter,' she said in a sing-song voice. 'He told me.'

We all looked at her in surprise. 'It's more than he told me!' I said.

'Too busy snogging you,' said Abby, going back to her book.

'That's enough of that, young lady,' said Mum. 'And it's high time you were in bed, Abby. You hardly had any sleep at your so-called sleepover. Run along and get into your pyjamas.'

'Found him!' said Dad loudly. 'Well, well, well, my little Holly. It looks as if you're going to be staying with the aristocracy.'

'What?'

'The gentry, my dear. I've found them. Our Brian and Gina are Sir Brian and Lady Clermont-Hayter. And no doubt, young Jonty, when his father dies, will inherit the title. What do you think of that? You'd better learn to curtsey!'

I told them it didn't affect me either way and that I was going to bed too. Between you and me, all this stuff about the gentry was actually making me nervous. All the boys at the school where Dad teaches are well off, they have to be to afford the fees. Mostly they're like other people – some nice and some not, but I do sometimes resent their attitudes. It's not just envy. Mum and Dad are solid Labour voters, and basically disapprove of all right-wing sentiments, so of course it's rubbed off on me. But I didn't want to be reminded of it as far as Jonty was concerned. Right then I wanted only the company of my diary and Jonty's letters. He'd started when I left him behind in Barbados and somehow we'd carried on communicating by post – well, a couple of letters either way anyway. That was how we'd fixed up my visit. We'd put some really lovey-dovey stuff in the letters, quite embarrassing really, so I'd reached a point where I would actually have felt quite shy talking to him on the phone.

I got ready for bed and curled up under my duvet. I keep my diary right in my bed – I reckon Mum and Abby won't stoop to looking for it there. I hauled it up. It's one of those hardbacked exercise books you buy in Smith's. I write in it every day and decorate the pages with different coloured pens and bits cut out of magazines. You know the sort of thing. I take a lot of pride in it, but it is *strictly* for myself. I stick letters and photos in there too – it's got rather fat and difficult to close since Barbados.

I turned back to the day I first saw Jonty in Barbados. I'd been on the beach with the boys from Dad's school, little sister Abby and some of the other staff daughters. The boys were playing an impromptu ball game half in the water and half out of it and we girls were sunbathing at the top of the beach. I'd seen a lone boy – who wasn't one of ours, though he looked about the same age – hanging round the ball game as if he wanted to join in. And you know how boys are – it wasn't long before he was part of the game.

Barbados

Met a boy today – not from Beale College. I watched him join in our boys' beach game and then he came back up the beach with them. He didn't talk to me – I just watched him. He's called Jonty and he's got a nice smiley face – not particularly goodlooking, just nice. Tanned, like everybody. He's got ordinary brownish wavy floppy hair that gets in his eyes. (I'm not sure what colour they are yet.) He's quite tall and skinny but what I noticed most was the way he moves. Kind of elegant. When he runs he sort of flickers. He got pally with the lads very quickly. I could hear him making them laugh. He's got rather a posh accent, but then so have most of Dad's boys, and a nice croaky sort of voice. I hope I see him again tomorrow.

Of course I did see him quite a lot after that. He was staying in one of the ultra-smart hotels, but I heard him saying he'd been there so much he was bored with it. We should be so lucky! I didn't talk to him, but I did like watching him. It wasn't that he was particularly handsome or anything, just very confident and happy with himself. Some days later he appeared with the most gorgeous looking bloke I've ever seen – American and way out of my league, not least because he was a couple of years older than our boys. And then the hunky guy's younger sister came along and joined up with us girls. That was Linden. Her brother was called Red and they turned out to be the kids of Oliver O'Neill (only *the* most famous film director in the world). And *then*, of course, I met Maddy; not American, not rich, just amazingly beautiful – and well, the rest of that is Maddy's story. But it was because of Maddy, and that first barbecue, that I got to know Jonty and his family.

It still seems like a dream really. I fell completely in love with Jonty out there. His sister Dilly is nice too, but the oldest one, Flavia, is ghastly. So when I got the letter from Jonty asking me to come and stay with his family in the country, my pleasure wasn't completely undiluted.

Holly, my gorgeous Holly, PLEASE come and stay down here with me. I want to come up to London but the parents think I'm too young to be in Chelsea on my own. Unlike Flavia who is there most of the time. But Dilly's going off on some horse thing so they're happy for you to come and stay for the week while she's away. I don't quite see the connection – there are ten million rooms here – but hey, who am I to complain? There's not a lot going on down here in the country, but that won't matter if we can only be together. I miss you heaps. Please say you'll come,

Jont xxxxxxx

So I'm going. Jonty's mum rang my mum to say it was all OK. My mum asked what I should bring and his mum just said, 'Oh, the usual things. Riding gear and a tennis racquet might be a good idea. And I think someone's having a do, so perhaps a fancy frock to be on the safe side.'

That last item was what blew Mum apart. 'Oxfam shop,' she said. 'We might find something in one of the upmarket ones. Or something I can cut up and turn into a ball gown.' No trips to Monsoon for me then. Needless to say, we traipsed round every charity shop and secondhand shop in Hampstead and even Camden, but we didn't find anything. We looked at material in John Lewis – *gorgeous* silks and velvets – and paper patterns, but nothing seemed right, let alone the right price. Then Mum remembered that my cousin Daisy had been to a May Ball earlier in the year, so she rang Daisy's mum to see if I could borrow Daisy's dress.

Daisy's family is chaos, so although they said yes, of course, no one could lay their hands on the dress at that precise moment. In the end they agreed to post it to me at Jonty's house. So that was that little problem solved.

We looked up trains and coaches (cheaper), but then Jonty's mum rang again to say that Flavia was driving up from town on that day, so why not have a lift from Chelsea?

Why not indeed.

The night before I was due to go I rang Maddy. 'I'll come over,' she said.

'How?' I said.

'Bus,' said Maddy. She's so much more streetwise than me. I wouldn't want to cross our bit of London on public transport on my own, even if my parents would let me, but she couldn't care less. She got here in just over an hour as well. She went through my case item by item. 'Bikini, good. Jeans for riding, plus – ooh, proper riding boots!'

'Cousin Daisy's cast-offs.'

'Tennis racquet. Whites. Doing well, Holly. So where's the ballgown?'

'Funny you should mention that.'

'Well, you remember me in Barbados. I had to borrow one. And Dilly and Flavia had all the kit. Flavia wore the crown jewels, remember?'

'I wasn't there, Maddy. Though of course I heard about it.'

'Beware the fabulously rich, my dear. Remember, we're normal. They're not.'

'Thanks for those words of advice, Maddy. Anyway, Cousin Daisy is coming to the rescue again with the ballgown.'

'Let's see it.'

'They're posting it straight to Jonty's, but Daisy wore it to a May Ball this year and she's got good taste. It'll be fine.'

'Well, let's hope so!'

It was hot in the car. London was full of tourists and cyclists. I was jittery. Abby was bored. Mum was driving and Dad was getting cross with her. It wasn't a great start. We got lost in the little streets and one-way systems in Chelsea, though Abby cheered up because there were lots of pedigree dogs to point out. We got there half an hour late. Hot and bothered, and wishing I hadn't forgotten my sunglasses, I went up the twee (pretty, really) garden path with my suitcase and pressed the doorbell. Mum and Dad and Abby stood behind me like dorks. Nothing happened. I pressed again. After an age I could hear someone in flip-flops approaching the front door. It opened and there was Flavia looking pink in a bikini with shades pushed on to her head. She eyed us suspiciously. 'Yah?'

'Hi Flavia.' She looked nonplussed. An extremely short man came down the corridor behind her. I recognised Flavia's jockey boyfriend.

'Problem, Flaves?'

'It's the kid Jonty met on holiday. Don't know why she's here.'

'It's me, Holly, Flavia. I thought – Your mother said—'

Dad stepped forward. 'Flavia, your mother led us to believe you were driving home today and that Holly could have a lift. Is that still all right?'

'Suppose so.' She looked at us. I felt somewhat awkward, to put it mildly.

But there was no way I was going home again. I took a deep breath. ' 'Bye Mum, Dad, Abby. I'll watch telly while

Flavia gets ready. I don't mind waiting.' I waved back at them and simply pushed my way into the bijou residence with my case.

It got worse. Flavia virtually *ignored* me for the next couple of hours. I sat in front of the television in the dark front room, torturing myself with the worry that Jonty would act all snooty like his sister once he was on his home ground too, until I just had to come out and go to the loo. I ventured out into the garden where Flavia and her boy-friend were *having lunch* (without offering me any)! She didn't bat an eyelid – simply told me where the loo was. After about another hour there was a ring at the doorbell followed by shrieks and giggles from two other girls. I decided to go and see what was happening. One girl was about my age and the other about eighteen, like Flavia. They were both tall and blonde and skinny and both were festooned with about ten designer carrier bags each. Major clothes shopping had taken place.

'Got room for Tamara?' asked the older one. 'She's bought even more than I have but she doesn't take up much space.' She laughed unkindly.

'Suppose so,' said Flavia – her usual answer.

I decided to remind her of my presence. 'When are we going, Flavia?'

'Do we know you?' asked the older one.

'Friend of Jont's,' said Flavia in reply. 'Ma asked me to give her a lift.'

'Oh.'

'I don't think it's fair if I have to go on the train,' said the one called Tamara in a whiny voice. 'I think you should, Beatrice. You're older.'

The jockey appeared at Flavia's elbow. 'Problem, Flaves?'

'Yah,' said Flavia. 'We've got to get four people into my car.'

'That's not a problem is it?' said the jockey.

'It is with all these bags,' said Beatrice.

I couldn't stand it any longer. 'For heaven's sake!' I said. 'It must be a tiny car if it can't fit four people!'

'But what about the bags?' said Tamara. She really was stick thin, and her mouth hung open all the time.

The jockey actually came to my rescue. 'Go and dress, Dumpling,' he said to Flavia. 'I'll put these togs in the boot for you and then you can all fit in.'

'As long as you're careful!' said Beatrice imperiously.

In the end, everything fitted in. Apart from me – socially, that is. Flavia never thought to explain that I'd simply arrived earlier than she was expecting and that we were waiting for her friends to arrive before setting off. Honestly, the arrogance of the girl! How could my lovely Jonty have such a nasty sister?

Beatrice sat in the front with Flavia. I sat in the back with Tamara, who ignored me. Flavia drove at great speed. She obviously felt she owned the motorway – like everything else. I nodded off but was woken by gales of uproarious laughter as we swept into the gravel drive of a vast mansion.

'Jonty's got a *girlfriend*?' snorted Beatrice. 'I don't believe it!'

'I know, it is unbelievable, isn't it?' *Thank you, Flavia.*

'Whatever sort of girl could fancy that spotty little twerp?' said Beatrice, climbing out of the car. 'She must be frightfully dim, or short-sighted or something!'

The other two followed her. Flavia opened the boot and handed them all the ten billion bags. More giggles and sniggers. 'Sssh,' said Flavia, not realising that I'd heard it all. 'You've just been sharing a car with her!' As she waved them off amidst more guffaws, I saw Tamara glowering back at me. Flavia got into the car and roared away down the gravel drive at a hundred miles an hour.

Twenty minutes later we turned off the road past a lodge and through an ornate stone gateway. We drove for nearly a mile down an avenue of chestnut trees. There were fields beyond the chestnut trees. Some of them contained horses. At last we drove over a little bridge and rounded a bend. Before me was a stately pile, Jonty's home. And running to meet us were three droopy little spaniels – and Jonty.

Boy was I glad to see him.

THREE

I couldn't get out of that car fast enough. I flung myself enthusiastically into Jonty's arms, and we clung on to each other for what seemed like ages. He buried his face in my hair. 'Oh Holly! You just – smell wonderful,' he said, and then stood back, abashed.

'You don't smell so bad yourself,' I quipped, and then felt silly. We both looked down at our shoes for a moment while the dogs sniffed around us excitedly.

Embarrassed, he introduced the dogs. 'Meet Flopsy, Mopsy and Popsy,' he said. 'King Charleses. Popsy's the boy and I'm afraid he farts rather a lot.' There was no answer to that. 'Let's get your stuff then,' said Jonty, quite formally, pleased to have something to do. He grabbed my hand and we scrunched over the drive to Flavia's car. She'd left all the car doors open but she hadn't bothered to wait. He gallantly led the way into the house carrying my case, prattling away about all the things he had planned for us to do. I followed him with my tennis racquet, not taking in anything he was saying. He looked slightly different from my memory of him and I couldn't think why. Then I realised he'd had a haircut – some of his floppy wavy fringe had gone. It made him look both older and younger, if that's possible. The spaniels wove in and out, doing their best to trip us up.

The low evening sun had been dazzling, so it took a while for my eyes to adjust to the darkness of the hall once we'd gone in through the porticoed doors, the dogs skittering along after us. I don't know why I had expected anything else, but it was just like something out of *Country Life* (sole reading material at our local vet's surgery). The hall was about the same size as our entire house with a grey stone flagged floor and a polished oak table bearing a beautiful arrangement of pink and white roses and sweet peas. There were dim portraits on the oak panelled walls. Stairs curved up on either side and I looked up to see a balcony above. Downstairs, several doors opened on to corridors that led into the distance. It was unbelievable. Mum had been rather disparaging about the Hayters' taste in Barbados, but this was simply centuries of quality. It smelt of cool stone and beeswax and summer flowers. 'Wow, Jonty. What an amazing house!' (The word 'house' didn't do it justice.)

'Welcome to Clermont Chase,' said Jonty. 'A small place, but my own – at least it will be one day.' He said it with a laugh, but of course it was true. Blimey. I remembered joking with Maddy that I was going to marry Jonty and be frightfully rich. Well, one day *somebody* would.

Gina, Jonty's mum, appeared through one of the doors. She was carrying a clinking glass of gin and tonic. 'Oh hello dear,' she said, not unkindly but vaguely, as if she had forgotten I was coming. 'Show your friend where she'll be sleeping, Jonathan. I think Mrs B. has done the green room, you know – at the back, a couple of doors along from Flavia.' (Can you believe it?)

'OK,' said Jonty. 'Follow me.' And he lugged my case up one of the staircases. We walked round the balcony to the back of the house and a row of rooms that overlooked the gardens and the ornamental pool. Jonty opened a door – 'Oops, no, that's the yellow room,' and then another, the green room. Fancy not *knowing* all the rooms in your house! But it was fabulous. The full-length windows faced west so the sun slanted in on to the dark, glowing floorboards and the green and red Persian carpet, up over the four-poster bed with a dark green silk awning and bedspread and on to the gleaming surfaces of the oil paintings of various pastoral and hunting (yuk!) scenes. In the corner by the window was a table with another gorgeous flower arrangement – yellow roses this time, with red hot pokers and orange lilies.

'Who does the flowers?' I asked Jonty. 'Is it your mother?'

'Ma? You must be joking! No – it's Jill, Christopher's mum. She likes to practise on the flowers from our gardens.' He opened a door in the wall. 'Here's your bathroom. All mod cons at Clermont Chase.'

After the bedroom it was indeed very modern. Double basin, power shower. Lots of mirrors surrounded by filmstar lights. Fluffy towels. Sea shell full of tiny soaps. No expense spared. 'Who's Christopher?'

We went back into the bedroom. 'You'll meet him tomorrow. He's coming to play tennis with us in the morning. Oldest friend. I've known Christopher since I was two and he was three. Do you want to be left to – er – powder your nose? Wash your hands, that sort of thing?'

I couldn't get used to seeing Jonty embarrassed. 'OK. I'm

dying for the loo after that car ride, but I might get lost trying to find you again.'

'I'll meet you in the hall in twenty minutes, and then we'll go for dinner together. OK? Can you find your way down?'

'Hope so,' I said, and I was on my own. After Jonty had gone I sat on the amazing four-poster bed and bounced up and down a few times. I hung my clothes in the wardrobe and laid out my underwear in the paper-lined drawers. I ventured into the wonderful bathroom and could have spent hours playing there. Actually I did have a quick wash before changing into fresh clothes and then went and stood by the open window. The sun was setting over the gardens and the ornamental pond and the woods in the distance. The Forest of Arden perhaps – this was Shakespeare's county after all. I could see walled gardens and greenhouses off to the left and stables off to the right. There were land-scaped hills with a glimpse of more water further off and a few small buildings dotted around – summerhouses and follies. I could just hear the sounds of tennis being played but the court was out of sight. I looked at my watch. I still had five minutes. Just time to write my diary. I pulled it out and sat with it in the window seat.

Sunday afternoon
Wow. What am I doing here? Me, Holly Davies at Clermont Chase, home of Sir and Lady Clermont-Hayter?? With a four-poster bed and my own posh bathroom! The journey here was ghastly, but it was worth it in the end. Jonty's got all sorts of things lined up for us to do – mostly riding and playing tennis. That's fine by me, as long as we get time by ourselves to just be. He's being lovely – not a bit like Flavia. More later. Now I have to go and dine!!!!!!!

I suppose that after everything I'd seen so far I was expecting us to eat in a great dining hall with butlers and silver and stuff. I was wrong, certainly for tonight. The kitchen at the back of the house was where the Hayters spent most of their time. It was actually quite normal – in a large 'country-style' way, with pine (or oak, probably) units and floral curtains and a big efficient looking cooker as well as an Aga and a microwave, and a vast American fridge. There was a utility room off it – Jonty showed me while he fetched ice for my coke – with an even vaster freezer, washing machines (two) and tumble driers (two).

We sat round the kitchen table, Brian (his dad), Gina (his mum), Flavia, Jonty and me. Apparently Gina hardly ever cooks, preferring to stuff the freezer with food from M&S and Waitrose. Her mother never cooked, because there were always staff. Gina told me she was taught domestic science at school but she always found it a 'frightful bore'. Tonight our meal had been left for us by the famous Mrs B., Jonty's one-time nanny but now general housekeeper and mother-figure to the entire family, it seemed. Brian was wildly appreciative. Nursery food had never lost its appeal for him and he tucked in enthusiastically to tomato soup (tinned, I'm sure), baked potatoes and cauliflower cheese followed by apple crumble and cream. 'Mrs B. is a *superb* cook,' he informed me between courses. 'Gina's marvellous in the kitchen too,' he added loyally, 'but Mrs B. always starts with the raw ingredients.' (Whereas Gina starts by opening the packet, I thought to myself.) He dabbed at his mouth with a napkin. 'We're very lucky to have her.'

Flavia, who had been silent up until then, suddenly barked 'Yah?' I realised she'd been palming the cordless phone as she ate. 'Oh,' she barked again, disappointedly this time, 'it's you. Ma – Cordelia.' She passed the phone across me to Jonty's mother. Cordelia (Dilly – Jonty's nice sister) was passed all round the table and finally to me.

'How's it going, Hol?'

'Dilly! I've only been here an hour.'

'I thought Flavia was driving you up at lunch time.'

I gave Flavia a sidelong glance, turned away from her and lowered my voice. 'Well, that's what I thought, but we gave two girls a lift.'

'Oh God. Beatrice and Tamara I bet. They never come when they say they're going to. Silly twits, the pair of them. Did they have loads of shopping?'

'Well, yes, they did actually.'

'That's what they do. Shop. Scarcely a neurone between them. Anyway. Don't let them get you down, or my darling sister. I have to go – by the way, have you seen James lately?'

James was one of Dad's boys on the cricket trip. He and Dilly had a bit of a romance in Barbados. 'I have, as it happens. I told him I was coming to stay here and he was very jealous and sends his love.'

'Hmm. Better write to him I suppose. OK, must dash. Byeee!' Phew. Dilly was a breath of normality in this un-usual household.

The others were tucking into the apple crumble and cream by then. As I ate mine I looked round the table surreptitiously. Flavia – horsy face and frizzy red hair; Gina, source of the horsy features but goodlooking in a suntanned, leathery sort of way; Brian, balding, but pleas-ant faced; and my lovely Jonty – also suntanned, light brown, slightly wavy hair and the same crinkly, smiley face as his dad, loose limbs akimbo as he sprawled in his hard kitchen chair. Jonty caught my gaze. He scraped his chair back noisily. 'I'm going to show Holly round the estate,' he said, getting to his feet. I stood up too and carried my plate to the sink. 'Don't worry about those, Holly. Mrs B. will see to them in the morning. Come on, let's go.'

I could hear Flavia snorting as we went down the passage to the back door. 'Practically' (she pronounced it 'praktik-leh') 'dark!' she said, as if it mattered to her.

The spectacular sunset was reflected in the ornamental pool as Jonty and I sat down beside it. A small fountain tinkled away in the centre and I could see some huge goldfish darting amongst the water lilies. Jonty put his arm around me and I leant against him. It was strange being out there just with him, and hardly anyone else around. In Barbados he always seemed to be off doing things with his family, just like I was with the cricket team – we were always being pulled in different directions. Now we sat there, gazing at the rippling sunset. I'd been there over an hour and we hadn't even kissed yet. I glanced up at Clermont Chase. 'Look Jonty, the windows are all on fire in the sunset!'

'Aaggh! My butt is on fire!' laughed Jonty (shattering the romantic mood somewhat). He leapt up and ran round like a kid being an aeroplane. I imagined all the frogs on the lilypads plopping straight into the water to escape. But it looked so brilliant I got up and ran around with him, both of us racing around with our arms outstretched as we went. 'Follow me to the topiary garden!' called Jonty, so I whooshed after him to a lawn surrounded by tall shaped hedges. It was dusk in there, and you could feel the cool air coming up from the grass.

We stopped and stood, feeling the change in the light and the temperature. Then Jonty walked towards me. 'No prying eyes here,' he said as we stood facing one another. He picked up my hand and toyed with my fingers. 'I feel a bit shy, all of a sudden,' he said.

'Me too.' I looked down and my hair fell across my face. It's dark and long and usually I tie it back, but I'd taken out my ponytail when I changed for supper. Jonty reached forward and pushed it back. Cue for a kiss, standing where we were in the twilit gazebo. It was lovely, but strange too, knowing that we had a whole week ahead of us. No one was going to try and separate us.

Total freedom was kind of scary. I think Jonty felt the same way, because before too long he announced that he was getting cold and there was something we could watch on TV, unless I wanted a game of pool in the games room. The *games* room! Or play a computer game, or listen to him on his electric guitar . . . We headed indoors. I could still hear people playing tennis. 'Jonty, who plays tennis at this time of night?'

'That's probably Christopher and his brother. They can use the court whenever they want. Christopher's got a tournament coming up. You'll see how good he is when we play tomorrow. By the way, Tamara Hilton will make up the four. I haven't seen her for ages, but it means we can play mixed doubles.'

Sunday evening
This is totally amazing – the bed, the room, the house, the grounds, the King Charles spaniels – everything! Jonty is brilli-ant, really sweet and really shy compared with when we were in Barbados, which is cute (and rather sexy in a way). I wish Dilly was here because she's so normal, but no good wishing. Flavia is a complete witch and the parents are OK but just so different from anyone I know. Tomorrow I get to see Tamara again, yuk,

and meet the mysterious tennis player. I'm knackered, so night night diary. More tomorrow.

FOUR

There's one thing I hate about staying in other people's houses, and that's not knowing what to do first thing in the morning. You wake up and listen to what's going on, and if it's all quiet you stay put. I'm terrified of going downstairs and making the dogs bark or setting off a burglar alarm or catching the dad in his underpants or something. At least I've got my own bathroom and loo – I don't have the problem of bursting in on Brian or Flavia on the toilet. Eugh. So. I listened for a bit and didn't hear anything. Then I thought I might as well get up and have a shower. Didn't think to look at my watch. Had a shower, shaved my legs. Dressed in jeans, then remembered about playing tennis. Put on shorts (khaki as it happens) and a white top and trainers and went to open my curtains and view the estate . . . *Then* I remembered to look for my watch. It had dropped on the floor by the bed. It was half-past ten! So late! How embarrassing!

I shot downstairs, went through a wrong door or two and, after catching up with the dogs, who'd come to sniff me out, finally made it into the kitchen. No one batted an eyelid. Jonty was there, in riding boots. Flavia was there in her dressing gown, hair all over the place, looking more witchy than ever. Gina was just off to the estate office. She said briskly, 'Morning Holly. Help yourself to breakfast because no one else will! Do have fun playing tennis. See you all later!' and whisked off.

Jonty stood up, not quite sure how to greet me at his family breakfast table. I saved him the trouble of hugging/kissing me by sitting down and pouring cereal into the empty bowl that was there. 'Jonty, why didn't you wake me?' I asked.

'I thought you'd probably like a lie-in,' he said. I could see already that Jonty's life was dug in to its own momentum and routines. There was no way my short stay was going to alter years, decades, centuries of life at Clermont Chase.

'Have you been up for ages?'

'I wanted to go out with the horses this morning. There's a new three-year-old our trainer's trying out.'

'Were they the horses I saw in the field by the drive when I arrived?'

Flavia snorted but Jonty cut in. 'Oh no. Those ones are our hunters. This one's a racehorse. He's with the trainer in Lotbourne.'

Flavia had to have her sneer. 'I suppose Bea and I *could* go hacking on the race horses, but I think we'll just stick to dear old Arnold and Sylvester this time.'

She'd lost me there. 'Horses,' said Jonty. 'Schwarzenegger and Stallone. Arnie and Sly. I'm afraid I was allowed to name then when I was about eight.'

'Cretinous, even then,' said Flavia.

'Well *you* named the dogs!' retorted Jonty. 'You can't get much more pathetic than Flopsy, Mopsy and Popsy, can you?' The dogs heard their names and proceeded to shuffle along the floor towards Jonty. A terrible smell emanated from the appropriately named Popsy.

The dogs' attention was diverted by the arrival of Beatrice and Tamara. 'Ciao!' Their voices preceded them from the door at the end of the passage. 'We're here!' (Duh.) Then they appeared in the kitchen – and their appearance was pretty diverting too. They had been dropped off by car, but Beatrice was in riding gear – not that unusual in these parts. Tamara on the other hand was decked out in the total tennis *outfit* – a silky, dazzling white track suit and an expensive-looking designer-label tennis shirt, the latest white trainers and *two* tennis racquets in the double case. She even wore a clip round her waist for tennis balls.

Jonty grinned and caught my eye. 'Say hello to my friend, Jonathan,' said Flavia. 'You remember Beatrice, don't you?' She didn't bother to introduce Tamara, but since the dopey girl was gawping at Jonty anyway, there probably wasn't much point.

'Of course I do,' said Jonty, collecting himself. 'Hi you two! Long time no see!'

Not that Beatrice and Tamara said anything to us of course.

'You've already met Holly, haven't you?' said Jonty. Silence.

'Er, hi,' I said, quietly, on account of feeling invisible.

Flavia stood up and yawned. 'Better dress I suppose. Make some coffee, little brother. Would you like some?' She addressed Beatrice (not me).

'Yah,' said Beatrice.

Jonty's very obliging. He made coffee in a cafetière (I'm not sure that I'd know how to) and dumped it in the middle of the table with some mugs. Then he told Tamara that it was time to meet up with Christopher. 'Are you going to come with us now or follow on when you've had coffee?' He bent under the table to drag out a pair of trainers.

'Don't drink coffee,' was Tamara's only answer. (So rude!)

Jonty was patient. 'So you'll come with Holly and me now?' Completely unselfconsciously he pulled off his riding boots and jeans and put on a manky old pair of shorts and some trainers.

Tamara winced. 'No.'

I wanted to scream, but Jonty's obviously used to people like this. 'See you at the court in about five minutes then?'

'Yah.' Good old Tamara. I'm amazed she and Beatrice and Flavia ever manage to hold proper conversations.

The day had started hazy but it was beginning to heat up as Jonty and I made our way to the tennis court that was hidden round the side of the house behind the rhododendrons. I could hear someone practising a few serves as we approached – I would never have found the court on my own, it was that secluded. Obviously it wasn't a problem with Jonty leading me by the hand. I was beginning to feel curious about Christopher. I imagined he'd look like a famous tennis player – Tim Henman perhaps. And of course he'd be brilliant – I was OK hitting a tennis ball around with Dad and Abby, but suddenly I realised I was rubbish really. Tamara would probably be well coached too. All that gear – she wouldn't have it if she was totally useless. Would she?

'We'll knock up a bit, first,' said Jonty, 'and then decide how we're going to play. We can always swap about if we're too badly matched.' I began to feel a bit anxious.

The noise of racquet on ball was suddenly right beside us. We'd reached a tarmac court surrounded by a mesh fence. It was nice and flat, but the lines were faded, especially around the service areas, and there were a few holes in the net. Christopher was picking up balls in the far corner with his back to us, but I watched as he straightened up and waved and came over. I saw another lanky lad who looked just like the boys in my class – hair so short you could hardly tell what colour it was; T-shirt and baggy shorts; grubby trainers. Nothing special.

'Christopher, hi!' said Jonty. 'This is Holly. Tamara's not here yet.'

Christopher loped over to greet us. 'So you're the famous Christopher!' I babbled, gushing nervously. Christopher looked at me, but he didn't reply. His jaw simply dropped. He glanced at Jonty questioningly.

'Heard you – playing – man, but never seen you in the flesh,' said Jonty. 'And I always seem to be telling Holly about you.' Christopher looked at the ground suddenly. He grunted something but didn't seem able to raise his gaze and look me in the eye. I wondered if the guy actually physically *couldn't* speak, and I hadn't been told, but Jonty punched him on the shoulder and said, 'Let's knock up. Whichever girl is more useless gets to play with you.' He whacked his racquet against a couple of balls lying on the ground and bounced them up to waist height. Clever, that. Took my mind off the insult. 'Come on, Hol! You play with me anyway until Tamara comes. We'll keep old Christopher here on the run.'

I realised early on that it was hardly worth my while joining in. Jonty and Christopher hit the ball low and hard to the baseline. From time to time they came up to the net and slammed the ball so fast I didn't have time to see it. Once or twice it arrived in my side of the court, but my nought to sixty acceleration is poor, and by the time I'd run for the ball it was too late. One time it hit me on the head and another on the backside. 'Perhaps I'd better sit out until Tamara comes,' I said, never thinking I'd actually look forward to her arriving on the scene. I didn't wait for a reply, but sat down near the mesh door of the court and took a swig at the bottle of Evian we'd brought with us. I watched the boys. Jonty was a good sportsman, and he played tennis as beautifully as he did everything else. But it was easy to see that Christopher had the makings of a champion. He might have looked like the boys at my school, but whereas they droop around not quite knowing what their legs are for, Christopher bounced and darted all over the court. He was always there, almost before Jonty had returned the ball, and his reactions were bullet-fast. Jonty started to flag, just a little, after five minutes of this, but Christopher was clearly only just beginning to warm up. I didn't know whether I wanted to be more useless than Tamara or not!

And here she was, along with Flavia and Beatrice, now both in full riding gear. The two older girls didn't stop. Her duty done by Tamara, Flavia led Beatrice off to the stables and the joys of Arnie and Sylvester. Tamara said 'Ciao' to the boys, who carried on playing, before peeling off her tracksuit trousers to reveal a tiny skirt, frilly knickers and the skinniest little pair of legs you've ever seen. Their rally over, Jonty and Christopher came to join us at the net post. Christopher actually managed to growl 'Hi Tamara.' Needless to say, Tamara didn't respond.

Jonty – I do love him for being so kind – said, 'You play with me then, Tamara, and we'll see how we go. Nice racquet,' he added, as she slid one of them out of the double case.

'Yah,' said Tamara, and trailed silently after him to the baseline.

I had as much trouble getting a word out of Christopher, though I'm sure in his case it was shyness rather than rudeness. He just wouldn't look me in the eye. I prattled away – 'Wow, hope I don't let you down by being atrocious. I don't really play, you know, just at school and with my dad, I've never played a real match before' – etc, etc. He just nodded and pointed to where I should stand. Aagh! Right by the net.

We knocked up a bit more. Tamara's stupid little knees pointed inwards when she ran and she never got to the ball once. I started to feel mildly superior as I returned Jonty's kindly angled gentle shots, but then the boys decided we should play a game. Christopher spun his racquet and Jonty called out 'Smooth' as it landed.

'Smooth it is,' said Christopher. He had no problem talking to Jonty, though he spoke quite softly.

'OK,' said Jonty. 'I'll serve first. OK, Tamara?'

'We'll stay this end,' said Christopher. He walked over to the right-hand corner, and gestured me to the net again with his racquet.

Jonty sent a sizzling service that squealed past my elbow. Christopher returned it to Tamara who simply stood and watched it, saying 'Eeuuu.'

Jonty swapped sides and I moved back to receive his serve. He sent me a gentle one, bless him, and I also hit it at Tamara, who missed it completely again, and said 'Eeuu.'

Jonty swapped sides again and served another sizzler to Christopher. Christopher made sure he returned it to Jonty this time and the two of them got quite a rally going while I crouched at the net feeling terrified and Tamara stood upright looking all around her. A volley came straight at me and I wopped it back instinctively. 'Well done!' yelled Jonty. He was racing all over the court while Tamara carried on standing there. Christopher and I won that game. We won Christopher's serve too. We even won mine – my service isn't very stylish but I can get it in.

And then it was Tamara's turn to serve. This was how she did it. First she removed a ball from the ridiculous clip she had round her waist. She held it up against the racquet. Then she brought both arms down in a circular motion, drew the racquet back dramatically, threw the ball a centimetre into the air and, piff, hit it into the net. A little scowl crossed her spoiled features as she frowned at her racquet and geared herself up to try again. But on her second serve she did exactly the same, except that she missed the ball altogether. It was hilarious, especially with Christopher bouncing and swaying, knees bent, in a very professional manner as he waited to receive it. We won that game too, to love (in other words, they didn't get a single point). In fact Christopher and I won the whole set to love. It was hardly due to me, but at least I hit the ball a few times – unlike Tamara. But was she abashed? Not a bit of it. At the end of the set she sat down with a bottle of water and pulled her second racquet from the case. As if it would make any difference! Jonty threw himself down beside me. 'Well played, my lovely!' he said, pulling my ponytail affectionately. Another resounding silence from our respective partners.

So we solemnly played a second set, the boys doing what they could, Tamara wallying about in her knock-kneed, mimsy fashion. I don't think she hit the ball once, not ever. Christopher and I won this set six-love, too. 'I'm whacked,' I said. 'Why don't you two boys have a game without us. We'll observe and learn, won't we Tamara?' I was trying to be friendly, honest I was, but she looked at me wordlessly, as usual, same vacant expression, mouth hanging slightly open. She sat down next to me and we were spectators as the boys played quite a reasonable game. Christopher won most of the points, but Jonty usually made him work for them.

I didn't know what to do with Tamara. I've just never met anyone like her before. However hard I tried, she blanked me. A phrase that amused my parents went through my head – 'Not quite our class, dear' – and I honestly think that's how she saw me. I'm used to posh people; after all, Dad teaches in a public school and I get to see the boys and their parents all the time, but here I was on a nice sunny day sitting by a tennis court next to a girl my own age and we had nothing to say to each other. I racked my brains, and suddenly I remembered my conversation with Dilly the night before: 'shopping – it's all they do,' was what she'd said. 'And barely a neurone between them.' Shopping. I took a punt. 'Harvey Nix is much better since they got that new bit,' I said casually. (I was winging it, but I've watched *Absolutely Fabulous*.)

Bingo!

'Yah. Tons. Went there yesterday. Bought a top.'

'Great. What make was it?'

'Calvin Klein actually.'

'Ooh. What colour?'

'Difficult to say really.' (She said 'ralleh'.)

More silence, but you can't accuse me of not trying. I went back to watching the boys.

Midday, and it was too hot to do anything. We trooped back to the kitchen, pausing of course for Tamara to zip her racquets into their bag and gather up her classy track suit before heading into the cool of the rhododendrons. Jonty was very efficient in the kitchen, rustling up a big jug of squash with ice for us all and then digging out crisps and bread and cheese, a bag of salad, a tub of hummus and some tomatoes, with pots of yoghurt and peaches for afters. I was impressed. 'Does your dad realise that you're a mean hand in the catering department, Jonty? Who needs Mrs B.?'

'I choose to keep those particular lights hidden under a

bushel,' said Jonty. 'Anyway, it's Mrs B. that needs us. And hot stuff and puds are what she's a whizz at. Can't match her there.' There was no irony in his voice.

'We have au pairs for cooking,' said Tamara, 'but Mummy always tells them what to do.' No irony there, either. 'Last nanny left when Bea was fourteen.'

Didn't these people do *anything* for themselves? I looked over at Christopher but he was eyes down as usual. We ate our way through the meal. No one said much – most of the noise came from the ice cubes in the squash jug and the rustling of crisp packets.

Christopher was the first to get up. 'I'm going home, man,' he said to Jonty. 'Promised Mum I'd do the lawn today. She'll be on at me if I don't. I'll be back this evening with my brother, if that's OK.'

'Sure,' said Jonty. 'Wish we could all go for a swim as well, but I'm afraid the pool's still out of action. Ma's got the guy who does it working on something else at the moment.'

'See you,' said Christopher.

'Yeah, see you later,' Jonty and I said together.

Tamara was silent. But not for long. When Christopher had gone she drawled at Jonty, 'You could swim at Bury Hall.'

'Where's that?' I asked. 'Is it a sports centre or something?'

Oh naive me. 'It's Tamara's house,' said Jonty. 'Thanks Tamara. Might take you up on that sometime.' He stood up. 'Have to make do with a shower right now, though. There's one in the downstairs loo if you want, Tamara. See you both back here in quarter of an hour?'

'And then we'll see my sister and the horses, yah?' said Tamara.

*

I whizzed up to my *own* bathroom for a shower. What bliss! Afterwards I changed and sat down with my diary for five minutes.

Monday afternoon
Played tennis this morning with Jonty, the ghastly Tamara and the silent Christopher. He's OK (Christopher, that is). Not ugly or anything. And ace at tennis. But he doesn't say a word. Not to me at any rate. Which is a pity, because sometimes I think Jonty and Tamara are from a different planet from me – what with nannies and gardeners and horses and tennis courts and private swimming pools – whereas I get the feeling that Christopher leads a slightly more normal life. Still, at least Jonty's behaviour is normal. He's so patient with those awful girls, though. Sometimes I wish he was a bit nastier – I end up feeling a total cow because I just want to hit them!

Ho hum. We're off to see the horses now. They've said I can have a ride if I want, but I suspect we're looking at classier horses than old Crisp at the riding stables! Or that trekking pony I loved so much on the school trip – Bonker? Conker? Question is, do I put on riding boots?

More tonight!

We met up in the kitchen. Tamara sat there turning through a copy of *Hello!* magazine. She'd obviously spurned the shower in the downstairs loo (I'd seen it earlier – it was a bathroom really, with the shower in a proper cubicle, heated towel rail, etc), not that she'd exerted herself enough to work up anything approaching a sweat. Just looking at her in her OTT tennis gear made me feel irritated. I wanted Jonty to come and give me a hug right then, but he didn't. So I went and put my arm round his waist.

'OK, you two,' said Jonty, taking control. (*Not sure that I like being 'you two' with Tamara.*) 'Let's go and find the horses. Follow me.' Neither of them wore riding boots, so I just hoped we weren't actually expecting to *ride*.

'I know the way,' said Tamara unnecessarily – I think she was trying to get back at me somehow by rubbing in the fact that I was an outsider. 'Unless the stables have moved in the last year, that is.'

I wasn't having her queening it over me, and I certainly didn't want her sucking up to Jonty. So I grabbed him by the hand and wouldn't allow him to shake me off. 'You'll have to lead me,' I said. At least that way I wasn't the one trailing behind.

We cut across the fields to the side of the drive and then on to another lane that led off the road. The fields were full of molehills and nettles, and I got stung once or twice. I kept quiet though, because I realised that Tamara must be getting stung too, and muddying her white trainers – and she wasn't fussing. A sort of doggedness there. The lane led to the stables. There was dung in the road and horseflies. We walked down to the yard where Beatrice and Flavia were unsaddling Arnie and Sly. They were giggling and chatting with the stable lads. Flavia was tossing her jockey's name into the conversation at every possible opportunity. It never meant anything to me, but Beatrice and the lads were obviously impressed. So was Tamara. She overheard the conversation and said, 'So your boyfriend, yah? – the one we met? – he's *the* Gil Smith? Cool.'

'Never mind that he's pint-sized and ugly and doesn't have a chin,' said Jonty to me under his breath. It was good to have him back on my side again. The other three girls were yahing and snorting at each other, so Jont took me on a tour of the horses. There were six of them. Arnie and Sly looked big to me, but Bluebottle (black) and Gorse (dun) were vast and Winslow (chestnut) and Shakespeare (dapple grey) were even vaster.

'They're huge,' I said.

'They're only hunters,' said Jonty. 'D'you fancy a ride? They're not neurotic, these fellows, but they go like the clappers once the chase is on.'

'Do you have anything – er – smaller?' I asked.

'Oh, but it's great being high up,' said Jonty, 'don't you think?'

'I wouldn't know.'

'But I thought you rode, Hol. You said you'd ridden quite a bit.'

'Depends how you see it. I had some riding lessons when I was little. And I've been trekking a few times . . .' I started to trail off. 'But I was quite good at it,' I added lamely. 'And I've brought my riding gear. Well, it used to be my cousin's . . .'

Jonty was looking at me. 'Ah,' he said. He thought for a while. 'Don't worry,' he added kindly. 'If you want to ride, you shall. There are quite a few younger kids who've just started to come on the hunt – I'm sure we can borrow one of their ponies. Ma can ring round tonight. We'll get you fixed up. A riding picnic's one of the things I've been looking forward to. There's this place I really want to show you, but you can only reach it on horseback – it's a bit too far to walk.'

Flavia, Beatrice and Tamara joined us. Tamara was patting the horses and being all soppy with them. 'How's my gorgeous Bluebottle?' sort of thing. I can't believe she can ride a horse that size, though she's a bit taller than Flavia.

Gorse bent his head down to Flavia and nuzzled her

shoulder. 'Gorse, my baby,' said Flavia. 'Are you missing Dilly, then?'

'Does Dilly ride that great beast?' I asked, impressed.

'He's Dilly's horse,' said Flavia. 'She might not object if you rode him.'

'Holly was hoping for a smaller pony,' said Jonty quickly.

'Oh,' said Flavia. It came out as a bark.

'There's always Nibbles,' said Beatrice, with a sneaky grin.

'Nipples?' I asked, incredulous. (It's the way she talks, honest – like the Queen.)

'*Nib-bles*!' Tamara enunciated patiently, as if I was very young indeed. 'Used to be my pony, but I've outgrown him and no one rides him much these days, poor darling.'

'Sounds more my cup of tea,' I said.

Tamara was getting quite chatty now. 'You could come over to Bury tomorrow, Jonty,' she said. (I had to assume I was included in the invitation.) 'Have a ride and a swim.'

I could see Beatrice and Flavia looking at her, appalled. 'Are you inviting *those* two over to Bury?' Beatrice asked her rudely.

'Flavia could come too.' Tamara wasn't backing down. 'I don't see why I shouldn't ask people over. You always do.'

'Yes, but—'

'Cool,' said Jonty. 'We'll come, won't we Holly?'

FIVE

Tuesday morning, early
I have to sort my thoughts out. It's good to write them down.
   There's this whole world that I don't understand. I have a dad

who's a teacher, a mum who's a part-time nurse. I have a younger sister and a cat and a guinea pig. We live in a three-bedroomed house with a small garden. My friends live fairly close. We can hang around together, go window-shopping, go to the swimming pool, go horse-riding even – whatever – all for a price, but not that much. If we go swimming we can't go for a pizza; cinema, can't go clubbing; buy two tops, can't afford shoes. We share the chores (well, Mum does do most of the housework, but I try and do my bit – sometimes) and there's certainly no treasure like Mrs B.

And here I am with people who can't begin to understand my incredibly ordinary life. I said earlier that I think Christopher probably does, but he doesn't seem to want to speak to me, so how will I ever find out?

Actually that's not quite true. Jonty wanted to ride yesterday evening, and there isn't a horse for me. And then Christopher wanted to knock up with Jonty because his little brother was doing something else. So I ended up playing tennis with Christopher. Well, hardly *playing exactly*, but he told Jont it was good practice for him to place shots where I could get them, and it was certainly good practice for me. I was running around like a maniac, so it didn't matter that he barely spoke – I was too puffed to chat anyway. I think I was right before, and he's just shy with me. Can't think why.

Today we're all going over to Bury for a ride, followed by lunch and then a swim. It's all rather jolly hockey-sticks (not that Tamara and Beatrice are jolly anything) and organised, but hey, I am in another world. Jonty's still incredibly cute – though I wish he'd be a little less cute with T – it makes me think he's not picky enough. J and I had a nice smoochy time last night watching TV in a room on our own. Good job no one came in.

Went up to bed fairly early – Jonty will have got up early again to go and ride his racehorse at Lotbourne. (I hate to admit it, but

Jonty is quite set in his ways. He won't not ride, just because I'm here. The horses and the life that goes with them are simply in his blood in a way that I wouldn't have thought possible. It's the bit I understand least about him, *and I kind of wish he'd be a bit more flexible.) I'm not sure what we'll do between breakfast and going to Bury, but I'm not going down there until I hear Jonty come in. I don't want to be stuck with any of the others over the Sugar Puffs. Right, I can hear him coming in now, so down I go. It's 10.30 again – v. slothful but what the heck.*

Flavia drove us to Bury Hall. It's a gorgeous house. Not as big as Clermont Chase, but with far more modern bits built on at the back, including this incredible pool – indoor, with huge glass sliding doors that you can open. Tamara was dressed for riding in jeans and a top, but Beatrice was in full sun gear and shades. She and Flavia went straight off to tan themselves on the patio outside the pool. Jonty and I followed Tamara, laden with tack, to the field where the ponies were. I spotted Nibbles miles away, a stout little bay pony with a pretty face, like a New Forest pony. The other two were considerably larger. 'They're not hard to catch,' said Tamara casually.

'Jonty!' I hissed. 'I can't catch a pony! Help me!' Tamara was already off after her pony, Skippy, who looked a bit lively to me, but good old Nibbles stood stock still, nibbling the grass.

Jonty walked up to him and slipped the halter over his neck, making it all look so easy, and walked him back to the yard. He put the saddle on and tightened the girth. He helped me fix the chin strap on my hard hat and gave me a kiss, making me feel a bit weak. 'OK then. You want to get on?' He stood by to help, but I knew he wanted to get going.

41

'Sure,' I said. It was a while since I'd done this – but I reckoned that it was probably something you didn't forget – like riding a bicycle. It isn't. I put my right foot in the stirrup, didn't I, and then realised that I'd end up facing the wrong way if I carried on. And then I couldn't untangle my foot. I was going to have to admit that I hadn't got a clue. I was sure I'd be all right once I was on his back. Tamara was already cantering around – show-off – and Nibbles looked like he wanted to join in. 'I'm sorry, Jont,' I said. 'I don't seem to be much good at anything, do I?'

'I can think of lots of things you're good at.' Jonty grinned as he helped me on to the pony's back. 'There. OK now?'

'I think so,' I said nervously. And Jonty was off again to saddle the big white – sorry, grey – pony.

Well, I stayed on. Some of those early lessons came back to me. Shoulders, hips, heels. Rise to the trot. Show who's boss. Well, the boss was definitely Nibbles. Mostly what Nibbles wanted to do was eat. The other two were up ahead looking dead professional. Annoyingly, Tamara looked a lot better on horseback than on the tennis court, but she still seemed strangely lethargic. I should have known that Jonty would look dashing on a horse. I remembered all over again why I fancied him. I almost wished I could be a damsel in distress.

Jonty twisted around in his saddle to check on me. I imagined how I must look, my feet almost touching the ground on this fat little pony – just like a Thelwell cartoon and not the slightest bit romantic. Jonty waved and then turned back to Tamara. Nibbles plodded along behind. But I was enjoying myself. We ambled through the woods, Nibbles and I. Every now and then he did a little trot to keep up with the others. I just clutched on to the reins with one hand and the saddle with the other until the trotting was over. We had to cross a stream at one point. I watched in horror as Jonty and Tamara jumped it, though luckily old Nibbles wasn't half as ambitious and simply picked his way through it, surefooted amongst the rocks and stones. It was beautiful, with dragonflies hovering over the water.

It was only a short ride (by their standards) because Tamara wanted to do some jumping. I'd had enough by the time we got back to the field, so I slipped off Nibbles, all on my own, and even managed to remove the saddle before letting him go and graze again. Jonty and Tamara were going round a little course of jumps. Tamara was efficient, but Jonty just seemed to fly. It's funny, isn't it, all these skills that you don't rate until you try them yourself? I could feel snooty about Tamara and Beatrice and Flavia because I felt they were so utterly deficient as human beings, but their ability to manage these great beasts certainly raised them a bit in my esteem. As for Jonty – he was a cool human being *and* an ace rider. I narrowed my eyes as I observed him with Tamara. I didn't want him being any nicer to her than was absolutely necessary.

We were all hot and thirsty. Tamara's mother was there when we got back. I'd expected someone thin and languid, if I'd expected anything at all, but she was short and bossy with thick glasses and wearing an extraordinary outfit – a velour sundress in jade green.

'Jonathan, dear! How nice to see you again after all this time. Goodness, you're a fine young man now!' She peered at me over her spectacles. 'Introduce me to Dilly's little friend. Holly, is it? Welcome to Bury Hall, dear.' I couldn't make her out at all. 'There's bread and salads on the patio table. Help yourselves and then come over to the barbecue.' Crikey. This was a bit like a military operation.

Jonty loved it. 'Ace food, Mrs Hilton.'

'Call me Judy,' she simpered. 'I know how hungry you big boys get.' Clearly her skinny girls don't get hungry. She hovered over us while we filled our plates. Then I saw her game. 'That's right Jonathan, have as much as you want. Holly – these are the less calorific ones. I like my girls to eat sensibly for me, so I make sure there's always something they won't turn their noses up at. Tamara – I've done some vegan burgers for you, dear. Flavia and Bea, I think you'll find something you like over here.' Fuss, fuss, fuss.

The food was great and the puds were amazing (not that Tamara went anywhere near them). As usual, no one said much, except for Jonty and Mrs Hilton – Jonty congratulating and Mrs Hilton clucking. Flavia and Beatrice snorted a bit and Tamara whined once or twice. I just stuffed myself. When we'd finished, Jonty was effusive with his appreciation but the girls went back to the serious business of sunbathing. I stripped off to my yellow bikini and joined them. Barbados gave me a great tan and I was quite happy to show it off. Flavia is so fair-skinned you wouldn't know she'd been anywhere exotic and the Hiltons had spent most of the summer so far with their grandmother in Scotland, so they were gratifyingly white too. Which meant Tamara was white *and* skinny. In fact, Tamara in designer swimwear was a truly grisly sight. Beatrice and Flavia weren't much better. In the bikini stakes I felt self-confident again. Jonty came and sat shoulder to shoulder with me – he had a gorgeous Barbados tan too. It gave us a bond. I found myself giggling ostentatiously. I wanted Tamara to know that Jonty was *mine*. I wanted her mum to know that I wasn't 'Dilly's little friend' – I was the *girlfriend* of Jonathan (now a young man).

What's more, I was brown and healthy-looking and not anorexic like her horrible daughters – even if I couldn't ride a horse. Believe me, I'm not usually catty, but this lot had that effect on me.

We had a swim once our lunch had gone down and then went out to sunbathe for a bit longer. Mrs Hilton brought home-made lemonade for us – 'far better for you than all those e-numbers, dears. I think the right food's *so* important, don't you?' Flavia and Bea disappeared off, for a cigarette I suspect. Jonty and I had another swim – just the two of us, which was great, and then it was time to go home to Clermont Chase. I was glad to say good-bye to the Hiltons. Nice house. Shame about the owners.

Jont and I separated for showers before supper. I like this little gap of time to myself in the evening. I'd never norm-ally shower at this time, but after all our various exertions it seemed a good idea. I might even try and keep it up when I get home. Good diary-writing time, too.

Tuesday afternoon
Went over to Bury, Tamara's house, for a ride and lunch and a swim today. I managed to ride T's old pony, Nibbles, without falling off, so I'm quite pleased with myself. Mrs H is a terrible fusspot but she gave us a good lunch and J and I were able to shake T off for a bit in the pool. She was with us all the rest of the time. She's really, really ghastly and whiny and I don't know what J sees in her. What am I saying? I don't think he does see anything in her, but she obviously fancies the pants off him and he doesn't seem to mind. I couldn't stand it if someone that repellent fancied me – I'd want to tell him to bog off. But J just isn't like that. I do sometimes wonder about him being so laid back and nice to everyone. I mean, it's what I like about him –

but if I'm honest, it's what I don't like about him, too. It was different in Barbados. I thought he was nice to me because I was special. Now I'm not sure. Maybe that was just his manner, and I misinterpreted it. Still, there are worse faults than being nice, I suppose!

I get another game of tennis with Christopher after supper tonight. It's quite a neat arrangement. I wish Jonty was as jealous of C as I am of T, but I couldn't do that to him, and anyway I don't fancy C and he barely says a word to me and still won't look me in the eye. Why not?

Supper was microwaved stuff that didn't taste of anything, with ice cream for afters. Gina wasn't around, so the other three did the microwaving. Brian smacked his lips as usual and said it was delicious and then Jont went off to ride, Flavia went to phone Gil, her jockey, and I went off to meet Christopher for a tennis practice.

Christopher was already there, surrounded by millions of tennis balls, serving them as hard as he could. 'That looks dangerous!' I called, ducking exaggeratedly.

'Huh,' he said, and gave the tiniest of smiles. Then he pointed me to the baseline and started potting some soft shots over for me to return. We did this for an hour. Sometimes he indicated with gestures that I should practise volleying at the net, or returning lobs from the baseline, but I couldn't get a word out of him. I gave up trying. I watched him instead. I learned a lot. I saw how quickly he took his racquet back, how he bent his knees, bounced about, never for one moment took his eye off the ball. And when I started concentrating as hard as he did it really started to show. When we came off he wiped his forehead on his sleeve and said (without looking at me), 'You're improving.' Then his mouth clamped shut.

'Thanks,' I said, thinking he was going to go off home. But he came with me.

'Got to fetch some flowers for my mum,' he said. (Hey, long sentence.)

I saw my opening. 'She does all the fantastic flower arrangements, doesn't she?' I said. 'She's a real artist.'

'Yes,' said Christopher.

He saw me looking at him questioningly. 'Yes, I mean she is a serious artist. That's what she does. Gina pays her for the flower-arranging. It all helps.'

What do you say to that, from someone who has barely uttered a word until now? 'What sort of thing does she do?' I tried.

'She's a – feminist artist,' he said, his eyelids lowered. 'You'd have to see for yourself.'

'I'd love to,' I said, wondering what on earth he meant.

We walked on in our more customary silence. There was Jonty. 'Christopher, hi! You coming in for a drink? I know Ma's got some flowers for you to take home.'

We all went down the passage to the kitchen. Flavia, Gina and Brian were sitting over gin and tonics. They were talking quite heatedly. Jonty fetched us Cokes and we joined them.

'I blame their mother,' said Flavia. 'She's so hung up about "the right" food. No wonder Tamara has eating problems.'

'She's a perfectly ghastly woman, I agree,' said Gina, going over to the sink that was filled with flowers and starting to roll huge bunches of them in newspaper.

'She's not ghastly,' said Jonty stoutly. 'She said I'd grown into a fine young man.'

'Well, she would,' said Flavia. 'She's so desperate to get

her girls married off to fine young men that she's getting to work on you already.'

'And she's a good cook,' said Jonty.

'Precisely,' said Flavia. 'That's the problem.'

'I know Tamara's unhappy at school,' said Jonty. So that's what they'd been talking about. 'She gets bullied.'

Hardly surprising, I thought uncharitably, and then wished I hadn't.

'It's a jolly good school, by all accounts,' Brian said, looking up from the paper.

'Bea loved it,' said Flavia.

And then, without thinking, I said something really stupid. 'I think I'd be unhappy if I had to go to boarding-school.'

'Oh no, no, no,' said Brian, dismissing the concept out of hand. 'Good for the character. Never harmed anyone. Good practice for the real world.'

I wondered how I could change the subject – I'd temporarily forgotten I was in a room full of people who went or had been to boarding-school (apart from Christopher) and I didn't want to get in any deeper. But Brian had started and he was determined to carry on. 'Of course, it has to be one of the better ones. Some of them are worse than useless.'

'*I* sometimes wish I was at day school,' said Jonty. 'Like Christopher. Then I could ride every day.'

'But there aren't any decent ones locally,' Brian blundered on, ignoring the fact that Christopher must go to one that wasn't decent if that was the case.

'My dad teaches at a private day school,' I said helpfully.

'Oh, well, fine if you live in London,' said Brian. 'But not out here.'

'I suppose a good education is important,' said Jonty, trying not to side with anyone.

'Of course it is,' said Brian. 'Absolutely crucial.'

'It is if you want to go to a good university,' said Gina.

My mind was racing. I'd heard this argument so often, though from a different point of view. Dad loves the school he teaches at, but he has no qualms about sending his children to the local state schools. He says we're clever anyway, and it's better to be with one's peers of all sorts; there's more to learning than just academic subjects. And I do want to go to a good university. Dad went to Oxford from a state school. I wanted to say so many things. I didn't want to put my foot in it again but I couldn't let them get away with this sort of talk. 'I go to a comprehensive,' I said bravely. Silence.

'Well, I don't expect your parents mind too much about what university you go to,' said Brian, trying to be kind.

I wasn't having it. 'They jolly well do,' I fumed. 'I want to go to Sussex or Edinburgh.'

'Exactly,' said Brian.

I could feel myself getting worked up. 'Oxford and Cambridge aren't the only good universities you know. And surely it isn't necessary to tear eight-year-olds away from their mothers just to perpetuate the system,' I said, echoing my father. 'Little kids should be at home. Tamara should be at home if that's where she wants to be.' I couldn't believe I was sticking up for her.

'Goodness me,' said Gina. 'Where *would* we all be if we simply let our children do what they wanted?' To be fair, she wasn't trying to put me down, she was trying to end a conversation that she could see was getting out of hand. 'Here are the flowers, Christopher. You'd better get them to Jill before they start to wilt on us. Shall I get some carriers for you? Now, Jonty, Holly, wasn't there something you wanted to watch on television?'

As Jonty hurried me off for another kissing session on the sofa (Gina isn't stupid) I heard Flavia saying to her father, 'What exactly do they *do* at a comprehensive?' I felt slighted and hurt, and I dare say Christopher did too, even though I knew they didn't mean to be insulting to either of us personally. Mum always says it's best not to get caught up in debates about education. Everyone always likes to think they're doing the best thing for their children.

Jonty isn't stupid, either. 'Sorry about that, Holly. Pa and Flavia live in the dark ages. Ma doesn't. Part of the reason she didn't want that conversation to carry on was because she took me away from my prep school. I loathed it. Pa didn't forgive her until I was ensconced where I am now. He thought she was turning me into a wimp.'

'You're not a wimp, Jont. You're . . . just right.'

'I know,' he said smugly and pushed me back on the sofa. He sat up again. 'Bit worried about Tamara though. She does look anorexic.'

'I'll say,' I said too quickly.

'Oy, Holly, don't be mean!'

'Sorry,' I said, but again I couldn't let it go. I should have done – he'd as good as told me he felt sorry for her. 'You don't *like* her do you?'

'What do you mean, *like*? She's OK.'

'She's not OK. She's wimpy and whingey and spoilt.'

'Hey, Holly! Miaow! She's not that bad!'

'She is,' I said. 'And she fancies you,' I added. There, I'd really done it now.

'Naturally,' said Jonty. 'No one is impervious to my charms!' He pushed me back against the sofa again, but somehow the moment had passed, and all of a sudden the football on the TV seemed to interest him more than I did.

*

I wrote my diary before I went to sleep.

Tuesday night
I'm not a happy bunny. I think I've blown it. They were all sneering about comprehensives and I made an idiot of myself. Jonty obviously likes Tamara and I'm stuck here for days yet. I feel so miserable. I love Jonty, he's so fantastic, but I can't seem to fit in. They make me feel so inferior – and bitchy too. All of them. Christopher actually spoke to me tonight. Apparently his mum is a 'feminist' artist. At least he's not a spoilt rich person. I'd like to go to his house and see his mum's work. We're off on some outing tomorrow. Can't remember where.

SIX

The outing was to Stratford-upon-Avon. Jonty woke me with a cup of tea. He hadn't noticed that I don't drink tea, but never mind. He tried snuggling in with me, but since he was still in riding gear it wasn't very comfortable. Flavia also decided to station herself outside the door and shout to Gina so that we were aware of her. 'Mother? You want to leave soon don't you? What's the weather going to be like? Shall I hurry Jonty up?' She moved even closer to my door and yelled, 'Jonty! Come and have breakfast! Now!' Cow.

Jonty shot out and I got up in record time. Shame. I've enjoyed my leisurely mornings up until now. I arrived at breakfast feeling as if I'd already done something wrong. Not a good start. But Gina was all smiles today. 'Right. Cooked breakfast this morning. What would you like

Holly? Jill's given me some eggs from her hens, so I'd recommend a boiled egg. Or would you prefer scrambled?'

I thought about Gina's cooking. 'I'd love a boiled egg.'

'Me too,' said Jonty.

'Flavia?'

'Yah.'

Gina had poured the orange juice into a jug. There was toast cooling off in a toast rack. She put a pan of water on to boil and sat down with us. 'Now today the Estate Office can go hang because today is polo day and I also want to be a good hostess and show Holly some of the sights. So – ' she stood up to check the pan of water and carried on speaking as she lowered the eggs in – 'we're going to Stratford. Sightseeing first, before all the grockles arrive. That's for you two while I get my hair cut. Picnic lunch by the river at Charlecote – ' she patted a picnic hamper. 'Afternoon watching polo, supper in the theatre and then *As You Like It*?'

'Wow!' I said. 'It sounds wonderful.' It did. I'd never been to Stratford-upon-Avon. Maybe it wasn't so bad staying here after all. And a day without Tamara! Gina doled out the boiled eggs. 'I want to be off before ten,' she said. 'Be out by the car – we'll take the Range Rover.' She went out of the kitchen, trailed by three hopeful dogs. Flavia made her egg into a sandwich and wandered off with it, leaving Jonty and me alone with our nursery breakfast of soft-boiled eggs and toasty fingers. I wanted to say something about the joy of a whole day without Tamara for a change, but I thought better of it. I was going to be my usual friendly self today, not the catty person that Tamara made of me. I half-wondered too if they were compensating for putting me down last night, but somehow I doubted it. I don't honestly think they're conscious that they're doing it.

'Do you think I should wear something different, Jonty? I'd no idea we were going to the theatre as well.' I was wearing shorts and a top.

'Ma won't mind. Dad likes my sisters to dress up, but he's not coming. Flavia will probably get tarted up for the polo, though. Yeah, go on, wear one of your skirt things. I'm just wearing *clean* shorts, a *clean* T-shirt and my less scruffy trainers.' We went our separate ways to change. Someone came to the door while we were going upstairs and Flavia answered it, but I never found out who it was.

Flavia didn't come with us – she was meeting up with Gil and joining us for the polo – so Jonty and I sat up in the front of the Range Rover with Gina. She drove fast but I felt safe with her – it was fun being so high up. We arrived in Stratford ahead of the rush of coaches and Gina went to have her hair done while Jonty took me off round the sights. It's a pretty town but I couldn't believe how touristy it was. Everything was half-timbered. Everyone was cashing in. We went to Shakespeare's birthplace and I tried to imagine it as it must have been but I couldn't make the leap. Does everyone have this problem with historic houses? I could imagine him peeping over the window-ledge at the house over the road, and maybe crawling up the stairs, but nothing else made me feel he'd really lived there. (Anyway, was Shakespeare ever a *baby*?) Jonty'd been loads of times before, so he was past that stage. 'Cool shop here,' he said. 'Have you got to buy presents for anyone?'

'Not really, I brought them all things from Barbados. I'll get some postcards to send to my friends though. Shall we do one together for Maddy?'

'Aah. Gorgeous Maddy.'

'Jonty!'

'Well, she was pretty, wasn't she?'

'Jonty! Ahem! Are we forgetting something here?'

'Well, you're pretty too, but you know what I mean.'

'And how would you feel if I went all starry-eyed about Red?' (Red was Maddy's boyfriend in Barbados, and yes, he was amazing-looking.)

'Well, we can't all look like film stars.'

'My point precisely.'

'Only joking, Hol. Lighten up?' He tilted my chin up so that I looked him in the eye. 'We're going to enjoy today, OK?'

'OK. I just get a complex if you start fancying other girls. Especially blondes.'

'Well, I won't today.' This wasn't quite the answer I required. 'It's just us. No skinny Tamara, no bossy older sisters and no lovesick Christophers.'

'Lovesick? What do you mean?'

'D'you mean you hadn't noticed?'

'Noticed what?'

'That he blushes and goes completely tongue-tied when he's around you?'

'I just thought he was . . . I just thought he was a silent sort of guy.'

'Christopher? Oh no, Ms Davies, that is the effect you are having on him.'

'I don't know what to say. Has he said anything to you?'

'What do you think? Course he hasn't. But I can tell he's jealous as hell. We blokes know these things. Isn't it great? Usually I'm the one who's envious of him.'

'So where does this leave me?' We were standing in the little garden just before the shop. Jonty threw his arms around me and sweetly touched his lips against my

forehead and my nose before kissing me. People were looking at us.

'As my very own gorgeous Holly who has a beautiful face,
huge eyes, lovely hair and a fabulous body.'

'Jonty!'

'I don't care! Stop worrying about other people!'

Oh my God – I just knew he was about to do something
embarrassing. He was. He went down on one knee and
started spouting Shakespeare: 'Shall I compare thee to a
summer's day? Thou art more lovely and more temperate,
et cetera . . . There, do you believe me now?'

A couple of American tourists in Bermuda shorts and
baseball caps started to clap. I was blushing frantically.
Jonty adored playing to the gallery. At least he hadn't
swept me up in a tango like he did with Maddy in Barbados.

'So just remember, OK? Now, let's go and buy a postcard
for the stupendously ugly Maddy. Then we can go and have
a drink in that coffee shop and wait for my mother.'

I was intrigued by the idea of Christopher liking me, but I
didn't understand it, and I certainly couldn't talk to Jonty
about it. And since any bloke would fancy Maddy, and he
did call Tamara skinny, I tried to banish all jealous thoughts
for the day.

We were having milkshakes and blueberry muffins when
Gina arrived and decided to have exactly the same herself.
She was a weird lady, and certainly a peculiar sort of
mother, but there was something a bit wild and bohemian
beneath her steely exterior and I felt that I could grow to
like her. Strange, because I'm not used to seeing grown-ups
as people! When she had finished she looked at her watch.
'Goodness! Is that the time? Would you two mind awfully
if we gave Charlecote a miss and had our picnic at the

polo? I promise we'll have our supper by the river. I'll ring now and reserve one of the riverside tables.' She pulled a phone out of her bag, and steamrollered the restaurant into reserving a special table. I couldn't imagine my mum doing that!

Then we emerged into the midday heat and walked to the Range Rover which was like an oven until the air-conditioning came on. Gina drove us to the horses. I've never been to anything horsy before. We parked in rows in a field, where loads of people had already set up their picnics, with champagne and salmon and everything, all balanced on little picnic tables. Most of them were quite smartly dressed and looked incredibly posh (I think I even recognised a minor royal – 'Almost certainly,' said Jonty – exciting or what?), so I was glad I'd made a bit of an effort with my clothes. The atmosphere was very friendly though. Gina buys a good picnic. She spread out one of those waterproofed tartan rugs and sat us down with all sorts of quiches and pies, French bread, French cheese, grapes, peaches. There was even chilled white wine which she pressed on us (not least because the only other drink she'd brought was tea in a Thermos). Then we went our separate ways, Gina to find Flavia, Gil and a polo pony that used to belong to them. Jonty and I pushed our way through the crowds to find a good place to watch. The wine had gone to our heads a bit, so we clung to each other and were glad when we found somewhere to settle. We sat back to back on the grass and dozed gently until the match began. It was blissful.

We were brought to our senses by the sound of a bell and the commentator clearing his throat over the PA system. There was going to be a 'practice match' followed by the main one. Jonty explained that there were only four players on each side. There were yellow posts at either end and the teams hit a white ball around with the side of a long wooden-ended cane stick. I couldn't quite work out what was going on, but it was fun to see how the ponies bunched up until one managed to ride free. I decided to root for the yellow team and joined in the ra-ra-ra-ing and cries of 'Good shot!' from time to time. The bell rang every time someone scored a goal and they changed ends, so it was hard to keep up. They played four 'chukkas' – seven-and-a-half-minute 'quarters'. When the yellow team won 4–3, I was jumping up and down with the rest of them!

Then a whistle went and the commentator asked the crowd to come and 'tread in'. 'Follow me,' said Jont, and everyone went on to the pitch to tread the divots back in! 'You ain't seen nothin' yet,' said Jonty. 'They were just juniors. The next lot will blow your socks off.' Actually, the players alone blew my socks off. They were really sexy, especially a couple of Argentinians, what you could see of them under the grilles of their helmets.

Jonty suddenly recognised one of the horses. 'That's Pink Gin!' he said. 'Great – this will be a really cool match. Pink Gin was once one of our racehorses. Watch out for him, he could turn on a pound coin!' He was right, the second match was far more exciting. The horses thundered backwards and forwards, the mounted umpires chasing after them with their whistles. I just prayed that no one would fall off near us! Pink Gin's side won and Jonty, Gina, Flavia and Gil went mad when the players went up to fetch their prize champagne. The five of us trooped back to the Range Rover – for a few moments I felt quite elated and part of it. Then Gina drove us back into Stratford for our evening at the theatre. It was a lovely pink sort of evening – I was beginning to feel like someone in a film.

As soon as Gina swept into the theatre restaurant it was obvious that she was known. No one could have mistaken her for another American tourist. We don't eat out much at home beyond the odd pizza or Indian – and even that seems expensive when I sneak a look at the bill. Dad gets thrilled when the staff at our local Indian recognise him. Now the waiter led us to a table which was right by the river. Swans bobbed about on the water, hoping for crusts. We waved regally at passing cruisers and some of the other boats that slipped past, quietly shattering the reflections in the river. Gina said we could choose what we liked – have all three courses if we wanted (with Mum and Dad it's always starter *or* pudding) and any sort of drink, though not alcohol if we wanted to stay awake for the play.

She needn't have worried about me staying awake for the play. I was spellbound from the moment Orlando walked on to the stage. He was *gorgeous*! Really tall with dark curls and dark melting eyes. We had such brilliant seats (front row of the dress circle) that I could drool over him at close quarters. As if the polo players hadn't provided enough excitement for one day I fell completely in love. (At a distance, naturally. Sort of getting my own back for Tamara I suppose.) Forgetting about Jonty sitting beside me, I even felt jealous of Rosalind! Of course, they were all Sirs and Ladies, high-born gentlefolk with servants and big houses. How strange that Gina and Jonty should be living relics of all that. Still, Shakespeare had to work for a living. My thoughts were short, ragged things – my head was really taken up with the play. In the story Rosalind (a blonde, please note) sees Orlando wrestling and falls passionately in love with him (I'm not surprised), and he with her (damn). Orlando has been banished to the Forest where Rosalind and her cousin Celia (dark-haired) have also fled (well fancy that), dressed as a shepherd and a shepherdess. So then there's lots of cross-dressing fun in the woods until the end when Rosalind finally comes out as a girl and she and Orlando get hitched, along with Celia who has strangely fallen for Orlando's horrible brother. It was fabulous, and I loved every minute of it. *I* wanted to wander through the woods in a beautiful long dress and find my name carved on the trees. In fact I wanted to *be* Rosalind, *now*. Or the actress that played her every night.

Jonty had enjoyed the play too. As the actors took a final curtain call he gave a happy sigh and squeezed my hand. 'Enjoy it?'

'I'll say.' I leant over to Gina. 'Thank you so much Gina. It was wonderful.'

'It was a pleasure,' said Gina graciously. 'The bard rarely lets one down. I must say, I thought Orlando was frightfully handsome, didn't you?'

'He was gorgeous,' I said.

'Reminded me a bit of Christopher,' she said.

'Mother!' Jonty said. 'He looked nothing like Christopher.'

'He's had that awful prison haircut for so long that you forget he has curls,' said Gina. 'You both had curls when you were little and then yours turned to waves but Christopher's got curlier and he had them shaved off. Mothers adore curls.'

'M-u-um!' said Jonty, getting to his feet, 'you're embarrassing me! How can I maintain my sophisticated macho image in front of Holly if you insist on talking about my lovely curly hair?'

'I was talking about Christopher's really,' said Gina.

I leant my head on Jonty's shoulder on the way back, imagining that he was Orlando, I'm afraid. I was sleepy as we drove home through the lanes, but Gina had given us a good day and I felt at ease with the Hayters again.

When we got back, Flavia and Gil were sitting up with Brian in the kitchen talking about the polo. Unlike me, Gina and Jonty knew what they were talking about and wanted to join in, but I wanted to go to bed. Jonty slipped out to kiss me goodnight. 'Fair Rosalind,' he teased. 'I know you wish I was that girly Orlando, but I'm glad you're you.' We kissed. 'Night, gorgeous,' he said, and then went back into the kitchen to join in the polo talk.

I made my way upstairs to the back of the house. I knew the way so well now. I opened the door to my room. It must have been Mrs B.'s day to do the bedrooms because it was all tidy, with my clothes in neat piles and the bed temptingly folded back. And the flowers were different. On the bed was a little pile of post and a parcel. The ballgown! Good old Daisy.

I'm one of these people who likes to save their treats, so I washed and changed into my nightie before starting on the mail. There was also a letter from my parents, carefully addressed to Ms Holly Davies, c/o Jonathan Clermont-Hayter, etc, and what looked like a letter from Dilly. Bumper post!

> 31 North Hill Road
> London N.

Dear Holl-doll,
Thought you might like a letter, though I'm sure you're not the slightest bit homesick. I suppose this is all good practice for the French Exchange next year. I hope you're having a lovely time – the countryside must be so green and cool in this weather. Do they have a swimming pool? (Shouldn't be surprised!) I'm dying to hear all about it.

Do be polite and thank for things, won't you? If there's any possibility of going to Stratford, jump at the chance. I've heard there's a terrific RSC performance of *As You Like It* on at the moment. If someone could get you there we'd be happy to pay for you and Jonty to see it (groundlings only, I'm afraid). I know you'd love it. See what you can do. Daisy has said she'll get the ballgown to you. If I've got the address right it will reach you at the same time as this.

Lots of love, darling. See you on Sunday,

M

How's life with the aristos then? Make sure they treat my little Holl-doll with the respect she deserves. You might not be an heiress but you have beauty and brains, a rare combination that Jonty obviously has the good taste to appreciate. Look forward to having you home again, sweetheart. Abby misses you and so do we.

Dx

Dear Holly,

Daddy has drunk a whole half bottle of wine so I think he feels a bit soppy. I hope you are having a nice time. I can't think what to say.

Lots of love from your adoring sister,

Abby

Aah. That letter did make me feel a bit homesick actually. Good old Mum. I felt almost disloyal for going to that very play and sitting in the most expensive seats when paying for them and for dinner must have meant so little to Gina. I put the letter firmly back in its envelope. I wouldn't want my hosts reading Dad's little contribution.

Second letter. From Dilly.

Hi Hol! Thought you might need a letter from me to get you through the week with my frightful family. I know you don't think Jonty's frightful, but you know how I feel about my little brother and perhaps you'll be of the same opinion by now. (Don't mean it really. He's quite cute, as little brothers go. Better than he used to be anyway.)

TIPS FOR VISITORS

Big sister: Keep out of her way. I can't stand her most of the time – she thinks she's so superior just because she's the oldest. I'm afraid you can't trust her to be nice.

Little brother: Typical male, arrogant and a pain. Only interested in sport. Charms the pants off old ladies. But you like him anyway, so I'll shut up.

Father: Fine and good natured as long as you don't engage him in conversation about a) politics b) education c) the EU d) the welfare state and e) blood sports.

Mother: Some of my friends don't understand Ma because she's not very mumsy and has some weird ideas. We get on fine because she mostly leaves me to my own devices. She'll like you, I know, because you've got a mind of your own.

Granny: You might or might not meet her – she was still away when I left and I'm not sure when she gets home. Granny doesn't understand the word 'can't'. She does what she wants and expects everyone else to do the same. She's quite cool as grannies go.

You can tell I'm bored. The others on this course aren't very interesting and the one guy I liked has gone off with a blonde bimbo. Don't you hate them?

Have you met Christopher yet? And his younger

brother, Toby? And his mum, Jill? I love Christopher to bits, always have done. He's been a bit like a brother to me so I don't fancy him. You might though – if you weren't going out with Jonty that is. He's deep, is Chris, so promise me you won't mess with him. And an ace tennis player too. I'd marry him if he was rich, but he's not, so he's safe from me!

Toby must be about twelve by now – looks identical to the way Chris looked before he shaved his hair off. He's a bit of a pain.

Jill: Wacko lady. Single mum, poor as a church mouse but brilliant artist. Granny buys her paintings but Mum's too embarrassed to have them on the wall. Have a look at them and you'll see why! (Does the name Georgia O'Keefe mean anything to you? Chris explained it all to me once.)

Who else? You said you'd been forced into the company of Tamara Hilton, Flavia's friend Beatrice's younger sister. Aagh. Poor you. I've never had to take any notice of her because she's Jonty's age (i.e. yours) not mine, but I can't stand either of them chiefly because they're so thick (huh – and thin!). Their house is quite nice and they've got a better pool than ours, especially since ours is out of action. Anyway, advice: avoid at all costs. It's supper time. Must go. Honestly, this is almost as bad as school except that there are boys, if you can call them that.

Love, Dilly.

My eyes were rolling up into my head I was so tired. The parcel could wait until morning – I couldn't be bothered to get out of bed and try a dress on anyway. I turned out the light and fell asleep.

SEVEN

It was Thursday already! I woke up knowing I had a treat in store, though when I checked my watch and realised it was 10.30 *again* I leapt out of bed like a scalded cat. I catapulted into the bathroom, had a shower, and then remembered my 'treat'. The ballgown! I shot back into the bedroom in my towel and tore open the parcel. Wow! Cousin Daisy could afford Monsoon! It was a full-works ballgown in fuchsia pink silk. The towel dropped off and I stepped into the dress. I paraded around feeling like a princess, my long dark hair tumbling down my naked back. I did a twirl in front of the mirror. I felt fabulous. I felt like Rosalind! I could see my name inscribed on all the trees of the forest already. Jonty would go ape!

The 'do' was tonight – wasn't it? No one had mentioned it, though I had seen the invitations, three of them, to Gina and Brian, Flavia and partner and Jonathan and partner, all gilt and deckled edges, tucked into the mirror. 'Black tie.' That meant evening dress, didn't it? The ball was in aid of some junior polo team. I shimmied out of the ballgown, enjoying the swish of the silk as it curtseyed to the ground. Shorts felt very mundane after that and it seemed almost criminal to scrape my hair back into a ponytail – I'd throw all the conditioners and stuff at it when I washed it for tonight. Exciting!

I was relieved to hear voices in the kitchen as I approached. Don't know why I worry so much. No one actually *cares* when I come down for breakfast – unlike at home where I can hear Mum and Dad saying, 'Isn't it time

Holly was up? She's wasting the day!' most weekends! I pushed open the kitchen door. Jonty, Flavia and Gil were in there with Brian, still discussing the polo as if they'd never been to bed. Jonty came over to greet me. He was looking good this morning in a whiter than white T-shirt and pale Gap shorts and sun tan. The sunlight coming in through the kitchen windows caught the hairs on his arms and legs. He's not *hairy* hairy, just right. I couldn't wait to see him all dressed up tonight. Maddy said he'd looked pretty cool at the dance in Barbados. Envy, envy. Still, I was going to look darned cool too in my fuchsia silk. 'Morning, gorgeous! Rescue me from yet another blow-by-blow account of yesterday's match!'

'That's not fair,' said Brian mildly. 'I had to miss it.'

'Anyway,' said Flavia, 'it's interesting, isn't it Gil?'

'Problems Flavia?' said Gil, who'd actually taken the opportunity to glance at the paper.

'Yah,' said Flavia. 'My baby brother's accusing us of being boring.'

'Ahuh!' Gil did a funny sort of laugh.

'Eat!' Jonty pushed a plate in front of me. 'Jill dropped round some croissants she picked up from the bakery in the early hours of this morning. She's getting Granny's cottage ready for her.'

'Granny back today then?' asked Flavia.

'Yup,' said Jont. 'She's been terrorising Tuscany for far too long.'

'My friend Zoe went to Tuscany this year,' I said. 'She's pretty terrifying. Does your granny like a good argument?'

'*Oh* yes,' said Jonty. 'Nothing better.'

'Perhaps they met up,' I said.

'I doubt it, dear,' said Brian, diplomatic as always.

'Let's talk about something else,' said Jonty quickly.

'OK,' I said. 'Guess what was in my parcel?' I grabbed his arm. 'I have got *the* most fabulous dress for tonight.'

It worked. 'Must fly,' said Brian, unruffled, and left, just as Gina came in.

'Tonight?' said Jonty.

'Isn't it the dance thingy tonight?' I said.

'Yeah, it is,' said Flavia, interested, 'but Holly's not invited, is she, Jonathan?'

'I thought Jonty was invited,' I said. 'With partner.'

'He is, dear,' said Gina smoothly.

I looked from Gina to Flavia to Jonty. There was a deafening silence.

'So—'

Jonty couldn't look me in the eye. 'I have to go with Tamara,' he said.

'You *what*?'

Stupid old Flavia said, 'Well, I was the one who organised the tickets, so when Beatrice said her miserable little sister wouldn't shut up until someone got her a ticket I had to say she could go with my brother, didn't I? Can't imagine why she should want to. Jonty never told me he was going with Holly. And anyway, Judy Hilton's paid me for the tickets already.' Her voice was rising into a steady whine.

'Problems, Flave?' Gil looked up from his paper.

'No,' Gina cut in. 'Never mind, Holly. There'll always be another one. Judy Hilton seemed set on this for Tamara, I'm afraid – something to do with a dress the child has spent vast sums of money on. But you can spend the evening with Granny instead. You'll like that.'

My jaw dropped. I knew I was about to cry. What about *my* beautiful dress? Daisy had gone to all that trouble to find it and post it.

Jonty tugged at my arm. 'Come on. It's not important.

It's only a naff old dance for the polo club. Bring your croissant. Come outside with me. It's a brilliant morning out there.'

Once outside, Jonty marched me away from the house as quickly as possible. I thought he was going to grovel and apologise, but he really didn't think there was anything at issue here. He simply said, 'Sorry about all that. At least we've managed to spend most of the time together. One evening apart won't kill us.'

'But Jonty!' I wasn't having all this matter of factness. 'Jonty – why won't you let me tell you how I feel?'

'Because it won't make any difference?'

'Why won't it make a difference?'

'Because, between them, my family have made the decisions already, and there's no way they'll budge. If Flavia's done her friend Beatrice a favour by getting a ticket to keep her sister quiet, she won't go back on it.'

'But what about me? I was really looking forward to it. I've had a dress sent to me specially. I wanted to go with you, because you're my boyfriend.'

'Believe me, you're not missing anything. I go to loads of these things, with Dilly usually. Everyone dressed up like idiots. Loads of giggling girls. Crap band. Vile wine.'

'You go with Dilly?'

'Well, there's this partner thing. Dilly doesn't have much time for me on a regular basis, but I can dance and I look older than fourteen. Once we're in, she abandons me and goes off to pull on her own – someone else who's been dragged along by a sister.'

'And what about you?'

'I block my ears against the crap band and get tiddly on the vile wine. I can do it without throwing up now.'

He really didn't see it. 'Well, it would have been a real

treat for me. I've never done anything like that before. I've never been to any sort of dance apart from the Christmas disco at school. And that's in the afternoon in a fully lit classroom. And now you won't see me in the dress. I look OK in it.'

'Bet you do. Can I have a private showing?'

'That's not the same thing, and you know it.'

'You get to go to Granny's, and that's far better.'

'You are joking?'

'No. Granny's a gas. You'll see.'

'Hhhhmph.'

'Come on, let me take you on a tour of the Clermont follies. Some of them are nice and secluded, and we won't be disturbed.'

Well, despite my disappointment, he *was* looking sexy. I wanted to make sure it was me he was interested in and not Tamara. Folly number three was actually an old dovecote and it was cool after the heat outside. It was only about twelve feet across. We stood in the middle of it, rays of light coming in through the holes for the doves in a conical roof. Jonty put his hands on the bare bit between my shorts and my top. He's got big hands and I've got a little waist. They almost went right round. He pulled me to him for a kiss. We're good at kissing now – we can sort out our teeth and tongues without getting embarrassed or giggling. We can do it for hours. My legs started to feel all weak. Jonty's must have been as well. 'Let's lie down,' he said. The ground was dry. 'I'll take off my T-shirt – give us something to lie on.'

Somehow Jonty with a bare chest and shorts was even sexier than Jonty in swimming things (probably because he'd taken his T-shirt *off*). I laid my head on his chest. His skin was silky and brown and smelt of nice shower gel. He was with *me*, not riding or anything else country estate-ish, and being nice to me alone, *not* the world at large. He was being the Jonty I loved again, for the time being. 'Love you,' I said.

'Me too,' said Jonty, twisting a strand of my hair round his fingers.

Some time later we came out squinting into the sun. Jonty had suddenly remembered that Jill was also doing a barbecue lunch for us all, including Christopher and Toby, because she'd been over at Granny's cottage.

'That seems incredibly nice of her,' I said.

'Well, Ma finances her quite a bit, so she likes to repay her in various ways. And, as you've probably noticed, Mum's a lousy cook. And hey, it's a lovely day.' He looked adoringly down at me. 'Isn't it?'

'Sure is,' I agreed. 'Your T-shirt's covered in dove poo.'

'And you think I care?' He swung our clasped hands.

I was happy, very happy. I actually thought, 'I am happy right now – I must remember exactly how it feels.'

The smell of barbecuing drifted towards us. Jill had set up a table on the grass by the door near the kitchen. Gina was there with Christopher and Toby. No sign yet of Flavia and Gil.

'We've been with the horses,' lied Jonty. 'Better wash before we eat.' He hustled me indoors before I had time to take in Jill and Toby, let alone Christopher. 'I think you look great – kind of wild and mussed up, but maybe you'd better go and check in a mirror. You might want to tidy yourself up a bit.' He squeezed my hand. 'And I don't want to be there when the Flavour turns up – she won't corroborate our story about being with the horses.'

'No one will mind, will they? That we've been messing around in the dovecote?'

'Nah. Don't suppose so. Just don't want comments. See you out there pronto.'

'See ya.'

I was a mess. My hair was all tangly and my clothes were covered in grot from the floor of the dovecote. I also had a mark or two on my neck. Oops. Luckily I had a similar (clean) pair of shorts and I put on a longer top. I brushed my hair out and arranged it carefully. There. I'd just had a wash and brush up before lunch. Don't know why I cared what they all thought. What did they expect me and Jonty to do? But aagh! Christopher was there, and his little brother with the curls-like-Christopher-used-to-have. And the feminist artist! I found myself hitting the mascara and just the teeniest bit of lipstick. Yes? No? This was daft. I don't fancy Christopher in the slightest. It's just – after what Jonty said. Nah. Jonty probably had his own agenda for saying all that. Something to do with Tamara perhaps. Don't want to think about her. Damn! Why did I have to start thinking about her? Just don't, Holly. Just don't. It'll make me feel all bitter about tonight, and I thought I'd forgotten. Go downstairs, Holly. Sort out the barbecue first.

The barbecue was brick-built into a wall and there was a long garden table with benches and a parasol. Jill had knocked up salads and sauces as well as kebabs and chicken. Gina introduced me to Jill as if I was one of her own friends. I liked that. 'Meet Holly,' she said, 'from London. Holly is a young woman with a mind of her own, unlike so many others I could mention.' I blushed, hoping it was intended as a compliment. I looked at Jill appraisingly. She had wild curly grey hair and vivid blue eyes. She looked brown, as if she spent a lot of time in the garden. She wore some large blue glass beads (exactly the same colour as her eyes), blue denim jeans, a man's white shirt and espadrilles.

'Hi Holly,' said Jill. 'I've heard a lot about you.' That was worrying. Now I knew why Christopher had cringed when I said the same thing to him.

Toby pushed in and shook my hand in a very grown-up way. He must be about the same age as Abby. He said 'Hi!' and then turned to Christopher. 'OK, Chris, you win. She does look like J Lo only prettier.'

'All right, Toby, I think we'll do without the personal comments,' Jill said briskly.

'And you're a real Babe yourself,' I said to Toby.

'Oh, thanks,' he mumbled.

'You've seen the film, of course,' said Jonty.

'Should have been ready for that one, Tobe! Thanks, guys,' said Jill. 'We do our best to squash him, don't we Chris? But we rarely succeed.' Chris was doing manly things to the barbecue and didn't respond. Flavia and Gil turned up then. True to form, Flavia didn't even acknowledge Jill, but sat at the table and grabbed a couple of cold beers for herself and Gil.

'Is Pa coming?' Jonty asked Gina.

'A bit later,' she said. 'Probably just as we're finishing.'

'Well, we're ready to roll now,' said Jill. 'Chris has put the chicken out, and some of the kebabs are ready. Come and help yourselves, everyone.'

We scoffed the lot. I was feeling content despite the ball fiasco. Jonty sat close by and fiddled with my hair or stroked my hand which reminded me all over again of the dovecote and made me smile. Flavia and Gil had been silenced by food. Toby and Chris cleared off to play tennis. I couldn't possibly have been so energetic after a meal in

71

that heat, but nothing seemed to stop them. Jill started to clear up but Gina brought out coffee and stopped her. The six of us were sitting round the table drinking it when Brian turned up.

'No food for a hard-working man, then?' He sounded genuinely peeved.

'Hard work, was it?' Gina asked.

'Well, you know what these meetings are like. And they never give you food, just inferior instant coffee. This looks nicer.' He pulled the cafetière towards him.

'I'll fetch you a cup,' said Jill, getting up before Gina could stop her.

Brian sat down and looked round at us. 'Bet you've all had a better morning than me.'

'Yah,' said Flavia.

'At least we're keeping the horses fit,' said Gil. 'I don't believe for a minute that they can really ban us.'

'What's all this about, Jonty?' I whispered.

'You don't want to know,' Jonty whispered back, but Brian had heard me.

'What's it all about? I'll tell you what it's all about! It's about damn-fool politicians in London thinking they can alter the way we've lived for centuries. They think they have the right to pass legislation on anything at all, never mind that they don't understand the first thing about rural matters, simply because some pressure group or other have decided that it's cruel. Oh, they eat meat, wear leather, use cosmetics – drink *milk*, eat *eggs*, for goodness sake and there's a thing – and think they can make *laws* about what is and what isn't cruel down here in the country.' The normally placid Brian was getting quite red in the face.

It dawned on me that they were talking about hunting. *I*

think hunting is cruel and disgusting. I could feel my heart beginning to thump.

Gil joined in. 'No more than you'd expect, is it Brian? I mean, these sentimental prats haven't got a clue have they?'

'Don't see the harm in riding to hounds,' wheedled Flavia.

'It makes my blood boil,' said Brian. 'Where's their sense of beauty? And history?'

'It would be a shame if all the old traditions disappeared,' Gina joined in. 'There's nothing quite like the sight of the hunt going by.'

I was huffing and puffing. Jonty gripped my hand. He has a natural instinct for danger, that boy.

'Never mind how it looks,' said Gil. 'What can beat closing in for the kill? That moment when you know you've *got* the beggar!'

'Well, personally I prefer shooting,' said Gina. 'But that's only because I like to do the business myself and eat what I kill.'

'You've got a point there, Ma,' said Flavia. 'But Grandfather never lets me come on a shoot when we're staying.'

'That's because the Hayters know that shooting is for the men,' said Brian.

'Really Brian!' said Gina. 'In my family we don't leave everything to the men. I've always encouraged my girls to get out there.'

'More's the pity,' grumbled Brian.

I couldn't believe what I was hearing. I tried to think of an innocent sounding question that would expose them all for the bloodthirsty dimwits they undoubtedly were. I smiled but my lip was wobbling. I ignored Jonty's restraining hand. 'So what harm have foxes ever done you?' That would stall 'em.

Wrong question. 'Oh, only ravaged a few tens of new-born lambs and decimated a hen house or five,' said Gina, suddenly defensive and icy. 'And of course they don't eat what they kill – just maim and tear a few heads off and innards out. Nothing much.'

'They're animals,' I said staunchly. 'They don't know any better. But then, hunting's all about behaving like animals, isn't it? Stupid, stuck-up animals, who also don't know any better. Thinking that hurtling around on horseback after a poor defenceless fox, chasing it until it's exhausted and then watching the hounds ripping it apart is *fun*!' I wished I had Zoe on hand to be eloquent for me but *my* blood was boiling now. All the hurt about the ball, the arrogance, Jonty and Tamara, horrible Flavia, made me see red. I didn't care what I said.

Gina tried to placate me, but it was too late. I turned on her. 'What is it with all of you,' I yelled. 'You're all just so sure that you're *right*. Well, you're not!'

'Holly!' said Jonty desperately. 'Please, don't. You simply don't understand . . .'

I brushed him aside and started marching towards the house. 'Enjoy your silly ball,' I said. 'I don't give a stuff. Why should I want to spend my evening with a load of braying hooray Henrys anyway!'

'Holly!'

'Oh leave her, Jonathan,' I heard Flavia saying as I pushed past a questioning Jill.

I vaguely heard Gina telling Jonty that they hadn't meant to upset me, but I was too angry to care as I stormed up to my room and flung myself down on the bed in floods of tears.

*

I suppose I'd half hoped Jonty would follow me. But he didn't. After ten minutes of hysterical crying I sat up and took stock. Daisy's beautiful ballgown hanging on the back of the wardrobe door didn't help. I started feeling sorry for myself and cried all over again. Still no Jonty. I reached for my diary.

Thursday afternoon
I really have blown it this time. Just when Jonty and I were really getting the hang of being boyfriend and girlfriend, just when he could make me go weak at the knees with a glance – I have to go and ruin everything by blowing my top and being rude and ungracious.

Well, it's all their stupid fault. They don't understand any-thing normal. How can they kill foxes and shoot beautiful birds for sport? I hate them and everything they stand for. Sorry, Jonty, but that's the way it is. What am I doing here anyway? And how dare they offer me a ball – a BALL for God's sake, and put me and my family to all the trouble of finding a ballgown – and then just withdraw the offer? Where do they get off? The unbelievable arrogance!

I sat for a few moments and gazed out of the window at the beautiful grounds bathed in afternoon sunlight. It must be about four. The barbecue had started quite late. The trees outside my window rustled in the breeze and leaf shadow patterns danced on my floor. It was soothing. I opened the window wider and leant out. The Hayters were all round the corner – I could hear talking but no words. Late summer scents of cut corn and distant bonfires drifted in.

I felt cut off. Cut off from my own familiar world of London streets and privet hedges and the lido, our strip of London garden, litter, booming cars . . . I thought about

Mum and Dad and Abby, and the tears came to my eyes again. I was homesick, goddammit!

I've just discovered homesickness! And naming it makes it feel a little less bad, though I'd give anything to be beamed back home right away and not have to face any Hayters ever again. Even Jonty seems like someone who happened in a dream. As it is, I suppose I'll have to apologise. Ask if I can use a phone to get Mum or Dad to come and fetch me. I'm sure the H's will all be glad to see the back of me.

Wallowing in self-pity, I lay back on the bed again. Exhausted, I fell asleep.

EIGHT

There was a tap on my door. I heard it through my dreams. There it was again, louder.

'Holly? Holly, can I come in? It's me, Jonty.'

'Hnnurfokay.'

The sun had moved round and my room was dim. 'I came to say that I've got to leave now. And Hol, I'm really sorry. You just don't get on to the subject of hunting with my family. I should have warned you.'

Of course, Dilly already had warned me. I sat up. Jonty was wearing a tuxedo. He looked fabulous. I was speechless. He leant over me. He smelt freshly showered and – fabulous. He bent to kiss me, tipped up my chin and looked into my eyes. 'Am I forgiven?'

But before I could pull him to me there was a rude beep from outside. 'Have to go – sorry. Flavia's driving all of us over to the Hiltons. Jill will come and pick you up in about half an hour to take you over to Granny's. As I said, you'll have a better evening than me. Bye! Must fly! Princess Tamara awaits!'

He shouldn't have said that. It conjured up a picture of skinny Tamara in a ballgown lying back rapturously and waiting for *my* Jont. Just when I was beginning to think I could forgive at least *him* amongst the hated Hayters.

Jonty was gone. They were all gone. And Jill was going to take me to see a strange grandmother I'd never even met. She was bound to be just as bad as the rest of them. A woman who could terrorise Tuscany.

I went into my bathroom for the quickest of showers, appreciating the luxury all the more since I was leaving as soon as possible. I changed again into jeans and a clean top. I pulled my grubby old hair back into a ponytail and then remembered the marks on my neck and thought better of it.

I could hear the doorbell jangling in the distance. There was a key in the lock and then Jill calling, 'Holly? Are you ready to come to Dorothy's? She's expecting us.'

I ran along the corridor and down the stairs to Jill. I didn't want *her* thinking I had no manners. 'Thank you for picking me up.'

'No problem! I had to fetch some things for Dorothy anyway. Are you all right? Christopher said he thought you'd been upset. I know it's hard, Holly, but don't let these wonderfully archaic people get you down. Accept them for the marvellous eccentrics they are. It's not always the values that count – families like the Clermont-Hayters can't really help those. But your Jonty and his mum are both generous and warm people. Gina's my friend. She wouldn't want to upset you.'

We got into her car, a tatty Deux Chevaux. A large potted plant took up the whole of the back seat.

'I feel a bit awkward about spending the evening with an old lady I don't know,' I said.

'Treat it as an experience,' said Jill, smiling. 'Believe me, an evening with Dorothy won't be a hardship. I'll call by again during the evening, and if you're fed up you can either come back with me and the boys or I'll drop you back at the Chase.' We had arrived.

Granny/Dorothy's house was like one of the follies. I hadn't seen it on my tour of the grounds because it was so hidden away. Jill drove into the drive and together we went up to the deep pink front door, Jill clutching the pot plant. The door opened as we approached and an elegant, white-haired, suntanned, upright elderly lady greeted us. She was obviously Gina's mother, but less horsy to look at.

'Come in, come in both of you. I've laid the table on the veranda and the antipasto and the wine are all waiting for us. I hope you'll have a glass of wine with us Holly. A little never did anybody any harm, did it Jill?'

'Thank you,' I said and followed the two of them through Dorothy's extraordinary house. Several surprisingly big rooms were connected with little flights of stairs up and down. The walls were white and hung with huge, strange paintings of pink hills, some with little reddish towers on them, others with strange brown or black forests and peculiar little lakes and caves. I'd never seen anything like them before. They were strikingly beautiful. I stopped in front of a pinky-brown landscape with deep clefts and valleys and a golden-brown thicket of trees.

'She's a genius, isn't she?' said Dorothy. 'Dear old Brian can't cope with them in the Chase, so I have the ones Gina's bought as well – not that I mind.'

A flush crept up my neck. *Feminist paintings*. These were Jill's paintings. And they weren't landscapes – as such. They were nudes. Thank goodness I hadn't said anything.

'We'll talk about my Tuscan buyers later, Jill,' said Dorothy. 'Suffice to say that I know I've got definite commitment on at least four of them. Your Christopher's wheeze of putting them on the website worked. Now they can't wait to come and see them. Isn't technology wonderful – don't you think, Holly? And now all you young people have the Internet at school, don't you?'

'Yes, Dad lets me use it on his computer for my homework,' I said. 'We want to get a scanner too. I'd never thought of selling art that way. I suppose it makes sense.'

'With an international star like Jill here, yes.'

'Don't make me blush,' said Jill, blushing. 'I don't think I'd be relying on yours and Gina's kind patronage if I was really an international star. But it's nice to know that everything's in place if I suddenly become one. I can't quite imagine it somehow.'

'No such word as "can't", Jill,' said Dorothy. (Just as Dilly had predicted!) We were out on the veranda which ran along the back of the house. It looked out over the garden. There was an outdoor table laid with little dishes of Italian food, three wineglasses and a bottle of wine.

'Just these little bits for me, Dorothy,' said Jill. 'I have to get back to the boys in a minute.'

'Good,' said Dorothy with a smile. 'Then I can have Holly all to myself. And there'll be all the more pasta for us. It's fresh, you know, Holly. I bought it in Italy this morning. Isn't that incredible?'

I sat down and helped myself to olives, which I *love*, three different sorts. It all seemed very sophisticated. Dorothy poured a little wine into my glass. She lit nightlights in

a couple of lanterns. It was lovely. Jonty was right. I was
having a nice time. I kind of hoped he *wasn't*. Jill drained
her glass of wine, crammed a couple more artichoke hearts
into her mouth and stood up. 'OK, I'm off. I have to go and
get supper but I'll call by later, Holly. Bye! See you!' And I
was on my own with Dorothy.

'I'll just go and put the pasta on, dear,' said Dorothy. 'It's
fresh, so it will only take three minutes. You sit back and
enjoy the garden. Have a little more wine if you want, but I
don't want Gina accusing me of getting you drunk. I have
the same arrangement with Cordelia.'

I sat back and relaxed. Wow. Dorothy was something
else. Some granny! I liked the way she treated me like a
grown-up, a bit like Gina in a way (except I'd blown it with
Gina, hadn't I?), as if she didn't know how to be a motherly
– or grandmotherly – sort of person. The garden was quiet
and gorgeous. The sun was setting. It was all rather romantic. The perfect setting for a fuchsia pink ballgown in fact. I
was just starting to feel *bitter* again when Dorothy returned
with a dish of pasta and a bowl of salad.

She put them down on the table between us. 'There
we are dear. Pasta (she pronounced it "parsta") and pesto
straight from Tuscany. And salad from Jill's garden. What
could be nicer?' She started to serve it out.

I was about to say 'Nothing could be nicer,' but it kind of
stuck in my throat. We ate.

'I like to eat early,' said Dorothy. 'Then there's a lot of
evening left. Evening is the best time of day for me. Evenings should be devoted to relaxation and pleasure!' She sat
back and drank her wine. Then she regarded me over the
rim of her wineglass. 'I think you're not speaking your
mind Holly. You can, you know. I have an inkling that all
is not well.'

(Yeah – that I've been hideously rude and ungracious to my hosts.)

'Have you ever stayed away from home before?'

I thought. 'I've been on school trips. And I've stayed with friends. But mostly I've been away with my family.'

'And you go to a day school, I gather.'

'I would hate to go to boarding-school.'

'Would you? I adored it. Still, no one should have to live away from home until they're ready. There's a time for everything. But I think it's good to stay with another family once in a while – if only to reassure you that yours is the best.'

'I – I wouldn't say that.' I didn't want to be cornered into saying anything bad about the Hayters. Not by their grand-mother!

'Of course they are, dear. Everybody's family is the best. And so it should be! Now, Jill left me a summer pudding. Would you be an angel and fetch it from the kitchen? Everything's there on a tray.'

The kitchen was painted in mellow Tuscan colours (I imagined) – deep blue and rose – and mercifully free of Jill's paintings. I carried the tray into the garden. 'I like your kitchen, Dorothy. It feels Italian.'

'It's meant to. Some of my house doubles as an art gallery, but not the kitchen! I don't cook – not worth it for one. But I eat like they do on the continent. Simple food, best qual-ity ingredients. And of course I can knock up pasta and salad like the best of them. More than can be said for my daughter, but she hasn't had the freedom I've enjoyed.'

We ate the summer pudding with thick cream. It was divine. When we'd finished Dorothy made a little pot of espresso and brought it out on to the veranda. She sat down and looked at her watch. 'There. It's only seven-thirty and we have the whole evening ahead of us.' She sighed with pleasure but I couldn't think of anything to say. I couldn't forget the ballgown on the back of the door and Jonty in his evening gear dancing the night away with Tamara.

Dorothy looked over at me. She said tentatively – 'So that silly granddaughter of mine gave the Hilton girl your ticket for the ball, did she?' (Obviously she knew the whole story.)

'Well, the Hiltons are her friends. Jonty said I wasn't missing anything.'

'All very well for him!' said Dorothy. 'Were you looking forward to it *very* much, dear?'

'It's just that I've never been to one before. And we had to go to a lot of trouble to borrow a ballgown, you see. We were going to try and make me one, but there wasn't time.'

'Oh goodness. What a mercy you didn't!'

'Never mind. I *can't* go and that's that.'

Oops. I'd said the magic word. The word that couldn't fail to trigger Dorothy into action.

'*Can't?*' She scraped back her chair and stood up. 'There's no such word! You *shall* go to the ball, if that's what you want! I'd *love* to play fairy godmother.'

'I – I—' Oh blimey. What was she planning? She was drumming her fingers on the table.

'Now, let me think. It's the polo club, isn't it? Goodness, that's just old Felicity doo-dah. I can speak to her. She won't actually go to the ball until it's over, when her Freddie makes the speeches. Hmmm. What's her number?'

'Please, Dorothy – I – I mean Jonty's there with Tamara now. I wouldn't have a partner. And he might not want me there.'

'Nonsense. Anyway, I've thought of that. There's Christopher. It's high time he did something other than play tennis. Pass me my mobile, would you dear?' Aagh. Poor Christopher.

I passed it to her reluctantly. I felt both gloomy and excited, if that's possible. I was almost positive this was going to be a fiasco.

'Jill? Dorothy. Poor Holly feels like Cinderella here, and I thought I'd play fairy godmother. What's Chris doing tonight? He'd be up for a ball, wouldn't he? Has he got the outfit? I've still got Charlie's here, somewhere. Could you pick up Holly's dress? Oh, all right – you come here, pick up Holly and the penguin suit for Christopher, take them both to the Chase to change and then drive them on. That's fine. I'll phone Felicity now.'

I couldn't bear to listen. 'Just going to the loo,' I mouthed, and tiptoed indoors, under the gaze – or whatever – of Jill's nudes, to find one. I already had a nervous stomach-ache. I sat on the loo and thought. I had the dress. Shoes weren't too good. Trainers, some Birkenstock-style sandals and another pair of flat sandals from Greece. They'd have to do. I needed to do something about my armpits (major problem with dark hair). They were a bit stubbly for a fancy frock. My legs were OK. Would there be time to wash my hair? I looked at my watch. It was 7.45 already. Probably not. Jill had to get here and *then* drive us to the Chase and *then* we had to change and *then* drive over – we wouldn't be there before nine even if we hurried. I finished and wandered back to Dorothy, still thinking. What about jewellery? What about my hair? I should have had all afternoon to prepare for this, dammit.

Dorothy greeted me with a smile. 'That's all settled then. There will be a pair of tickets with your names on, waiting at the entrance. Just help me carry our plates into the kitchen and Jill will be here before we know.'

She was right. Jill arrived in no time at all. Christopher was with her and so was Toby. Christopher was silent as usual and white as a sheet. He wouldn't look at me. Toby was the opposite. 'It's me you should have asked, Holly. I'm a wicked dancer. Christopher can't dance to save his life.'

'Shut up, Toby,' said Jill. 'Course he can, Holly. Very light on his toes is our Chris.' Christopher's face was like thunder. He was clearly deeply embarrassed. Oooh, this was getting awful. I could have enjoyed a nice quiet evening with Dorothy, watched a bit of TV and then gone back to the Chase to bed. But no. I had to go and open my big mouth. I just had to let on that I was miffed.

'Run up to Charlie's old room, Christopher,' said Dorothy. 'It's all right, it's not haunted – Charlie is happily playing on that golf course in the sky, dear. Look in the closet and you'll see the DJ straight away. There's a bow tie there and a cummerbund too.'

Christopher couldn't escape quickly enough. 'But I'm not sure about a shirt,' Dorothy muttered.

'Never mind,' said Jill, 'I'm sure we can nick one of Jonty's at the Chase.'

'My dear!' Dorothy pretended to be shocked.

Christopher came down with the suit over his arm. It was still wrapped in polythene from the dry cleaner's. 'I had everything cleaned before giving it to Oxfam,' said Dorothy (I didn't think the Hayters had heard of Oxfam). 'But then I couldn't bring myself to give some things away. Jonathan might grow into them one day. Or you, Christopher! I think that suit will fit you perfectly. Just try the jacket on, do, before you go off. For my sake.'

Still silent, Christopher slid the jacket out from under the polythene. It was a very posh one. He put it on over his

T-shirt. Dorothy was right, it fitted beautifully round his shoulders and back. Hmmm. He looked *rather* tasty in it – apart from the scowl!

'Wow,' said Jill. 'Very dashing, Chris. We should dress you up more often. You were pretty as a girl when you were little – and I always encouraged you to wear bright colours – but you don't half look good in a suit!'

'You'd better get a move on,' said Dorothy. She was clearly loving this. 'I'm afraid I'm too tired after travelling and I've drunk too many glasses of wine to follow later, but I shall want to hear all about it, Holly. Now run along and enjoy yourselves.'

'Thank you so much for making it possible, Dorothy,' I said, beginning to wish she hadn't.

'Glad to be able to wave my magic wand,' said Dorothy. 'And thank you for keeping me company. I'll try and hang on to you for a little longer next time!' She waved us off.

Christopher kept his head down and went to sit in the front seat of their car, leaving me to scramble into the back with Toby. 'That's not very polite to Holly,' said Jill, but Christopher was past caring. Oh great.

We skidded over the gravel and piled out of the Citroën. 'Use the downstairs shower room, Chris, like you usually do,' said Jill. 'Can you be ready in ten minutes, Holly? I know it's a lot to ask of a girl, but we don't want to turn up there just as it's winding down.' I set off up the stairs. 'Come on Tobes. Grab a Coke if you want and we'll watch TV.'

I shut the door of my room behind me and sat on the bed to gather my thoughts. The dress hung invitingly on the wardrobe door. I tried to convince myself that the evening ahead could be fun. It would be if Christopher cheered up – and if Jonty was OK about us turning up and if the other

Hayters didn't spoil it in some way. Not much to ask, really. Huh!

I went into the bathroom and stripped off. I tipped my head up and brushed my hair vigorously. I sprayed it with Happy. I held it up on top of my head and then saw the state of my neck. I'd have to wear it down. So I made a few little plaits – I could tie them back to look pretty. I had the quickest of showers and then stood in front of the mirror over the basin to attack my armpits. The razor had seen better days. Ouch. Damn. Blood everywhere. I didn't have another one. Jonty would have one. We were the only people in the house and I was the only one upstairs so I boldly wrapped my towel round me and went down the corridor to Jonty's room. He didn't have a whole bathroom like mine, but he did have his own washbasin and he did shave – sometimes. I went in. His wardrobe was open and the whole room was a mess of PlayStation stuff and plastic aeroplanes and computer magazines. There was a photo of us together in Barbados by his bed. I was tempted to root around a bit with him not there, but a razor was the thing. Ha! And there was a whole packet of disposable ones above the basin. And some proper shaving cream. I decided to have another go at my armpits then and there. I tucked the towel firmly round me, ran a basin of hot water, squidged out some shaving cream and tried not to cut myself any more. Ouch again. My armpit was spurting blood. I lifted my arm and leant right towards the mirror to inspect the damage, tongue caught between my teeth in concentration. And then, in the mirror, I saw someone come in. Oh my God. It was Christopher. But he didn't rush out again. He froze. Of all the times to choose.

'I was looking for a shirt,' he said lamely.

'Obviously,' I said, since he was wearing the whole outfit

(apart from the DJ), including braces, bow tie dangling round his neck, and cummerbund, without one. 'Carry on. Don't mind me,' I said, also lamely.

Then he looked at me properly – me in a shower cap, neck dotted with purple marks turning green, wrapped in a bath towel, froth and blood oozing out from under my arms. 'Ooh, you're bleeding,' he said.

'Cut myself shaving.' I tried to catch his eye.

And then, he pointed to his chin. 'So've I!' he said, and quite unexpectedly gave a loud hoot of laughter. 'Bloody useless at being posh, aren't we Holly!' He sat down on Jonty's bed in his shirtless outfit and laughed until the tears ran down his cheeks.

I wanted to be cross and say 'Less of the "we"; you speak for yourself!' but he was so hysterical with giggles I couldn't bring myself to. I sat down next to him and laughed too. Then I asked, 'Why was it you came in? Other than to spy on a lady at her toilet, that is?'

'*Toilette*!' he was still chortling. 'A lady at her *toilette* if we're being *poshe*. I didn't reckon on finding you in Jont's room. I was looking for a shirt, as I said.' This was more words than he'd spoken to me the whole time I'd been here. It was more of a transformation scene than any in Cinderella. And then he carried on! 'This outfit hasn't got one – as you can see – and I need a nice white shirt, preferably with pleats and frills, to go with the bow tie and cummerbund. Honestly Holly, I think all this dressing up stuff is complete pants—'

'Oooh, paa-ants!' I said in a silly voice. I stood up. 'Now stop moaning, Chris. Granny Dorothy has ordained that I shall go to the ball and you can't duck out of taking me. So let's find a shirt.'

Well, we looked through all Jonty's wardrobe and then

through his drawers, but not a white shirt was there to be found. Then Christopher pounced on one that Jonty had bought in Barbados. It was a 'tropical' shirt, red, covered in yellow bananas. 'Banana!' I yelled. Christopher looked at me blankly. 'Sorry. Silly game we played in Barbados. Every time you see a banana you shout "Banana".' I trailed off.

'Obviously you had to be there,' said Christopher. And then, 'I like you calling me Chris. Not many people here do.' He held up the shirt and gave an evil grin. 'I'm going to wear this. Let's see how many people say something.'

I wasn't sure. What about me in my fuchsia silk ball-gown? Did I want to be with someone in a tropical shirt with bananas on it? Chris was putting it on. 'Help me with the bow tie,' he said. 'It's got a clip at the back.'

'Sit down, then. You're far too tall for me to reach. There.' I clipped it on. He stood up for me to admire the effect. Actually, his tennis-player's body would have looked good in anything, I realised. Yup, it looked good in the gear, even the silly shirt. 'Try it with the DJ.'

There was a clattering of claws along the corridor. The three spaniels had come to look for us, followed by Jill's voice. 'I hope you two are ready. We should have left five minutes ago. Do either of you need a hand?'

'We're fine, Mum. Down in a minute. Go and get your dress on, Holly. I'll wait outside your door and keep Mum posted.'

I scuttled along the corridor. I didn't really want Jill, or Toby for that matter, knowing that I'd been consorting with Christopher dressed only in a bath towel. I whizzed under the shower again, put on some underwear and the Greek sandals and stepped into the dress. Fabuloso! I felt pretty princessy, I can tell you. I couldn't do it up but I whacked on some make-up and a little necklace and earrings Josie had bought me in Camden Market. I looked in the mirror. My hair fell satisfactorily over my neck and the little plaits looked partyish enough, except that I only had a towelling hair thing to tie them with. The dress would look great when it was properly zipped up. Oops, no it wouldn't. I couldn't possibly wear it with a bra. Bra off – please don't come in Christopher. Dress on again. Jewellery looked nice against my tan. All in all, not bad for a first ball. I had a sudden repeat lurch of homesickness. Dad should have been waiting out there with his camera ready to take the 'Holl-doll's first ball' piccy for the album. Concentrate Holly. I tried to do the zip up. I struggled but I just couldn't do the last couple of inches.

'Come on!' Jill's voice.

A knock on the door. 'Are you ready Holly?'

Damn. I opened the door. Chris was loitering there. 'Chris? I'm going to have to ask you to do me up. Cliché and all that, but I just can't do it myself.'

'That's cool,' he said. 'No problem. *Ni probleme*. Turn round.' And then he giggled again. I stood there waiting for him to finish the zip, feeling exposed. He did it up – there was a little pause and then I felt his fingers gently touch my back. Just once. Nothing more. 'There, all done. Wow! That's quite a dress!'

I sensed a hesitation in his voice. 'It is OK isn't it? I mean, it's a ballgown for a ball, isn't it?'

'You look great,' he said, ever so slightly non-committally. We went down the stairs together. There I was *walking down the stairs* of a stately home in a gorgeous ballgown! What a photo-opportunity. Jill and Toby emerged to watch our entrance.

'Wicked!' said Toby.

'I say,' said Jill. 'That's some dress!' She suddenly plucked a few flowers from one of her arrangements. They were exactly the same colour as the silk. 'Corn cockles,' she said. 'No one will miss them. I'll tuck a few into your hair-band. There, gorgeous.' She suddenly clocked Chris's shirt. 'Christopher! You're not sending the whole thing up, are you? This is a formal ball – and you know what old Felicity do-dah and her polo club are like.'

'All I could find, Mum.' Chris gave a shrug and a smile.

'At least you've cheered up.'

'I think it's cool,' said Toby. 'Wish I was going. I'd wear a – a wetsuit or something.'

'That's not the attitude at all. Come on, let's at least get there before it ends.'

Well, what a turnaround. Silent old Chris laughing and being friendly. He wasn't lovesick at all – was he? This time Chris let me sit in the front, but I could feel his eyes on my bare back the whole way there.

NINE

Jill dropped us outside the gates. The venue was the Pump Rooms in one of the small towns. It was all very Georgian and Jane Austen. I wish we'd arrived in a carriage and been greeted by torch-carrying footmen, but never mind. Jill shoved us out of the Deux Chevaux on to the street. 'Back at midnight,' she said, laughing. 'They always end very promptly here – caretaker's an ogre. Have fun!' We were on our own.

This was weird. Jonty was in there somewhere, with all the other Hayters plus Tamara. He didn't know I was coming. I was with Christopher. Christopher, who was, Jonty thought, in love with me. Chris who had suddenly untied his tongue. I remembered Dilly's letter – '*Promise me you won't mess with Chris.*' I wasn't, was I? I looked sideways at him. He was shooting his cuffs and wriggling his neck and chin the way blokes do to accommodate the collar and bow tie. He looked nervous and – well, pretty gorgeous really. Why hadn't I noticed before? Was it because I'd seen him laugh for the first time? Or because he'd sided with me – '*We're* no good at being posh'? He didn't seem fazed by seeing me half-dressed. I guess Jill made sure he had a good attitude to women.

Boy, was I confused. My instinct was to take his arm. But Jonty was in there. *My* Jonty. Christopher nodded to me and gestured the way forward with a wave of his hand. 'Shall we?' he said, and crooked his arm for me to take.

But then he spoilt it by saying, 'I'm gonna go in there and get *smashed.*'

'Christopher!'

'Well, what else am I supposed to do? Jont's going to come and take you away – and I'll have two and a half hours until Mum comes to pick us up. The wine is allegedly horrible, but free. I haven't got a tennis match tomorrow.'

'Chris!' We were just outside the entrance.

He turned to me and put his hand over the arm I had tucked into his. 'Yes?'

'I – Perhaps it won't be like that. Jonty's with Tamara.'

'Oh great. So I get to *act* the boyfriend?'

'No – I just meant – Maybe everyone dances with different partners?'

'It's not a school dance, Holly. Jonty's told me the score. You either go with your girlfriend and snog the entire time or you go on the pull. At least, the girls try to and the boys mostly go on the booze. So what's new? It's the same with the toffs as with anyone else.'

We were in. A woman sat at a table. 'Yes?' she said. 'And who are you?'

'You're holding tickets for Miss Holly Davies and Mr Christopher Green,' said Chris.

'Oh, yah,' said the woman, opening an envelope. She fished out the tickets and handed them to a man who looked like a bouncer. We followed him up some steps to a pair of double doors. He threw them open with a flourish. 'Miss Holly Davies and Mr Christopher Green,' he announced – to a room empty except for a skinny figure sprawled in a chair at the back who looked exceptionally like Tamara in a slinky dress. She got up and came over to us where we stood by the doors.

'Oh my God,' she said, with unmistakable malice. 'A meringue. A magenta meringue. That is *so* two years ago!'

I flinched, visibly, I know. I wanted to turn and flee. Chris gripped my wrist protectively. 'Look at *me*, Tamara. You don't think *we* take a polo club bash so seriously, do you? Anyway, where is everyone?'

'Eating,' said Tamara. 'Disgusting. I ate some to please Mother, but I got rid of it. You'd better not let Jonty see you two together. He's been going on all evening about "I wonder what Holly's doing now?" ' (whingey voice). She sighed. 'I wish I hadn't come. I only did it so's I could wear my Donna Karan.'

'Where is Jonty?' I asked.

'Why should I know?'

'Because you came here with him as his partner,' I said, and had to add, 'making it impossible for him to bring me.'

Christopher tugged at my arm. 'She's a waste of space, Holly. Let's go and find the bar.'

'Suit yourselves,' said Tamara, and aimed herself in the direction of the loos. The dance was about to start again.

Without us noticing, the band had slipped back into their seats. They launched into something a bit smoochy. 'For you two alone!' called the bandleader.

'What, us?' I asked.

'There's no one else around,' said Christopher.

'OK, then. Come on,' I said, and pulled him into a waltzy sort of dance.

'OK,' said Chris. 'But just remember, you started it.'

He put his hand on my back, my bare, bra-less back, and interlaced the fingers of his other hand in mine. He pulled me in towards him, so my head was crushed against his banana-clad chest. I've never been taught this sort of dancing, but Christopher led, nudging my leg back with his. He could dance – Toby was lying. What's more, it was *incredibly* sexy. All this time, and I never realised ballroom dancing was sexy!

'Count!' said Chris. '*Back*, two, three. *Turn*, two, three. *Forward*, two, three. That's it! And again!'

Hey! I was dancing! I could do it! But it was Chris teaching me, not Jonty. And it should have been Jonty. We were still the only two dancing, more or less the only two in the whole room. The band slowed the tempo down. I was getting the hang of it! I kind of forgot who Chris was and just got into the dancing, spinning round the floor in my silk ballgown. But then I was aware of his hand just stroking my back, ever so gently, his fingers reaching up into my hair. I risked peeping up at him. His eyes were shut.

The song came to an end. The room was filling up. We stopped. Christopher seemed to wake up with a jolt. 'Need

a drink,' he said gruffly. 'I'll look out for Jonty. See you!'
And he disappeared, leaving me in my 'magenta meringue'
in a room that was filling up with girls and women in long
slinky dresses, short cocktail dresses – strappy little *décolle-
tée* numbers, but not a traditional ballgown between them.
Oh dear.

I spotted Flavia and Gil. I tried a little wave, but they
blanked me. I saw Gina and Brian and ducked. I didn't
fancy talking to Gina right now. Chris wasn't coming
back, it seemed. Where was Jonty?

I pushed through the dancers towards the room Chris
had been heading for. There was a bunch of extremely
drunk looking teenagers, my age and a bit older, on seats
by the bar. Some of the girls were on the boys' laps – they
seemed to have forgotten that they weren't somewhere
private. A small group of lads had their backs to me.
Christopher was with them and they were all smoking
their heads off.

'Hey man, you look *so* cool,' one guy was saying to him.

'Yeah, in my shirt! Why didn't I think of that!' It was
Jonty speaking! He sounded uncharacteristically sarcastic.

'So where's your bird?' someone was asking Chris.

'Around, somewhere,' I heard him mumble.

'What about yours, Jont? What have you done with
her?'

'Dunno,' said Jonty. 'Don't care, stupid cow.' He sat leaning right over, his head hanging down. He was pretty far
gone. Was he talking about me? I stood on the fringe of
their circle. I'd known tonight was going to be a fiasco. But
this bad? Could it get any worse?

It could.

Chris went right up to Jonty. 'I hope you're not talking
about Holly,' he said.

'Why should you care?' said Jonty nastily. 'Oh yes, of course. You fancy her, don't you? Well, hands off, because she's *mine*.'

'So why d'you agree to bring Tamara tonight?' Chris's eyes were blazing. 'You knew Holly wanted to come.'

'Oh – *because*.' Jonty shook his head and took another drag on his cigarette. (He wasn't a very convincing smoker.) 'Sisters, you know. Anyway, Holly didn't mind.'

'She did,' said Chris. 'That's why I've brought her. Your grandmother set it all up.'

Jonty sat up. 'You *what*? Holly's *here*?'

I didn't know what to do. Jonty was wrecked, a mess. At least I wasn't the stupid cow. But Chris was in fighting form. 'Yes, she's here. And she's been dancing with me. You don't deserve her, Jont.'

The other guys were backing off. It looked as though Christopher and Jonty were spoiling for a fight. Over me.

I was paralysed. Should I go over to Jonty, my boyfriend? Up until an hour ago I hadn't felt anything at all for Chris – had barely exchanged a single word; now I felt we had a bond which I didn't want to betray. What's more, he was stone cold sober. Jonty wasn't.

But then Tamara returned. The dress was to die for, but her face looked terrible. She hadn't sussed out the situation at all. She went up to Jonty. 'I suppose, now *she's* here, you won't want to be with me any more.'

'Never did in the first place,' said Jonty. He *really* wasn't himself – one of the nice things about Jonty is that he'd never hurt anyone intentionally.

'You can at least give me a cigarette,' said Tamara.

'Help yourself,' said Jonty. Then he spotted me. 'Holly!' he said. 'My gorgeous Holly! You look so – so— '

'Ridiculous,' muttered Tamara.

' – pretty!' said Jonty. He started staggering towards me. 'I just want to—'

I stood frozen to the spot. Chris was beside me, his fists still bunched. Then he suddenly relaxed. He grabbed Jonty by the shoulders. 'Hey, man. Back off. You know what happens next, and you don't want to throw up on Holly.'

'Yes, yes. Sorry, I'm sorry, sorry man.' All the fight had gone out of Jonty and it was now as clear to me as it had been to Chris that he was about to be sick.

'Take him outside, Tamara,' said Chris. 'It's the least you can do.'

I wasn't so sure about this. 'But—'

'Trust me,' said Chris. 'Jont will throw up and then he'll have a nice little sleep and he won't remember anything about it.'

'But he's my boyfriend – I ought to look after him.'

'I think not. Just flatter yourself that he got into that state missing you. Anyway, Tamara's used to people throwing up.' Tamara was guiding Jonty out through the door. She hadn't fussed, despite the Donna Karan. Most of me didn't like it, but a part of me was glad to let her look after him. After all, she'd made him bring her.

I turned to Chris. 'This is a mess, isn't it? What is it people say about wishes? "Don't make them because they might just come true"?'

'Huh,' said Chris, and looked away.

It was foul where we were. Mostly dark and smoky with a few unpleasantly bright spotlights, and sticky underfoot. The people sitting around were oblivious to the rest of the ball. 'What shall we do now?' I asked.

'Well, we could go back in and dance, but I think it's wrinklies-time in there, judging by the music. Or we could grab some crisps and drink and go and sit outside. There are lawns out the back. It's still a nice evening.'

'OK.' (Well, what would *you* have done?) I found an exciting bottle of unopened fizzy mineral water and Chris spotted a whole new tube of Pringles that had rolled on to the floor. 'Lead the way,' I said.

We made our way back towards the dance hall, where French windows opened down the side to a terrace and then, lower down, a lawn. It had been made very pretty with strings of fairy lights and a few outdoor candles stuck into the ground. There weren't many people out there because there was nowhere much to sit. We headed for the steps that led down to the lawn. 'I don't want to dirty Daisy's dress,' I said.

'They had loads of paper napkins in there. I'll get you some.' Chris nipped back inside for a pile of them and made a little seat for me. 'Now you're going to say you're cold, aren't you?'

'Well, now you mention it . . .'

'Have my jacket – Charlie's jacket.' He peeled it off, revealing the banana shirt in its full glory. 'Comfortable?'

'Very.'

We sat in companionable silence for a while. It was almost dark. The flowers in the herbaceous borders glowed in the twilight and the stars were just appearing. My beautiful dress fell in silken folds round my feet. I began not to care that it wasn't quite the right sort of dress, I felt good in it again. I hoped Jonty was all right. I half wished I'd never come, but sitting here with Chris was OK – different, anyway.

'This is really weird, Chris. I can't believe we're sitting here *talking*. You've barely spoken a word to me all week – until tonight.'

'Ah, well, silence is good too, you know. We've just had a very pleasant silence.'

'You know what I mean. Why wouldn't you talk to me those first few days?'

'Oh, just shyness, I expect.'

'I always talk too *much* when I'm feeling shy.'

'Drop it, Holly. You know perfectly well why I was shy. Don't make me say it. I don't want to spoil things for you and Jonty.' He took a swig from the bottle of mineral water.

'I'm scared I've spoilt things for myself with all the Hayters. I was so rude to Gina earlier. I'm completely out of my depth with them, you know. Everything about them, all their – their assumptions – they're just coming from such a different place from me. I think I'm OK – professional parents, nice enough house, just been to Barbados – but they make me feel like – well, to use your word – pants. Completely insignificant.'

'You wanna talk about the Hayters? OK, we'll talk about the Hayters. But don't forget that Jonty is my mate. Dilly is my mate, and Gina and particularly Dorothy are my mum's mates. We don't come from the same place at all either, and I dare say our place is a good deal further away than yours, but you have to see things from other people's point of view. That's what Mum's always taught us.'

'Your mum's quite a lady, isn't she? I like her.'

'Mum's cool. She's brilliant at her work – if you like that sort of thing, but not at earning money.'

'What happened to your dad – do you mind me asking?'

'Ah, well, we don't see him. Mum left him when we were babies and he went to Australia. Mum's not that bothered about men. I mean she likes us, but she's an artist first and she doesn't want to have to look after a man or be bossed about by him.'

'You're very cool about it all.'

'Have to be. Anyway – that just happens to be how my family is. Mum doesn't embarrass us beyond the subject of her painting. But I'm proud of her. It would be so excellent if she got the recognition she deserves. That's partly where Gina and Dorothy come in. They buy Mum's paintings at prices they think they're worth. They both know about art and they think it will be worth a lot more one day. But they know it's not enough for Mum to bring us up on, so they pay her to do other things as well—'

'Like flower-arrangements and cooking?'

'Yeah. They're pretty good to us. "Philanthropic" is the word Mum uses.'

'And your mum doesn't mind?'

'Why should she? It means she can get on with what she wants to do. And they genuinely appreciate the other stuff she does for them. And she likes them. You've met Dorothy – she's great. She and Mum get on really well.'

'Wow. The people I met in Barbados made me feel boring. Now you do too.'

'Believe me, boring is good.'

'I've heard that somewhere before, too. Now I feel even more terrible about mouthing off at Gina. I know she's OK underneath. She was great yesterday when we went to Stratford. She's not like other mothers.'

'There's nothing to stop you apologising to her. Mum's very keen on apologising. She's always losing her rag with people and then ringing up the next day. She says people soon stop minding – and you can sometimes say what you really mean.'

'My mum and dad are the opposite. They always say, "Least said, soonest mended." Trouble is, I get so *angry* sometimes. Especially when I know I'm right.'

'If you ask me, you should probably be brave and apologise to Gina. She likes people speaking their minds. Brian's more – well, deadly dull really. Mum doesn't have a lot of time for him. And Flavia's just appalling. I think they've all given up on her. Don't know what Gil sees in her.'

'Money?'

'Holly! Hope that's not all you see in Jonty?'

'If I did, I'd hold it against him!'

'Wish you'd hold it against m—'

'Don't wish – it might come true.'

'Only joking.' There was another long pause. 'Holly?'

'Yes?'

'Can I tell you something? I'm not sure how to put it – you mustn't get me wrong.'

'What are you on about?'

'I want to tell you something.'

'Go on then.'

'OK. Deep breath. Hang on, I'll have another swig of water.' He tipped up the bottle. 'Right. Here goes.'

'As soon as I saw you, I felt something I'd never felt before. I just fancied you so much I didn't know what to do.'

'This *is* going to make things difficult, Chris—'

'No, hear me out. It was pure lust. Pure lust, Holly! Nothing sweet and innocent at all! Up until then I'd look at girls and wonder if I fancied them. I didn't fancy Flavia – who could, apart from Gil? I love Dilly and she loves me, but there's no chemistry between us. I thought there must be something wrong with me.'

'Dilly adores you,' I said.

'I know,' he said coolly.

'What about the rest of the world? Film stars, models, people on telly? School? *Loaded, FHM*? That's what all the boys in my class drool over. Surely you don't base everything on your experiences with the Hayter family, you sad person?'

'Course not. But you don't understand – these things run through my head the entire time. Especially with Dilly, you know. We're close. And I kind of thought things ought to happen, but they didn't.'

'Seems to me that she's more like a sister, anyway.'

'Maybe, but I'm trying to tell you something important Holly.'

'That you're a normal guy. Big deal.' I knew it was unfair of me, but I suppose I'd kind of been hoping for a declaration of undying love.

'It's more than that Holly, and you know it, but what's the point in making it worse if you're going out with Jonty? I could say, "Oh they're miserable upper-class twits, the lot of them. Forget him and go out with me." But I don't think that. Jont's my best mate. You're his girlfriend. Best friend's girlfriend – big no-no. End of story.'

'I love that film, don't you?' I said. 'I just love the ending when Louis Armstrong says "end of story"!' I waved my arms around, and the jacket slipped off my shoulders.

'End of story is *not* a concept I love, no.' He turned to me. 'Put the jacket back on, Holly. I might not be responsible for my actions if you expose your flesh to me any more tonight, I behaved very well in Jonty's room, didn't I?'

'I suppose you did. I assumed it was because the flesh on view was mixed up with shaving foam and blood – *very* seductive.'

'I'm used to all *that*. Mum's not a great one for shutting the bathroom door. See what I have to put up with? She doesn't want me putting women on a pedestal. Trouble is, she knows me too well. She knew straight away how I felt about you.'

'Mothers are like that.'

'Anyway, I meant when you asked me to do your zip up.'

I remembered the pause after he'd done it up and then the touch of his fingers, and I realised as if I'd seen it that he'd kissed them and planted the kiss on my back. 'OK, you behaved very well.'

Chris suddenly stood up. 'I think I'm going to find some alcohol.'

'You said that before.' I stood up too. This conversation had been so inconclusive. Was he trying to tell me that he was actually in love with me? What did it make me feel about Jonty? I didn't want to be left alone. There was no one near us. All the noise was coming from inside. It sounded as though someone was giving a speech. I wondered what the time was, but I didn't have my watch on. It must be nearly midnight. I reached tentatively for Chris's wrist and the jacket fell off again.

My hand touching his arm changed everything. It was like a flash of electricity. Chris turned on his heel and pulled me to him. He bent and kissed my shoulders and before I knew it he was kissing me on the mouth. Serious kissing, the sort I'd only just learnt with Jonty. But it came from me as much as from him. There was a burst of clapping from the hall (kind of appropriate), but a few seconds – or a few light years – later we heard voices coming down from the terrace towards us.

'You'd better not have lost it, Tamara.'

'Well you shouldn't have lent them, Bea, if you cared that much,' Tamara wailed. 'We were standing about there, where that couple are *eating* each other. Jonty made a pass at me and—'

'What's the matter? Do you know them or something?'

'Come on, Bea. You couldn't mistake *those* clothes, could you?'

TEN

Chris asked Jill to whizz me back to the Chase and let me in in the hope that I could simply creep upstairs to bed. He pretended I'd had too much of the vile wine. I left my sandals at the bottom of the stairs so they would know I was in and shot up to my room. I was terrified of meeting any of them, but I heard them all come in later, so that at least was lucky.

Diary, I needed my diary. I turned off the light in my bedroom and sat in the bathroom with just the shaving light on. I didn't want anyone thinking I was awake and knocking on my door.

Thursday night/Friday small hours
Aaaagh! Complicated day! Seems to have gone on for ever. I'll go through it bit by bit. Maybe find some sense in it all.

1. Woke up all excited about Daisy's ballgown (if only I'd known). Then Flavia, such a sweetheart, told me I wasn't invited and Jonty told me I'd have a better evening at his granny's. Kuh! (But how right he was!)

2. The dovecote interlude. Hmm. Possibly I'm becoming a bit of a slag in my old age. Anyway, I have to remember that it's great with Jonty. It's nice that he hasn't had a proper girlfriend before and I haven't had a boyfriend – we kind of make it up as we go along (hope no one reads this). Then we had to stop (probably a good thing) because Jonty remembered

3. the lunchtime barbecue. Saw Jill for the first time. She's amazing. The most alive woman I've ever met. Chris still silent at this point. (Perhaps it would have been better if he'd never opened his mouth – see later!)

4. The part I'd rather forget. See last entry. No excuses really. I acted like a four-year-old. I will have to apologise tomorrow. Think I know what to say now.

5. Dorothy, and Jill's paintings. Interesting. More later.

6. And then CHRIS. I don't know what I've done. Dilly told me not to mess with him, and I have. I kind of led him on. I think. And then we had this kiss that went on and on for ever and set off all sorts of fireworks inside me. I felt completely 'ravaged' (tho' I'm not quite sure what that means).

Right Holly. I have to get my head round this somehow. Tomorrow is Friday and then Saturday is my last day, assuming they don't send me home for bad behaviour! I need never see Chris again, though God knows, I want to. I could go home tomorrow and never see any of them again. I could sneak down and ring Mum and Dad now. But I know what they'd say.

Decision time.

Jonty will know by now that Bea and Tamara saw me with Chris, but I know he made a pass at Tamara. I do love Jonty, but compared with the effect Chris had on me – well, perhaps it's a bit mundane. Jonty and I could both say last night was all a terrible mistake and carry on where we left off. Or we could say it's not working, just try to be friends and have a nice last two days. I keep remembering Chris kissing me, and the way he held me. He was just so – passionate, I suppose. As if he'd really kept his feelings bottled up and they were all coming out.

I decided to sleep on it. It was tempting to ring the parents, but they would only tell me it's no use running away from problems.

*

When I woke up I knew that the first thing I had to get off my chest was apologising to Gina. I'd been worrying about it all through the night. At seven o'clock I got up, showered and finally washed my hair. Then I dressed and waited by the door for sounds of people going downstairs. I heard Gina and Brian talking, gave them five minutes, took a deep breath and went down. Brian was eating cornflakes in the kitchen. Gina was standing by the kettle.

'Gina,' I came straight out with it. 'I got up early because I wanted to apologise for my behaviour yesterday. I was childish and ungrateful. I hope you'll forgive me.'

'Forget it,' said Gina, peremptorily. 'Cup of tea?'

'Thank you,' I said. I piled loads of sugar into it and quite enjoyed it.

'Granny enjoyed your company very much last night,' said Gina. 'You must see her again before you go. I gather she sent you to the ball?'

'Yes. It was very kind of her.'

'Silly of me not to realise you'd mind. I should have stepped in and not been browbeaten by the terrible Hilton woman.' (Now she was apologising to *me*!) 'I feel rather sorry for poor old Tamara though. Little vixen, but you know she has an eating disorder? And so young.'

'Her mother does seem rather obsessed with food.'

'Exactly. And appearances. And money. He's in business, of course, and hardly ever there.'

Brian looked up, smiling. It seemed he'd forgiven me too. 'Now, now chicken,' he said to Gina. (*Chicken?*) 'Old money you might be, but we all stoop to business these days.'

I didn't know what he was talking about.

'It's Gina's business talent that keeps this place going, you know,' he said proudly.

'I'm sure Holly's not interested, dear,' said Gina. She

turned to me again. 'Brian loves to wind me up. I expect Jonathan will be late this morning. I gather he hit the wine rather hard at the bash last night. Still, he has to learn.' (See what I mean about not being the usual motherly type? My parents would have gone ape.) 'I'm glad you're a sensible girl Holly.' (Little did she know.) 'I think he and Tamara have some more riding planned for you for this afternoon – followed by a swim, I dare say. It's a lovely morning. I'd go and sit outside if I was you. There's a pile of magazines in the lobby if you want.'

It seemed like a good idea. I picked up some magazines and took them into the gazebo. Huh! Gina isn't stupid. Well, I knew that, but she doesn't suggest things without a reason. The magazines were *Horse and Hound* and *Tatler* and *Country Life*. And every one of them contained articles on the pros and cons of hunting. I felt compelled to read them. And I learnt a lot. Now, I'll *never* approve of killing animals for sport, but I do see that a complete ban on it would change all sorts of aspects of country life, and not just the nice red jackets and steamy breath on the frosty air etc, etc. All the hounds would probably be put down. There would be no more point-to-points. The Pony Club, which is linked to the hunt, wouldn't be able to survive. Other game sports would also have to be banned. Including angling. And my dad *loves* fishing. Face it, Holly, you should have kept your big mouth shut. Oh well, at least I understand the issues better now. I tried to remember what Zoe had said in the school debate on the subject – I know she was all for banning it. Perhaps we should have another one.

I rubbed my arms that were suddenly goosepimply. That bright start to the day had been untrustworthy. Clouds were coming up round the horizon and the trees shivered in the breeze. I felt tired – like you do when you've got up too early. Yesterday had been a funny old day. I went in, putting my head round the kitchen door to tell Gina that I was going to write some letters in my room. She nodded at me over her newspaper. 'I certainly don't expect to see Jonathan or Flavia for a while,' she said. 'I'll tell Jonathan where to find you if he asks.'

'Thanks,' I said, all politeness now. I was grateful to Gina for letting so much water go under the bridge.

In my room I snuggled under the duvet with my diary and tried to marshal my thoughts again. I might have apologised to Gina, but I still had Jonty to sort out. And Chris. Tamara's whingey voice saying 'Jonty made a pass at me' . . . Do you know, I hadn't really registered that statement before – I'd been feeling so guilty about Chris. But now it hit me with its full force. Had Jonty *really* made a pass at Tamara? How *could* he? After our time in the dovecote. But then I'd got off with Chris hadn't I? Though that was different. No it wasn't. Yes it was – Tamara just wasn't fanciable. But then maybe Jonty would think the same about Chris. Nah. I couldn't believe Jonty would have made a pass at Tamara unless he'd been completely out of it. Ooh dear. He had been out of it. Probably, knowing Jonty, he'd just been nice to her. And she'd reckoned that was making a pass. Hmmm.

And I suppose Jonty *would* have been told about me and Chris. Bea. Flavia. Jonty. It was a short route, possibly taking in Gina and Brian along the way. I'd hated them all so much last night I hadn't cared. And I suppose Jill and Dorothy would know by now too. But then I remembered Jill's advice about seeing things from other people's point of view. Gina and Dorothy no doubt regarded adolescent antics from a distance. And what's a kiss at a dance, either way? OK, a lot from my point of view, but not from theirs.

Why is life so difficult? I couldn't really be bothered to write my diary. I'd agonised about most of this stuff last night. A little zizz seemed more appealing. So a little zizz it was.

There was a discreet knock on my door. 'Come in,' I said, swinging my legs over the side of the bed as if I hadn't been asleep. (Why do we always pretend we haven't been asleep? It's the same if I fall asleep babysitting. I always pretend to be wide awake when the parents come home.) It was Gina.

'We've just had a call from Judy Hilton, dear. Apparently Tamara's gone missing. She didn't say anything to you at the do, did she? No funny plans to go off with some boy or anything? I wouldn't want you to tell tales about your friend, but Judy is just a little worried. They think she might have been out all night. She left her mobile behind, which isn't like her.'

I rubbed my eyes, trying to take all this in. My friend? Some boy? There was me thinking they knew everything and hoping they didn't care, but they knew *nothing*! Less than nothing. And, in Judy Hilton's case, hardly seemed to care either. 'Just a little worried'? My parents would have been out of their *minds*!

'What does Jonty think?' I asked. 'I mean, he was with her last night more than I was.'

'Oh, was he dear? I rather thought I saw her trailing round after you and Christopher.'

That one moment. How easy to misread a situation. Then I had a thought. 'Didn't you say she and Jonty were planning a ride?'

'Yes, I did, didn't I? That must have been when we stopped off at Bury on the way.'

'Might she have gone out on her pony? With Jonty even?' I didn't really want to know the answer to this question.

'Not with Jonathan, no. He's still dead to the world. But I'll suggest they check the ponies. Now I come to think of it, she and Jonathan were talking about a ride through the forest. It's tricky in places and Jonathan was wondering if you'd be able to manage.'

Thanks, Jont.

'Can I do anything?' (Not that I was hugely keen to unearth Tamara, you understand.)

'No, no. You carry on with your letter-writing. I'll rouse Jonathan. High time he got up. Maybe he can shine some light on the situation.' She backed out of my room and shut the door, leaving me to my 'letter-writing'. (I'd forgotten about that.)

I got up and looked out of the window. The day had turned nasty. It was wet and unseasonably cold, as it can be when September isn't all that far away, I've noticed. Sharp little reminders that the autumn term starts in just over a week. Huh. No tennis for Chris today then. I suddenly thought of Alex and her tennis tournaments. Maybe Chris has already come across her or some of her ten billion brothers. Quite possibly, I suppose. Oh Chris, Chris. What did I feel about all that stuff last night? How would I feel in two days when I'd said goodbye to both Jonty and Chris?

I wondered if my relationship with Jonty was a bit one-sided. Had I fancied him more than he fancied me? Did I *like* him more than he liked me? A new and worrying thought, that, best tucked away. It really was vile outside. Not a day for a riding picnic.

As if my brain had conjured up the image for itself I

spotted Jonty striding across the wet drive in his riding gear plus a navy blue cagoule. I was going to yell down to him, but he looked very purposeful and the trees rustling in the wind made quite a racket to shout over. I wondered where he was going. Could this have anything to do with Tamara? Was he in fact striding purposefully after *Tamara*?

Rrrrrahrr! Diary. I needed to vent my spleen.

Friday morning
God I hate Tamara. Unfanciable, did I say? Unappealing, unattractive. Unlovable? *Too right she is! What can Jonty possibly see in that skinny little zip turned sideways? Blonde she may be, but her stupid face with her mouth always hanging open is witchy and ugly. No wonder people bully her. I would. And she thinks she's so great just because she lives in a big house and can ride a horse.*
Hate Hate Hate.

And I drew a little picture of her on the ground with pointy things sticking out of her and drops of blood.

There. That felt better. I decided not to hide in my room any more. Anyway I was thirsty. And I was just a teensy bit curious to find out what was going on.

Flavia and Bea were in the kitchen. They were making coffee and ignored me completely. I poured myself some orange juice from the fridge and sat down with the paper. They were tittering and joking about Tamara. 'Stupid kid!' said Flavia, with a snort.

'Drivelly attention-seeking as usual,' said Beatrice. 'Honestly, she'll try anything. Not eating. Eating and throwing up. I don't understand it. She gets whatever she wants. That dress last night cost over a thousand pounds.'

'Hah!' said Flavia. 'What a waste of money!' And they both cackled.

'Come over to mine,' said Bea. 'Mother's doing salmon for lunch because the Page-Joneses are coming over. She's furious already that Tamara isn't there, so she'll be really glad to see you.'

'Page-Joneses?' said Flavia.

'You know. Twin boys. Non-identical. Mother adores them.'

'Oh yah!' Flavia remembered. 'Bags the goodlooking one!'

They went off, still without acknowledging me. I could hear their conversation trailing into the distance. 'That's not fair,' Beatrice was saying. 'You've got Gil!'

I sat there for a while not quite knowing what to do. The older girls had left. Gina was working. Brian was doing whatever he did to fill the day – arranging to massacre another lot of defenceless wild animals probably. I wanted to see Jonty and make sure we were OK – still friends, that is, even if we had both transgressed – though now I wasn't sure any more how much he knew about me and Chris (or whether he had actually transgressed himself). I wanted to see Chris too, but I was scared. Best not to see him alone.

The telephone rang. I looked around stupidly for someone to answer it, and of course there was no one but me. I picked it up gingerly. 'Hello?' I said tentatively.

'Hol, it's me, Jonty.' He sounded out of breath. 'Look, I'm ringing from a phone box outside the Green Man pub. I've found Tamara's horse. But not Tamara. I think she might have had a fall. I need someone to help me look for her – on horseback. You can't get through the woods quickly on anything else. The ground's really slippery. Is Flavia there? Or Ma?'

'No,' I said. 'Flavia's gone to Bury with Beatrice. You could ring her there.'

'Damn,' said Jonty. 'My money's about to run out. You'll just have to get help Holly. Look – I'll – I'll— ' And the phone went dead.

Help? Me? I was on my own and I didn't know anyone's phone number. I couldn't even ride a horse properly. For some reason I remembered Maddy saying one of her friends had to find a lost child on holiday and how calm she'd been. Unlike me! Help! *I* needed help. All this for toffee-nosed Tamara. Use your *brain*, Holly.

Jonty was outside in the pouring rain by a pub called the Green Man, with two horses. Tamara was possibly lying in a ditch somewhere. (A very small, mean part of me rejoiced.) If Tamara was injured she'd need medical help. Aaaaah. What should I do?

Deep breath. I rang Directory Enquiries and got the number for the Hiltons at Bury. I rang them but amazingly I got the answer service. Could they really not be answering the phone because they were having a lunch party – with Tamara missing? Still, they didn't know she might be injured. They just thought she was seeking attention again.

To be honest, the next call I made was to Mum and Dad. I needed to hear their voices. I got Mum. 'Mum,' I wailed, before she had a chance to chat. 'You've got to help me. There's this girl who's gone missing and she's probably fallen off a horse and it's raining. I'm on my own but I've got to get help for her.' I told her about my call from Jonty.

'Calm down, sweetie,' said Mum in her gorgeous Scottish voice that I was missing like anything. 'You need to do 999 to alert the emergency services, and you need someone to go out to Jonty with a mobile phone. Surely there are plenty of mobile phones knocking around in that house?'

'I wouldn't know where to look, Mum. The girl who's hurt left hers at her house, but no one is answering there.'

'Is there anyone else you can ring? Friend? Housekeeper or something?'

'Of course, Mum. I was so flustered I couldn't think. I don't know where Mrs B. is today. But there's Granny. And there's Jill.'

'Jill sounds possibly more use than Granny.'

'You haven't met this granny. But you're right. I'll ring Jill. Except I don't know her surname or the name of her house. This is mad. I know. I'll ring Dorothy and then— '

'You've lost me, darling, but I think you should get on. Let me know what happens. Love you loads, byee.'

Directory Enquiries again. Dorothy Clermont, Clermont Lodge. Please don't let her be ex-directory. Amazingly she's not. I rang her.

'Hello dear. I'm resting up in bed today I'm afraid. All that travelling. Jill's number, you say? Of course dear, Jill Green, I know it off by heart. Here you are – I'll ask you about the ball another time.'

Great. Jill would know what to do. The phone rang a long time. Toby answered. 'Holly!' he said. 'What did you do to my brother last night? I— '

'Toby, this is a bit of an emergency. Is your mum in?'

'I thought you'd be wanting to talk to my brother not my mum.'

'Toby – Can I speak to Jill please?'

'No, you can't. She's not here. But *Chris* is. Shall I get him?'

'I suppose you'd better.'

'I could hear him calling, 'Chri-is! It's for you-ou! Guess who's on the phone!'

Then Chris. 'Holly!'

'Chris – there's a bit of an emergency. I need help.'

'What's up?'

I told him.

'I'll come over with my mobile. Jont's useless with his. If he hasn't left it behind he forgets to switch it on. Then we can go over to the stables. Tell you what, meet you over there in ten minutes. You know how to get there, don't you? Maybe one of the lads will be able to help, too. Call 999 and tell them we'll keep in touch. See you.'

I called 999 and spoke to a really nice guy. He said they did have a couple of doctors who rode, but if Tamara was badly injured she might need a helicopter. They were sending someone over to the Green Man. Jonty should have rung them first really. Still, he hadn't known he was going to get a wally like me, had he? Wally Holly.

Enough self-pity. I ran over to the stables, through all those wet nettles and muddier-than-ever molehills. My cross-country run got me there at the same time as Chris who'd ridden down the road on his bike. We were both very wet.

It was lunchtime and there were no lads about. 'I'll take Shakespeare,' said Chris, rooting around in the tack room. (Where were those lads? Nothing was locked. Lucky in some ways.) 'Do you want Gorse?'

'Chris – ' I should have foreseen this. 'I – couldn't ride one of those great—'

'Take the bike then,' said Chris, swinging himself up on to the huge dapple-grey. 'Follow me to the Green Man. Then perhaps you can station yourself in the telephone box or something.'

So I got on Chris's bike (large, with crossbar), and followed him out into the lane.

*

The pub was opposite a bridle path that led into the woods. It was only about fifteen minutes of hard cycling away. Luckily there wasn't much traffic on the roads. I felt very vulnerable following a horse on a bike, and visibility was lousy. An ambulance was already parked in the pub car park. We rode – in our various ways – up to it.

'You the lass that rang us?'

'Yes.'

'No one here seems to be able to tell us anything.'

'I can,' said Chris. 'I think I can piece things together. There's this clearing which we called Foxhole – in the middle of the wood where Jonty and I used to ride when we were a bit younger. It's a difficult ride, which made it kind of private. Jont and I once saw a fox hiding there as the hunt went by on the path above – they couldn't reach it.' The ambulance man coughed. He wanted Chris to get on with it. 'I think Jonty wanted to take Holly there today. Unfortunately – ' here he grinned at me and the ambulance man – 'Holly's riding skills aren't up to it. But Tamara's are. I suspect she knew that Jonty would have to come and find her there without Holly.'

'Bit of an attention-seeker then, this young Tamara?'

'I'll say,' I said.

'I'll go looking,' Chris said. 'Give me a number to ring when I've got something to report.'

'We've got chaps in there looking,' said the man. 'But they didn't have much to go on. Your mate must have gone back in with both the horses. Unfortunately it's so muddy you can't tell which are the fresh hoofmarks.'

'Perhaps he hoped Skippy would lead him to Tamara.'

'I think she really loves that pony,' I said, thinking perhaps it was the only living creature that might return the affection.

The three of us crossed the road. I was going to station myself in the phone box where I could see up and down the road, into the pub car park and into the woods. We all exchanged phone numbers. I had a pocketful of coins and I felt quite important all of a sudden. Chris went off into the woods. Before today I hadn't even known he could ride, but I suppose it shouldn't have been a surprise. The ambulance-man went back into the car park to await instructions.

I stood in the phone box for a while. I was cold and damp and the rain drummed on the roof. Twenty minutes later nothing had happened, but the clouds had lifted a little and the rain had practically stopped. I wandered outside as far as I dared from the phone box and gazed into the woods. They were dripping and full of birdsong, but no clues as to where Tamara, then Jonty and now Chris had disappeared.

There were two huge conker trees at the beginning of the path. (Even I can recognise a conker tree at this time of year.) One or two early conkers had fallen on the ground. I stamped on one, out of habit, just to see the lovely shiny brown conker inside. There it was. I picked it up and leant against the tree. Then I saw our clue! Carved into the bark – the vandal! It was fresh. Tamara 4 Jonty. Well, that was pretty unambiguous! Perhaps she'd seen *As You Like It* too! Quite romantic as well, I had to admit. Perhaps the silly girl had done it on other trees and left a trail.

I nipped back into the phone box and rang Chris's mobile. It took a few rings before he answered. 'Hi Chris! Any news?'

'Nothing. It's very wet and slippery. Poor old Shakespeare is having to work hard.'

'I've got a clue, Chris.'

'What's that? Hey – hang on! I've just seen Jonty! *Jo-ont!*'

he shrieked, deafening me on the end of the phone. 'Hol, I'll ring you back. I need two hands to gallop.'

I put the phone down. A few minutes later it rang. I grabbed it. 'Holly, hi. It's Jont.' He sounded flat and out of breath.

'No sign of her then?'

'Nope. Skippy doesn't seem to have a clue either. He just doesn't like rain and fluttering leaves much.'

'Are you going to your Foxhole place?'

'I think that's where she was heading, but she's not there, I've checked. Anyway, Chris said you had a "clue".'

'Well—' it was more embarrassing explaining it to Jonty. 'Just here at the entrance to the wood there's a tree with your and Tamara's names carved into it. I wondered if she'd left a sort of trail. Didn't realise the silly cow was that stuck on you.'

'Huh. Neither did I. And I think we'll have a bit of an embargo on nastiness about Tamara, Hol. She could be dead.'

Blimey. That made me feel terrible. 'Sorry,' I said in a small voice. 'Well, I hope the clue helps you to find her.' I put the phone down. Remorse was hitting me by the bucketload, even though she was horrible. I felt about two inches high. She tried to nick my boyfriend, dammit, why should I be all-forgiving? I slumped down on to the floor of the telephone box and waited.

About half an hour later there was a flurry of activity in the car park. A couple of police cars joined the ambulance and then they all drove away. A little later I could hear a helicopter circling. Perhaps they'd found her. I tried ringing Chris's mobile again, but all I got was a stupid woman telling me that the Vodaphone I was ringing was switched off. What was going on?

Half an hour after that I climbed on the bike and cycled back to Clermont Chase. There was still no one around. I went up to my room and had a long hot bath.

ELEVEN

I was warm and dry again at last. It was still pouring with rain outside, but I blow-dried my hair and put on a jersey for the first time this holiday. I was beginning to feel marooned in my room in an empty house yet again when I heard Flavia's Mini on the gravel and Jonty and her talking.

'She's even more stupid than Beatrice says she is,' Flavia was saying. 'Idiotic to do a dangerous ride on your own without telling anyone where you're going. One of the first things you learn in Pony Club. And then to leave your mobile behind!'

They went out of earshot before I could hear Jonty's reply, but I was inclined to agree with Flavia. That was a first.

I wasn't sure how I was going to deal with Jonty – for all sorts of reasons – but curiosity got the better of me. I thought I could at least offer to make them some tea and toast. I went down to the kitchen. Jonty and Flavia were both by the Aga with their backs to me. Flavia was in fact putting the kettle on and Jonty was stripping off his wet clothes and hanging them over the rail. He was down to his boxer shorts when I walked in. 'Hi!' I said, to anyone who cared to listen.

Flavia of course didn't respond, but Jonty said, somewhat discouragingly and still with his back to me, 'Oh, Holly. It's you.'

'Well?' I said. 'What's happened? Did you find Tamara?'

Jonty turned around. I felt quite scared of him, even in his boxers with wet hair. 'I'm surprised you're interested,' he said, not looking me in the eye.

I could see he was exhausted. Last night's antics probably got him off to a bad start anyway. It was awful not knowing how much he'd been told about me and Chris. What if Chris had blurted it all out while they were riding together? Though I suppose I'd be flattering myself to imagine that I was their main topic of conversation just then. 'I was trying to help you find her,' I reminded him. 'I wasn't squatting in a damp telephone box in the middle of nowhere just for a laugh, you know.'

'OK, sorry,' said Jonty.

'I only want to know what happened. To you and Chris as well.'

'Let me get some clothes on and I'll tell you,' he said. But he still wasn't looking me in the eye. That was a very bad sign indeed.

'I've just made tea, Jonathan,' said Flavia to his departing footsteps.

'I'll be back in a sec— ' his voice floated down.

Flavia banged some crockery on to the table. I fetched cutlery. 'Ruined their lunch do,' said Flavia, not exactly *to* me, but at me. 'You can imagine – phone call from the hospital. Page-Joneses decided to go home.'

'So she's all right? Tamara's OK?'

'Depends what you call OK. I imagine what you call OK and I call OK aren't quite the same.'

Oh, very helpful, Flavia. 'I only asked,' I retorted, petulantly. I picked up a knife and put it down again. I seemed to have spent a lot of time in this vast house feeling trapped. Fortunately Jonty came in soon after that.

'That's better,' he said. 'I feel a bit more human now.' He poured himself a cup of tea.

'Can I have one?' I asked, desperate not to appear stand-offish. He poured me one and I loaded the sugar in again. Stirring it gave me something to do.

'OK,' Jonty began. 'Well, as soon as Mum said Tamara had gone missing I knew she'd have gone to Foxhole. We were talking about it last night. I said I wanted to take you there and she asked if she could come. Thing is, it's too far to walk, and possibly too exciting a ride for you.'

'What do you mean?'

'Well – we hunt, so hedges and streams are all par for the course. I've done it for a couple of years now and Tamara's been once, though Chris and I discovered Foxhole when we were kids.'

'He told me. Anyway, never mind the whys and where-fores. Tell me about Tamara now.'

'OK. Well, she'd fallen off jumping a stream. You got it right about her leaving a trail of vandalised trees. We followed it and found her lying half in the water with her leg broken under her. We could see the bone sticking out. She kept passing out with pain. We called the ambulance people. They landed a helicopter as close as they could but it was still about a mile away. So they had to stretcher her to the helicopter and then airlift her to Birmingham. I'd left Skippy tied up so Chris and I had to ride Arnie and Shake-speare back to fetch him and then come back to the stables. The police wanted statements from us and then they drove us to the hospital.'

'The *police*?'

'Yes. The whole incident was pretty serious. They wanted background. All a bit embarrassing really.' He looked away. 'All that carving on trees. Somewhat unbalanced, our Tamara.'

'Yah!' said Flavia, her only contribution so far.

I found myself suppressing a smile. Oh, what had happened to Jonty's sense of humour. Wasn't it ever so slightly amusing, Tamara carving their initials on trees? Apparently not.

'I've never seen anyone in so much pain. We thought she was dead at first. She just looked like a bundle of bones, all muddy.'

'She is just a bundle of bones.' Jonty looked up at me fiercely. I cringed. 'I mean it. I – mean – I don't mean it unkindly. It's a fact.'

'It's all her own fault!' said Flavia. 'And if you're anorexic your bones are bound to snap more easily. Oh well. She's certainly got the attention she wanted now.'

I saw Jonty's thunderous expression and decided to keep my mouth shut. Flavia left the kitchen just as Gina was coming in.

'Any news on the Hilton girl?' she asked cheerily. 'Oh, and Jonathan, you know you said you'd ride over to Granny's this evening don't you?'

'They found her,' I said. 'Jonty and Chris found her in the woods.'

'Was she all right?'

'No,' said Jonty dully, as if he didn't want to have to go through the whole thing again. 'She was badly injured. She's in hospital now.'

'Well,' said Gina, 'all's well that ends well. Why don't you two go and watch TV or something while I do supper? We should eat early tonight if you're going to Granny's, Jonathan. I'll drive you over if it's too unpleasant outside.'

'Shall we go and watch TV then?' I asked shyly. It was as if I didn't really know Jonty any more.

'Might as well,' he said, and shouldered his way through the door ahead of me.

We sat down without even turning the TV on.

'Please talk to me, Jonty,' I said. 'I can't bear this. I know a lot has happened, but most of it isn't my fault. It all started to go wrong with tickets to the ball.'

'And you made such a fuss. I'm used to it with my sisters, but not you, Holly.'

'Well, I'm sorry. But it's not my fault your grandmother fixed it for me to go with Chris, either. I had nothing to do with that.'

'Nor did Chris, poor guy. He loathes that sort of thing.'

(Hmmm. What had Chris told him then?) 'It was all a fiasco, as you probably heard, not least me being over-dressed in a ballgown.'

He smiled then. 'You looked gorgeous. 'Fraid I was too far gone to do you justice. I don't remember much after I saw you. Exhausted from giving Tamara a good time.'

'Jonty! What do you mean by that?'

'Well, poor kid.'

'She's the same age as us.'

'Yeah, but you wouldn't think it, would you?' He shook his head. 'It's just that everybody's horrible to her and then she makes it worse. I just wanted to be nice to her, see if it made any difference.'

I felt angry all over again. 'So where do you get off on that, Jonty Hayter? Because you saw what happened. She fell crash bang wallop in love with you – and then she only goes and tries to top herself!'

'She wasn't trying to *kill* herself. It was the old attention thing again.'

'So why did you do it? Isn't it enough having me in love with you?'

'Are you?' He narrowed his eyes at me – at least he was looking me in the eye.

But I hesitated, didn't I. 'Jont – one of the things I – like – about you is the fact that you're so softhearted. But *her*! Why *her*?'

Now Jonty was cross again. 'You just don't get it, do you? You've met her mother and her sister. Her father isn't at home much, but she's bullied rotten at school. She told me some of the things the other girls do to her – not speaking to her for days, leaving her out of everything, hiding her underwear, her prep, her shoes. It's torture. And at home nobody listens to her either. They just spend money on her.'

'More than happens to me.'

'Holly! You know there's no comparison.'

I was stung. '*Anyway*,' I said, like a kid, 'you called her a stupid cow last night.'

'The less said about last night the better, I would have thought,' said Jonty coolly (my gorgeousness clearly a thing of the past), standing up in response to a shout from Gina. 'But she is a stupid cow – for not realising what she's doing to herself.'

I trailed after Jonty into the kitchen. I hated myself. I hated this whole place for what it was doing to me – making me so jealous, so unsympathetic, and such a traitor.

Supper was rather a silent affair. Brian was away overnight apparently, so we didn't have him complimenting the chef all the time. It was something rather elaborate from M&S. Flavia was reading. Jonty told Gina in a bit more detail about the events of the day. Gina was very matter-of-fact about it all. 'Mother like that, hardly surprising,' sort of thing.

Flavia left the table with, 'Well, she succeeded in ruining her mother's day – and Beatrice's for that matter.'

I didn't say anything apart from 'Would you mind passing me the salad,' and 'Yes please' and 'Thank you'. It was raining again. Gina offered Jonty a lift to Dorothy's and went upstairs to change her shoes before leaving. I waited in the hall with Jonty. Clearly I wasn't invited to Dorothy's with him, but nobody gave any explanation. I tried to think of something positive to say about Tamara. I didn't want Jonty thinking I was a total bitch.

'Perhaps,' I ventured, 'it's a good thing Tamara's in hospital—'

I was going to say, so they can sort out her bulimia, but Jonty didn't give me time to finish. 'Oh yeah, so you don't have to be bothered with her before you leave!' he snapped. 'I expect that kind of snidey crap from Flavia, Holly, but there was me thinking you were kind-natured as well as strong-minded. I was wrong, wasn't I?' We heard Gina coming down the stairs. 'We'll talk in the morning,' he said. 'Perhaps we should both sleep on it—' and he was gone.

Alone again. It was only seven o'clock. I thought of Dorothy and 'the whole evening ahead of us'. What sort of evening could I have? I certainly didn't want to spend it with Flavia. Or Gina. And I didn't particularly want to spend it with my diary again either. I sat in front of the TV for a bit. I like Friday-night TV – shows what a sad person I am. After a while I realised that I couldn't see the screen properly because the sun was reflected in it. I went to close the curtains and saw that the tattered clouds had pulled back on a spectacular evening. Everything was shining.

I had an idea. I went over to the phone in the corner of the room. (Phones in most rooms here.) After this morning I had the number of Chris's mobile off by heart. I dialled it. Uh-oh. 'The Vodaphone you have called is switched off . . .' Did I dare to ring the phone in his house? What if Jill answered? Perhaps I could offer to cycle Chris's bike back for him, since I had nothing else to do. That sounded normal didn't it? I fetched the number from where I'd pinned it by the kitchen phone and tried again.

Chris answered. Phew! 'Chris – could I come over? I'm on my own again – Jont's at Dorothy's – and I need to talk to someone.'

'Oh. OK then. I suppose. It's quite a long walk though.' He didn't sound that enthusiastic. 'Actually, you could do me a favour and cycle my bike back.' (He'd thought of it too.) 'It'll take you about twenty minutes. Mum's out collecting Toby, but I expect she could drive you home.'

'You sure?'

'Yes, why not.' (He was sounding keener now.) 'I'll tell you how to get here. Maybe you'd better write it down.'

I left a note saying that I was returning Chris's bike for him and that Jill would bring me back. I was kind of past caring what they all thought anyway, but I didn't think another runaway teenager was a good idea. I borrowed Jonty's cagoule from the rail on the Aga in case it rained again. I had to bounce the bike up and down a few times to shake the water off it. I swung my leg over the saddle, wobbled a bit and then set off, my backside instantly remembering the pain of it as I pedalled down the drive with Chris's instructions folded in the pocket of the cagoule.

It was a brilliant evening. The bike made a very satisfying

swishing noise along the wet road. The birds were all singing and the sky was full of jazzy pink and gold vapour trails.
It smelt fresh and rainwashed. I only met one car the whole
way there, and that was a little old lady driving very slowly,
thank goodness. The Greens' cottage stood alone. It fronted
the road but a path led round to the back. I wheeled the
bike round. No Deux Chevaux in sight. The cottage made
an L-shape with a long, low wooden barn – Jill's studio I
guessed. The outside walls were covered in climbing plants
and the garden itself contained nothing but vegetables and
herbs – and chickens. I could see lavender and marigolds
between the marrows and tomato plants. The fields beyond
stretched away to the west into a gentle valley. I leant the
bike against the wall.

I knocked on the cottage door. I could hear Chris making
his way downstairs. My heart was thumping in my chest. I
hadn't quite thought this venture through. There had been
so many unanswered questions and emotions flying around
when I'd last been alone with Chris. Not to mention that
kiss. I found myself remembering it as I stood there. The
taste of his mouth. Where was he? I knocked on the door
again and was surprised how quickly it opened.

'Did you knock before?' said Chris. 'I had some music on
and then I came downstairs where the tumble drier was
making a racket. Still,' he beamed, 'at least I've got some dry
clothes to wear.' He ducked outside the low front door and
stood facing me. He had bare feet under his loose jeans and
a top that had obviously just been pulled from the drier. I
could smell its warm, pleasantly synthetic scent from where
I stood. His hair was still damp from being washed and
towelled dry. I could see traces of the famous curls. And the
big dark eyes with the sunset shining in them. Orlando. I
did a naughty thing. I reached up and pulled his head down

to kiss me. I hadn't planned it. It was just that he was irresistible in that tousled state.

After a while he pulled back and wiped his mouth with the back of his hand. 'I don't think we should stand here. I don't know when Mum and Tobes will turn up. Come indoors.' I followed him into the cottage.

My first impression was that it smelt lovely – of beeswax and woodsmoke and flowers, with slight laundry and shower smells in the background. Chris turned, ducking again under the low lintel into a sitting room where a sofa covered in a Welsh blanket faced a log fire. 'Mum lit it when I came in soaked,' he said. 'Do you want to take that cagoule off indoors?'

I pulled it off over my head, trying not to take my T-shirt off with it. Mistake. I should have remembered Chris's re-actions to bare flesh. It was like the starter's gun had gone off. My arms were still tangled in the cagoule when he pulled it off for me and held me in a clinch before I could fight back – if I'd wanted to. We kind of subsided on to the sofa. This wasn't like cuddling up in front of the TV with Jonty. This was more like – a – match, a championship match. Huh, a love match. Jonty was laid back and casual, fluid and smooth, but Chris gave it all he'd got. Not that I was really comparing them, you understand. Our T-shirts were getting rucked up when Chris sat up suddenly and listened. I heard it too. Jill was back. 'Come into the kitchen,' he said. 'I'll make some coffee and tell Mum why you're here. You don't need to go back straight away do you?'

I laughed ruefully. 'I actually came here to talk, Chris. True to form, we've hardly spoken a word yet!'

He gave me a sort of smiling frown. 'And, of course, you brought my bike back. I just don't want Mum muscling in on you. I'll tell her I'm giving you a tour of the studio. She'll leave us alone then. She hates showing off her work. And I know Toby wants to watch something on TV.' He hauled me into the kitchen just before Jill and Toby came in the door.

'Ooh, I didn't know we were expecting company,' said Jill. 'Hello, Holly.'

'Holly brought my bike back,' said Chris. 'They've all deserted her at the Chase.'

'No manners, have they, these aristos,' said Jill, hanging up her coat. 'Only joking. I'd forgotten Dorothy was expecting Jonty tonight. She likes to have the kids on their own. She and Jonty play chess on Fridays when he's at home.'

'I thought I'd show Holly the studio while she's here.'

'Fine, fine,' said Jill. 'I haven't eaten yet, so I'll fix myself some food and perhaps we'll have coffee together later?'

Chris hustled me off. There was a way into the studio through a bolted door. The door rattled and squeaked back and we were faced with this huge barn area, the bare walls painted white and hung with more of Jill's paintings. I was struck again by how beautiful they were, but quite frankly, if you've just got off with a boy, you don't *really* want to find yourself looking at enormous paintings of female bottoms and breasts with him. Chris is used to the paintings, of course, but I'm not. He had his arm round my waist and ran his hand up and down the side of my body, tweaking under my T-shirt as he passed the gap. 'Your skin is so *warm*,' he whispered.

'Chris!' I barked. 'Just show me the paintings, and then I want to talk.'

'You sure?' he said, right into my ear. I could feel his breath. 'Do we have to talk?'

We'd reached the end of the barn. There was a separate

section here as if someone else used it. Well, someone else must have used it, because the art was quite different. The pieces were mostly 3-D, some made in metal, others in strange rusty fabric pulled taut over wire frames. There were a few paintings – they were abstracts in purples and bronzes, full of movement. My eye was caught by an unfinished painting on the easel – a flash of bright pink and bronzy black. The top of the black was dotted with more bright pink in flower shapes. The whole thing was vivid with life and energy, like someone dancing. The colours were very different from Jill's but there was the same strength and confidence.

'Does your mum share this studio with another artist, then?' I asked, trying to ignore his hand resting on my hip.

'In a manner of speaking, yes, she does.'

'And what's that supposed to mean, Christopher Green?' I asked, smiling at the rhyme.

'It depends whether you describe the other person's work as art or not.'

'I think it's fabulous. Of course, I like your mum's work too,' I said, not wanting to offend him. 'Do Gina and Dorothy buy and sell the other artist's stuff too?'

Chris actually let go of me for half a second and laughed out loud. 'It's *my* stuff, Holly! GCSE work!'

'Wow. It's brilliant.' I was silenced. I suppose you might expect an artist's son to be an artist too. I just didn't expect a silent fifteen-year-old tennis player to be one.

'Good art department at my school,' he said modestly. 'Honestly. It makes Mum laugh seeing people pay out for private education when there's an art department like ours on their doorstep. It's one of the best in the country. Good for sport too, so that's me covered.'

'What do you want to do later?' I asked.

'Dunno. What about you?'

'Dunno either. English at university probably. My school's really good on English. And history.'

'Hol, do you still want to talk – or can we go and find Mum's studio couch?'

'I do want to talk. About Jonty and Tamara and stuff. Jonty's really angry with me and I want to know how much he knows about last night.'

'Ah. Perhaps we'd better find Mum's studio couch anyway.' We sat down a little way apart from each other. 'OK. As I see it, Jonty takes Tamara to dance so she can show off new designer dress. Jonty would prefer to take girlfriend, but no big deal, he knows she's well taken care of by the extraordinary Dorothy. Jont, being Jont and a big softie, is nice to Tamara because it comes more easily to him than being nasty. Tamara, who has never had anyone be nice to her, as far as I can tell, reacts like an ill-treated stray dog and latches on to him bigtime. Jont finds it a bit of a strain, especially as she keeps eating and then running off to the loo to make herself sick. In fact he finds it rather distressing and turns to the vile wine to pass the time while she's off in the Ladies. Surprise entrance of Christopher and Holly, Holly looking particularly stunning. Tamara is devastated. Jonty doesn't know how to handle the situation and is too far gone to do much about it anyway. (Jonty told me all this this morning – I got it wrong too.) Now, this is the tricky part, and I haven't been entirely truthful with Jonty about it. When Tamara saw us together, she flipped. Jonty had just turned on her because he couldn't handle both of you, remember? (Though the poor girl had looked after him while he threw up anyway.) Because then she saw that you – the girl he spurned *her* for – couldn't care all that much about *him*.'

I didn't like this at all. 'Oh dear. So she ran away?'

'Not sure when. She went home with her sister and changed, but they think she slept in their stables. Skippy's the only one who understands her, sort of thing. By the way, Beatrice told Flavia about us. Flavia probably couldn't care less but she did mention it to Jonty in a vague sort of way. So when Jonty asked me about it – challenged me about it – I said I was keeping you warm or something corny like that.'

'You *were* keeping me warm. That wasn't a lie.'

'But I told him you didn't mean anything to me, and that *was* a lie.'

He gave me a puppy-dog look and was about to lunge at me again, but I stopped him. There was more I needed to know. 'So Jonty isn't angry with me because of you?'

'Don't think so. But searching for Tamara today was really distressing, really traumatic, especially for Jonty. I'm sort of over it now I've been home and – and you're here. We thought she was dead. She just looked like this little crumpled heap of bones, all muddy—'

'That's what Jonty said.'

'It was scary. I called the ambulance people straight away, so at least I had something to do, but Jont slid down the bank to check whether or not she was still breathing. Her bone was sticking out through the mud. It was horrible – like those pictures you see of corpses in the trenches, in the First World War. She kept coming round and whimpering and then fainting again. It seemed ages until the medics arrived. And then it was awful watching them get her on to the stretcher, though they'd given her something by then. Jont kept saying, "Poor kid – this is all my fault." Actually I kind of suspected it might be all our faults, but I kept quiet about that.'

'Ultimately it's her family's fault, Chris, not yours or mine or Jonty's. Sending her away to a school she hates. Buying her off with designer dresses instead of affection. Food as power. But I'm beginning to see why Jonty was so angry with me. I've been horrible about Tamara. Actually, I think he's cross with himself too, for letting Flavia bully him into taking Tamara to the dance last night. After all, none of this would have happened if he'd taken me.'

Chris leant over and rubbed his face against mine. 'But then none of this would have happened either, would it?' He kissed me. 'We'd better go. Otherwise Mum might stalk up on us and catch us all unawares, and that would be embarrassing.'

'Can we look at your paintings again, now I know who the artist is?'

'OK.'

I stopped in front of the easel. 'Is this a GCSE one?'

'You know it isn't.'

'So when did you paint it?'

'Earlier on.'

'It's me, isn't it?'

'Of course it's you.' He looked down at me with melty eyes. 'You are the only image I have in my head right now.' He touched my forehead with his lips and we went off to find Jill.

Jill was watching TV with Toby. They were very engrossed. She looked up with a start. 'Oh, Holly, I said I'd give you a lift back didn't I? Would you awfully mind waiting until this is over? It's quite long I'm afraid.'

'Ssshhh, Mum!' Toby admonished.

'It's OK, Mum,' said Chris. 'We'll walk back. It's still a nice evening. I'll wheel my bike. See you later.'

'Bye Jill,' I whispered.

TWELVE

Friday night
I've just walked back across the fields with Chris (and his bike). It was the most romantic walk I've ever had in my life. The sky was still rosy and the stars were popping out. And then a huge moon came up, all golden and strange. No one was around, we were completely alone. We kept stopping to kiss and Chris told me over and over again that he was crazy about me. He is so sexy. I can't think how I didn't see it at first. It's partly his eyes. He never looked me in the eye at the beginning of the week. And his sinewy strength. We jumped over straw bales and rode around on his bike together like kids. We lay down and hugged and rolled down a slope still hugging, over and over.

But now the awful bit. He said goodbye before we got here because we didn't want to bump into Jonty. And it was really goodbye. He's going to a tennis tournament somewhere tomorrow – all weekend. So I might never see him again. It's over. How could we carry on? We both cried. I'm crying now as I write. I can't bear it. He said that I had to do what I wanted, but that he would never tell Jonty. Their friendship goes back for ever and it means a lot to them both. So of course I won't tell him either. Chris thinks Jonty won't be angry with me about Tamara any more tomorrow. Says he never stays angry for long. He (Chris) understood my feelings about privilege too, though he says that he and I are every bit as privileged, far more than Tamara. I know what he's saying, but he's grown up with the lords of the manor, people with just so much more money. I haven't. My parents are old lefties. Jill probably is too, but maybe she's had to put her politics on one side a bit.

Tomorrow is the last day of this strange holiday. Tomorrow I will pretend Chris never happened and concentrate on me and Jonty, who is, when all is said and done, a sweetheart.

Oh yes. And Chris does know Joel, one of Alex's brothers – in fact he'll be in the tournament tomorrow. Small world, huh?

I don't know how I slept. I kept wanting to get up and run across the fields to Chris's. I wanted us to be together all his last night, not apart. When I woke up it was bright outside.

I sat up in bed for a bit of positive thinking. Today was my last day. I wanted to stay friends with Jonty. I certainly didn't want him thinking so badly of me. I hopped over to the mirror and looked at myself hard. Actually, I didn't altogether like what I saw. Holly Davies. Slag. Comes to Clermont Chase to stay with Jonty, my holiday romance. And gets off with his best friend. Not to mention being rude to his family and unkind about a girl with a serious eating disorder, simply because she happened to fancy my boyfriend. Jont knew Chris fancied me, but he didn't let it bother him, did he? Because he trusted me. And I'd betrayed that trust. And Dilly's trust too. *Don't mess with Chris*.

I had a shower and washed away some of the self-disgust. Jonty's family *were* pretty difficult to deal with. Tamara *was* a pain. Chris had fallen in love with *me*. It might sound trivial to blame it all on the ball tickets, but I had been seriously disappointed. Really it boiled down to our different values. Meals out, expensive theatre seats, ballgowns – Davieses and Clermont-Hayters put different values on them. Where Greens stood in all this I don't know. There was Jill, hugely talented, struggling and juggling with flower-arranging and cleaning to keep her family afloat while Hayters see her art as a valuable *investment*. It's all a mystery to me.

I tried to extract what was important here. Jonty-and-Chris was important. They understood one another. Were friends without jealousy. I didn't want to leave scars on that friendship. My self-esteem was important too. I wanted the Hayters to rate me – I didn't want to give them any reason to feel superior. OK, we weren't rich, but I was every bit as good as them.

So. Today. Today I had to make my peace with Jont. No Chris or Tamara to get in the way. It was half-past ten. *Again!* Time to get started.

'Morning Holly.' Brian.

'Hello dear. Sleep well?' Gina.

Silence. Flavia.

'Hi Hol.' Jonty. At least he was speaking to me.

'So what's on the cards for my last day?'

'Granny. She wants to take you and me on a picnic to Charlecote. Her house at 12.30. Which gives us an hour or so to go on the quad bikes.'

'Quad bikes! You've got quad bikes?'

'Yeah, well, we got them a couple of years ago so the excitement's worn off a bit. Granny reminded me that you might enjoy them.'

'Wow!'

'They're in the garage. But they won't run away while we have some breakfast. I've only just got up. Didn't fancy riding this morning somehow.'

'Well don't expect me to come,' said Flavia.

Jonty flashed me a grin. As if. 'It's OK Flaves. We can manage.' Perhaps he'd had a bit of a think too. And Chris said he never stayed angry for long.

We walked over to the garage. We didn't hold hands or anything. Jonty shot me sidelong glances.

'I'm really sorry—'

'I'm really sorry—'

We both spoke at once. 'Me first,' said Jonty. 'I'm sorry I gave you such a hard time about Tamara. It was just seeing her like that, thinking she was dead and that it was my fault for treating her as badly as everyone else.'

'Wasn't your fault, Jonty.' I came *very* close to saying it was mine. But then I stopped myself. It wasn't my fault either. As I'd said to Chris, the problem went far deeper than that. 'I'm sorry I was so mean about her. Guess I felt kind of insecure.'

'Friends?' he said, holding out his hand.

'Friends,' I said, and took it.

I wish I'd known about the bikes before. Now *they* are rich people's toys I can really get to grips with. I've always wanted to have a go. Jonty and I put on the helmets and tore noisily across their land with no one to irritate. It was fast and smelly and exhilarating, just what we needed. We careered round like kids, delinquent kids. And when we finally got off them, our whole bodies vibrating and our ears ringing, Jont was full of admiration. 'Can't believe you've never done that before, Holly! You were wicked at it.'

Well, I thought, it's not like tennis or riding – you don't need years of practice. Just energy and a sense of fun. We peeled off the helmets and overalls. 'I'll miss you,' said Jonty.

'I'll miss you too,' I said truthfully.

Dorothy drove a small Mercedes people-carrier. It suited her somehow. Our picnic had been ordered from the local delicatessen and packed into a number of coolbags. Hey, this was stylish. The day had started grey but now it was beginning to brighten up. 'This is good,' said Dorothy. 'It means that most of the tourists will have chosen to go somewhere indoors.' I thought it was quite strange to be visiting a country house for a picnic when you had an entire tourist-free estate of your own, but Dorothy seemed keen on the idea of a day out. She pulled into a parking space under the trees and gave us each a rug and a coolbag to carry. 'Now, isn't this fun?' she asked us. 'I'd have ended up watching the cricket on television if I'd stayed at home. Much better to sit by the river and watch the deer. You might like to go round the house together after lunch while I take a nap, but it's not obligatory.'

Over lunch Dorothy asked us both about yesterday.

'Didn't Jonty tell you last night?' I asked.

'No dear. Jonathan didn't want to talk about it last night – did you Jon?' (Jon, that sounded more grown-up than Jonty.) 'Anyway, we had a chess championship to concentrate on.'

I began, 'Well, the first I heard of it, Gina knocked on my door at about nine in the morning and said that they'd heard from the Hiltons. No one seemed very worried at that point. My parents would have been frantic.'

'Mother woke me up a bit after that,' Jonty joined in. 'Tamara'd been telling me at the polo-club bash about how she didn't want to go back to school next term – in between dashing off to make herself throw up. She kept saying, "No one will listen to me." I guess that's the main problem.'

'Imagine,' I said, 'having to go away from home to a place where people bully you mercilessly. Why do they make her go?'

'No imagination!' said Dorothy. 'They can't imagine what it's like for her.'

'Well I can,' said Jonty. 'Remember my awful prep school, Granny?'

'Of course I do, dear. Your poor mother was desperate. I had to insist she took you away.'

'Thank goodness you did.'

I'd forgotten that Jonty'd had a taste of what Tamara was going through. And I suppose even I had had a taste of homesickness this week. Maybe I should have used my imagination a bit more on Tamara.

'She doesn't help herself, though,' said Jonty. 'In fact she's not very bright, not even very likeable. She's only interested in clothes – and her pony, of course.'

'Jonty—'

'You're quite right about her, Holly. She's a complete pain in the neck. She just doesn't deserve to feel so lonely. Do you know, Granny, when we first found her, and thought she was dead, I was almost glad for her. I thought at least she wasn't miserable any more. Still. Maybe she'll get the attention she needs now.'

'The doctors are bound to see that she's anorexic and try to do something about that,' said Dorothy. 'And she might have got her wish about not going back to school.'

'That's the thing about wishes, isn't it?' I said.

'What is?' said Jonty.

'You know, like I said—' but then I stopped, because it was Chris I'd said that to.

'I heard that helicopter,' said Dorothy. 'I wondered what was going on. Of course, Holly had rung me, so I knew something was up.'

'You rang Granny?' Jonty asked. I realised there were lots of things he didn't know.

'I had to start somewhere. You just told me to get help. I

didn't know where to begin. I didn't know anyone's names, let alone their phone numbers.'

Jonty sat back and looked at me with something like respect. 'I really do owe you an apology, Hol. You know, I forgot all that part. You must have organised the emergency services and Chris and everything.'

Dorothy poured herself a large glass of wine and regarded us with a half smile on her face.

'Well, I was impressed by the fact that you'd just gone out there.'

'It seems that Tamara has quite a lot to thank you both for,' said Dorothy. 'Now, run along you two. I fancy a little nap in the sun, and I don't want to have to listen to you apologising to each other all afternoon.'

Jonty stood up. 'Oh all right, Granny. Back in an hour, OK?'

'That's fine dear,' she said, and leant back against a tree with her newspaper.

'Come on, Hol,' he said, pulling me to my feet. We set off holding hands. I had the distinct feeling that this was the precise scenario Dorothy'd had in mind.

We wandered up to the house. 'Do you want to go in?' Jonty asked.

'Not particularly,' I said. 'It's nice just wandering here by the river. Gosh, imagine owning all of this.'

'I don't have to imagine,' Jonty said, and I felt foolish. 'Holly, I can't *help* who I am, or what I was born into, you know.'

I looked at him standing by the river. He was wearing baggy trousers and a T-shirt – a boy like any other – but then my brain conjured up a strange vision of ten or fifteen Jon Hayters going back for centuries: lanky young men with a flop of hair and a ready smile, and a look in their eyes that told you how secure they were in their lineage, both past and future. I imagined them standing there, in tabards and ruffs and cloaks and Edwardian suits. I tried to imagine being Jonty, tried to imagine living in a house and grounds that generations of my family had owned. I know that families like Jont's are rare these days – they have to find other ways of keeping the estate going, like Gina and her art buying. But it's just a different world.

'Hey!' He snapped his fingers in front of my face. 'Where've you been? You went off into a daze just then!'

'Nowhere,' I said. 'Right here.'

'It's changed, hasn't it?' he said wistfully.

'I suppose it has.'

'You fight against me Holly. You fight against my family and the system I live in. I want you to relax and enjoy it, but you can't quite, can you?'

'I do want to, Jont. I try to imagine living your life, I do, but you have to imagine mine, too.'

'I'd love your life. Nice normal parents. Friends living in the road. School round the corner. Comfortable with people up and down the social scale. My life will improve when I get a car and I'm allowed to use the London flat, but until then I have to make do with the Christophers and Tamaras of this world.'

'Nothing wrong with Chris!' I felt he needed defending.

'You said it!' Jonty laughed, and I wondered again how much he knew. 'Chris is the one who keeps me in touch with the real world. Actually, Jill's probably the one who keeps me in touch with the real world. She does the same for Mum. And Granny.'

'I love Dorothy.'

'Well lucky old Granny. You don't love me any more, do you?'

'Jonty!'

'I'm not bitter about it. I just know it's not how it was in Barbados.'

'Jont—'

'Yes?'

'Can I say that I love you for being my first boyfriend?'

'Gee, thanks.'

'No, I mean it. I'll never have another first boyfriend.'

'You mean, I can't be the first and only?'

'No,' I said, too quickly and too definitely.

He gave me a long, cool look. 'I'm not going to ask, Holly, because I don't want to know. I want it to be like it was before, but I know it can't be.' Then he leant over and gave me the tenderest of kisses.

'Hold my hand,' I said, as we walked along the river path. 'For old times' sake?'

He held it. 'So as not to disappoint Granny,' he said.

So that's how a relationship ends.

When we got back Dilly was there in the kitchen.

'Hi Holly! I couldn't be bothered to wait until tomorrow to come home. Seemed crazy to miss you. You don't mind sharing her do you, little bro?'

'What can I say?' said Jonty gallantly. He ruffled my hair. 'I promised I'd play tennis with Toby tonight anyway.'

'Chris not here?' asked Dilly.

'No,' I said, 'he's playing in a weekend tournament, somewhere in Hertfordshire I think.'

'More than I knew,' said Jonty. But he was laughing. I think we were both glad Dilly was home. Jonty disappeared off to change.

Dilly got two Cokes out of the fridge and handed me one.

We sat down at the kitchen table. 'So. What's it been like? You and Jonty still like this?' She linked her little fingers.

'Pretty good,' I said non-committally. 'This place is really beautiful.'

'Pity the pool's out of action,' said Dilly. 'Only thing that makes it bearable in hot weather. Can't think what you've found to *do* here. Still, won't ask.'

'We swam at Bury,' I said. Then, 'I suppose you've heard the Tamara saga?'

'Nothing but,' said Dilly. 'Silly idiot. Fancy going off in conditions like that without taking a phone with her. She's not even much of a rider.'

'Better than me,' I said. 'Though that's not hard!'

'I thought you rode.'

'Pony trekking riding. Not like you lot. I panic if the horse so much as canters!'

'Good job you're not here in the hunting season then,' said Dilly.

I kept quiet this time.

Saturday night
My last night. This time tomorrow I'll be in my own little bed, and I can't wait. Can't wait to see Alex and Zoe and Josie and Mum and Dad and Abby. Didn't think it was possible to miss them so much.

It was great seeing Dilly, especially as Jonty and I have basically broken up. Of course she wanted to know what I thought of everything. She kept saying 'So what did you think of blah?' – Chris/Bury/Stratford/everything. I answered carefully. She so much wanted me to love it all. Which of course is what Jonty wanted me to do too. Oh well.

Chris, where are you now? Staying with a tennis person in St Albans, but I can't picture it. Are you thinking about me as much as I'm thinking about you? I must contact Alex as soon as I get home and get a message to you through her brother.

Tomorrow this will all seem like a dream, a play.

THIRTEEN

Dilly came crashing into my room at 8.30. 'Get up Holly. Come down and have breakfast with me.'

'Uh? What's the time? It's too early!'

'No it's not. Jont went out hours ago.'

'Hours?'

'An hour and a half.'

'So he's on a horse again. I thought the hunt for Tamara had put him off.'

'Jont? Nah. There's this new horse that he really likes. But he wanted to be back to take you to the coach station. Thought I'd pass on that one myself.'

'Any news on Tamara?' I got out of bed and went into the shower. Dilly carried on talking.

'Flavia says they're keeping her in. Horrible old Beatrice can't see what all the fuss is about. Their dad has actually come home from Bahrain or somewhere to see Tamara.'

'Good.'

'What do you care?'

'Well, perhaps all that attention-seeking actually means she needs some attention.'

'True. Hurry up in there. I'm used to eating at 8 o'clock sharp on the course. I'm starving!'

'Go on down then. Mine's an orange juice!' She went. How much easier the week would have been in some ways with Dilly here. Then again, she wouldn't have let me near Chris!

Jont and Dilly were already troughing away when I got downstairs. The table was littered with cereal packets and yoghurt pots and juice cartons. More evidence of Dilly being at home. 'Pity you're off today, Holly. I was just thinking, I could have given you some proper riding lessons. Then, next time you stay, you could follow the hunt with us.'

Jonty was looking at me to see what I would say. 'I'd love to be able to ride better,' I said cautiously. 'Jont and I never got our picnic at Foxhole, did we? And I can't put all the blame on Tamara.'

'No,' said Jonty, equally cautiously, 'we can't put all the blame on Tamara.'

'So?' said Dilly. 'We've got, what, two hours. What shall we do? At least come and say hello to the horses. Tell you what, I'll put you on Gorse on a lead rein and we could all ride over to Granny's. What do you think Jont?'

'Don't mind,' said Jonty. 'What do you think Holly?'

'I think I'd feel safe enough. I'd better change though.'

Dilly helped me up on to Gorse. I felt so high above the ground. 'Go slowly, won't you?' I pleaded. Jonty went on ahead on Shakespeare and Dilly led me on Bluebottle.

'We'll just walk,' she said. 'Gorse will follow Bluebottle. They're great friends.'

'Do horses have friends?'

'Course they do.'

By the time we came to dismount at Dorothy's I was mighty proud of myself. Jonty was already in there eating chocolate Hobnobs. 'Granny!' shrieked Dilly.

'Cordelia, darling.' Dorothy hugged her warmly. 'How lovely to have you home. And what fun to have you two girls together! You will come again, won't you Holly? Do you know, Cordelia, I had to play fairy godmother to your friend here, and send her to the ball?'

Jonty looked at his watch. 'We haven't got long, Granny. You'll have to gossip another time.'

'Jonathan! I don't gossip!'

'No, of course you don't, Granny. But Holly's coach won't wait, and we've got to get her back in one piece on Gorse before we can even drive to the coach station.'

'All right my dears,' said Dorothy. She came over to me and gave me a hug too. 'Goodbye Holly. I've so enjoyed meeting you.'

'Not half as much as I've enjoyed meeting you,' I said. 'It's been great having a fairy godmother!'

'Even if my spells didn't always quite work out as intended, eh?' Dorothy chuckled to herself, and waved us off to the horses.

'What was all that about spells?' Dilly asked.

'Oh, just Granny being daffy as usual,' said Jonty.

Gina drove us to the coach station in the Range Rover. The coach station was concrete and tawdry and smelly. It was crowded with the old and the poor, people with carrier bags and clapped out old buggies and too many children. Gina gave me a brief hug. 'Goodbye Gina,' I said. 'Thank you so much for having me, and taking me to the theatre and everything.'

'Goodbye dear, come again,' she said in return, but I could see that already she was vague about me. How long before she'd find it hard to remember which one was Holly? She got back into the car and made herself comfortable with the Sunday papers.

Jonty carried my case. I was anxious about finding the right coach and getting a seat. I've led a sheltered life – it was my first long journey alone. Jonty checked all the numbers on the coaches, the bus stops and my ticket for me, and we found the one to London eventually. 'We make a good team,' I joked.

'Yeah,' he said. 'I think we met too young. I mean – this is husband and wife stuff. We'd be good at that wouldn't we?'

'Yup. Couple of little kids in tow.'

'Charlie and Georgina!'

'Sam and Ellie more like!'

'And we'd give them all the attention they wanted, wouldn't we?'

We looked at each other, not knowing whether to carry on laughing or start crying. Jont put my case down and threw his arms round me. Big, huggy squeeze. We straightened up. 'OK,' he said, 'here's the deal. In seven years' time, to the day, to the minute – it's twelve noon – we'll meet at – at—'

'Somewhere that's neutral territory – that'll still be standing. I know, on the steps of the National Gallery!'

'Done,' he said, and slapped my hand.

We handed over my case to be loaded into the boot of the coach. 'I can e-mail, can't I?'

'I could live with that.'

'We might end up at the same university,' I said, climbing into the coach.

'That would be the best!' called Jonty.

'Bye! Thanks for having me!'

'Bye! Thanks for coming!' And he ran off, his flickering stride a joy to watch.

As our tatty coach revved up for the journey to London I saw the sleek Range Rover pulling away, heading back down the leafy lanes to Clermont Chase.

EPILOGUE

Ah, the bliss of being home again! Mum, Dad and Abby were all there to meet me at the coach station. We had homemade lentil lasagne – which I love – for supper. My bedroom seemed tiny but so much my own. Abby and Dad wanted to know everything, but Mum, bless her, was all for me having a long bath and getting a good night's sleep first.

I woke up with a cold. Odd to have one in the summer, but Mum thought it might have something to do with getting wet and hanging out in damp phone boxes.

Anyway, I was better by the time we started planning our end-of-holiday sleepover. Strangely enough, Alex and Zoe were both vying to have it. 'We're having it at Zoe's,' Alex said when she rang. 'But only because she's got more room.'

'Fine,' I said. 'I'm surprised you ever wanted it at your house. You usually can't wait to get out.'

'Ah, well I might just have a lot to tell you,' she said. 'But not a word until Sunday night, OK? It's not fair if we all tell each other everything before Josie gets back.'

Zoe rang to confirm. 'My place,' she said. 'I've got loads to tell you all. What about you, Holly? Oh no, I can't ask yet can I? Can't wait for Sunday!'

The rest of the week passed with buying shoes and stationery, a visit from my little cousins, taking Abby to the cinema. I sensed the summer ebbing away. Maddy called. It felt funny telling her that my Barbados romance hadn't lasted but she was very matter-of-fact about it. 'Can't last, can it?' she said. 'You're in different places.'

'But that wouldn't matter if we really loved each other, would it?' I was actually thinking about Chris.

'Course it would,' she said. 'You can't stay a nun, can you? We're too young to get serious about anyone. There are far too many exciting new people to meet.' I wasn't so sure. I missed Chris like hell. But then I'd missed Jonty before. Maybe I'd have to talk to the others about this.

Josie rang at last on the Saturday night. It was late, after eleven. I snatched up the phone – I'd been expecting her to call since six. She was all squeaky. 'Hey, Holly, you'll never guess what . . .' (but no lisp). I persuaded her to save it for tomorrow night – partly because I wanted a little more time to think about my week in the country before opening it up for inspection and comment from the others.

We all turned up amazingly punctually at Zoe's. Because her mum's American they have a huge freezer jampacked with food. We had burgers and chips and salad, with Haagen Daz – about five different flavours – for afters. Zoe practically has her own flat in their basement. They used to let it out, but now it's Zoe's and it's brilliant. 'OK, who's going first?' said Zoe.

'Me!' said Alex and Josie simultaneously.

'Let's go in alphabetical order,' said Zoe. 'That'll put me last, which suits me fine, but I don't think Alex is going to be able to hold out much longer.'

'This is all such a surprise,' said Alex. 'First of all I want to thank my agent, and my two cats, and of course the weird guy in the cyber-café, without whom . . .'

'Get on with it!' shouted Josie.

'Well guys, you have to remember that this is all very new and exciting for me . . .' Alex was away. Seems like the last couple of weeks have been a bit of a steep learning curve in the ways of womanhood for her.

I was next. Trouble was, as I recounted my story I realised that I came out of it all rather poorly, my pique over not being invited to the ball seemed so petty compared with Tamara's misfortunes. And as for getting off with Jonty's best friend . . .

But then Alex butted in. 'Is there any chance that your tennis-playing Chris Green was in Hertfordshire last weekend, and that he is in fact the same tennis-playing Chris Green that my brother Joel knows?'

'Why yes! Of course! I knew there was a connection! I completely forgot to ask you. I'd meant to try and get a message to him through you, until I realised that it would have been too late.'

'You know of course that this puts a completely different complexion on things, don't you?' said Alex gravely.

'Why?'

'Because Joel's tennis-playing Chris Green is *gorgeous*. Quiet. Smouldering eyes. With dark curly hair. I haven't seen him since last year, but I liked him then, even before I understood what you lot saw in boys.'

'No curls now,' I said. 'Shaved head, practically.'

'I wasn't talking about his *head*,' said Alex.

'Oh shut up.'

'Go on Josie,' said Zoe, 'your turn.' Josie arranged herself comfortably, settling in for a long story (while Alex muttered in the background, 'his armpits, *naturellement*').

Josie's story was just as complicated as mine, if not more so. She didn't see it herself, but I reckon she came out of it even worse than I did. She did recognise that best friend's boyfriend (as opposed to best friend's girlfriend) is a complete no-no. But she said it wasn't quite like that.

As for Zoe. Well, true to form, Zoe's week doing

Community Theatre had had a profound effect on her. No straightforward fluffy romance for her. Hers had encompassed race and culture and, well, Life, really. Still, mine had raised questions of class, and attitudes, among others.

. . . And my few hours with Chris. If they weren't true romance, then I don't know what is.

Alex

ONE

God, I hate boys! This morning's little episode is typical of life in a house full of brothers.

'Get your great butt out of there, Al!'

'Yeah. Come on, Al. Bet you're reading in there!'

I am, as it happens. I'm reading *Have You Started Yet?* by Ruth Thomson. Leaving it in the loo is as close as Mum gets to telling me important girly things. And why isn't she here now, protecting me from my annoying twelve-year-old brothers? Can't a girl even go to the loo in peace? I know that if I stay in here long enough they'll start fighting each other in a mild sort of way and forget about me.

Needless to say, I *haven't* started yet, though all my friends did, ages ago. But I've had these funny tummy-aches lately, and I've got a ferocious spot bleeping away like a Belisha beacon on my nose, which makes me think it might be about to happen at last. All when I'm about to play in a tennis tournament, of course, and wearing lovely virginal white from dawn till dusk. Probably won't. God missed me out when he doled out the feminine attributes, I think. I beg your pardon? Boobs? Surely not. Hips? Straight up and down far more economical. Means you can wear your brothers' hand-me-downs for a start. Oh, and even the name – Alex. No one need even *know* you're a girl.

I'm number three in a family of five. Phil and Joel, seventeen and nearly sixteen. Then me, a girl. Parents thought, oh how nice, let's try for another girl. And what do they get? Double whammy – twin boys. Jack and Sam. Such a blessing. Apparently Mum sank into a deep depression after that and never really came out of it. No, really. She's very depressed, my mum, and fat with it. We don't get on. Dad's great, but Mum? Give me a break. I do try sometimes. But she's no use at all.

I waited for the boys to go away before I emerged from the loo. It was my turn to go to Tesco with Dad. I wanted to stock up on emergency supplies, just in case, but somehow I didn't feel I could involve him. When the coast was clear – i.e., when three of my brothers were squabbling over TV channels – I rang Zoe, my friend and salvation. 'Zo – I need a friend. You going over to Holly's tonight?'

'Of course,' said Zoe. 'Aren't you?'

'No, I'd prefer to relax indoors in the company of my charming family. Of course I am! I've got to go to Tesco with my dad first, though.'

'Mmm. That's exciting. So why do you need a friend?'

'Zoe?'

'What is it Al? What's with the long pauses?'

'Er—'

'WHAT?'

'I think something might be happening that has not been happening before – period-wise.'

'You *think*?'

'Well. I don't know.'

'Listen, you'd sure as heck know if something *had* happened.'

'You mean, it might look as if I'd sat on something?'

'Yeah. Like a squirrel. And killed it.'

'Hey! It's me that makes the jokes! Remember?'

'I'm not joking.'

'Well, OK. It's just that I've had these weird stomach pains, and I'm fearing the worst, since I'm just about to spend a week wearing white.'

'That would be typical. You probably are about to start then. Hey, Al! Welcome to the world of womanhood. Of having a good excuse for being off games and blaming PMT for being grumpy.'

'You wouldn't come shopping with us and pretend the stuff's for you, would you?'

'Sorry, can't do it. Got to see Granny – White Granny – before I'm allowed out for the evening. But I'll bring a nice little selection along with me tonight if you like. How's that?'

'You're a star. Thanks. See you at Holly's then.'

'See you at Holly's.'

I could have asked Holly or Josie rather than Zoe – especially Holly, as she lives closer and her mum's a nurse, after all. But Holly just wouldn't understand me not wanting to ask my own mum – she gets on so well with hers. Actually, Zoe and her mum get along fine too. It's just that Zoe's more sympathetic. She knows a lot about life's little ups and downs.

Holly, Josie and I go back a long way – we were all at junior school together. Zoe came on the scene more recently. I first met her through the twins. Her younger brother Tarquin (yes, Tarquin) is one of their best mates. Believe me, to break in on the twins' little world you have to be quite a personality. And Tarquin is certainly that. So's Zoe. It was great knowing her the day we all started at our comprehensive school. Holly and Josie are both normal looking – you know, medium height, hair tied back, the right clothes. Whereas I was this great beanpole with short sandy hair. Dressed like a boy. Wanted to be a boy at that point – it made life so much easier in our household. And there was Zoe. Tall as me, and dark (her dad's English and her mum's black American). I almost had a crush on her at first. Not really, it was just that she was an exotic new girl and I felt proud that I knew her already. And she laughed at all my jokes. The others do, too. But they take them for granted. Zoe laughed at everything afresh. It did my ego a lot of good.

Holly was having a sleepover. She wouldn't quite tell us why. But that was cool – I'm always happy to meet up with the other three. Especially since I haven't seen that much of them this summer holiday. Zoe's been in Italy. Holly went away for what seemed like weeks to *Barbados* – lucky thing (with her dad's posh school cricket team). And Josie was off on some music course.

I'm not sure what I've been doing, apart from watching telly and reading a bit. And going up to the Club. The Club is our tennis club, and even calling it a club is a bit of a joke. It's hidden away behind the allotments, with only three courts and not many more members. It's kind of scruffy as well as small – *exclusive* is how we think of ourselves. Seriously, we always have one junior player in the local county finals, if not more. Dad's on the committee. Mum was too, apparently (though I can't believe it), and with five of us kids playing, the Dunbars are core members. I go up most nights. There's always someone I know there (even if it's only a brother). I see more of my tennis friends than my schoolfriends in the summer holidays.

Back to the sleepover. Dad and I unloaded the shopping. I left my brothers to put it away and ran up the road to Holly's (having sneaked out with a few cans of shandy Dad had bought me). It was so late I didn't have time to change out of my sweats from playing earlier – not that any of them would hold it against me. I like going to Holly's house: she and her little sister never seem to quarrel and there's always loads of food on offer – two major points of difference from mine. Holly's mum always shows an interest too, and that's another difference.

So there we were: Zoe, Holly, me and Josie. Josie's a bit silly sometimes, but basically she's OK. She's just had a brace fitted – it's really uncomfortable, apparently. Certainly makes her speak strangely. Holly made us wait until we'd watched *Titanic* and eaten pizzas before she told us the reason she'd gathered us all together. We'd made up beds in their living room, and we were preparing to talk into the night the way we always do – usually about boys if the others have their way, though as you can imagine, boys aren't my favourite topic of conversation. I have enough of them at home.

This was Holly's plan. It was very bizarre actually. She'd met some girl in Barbados who knows someone Josie knows, and four of them who are friends had made this sort of pact at the beginning of the summer holidays to have holiday romances and then report back on them at the end of the holidays. 'And I thought we could do the same,' said Holly. 'It would be brilliant. What do you think?'

'Why?' was my first question. I didn't see the point, personally, especially as Holly's already met some rich guy in Barbados and now she's off to stay with him at his country estate.

The others thought it was a cool idea. Josie's going to Cornwall and she seems to think she might find romance, brace and all. Zoe's not even going anywhere, though she'll be checking out a local Community Theatre Project, so she said she'd try her best to have a romance too. I tried telling them that romance wasn't quite my thing, but when Holly's enthusiastic about something it's infectious and I didn't want to let her down. I'm just playing in a tennis tournament, Mapledon, like I do every year, but I said – yes, OK, I'd try my best too.

Romance, eh? Some girls in our class seem to do and know it all, but that doesn't include us. Posh Boy is Holly's first real relationship so now she's hugely keen on 'lurve' and can't stop talking about it. Josie's just as bad. She goes to a girls' school (her parents took her away from our comprehensive after the first year), which seems to make her more interested in boys than ever, but I suspect she's all talk and no action. Zoe is the opposite. She doesn't talk at all, but she could have any boy she wanted. As for me, I'm a 'late developer'. Perhaps, if I am about to enter the 'world of womanhood', Zoe will talk a bit more. I need someone to, because I wouldn't know where to begin, not from a practical point of view anyway. Just fourteen and never been kissed! I am actually the baby of the group – so I do have some excuse. Zoe's nearly fifteen but I only had my fourteenth birthday earlier this month.

Zoe chose a moment when Holly and Josie were in the kitchen to thrust a carrier bag at me. 'How are you doing?' she asked.

'Nothing yet,' I said.

'Well, here's your very own supply of goodies, just in case.'

'Thanks Zo. Wow! I can't believe you lot all know what to do with these things. I'm not sure that I want to learn. Life's nice and simple at the moment.'

'No choice, darling.'

'I just can't bear the thought of growing up like my mum.'

'Grow up like your dad, then. You look more like him.'

'Dads don't have babies.'

'They probably will before long. Then you can find this cute guy to have your babies for you while you get on with all the fun things in life.'

'That would make sense. I'm sure it was having babies that made Mum fat and depressed.'

'Lighten up, Al. It's not like you to get all gloomy!'

'See? Aaagh! I'm turning into her already!'

Two

When I got home next morning it was nearly lunch time. I whizzed straight upstairs and shoved the wretched things Zoe had given me into a drawer. There was a loud knock on my bedroom door.

'Alexandra! What sort of time do you call this? I don't suppose it occurred to you to let us know when you were coming home, did it?'

My mum. Usually I know she's approaching by the slip-slopping of her slippers or the wheezing as she comes up the stairs, but I was obviously too busy rustling plastic bags to hear her. What she said was typical, by the way. She always picks on me. But I was stung, because I'd told Dad last night exactly what time I expected to be home this morning. 'I told Dad. It's not my fault if he doesn't tell you.'

'Oh well. I'm not surprised. Nobody tells me anything. I'm just expected to run around after you all, provide the meals . . .'

(Yawn.) 'Yeah, yeah.'

'Don't talk to me like that, Alexandra.' She always says this, without much conviction.

'Calm down, Mum. I did actually do the shopping with

Dad last night. It's Phil's turn to help with the lunch, isn't it? Did anyone ring while I was away?'

'Yes. Several people.'

'Who?'

'I don't know, I really don't have the time to be your social secretary.' (She always says this, too. In fact, one of the boys usually gets to a phone first in our rabbit warren of a house.)

'Is Phil in?'

'I expect so.'

I dodged round her and knocked on the door of (oldest brother) Phil's room. He was watching Saturday morning kids' TV. 'Philip! Grow up!'

He punched out at me lazily. 'Grow up yourself, kid.'

'Not a kid. Anyway, it smells like a tart's boudoir in here. These *laboratoires* don't need to test their products on animals – they've got you.' I picked up the offending tester bottle. 'Mmm. "Tester". Short for testosterone. Are you practising for the lovely Lana, tonight?'

'None of your business. And since when you have been interested in toiletries anyway?'

'Toiletries! Phil, what sort of a word is *toiletries*? You *are* practising for Lana.'

'You're annoying. Go away. What did you want?'

'Well, I knew that you would have been inches away from the phone from the moment you woke up – so I wondered if anyone had rung for me.'

'Yes.'

'Well, who?'

'What's it worth?'

'Now who's being annoying?'

'Lucy. And Paddy. And Richard.'

'And? What did they say?'

He smirked at me.

'Oh, all right. What do you want me to do?'

'Help Mum with lunch?'

'That's not fair! I did the shopping with Dad last night.'

'That's a *nice* job.'

'OK, OK! Just be prepared for me to extract favours from you, too, in exchange for messages.'

'Lucy – ring her. Paddy – ring him. Richard – do you know where Lucy is? Now go and help Mum. Get her off my case. She's been whingeing on at me all morning.'

'Your methods stink. And so do you!' I slammed the door on his laughter. Actually, Phil is OK. He calls me his 'favourite brother' (ha ha), but he is definitely *my* favourite brother. The twins have always been the bane of my life and Joel, the nearly-sixteen-year-old one, is good-looking apparently (despite the bleached hair), brilliant at everything and a bighead. I sometimes wonder if we share the same parents. Mum certainly treats him differently from the rest of us – she lets him get away with murder. It's particularly harsh because although we're nearly two years apart – his birthday's in October and mine's in August – we're only a year apart at school.

I told Mum I'd help with lunch, though I don't know why she bothers at weekends. We'd all much rather grab a sandwich. Then I phoned Lucy.

Lucy is my tennis partner. My life at the Club is quite separate from my life at school. I'm no one special at school but everyone knows me at the Club. Chiefly because I'm a Dunbar, and it's hard to miss us, even if we are known collectively as 'the Dunbar boys'. As for my Club friends, there are four girls (including me) and four boys in my particular 'crowd': Lucy and me and two girls called Rosie and Harriet; then Paddy and Richard, Neil and Raj (pair of clowns). We've all been taken there by our parents since we were babies.

'Lucy, hi. Has Richard phoned you?'

'Yes, he ran me to ground. He's trying to arrange a practice match tomorrow evening for you, me, Paddy and him.'

'Does it have to be that formal? Can't we just go and knock up like we usually do?'

'He says he wants to practise specifically for the mixed doubles. But I think he really wants a sneak match *against* Paddy, rather than always playing *with* him.'

'That's really stupid. They can knock up any time, like us.'

'Oh, I don't know what his tactics are, Al. I'm not a mind-reader. I just said I'd check with you. Do you think Paddy might object or something?'

'I just don't want to *assume* that Paddy's my mixed doubles partner this year.'

'Why on earth not? He has been for the last three years.'

'I know that. It's just that he hasn't actually mentioned it. I'm worried that he might prefer a *girly*-girl this year.'

'What are you talking about? Why *should* he mention it? He probably assumes you'll be partners like you always are. You *won* the under-14s at Mapledon the year before last – why'd he want to spoil a good thing?'

'Last year we did uselessly.'

'That's because you had to play in the under-16s with him. And because you had to play against *Joel*.'

She was right. And I didn't want her to start on the subject of Joel or I'd never get off the phone. (All the girls, without exception, fancy Joel. They just don't realise what a pig he is.)

'OK. I've got to call him back anyway. I'll ask him about tomorrow night. I'm on for it.'

As Lucy pointed out, Paddy and I have been partners for ages. We play tennis and I make him laugh. But he's been behaving slightly differently this year, and I don't know what it means. He's older than I am so it could be that he's beginning to find me tiresome. People do sometimes tell me to 'grow up'. Anyway, I daren't take our mixed doubles partnership for granted, whatever Lucy says.

'Paddy – you rang.'

'Yes, but it doesn't matter now.'

'What was it?'

'You are – playing – next week, aren't you? Mapledon?'

'Yes, of course. You know I am.'

'Just checking.'

'Duh-uh. *You* are, aren't you?'

'Yes.'

Honestly. He's as bad as my brothers. (The difference is, Paddy and I like each other.) 'Fancy a knock tomorrow night with Richard and Lucy? That's if you're not off snow-boarding in Timbuctoo.'

He didn't rise to it. 'Yup. OK.'

'See you about seven? Lucy reckons the adults will be off the courts by then.'

Mum was noisily plonking things on the table, making the point that I'd been on the phone instead of helping her. Slip-slop, plonk – a pile of plates. Slip-slop, plonk – a jug of water. Slip-slop, plonk – the breadboard. 'It's OK, Mum. I'm here now.'

'You're here *now*,' she grumbled. 'But if we all had to wait for *you*, lunch would never happen.' She carried on in this vein, but I blanked her out. The others rolled in: Dad from the local library, where he likes to spend Saturday morning; Phil from watching telly; Joel barely awake and in his dressing-gown; and Jack and Sam, together as always, fighting as always. You can see why I get fed up when Mum picks on *me*.

Dad is the complete opposite to Mum. They're from different planets. I can't imagine how they ever got down to producing the five of us (a ghastly thought – oh well, at least they only had to do it *four* times). Dad works in engineering design and he loves his work. I know he's popular there because I've been to his office and met his work-mates. He plays tennis every Sunday – come rain, come shine – and he coached all of us himself. He's a great stalwart of the club, too, organising tournaments and barbecues and quiz-nights to raise funds. His latest little money-spinner is our Tennis Club Diary. He designed it himself with a handy tennis hint on every page and lots of spaces to fill in things about the matches you're playing. It's a bit naff, but typical of his enthusiasm and I try to fill mine in every day just to please him (which is daft really, because I'd die if he read it). I adore my dad and he always sticks up for me, which kind of compensates for Mum. He treats me like one of the boys in other ways, which is great. He allows me the same freedom and has the same high expectations of me. When it comes to going out to work he'll want me to smash through every glass ceiling there is, unlike Mum, who fell at the first post. Pardon my mixed metaphors.

I hung around long enough after lunch to make sure Jack and Sam were doing the clearing away and then went up to my room. I needed to get to grips with this period business. I was becoming obsessed with the idea now that I might start during the week of the tennis tournament. Zoe warned me that the curse operates on sod's law, so that I was almost bound to start when it was least convenient.

I sorted out my whites. White socks. White tops. White baggy shorts. And a *navy-blue tracksuit*, of course. Pray for cooler weather and I need never take it off! There was my answer. I checked out my white underwear, including my 32A bra (wretched thing, I only wear it because school shirts and tennis gear are so see-through), and lugged the whole lot downstairs to the washing machine. Jack and Sam were still in the kitchen and couldn't pass over an opportunity to comment on my more intimate garments. 'Why do you bother with a bra, Al?' (Jack).

'*I* might as well wear one!' (Sam). He snatched it before I could stop him and paraded round the kitchen, holding it in front of his chest and pointing his fingers into it, Madonna-style. God, I *hate* them! They are *so* gross.

I finally got it off him, and my days-of-the-week knickers off Jack, and stuffed them into the washing machine. Mum came slip-slopping in when it was all over, the twins looking as if butter wouldn't melt in their mouths, and told me to let them get on with the clearing up please. Give me strength.

Saturday afternoon and evening stretched ahead of me, with nothing on the horizon until Sunday evening, so I was glad to be called away from sorting out my tournament gear to speak to Rosie on the phone. (Quick reminder – Rosie and Harriet are the other doubles pair from the Club.) Harriet's away until tomorrow, so Rosie was at a loose end, which suited me fine.

'Make me laugh, Alex,' she said. 'I'm all sad and lonely because I met this boy on holiday and he's still out there and I miss him.'

'Oh not you, too! All these holiday romances are making me sick. Didn't you have anything better to do?'

'Well, we did swim, and er . . . play table tennis, and—'

'Where have you been, exactly?'

'Camping in France. He lives quite near here, though. Says he'll come and watch me play next week – when he gets back. I'm ever so rusty. You don't fancy coming up to the Club later on, do you?'

'Don't mind. Just let me wait for my wash to finish so I can hang it out.'

'Doesn't your mum do that sort of thing for you?'

'Easier to do it myself. She's got five men to look after!'

'That's not the attitude.'

'Try telling her that.'

Joel came up to the Club with me – a mixed blessing. Rosie had eyes only for him at first. And she looked tanned and beautiful, so Joel deigned to speak to her, while I stood twiddling my thumbs. When she finally turned to me, Rosie said, 'Hey, Alex, you look different!'

Joel gave a derisive laugh and went into the pavilion to check the noticeboards. 'What do you mean?' I asked.

'Not sure. Has your hair grown or something?'

'I don't know. Perhaps the daily Baby Bio treatment is starting to take effect.'

'Oh Alex! You're so funny.' (It's easy to make some people laugh.)

Four men were just leaving one of the courts, so we went over to bag it. One of the 'men' was Paddy! I saw that another was his father.

'Hi Paddy!' Rosie and I both said.

'Hi girls,' said Paddy.

'Why didn't you say on the phone that you were coming up today?' I asked him. I didn't like Paddy going mysterious on me.

'Last minute thing,' he said. 'Dad needed someone to make up a four. How are you, Rosie? You're looking bronzed and beautiful.'

'I've just come back from France,' she said.

'She's all aglow because she's in LURVE,' I said, paranoid that Paddy might be on the lookout for a more glamorous partner.

'Is that what happens to people?' he said. 'They get radioactive?'

'Well, girls glow, but boys *sweat*, don't they?'

'Stop it, you two,' said Rosie. 'Go home, Paddy. Let me have Alex. See you on Monday?'

'You *are* playing in the tournament, aren't you Paddy?' I asked innocently.

'Of course he is,' said Rosie impatiently.

'Well, if Rosie says I am, then I guess I must be,' said Paddy, setting off after his father. 'See you tomorrow, Al!'

I reckon that point went to him.

SATURDAY

Winning is a state of mind. So is losing.

EVENT/S	VENUE	WEATHER CONDITIONS	PHYSICAL HEALTH
Practice	Club	Fine	Rubbish

OPPONENT
Lucy on court, but Paddy really, because he's being odd.

TACTICS
Make him realise he's being odd.

EQUIPMENT
Sarcasm, humour.

COMMENTS
Wish he'd just say straight out that he wants us to be partners as usual.

TOMORROW'S MATCH
Practice: Me and Paddy v Lucy and Richard.

I went up to the Club for our practice as planned on Sunday evening. Joel and Phil came too. Harriet was home from holiday and she and Rosie were sitting round chatting with Richard and Lucy. The arrival of my brothers instantly distracted the girls, so Richard came over to me. I hadn't seen him for a while. When he and Paddy first played doubles together they looked hilarious because Richard was a tiny black boy and Paddy was a huge white boy by comparison. Now Richard has just about overtaken Paddy in height. He's extremely good-looking, deadly serious about his tennis and gets very angry with himself when he makes mistakes. He's a good partner though, and he never gets cross with Lucy or Paddy.

'Hi Alex! How you doing, man? You look different. Is it your hair or something?'

'No, Rich. Same old Al. Still look like a boy, only funnier. Where's that Paddy? Shall we go and start? – or we'll never drag Lucy away from my horrible brothers.'

Richard and I went on to the lower court. I was facing the entrance to the Club so I saw Paddy arriving on his bike. He nodded apologetically to us as he got off and then went to detach Lucy from the group around Phil and Joel. Watching Paddy talking to the girls I started to panic all over again. What if he didn't want me as his partner any more? Why hadn't he asked me? I could see the girls flirting with him. It came so naturally to them. Lucy was still at it as they came on court. I hoped she wasn't going to bring up the subject of partners. 'Come on you two,' I shouted, before she had a chance. 'Or we won't finish before dark.'

'Yes, we will,' said Paddy, joining me. 'We'll wipe the floor with them in no time.'

'You wish,' said Richard. 'I'm spinning now and we'll start in five minutes flat. Rough or smooth?'

'Rough!' called Paddy.

'Rough it is!' said Richard, and we were off.

Though I say it myself, Paddy and I make a pretty good team. We just seem to anticipate each other's moves and know precisely when to take or leave a shot. Pit us against Richard getting cross with himself and Lucy being apologetic and we're almost bound to win.

I know Paddy and Lucy so well, it's hard to be objective, but I'll try and describe them. They're both nice looking. Lucy has frizzy dark hair which she ties back. She's got a pretty face with wide brown eyes and a friendly expression. She's shorter than I am (most girls are). Paddy is about the same height as me at the moment, though I expect he'll be several inches taller soon. He's quite stockily built – not long and lean like a lot of tennis players. His hair is light brown, a bit darker than mine maybe, but while I've got bog-standard grey-blue eyes, Paddy's absolute best feature is his dark blue eyes and long, sweeping eyelashes. (We tease him about them. Lucy says they make him look like a giraffe!) He doesn't look that different from when he was a little boy, just bigger. He cycles everywhere and does weights, so he's very fit physically, fitter than the rest of us. Richard's had coaching for most of his life, but Paddy's had very little. Like me, he was taught by his dad, so he's fast but not as stylish as, say, Joel and Phil, who've had loads of professional coaching on top of Dad's.

Paddy was right. We won. It was dusk by the time we finished though, so we went and sat in the pavilion where Rosie and Harriet were still trying to chat up my brothers. Phil considers himself way older than my friends, and Joel's so superior, they weren't getting very far.

We got drinks out of the machine and sat down with them. To my horror, Lucy turned to Paddy and said straight out, 'So, Paddy. You and Al are on good form. I take it you are going to be partners next week?'

Paddy flushed. I was waiting with baited breath for his answer when Joel butted in. 'I want to get back, Phil. You coming? And you'd better come too, Alex, unless you want to walk home alone in the dark. See ya, Richard, Paddy. And you girls. Good luck in the tournament. I'm playing in the Prestige Gold Cup next weekend so I can't do Mapledon this year. Bad form to make the final and then have to drop out.'

Snooty so-and-so. The Prestige Gold Cup is exactly how it sounds. Only extremely talented players need apply, so Joel likes to drop it into the conversation. I gathered up my stuff and trailed home after my brothers. It was the eve of the Mapledon tournament and I still couldn't be certain whether or not I had a mixed doubles partner. Wretched boys. Life would be so much easier if I simply was one.

SUNDAY

Anticipation is more than half the game.

EVENT/S	VENUE	WEATHER CONDITIONS	PHYSICAL HEALTH
Practice	Club	Grey	Still crap

OPPONENT
All my brothers except Phil. Why can't they leave me alone? I feel embarrassed enough without them making it worse all the time.
Mum. Because she never tells them off.
Lucy and Richard really.

TACTICS
Ignore brothers.
Wait for Richard to get cross with himself.

EQUIPMENT
None necessary.

COMMENTS
Hate boys. Hate having to think about periods.
Still don't know if Paddy wants to be my partner in tournament.
Tennis OK.

TOMORROW'S MATCH
Help! Don't know. Only singles and girls' doubles though.
Mixed won't start until Wednesday.

THREE

Monday morning. First day of the tournament. Players go in at about eleven, but most matches don't get under way until the afternoon. You've probably watched Wimbledon, so you know how a tournament works, but I always have to remind Zoe and the others. There's boys' singles and girls' singles: under-16 and under-18 are the only important ones. Likewise, boys' doubles and girls' doubles. Mixed doubles starts later on because there are fewer entries, especially in the younger age groups, when you get some real comedy pairings.

The tournament is held at Mapledon, a big club that's about five miles away. Dad drives us if he can get off work. Mum, incidentally, doesn't drive – she must be the only ever 'tennis mum' in history not to do so. More often we get lifts from friends and partners. Lucy usually takes me. Dad took us today because it was the first day and he wanted to check out the draw for Phil and maybe watch a few players in action so he could advise him. The twins played together last year in the under-12s but this year they'd be in the under-14s, and Dad also reckons it would be better if they didn't play together, so they're not here this year, which is great.

So, first things first. Woke up, rushed to loo. No sign of anything, certainly no dead squirrels. Packed emergency supplies into sponge bag, wore dark tracksuit and hoped for the best.

Twins being obnoxious at breakfast because the attention was on Phil and me. Dad chirpy because he wasn't at work. Mum sighing copiously over the amount of laundry that she was shoving into the machine. She'd already made packed lunches for the three of us. I know I should be grateful, but there's a snack bar at Mapledon where all my friends buy toasted sandwiches and crisps and drinks, and I'd much rather have the money than dull old sandwiches and fruit.

We picked up Phil's partner, Kieron (he doesn't belong to our club), on the way. Nobody said much, we were all feeling too nervous. My stomach was so full of butterflies I began to think that had been the problem all along.

As soon as we rolled into the car park at Mapledon it all came flooding back. Loads of big cars. Keen, sun-tanned parents dressed in sports gear and sunglasses, exchanging holiday news. An alarming number of ex-tremely small players, all apparently shorter than the tennis racquets they're carrying. Older players quickly find-ing their own space, where they lounge about as if they own the place. Or that's how it seems. The same feeling that I stick out like a sore thumb, belonging neither with the tinies nor the older ones, and never seeing anyone of my own age.

Then Lucy came roaring up and said, 'Have you seen the draw?' which of course we hadn't because we'd only just arrived, and she kind of skipped alongside us trying to remember it and scaring me silly, thinking I'd been drawn against the top seed in the first round.

The clubhouse was a hive of activity and competitive-ness, with parents and players gathered round the flip-charts where the draws were displayed. Comments were quickly relayed in loud voices and even on mobile phones.

Phil went off on his own and Lucy dragged Dad and me to the under-16s girls' singles board.

There's nothing random about the draw. It's calculated to ensure that the two best players entered get to play against each other in the final. A huge crowd was gathered there and I had to claw my way through to the front. Miss A. Dunbar. Every year I scan the list for Alexandra or Alex, but at Mapledon it's all very formal and old-fashioned. Here I'm Miss A. Dunbar, just like Wimbledon. Where is she, this Miss A. Dunbar? Hey! Dad called out from the back at the same time as I saw it. I was seeded! It looked as though I was expected to make it to the quarter-final. I looked more closely. My first match was against someone I'd never heard of – a Miss P. Chang. I ducked out of the crowd. 'Well done, Alex,' said Dad. 'That's excellent when you must be one of the youngest.'

Lucy had checked the doubles draw already, so I didn't need to fight my way over to that one. She wanted us to bag a practice court together. Dad said he'd go and sniff out the competition. There was no sign of anyone else from the Club, so I followed Lucy out on to one of the back courts. It was fortunately quite a bright, chilly, windy day. I reckoned I would be able to stay in my tracksuit all the time if I was lucky.

We giggled our way through a few stretching exercises. Meanwhile, the first and second seeds from the under-16s – Connie and Alicia – incredibly talented black cousins, came and starting knocking up on the court next door. They had all the professional gear, and wasted no time chatting (unlike us). 'We might have to play them,' Lucy whispered when we met at the net, 'if we get to the semi-finals.'

'As if!' I whispered back. 'I think I heard that they're both sixteen next month. Junior Wimbledon and stuff. We wouldn't stand a chance.'

'Probably won't get that far, anyway,' said Lucy. We hadn't played for long when I caught my name coming over the tannoy. 'Would Miss A. Dunbar and Miss P. Chang please go to Court Six. First Round, Under-16 Girls' Singles. Miss A. Dunbar and Miss P. Chang.'

Paddy came rushing over. He seemed almost as nervous as I was. 'Did you hear that, Alex?'

'Yeah, yeah,' I said, trying to sound casual as I put my tracksuit top on back to front. 'Miss *Pchang*, here I come. Sounds like a ball pinging off a racquet doesn't it?'

'Will you stay and knock up with me, Paddy,' asked Lucy, 'or are you going to watch Alex?'

'I'll knock up for a bit,' he said. 'And then we'll go and support Al. I've got a feeling old Pchang is quite good.'

'Funny how Alex's nicknames always stick, isn't it?' said Lucy.

Pchang and I reported in to the desk and then solemnly made our way to Court Six, followed in procession by both her parents and her coach. Dad came over to hug me and wish me good luck and said he might come over later. Pchang was a very silent girl. We knocked up and chose ends, and almost all she said was 'Sorry' from time to time. She wasn't bad at all – but I was better. The constant encouragement from her parents and coach began to get on my nerves which was good because it gave me an edge. I won the first set 6–4 but I was actually losing the second when my troops arrived: Lucy, Paddy, Dad, Phil and Kieron. Every time the Changs shouted encouragement, my lot shouted counter-encouragement. (In fact I could sometimes hear Paddy muttering 'pchang!' when she hit the ball really hard.) It was what I needed. I equalised and then went on to win the match. Pchang and I – her name was actually Philippa, I discovered (Phchang!) – shook hands and went off with our separate bands of supporters. I felt quite sorry for her. She didn't seem to have any friends at the tournament at all.

As we walked back to the desk, Kieron said to me, 'Hi, I'm Kieron.'

'I know,' I said. 'Kieron, you travelled here in the car with me this morning. And we've met tons of times before, dipstick!'

'Oy!' said big brother Phil. 'That's no way to speak to my partner!'

'Sorry,' said Kieron. 'But you were sitting in front, and I was a bundle of nerves. You must look different this year. Anyway, well done. Philippa was expected to win that.'

'Oh. Does that mean I wasn't seeded after all?'

'Think we might have got it wrong,' said Dad. 'But never mind – you'll get to the quarter-final, you see. You show 'em!' That's my dad, always expecting the best of me.

I gave our score to the desk and was told that the doubles were starting later in the afternoon, which gave me several hours off. Lucy had a bye (no match) for the first round which meant she was also free until our doubles match. We found somewhere to sit and eat our sandwiches (her mum makes them too).

'How about Kieron talking to you then!' she said after a gulp of Tango.

I had some too. I burped before replying. 'He obviously mistook me for someone who would be flattered.'

'Well, he is rather gorgeous. Old Phchang quite lost her concentration when he and Phil turned up.'

'Are you trying to say that's why I won the match?'

'No, no! Not at all. I was just going to say that maybe you *should* be flattered by Kieron taking an interest.'

'Watch my lips, Lucy.' I burped again. 'Boys do not interest me. OK? I am surrounded by them. I wouldn't mind *being* one. Though on second thoughts, they're all so disgusting that I'm glad I'm not.' Lucy gave me a disapproving look as if to remind me that burping was pretty disgusting, so I did it again, just to irritate her. 'Anyway, what's the hurry all of a sudden?'

'Dunno,' said Lucy. 'It's just that once you do start fancying boys, you can't help it, I suppose. And it's a laugh,' she added.

'Yeah,' I said. 'Like going to the dentist is a laugh.'

'You're a hopeless case,' said Lucy. 'Let's go and mingle, maybe watch the boys. I heard Paddy being called a few minutes ago.' I followed her without another word because suddenly – far more terrifying than any tennis match – the challenge of the 'holiday romance' reared its ugly head. I thought of telling Lucy about it, but she'd only jeer at me after that last conversation. How on earth was I going to carry it off? Kieron had been a bit interested in me, hadn't he? I couldn't think of anyone else. But no. It was impossible. It's just not the sort of thing I do. Where would I even begin? How could I have agreed to anything so utterly ridiculous?

We made our way over to the clubhouse. The whole place was heaving now. All the old hands were there. Another family large enough to rival us Dunbars are the Smarts. Tom and Louise Smart are the same ages as Joel and me. There are at least two younger ones and an older one. I've always found Louise annoying – she wiggles her bottom when she walks, making the pleats of her tennis skirt swing from side to side. Anyway, they have a big house with a swimming pool, close by in Mapledon, where the cliquey set get invited to barbecues. Joel's been, naturally. I don't think Phil's ever quite made it into the in-crowd – or the 'Smart set' as everyone calls it – but Kieron probably has.

'Uh-oh,' I whispered to Lucy. I'd just spotted Ethlie (known as Deathly Ethlie by all and sundry), a sad girl I wanted to avoid. She's one of those people who latches on and pretends you're her friend. We had to put up with her last year. Sounds mean, I know, but she follows us around like a little dog and laughs uproariously at absolutely every-thing I do, whether it's meant to be funny or not. I could say, 'I've got a hideous incurable disease and my grand-mother's just been run over by a bus,' and she'd titter and say, 'Oh no! Really? Ooh, you are funny, Alex!' Lucy and I immediately ducked out of sight like naughty six-year-olds.

We wandered out to the main courts in search of Paddy's match. The singles were in full swing now, and almost every court was occupied. We spotted Richard in the dis-tance, so we followed him and ended up in the right place. The game had just begun. Paddy's opponent was listed as R. Laxton. Richard sat on the bank with another boy, presumably a friend of R. Laxton's. We joined them. 'How's it going?' I whispered to Richard. I didn't want to distract Paddy.

'Nothing yet,' whispered Richard back.

'He and Robin seem to be pretty evenly matched,' whis-pered the friend. 'Hi, I'm Charlie.'

Charlie and Robin. They were new to me. They were similarly built, lanky boys, Charlie dark, Robin fair. I was about to carry on the whispered conversation, but I saw Paddy glaring at us, so I gave him a wave and shut up. It was a close match. Robin had style and Paddy had speed. It was probably going to depend on who was fittest – and in that department I'd put my money on Paddy any day. At 5–all Robin spent a lot of time picking up tennis balls and retying his laces while Paddy waited calmly for him to carry on. Charlie started talking again when they were changing ends at 5–6. 'Robin's my partner,' he said, 'so I want him to win, but the other chap's got a lot of power hasn't he? This could take a while.'

I was about to say, 'And Paddy's my partner,' but I didn't dare tempt fate. 'Paddy's from my club,' I said, 'so I want *him* to win. Is this your first year here?'

'We don't normally do this tournament,' Charlie said. 'In fact we're doing the Cup this weekend, too, so I seriously hope neither of us gets into the finals!'

'Is that the Prestige Gold Cup? That's a bit bad, isn't it?' I asked. 'One of my brothers has dropped out of Mapledon because he's playing in the Cup. Why doesn't Robin just let Paddy win now, if that's the case? Paddy's desperate to get to the final.'

'Don't blame us,' said Charlie. 'Our coach tells Robin and me what to do.'

'Is he called Batman?' I asked. 'Tennisbatman?' It was a pathetic joke, but Charlie guffawed loudly, making Paddy fluff a serve.

'Do you mind if I take that again?' Paddy asked Robin, frowning in our direction.

'Sorreee,' I mouthed, and then Lucy was tugging at my sleeve because our names had been called for the first round of the girls' doubles and we had to check in.

'I don't know,' she said. 'It's so unfair. Guys chatting you up all over the place, and you couldn't care less. That Charlie bloke obviously thought you were really funny.'

The thought popped into my mind that Charlie might *just* be another candidate in the romance stakes, but it popped out again very quickly indeed. My brain finds that sort of data difficult to process.

'I try my best to amuse. I want to go to the locker room first, Lucy. Will you check in for us? I'll be there in a minute.' I ran off, praying that it was too much fizzy drink making me desperate for the loo.

'You OK?' asked Lucy when I found her.

'I'm fine,' I said. I was, thank goodness. We were drawn against two very blobby girls who were far, far worse players than we were. And of course that meant that Lucy and I played atrociously. Our audience consisted solely of Ethlie. We scraped through the first set and we were 4–all in the second set when Dad turned up to watch, closely followed by a triumphant looking Paddy. Lucy and I were doing badly, returning stupid donkey-drops with even stupider donkey-drops that went in the net. We'd reached the point of snarling at one another. Dad and Paddy called me over as I was walking back to serve. 'Play *hard*,' said Dad. 'Bend your knees.'

'Run in to the net, Al,' said Paddy. 'Go for the kill! By the way, I won.' I gave him a thumbs up sign as I moved back to the baseline.

'Come on, Alex!' came another voice as I was about to serve. Charlie and Robin had stopped to watch. I served an ace and we went on to win 6–4 without dropping a single point.

'I could murder an iced bun,' said Lucy, after we'd all shaken hands and come off the court.

'So could I,' said Robin, surprisingly.

'I thought I'd go and watch Phil,' said Dad.

'I'll come with you,' said Paddy. 'He should win, shouldn't he? Are you coming too – er—?'

'Charlie,' said Charlie. 'I'm the partner of the guy you just thrashed, Robin. Is the Phil we're off to watch Phil Dunbar?'

'My brother, yes,' I said, following them and guiltily leaving Lucy to the mercy of Robin. She didn't look that unhappy about it.

'Wow,' said Charlie. 'So you're Joel Dunbar's sister, too, presumably?'

'Might be,' I said.

Charlie looked taken aback and then laughed. 'You get used to her,' said Paddy appreciatively. 'How do you know Joel, Charlie? He's not playing this week because he's in the Prestige Gold Cup at the weekend.'

'Everyone knows Joel, don't they?' said Charlie, warming to Paddy, though I don't know if Paddy was warming to him. I was glad Charlie glossed over the fact that he was in the Cup too. Paddy wouldn't have approved.

I linked my arm in Dad's and let the two boys walk ahead. Charlie was a very suave guy with thick, shiny brown hair and long tanned legs. Beside him Paddy looked stockier than ever. 'How's my girl?' said Dad. 'Glad you picked up at the end of your match. It would've been terrible to have lost to those two.'

'Shocking, wasn't it? I'm glad you all arrived and shook us out of our apathy.'

'Quite a little entourage you're building up. Who is this Charlie boy?'

'I dunno. Someone who knows Joel. I haven't seen him play, but Paddy managed to beat his partner, Robin.'

'Good old Paddy. It would be super if he won this year.'

Phil was playing on one of the main courts and there was quite a crowd watching him. As Dad and I tried to slide inconspicuously into the row of seats, people turned round to smile at us. Charlie, who ended up sitting next to me, was impressed. 'The Dunbars are obviously good people to know!' he said to Paddy.

Lucy and Robin turned up soon after, closely followed by Ethlie. Ethlie schmoozed up to Paddy while Lucy grimaced at me behind their backs. Brother Phil was winning easily, so Lucy and I climbed over the seats and went to the clubhouse to look at tomorrow's draw. 'Ooh, thank goodness we've got rid of Deathly Ethlie! She doesn't half give me the creeps.'

'Me too,' I said. 'Still, Paddy's got her now.'

'Paddy's always nice to everyone,' said Lucy. 'Which means that Ethlie will love him for ever, like a faithful dog.'

'Arf, arf,' I said, and we both giggled.

The first day's play had gone more or less according to plan, if you didn't count the little upset I'd created by beating Phchang. Tomorrow I'd be playing against one of the Blobs, and Lucy was up against Rosie, which was a bit tough on both of them – it's rotten playing against a friend in a tournament.

I was ready to go home. I suddenly wanted my own room and a break from all these people. My stomach was feeling odd again. Lucy rang her mum on her mobile and she offered to give me a lift home. I went to tell Dad just as everyone was clapping Phil for winning. Louise Smart had gathered a little group around her that included Kieron and the new boys, Charlie and Robin. Ethlie was hanging in there, no doubt hoping for a Smart invitation, but Paddy was on his own, not to be drawn.

Lucy nudged me. 'Ask him,' she said. 'Go on, ask Paddy about the mixed doubles now.'

'I can't, Lucy,' I said. 'He's in unapproachable mode. You

see? That's what I mean when I say he's acting strangely this year. He never used to be like this.'

'Shall I ask Richard to ask him?' she said.

'No, that's daft. Right now I just want to hope for the best.'

My room is my haven. There is possibly only one decent rule in our house – which you might even have noticed – and that is that all of us knock on each other's bedroom door, including the twins (who have separate rooms). It doesn't mean to say that someone won't knock and come crashing in straight away, but they will knock. After supper I lay on my bed to think. I put on my *Jungle Book* CD and gazed up at the ceiling. All right, I know my taste in music is immature and it wasn't a hundred per cent appropriate to my mood, but never mind.

I always feel like this when I've been with a large group of people. I find myself wondering where I fit in with them and whether they like me or not. Louise Smart usually ignores me, so that's nothing new. Ethlie's a pain. I don't *want* her to like me. But Charlie and Robin – the new guys – had been friendly. I smiled at the memory of Kieron introducing himself to me. Kieron who's been Phil's partner for ages. Idiot! Something has definitely changed this year. Perhaps it's me! All those people saying I *look* different. I don't really *feel* different. *I* don't think . . .

I stood up and went over to my mirror. To be honest, I don't look in it very often. It's not as if I wear make-up or anything. It's true, my hair, which always goes fairer in the summer, is a bit longer. My fringe has grown so much, I have to hold it back off my face with a hairband or clips. And it's just about long enough at the back to scrape into a silly little ponytail. You can see I've got eyebrows and cheekbones now! Maybe that's why people think I look different. I pulled my T-shirt into a bunch at my back and regarded myself closely. Perhaps I do go *in* a bit more at the waist than I did before (I certainly don't go *out*, up top). Perhaps Alex Dunbar is a girl whether she wants to be one or not. That could be a plus in the holiday romance allure and seduction stakes. Help! What have I let myself in for here? Two boys being friendly is a zillion miles away from actually 'having a romance'.

My big gorilla poster grinned knowingly down at me from the wall. Time *he* went.

MONDAY

A good tennis player is like a good orchestral musician: rhythm, timing, pitch and harmony are all crucial to the performance.

EVENT/S	VENUE	WEATHER CONDITIONS	PHYSICAL HEALTH
U-16 singles	Mapledon	Bright but chilly	Unpredictable
U-16 doubles			

OPPONENT
Phchang (singles).
The Blobs (doubles).

TACTICS
Didn't mess about (after bad beginning).

RESULT
Won both matches.

EQUIPMENT
Dark tracksuit proving useful.

COMMENTS
Good to see people again. Kieron introduced himself to me! Two new guys, Charlie
    and Robin – v. friendly. Ch thinks Joel's cool so he must be a bit of a prat.
    STILL not certain about mixed doubles. This is getting silly, but for some
    reason Paddy makes me nervous when we're not playing.

TOMORROW'S MATCH
One of the Blobs for singles. Two unknowns for doubles. Should be an easy day.
Lucy has to play Rosie (poor both of them).
Paddy has to play Richard (also poor both of them).

FOUR

Tuesday. Day Two. Mum was in a particularly filthy mood this morning, even though Dad had left for work and the twins had gone off somewhere (Joel was still in bed) so only Phil and I were having breakfast. I wondered if the tournament had something to do with it. Too many packed lunches perhaps. We weren't needed at Mapledon until midday, so it wasn't even that early. She wearily offered us a cooked breakfast, which neither of us wanted, and huffed and puffed as she made our sandwiches.

'You all right, Mum?' asked Phil cautiously.

'Why shouldn't I be?' she asked, somewhat ungraciously, I thought. Phil and I both shut up and refrained from saying, 'Because you're sighing even more than usual,' and got up from the table to put our things in the dishwasher.

'Kieron's offered us both a lift today,' Phil said, once we'd made ourselves scarce.

'That's OK, Lucy's picking me up any minute now,' I said.

'Kieron seems unaccountably interested in you – did you notice?' Phil asked.

'Was "unaccountably" his expression, or yours?'

'I don't understand you, Alex. Most girls would be really chuffed.'

'Well, I'm not most girls, am I? I'm your favourite brother, remember?'

'Maybe it's time you started being my favourite sister.'

'Your *only* sister.'

'Shut up. You know what I mean.' He punched me on the shoulder.

*

Lucy and I went straight to the clubhouse. I felt as if we'd been coming to Mapledon for weeks already. There were fewer parents today. There is a certain type of professional tennis mum who attends these tournaments. She is always tanned, always wears sunglasses and is permanently glued to her mobile. There is another sort – floral and harassed, usually with millions of small boys – but she is quieter and less in evidence than the first sort. Mrs Smart – 'call-me-Janice' – is one of the first sort, the professional ones. Not only does she organise her own brood very efficiently, she likes to have a handle on all the other 'young people' as well, at least the suitable ones, e.g. Joel.

Louise annoying-bottom-wiggle Smart and her mother were surrounded by quite a few players. They were talking about the possibility of a swim that evening and a big barbecue towards the end of the week. It was a toss-up between the Thursday and the Friday. Louise plumped for the Thursday because more people would still be left in the tournament. So it was put about that the Smarts were having a barbecue party on Thursday evening. It was the sort of general invitation that carries its own subtle rules – the sort that I assume excludes me. The so-called 'Smart set' know who they are.

After checking the board, Lucy and I walked over to the outer courts. Nice coolish day. Nothing odd about keeping tracksuit bottoms on, certainly not at the level of tennis I'd be playing. We polished off our sandwiches and then ambled on court for a knock-up and a gossip. Lucy finds me very frustrating, I know.

'I really – like Kieron – don't you?' she said between strokes.

'He's all right,' I said. 'Bit of a bighead.' I wasn't ready to tell Lucy about the romance project – not yet anyway.

'What about – Charlie?' she said.

'He's a – prat,' I said, whacking the ball for emphasis. I wanted this conversation to end.

'I thought you liked him. Anyway, he's not a prat,' she said. 'He's – fit.'

'That doesn't stop him being a prat. He's a fit prat, but he's only interested in me because I'm Joel's sister.'

'You're lucky. I wish I had a brother to make people interested in me.'

'You really don't wish you had brothers,' I said. 'Anyway, I want people to be interested in me for myself, not because of some pain of a brother.'

We were interrupted by Phil and Kieron. 'I hope you're not talking about me,' said Phil. 'Thought we'd come and knock up with you, give you a run for your money.'

'Blimey,' I said. 'To what do we owe this honour?'

'Well, it certainly wasn't my idea,' said Phil, herding me down the other end with Lucy, 'but I'm sure it will improve your tennis.'

I love playing against the boys. It raises my game like anything. I had some great baseline rallies with Kieron.

'She's practically as good as you!' said Kieron to Phil.

'Rubbish!' said Phil, hitting a hard, spinning shot on to my backhand.

I wasn't having that. I went up to the net and started sending volleys at him, fancy ones, leaping and turning ones. I beat him nearly every time. Then, when my back was turned he childishly whacked a ball straight at me. It hit me on the arm.

'Ouch!'

'Should have volleyed that one, shouldn't you!'

'Phil!' The pain had brought tears to my eyes. 'You hurt

me!' Honestly, boys just can't help being competitive. Even Phil can't cope if I win occasionally.

'Hey, are you all right?' Kieron was all concern.

'Course she's all right,' said Phil gruffly, possibly feeling just a teensy bit foolish.

'There's a great red mark!' said Kieron. 'Charming brother you've got!' He smiled sympathetically at me. I caught Lucy at the edge of my vision looking all wide-eyed.

Announcements were coming over the tannoy. We stopped to listen. 'Better go, Kieron,' said Phil. 'Sorry, Al. Didn't mean to hurt you,' he said. And punched my arm – just where he'd hit it with the tennis ball.

'Ow!'

'Oops. We'll be off then,' said Phil. 'Really didn't do *that* on purpose, Al.'

'See ya!' said Kieron.

Lucy came over to inspect my wound. 'Wow. That must have been worth a bit of pain, just for Kieron's sympathy! Did Phil hit the ball at you on purpose, then?'

'Oh yes,' I replied. 'Like I said – brothers! Boys! Who needs 'em?'

'Well, at least he didn't *punch* you on purpose.'

'No. But why are you so protective all of a sudden?'

'I just didn't believe someone as nice as Phil could be such a bully.'

'You ain't seen nothin', then. That *is* nice compared to Joel and the twins, who have horribleness down to a fine art.'

I had to go off to an outer court with my opponent, one of the Blobs from yesterday. Blob Two was our only audience. I remembered Dad's words from the doubles, and ruthlessly set out to win every shot. Which I did, more or less. Blob One spent a lot of time drinking water and wiping her brow when we changed ends, and Blob Two spun out the business of moving the little tabs that show the score, but I still won 6–0, 6–0 in little more than half an hour. Humiliating for her, but not a lot I could do about it. We shook hands and wandered off to report. Lucy appeared almost immediately because we had a doubles match to play. 'Lucky I'm not too exhausted,' I said. 'Do I get time for a drink?'

'Yes, of course,' said Lucy. 'But they know it's practically a walkover. These two are even worse than the Blobs. It'd better be a walkover because I've got my match against Rosie later this afternoon, worse luck.'

'Yeah, that's a tough one.'

As predicted, the doubles was a piece of cake. We didn't give them a chance. Lucy faltered momentarily when she saw Robin and Charlie stop to watch for a few minutes, but the whole thing lasted about the same time as my singles match.

'Not a bad way to warm up, I suppose,' said Lucy as we came off. We went ahead to report, and our opponents followed. It was still early.

'How soon do you think you could play your singles against Rosie?' the woman on the desk asked Lucy.

'Straight away if I can just grab a bottle of water and go to the loo first. Wish me luck, Al. Glad I haven't had too much time to think about it.'

'Break a leg,' I said as she disappeared into the club-house.

Ethlie materialised beside me. She always comes too close and invades your personal space. 'How did you do?' she asked me excitedly.

'I won,' I said. 'And then we won.'

'Oh no! Really?' (*Why* does she always say that?) 'Who's your partner for the mixed doubles?' she asked, when our score had been logged in. 'No one's asked me – I don't seem to be very popular with the boys, but there are so many to choose from this year.'

'Dunno,' I said nonchalantly, wishing she'd spontaneously combust. I didn't want to admit, even to myself, that I belonged in the same partnerless category as Deathly Ethlie.

'D'you think one of the new guys – Charlie or Robin – might play with me?'

A horrible image of two sleek tigers tossing a scrawny little terrier between them filled my mind, but I refrained from communicating it. 'Dunno,' I said again. I could see her ears pointing, I tell you. 'Ask them and see.'

'Oh no! Really?' she tittered. 'Anyway, I'd much rather watch the girls. Shall we see how Rosie and Lucy are doing?' she asked, as if the pair of us had a jolly action-packed afternoon all mapped out.

Damn. That's where I was heading anyway, and I didn't want Ethlie doing her limpet act. 'Must just go to the loo,' I said in an effort to lose her. 'You go on.'

'I wouldn't go off without you!' she said. 'Don't worry, I'll wait.'

Argh! I went to the loo anyway. I'd got used to the turmoil that was once a well-behaved gut, but I couldn't altogether relax. I eavesdropped on at least two conversations to eke out the time down there. Both were interesting, and both kept me locked in the loo until the speakers had gone away. The Blobs were discussing my earlier singles match. Blob One was saying, 'I really should have won. She wasn't supposed to get beyond the first round.'

'It was a shame you were having a bad day,' Blob Two said

supportively. 'I'm sure you would have beaten her hollow on a good day.'

'You wish,' I said to myself as the door closed behind them. But then I heard Louise Smart's distinctive cut-glass voice.

'Guard the door for me, will you?' she said to whoever it was. She carried on from inside the cubicle. 'You are coming tonight, aren't you, Claire?' (I don't know Claire, but I pictured the girl with smooth dark hair I'd seen with Louise earlier.) 'You must see this Joel Dunbar guy, he's gorgeous. It means I'm going to have to ask Phil and the sister, so he simply can't get out of it, but he's worth it.'

'Isn't he here this week then?'

'No. He's in the Cup this weekend.'

'With Chris Green and co.?'

'That's the one. We'll have to go over there and watch them,' said Louise, flushing the loo and emerging. I couldn't hear much after that against the sound of the cistern. Didn't need to really, did I? So, I was about to receive a Smart invitation. Lucky old me. Maybe I should say no, and persuade Joel not to go either. Nah. Wouldn't work. I came out. Oh God – there was Ethlie.

'Thought you'd died,' she said cheerfully. (I wish *you* had, I thought.) But then I was saved by the tannoy. Ethlie was called to play a doubles match and I was able to go and watch Lucy without her.

Lucy and Rosie had gathered quite a crowd. I looked on from a distance for a while to gauge how it was going. Lucy, who was serving well, seemed to have the edge on Rosie right now. I decided to stay back until the end of her service game. Wouldn't do to distract my friend and make her do a double fault. When she won the game I moved closer to hear the score. It was 7–6 to Lucy and still the first set.

My friends from the Club were sitting right at the front. I don't think I would have liked that if I'd been playing another Club member, but they were being very quiet and unobtrusive. I sat on the bank behind with Charlie and Robin. We were out of the players' line of vision there. 'Hi guys!' We spoke in whispers.

'How did you get on?' asked Charlie.

'Six–love, six–love against the Blob. Same against the Ugly Sisters. What about you?'

'Haven't played yet,' said Charlie. 'I think I'm against that guy over there – if he's R. Vishindi. Is he good?'

'Terrible,' I said.

'Really?'

'Course not. He's probably a bit better than Neil there and not quite as good as Richard, who's playing Paddy on Court Three – depending which side of bed he got out of.'

'Temperamental then?'

'Hey, these are my guys! I'm not giving away secrets!'

'What d'you mean, your guys? Are you going out with *all* of them?'

'Don't be daft. They're from my club, that's all.'

'The Miss A. Dunbar fan club? Can I join?'

I giggled.

'Ssh, you two,' said Robin. 'They're playing a tie-break.'

I looked over and saw Lucy glaring at me as she picked up some balls from the corner of the court. I shut up.

Lucy won the tie-break and they launched into a second gruelling set. You don't want to lose when you play a friend, but you don't quite want to win either! Robin, Charlie and I moved back even further, so we could carry on chatting without disturbing the players. Robin's mobile went off at one point, so it was a good thing we did.

'Robin's girlfriend,' said Charlie. 'Jealous. Won't leave

him alone. Switch it *off*, Rob! You're distracting everyone now.'

Robin smiled. He was a good-natured bloke. 'Better than having to listen to you two chat each other up all day.'

Charlie and I both protested. 'She's funny,' said Charlie. 'I can't help it if she makes me laugh.'

'We can go and watch Paddy playing Richard if you want,' I said. 'Then you can imagine Raj being somewhere in between, and see for yourself. I usually try and watch Paddy anyway.'

'Is Paddy your boyfriend then?' asked Charlie.

'NO!' I said – too loudly. Rosie glanced over crossly this time. Charlie and I got up to go. Robin gestured that he was staying. 'I have boy *friends*, not a boyfriend! I'm just one of the lads, me.'

We wove our way across to where Paddy and Richard were slugging it out. Paddy waved at me, but he eyed Charlie suspiciously. I don't think he knows what to make of him.

At that moment it started to rain. Players all over carried on for a minute or so, but then the heavens opened and everyone rushed round the courts gathering their racquets and tennis balls before joining the mad dash for the clubhouse.

It was like an overcrowded party with everyone crammed in there in their damp tracksuits. I found myself washed up against Phil and Kieron and Louise Smart mid-conversation. 'Good,' said Kieron. 'So that means Alex will be coming.'

Louise looked embarrassed. 'Oh, of course,' she said.

'What?' I asked. 'What am I coming to?'

'For a swim at my house this evening,' said Louise. 'Presumably you and Phil and Joel can all come together?'

'Shouldn't count on Joel doing anything,' I said.

'Oh surely you and Phil can persuade him? Can't you?' Louise was pleading.

'We'll do our best,' said Phil. 'I'd like to come.'

'The weather will need to be a bit better before I go swimming,' I said, wanting her to beg.

'Don't feel you *have* to come—' Louise started to say.

I was enjoying this, not that swimming was actually my recreation of choice at this precise moment. 'Oh no, I'd love to come, Louise. Thanks so much for inviting me. Anyway, it looks as though the rain's easing up already.'

I started to move away because I'd spotted Paddy heading in my direction. 'Bloomin' rain,' he said grumpily, when we managed to get close enough to speak. 'I was just getting into my stride against Richard there. Beginning to needle him, go for his soft spots, make him riled with himself.'

'Steady on,' I said.

'And then we have to come off and be nice to each other.'

'Well, you are partners the rest of the time.'

'Yeah, but I want to *win* this year.'

'I know. Calm down, calm down.'

'Oh go on, just make a joke of it like you do about everything, why don't you.'

'Well I'm sorry,' I said, confused. Paddy's usually so cheery. I'm not used to seeing him frustrated and cross.

'No, I'm sorry,' he said. 'Shouldn't take it out on you.' He raised his head to apologise, the old giraffe-lashes fluttering like mad. Then he looked over my shoulder. 'Charlie-boy's after you again. Excuse me if I go and vent my frustrations on something that doesn't answer back.' He set off, but Charlie waylaid him.

'Hey! Hear you're coming to the swim, Alex. Are you coming too, Paddy?'

'What swim?' asked Paddy.

'At the Smarts',' said Charlie.

'They don't invite people like me,' said Paddy, sounding a bit brusque, and went on his way.

'But they do invite people like you?' said Charlie to me.

'Oh, Lousie only invited me because she wants my brother Joel to come,' I said.

'Lousie? Oh! Ha! I see, *Louise*!' Charlie guffawed.

'Not that I shall encourage him, of course.'

The rain had stopped and people were going outside again. Lucy passed on her way back to her match. Robin was with her. (I think the girlfriend on the mobile is fighting a losing battle.) '*You're* coming to the Smarts' tonight, Rob, aren't you?' said Charlie. 'Alex is.'

Lucy looked incredulous. '*You're* going to the Smarts', Alex?' she said. 'Blimey. You must tell me why, sometime. Anyway, must fly. Got a match to win.'

'How's it going?' I asked.

'Fine,' she said. 'But I think I'm better off without you and Charlie being there. Wish me luck!' She went off.

'Louise did mention it to me,' Robin was saying to Charlie. 'But I'm not sure I'll come. I haven't been fishing for an invitation like you have. I don't really know the girl.' He set off after Lucy. 'Told Lucy I'd carry on watching her. You coming?'

'No, we've been banned,' I said.

It was a strange afternoon. I wanted to watch Lucy's game against Rosie, but Lucy had given her orders. Normally I support Paddy, but I knew that if Charlie came along we'd end up laughing and joking and putting him off. So I found myself wandering around the courts with Charlie until my friends' matches were all finished.

I learnt a lot about Charlie. He and Robin are at school together. Charlie's home set-up sounds pretty similar to the Smarts', though they have a tennis court rather than a swimming pool in the garden. Charlie plays with his dad, like I do. He's got two older sisters who aren't that interested in tennis any more, but it's clear his entire family dotes on him – which might explain the self-confidence. He says they talk about girls all the time at school, but he doesn't know many apart from his sisters.

We almost missed the call for his match against Raj. In fact it was Raj's name I recognised first. 'You'd better come and watch me then,' said Charlie, 'since the others have banned you. And you'd better be supporting me because all your friends will want Raj to win, won't they?'

I went to the clubhouse with Charlie. Paddy and Lucy were there buying drinks for Richard and Rosie and trying to hide their glee, but it was obvious from Richard's and Rosie's faces that they were the losers. Horrible, all round. It didn't seem tactful to stay.

This was the first time I'd seen Charlie play and I was curious. Raj is good – most people find it hard to beat him. But Charlie – Charlie was a top player. Wow. He was in another league. How could he not get to the final? How, if they both made it to the semi-final, could he not beat Paddy? I didn't like to think about it. Sneakily I found myself looking for weaknesses so that I could tell Paddy. But there were none. Charlie's play was flawless.

One-by-one my friends – Raj's friends – came to watch. Lucy arrived with Robin. Some sort of chemistry is definitely at work there. I almost hoped Paddy wouldn't turn up to this match. He wanted to win the championship so much – seeing Charlie would only depress him.

Charlie was making mincemeat of Raj. I wanted to shut my eyes – hide behind the sofa. Charlie served ace after ace. When Raj did manage to return, Charlie slammed the ball on to his weak backhand, scooting up to the net to finish with a flash volley – the few times Raj actually managed to get a rally going. Poor Raj fought back as hard as he could, but Charlie was utterly brilliant. I heard Phil and Kieron behind me. 'That kid shouldn't be in the under-16s, should he?' Kieron asked me.

'He's fifteen,' I whispered back.

'Glad I won't have to play him, then,' said Phil.

'Joel will in the Prestige Gold Cup,' I said.

'What's the kid doing here if he's in the Cup? Not that it's any of our business. Probably best to keep quiet about it. Still. Do Joel good to be brought down a peg or two,' said Phil. He looked at me. 'You OK, Al? Sorry I whacked you earlier. Don't know what came over me. Very juvenile.'

'Some mistake, surely?' I said. 'Can this be a brother apologising?'

'I had a go at him for hitting a girl,' said Kieron.

'I have the dubious privilege in my family of not being treated as a girl,' I said.

'So Phil told me. Weird family.'

Charlie served four aces in a row and won the match. Paddy appeared with Ethlie as we were clapping, though I could see the others from the Club looking more inclined to boo.

'Hello everyone,' said Ethlie brightly, as if we might be glad to see her or something. No one returned her greeting because Charlie was being congratulated by Robin, and Phil and Kieron don't do that sort of thing. It was left to me.

'Oh, hi,' I said, pretending I'd only just noticed her.

'Guess what!' she said, glancing winsomely (oh, hideous sight) back at Paddy.

'They've just posted the mixed doubles list. People are putting their names down.'

'Well, I know who I'd like as a partner,' said Charlie, smiling broadly at me.

'Time to go,' said Phil with the usual Dunbar immaculate timing. 'You might as well come with us, Alex, since we're all going on to the Smarts'. See you, guys!'

FIVE

Please be there. Please be there. 'Zoe?' Phew.

'Zoe, I've been invited to a swimming party.'

'Lucky old you. What's the problem?'

'Have you forgotten?'

'Oh! Has it finally happened?'

'Well, no, actually.'

'Don't worry then. Not about swimming anyway. Cold water seems to stop things. Hanging around in a swimsuit might be more of a problem.'

'It's not the warmest evening.'

'Exactly. Make your excuses and get dressed I would. Now enough of that, it's yukky. How's the tournament going? How's the *romance*?'

'What romance?'

'Don't tell me you've forgotten already. Blimey, you're the one with a short memory. Holly's idea?'

'Only joking! How could I forget. It's loony expecting me to do this. Not that romance isn't being shoved down my throat every minute—'

'What do you mean?'

'Well, Lucy, my partner, is forever saying, so-and-so fancies you, hadn't you noticed. Then there's this guy called Charlie who thinks all the boys from the Club are my boyfriends.'

'Sounds a riot.'

'It's cool. But do I absolutely have to have a romance? I said I would, didn't I?'

'Pledged.'

'Oh dear. You know I don't have romantic leanings.'

'Well, you'd better start now. Sounds as though you have plenty of choice.'

'Aagh! I dunno, Zo. Anyway, got to go. Phil's hovering. Our lift to the swim is due any minute now. Thanks for the advice! I'll call you again and you can tell me your stuff. Byee!'

Phil was in big brother mode. 'Get your act together, Alex. Kieron should be here by now.'

'Where's Joel? Have a go at him, not me. He wasn't around for supper. Is he even out of bed yet?'

'Good point.' Phil went in search of Joel and I ran up to my room. It wasn't that warm outside – I could wear my jeans and a vesty top. Take a sweatshirt. As for swimming things – well, not much choice really. Same one I had last year. Speedo, bright blue. I bundled it up in a beach towel and shoved it in a Tesco carrier bag with my sweatshirt along with a wrapped sanitary towel and a hairbrush.

The doorbell rang. I wanted to bypass Mum, so I ran to open it.

'Are you all ready?' said Kieron. 'You look nice.'

I tried desperately to think of a funny response to the compliment, but none came. 'Er, yes. Thanks. I'll call the others.'

Joel arrived on the scene looking as though he really had just got up, his bleached hair all tousled. He dangled a pair of swimming shorts on his finger. No towel. 'Use yer bag, Al?'

'Get your own.'

He didn't.

'I think Phil has high expectations of this swim, don't you?' said Kieron to me with a smile.

'Oy,' said Phil. 'Leave it out. Just because I'm not a scruff like my little bro.'

The three of us followed Kieron to his mum's car. Kieron sat in the front with her and we three Dunbars bundled into the back. 'Ouch!' said Joel. 'You got a hedgehog in here?'

'Get off my hairbrush, slaphead!'

'Shut up, you two, or Mrs Mallory will think we're always like this,' said Phil, embarrassed.

'Speak for yourself,' I said. But we continued the journey in silence.

'Shall I pick you up at ten-thirty?' said Mrs Mallory as she disgorged us on to the pavement outside the Smarts' (mock) Tudor mansion.

'OK for you guys?' asked Kieron.

'Fine for me and Al, thanks,' said Phil. 'We're playing tomorrow.'

Joel looked uncertain. 'I'll wait and—'

'– see if you get a better offer,' said Kieron. 'That's not a problem, Joel. Thanks, Mum. See you later.'

The swim was in full swing. It was a decent-sized pool in a little fenced-off area of its own. Joel immediately pulled his T-shirt down at the front, stripped off his bottom half and changed into his swimming shorts right there, to hoots and squeals from Louise and her friend Claire (the girl I'd heard her talking to in the loo). Phil and Kieron nabbed the oldest Smart. 'Hi guys, how's it going?' he said.

'Where do we change?' Phil asked him.

'Go back indoors. Guys in my room. Girls in Louise's.'

'Where's that?' I asked. I didn't like the sound of this.

'Across the landing from mine. You'll see.'

Louise's room was really tidy apart from the piles of clothes where people had changed. One wall was completely covered in posters – and none of them were of gorillas. She had fitted wardrobes, her own basin and a mirror surrounded by film-star lights. Luxurious but quite old-fashioned compared with, say, Holly's or Zoe's, but then I always knew my friends had more style than the Smarts. Just less money! There was no one else around, but I felt self-conscious. What if someone came in when I had nothing on?

I was standing in the middle of the room clutching my carrier bag when the door flew open and Claire and Louise did come in, on gales of hysterical laughter. They were very wet, with sarongs over their bikinis.

'Did you *see* Joel changing?' squealed Louise.

'He doesn't mind what people see, does he?' said Claire.

'That's because he knows they'll be impressed,' said Louise, giggling. And then 'Oops! Sorry Alex. Didn't see you there!'

'Can you tell me where the loo is?' I asked. *I'll get changed in privacy thank you very much.*

'At the end there!' Louise just about managed to point me in the right direction before collapsing into giggles again. I heard her saying, 'Oooooh! That's Joel's sister. Do you think she heard me? What if she tells him?'

Fat chance, I thought, locking the door. He's bigheaded enough as it is. It was a tiny loo. I struggled out of my clothes and into my Speedo. No mirror to check how I looked. I wrapped my beach towel round my shoulders and unlocked the door. No one around. The boys must have gone on ahead.

It was kind of scary in the garden. The evening sun was making long shadows on the lawn and there was a lot of drinking and smoking and snogging going on amongst the older ones. I couldn't see anyone I knew well enough to speak to. Remembering what Zoe had said, I wanted to get into the water as quickly as possible, so I went through the gate to the pool, dumped my bag and towel and dived in.

Actually it was gorgeous. The water was just the right temperature – really refreshing. I surfaced and looked around me. Joel was at the shallow end, holding on to the bar behind him and showing off his six-pack to advantage while the girls played 'splashy splashy' with him. Phil and Kieron were mucking about with an inflatable shark with some much younger kids. As I swam over to join in the shark game, the boys went off to help splash Joel. The little kids were pleased to see me. 'Who are you?' they asked. 'Will you help us get on the shark?'

'I'm Alex,' I said, 'Dunbar.'

'My big sister loves Joel Dunbar,' said one of the little girls, who looked just like all the other Smarts except that she was wearing arm bands and huge swimming goggles.

'She must be mad, then,' I said. 'Come on, who wants to be lifted on to this thing? Shall we see how many we can get on it?'

'She is mad,' said the littlest Smart. 'I think boys are yuk.'

'And so do I,' I said. 'What did you say your name was?'

'I'm Scarlett,' she said. 'Scarlett Sarah Smart. Triple S. My middle name's Sarah in case I get fed up with the Scarlett.'

This was more information than I required, but it was

good to talk to at least one Smart who didn't immediately give me an inferiority complex. I climbed on to the shark with difficulty and complete loss of dignity. (Have you ever tried it?) Once I was on I was able to haul Scarlett up in front of me. I leant back to lift up the other kid, when – Wuh! the shark shot out from between my legs and catapulted us both backwards into the water.

'That was brilliant!' shrieked Scarlett, unfazed.

'I want a go! I want a go!' cried the other kid.

'I didn't do it on purpose, you know,' I said.

'Well, you've just invented a new game then,' said the other kid. 'My turn now.'

So I struggled on to the shark again, lifted up the other kid, leant backwards and – Wuh! out shot the shark again. It was fun playing with these two. Certainly more fun than wimpy splashing games with Joel. We did it quite a few times. My extra weight made the shark shooting out far more spectacular than if it had just been the kids. In the end, 'call-me-Janice' came and hoiked Scarlett and friend out of the water because it was their bedtime. I was quite disappointed. 'And who are you, dear?' she asked, patronisingly.

'Alex Dunbar,' I muttered.

'Oh, Joel's little sister!' she said, standing on the edge of the pool, Scarlett clinging to her leg. 'Joel!' she trilled. 'Joel, your little sister's looking rather cold!' Gee, thanks.

'I don't think he'll be very interested,' I said. 'I'm fine. I'm getting out now, anyway.' I hauled myself out and stood up. *Little* sister indeed. I towered over 'call-me-Janice'. Where was my bag? I needed my towel and clothes. Not only did I feel exposed in my unglamorous swimsuit and goosepimples, I remembered Zoe's advice. I looked around. I was sure I'd left it there, by the hedge.

Then I remembered following Mrs Smart's glance to where Joel sat surrounded by admirers – wrapped in *my* towel. I heard him playing to the gallery. 'Sorry folks – the sex with a shark entertainment has sadly drawn to a close. And – oh, excuse my goosepimple – it's a sister. In fact I think I can spy *two* goosepimples!'

A red haze came down over my eyes. I strode over to him. 'Joel!' I shrieked. 'You BUM! Give me back my towel!' I saw the Tesco bag and then saw that he had tipped everything out of it. Everything.

'Which towel?' said Joel. 'This one –' he held out the beach towel, tantalisingly – 'or this one?' You can guess what he held up then.

Amidst the ensuing laughter I moved exceedingly fast. I smacked him and grabbed my towel almost in one move. While he was still reeling, I snatched up my bag, stuffed everything back and ran to the house, my eyes smarting with tears. Louise and Claire weren't the only ones I'd recognised amongst my mockers. *Charlie* had been chortling too. And I thought he was my friend. Not any more. I never wanted to speak to him again.

I locked myself in the loo again and peeled off my wet swimsuit. It was not a comfortable operation. I dried myself and dressed and then didn't know what to do. I looked at my watch. It was nine-thirty. Could I stay in here for a whole hour?

Obviously not. I heard voices coming up the stairs. I was used to eavesdropping on Louise now. 'That Joel,' she said. 'You have to laugh, don't you? I know he's cruel, but he's just so funny when he gets going.'

'I thought he was a bit mean,' Claire said. 'His poor sister. I would have died.'

'Well—' said Louise, and then they shut the bedroom

door and I was spared the end of her sentence. But then she came out again to go to the loo. She rattled the doorhandle. 'Yoo hoo!' she said. 'Is someone in there? Hurry up, I'm desperate!' So I had no choice but to emerge. Boy, did I want to go home. Without a word to Louise I went downstairs. I found a room with a telly in it, switched it on, and sat in front of it. Most things I can make a joke of (just like Joel, I suppose) but this situation was without comedy as far as I was concerned. I felt utterly, utterly humiliated. The tears started to flow again.

After a while, someone came into the room behind me. It was Kieron. 'Alex?' he said. 'I've been looking for you.'

'Can't think why,' I said.

'Just wanted to see if you were OK. I don't understand why your brothers turn into such pigs around you.'

'Joel's always a pig.'

'Maybe. But Phil's my mate. He's OK.'

'I know. Phil is usually OK. Don't know what got into him this morning.'

'Jealousy I expect.'

'Don't know what he's got to be jealous of.'

'You, of course. He didn't like me paying attention to you.'

'Only this morning he told me to stop acting like a brother and start acting more like a sister. He can't have it both ways.'

'Confused, obviously.'

'Anyway, Kieron. It's all right. I'm used to it.'

'Well, you shouldn't be. What do your parents say when your brothers tease you?'

'Honestly, it's only Joel. The twins are just stupid and Phil's the good guy normally. They wouldn't do it in front of Dad – or Mum. You know what families are like.'

'Well, I've only got one older sister, and I wouldn't *dare* treat her like that!'

I paused. For a brief moment I wanted to tell Kieron about how useless Mum was. How she never stuck up for me, or stopped the boys taunting me. How the sun shone out of Joel's bottom as far as she was concerned – he could do no wrong. But I didn't.

'Kieron? You're a cool guy. Why are you being nice to me?'

'Because, just like in the movies, my friend's kid sister is turning into quite a babe.'

'Oh stop it.'

'There. Made you smile. No, you're OK, Alexandra Dunbar, and don't let anybody tell you otherwise.'

I laughed and played air violin.

'You're your own worst enemy,' he said.

'No. Joel's worser.'

'Worser? No such word! Anyway, it's nearly time to go. Are you coming out to hold your head up in front of those idiots or do you want to lurk in here until my mum comes?'

I didn't know.

'Come on. I'll protect you.'

'OK!' Suddenly the world seemed a better place. Kieron was kind and nice and wanted to make me feel better. Maybe, *maybe* – this was how a romance began. I didn't think so, but what the hell! 'You're on. Kieron, *darling*!' I linked my arm in his.

'Steady on,' he said, and we went out into the garden.

'Kieron! Your mum's here!' someone yelled almost as soon as we'd gone outside and found Phil (who hadn't got lucky on this occasion).

'OK Phil, Alex?' said Kieron. 'Not sure we should give Joel car-space, frankly.'

'What do you mean?' said Phil.

'If you weren't there it's better that you don't know. He was extremely unfunny at your sister's expense.'

'Oh well, that's nothing new,' said Phil. We'd reached the car.

'You come in the front, dear,' Kieron's mum said to me. 'Don't see why you should be squashed in the back with those two.'

Ah. A friend and sympathiser! No wonder Kieron showed a bit of respect.

'What about Joel?' I said.

'What about him?' said Kieron as we all saw him running towards the car. 'Drive on, Mother.'

TUESDAY

Always stay on top of the game whether you are winning or losing. If your opponent drags you down you have not only lost the game but the pleasure of playing.

EVENT/S	VENUE	WEATHER CONDITIONS	PHYSICAL HEALTH
U-16 singles	Mapledon	Grey and rainy	Unpredictable
U-16 doubles			
Swim at Smarts'	Smart Towers	Cleared up	!

OPPONENT
Blob One
Ugly Sisters (doubles)
Joel

TACTICS
Ruthless both times.
None

RESULT
Won both matches.
Humiliation. I definitely lost.

EQUIPMENT
Dark tracksuit still proving useful.
Blue Speedo – inappropriate.

COMMENTS
Tournament OK. Me, Lucy and Paddy both through to next round. Also Charlie and
   Louise and Tom Smart. And others who I can't remember. Charlie v friendly all
   day but I've gone off him <u>big time</u> since he was one of the people jeering with
   Joel. MIXED DOUBLES DILEMMA. What shall I do? Charlie virtually asked
   me to partner him. (Definitely won't now.) Deathly Ethlie was homing in on
   Paddy. HELP! Paddy is <u>not</u> his usual self.
PS Kieron is so nice. He'd be perfect for the romance I suppose. But the thought
   of actually kissing him – kissing anyone properly – is just too scary.

TOMORROW'S MATCH
Singles and mixed doubles (if I have a partner).
Singles v Unknown (her name's Megan Birchill).
Mixed doubles. Partner: Unknown. Opponents: Unknown.
A days of Unknowns for me.
Lucy v Ethlie.
Paddy v First seed (Paul Sisson). Tough one. Paddy can do it!

Joel arrived home about an hour after we did. Mrs Smart
had given him a lift herself. I heard him ranting at Phil
about being left behind. I heard Mum weighing in too. I
heard the phone ringing and Dad saying he was sorry but
Alex had gone to bed. I went to sleep feeling OK – but I still
had *no* idea what I was going to do about a mixed doubles
partner, or a romance.

SIX

'Hello?'

'Hi, it's me, Lucy – how was the swim last night? D'you
feel like coming to the Club this morning? I want to hear all
the gossip.'

'No you don't. But I'll come anyway. I've never set eyes

on this Megan Birchill girl I'm playing today, so I need to be prepared.'

'I'm against Ethlie, and there's no way I'm losing to *her*.'

'Arf arf!'

'And the mixed doubles start today. Hey, guess what! Robin rang last night and asked me to be his partner.'

'And what did you say to him?'

'Well, "No", of course. I've got a partner, haven't I?'

'More than I have.' I looked at my watch. Ten o'clock. 'I've got to do a bit of house stuff. See you up there in half an hour.'

I could hear Mum approaching. Slip-slop, sigh. Slip-slop, sigh. 'I suppose I'd better do your sandwiches then,' she said wearily.

I wish she'd just give me money. 'It's OK, Mum, I'll do them. I'll do Phil's as well, if you like.' Anything to get her off my back. I didn't want her to stop me going out.

'Would you, dear?' Mum's round face positively lit up.

'Yeah, fine.'

'Well, well. That's a first.'

'It's not, Mum, and you know it. Precious Joel might not do anything to help, but I do loads.'

'Poor Joel. He says you all drove off without him after the swim.'

'Only what he deserved. He was vile to me last night.'

'Oh, I'm sure it wasn't on purpose.'

See what I mean?

'His word against mine, Mum, and I know who you'll believe. Now, excuse me. I want to make two packed lunches.'

'I wish you and Joel would get on. I would have loved an older brother when I was your age.'

'Maybe, but *two* older brothers, not to mention two

younger brothers, is a wee bit over the top.' I spread the bread and laid cheese slices on.

'Are you sure Philip likes cheese slices?'

'If he doesn't, he should make his own sandwiches.' *Go away, go away.* I was saved by the twins. They burst into the kitchen, squabbling, so Mum had to go and sigh at them for a while. I stuffed the sandwiches into a carrier bag, grabbed a couple of apples and filled a bottle with squash. That would have to do. 'I'm off out for a bit now,' I called, picked up my racquet and made a dash for it.

'I really like Robin.'

'You really liked Kieron yesterday.'

'I know, but that was sort of "from afar".'

'I think Kieron's nice.'

'Excuse me? Would you mind repeating that? Did Alex Dunbar actually say she liked a boy?'

'I like loads of boys. But Kieron was – sort of – well – nice to me last night.' I looked away, remembering. 'Tell me about Robin, I know you're dying to. I also know he has a jealous girlfriend who phones him all the time.'

'Emma.'

'So he's told you about her?'

We made ourselves comfortable on the seat outside the pavilion. 'Yes. He's fed up with her. Said he wanted to get to know new people.'

'Like you.'

'Exactly. He went on about how he'd watched me playing and how our styles would go well together, but I knew that was all bull.'

'Are you going to go out with him?'

'Alex!'

'Well, that's what all this is leading up to, isn't it?'

'I don't know yet. We just had a nice long chat, that's all.'

'I dunno. It all seems like a silly game to me. You like him, he likes you. So why don't you just cut out the middle bit and go out together?'

'Because the middle bit is what's fun. I despair of you sometimes Alex.' She stood up. 'We'd better knock up if we're going to.' We walked on to the court. 'Anyway. I'm quite looking forward to the mixed.'

'Huh. So would I be if I was in it.'

'What do you mean?' Lucy hit a ball to me.

'*I* still don't have a partner, remember?'

'Seems to me that you have a choice of at least two. Three if you count Robin.'

'So who's number two?'

'Didn't Charlie say he wanted to be?'

'Not in quite so many words. Anyway, I'm right off Charlie.'

'Paddy seemed to think Charlie had already asked you.'

'Well he didn't. Did you talk about it with Paddy then?'

'Yes. He seemed a bit down, actually.'

'Can't help that. He should have asked me himself.'

'You're impossible.' Lucy practised a couple of serves on me. 'So what has Charlie done to blot his copybook and how was Kieron "nice"?'

'It's a long story. As I said, you don't want to hear it.'

'Meanie. You know that makes me all the more curious.'

'It's just that at the swim last night Joel went in for a particularly unpleasant form of ritual humiliation of his sister and Charlie found it as amusing as the rest of Joel's cronies.'

'What did Joel do, for goodness sake?'

'Oh, just tipped out my bag and held up its most *intimate*

contents for all to see and laugh at. Hilarious really. I was so upset. Which isn't like me, I know. So I went off in a grump and Kieron came and found me and tried to cheer me up.'

'I said he fancied you.'

'Nah. He's far too old. But he said I'd turned into a "babe".' I vaguely hoped that Lucy would pounce on this piece of information as a definite sign that romance would surely follow. I waited for her reaction.

'Wow! I'm jealous. Not that everyone hasn't been saying the same thing. You know – "I say, the Dunbar girl has *grown* up a lot hasn't she?" nudge, nudge, etc . . .' (No, I wasn't getting any help here.)

'I don't *feel* any different.' I slammed the ball as hard as I could. It landed in the net. 'Who, exactly, has been saying this?'

'Oh I don't know. People.'

'Anyone would think that it was unusual to grow up at our age.'

'Yeah, yeah.' Lucy wore her despairing look again. 'But Paddy and the mixed doubles thing is important. You really don't want him to end up with Deathly Ethlie, do you? Nab him as soon as we get there. Ring him, *before* we get there.' She was right. Forget holiday romance. The partner business *had* to be resolved.

The first people we saw when we arrived at Mapledon that Wednesday morning were Charlie and Robin. I hadn't managed to get hold of Paddy on the phone, though believe me, with Lucy standing over me I had tried. I cut Charlie dead, the toad, and ran off to look for Paddy. Absolutely no time left for misunderstandings now.

I found him – with Ethlie! Maybe it was too late already. 'Paddy, could I have a word?' I asked, finding that I felt really nervous all of a sudden. Paddy actually looked relieved to be rescued.

'Excuse me, Ethlie,' he said. So polite, Paddy, bless him. He turned his back on her. 'What is it, Alex? Is something the matter?'

'It depends.'

'Depends on what?'

'On what you've been talking to Ethlie about.'

'Her options! Her GCSE options, if you must know!'

'Not partnership options?'

'Alex!'

'Be my partner?'

'In the mixed doubles? Well—' He paused, horribly.

'Oh. Never mind. If you've already asked someone – never mind.'

'I haven't, Alex. It's just that—'

'As I said, never mind. Doesn't matter.' I headed off.

'Alex!' Paddy called after me. 'Of course! I'll put our names down, shall I?'

And do you know what? I went back and threw my arms round him.

'Hey! It's no big deal!' he said, going pink.

'Thanks mate,' I said, and punched him on the shoulder.

They were starting to call players for the singles. I wanted to find Lucy again before her match against Ethlie and I wanted to check out the mysterious Megan Birchill.

I found Lucy being wished good luck by Robin, with much twinkling and giggling on her part. Now the mixed doubles was safely sorted I had a sudden brainwave about the romance. I could cheat! It would mean letting Lucy in on it, but never mind. I waited until Robin had moved away. 'Hey, Lucy. Want to do me a favour?'

'What is it this time? Don't tell me you haven't had the

guts to ask Paddy. I don't know what's got into you this year.'

'Nothing's got into me. It's him who didn't ask me in the first place. Anyway, I have and he's said yes. Though he was still a bit iffy.'

'So what's this favour then?'

'Do you want to have a romance for me?'

'*What*?' Loads of us were converging on the desk. It wasn't easy to hold a conversation.

'I'm meant to be having a romance and reporting back to my friends – Zoe and that lot,' I said, as if it was something I did every day. 'It's just that you look as if something might happen with Robin anyway and that would spare me and you could just give me the details and I could pretend it was what happened to me.'

'You're mad, Alex,' said Lucy, raising her voice across the crowds. 'Go and have one of your own, for goodness sake. Right now we've got matches to play. Good luck!'

I vaguely recognised Megan. I'd seen her around, but she looked older than most of the under-16s – big and shambling, with a Janet Street-Porter voice. Her whites were definitely less than white and her trainers were at least last year's. She was even taller and noisier than me! 'Hi Alex, how you doing?' she said when we met.

'How did you know which one I was?' I asked.

'You're a Dunbar aren't you? I've met your brothers.'

'I apologise right now for anything they might have said or done.'

'No need. Joel's the cute one, isn't he? And Phil's the nice one?'

'You could describe them like that I suppose. And I'm the female one.'

She laughed. 'You come here every year, don't you?'

'Well, yes. It's what we do. I don't even think about it.'

'My PE teacher made me come. The local authority pays for me. Hi Charlie! Hi Robin!' she said. I looked up to see the pair of them. I blanked Charlie again, the treacherous one. 'Do you know those two?' she asked as we walked on.

'Just met them this week,' I said.

'They're cool,' she said. 'Nice to have guys who aren't part of the usual crowd, not to mention the Smart set. Wouldn't say no to an invitation there though. Their house is supposed to be dead posh. Not special friends of yours are they, the Smarts?'

'No,' I said. 'Though I think Charlie would very happily be part of the Smart set. He's already a member of the Joel Dunbar fan club, which makes me think he must be a few sandwiches short of a picnic.'

'He told me he was a member of the Alex Dunbar fan club yesterday. I thought he was a friend of yours.'

'*Was* is the operative word there.' We'd reached our court. 'Let's knock up quickly and get started, shall we? Anyone in the mixed doubles has got at least one more match today.'

'Don't think I want to win this,' said Megan. 'The winner gets to play either Louise Smart or Connie King, don't they?'

'Oy, don't be so negative! In this match you get to play the terrifying Alex Dunbar, who's far better than either Louise or Connie. Allegedly.'

Needless to say, I won. I shouldn't have done because I was playing so badly. I was easily distracted by each and every spectator, especially Charlie and Robin, and Paddy. There were questions I wanted to ask Paddy, and Charlie seemed to want to communicate something to me – he kept doing telephoning gestures. Phil and Kieron appeared, too, Kieron waving and smiling. Even Tom Smart passing by made me lose my concentration. His dark hair had gone all bleached and spiky, like Joel's, overnight. Must have done it at the swim. Fancy wanting to look like Joel!

My brain kept going back to this romance thing and my 'pledge'. I'm always up for a challenge – I don't want to be the wet one of the group.

'Thanks,' Megan was shaking my hand. We'd finished. All our spectators had gone off to play their own matches. 'I really enjoyed that. I didn't expect to get a single game off you. I never thought we'd still be going an hour and a half later! The taxpayers don't get any return for their investment, but that's their tough luck. And you get to pay for the drinks!' She rattled on as we headed for the clubhouse. 'Who's your partner in the mixed doubles?'

'Paddy Gardner.'

'Don't think I know him. Do you know mine, Max Freeman? He's only playing in the mixed for a laugh. He's quite good, but not a serious player. Music's his thing. And girls. Excitable, is Max. You'd like him. I'll introduce you.'

I refrained from asking what made her think I was interested in an excitable guy. Partly because, yet again, I was pondering, maybe here was someone I could have a romance with if Kieron didn't work out – now Charlie's so definitely off the list. Aagh! This is so not me!

I bought the drinks and we went over to look at the draw for the mixed. Paddy and I were up against fellow Club members Harriet and Neil straight away. Shame. Hey! Charlie was playing with Louise Smart, and they were first seeds. Not surprising – someone must have clocked Charlie's play, and Louise is brilliant (annoyingly). Hmmm.

Charlie and Louise, eh? What about the Alex Dunbar fan club? I wasn't jealous. I hate Charlie, don't I?

Get a grip, Alex. I really was all over the place this morning. When Megan left I decided to take my sandwiches and watch Lucy playing Ethlie, though knowing Ethlie she'd think I was there to support *her*. I went over on my own, passing Charlie's match on the way. Robin saw me and joined me. 'You going over to watch Lucy? I'll come with you.'

Lucy has great concentration. She smiled at me and Robin – especially at Robin – but she didn't alter her game. Robin checked his mobile was switched off and sat back with a smug expression on his face. Emma was now an ex-girlfriend it seemed.

'Did you find a partner for the mixed?' I asked him, between games. 'Yes,' he said wistfully. 'Lucy's already got a partner, so I agreed to play with Louise Smart's friend Claire. Louise asked Charlie last night, you see. That's when he called you.'

'Called me? What do you mean?'

'Last night. Quite late. We wanted to be quite sure first that you and Lucy couldn't be our partners. You two were the ones we wanted. But then Lucy told me she already had a partner.'

'Someone did ring last night after I'd gone to bed – I heard my dad telling them. But messages only get passed on at a price in our house. So that was Charlie, was it?' *But I hate Charlie. He laughed at me.*

We shut up. The score was one set all. Ethlie, despite her unattractive personality, is quite a good player. She's left-handed and she's got a very solid backhand. The trick is to get her up to the net and alternate hard shots with lobs – she's not much of a runner. Robin and I agreed that that was a good tactic, and I whispered it to Lucy when they were resting before the final set and Ethlie had her back turned.

The sun came out and it was turning into a beautiful late-summer day. (I didn't want it getting too hot.) Lucy followed our strategy and won the third set easily. When they came off Lucy went dreamily over to Robin. You could practically see the hearts and flowers dancing in the air between them. Blimey. I'd definitely use Lucy's romance if I couldn't concoct one of my own.

'Hello, gorgeous!' I jumped. It was Kieron. He was addressing me. 'And how are we this morning?' He gave me a penetrating look.

'Fine now,' I said. 'Thanks.'

'That's all I wanted to hear,' he said. 'Thought I'd catch you before Phil and I go on. Must dash. See you.'

'Alex? Al?' It was Lucy. 'Excuse me?'

'Sorry, I was miles away.'

'Obviously. I think you're *in* there.'

'Where's Robin?'

'Gone to find Claire, more's the pity. They want to get going on the mixed at three-thirty apparently, but most of the boys' matches seem to be still going on. I suppose they're quite close at this stage, like mine was. Thank goodness Richard's out of it – he won't be too tired. Paddy's got a tough one, hasn't he?'

'Yup. He's playing the first seed. Actually I'd forgotten. He was probably really keyed up this morning.'

'But you're sorted for the mixed now?'

'Yes. But not in other ways, Luce. My brain's all over the place today.'

'Glad I'm not playing with you till tomorrow then. What's the problem?'

'Let's go and sit over there.' There was a white plastic garden table and chairs over by the practice wall. We laid claim to them, discouraging anyone from joining us.

'OK. Out with it.'

'There isn't an "it" really. It's just that I'm still furious with Charlie for ganging up against me last night, and I don't think he's even noticed. Paddy's still acting odd – unfinished sentences and stuff. And Kieron's being dead kind, but I don't quite know what it's all about. I asked him last night – I think he just feels sorry for me.' I let out a sigh. 'And I'm meant to have this romance.'

'You make it sound like an exam or something!'

'I see it's not like that for you and Robin.'

'He's so cute, isn't he? Pity you're off Charlie – we'd have made a good foursome.'

'Stop it, Lucy. I wouldn't have wanted to have a *relationship* with Charlie, even if I did still like him.' (I didn't want her jumping to conclusions.)

'OK. So Charlie's in disgrace and has disqualified himself in the romance stakes. Which leaves Paddy and Kieron. Which one shall it be?'

'*Paddy*? You *are* joking?'

'Don't see why I should be. He's a top bloke is our Paddy. You get on well, know each other's shots, so to speak.'

'Paddy is my *mate*.'

'OK, OK. No need to get all vehement about it. So that leaves Kieron.'

'And Max.'

'You are so full of surprises, Alex Dunbar. "No romance! No romance!" you cry, and then you suddenly come up with an unknown contender. And who is Max?'

'Oh, no one. It's silly. He's Megan's partner – only here

for the mixed, and she said we might get on. You can see what a state I'm getting into. Anyone's fair game.'

'Except Robin.'

'OK. Not Robin.'

'Kieron then,' said Lucy.

'OK,' I agreed. I sat up. '*What* did I just say?'

'Romance with Kieron. Go for it.'

SEVEN

'Hi babe!' The voice came from behind us as we headed for our first mixed doubles match. Paddy looked round sharply. It was Kieron again.

'Hi Kieron,' he said.

'Since when have you been a babe, Paddy Gardner?' said Kieron. 'I was addressing Miss A. Dunbar here. Good luck both of you, anyway.' He waved his racquets cheerfully as he turned left and we turned right. My knees felt quite weak. How was I ever going to do this romance thing with him?

'Nice guy, Kieron,' said Paddy. He'd just beaten the first seed to a place in the semi-final and was in a magnanimous mood.

I wanted to change the subject. 'Wish we weren't playing Harriet and Neil in the first round.'

'Do us good,' said Paddy. 'We know their weak points. We know we're better than they are. It'll give us con-fidence!' He gave me an encouraging smile as we went on. Harriet and Neil were already there.

'Just our luck having to play you two,' Harriet grumbled.

'Our sentiments precisely,' I said.

Actually, Paddy and I *are* good together – I'm reminded as soon as we start knocking up. He bounces around at the net but he always knows when to leave the shot for me. We always sense when one or other of us is tired or in need of a confidence boost. We get quite giggly sometimes. I can always make Paddy laugh. *Could* always – I haven't been so sure of him this week, as you know. Perhaps playing a match together will make everything all right again.

'Down the middle,' Paddy whispered, once we'd started. 'It works every time.' It was true. Neil and Harriet were fine at hitting the ball when it came into their court but very bad at knowing when to take or leave a shot. Harriet got riled if Neil poached and Neil got equally cross if he left it to Harriet and she didn't get to the ball. So playing down the middle shook up their personalities as well as their game. It wasn't long before they were barely speaking to each other and then only in monosyllables.

I enjoyed myself because it was a good hard-hitting game. I got a bit hot in the old tracksuit bottoms, but Paddy and I were beating them. Hardly anyone came to watch because they were all busy, though Phil and Kieron were spectators for five minutes or so. Kieron's presence didn't affect my game so long as I didn't think about the 'other stuff' (not even the word), and I was concentrating too hard on playing for that.

We won, of course. Paddy shook my hand and patted my back as you always do after a match. And then I couldn't help thinking about the 'other stuff'. I found myself looking at Neil in a different light when he did the same – after all, as I'd said to Lucy, everyone had to be fair game if the romance challenge was to come off. Neil's a mate, so I don't look at him critically usually – don't usually notice that he's got a terrible skin . . . Hey! This romance thing is not good!

I don't want to notice bad things about my friends. Needless to say, I struck Neil off my list of potential romancers.

Back at the board, Paddy and I looked at how our Club had fared in the mixed. Lucy and Richard were through, though Rosie and Raj had been beaten by Claire and Robin. Lucy and Robin were busy congratulating one another at that very moment. Lucy came over and pulled me away from the crowd.

'I'm not going to give you a lift tonight!' she said.

'Why ever not?'

'Because you're going to go with your brother and *Kieron*. Remember?'

'Ssh! He'll hear.'

'He's not around – I checked.'

'Lucy – you won't tell anyone, will you?'

'Not even Robin.'

'Especially not Robin. And I don't want Paddy knowing either.'

'Ooh. Touchy. Don't worry, girlie, your secret's safe with me.'

'What secret?' asked Robin, coming to join us.

'Nothing you need worry your pretty little head about,' said Lucy, steering him away. 'Run along now Alex, and find your big brother.'

I stuck my tongue out at her. 'I'll get my coat,' I said, and went off to find Phil.

Phil and Kieron were playing a match. Mens' doubles. Great to watch. While I was waiting for them to finish, Megan came to join me with a guy I hadn't seen before: the famous Max. 'How did you get on?' I asked.

'We lost,' said Megan glumly, 'to Charlie and Louise Smart. They chewed us up and spat us out.'

'I'll tell you the good part, though,' said Max. 'We got a Smart invitation out of it. It was Charlie actually – when we were shaking hands he said to Louise that she ought to invite us to the barbecue tomorrow to kind of make up for totalling us. Nice guy, Charlie. Dead posh but doesn't act it. Anyway, Louise had to say yes. She must know everyone's heard it's a free-for-all.'

'Is it?' I said. 'I was always under the impression that the Smart set was rather exclusive.'

'Nah,' said Max. 'People like that love to feel they're at the centre of things. That's why they have parties. I'm going, for sure. And I'm making Megan come.'

'Well, I'll go if you go, Alex,' said Megan to me. 'Better still, you can give me a lift. Can I come round to yours first? I don't want to go home in between. I'd rather get Dad to take over for the whole evening.'

What could I say? 'OK,' I said weakly. People don't usually drop in to my house but I'm not used to being steamrollered like this.

'We're off now,' she said. 'In fact we're out of the tournament, but we're both coming to watch tomorrow. Nothing better to do. See you!'

So if it was to be Max, I'd see him again tomorrow and at the party. He might be just about possible if all my other attempts failed. What you'd call a fun guy. Hmm. But Phil and Kieron had just won. It was time to practise my charms on Kieron.

'Would you like to sit in the front, Alex?'

'Let Phil have a go. I don't mind going in the back with Kieron.'

Phil: 'Great, thanks. Don't mind if I do.'

Kieron: 'Are you sure, Alex? I'm a bit rank after that doubles match.'

Me: 'Well that makes two of us. My shirt's still superglued to my back.' *That's not very seductive.*

Then of course, Phil: 'Why didn't you take off your trousers if you were that hot?'

Me: silence. I'm desperate for something to say to Kieron. Something with a hint of romance. Zoe, Lucy, where are you when I need you? I blink at him in a manner I imagine to be appealing.

'You OK, Alex? Something in your eye?'

'No. I'm fine. Ermm. Nice of you to ask.' I racked my brain for a compliment to pay him. 'I like your – your—' Everything he was wearing was quite unremarkable. But as he smiled I noticed that he had nice, even, white teeth. '– teeth.'

'Sorry, what was that?' Kieron asked. He laughed uproariously. 'It sounded as though you said "I like your teeth"!'

'No, silly!' I said. (Help, what could I substitute?) 'I said, "I like this seat"!'

'Good,' said Kieron. He gave me a funny sidelong look. 'But I'm afraid you're going to have to get out of it soon.'

'Why?' I asked, alarmed. Had I completely blown it? Was he ejecting me from his car?

'Because we're nearly home, klutz,' said Phil.

I'm not cut out for this, I'm really not. I rang Zoe to ask if I could back out of the deal, but she said absolutely no way. She was doing her best against the odds and I had to persevere too. She asked if I was all right and if I'd used up all the supplies yet. I said no, because I hadn't started, but I wished something would happen – I was getting terribly hot wearing trousers every day. That's what the emergency supplies are there for, birdbrain, she said. Use them just in case! It doesn't matter if you need them or not! Daft thing, keeping your long trousers on! See? This is the sort of stuff my mum should have told me! Then I rang Lucy and told her how I had completely failed to entice Kieron. She said she'd meet me up at the Club tonight. Tomorrow we had an early start at the tournament because so many of the people still in – and that included both of us – had three matches to play.

'I can't do it, Lucy. I just don't know how to play this romance game. I did that fluttery eyelash thing that you do with Robin, and Kieron just asked if I had something in my eye. I mean, he was still nice to me, because he's a gentleman, basically, but he's starting to give me strange looks.'

We weren't even pretending to play tennis. Lucy'd had a more strenuous day than I had, but we were both saving ourselves for tomorrow.

'Let me think about it,' said Lucy. 'I'm sure we can come up with a plan. I'm trying to think what happened with Robin and me, but that was different because we simply fancied each other. We need a bit of a plan anyway, because tomorrow's long and complicated, isn't it? Three matches and a party.'

'Ten a.m. start. Do you realise I'm up against Louise Smartypants in every single semi-final?'

'At least we're *in* every single semi-final. Paddy too. The Club kicks ass again!' Lucy stood up and cheered. 'Actually, our lads don't have their semi-finals until Friday.'

'I've just remembered. Robin and Charlie can't play on Saturday, can they, because of the Prestige Gold Cup?'

'I know,' said Lucy. 'Robin feels terrible about it. He's really glad Paddy knocked him out now.'

'They're both still in the doubles and the mixed doubles. What'll they do? How are they going to get out of it?'

'Robin thinks the competition is better than them, but I'm not so sure. Nobody's better than Charlie in the under-16s. Their coach only sent them to get practice – he didn't think they'd get this far.'

It did seem unfair on our boys. And us, for that matter. 'The singles is the worst. Paddy has to beat Charlie to get into the final,' I said. 'And he's so desperate to win this year.'

'Maybe Charlie will lose on purpose.'

'That's almost as bad. Still, if he can't play on Saturday maybe he'll have to. Then it will be Paddy against Tom Smart for the final.'

'Ruddy Smarts. By the way, have you heard? Absolutely everybody's going to their barbecue tomorrow night. Sort of mass decision. People are just going to turn up.'

'I know. Even Megan and her friend Max. She wants to come back to my place first.'

'Lucky old her,' said Lucy. 'You don't usually let me in, however much I want to see the gorgeous Joel in his natural habitat.'

'Robin is a lot more gorgeous than Joel, believe me. And he doesn't put Domestos in his hair. I did try to put Megan off, but it didn't work. Means I'll have to introduce her to Mum and everything.'

'It's going to be so cool being at a party with Robin. Maybe you'll get somewhere with Kieron too. Nothing like a bit of fruit punch and a few burgers round the fire to get things moving.'

'Maybe.'

*

'Mum, would it be OK if I brought someone round to-morrow night between the tournament and going out to the Smarts' barbecue? Obviously you won't have to feed her.'

'Are you all going to this barbecue? Joel and Phil as well?'

'I expect so. I don't think there'll be a problem with lifts there and back.'

'Oh well. That's fewer people for supper then. Yes, dear. You know I like to meet your friends.'

Yes, but they're not that thrilled about meeting you. 'Thanks.'

A party and a romance. Who was it to be? Time was running out. Kieron was number one candidate. Who was number two? Max? Charlie? No. Not Charlie.

I had to make myself more attractive. To the old dressing-table on the landing. There are actually some odds and ends of make-up in there from the days when Mum wore it. Believe it or not, Joel and I used to play with it for dressing-up ten million years ago. I would enjoy reminding him of that one day. Yup – here it is. Little make-up bag with a Mary Quant daisy on it. Gosh, this takes me back. One lipstick. Mascara. Eyeshadow, green. Extremely small bottle of duty-free Je Reviens that must go back to the seventies at least. *Never mind.* I took the whole lot to my room and shut the door.

Now, my friends all wear make-up. Josie wears loads. Holly and Zoe probably do too, but they are more subtle. Lucy doesn't put it on most of the time, but she will if it's a party. Zoe's made me up once or twice for a laugh and it looked quite good.

I started with the lipstick. I didn't put much on, but I

went over the edges so I still looked like a clown. Hey ho. Nothing ventured, nothing gained etc. He who dares . . . Then the eyeshadow. Green isn't really my colour. Doesn't go with sandy hair. Still. I just smoo-oothed a bit on. The light wasn't very good in my room. Never mind. This was just an experiment.

Then the mascara. It was ancient. I rattled the stick round the tube a few times. Right eye. Carefully does it. Fine. Left eye . . . Damn. I jabbed it in my eye by mistake. That made my eyes water and I blinked. A lot. Oh no. Now I had great black zigzags going down my face in rows. I looked like a whole troupe of clowns.

Knock knock.

'Don't come in! Who's that?'

'Kieron.'

Oh yeah? What sort of tricks was Joel playing on me? Maybe he'd like to be reminded right now of happier days playing with the make-up bag. Would he, huh. With a stream of expletives I hurled open the door.

'OK Joel, you *** scumbag! What is it this time, you *** toad?'

It *was* Kieron. I should have realised something was different. Joel wouldn't have waited for me to open the door.

Kieron did a sort of choke-hysteria giggle before returning to his gentleman-like ways and apologising – he thought he'd been directed to Phil's room. He was returning the sunglasses Phil had left in the car.

'No.' I acted all dignified and cool and stepped outside my room. 'Phil's in here.' I knocked on Phil's door politely. Phil opened it, took one look at me and cracked up. Then he saw Kieron. 'What's going on?'

'These were in the car, mate,' said Kieron. 'One of the

twins left off watching telly just long enough to open the door and tell me where I could find you.'

'More than one clown in this family, then,' said Phil, looking at me and doubling up again. 'Come in, big K. We don't often have visitors. Go and wash your face, Al. You look hideous.'

I kept thinking, *Kieron is here. Perhaps he really did come to see me. Perhaps Phil's sunglasses were just an excuse.*

'Let me come in too, Phil,' I asked. Perhaps someone as sophisticated as Kieron would be impressed by my enhanced beauty. I lowered the mascara-clogged eyelashes again.

Phil was not impressed. 'Only if you do something sensible with your face. I'm not having you embarrassing me in front of my friends.'

'Oh.' That said it, really. I didn't see Kieron objecting to Phil's high-handed behaviour on this occasion.

I slunk off to the bathroom, humiliated again. I locked the door, switched on the shaving light as well as the overhead one and inspected my face in the mirror. I did indeed look ridiculous. And Kieron had seen me looking like this. Sense of humour failure again. It's hard to make a joke about being seen looking completely batty by a guy you're trying to ensnare. *Give up Alex. Give up.*

Of course soap and water are barely adequate for removing large quantities of ancient mascara. Mysteriously there was some baby lotion in the bathroom cupboard, so that helped. Why can't my heap of a mum even do straightforward make-up things like other women? Has she no self-respect? Perhaps she doesn't like looking in the mirror. I'm beginning to know the feeling.

I slipped back into my room and pushed a pile of books up against the door. My gorilla grinned down at me. I ripped him off the wall. I moved my mirror into the light.

I tied my hair back and clipped the straggly bits. Then I dipped my finger into the eyeshadow again and smeared just the tiniest bit on to my eyelids. I checked at every dab. A bit green (I could imagine Lucy saying that – It's OK Al, just a bit *green*). I applied the mascara again, ever so lightly – stroke – stroke – stroke – right eye. Stroke – stroke – stroke – left eye. I ignored the lipstick. I regarded myself in the mirror. *Not bad*. It wasn't bad. I'd try it. At the risk of further humiliation, I'd go downstairs like that.

I heard Kieron leave. He called out, 'Cheerio Alex!' as he went downstairs and I heard the twins letting him out. I went down. Everyone was milling around in the kitchen. The twins were hyped up from what they'd been watching on TV. Dad and Mum were involved in some gritted teeth wrangling, nothing unusual. Phil said, 'So what was all the face paint about?' but I said, 'None of your business,' and turned to Joel instead. 'I suppose you've seen Tom Smart's hair?'

'Yeah, course,' said Joel. 'I helped him do it last night after *you* lot left me behind.'

And Mum said, 'Poor Joel, that really was too bad.'

Nobody mentioned my eyes.

Until later. My turn to help Mum tidy up the kitchen. What a surprise! 'I rather like your subtle eye make-up,' said Mum, noisily putting things away. 'I hardly noticed it at first, but that's the way it should be. My, my, how you're growing up all of a sudden.' She looked sad.

I was gobsmacked. 'Just experimenting,' I muttered.

'Oh, I recognise the make-up.'

'Sorry. I should have asked.'

'No, no! I kept it because you children used to love playing with it. Heavens, I've no time for make-up.'

'Why not, Mum?' I ventured.

She appeared not to hear me. But I'd just had a conversation with her! I went to bed feeling curiously elated. Despite everything.

WEDNESDAY

You and the opposition are two parts of a single whole.

EVENT/S	VENUE	WEATHER CONDITIONS	PHYSICAL HEALTH
U-16 singles	Mapledon	Grey, sunny later	Unpredictable
U-16 mixed			

Romance (have you ever heard of anything so daft?)

OPPONENT/VICTIM

Megan Birchill. Unusual unknown! I really liked her.
Neil and Harriet (I hate having to play other Club members).
Kieron (in the romance event).

TACTICS

None in the singles – should have had.
Mixed – played down the middle.
Romance – Blinked a lot. Paid compliments.

RESULT

Won
Won
Failed utterly.

EQUIPMENT

Dark tracksuit proved useful but hot. Know what to do now after talking to Zoe. Wish I'd realised before.
Ancient make-up (not so bad second time round).

COMMENTS

At least the mixed got sorted. Paddy almost back to his usual self once we were playing. That's what I've been missing! The old Paddy.
Megan is an amazing girl. She makes things happen.
Trying it on with Kieron was just so stupid. I'll have to think of someone else. Or give up.

TOMORROW'S MATCH

Singles, doubles and mixed doubles
Singles v Louise, worse luck.
Doubles v Louise and Claire, worse luck.
Mixed doubles v Alicia and bloke.
Lucy's got to play Alicia in the singles.
Paddy has a day off the singles before playing Charlie on Friday.
Smart barbecue and all that that entails.

EIGHT

I didn't feel too good on Thursday morning. My legs ached and my eyes felt gritty. I put it down to too much tennis and mucking about with mascara. Lucy picked me up at half past nine. On top of the early start, the prospect of *three* matches was almost more than I could bear. I'd taken Zoe's advice so at least I wouldn't be getting overheated.

'Well?' As soon as I got into the car Lucy twisted round to question me.

'Well what?' I replied blearily.

'Kieron!' she hissed. 'What are you going to do today?'

'Nothing at all,' I said. 'He came round last night.'

'Wow! I didn't think you had visitors.'

'We don't. He was dropping something off for Phil.'

'Bet that was just an excuse.'

'Unlikely, but even if it was, the sight of me with weird make-up all over my face didn't exactly bowl him over.'

'How did that happen?'

'He knocked on my bedroom door thinking it was Phil's, and I let him in, thinking it was one of the boys winding me up. Trouble was, I'd just been experimenting with Mum's old make-up and blinked mascara all over my face – as well as bright red lipstick.'

'Mmm. Attractive.'

'Exactly. I'm giving up on Kieron. I might want to keep him up my sleeve for a few years' time.'

'So who are you going to have your romance with?'

'I don't feel like having a romance with anyone. I feel lousy today for some reason. Three matches will keep me busy. Maybe I'll have thought of another victim by tonight.'

'I'm looking forward to tonight.'

'I'm not. I'm only going because Megan has bulldozed me into it.'

Lucy and I were soon started on our singles semi-finals. Although it was an early start for the under-16s and there weren't many spectators, we had proper umpires and there were some local reporters and photographers around. Dad makes it to the Friday afternoon semi-finals – under-18s and boys (unfair), and of course he makes it to Finals Day whether we're in it or not, but he couldn't come today. Joel threatened to make an appearance in the afternoon, but I can't say I was particularly thrilled about that.

Lucy looked tiny as she followed Alicia to their court. Both Alicia and her cousin Connie are close to six foot. And professional-looking. I didn't envy Lucy.

I didn't envy myself much, either. Two matches against Louise Smart in a day, and a third in the offing. I'd be gutted if she won all of them, though it wouldn't surprise me. Whatever you think of the Smarts, they are ace tennis players. I expect even Scarlett totes a little tennis racquet about – and beats the other three-year-olds into the ground.

Louise looked the business this morning. Her gear was brand new and she wore her hair tightly pulled back. Her bottom wiggled even more bossily than usual. I noticed that she wore eyeliner and lipstick. 'Are you ready, Alexandra?' she asked, condescendingly I thought. But I wasn't going to let her win before we'd begun.

'Oh, more than!' I replied more enthusiastically than I felt. 'I've been looking forward to this match.' (Dad's training – *never act defeated. Even when you're one set and 4–5 down, there's still a possibility of winning* – it was also today's handy hint in the tennis diary.)

Actually, at one set and 4–5 down, there didn't seem much chance of me still beating Louise Smart. I'd given her a good run for her money, but I wasn't on top form today. She won 7–5 6–4. A respectable score, but annoying all the same. She isn't necessarily better than me.

Lucy appeared, looking distinctly hacked off. Her thumbs down gesture confirmed that she'd lost, too. To make matters worse, the organisers wanted to start the girls' doubles semi-finals as soon as possible – the boys were already playing their third round, and that way we'd all be free for the mixed in the afternoon.

We made our way to the clubhouse. I wasn't going to miss out on my loser's drink. I needed it. Lucy sat with us without saying anything, her mood made even blacker when Claire turned up all fresh and keen. She couldn't really forgive Claire for being Robin's partner. Claire's OK actually. 'Hi guys!' she said. 'Are we all ready to play? They want us to start as soon as possible.'

'Don't you think we ought to pace ourselves?' I asked. 'We've all got mixed doubles matches after this.'

Claire was ready to agree, but Louise had other ideas. 'The mixed isn't really important, is it?' she said.

'Thanks a bunch,' retorted Claire. 'You're only playing me and Robin.'

'Just a bit of fun,' said Louise briskly. 'I want to finish everything and get home as soon as possible. We've got this barbecue tonight.'

'I know. Thank you for inviting us,' I said wickedly.

'Really looking forward to it,' Lucy added, perfectly aware that Louise could hardly say she didn't want us to come.

'So we'll go and check in, shall we?' said Louise.

'I suppose so. You do it. We'll see you in ten minutes, OK?' I wanted to talk tactics with Lucy.

'I haven't even had a chance to find Robin this morning,' Lucy wailed. 'My match with Alicia was awful. I never even got going.'

'Mine wasn't much fun either.'

'You looked as if you were winning yours. I didn't realise Louise had beaten you at first.'

'Well, she did. And I don't want her winning again. So we've got to play on Claire. She's surprisingly steady, but nowhere as good as Louise.'

'I expect they'll be playing on me.'

'We won't give them a chance. Come on, Luce. It's a challenge. You know me and challenges.'

'Don't I just. Except that you've given up on Kieron.'

'Not for ever! Just for now. And I have others lined up.'

'OK. Club members rise to the challenge! I won't let you down if you don't let me down.'

We lost to Claire and Louise too. 6–3 6–3. It was all over in under an hour.

In disgust, Lucy and I went to the farthest possible court to rake over our woes. 'Oh well,' she said. 'Sorry partner, and all that. You deserved better.'

'They were going to win, whatever. Think of it as conserving energy. At least no one saw us.'

'I console myself with the thought that the fewer matches I'm in, the more time I have with Robin.'

'So what *are* Robin and Charlie going to do after Friday? D'you think they will lose on purpose? Paddy would be so gutted if he only won because his opponent let him.'

'Well, only one couple can go through in the mixed. Where are they in the doubles?'

'I know they're not in the same half of the draw as Paddy and Richard.'

'So it's quite possible that Charlie might be in all three semi-finals.'

'Or Robin in two and Charlie in two,' I said. 'I'm sure the organisers wouldn't be very happy about this if they knew.'

'Well we're not the ones to tell them.'

There was nothing anyone could do about it now. In the distance two people were walking towards us, Megan striding and Max bounding along beside her. They threw themselves down on the grass next to us.

'So you're the famous Max are you?' said Lucy with a wry look at me.

'How's it going then?' said Megan, not giving Max a chance to reply. 'Got my party gear in my bag.' She patted it. 'I know I could have worn what I'm wearing now, but I like tarting myself up and Dad's given me the evening off. Still OK if I come to yours, Alex?'

'Yes, fine,' I said weakly. 'Actually, the day has been poor, so far, hasn't it Lucy? We've both lost two matches.'

'I don't hold out much hope for this afternoon either,' said Lucy. 'Robin and I are against Connie and partner and Al and Paddy are against Alicia and hers.'

'Who are Connie and Alicia?' asked Max.

'The Venus and Serena Williams of Mapledon,' said Lucy despondently.

'Oh yes, I've seen them,' said Max. 'Why are you both so gloomy?'

'I don't know,' I said. 'Losing might have something to do with it.'

'Hormones, probably,' said Max sagely.

'And what would you know about hormones?' Megan asked him.

'I might be male, but I too have hormones,' said Max. 'Anyway, I spent ten days cooped up with a whole load of girls recently. I understand these things.'

I kept quiet. What if he was right?

'Can we move on to more cheerful matters please,' said Megan, 'such as which matches to watch this afternoon?'

'Well, all the under-18s are pretty good at this stage. Or under-16 boys' doubles – you could watch any of the boys from the Club, they're all likely to win today's matches and go on to the semi-final tomorrow.'

'Why aren't you watching them?' asked Max. He had a bright, intent look which I actually found quite appealing (but, oh dear, not romantic. Try, Alex. *Try*.).

'We're sick of tennis!' I said. 'When you've lost two matches and you're contemplating losing a third you go off it a bit.'

Max stood up. 'I'm going to have a wander round. Does anyone want to come with me?'

Lucy raised her eyebrows at me. She tilted her head in Max's direction. It was the most animated I'd seen her all day. I really didn't feel like moving, but the word 'challenge' kept haunting me, and Lucy wasn't going to let me off the hook. 'I'll come with you, Max,' I said. 'I've played in the Mapledon tournament practically all my life so I ought to know my way around.'

The first match we sat in on was Phil and Kieron. 'That's my brother playing there – one of them. His partner's called Kieron. Kieron's nice, but I don't really want to see him right now.'

We moved on. *Great*. There was Joel watching us with a sneaky grin on his face. I'd forgotten he was coming. 'Aren't you going to introduce me to your friend, little sis? Is this who the OTT make-up was for? Phil and Kieron were telling me about it on the way here.'

I blushed. Horrible brothers. 'Max this is Joel. Joel this is Max.' I hastily led Max on.

'What was all that about? Could this have something to do with why you don't want to see Kieron?'

'Oh, just my nasty brother trying to embarrass me.'

'Looks as though he succeeded.'

'He always does.'

All four matches for the under-16 boys' doubles were being played on adjacent courts. There was a lot of interest. Paddy and Richard were winning. 'Who's the guy at the net this end?' asked Max. 'He's so speedy.'

'That's my partner, Paddy Gardner,' I said. I felt quite proud. 'And Richard, Lucy's partner.'

Max watched a bit more. 'Is Paddy tipped to win the under-16s?'

'He'd love to,' I said, 'but see what you think of the competition. It's good to hear what an outsider thinks. Paddy's got to play Charlie in the semis and if he gets through that he'll either have to play Leon – that guy serving over there (brother of the famous Connie), or Tom Smart (whose barbecue you're going to tonight).'

Max watched all the contenders carefully. 'I would have thought Charlie was the only one who'd give him any grief. Is he really under sixteen?'

'Yup. Not fair is it?'

Max watched some more. 'Though I would say, his left knee is giving him just a tiny bit of trouble. Watch him run. There! See what I mean?'

He was right. The slightest of movements to save that knee. Charlie was a joy to watch anyway – he had a distinctive way of spreading the fingers of his left hand as he hit the ball. It was almost like watching a dancer. Hang on, I hate Charlie. Charlie jeered at me with Joel.

Charlie spotted me. He waved as if nothing was wrong between us, as if I hadn't been avoiding him or blanking him for a day and a half. He even mouthed something at me, but it was unintelligible over that distance, and I wasn't going any closer. If it was that important, he knew he could get a message to me via Robin and Lucy.

'So Phil and Joel are your brothers. Paddy and Richard are yours and Lucy's partners. Kieron is someone you don't want to see. Charlie is someone you obviously don't want to talk to, even though *his* partner has something going with *your* partner . . . There's more than meets the eye at this tennis tournament – real "mixed doubles". You must fill me in some time!'

We sat down where we could watch the four matches that were all in their finishing stages. 'So what about you and Megan? I only met her yesterday, but I like her.'

'Well, first of all, there is nothing whatsoever between us. I'm not in her league.'

'What do you mean?'

'Megan, as you've probably noticed, is kind of larger than life. Her mum died when she was about ten, and she more or less brings up the two younger ones. They're off on playschemes this week – that's why she's high as a kite to be out of the house. School holidays are a complete pain for her.'

'I didn't know.'

'Why should you?'

'It's just that I hear something like that and it makes my problems pale into insignificance. I can't imagine actually having to *look after* my brothers.' I glanced at my watch. 'Max, I'm going to get called quite soon. But before we go – you are going to be at the barbecue tonight, aren't you?'

'Sure thing.'

'I'll tell you more about the complications then. And Max?'

'Uh-huh?'

'Since you're such a great guy I might just have to ask you to do me a *massive* favour. I won't tell you what it is now, because it might not happen. But be prepared. OK?'

Lucy and Megan were approaching. I slipped away. I felt rather sick – I thought a solitary muffin and a cup of tea might help.

I sat myself in a corner of the clubhouse and prayed that no one, e.g. Ethlie, would come and bother me. I didn't want to lose a third match or let Paddy down but I had a really unpleasant pain in the pit of my stomach. Nerves probably. I made myself invisible and watched the world go by. There was a lot of activity round the board as the semi-finals took shape. Joel came and studied it for a while but he didn't notice me. The first mixed doubles matches were called as the other doubles players came off. I was lucky to have as much time as I did between matches. Mrs Smart appeared, looking queenly, and there was a sort of buzz round her for a while in anticipation of the barbecue. Scarlett was with her. She spotted me and ran over. 'Are you going to come to my party tonight?' she asked me and I just had time to tell her I was before her mother hauled her off again.

'P. Gardner and Miss A. Dunbar; L. Johnson and Miss A. Smith. To the desk please.' That was us.

'Hi there,' said Paddy. 'I wondered where you'd got to.'

Dad: Never let your partner think you're below par. 'I was preparing myself for the big match. You know, carbo-hydrates, feet up, positive thinking.'

'Great. Because we're going to win this one aren't we?' Paddy's learnt the same rules as I have, but I actually detected a look of concern in his eyes. Alicia and partner arrived. They both wore baseball caps and carried cyclists' bottles of water – very professional. We went over to warm up – not that Paddy needed to. As on other days the sun had broken through the clouds during the afternoon and it was quite hot. I took off my tracksuit before we started. (Thank you Zoe.) Paddy was on a roll. I felt reassured but also determined to keep him on this winning streak.

It was a tough game. Like Max, Alicia's partner had only been brought in for the mixed doubles. He was a flashy player – daunting at first, but comparatively easy to beat because he so often fluffed his shots and then ran through the gamut of self-hate moves. He threw his racquet to the ground several times, hit the ball hard against the wire mesh, cursed himself – all of which made the two of us feel more in control. I was aware of Paddy covering me, though. He didn't leave as many shots for me as he might have done, spared me from running across the court behind him. He's psychic, that guy! And never, ever a cross word. Only encouragement and praise. I mean, I do the same for him, but during that match I really appreciated it.

Towards the end my friends came to watch. Lucy's mum was there, so I knew our lift was in place as soon as we finished. I was less pleased to see Joel and Phil and Kieron amongst the spectators, but luckily by that time we were 4–2 up in the second set, with the first set in the bag. I couldn't have borne to go on to three sets.

'Vultures are gathering,' said Paddy as he came back to receive.

'It's the barbecue they're gathering for,' I said.

Alicia served a double fault. 'You are coming, aren't you?' I asked Paddy as we moved again. It would be a shame if he wasn't there.

'Not sure,' said Paddy from the net. We played a long point which Paddy won with a terrific cross-court volley. He walked back. 'I don't know all those people.'

'Rubbish! You know them as well as I do. You *know me*!' The game got tricky at that moment. If we got to deuce and they won it, we'd only be 4–3 up – a dangerous score. 'I'll shut up,' I said, remembering uncomfortably Max and the massive favour. Maybe I wouldn't want Paddy as an audience.

'Yeah, let's WIN,' said Paddy.

Six points later we had. But as we were shaking hands I suddenly knew I had to rush to the loo. I couldn't hang around to see whether or not Paddy was coming to the barbecue, I just had to get to the clubhouse. Megan, anxious about her lift, followed me.

'You OK?' she asked from the next cubicle.

'No,' I said. And then, 'Well, I'm fine really. I've just started my period. Good job I came prepared.'

NINE

I wasn't sure how Megan would react to my bizarre household. Seriously, I always visit my friends – I never bring them home. Maybe it's something to do with having an enormously fat mother. So I couldn't have been more surprised when Megan announced in her Janet Street-Porter voice as soon as we got in the door – 'What an amazing house! Doesn't it smell nice? – all lemony and clean! Ours always stinks of frying and cat food.'

Mum hove into view. 'This is Megan, Mum.' I wanted to fill Mum in on the facts I'd learnt about Megan, but it didn't seem appropriate.

'Great house, Mrs Dunbar,' said Megan enthusiastically. 'Really *homely*.'

'I'll take Megan up to my room,' I said, not wanting to expose her to the twins or Joel.

Too late, because Jack came down the stairs, deep in a Gameboy game. 'What's for supper, Mum?' he said, not lifting his eyes.

'Chilli con carne,' she replied.

'Aw,' said Jack. 'That means it'll be spicy doesn't it?'

'It'll be chilli con carne, yes,' said Mum.

'Can I have a sandwich?' he whined.

'Ooh!' Megan couldn't keep quiet. 'Hope you're not going to let him get away with *that*, Mrs Dunbar!'

Jack was silenced. Mum, already on her way to make him a sandwich, looked back, surprised.

'Sorry,' said Megan. 'None of my business, but I bawl mine out if they moan about the food.'

'Oh,' said Mum, flummoxed. 'It's just that Jack makes such a mess when he does his own sandwiches—'

'Come on, Megan,' I said. 'We don't have a lot of time.' She followed me up the stairs past Jack, who flattened himself against the wall with a look of something like respect on his face.

'Sorry,' she said, once we were in my room. 'Forgot you probably want to get to the bathroom. I get hideous periods. Do you?'

'Um. I don't know. This is my first one.'

'What? Oh, wow! Congratulations! Welcome to the world of womanhood!'

'That's how my friend Zoe put it,' I said, and suddenly burst into tears.

Megan sat on the bed beside me. 'Oh bad luck. It's not very good timing is it? Still, that's typical. Have to get used to it.'

I couldn't stop crying.

'Hey! There, there.'

I carried on snivelling. Poor Megan didn't know quite what to do. 'Won't be a minute,' she said, and then, to my horror I heard her running down the stairs, calling, 'Mrs Dunbar? Mrs Dunbar? I think your daughter needs you!'

Joel: 'So what's up with poor little Ally Wallie?'

Megan: 'Girl stuff. Where's your mum?'

Joel: 'Arranging the cushions at right-angles probably. What sort of girl stuff?'

Megan: 'None of your business.'

Joel (retaliating sarcastically): 'Sorry I asked.'

And then there were muffled females voices followed by Megan taking the stairs three at a time and Mum huffing and puffing behind her. And then they were both in my room.

Mum came and sat on my bed too. (She's so heavy I boinged up in the air a couple of inches.) 'Darling,' she said. 'Why didn't you say?'

'It only just happened, didn't it?' Megan said, genuinely excited on my behalf.

'I've had some supplies ready for you for a while,' said Mum. 'I'll go and fetch them. I've got some of those little disposal bags that you can buy these days, too. You'll want to be a bit discreet in this house full of boys.' And she shuffled out.

Far from easing up, I was now crying buckets.

'Are you in pain?' asked Megan.

'No!' I sobbed. 'It's complicated. I don't usually get on with my mum.'

'Well start getting on with her. At least you've got one.'

'I know,' I hiccupped.

Joel knocked on the door and put his head round immediately.

'What's going on?' he asked. Joel doesn't like not knowing what's going on.

'I told you before!' said Megan. 'It's none of your business. Go away!' I sobbed afresh. 'How did he earn his cool reputation, your brother? He's about as sensitive as a rhinoceros.'

'And that's unfair on rhinoceroses.' I managed a laugh.

'Hey, that's better!' said Megan.

Mum rustled in with a large Boots plastic carrier containing a brand-new sponge bag and much the same variety of things as Zoe had given me, as well as a little swing-top bin and a pack of scented purple plastic bags.

'Mum – why didn't you tell me you'd got all this stuff?'

She sighed. 'I didn't want to presume – or pry,' she said defensively. 'Anyway, here you are. Your friend Megan is probably more use to you now than I am. I must go and get on with that chilli.'

'That the boys don't want,' I said under my breath as she left.

'Why is she so fat?' asked Megan in her upfront way.

'Dunno,' I said. 'She wasn't always like that. Not in the photos.'

'Right, let's get ready,' said Megan. 'What are you wearing? My tennis gear's rubbish but I've got good party clothes. I've brought loads, so you can borrow something if you want.'

'Nothing pale,' I said.

'Oh, don't be ridiculous! Nothing much will happen if this is your first time. Anyway, that's what all this stuff your mum gave you is for. Remember that a quarter of the girls at the barbecue, not to mention the tennis tournament, will be in the same boat.'

'Yuk!'

'True. Though it might be an idea not to swim.'

'So how do you explain to people that you're not going in the pool?'

'*If* they're rude enough to ask, you simply give them a withering look and say, "Why do you think?", and if they still insist on not understanding, tell them, in gory detail. OK. Now, you'd look good in this little number.'

Half an hour later we sashayed downstairs. I was wearing a red-and-gold shot top of Megan's with a pair of her baggy trousers. She'd pinned my hair up and made up my face a little. I felt pretty cool. She looked much the same in a black-and-silver top.

'I've got some money for burgers,' said Megan. 'Have you got a corner shop?'

I hadn't thought of that – I wondered if the boys had. We went into the kitchen where Mum was ironing Joel's T-shirt while Joel looked on.

'Mum – we all ought to take something for the barbecue. If you give me some money I'll buy something for Phil and Joel as well.'

'Spare ribs for me,' said Joel.

'You'll have what I choose,' I retorted, 'unless you want to buy it yourself.'

Mum fetched her purse and gave me a tenner. 'I'll want change,' she said.

'Don't worry Mrs Dunbar,' said Megan. 'I'm the burger expert. It's what my lot get most days.'

'Doesn't your mother—' *Oh Mum, please stop right there!*

'She died,' said Megan, matter-of-factly. 'But Dad's feeding them tonight. I've got the night off! Ta-ra!'

My dad was just letting himself in when we got back. Joel looked at his watch. 'We ought to be off, Dad.'

'Give me a chance to turn round,' said Dad. Then he saw us. 'Hey, you two girls look nice. Anyone seen Alex anywhere?'

'Not funny, Dad. This is my friend Megan.'

'Hi,' said Megan.

Mum appeared with a coolbag to put all our burgers in. Dad gave her a kiss. 'Sometimes I wish you could drive, dear,' he said. 'I'm almost too tired to be a taxi-driver tonight.'

'Doesn't Philip drive yet?' asked Megan. 'I can't wait – only eighteen months to go! You ought to learn, Mrs D. I know the *best* driving instructor. Are we off then? Bye! Thanks for having me!'

Everyone was at the Smarts'. Tuesday night's swim seemed a long time ago, and I felt kind of safe with Megan. She gave me courage. It was even quite nice to arrive with Phil and Joel – people are pleased to see them.

Louise and Claire both leapt on Joel. 'Hey this is some party,' he said, making them titter (why?), and they marched him off for a swim.

'Airheads,' muttered Megan.

'You're not very impressed by my brother, are you?' I asked her.

'Not by that one,' she said, 'but I quite like this one!' She beamed at Phil, making him blush. 'Though I happen to know that a certain young lady named Lana is expected tonight . . . which means I won't get a look-in.' Phil blushed some more.

'How on earth did you know that?'

'Oh, I keep my ear to the ground,' Megan said. 'I'd better go and find Max. Hi, Kieron. You're looking very fine tonight!' And she was off into the throng.

Phil's eyes were darting around nervously. 'Lana's here, mate – allegedly,' he said by way of apology to Kieron.

'Go seek out the lovely Lana!' said Kieron. 'I'll content myself with the lovely Alexandra. How you doin' Al?'

'Fine,' I said.

'You look every inch a lady tonight.'

'You flatter me.'

'So the other night was just a rehearsal, was it?'

'In a manner of speaking.'

I was still hanging on to our coolbag with the burgers in, and Kieron was also clutching a carrier bag. 'Shall we go and dump these somewhere?' he suggested, and I followed him to the major (Scout camp size) barbecue that had been set up on the patio. We each grabbed a can of Coke while we were at it. We sat down together on a garden bench. 'So who's the lucky guy?' he asked. 'The one the rehearsal was for? You certainly got it right this evening – the hair, everything!'

'Kieron, you're so nice to me. Why?'

'Why not? Two years' time. It's a date, OK? Even if I have to fight off the competition.'

'OK, if you say so.'

Kieron leant over and kissed me on the cheek just as a stunning redhaired girl came over to us. He stood up to greet her. 'Ingrid, hi!' And they went off arm in arm, leaving me to put my hand up to my cheek. So that was Kieron well and truly off the list.

Where were Lucy, Max, Robin, Charlie even? Where was Paddy? It was time to investigate. I wandered towards the swimming pool, trying to put the other night to the back of my mind. I wasn't going to be beaten by Joel. At the gate Scarlett and her little friend spotted me. 'There she is! Will you come and play that game with us again? Please? Please?'

'Sorry guys. I've come to party tonight, not swim.'

'Aw.'

Joel appeared, dripping. 'Not coming in this time then Alex? Scarlett wants you to.'

'No,' I said. 'I told them I'm here to party tonight. Don't feel like getting wet.'

Claire and Louise appeared behind him. 'Why don't you want to swim, Alex?' he persisted now he had an audience.

'Why do you think?' I retorted on cue.

'Honestly, Joel,' said Louise. 'You're hopeless.' They were tittering again, but I had won. I held my ground and watched the swim for a while. Scarlett and friend had found another victim – though they weren't having nearly as much fun as they did with me. I felt quite calm for the first time in ages. Max would probably say it was hormones.

Calm, but hungry. Smells from the barbecue were wafting over – if my friends had any sense they were loading their plates with food. I was right. Lucy saw me and called me over to join her in the queue. Her, Robin – and Charlie. I didn't know what to say to Charlie. Lucy and Robin were chattering so much it didn't show at first – I talked to Lucy, and Charlie talked to Robin. We got through platefuls of food that way. I was even enjoying myself – just so long as Lucy and Robin stayed.

But they didn't stay. One of those irresistible dance songs floated over to us and Lucy hauled Robin to his feet and whisked him away. I was left with Charlie.

Charlie: 'It's taken me until now to realise why you weren't talking to me.'

Me: 'Well.'

Charlie: 'I wasn't laughing at you the other night.'

Me: 'What were you laughing at then?'

Charlie sensed that I was lightening up. I was. 'Oh I don't know. Joel's like you – he's funny, but that was uncalled for. I think I was laughing because someone had farted or something. Nothing to do with Joel. You know I tried to ring you later on, don't you?'

'Lucy told me, yes.'

'Robin and I had decided to ask you two to be our partners in the mixed doubles. You and Paddy hadn't signed up at the time, if you remember,' he added carefully, 'so it seemed like a good idea.'

'OK, OK.'

'So you're not cross any more?'

'No.'

'Phew. Shall we go in there and leap about with the others?'

'OK. Charlie? There's something I want to ask you before we go in where it's noisy.'

'Fire away.'

'Does everyone know that you won't be playing on Saturday?'

'We're not exactly shouting it from the rooftops.'

'So what's going to happen in your semi-finals? Are you going to lose them on purpose?'

'I'm assuming that the eventual finalists will be better than me.'

'But they're not, are they? Paddy, for one, would hate it if he felt you'd *let* him win.' Just the thought of Paddy's hurt pride really upset me.

'I suppose I hadn't thought of it in terms of individuals. Jeez – Louise and I are playing you and Paddy together aren't we?'

'Yup.'

'Actually that's not a problem. You'll win that.'

'What do you mean? Louise beat me today.'

'Maybe, but she's no better than you—' I started to protest. 'No she isn't, you know. I've watched you both, and I know these things. And—' he carried on as I started to protest again, 'you and Paddy are a fantastic partnership. You work really well together. Louise and I don't know each other at all. And though I'm good at the net,' he bragged, 'Louise isn't.'

'So you think we can beat you on merit?'

'I do.'

'Good. You'd better watch out then. What about the boys' doubles?'

'Robin's not as good as I am. Neil and Raj can win if they play on him ruthlessly.'

'Poor Robin!'

'Who do you want to win this match?'

'OK. But the one I'm really worried about is Paddy.' *Where was he?*

'I'm really worried about him too. I think he's going to beat me.'

'What's the order of play?'

'I think they'll let us do the singles while we're fresh. Probably mixed doubles last.' He stood up. 'Come on. You haven't made me laugh once this evening. Let's have a dance. Then I can make you laugh.'

It was dark and heaving in the room with the music: a converted garage – usually a games room with a table tennis table, Charlie told me. Phil and Kieron were in there with Lana and Ingrid. Joel had gone for Claire – which showed good taste on his part but not on hers. Even Ethlie was jigging away on her own. I like dancing, so long as it doesn't get smoochy. Eek. No. I couldn't do the romance thing with Charlie. Almost. But not. Almost – but how could I kiss someone if I didn't want to? It all seemed so alien. And where was Paddy?

I was saved from a slow number by the arrival of Max. Excitable Max with *bleached* hair! 'Your turn Charlie!' he said. 'What do you think of mine, eh?'

'What's going on?' I asked.

'Tom's got a production line going,' said Max. He did a twirl. 'Cool, or what?'

'Can't wait,' said Charlie and set off up the stairs.

'Scalp feels a bit tender,' said Max. 'Can we go outside in the fresh air? I think the fumes are making my eyes water.'

'Is Megan having hers done too?'

'No, she's just an onlooker. She said to tell you that's where she was.'

'It's quite cold out here, Max. Hang on while I get my jacket will you. I won't be a sec.'

'I'll be here, don't you worry,' said Max, seating himself on a fancy 'love seat' the Smarts had placed in a herb garden beyond the pool.

My jacket was upstairs so I visited the bathroom where the hair colouring was taking place. Much hilarity as Charlie stripped his top off ready to be the next sacrificial victim and presented his glossy brown locks for bleaching. Megan waved from the thick of it.

Max was waiting for me. You can guess what favour I wanted to ask him. My romance pledge was unfulfilled and I had this feeling Max and I could concoct something together that I could use to convince the others. 'OK sweetie, what is it?' said Max, running his hand through his hair in a camp way as I sat round from him in the love seat. In fact it was a sort of double love seat, made in the shape of a curved '3' rather than an 'S'. I was in the middle.

'Just listen then.'

'I'm all yours.'

'I made a sort of pact with three friends that each of us would have a holiday romance and report back on it. Only – I haven't had one. I'm useless at that sort of thing.'

At that moment Deathly Ethlie burst on the scene. 'Oh there you are, Alex!' she said, gripping my arm. 'I haven't seen you for ages!'

'I'm kind of in the middle of something at the moment, Ethlie. Can I catch up with you later?'

'Oh no! Really?' she said, predictably. 'All right then,' and she wandered off, laughing.

'Did you say something funny just then?' said Max.

'No, she always says that.'

'So how can I help you with your romance?' Max leered at me. 'Do you want us to be caught snogging or something? I'm game.'

'No!'

'Well what, then? Just a quick kiss? Naked? In the parents' bedroom?'

'Max!' I thumped him.

'You've never kissed anyone have you?'

'I—'

'Go on, I can tell.'

'All right. No. I haven't. There seems to be too much spit involved.'

'Tell you what. I'll teach you an actor's trick a friend showed me. It looks as though you're kissing but actually you put your hand in the way.'

'Show me.'

He grabbed the back of my head with one hand, put the other one over my mouth and pretended to kiss me passionately. It felt strange, especially as I was nearly overwhelmed by the smell of bleach. 'Excellent. Do you want to go and try it out on the dance floor?'

'Not yet.'

'You mean there's more? What else do you want me to do? No one's ever asked me to pretend to have a romance before. I could hold your hand?' He picked up my hand and stroked it. It tickled. 'Rip my clothes off?' He pulled his bleach-spattered T-shirt over his head. 'You could lie with your head in my lap – actually, no, that's not such a good idea.'

'I don't know. You see, that's the problem, I don't know what I have to do.'

'Hey!' Max was momentarily distracted. 'Here comes Charlie boy – a very fetching blond!'

Charlie strode out to the love seat. 'What do you think?'

'Cool,' we both said as he sat on my other side.

'What are you two up to?'

'I'm teaching her to kiss,' said Max.

'You *what*?' Charlie sounded quite shocked.

'Let's show him,' said Max. And so we went through the whole drama for him.

'That was useless!' said Charlie. 'I could see your hand! This is how you should do it!' And, from the other side of the love seat, he put one hand behind my head – and the other in my hair – and kissed me for real!

'Mmmmmuh – mmmmmuh!' I said struggling. 'You weren't supposed to do it *really*.'

'Oh well, if he's allowed to do it unprotected, then so am I,' said Max, and grabbed my head again.

'Oy!' yelled Charlie, 'I was enjoying that!' and tried to pull me back again.

At which point Megan arrived. 'Hey guys!' she said. 'Look who I've just found wandering around like a lost sheep.'

It was Paddy. But all we saw was his retreating back, and all we heard was his diminishing voice saying, 'I knew I shouldn't have come.'

TEN

I tried ringing Paddy as soon as Dad had driven us home (he didn't want Phil and me having a late night before semi-finals day, though I could have slept in until lunch time if I'd wanted). I wasn't sure what I was going to say to Paddy, but his mum answered and said that he'd gone to bed early on account of having three big matches the next day. She sounded proud.

THURSDAY

Never act defeated. Even when you're one set and 4–5 down, there's still a possibility of winning.

EVENT/S	VENUE	WEATHER CONDITIONS	PHYSICAL HEALTH
U-16 singles			
U-16 doubles	Mapledon	Warm	Curse, lousy
U-16 mixed			
Smart barbecue	Smart Towers		

OPPONENT/VICTIM
Louise Smart
Ditto and Claire.
Alicia and Luke
Kieron, Max, Charlie, Paddy – you name them.

TACTICS
None really.
None really.
None really.
Romance – Tried to get Max to pretend to have a romance with me.

RESULT
Lost
Lost
Won
Confusion

EQUIPMENT
Emergency supplies came in handy.
Megan's make-up and clothes.

COMMENTS
Too much to fit in here. Extraordinary day all round. Mum actually nice to me.

TOMORROW'S MATCH
Mixed doubles v Louise Smart and Charlie.
Paddy's big match against Charlie.

I lay awake for ages thinking about the weird day I'd had. First period. First kiss. Practically the first time I'd had a sympathetic conversation with Mum.

Kissing Charlie – which was *very* different from pretending to kiss Max – was all mixed up in my mind with Paddy turning up. In fact, as I drifted into a sleep that bristled with vivid dreams, Paddy was the one I was kissing. And then I'd jerk awake and sit up, trembling, every second and every centimetre of Charlie's soft lips on mine replaying itself. His face tilted and his eyelids closed in slow motion. The slight bristle of his chin grazed for an eternity. The awkwardness of our teeth briefly clashing lasted for excruciating aeons. (Not to mention the strong smell of bleach – it'll probably be linked with kissing for the rest of my life.) Then me, struggling to get away. Pathetic, naive girl. What must they think of me? It was only a bit of fun.

What had Paddy seen? Why did he act so – *hurt*? The others wondered what had happened to Paddy's sense of humour, but I know Paddy's got a great sense of humour.

'I think he's jea-lous,' Megan had said to me in a sing-song voice.

'What of?' I'd said.

'You tell me-he,' she'd said, in the same tone as before.

And then, before anything at all was resolved, there was Dad, car keys at the ready, prising Phil away from Lana, Joel away from Claire and me away from my group of friends.

'See you tomorrow,' said Charlie, cheerful and completely unfazed. Kissing was clearly just another game to him.

'We'll try and come on Saturday, won't we Max?' said Megan. 'Though I might have to bring one of the kids.' She gave me a hug. 'Good luck with – everything! Be nice to Paddy. I sense that something's going on behind those gorgeous deep blue eyes of his.'

All their words were going round and round in my head. I had to get to sleep – tomorrow's match was important. I really couldn't let Paddy down now. It all meant too much to him. And I had to be there for his match against Charlie. Ah. I didn't want to think about that. What if Charlie played badly on purpose and Paddy thought I'd put him up to it?

In the small hours I got up quietly to fetch some water and go to the loo. Mum appeared from nowhere. Scary because she's so huge. 'Everything all right, love?'

'Yeah, fine thanks, Mum,' and then she slip-slopped off back to bed. It was as if she had been acting on instinct.

I went to sleep after that.

'Nice girl, Megan,' Mum said, as she handed me my sandwiches in the morning. 'Fancy having to look after her family like that – she's only a kid herself.'

'Doesn't seem to get her down,' I said. Kieron was at the door to pick us up.

'Seems there were two lucky guys last night, then,' Kieron said to me.

'Oh shut up, Kieron, we were only mucking about.'

'Didn't ruin your make-up then?'

'What's all this?' said Phil, climbing into the car after me.

'Idle gossip,' I said. 'Nothing at all compared with you and Lana or Kieron and Ingrid.'

'Who?' said Kieron's mum, and both the boys were silenced.

I'd wanted to catch Paddy before his match with Charlie, but I was too late. They'd been on Court One in front of a surprisingly large audience, with several photographers making a nuisance of themselves. I caught Paddy's eye as I sat down, but he glowered at me. My God, he looked absolutely furious.

Down the other end, Charlie was a picture of concentration, despite the frivolous blond spikes on his head. No sense at all that he might be giving the match away. No sign either that his left knee was giving him any trouble.

But Paddy was playing a blinder. He was a fireball of energy – like Boris Becker used to be. He didn't miss anything. And he was hitting so hard, slamming shots at Charlie like bullets, as if he wanted to injure him. It was exciting stuff, and the spectators sensed it. Under-16 tennis wasn't usually this good.

Paddy took the first set almost before Charlie realised. The second set was going to be tougher. Charlie got into his stride, and he made good use of his height at the net. There was a game where Paddy couldn't get anything past him.

It was awful, I so much wanted Paddy to win. I sent thought signals to him, like I do when we play as partners. *Lob him. Lob him. Do an ace, now. Keep him running.* Maybe Charlie was simply too good for him. They only play best of three sets at this level. If Charlie got this set – well, anything could happen.

Charlie did take the second set after a tie-break. It was that close. Paddy wouldn't look at me as they sat down to rest between sets. I'd have to use telepathy again.

As everyone said, Paddy was incredibly fit. I happened to know he'd had a better night's sleep than Charlie, too (as long as he hadn't been tormented like I had). He just had to keep Charlie on the run, exhaust him, not give him a chance to win at the net, serve aces. The tension was hideous. Charlie was too good. No, Charlie *wasn't* too good. Give Paddy credit, I thought. At least think positive on his behalf.

Paddy had spotted that weak left knee. Again and again he made Charlie turn and run to the left. It was a cruel trick, maybe, but one that required a huge amount of skill on Paddy's part to make it come off. He made Charlie reach higher and higher at the net, forcing him to jump. Paddy's eyes were gimlet sharp, his forehead creased. It was as if he was fighting for his life.

Four–two. Paddy had broken Charlie's serve. In the next game the spin on Paddy's serve was so deceptive he managed to wrong-foot Charlie every time. I hardly dared to look, but I think the knee was beginning to play up under the punishment. Five–two. I had to leave, I couldn't bear the suspense.

Five minutes later, from the depth of the clubhouse I heard the cheer go up. Paddy had beaten Charlie, and I knew that Charlie had not willingly conceded a single point. Wow. What a performance!

I went out and watched the two of them shaking hands with the umpire and coming off court in a blitz of camera flash. Charlie spotted me first. He gave me an exhausted grin. 'As I said,' he murmured as he passed, 'I expected the finalists to be better than me. No question, Paddy *won*, OK?'

I couldn't help it. I rushed up to Paddy and gave him a hug. But it was like hugging a splintery wooden post – with barbed wire on it.

I stepped back quickly. Was he angry with *me*? Was it sheer anger that had made him win?

Paddy and Charlie disappeared into the changing rooms. Robin and Lucy were suddenly at my elbow. 'Did you see that?' asked Robin. 'I've never seen Charlie totalled like that before, not even by one of the men. That was genius play.'

'Yup,' said Lucy. 'Respect for Paddy gone up by one hundred per cent. Not that I didn't respect him before. I should think you're quite proud of your partner, aren't you, Al?'

'He's ignoring me, Lucy. It's awful.'

'Paddy? Why?'

'I'm not sure. Something to do with last night.'

'Uh?' Lucy saw I needed to talk. 'Robin – I expect you want to go and commiserate with your old mate, don't you? Talk up the next match and so on?' Lucy gave him a piercing look.

'Oh, OK,' said Robin. 'I'll be off then.'

'Far-distant court,' said Lucy, taking me by the elbow. 'I think there are things I should know. I was a bit wrapped up in Robin last night. Seems like I didn't get the whole picture.'

We sat down and I told her about last night. After all, she had something to do with it. 'Remember the challenge?'

I told her about Max playing along and teaching me how to do a stage kiss and then Charlie joining in.

'Ooh, so you made it up with Charlie did you? Great. So you *can* be a foursome with us. Not so sure about the bleached hair though.'

'I know. It was a perfectly nice colour before. It's quite cool though.'

'Didn't think you noticed these things.'

'Watch it.' It was nice talking to Lucy again. Megan had breezed in and out of my life like fresh air, but I've known Lucy for centuries. She knows the background. 'And no, Charlie and I won't be making a foursome with you and Robin. He doesn't take me seriously.'

'Unlike Paddy?'

'And what is that supposed to mean?'

'Oh come on Alex? Haven't you noticed the way Paddy looks at you these days?'

'With a face like thunder last time I saw him.'

'Has it never occurred to you that he might have feelings for you beyond being your tennis partner?'

'No.'

'And you can honestly say that you don't have *any* feelings for him outside the tennis court (you sad woman)?'

'Well—'

'Ha! You hesitated!'

'Well, I did kind of hope he'd turn up last night.'

'And he did.'

'Yeah, but he turned straight round and went home again.'

'Because he saw you canoodling with Charlie?'

'And with Max!'

'So that makes it better does it?' Lucy was laughing at me.

I protested. 'But I don't care about Max or Charlie! It was all only for this stupid romance thing anyway. I wish I'd never agreed to it. I've just made a complete and utter idiot of myself, and lost a good friend in the process!'

'You haven't lost Paddy. You've got to play a match with him this afternoon. Anyway, if he is angry, it can only be because he *likes* you, can't it?'

'You don't think – you don't think – that Paddy *likes* me, like that, do you?'

'Pea-brain! What do you think I've been trying to tell you *all* week?'

'Ohmygod! But that's awful! I mean – I never quite thought of that, until the Charlie kissing me thing, I suppose—'

'Make up your mind, would you? I know you don't *do* romance, don't think of boys "in that way" – you've told me nothing else. But I'm beginning to think the lady doth protest too much. You've been trailing blokes after you all week, and one in particular!'

'We're talking Paddy here? Tell me, because I'm getting confused.'

'YES!'

'Oh.'

I needed to be on my own. I told Lucy I didn't want to keep her from Robin any longer, and took a little walk into the car park. Only a few parents chatting on their mobiles or listening to the cricket there. Paddy, my friend and partner, was angry because he'd seen me apparently kissing Charlie. It only made sense if he had – feelings – for me. But he was my mate. How could I play tennis with him if I knew he felt like that about me?

I paced about. What would Megan say? She seemed to get to the quick of the matter before most people. Actually, Megan had said something last night – what was it? 'I think he's jealous' and 'something's going on behind those gorgeous dark blue eyes.'

I thought about Paddy's eyes for a moment. They are a gorgeous colour – kind of navy blue, and the giraffe lashes . . .

Oh dear. This didn't get any better.

I forced myself to think about something else. I wondered how the boys' doubles was going. Paddy (well, I *tried* to think about something else) and Richard were playing Tom Smart and a bloke called Toby; Neil and Raj were against Charlie and Robin. I suddenly felt all protective about our Club members. You expect people with years of expensive coaching to do well, but we're a bit home-grown, if you know what I mean. I decided to track down Neil and Raj before their match began and tell them to play on Robin and to exploit Charlie's knee injury. I found them at the snack bar. 'Hi Al! How you doin'?' Raj was very cheery. He'd gone blond the night before too.

'Great! You two going to win then?'

'Of course,' said Neil.

'Of course,' said Raj.

'Well, maybe not,' said Neil.

'No. Probably not at all.'

'In fact we're almost certain to lose,' said Raj.

'Right boys. I've got news for you. You *are* going to win, and here's how.' I drew them into a corner and told them. 'You owe it to the Club, OK?'

'Yes ma'am!' said Neil, clicking his heels. Their match was called at that precise moment, so off they went, joshing each other and laughing.

Then Lucy appeared. 'So who are you going to watch?' she asked.

'Well I'm not watching Paddy.'

'That settles it then. Let's go and watch Robin.'

'And Neil and Raj. They're going to win, you know.'

'Oh yeah?'

The boys' match went on for ever, and I was glad. I wasn't looking forward to my next encounter with Paddy. What's more, it all served to tire Charlie out, and I wanted him to be dying of exhaustion by the time it came to our match. Neil and Raj put up a really good show. They kept up the pressure on Robin. Lucy didn't know who to support in the end. All three sets were close but Raj and Neil hung on in there to the last: 8–6, 6–8, 8–6. Lucy was thrilled for them, but she was even more thrilled to be able to comfort Robin. He and Charlie came over to us afterwards. 'Two defeats down,' Charlie said to me, 'and I'm knackered.'

'You're not supposed to let me know that,' I said.

'It's obvious, isn't it? And I think this great surgical bandage round my knee might be a bit of a giveaway.'

'Are you OK?'

'What do you care? Paddy's after my blood anyway, so I don't stand a chance. Man, he was ace this morning. Think my coach ought to see him in action.' He turned his back on Robin. 'He's better than Robin.'

'Charlie! Ssh!'

'True.' He put his foot up on to a seat to ease his leg. 'Got to make him forgive me first. Could it be that Paddy is keener than we realised on a certain person not a million miles from here? Number one fan, in fact, of the club of which I'm a founder member?'

I blushed. 'I don't know, Charlie. I genuinely don't know.'

'Come on Charlie,' said Robin. 'A free drink awaits. We ought to go and claim it.'

'See you in a bit, Alex,' said Charlie. 'And just play on Louise OK? Leave my knee out of it. I might want to walk again one day.'

Paddy and Richard had lost. The mixed doubles semi-final couldn't be put off any longer. We were on Court Two, and quite a few parents had gathered to watch.

We filed on to the court. Paddy nodded at me. He didn't speak, just picked up a few balls ready to knock. Louise did her annoying hip-wiggle down to the other end, ponytail swinging officiously as she herded Charlie into position.

'Paddy – please tell me what's wrong,' I said.

'Let's just get on with the match, shall we?'

'Play on Louise,' I said. 'Keep it away from Charlie at the net.'

'Do you think I don't know that?' he said. If what everyone implied was true, and he did like me, he certainly wasn't showing any signs of it now. He was right really, there was nothing for it but to get on with the match.

Louise fancied Charlie. Since Joel was already spoken for, she was determined to turn on the charm for Charlie. So she was showing off to him and playing incredibly well. Paddy didn't trust our usual empathy, but roared instructions at me all the time: 'Over there!' 'Yours!' 'Leave it!'

'Run, for Pete's sake!' And it didn't work. We tripped over each other the whole time. I lost confidence.

Louise and Charlie won the first set. Both boys seemed to have found a second wind. I suppose mixed doubles is a bit gentler for them. But I had to say something to Paddy.

'Please relax a bit, Paddy. We're great together usually – don't spoil it.'

And then he looked at me. A beautiful, raw, dark-blue gaze, piercing me to the heart.

It brought tears to my eyes. I put my hand on his arm. 'You got it wrong, Paddy. Trust me?' Our eyes locked for a few moments. I smiled. 'Let's get on with the match shall we?'

So we won. OK, maybe Charlie had to lose, but we were the better team. Louise got tired of showing off, Charlie's knee wasn't great, and the famous Dunbar–Gardner partnership came into its own.

Dad was there, clapping away with the best of them. 'Two Dunbars in the finals. *E*xcellent result!'

Phil was with him. 'Well done, guys. You deserved to win that.'

'Get your gear together,' said Dad. 'Tonight something unprecedented is happening. Because the twins and Joel are out for the evening, the rest of us are going for a pizza.'

'What, Mum as well?'

'Yes, her idea. Not quite sure what's come over her, but I think we should take her up on it before she changes her mind, don't you?'

'See you tomorrow then,' said Paddy, with another of those looks.

So I left, without saying goodbye to Charlie or Robin, and with my 'relationship' with Paddy about as different as it could be from how it had been only three hours earlier. I felt all fluttery. At what precise moment does a friendship turn into a so-called 'relationship'?

ELEVEN

'You're very quiet Alex.'

'Sorry, Dad. A bit tired, that's all.'

'Too much fun last night,' said Phil.

'You're on dangerous ground, Phil,' I glared at him.

'Anyway, I'm very proud of you both,' said Dad. 'And everyone from the Club. I heard Paddy played well.'

'Paddy beat that Charlie guy,' said Phil. 'I only saw a bit of the match, but everyone was talking about it. And Charlie's as good as anyone in the under-18s.'

Please don't talk about Paddy.

'So why the pizza, Mum?'

'It seemed like a nice idea. You know, just to have a night off from cooking once in a while.'

'I'm all for it,' said Dad, giving Phil and me an isn't-this-great? look. It crossed my mind that we had no idea how Mum and Dad related to each other. They must have loved each other once. They were still together, weren't they?

'Maybe we should cook sometimes,' I said. 'You too, Dad. Rather than helping, perhaps we should give Mum more evenings off.'

'Ooh,' said Mum. 'I shouldn't know what to do with myself.'

'Watch *EastEnders*?' said Phil.

'Join a choir?' said Dad.

'Driving lessons?' I murmured.

FRIDAY

Know your partner's game as well as your own.

EVENT/S	VENUE	WEATHER CONDITIONS	PHYSICAL HEALTH
U-16 mixed	Mapledon	Sunny	Curse, bearable

OPPONENT
Louise Smart and Charlie.

TACTICS
Played ruthlessly on Louise.

RESULT
Won

EQUIPMENT
As before.

COMMENTS
I think I'm in love with Paddy.

TOMORROW'S MATCH
Mixed doubles v Phchang and partner.
Paddy also in the singles final against Tom Smart.

I went to bed as soon as we got back. Partly because of my bad night last night, but mostly to be on my own. I felt fine physically. As Megan had predicted, my first period turned out to be a one-day wonder and seemed to have fizzled out. I only had the next ten million years to look forward to. But it was as if my entire life had shifted. It wasn't only my body. It was Paddy. Mum as well.

As I lay there, I invented little scenarios for me and Paddy to star in. There was the one where our end-of-match handshake turned into a kiss in front of the cheering crowds. The one where we wandered off hand-in-hand to the woods by the car park. The one where we met at the beginning of the day and he told me that he'd been in love with me all summer.

In love? Was this me, Alex Dunbar, dreaming of love and romance? Things *had* changed! I found myself remembering little things about the way Paddy looked. He was certainly fit. Not tall, but taller than me, just. Lightish brown hair, slightly sun-streaked. Ordinary nose, possibly on the blobby side. Full lips. Smiley lips. Nice teeth (though I'd spare him any comments). Quite a fair skin. Possibly a freckle or two. And dark blue eyes with black curling lashes.

And the kindest, most steadfast, cheerful nature. Until yesterday of course, though perhaps a little anger in the right places was no bad thing. And he mostly took it out on the tennis ball. In fact, he was so gorgeous, why hadn't I noticed before? And if he was so gorgeous, probably there were queues of far more suitable girls just waiting to grab him for themselves.

PANIC!

Calm down, Alex, and go to sleep. I did.

Saturday morning. Finals Day – the big one. Perfect Finals Day weather, too. Late summer sunshine. For the first time in the tournament I had the confidence to wear tennis whites without covering them up with a dark tracksuit. About time I showed off my brown legs, anyway. Phil and I were both keyed up as we drove in with Kieron, though possibly for different reasons. Phil was worried about the tennis. I wasn't.

Paddy was nowhere to be seen. His match wasn't until two p.m. and our mixed doubles was much later in the afternoon. Phil and Kieron had to go off and play almost immediately so I was left to wander round on my own. Tom and Louise Smart were both singles *and* doubles finalists, so the Smarts were there in force, including the grandparents, all sporting a wide range of fashionable sunglasses, Scarlett included. Louise was making her presence felt, big time, swanning about as if she was champion already. I decided to go and watch the boys (Tom Smart and Toby versus Neil and Raj) rather than the girls (Louise Smart and Claire versus Alicia and Connie). Louise with her silly walk and bouncing ponytail is too annoying. I needed someone to talk to and I was missing Lucy and Robin and Charlie already. They were all at the Prestige Gold Cup of course. Dad, Mum and the twins would arrive as soon as they'd dropped Joel off there.

I sat on the end of a row to watch. The boys were having a niggly sort of match. No one seemed to be winning or losing. I went into a daydream about Paddy. I was dying to see him but dreading it at the same time. What if *I'd* got it all wrong? What if I was just imagining things? I was miles away when Paddy came and sat beside me. We were both in shorts and I suddenly felt embarrassed by the proximity of our bare legs.

'Who's winning?' asked Paddy (very romantic).

'Tom and Toby, just.' (Equally so.)

'Oh.'

'When's your match?' I asked, as if I didn't know.

'Two o'clock. Assuming this one's over.'

We both watched in silence as Tom served four aces in a row, followed by Neil serving four double faults.

'I'm too nervous to watch this,' said Paddy. 'See you later.' And he was gone before I could ask anything important, or even catch his eye. As he left, there was a roar of applause from the next court. It didn't seem fair on the boys to disturb them further by going to find out who had won the girls' doubles, but there was no need, because the entire Smart clan, looking sombre, filed into the back row to watch Tom and Toby cranking out a narrow win. The long faces meant that the title had been won by Alicia and Connie and that Louise had even more to play for in her singles against Alicia.

I saw my family arriving in force but they turned off to watch Phil and Kieron. It was time for the junior singles finals. The boys' and the girls' matches were on adjacent courts, so it was possible to keep an eye on both. The Smarts took up most of the standing space between the courts. There was no escaping the fact that they had a finalist in each. As the four players filed through a single gate I saw Louise in animated conversation with Paddy – she obviously had something exciting to tell him, because he was listening, despite his pre-match psyching up routine (that I would never dream of interrupting). Tom was completely relaxed. He looked fresh as a daisy. Poor Paddy.

My emotions during that game went through more highs and lows than I have ever experienced in my life. They had become as untrustworthy as my body! I was fearful for Paddy. I was proud of him. I wanted him to win so badly it hurt. He wasn't driven by anger like he was against Charlie, but then Tom Smart wasn't as good as Charlie, and he had just played a match even if it hadn't been very strenuous. While I was sitting there two men with Australian accents plonked themselves down next to me. 'Which fellow is it?' one asked the other.

'That one. Must be. Charlie didn't say anything about bleached hair.'

'Beaut backhand. Look at that.'

'He's fast.'

'You can say that again.'

They were talking about Paddy, but they were distracting him. He glanced up in our direction. 'Ssh!' I said to the two men.

'Apologies,' whispered the designer-stubble one. 'Good girl. You stick by your young fella. He's going places, I'd put money on it.'

They wrote a few things down and then slipped away. I felt all excited. Paddy was going to be a tennis star! *But if he's a tennis star he won't be interested in me any more.* I was up and down like a yo-yo. I just wanted the match to be over. Then again, I wanted it to go on for ever.

Paddy beat Tom in straight sets! Yippee! I ran over to congratulate him, but the two boys were surrounded by their families and other people too. To make matters worse, Louise won her match a few minutes later so the crowd of Smarts and others got bigger. Then, in front of my eyes, Louise and Paddy were pushed back on to the court by a group of photographers who wanted pictures of the two new junior champions. They were making them do all these ridiculous poses together. It was nauseating. And there was no Charlie to distract Louise either.

I gave up in disgust and went to find some Dunbars, not hard when someone as large as Mum is involved. They'd moved on to the under-18 boys' singles. For once the twins were totally rapt – I've never seen them sitting so still. Kieron was with them. 'Not a patch on Paddy and Charlie yesterday,' he whispered. 'Who won over there?'

'Paddy did and so did Louise.'

'Oh boy. Did he now?' Kieron craned his neck to see the photographers' antics. 'Paddy might not know it, but he is about to join the Smart set. "Call-me-Janice" loves winners – shame the loser had to be Tom.'

'Paddy loathes the Smart scene.'

'He'll have a battle on his hands then.'

I felt comfortable with Kieron and my lot. I decided to stay there until our mixed doubles was called. In between sets I heard a familiar voice. It was Megan, with a boy who looked about the same age as Jack and Sam. 'Hi guys,' she said in a stage whisper. They sat down. 'This is David. You have to keep your mouth shut when they're playing, David, or they shoot you.'

'It's OK, I know,' said David. 'Stop being embarrassing.'

Mum and Megan exchanged sympathetic looks.

Megan turned to me. 'This is going to go on for a while, isn't it? Do you want to wander about, fill me in on the gossip? David will be OK with your folks, won't he?'

'Yes, yes and yes.'

We slipped away. 'OK,' she said. 'Spill the beans. What's going on with you and Paddy?'

'Nothing!'

'I don't believe you!' She was using that sing-song voice again. 'A guy doesn't walk away in disgust from a friend who happens to be kissing two other guys simultaneously unless he fancies her.'

'I wasn't really kissing them.'

'That's how it looked to me. And to Paddy as well, I presume.'

'Well, I suppose it's not entirely true to say that *nothing* is going on. It's just that I'm not sure what.' We had arrived at the far-distant court with the table. 'Yesterday he wouldn't look at me and seemed to be incredibly angry.'

'Jealous, I told you so.'

'And his match against Charlie was completely amazing. He looked as though he was trying to kill him.'

'As I said. Jealous.'

'Then we had to play together and he was completely horrible to me at first.'

'Jealous.'

'Until – I just asked him to stop it. I told him he'd got it wrong and that he should trust me.'

'Jealous as a parrot.'

'Will you stop staying that! Anyway, it's sick as a parrot.'

'Same thing.'

I hit her, and continued. 'I didn't actually say *what* he'd got wrong, or *how* he should trust me.'

'And you think he doesn't know?'

'From the way he *looked* at me, I think he did. But I haven't spoken to him since then – apart from "nice shot" and "leave it" and that sort of thing. Our family went out for a pizza and he'd gone to bed when I phoned afterwards and today he wouldn't look me in the eye again when we saw each other.

'Ah. Was it a gooey look – yesterday?'

'I suppose it was.'

'Did it make your legs go all funny?'

'I suppose it did. Ooh, I don't know what to do, Megan. I've never had feelings like this before. When I first met you, all of three days ago, I was still one of the lads. And look at me now!'

She raised her eyebrows and gave me a knowing smirk.

'Enough of that. This is quite different. But I still need help!'

'Can't help. You've got your match with him soon. See how that goes. I shall be observing both your expressions very closely.'

'I'm feeling all nervous now.' I looked at my watch. 'It's four-fifteen. We'll have to start soon. The prize-giving's at six.'

Bang on cue: 'Under-16 Mixed Doubles finalists please. Patrick Gardner and Miss Alexandra Dunbar. Lee Barclay and Miss Philippa Chang. (Full names for finalists.) Court Three in five minutes please.'

'I'll come with you as far as the others. I'd better see that David's behaving himself.'

'Thanks. I can't believe how scared I feel.'

When Megan left me to go to Court Three on my own I felt like a lamb going to the slaughter. It was silly, because I'd beaten Phchang in the singles, and whoever Lee Barclay was he couldn't be as good as Paddy – this year's champion. (That was so cool!) Lee and Phchang were already knocking up. The umpire was up on her seat. We even had a couple of ballboys (girls). Paddy made a bit of a hero's entrance, the crowd parting and pointing at the new champion. He didn't look nervous at all. He came over to me with a wide Paddy grin.

'OK? This one's easy,' he said.

'Well done for winning – I couldn't get to you afterwards. Media frenzy.'

'We might be interviewed on local TV later!'

'Wow!' I'd tell him about Charlie's Australians later. He was so happy, his eyes were sparkling and his step was even more springy than usual. Just the sight of him made me feel weird and trembly.

We started our knock-up. I seemed to trip over my own feet a bit, but that's par for the course when you start completely cold. I should have been hitting against the practice wall rather than chatting with Megan. Paddy was flying, though, so my little errors didn't really show. Until, that is, we started playing. Paddy won his service game – no worries. Lee didn't quite get into the swing of his. But then I completely lost it on mine. Double fault after double fault. 'Never mind,' said Paddy. 'We can afford to lose one game.'

But I'd lost it. Not just the game – *it*. My telepathy had gone, for a start. I no longer had a clue what Paddy was going to do next. We kept bumping into each other, and when we did, well, the physical contact turned me even more to jelly.

'I'm so sorry,' I said to Paddy when the other two won the first set. 'I don't know what's come over me.' And then when he turned his sympathetic blue eyes on me I simply melted away.

He smiled a very small and secret smile. 'It's what I was afraid of at the beginning of the week,' he said almost to himself. And then, louder. 'Never mind! Twelve more games and the match is ours!'

In fact, eight more games and the match was theirs. The only ones we won were Paddy's service games. It was so humiliating. The applause from those who'd bothered to stay on was half-hearted.

'You were useless, Al!' said Jack as the family crowded round me afterwards.

'Paddy was brilliant! He should have a better partner,' said Sam.

'Thanks, boys, for your support,' I said.

'Keep quiet you two,' said Mum severely. *Mum*? 'You don't know what it's like out there for the big match.'

'And I suppose you do?' said Jack cheekily.

'As a matter of fact she does,' said Dad, weighing in.

'On this very court as a matter of fact,' said Mum, without sighing. My mouth was hanging open. 'With your dad. Wasn't it, dear?'

'How come we never knew this?' Phil was staggered too.

'No secret,' said Dad. 'Just a hideously long time ago. Never mind, Alex. You've done very well to be a finalist. I'm proud of you. And Paddy'll be up there getting his cup along with Phil. Our little club does it again!'

There were one or two matches still finishing off but the organisers were setting up the prize-giving on Court One. The cups and salvers and teaspoons (that's what I'd get) lay in shining array on the white-clothed trestle table. The local mayor was there, chain and all, along with the Mapledon Club worthies. I left my family to join the other finalists. As I passed Megan she said, 'Bad luck for losing. Think you might be a winner in other ways though. I saw the looks he gave you. His game was affected too, you know!'

'We still haven't talked.'

'Your chance will come. I'd better get out of the way before I'm mown down by gentlemen of the press. Go on. Go and claim Paddy before Louise eats him.'

I pushed through the crowd. Once we were all on court the proceedings began. Lots of speeches about talented youngsters and thanks to the ladies who provided the teas, etc. First the under-16s: Louise and Paddy (Mr Popular – the cheer for him was enormous); Alicia and Connie; Tom and Toby; Phchang and Lee. They all stood in a row with their cups and platters. Then the runners-up: Alicia went up again; so did Tom; Louise again and Claire; Raj and Neil; and then me and Paddy (still hugging his cup – up went the cheer again). He turned to me with a smile and lifted my arm in a sort of wave to the onlookers. The photographers went wild. Flash. Flash. Flash.

Then we all stood back and the under-18s (including Phil and Kieron) went through the same rigmarole. I was squashed against Paddy. He kept beaming at me, but this wasn't the time to have a meaningful conversation. I hoped that would come later. As we made our way off the court the two Australians were waiting for Paddy. They asked to be introduced to his parents and I lost him. Worse still, when he reappeared, Louise wiggled up to him, saying that the four singles champions were wanted down at the local TV studio. Her parents were going to give them a lift. I saw Ethlie running after them, still trying to be part of the action.

So there I was. All hyped up and nowhere to go. Megan and David had to catch the bus home. Dad was ready to take us. The week was over. It was all over. Carrying my tennis bag and my teaspoon I followed the others to the car.

TWELVE

'Mum, it's them. Come and watch.'

Slip-slop, sigh. 'I'm too busy with the supper. Phil was meant to be helping and now they've all gone off with your father to get Joel.'

'Come on Mum. Quick. It'll only last a second. I'll help you when it's over.'

Slip-slop, floomph (Mum sitting on the sofa). 'Oh, there's you and Paddy!'

It was. One of the cameras must have been a camcorder. I wished I'd set the video. There for all the world to see was Paddy smiling and me blushing as he raised our arms in front of the Mayor. Cut to the studio.

Oh great. There was Louise, sparkling vivaciously as she sat knee-to-knee with Paddy. The interviewer kept on about these players of the future, names to watch etc. He asked Paddy if the final had actually been his hardest match of the tournament. 'Definitely not,' said Paddy. His semi-final had been hardest.

Then Louise interrupted and said that her final had been her toughest, and the two under-18s were brought into the discussion before we were suddenly on to the next item about a traffic-calming scheme.

'The local paper was the pinnacle of news coverage in my time,' said Mum. 'TV news seems very grand.'

'Mum, how come you've never talked about this before? I knew that you'd played at some point, but not that you actually played with Dad at Mapledon.'

'Well,' said Mum. 'Look at me. As you can see, my tennis playing days are long gone.'

'Mum, nobody has to be – overweight – these days. They're always telling us that in PSE at school.'

Mum stood up abruptly (for her). She sighed again. 'Well, madam. You'll find out one day just how hard it is to raise a family and be all things to all people.'

'But Mum—' She was off, slip-slopping into the kitchen to bang things about. I followed her. 'Mum, if I stay and help, will you carry on talking to me, without "madam-ing" me. I am your daughter, you know.'

'All right, all right.'

'Could it be that you're – depressed? They tell us about that at school as well. Not to mention on daytime TV programmes.'

'Maybe.'

'Have you been to a doctor?'

'Alex! That's enough now.'

I felt dogged. 'I don't see why I shouldn't ask. It was something Megan said, Mum. She said, "at least you've got a mother". Which is true. And Megan hasn't. But I thought – don't get me wrong, Mum – I thought, well, I do have a mum but she doesn't seem all that happy to have me. I always thought you picked on me because you were – well – a grumpy personality. But if you *are* depressed, and you could get undepressed, well, that would be great.'

'If only it was that simple. Now I really must get on.'

'Mum! You're being defeatist before you've even begun. You know what Dad says about that.'

'No, what does he say?'

'Well, you can still win even when you're six–love five–love down, and stuff. He's got lots of things like that.'

The boys crashed in at that point: Dad, Phil, Joel, Jack, Sam. All demanding food. All talking about the day's sport. Noisy. Perhaps I know why Mum's overwhelmed. We had supper. I tried to tell them about being on the news, but they didn't hear. Joel, on a high from winning his matches, picked a quarrel with Jack. Sam joined in. Phil slammed out. Dad tried to stay cheerful.

'I'm going upstairs,' I said.

'It's barely nine o'clock,' said Dad.

'I didn't say I was going to bed. Just to my room. I'm tired.'

Just then there was a shout from the front room. 'I'm on the telly!' It was Phil. Everyone rushed in. 'Ooh look! There's Alex and Paddy.' There we were again. I so much wanted to see Paddy, to talk to him. To—

'Yuk! They're holding hands.'

'Is Paddy your boyfriend, Alex? Does he snog you?'

I saw red. 'SHUT UP!' I screamed. 'LEAVE ME ALONE!'

'Yes, leave the poor girl alone,' said Mum sternly as I ran from the room.

As I sat on my bed sobbing, I imagined Paddy with Louise and the Smarts. I could practically hear Louise chatting him up. After all, I'd heard her smarming round Joel and Charlie. They all love winners in that family. What if they'd asked him back afterwards? The phone rang. I shot out of my room to grab the cordless one on the landing. It was Lucy.

'Hang on while I take it into my room.'

'I just saw you and Paddy on the telly. Sorry you didn't win the mixed, but isn't it great about Paddy? I had a brilliant time with Robin and Charlie at the Cup. Wish I was still with them. After all, it is Saturday night. How did your day go? And I don't mean the tennis.'

'We still haven't talked, Lucy. It's crazy. Paddy kept being whisked off. I last saw him disappearing in the Smarts' car on the way to the TV studio with Louise all over him.'

'He was smiling very fondly at you on the telly. You were holding hands!'

'No we weren't! He was just making me wave. Lucy, do you think I should ring him? I don't know what I'd say, but—'

'Why not? Nothing to lose.'

'I'll die if they say he's still at the Smarts. Or if he wonders why I've rung.'

'Go on. Ring him now and ring me back. I order you to.'

I dialled Paddy's number and put the phone straight down. But Lucy would be waiting. I dialled again. Mrs Gardner answered. 'Hallo? Could I speak to Paddy please?'

'He's not here, I'm afraid. Those Smart people have taken him out for a meal. I wish he was here. There's an Australian coach who keeps ringing and I don't know when Paddy will be back.'

'Perhaps you could ring the Smarts on their mobile?'

'I wouldn't know the number – do you?'

'They might give it in their answerphone message.'

'That's a very good idea. I'll give it a try. And shall I tell Paddy you rang?'

'Yes, OK. Tell him – tell him to meet Alex up at the Club tomorrow morning – nine o'clock, please.'

'I will, Alex.'

*

'Lucy? He's only out to dinner with the Smarts! But I was brave. I left a message for him to meet me at nine o'clock tomorrow morning.'

'That's a very romantic hour!'

'It's all I could think of. Twelve hours from now.'

'Aren't you coming to the Cup tomorrow? Robin and Charlie get to play Joel.'

'Did Charlie tell you he'd sent his coach to talent scout? Paddy's mum says they've been ringing already.'

'Shows that Charlie's a nice guy. Not everyone would be so generous.'

'Something to do with his confidence. And I'll tell you something else about Charlie.'

'Something I don't know?'

'He's a damn fine kisser!'

'Alex! You *have* changed!'

'I was just thinking about it. I'm kind of glad he gave me a bit of practice. Now I'll know what to do with Paddy when I get him on his own.'

'Wonders will never cease, Alex Dunbar!'

'You were the one who tried to convince me that it might be fun.'

'And is it?'

'We'll see, won't we?'

SATURDAY

You can cover the whole range of emotions in a game of tennis, from anger and frustration to joy and to calm.

EVENT/S	VENUE	WEATHER CONDITIONS	PHYSICAL HEALTH
U-16 mixed	Mapledon	Sunny	Great (Emotional health, variable)

OPPONENT
Phchang and partner.

Summer Cool

'Just off to the club!' I took my racquet. This wasn't abnormal behaviour in our family.

'Hi!' Paddy was already there, face lit up, but nervous.

'How was last night?'

'My Smart night out? OK. It was a nice meal. "Call-me-Janice" and Louise talked non-stop. They want me to join Highcliffe tennis club.'

'Paddy! You won't will you?'

'Course not.'

'So what about the Aussie tennis coach? Has he rung again?'

'Not yet. It's quite cool, isn't it?' He looked me in the eye. 'So why did you want to meet me up here?'

'I – just wanted to talk. Sort a few things out.'

'Like what?' He was smiling at me.

'Well, I'm sorry I let you down yesterday.'

'That's OK.'

'Paddy!' He was being infuriating. 'You're really making me work, aren't you?'

'Yup.'

'OK. I wanted to go back to Friday, when I told you you'd got it wrong.'

'Uh-huh.'

'Grrrr! OK then. Thursday night. I'm not going to beat about the bush any more, so serves you right if I embarrass you.'

'I'm listening.'

'Thursday night. At the Smarts. You arrive. And I appear to be kissing Max and Charlie. The truth is extremely silly, but you'll have to believe me. I was on a dare if you like – more a promise – with some friends from school, to have a romance during the tournament.'

'Ironic,' said Paddy.

'As you well know, I have no experience in these matters at all.'

'No good at reading the signs?'

'No.' I narrowed my eyes at him. *What did that mean?* 'Time was running out, so in desperation I asked Max to *pretend* to have a romance with me. And you know what Max is like – he was up for it. And he was *pretending* to kiss me, you know, with his hand over his mouth, when Charlie came along and thought it was some sort of game he could join in and kissed me – for a laugh.'

'I knew all along that Charlie fancied you.'

'Not really, Paddy. It was just a laugh, honestly. And I didn't start it, OK?'

'I could have killed Charlie.'

'Now you have to tell me why.'

'At the risk of embarrassing you? OK, here goes.' He spoke without looking at me. 'I sort of fancied my own chances with you. But you never seemed to notice me, apart from as a partner. So I thought perhaps it would be better if we weren't partners for a bit.'

'I just thought you'd gone off me.'

'Nah.' He managed a quick grin at me then. 'I also

thought I might not play so well if I was concentrating more on the girl next to me than on the ball.'

'Precisely what happened to me yesterday.'

'I know!' he said, and laughed delightedly.

I thumped him. We were sitting on a bank by one of the tennis courts at the Club. A couple of extremely old people were playing on the farthest court. No one else was around. Paddy retaliated by throwing a handful of grass at me. I got up and ran round the back of the pavilion. Paddy, as I've often said, is fantastically fit, so it didn't take him long to catch up with me. He caught my wrists and leant towards me. He was still smiling but his dark blue eyes were looking into mine intently. I held his gaze for a few seconds before letting my eyelids close. His lips were incredibly soft and the way he held my face was just so tender. Of all the kisses I have had (three now) it was the sweetest.

We stood apart and looked at each other shyly.

'It's been a funny week,' I said, as we walked back to sit on our bank. Behind the pavilion is fairly unsavoury.

'For me too,' said Paddy. 'I was so angry on Thursday night and Friday morning. Looking back, I suppose that's why I beat Charlie. I never would have otherwise.'

'Never mind, the fact is, you did. You do know it was Charlie who put the talent scouts on to you, don't you?'

'Do you mean I have to thank the guy?'

'Apologise even.'

'Never!' He looked at me seriously again. 'Hey, I never thought it would turn out like this.'

'Me neither. It's good though. Now I have a romance to report back on.'

'You didn't just – this isn't just a dare, is it?'

He looked so panic-stricken I had to laugh. 'No. If it was a dare I would have put my hand over my mouth.'

'I'm glad you didn't.'

Our little rendezvous was soon brought to a halt by the Club members arriving for their Sunday morning session. That was when Paddy let on that he'd agreed to partner his dad.

'So I just have to make myself scarce now, do I?'

'Unless you want to stay and watch.'

'I don't know what I want to do now. I feel all—'

'Churned up? So do I! When can we get together again?'

'It's never been difficult. We've always had an excuse. Ring me this afternoon. I might have been dragged off to watch the Cup, but keep ringing, OK?'

'Try and stop me.'

I walked home, almost danced home, taking the route I knew my dad wouldn't use. I was greeted by various Club members on the way, cheery middle-aged men and women. They know me, even if I don't know them. They made me think.

When I got in, Joel had gone to the Cup, but the other boys were slobbing about in their various ways and Mum was slip-slopping and sighing her way round after them. My warm and generous mood was still with me.

'Do you want a cup of coffee, Mum?'

'What, dear?'

'Would you like to sit down and have me make you a cup of coffee?'

'Well, I don't know—'

'Sit!'

Who could refuse? I made some instant coffee for her and some instant hot chocolate for me and sat at the kitchen table with her. I'd had an idea. 'Mum?'

She looked at me warily. 'What is it now?'

'I want you to start playing tennis again.'

'That's all very well for you to—'

'I know you used to be good.'

'I don't think—'

'I'll play with you. We can go up to the Club when there's no one there. When I come home after school next term – no one goes up then. Please, Mum?'

'Why all this—'

'Because I know you'll enjoy it. And then when you've got your confidence back you can go and play on Sunday mornings with Dad. You ought to be up there with him.'

'Well, it's a nice thought, dear.'

'It's more than that, Mum. Just say you'll give it a try. Use one of the twins' racquets. Wear my spare trainers. No excuses.'

'All right. Maybe.'

Then Phil came in. 'What's for lunch, Mum? Are we going to eat before we go and watch Joel?'

'Oh dear, I'd better get a move on,' she said. 'We don't want to miss Joel, do we?'

Serve him right if we did, I thought. I went upstairs to my room.

I lay back on my bed. Happiness kept bubbling up. He kissed me! Paddy likes me! He's liked me all along! I guess I've got a boyfriend – I've had a holiday romance, even. More than a holiday romance, I hope. I don't have to say goodbye to Paddy like I would have had to to Charlie.

Charlie. He was kind of the catalyst in all this. The founder member of the Alex Dunbar fan club. Actually I did want to say goodbye to him, and thank him on Paddy's behalf. I decided to go along to the Cup with the others. It would be nice to see Lucy. And it would spare me the agony of waiting for the phone to ring.

Joel and his partner were losing to Charlie and Robin. Joel is a bad loser. Unlike Paddy, he hadn't noticed Charlie's dodgy knee. Joel plays lovely shots, but he's frankly too selfish to notice things about other people, even to take advantage of their weak points. I looked round the spectators for Lucy. Claire was there below us, supporting Joel of course, and she had Louise with her. Tee-hee. I wondered how Louise would feel if she knew that Paddy and I were – whatever we were. Wretched girl. She'd better keep her hands off him from now on. And then I spotted Lucy over the other side. I decided to make my way over when the players changed ends. I had lots to tell Lucy.

'Robin said he'd come and find me here,' said Lucy. 'It's a good place to see people. I just saw Chris Green.'

'Who's he?'

'Tennis heart-throb. He is gorgeous. Louise Smart has the hots for him.'

'Louise has the hots for everyone. Joel, Charlie. It was Paddy last night.'

'I knew it wouldn't be long before you mentioned his name. OK, so what's the deal?'

'We—' I grinned.

'Thank goodness for that!' she said.

'Thank goodness for what?' said Charlie as he and Robin joined us.

'Alex and Paddy finally got it on.'

'Lucy!'

'Thank goodness for that,' said Charlie. 'Lucky bloke.' I

looked at him questioningly. 'Can't deny I'm jealous,' he said. 'Snappy tennis player too.'

'He's really grateful about the coaching offer.'

'Glad to be of service,' said Charlie. 'Keep in touch won't you, Miss A. Dunbar? I might need some humour to lighten my life at school next term. Robin won't be much use.' Robin and Lucy were starting to say goodbye already, in an interactive hands-on sort of way.

'Of course, if you give me the address. Thanks, Charlie. For more than you realise.'

'As I said, glad to be of service.'

Joel appeared – unexpectedly as far as I was concerned.

'Hi guys. We're off, Al. Coming?'

'OK.' I unglued Robin from Lucy so I could give him a hug. 'Bye, Robin.'

'Maybe we'll visit you both at half-term?' he said.

Then Charlie. 'See ya,' said Charlie, '– before half-term I hope,' and I gave him a hug too. 'Easy does it,' he protested. 'I'm not Paddy!' And we were off.

'Bye!' Joel called after them. And, 'Bye, Chris, see ya next year!' He waved at someone in the distance.

'Who is this famous Chris Green?' I asked, intrigued now. 'I never manage to catch sight of him. Was he around last year? Dark curly hair?'

'That's the one. Do you remember him?'

'Only just. I vaguely remember thinking he looked nice.'

'Well, now he happens to be the coolest guy and an ace tennis player. Comes from the Midlands somewhere. Maybe I'd better keep you away from him – with your reputation!'

'Joel!' I hit him.

'Well – last year, gangly tomboy sister – Alex, is that a boy or a girl? This year – Kieron, Charlie, Paddy and I don't know who else!'

'No one else! Anyway – only keeping up with my brother.'

He laughed. And *that* was the first jokey conversation I have had with Joel since we used to play with make-up.

The day stayed good. As we came in the door, the phone was ringing. I rushed to pick it up, hoping it would be Paddy. It wasn't – it was Megan.

'Megan! I've got so much to tell you,' I burst out, but as I started running out of steam (about half an hour later), she said, 'Actually it was your mum I wanted to speak to. At least, I was going to put her on to my dad.'

'Mum?' I said, shocked. 'Mum, it's Megan's dad. For you.'

The others dispersed around the house, but I couldn't go too far away. I hung around the bottom of the stairs. Why on earth should my mother want to speak to Megan's father?

'Thanks,' I heard her say. 'Wednesday morning ten-thirty it is. You'll pick me up. Look forward to seeing you.'

Curiosity got the better of me. 'So what was all that about, Mum? What's Megan's dad got that my dad hasn't?'

'A driving instructor's qualification.'

I practically fainted. But then the phone rang again, and it was Paddy.

SUNDAY

Love tennis, love life.

EVENT/S	VENUE	WEATHER CONDITIONS	PHYSICAL HEALTH
Romantic encounter	The Club	Great	Great

OPPONENT
Paddy

TACTICS
Honesty

RESULT
Result!

EQUIPMENT
Heart

COMMENTS
Game, set and love match.

TOMORROW'S MATCH
Yay! And for ever!

EPILOGUE

I used to accuse Joel of being so self-obsessed that he never noticed what anyone else was thinking or doing, but now I think that I've been a bit like that too. It isn't all just about 'boys' and fancying them, is it? In fact I always had that empathy with Paddy, but I've noticed so much more about other people in this last week – it's quite spooky. Not that I now love all my fellow men and women or anything holy like that. I still think Ethlie's a pain in the butt, and I don't want to even try and understand how someone like Louise Smart ticks. It was Megan, I suppose. And having a glimpse of Mum and Dad as real people. I don't forgive my brothers for bullying and taunting me – Joel's old enough to know better. But the twins aren't. They need someone to tell them when they're out of order. That's all. I shouldn't let them get away with it.

And my family isn't that bad. I'd rather be a Dunbar than a Smart any day!

*

Paddy and I are having a brilliant time. We go to the Club a lot, because that's the easiest place to meet. It's not a going-out-on-the-town sort of relationship, and neither of us quite wants to take the other home. Yet.

I did think it might be possible to have the sleepover at our house (now there's a first), but Zoe said we should go to hers – she does have a lot more room and only one younger brother. I let on to her that I'd managed a romance, but we agreed to save the details until the sleepover even though I was itching to share it with her – of all people. I still couldn't believe I had something to report! Holly's back too, but we keep missing each other. The others are all in for such a surprise!

Zoe practically has the whole basement to herself in their house, and the food is real fabbo help-yourself-to-anything-in-the-freezer stuff. Her mum is not fat. Could there be some connection?

I'd been shopping in the last few days and bought some baggy trousers and little top like the one Megan lent me. I scraped my hair up too. Didn't want my friends thinking I was exactly the same unsophisticated Alex they knew and loved.

'Hey!' said Zoe. 'A new-look Alex, then?'

'Oh, not so different. You're used to me in trousers.'

'Yeah, but I've never seen the belly button before.'

'That's because it's new.'

Zoe gave me a hug. 'Oooh! Can't wait!' she squealed, just as the other two arrived. There was lots more squealing and hugging. We loaded up with food and went down into Zoe's room. 'OK, who's going first?' said Zoe. We decided to go in alphabetical order, perfect when you have an A and a Z. I felt as though I was making a speech at an award ceremony and that I ought to thank everyone who'd made my romance possible, but the others screamed at me to stop messing around and get on with it. So I did. I told them about Kieron and Charlie and Paddy (of course), but also about Megan and Mum and the fact that I now had as good an excuse for being grumpy once a month as they had.

Holly was next. Holly's so pretty that if something went wrong with one guy I'm sure there'd always be another there to take his place, though I couldn't quite work out what order things were happening in while she was staying at her boyfriend's stately home. She was beating her breast about some girl who sounded like a waste of space to me and I found myself daydreaming about Paddy and not listening – until the name Chris Green popped up. I tuned in, rapidly. 'Not the Chris Green who was playing in the Cup in Hertfordshire?' And it seems that it was! Oh well, no point at all in Joel introducing me if Holly's in the picture. I know my place in the pecking order.

Josie seems to have made a beeline for her best friend's boyfriend, which of course didn't go down well with the best friend, and it was all our fault for forcing her to have a romance when she was wearing a brace. Still, matters improved *enormously* later on, apparently. It must be fun seeing the same people on holiday every year. Not unlike Mapledon I suppose.

Zoe, after being frivolous in Tuscany earlier on, worked incredibly hard at the Community Theatre Project and met loads of really grown-up people. I sometimes wonder how she tolerates me as a friend when each time I begin catching up with her she leaps on ahead. I feel she's at least six years older than me. But the fact is, she does.

And so do the others, jokes and all. So does Paddy. And, do you know? I can't think of a single funny thing to say about it.

Zoe

ONE

MONDAY: Day One of the Project

'I really do not want to be doing this.'

'Neither do I.'

'Mum only made me do it so that I could check up on you.'

'Why don't we both bunk off then?' said Tark, my twelve-year-old brother, his face lighting up.

I pondered the idea. But I'm not in the habit of lying, and the thought of inventing dramas about what we'd done every day for a week was almost as bad as going on the drama course itself. 'Nah. We'll give it a try. And then if it's rubbish we'll bunk off tomorrow.'

Tark didn't put up a fight. Instead he yawned and shrunk down into his seat as the bus trundled on towards the Centre and a whole week of precious summer holiday devoted to the Community Theatre Project.

I have to admit I was ever so slightly curious. Curious about who did this sort of thing when they could be lying in the sun, down at the lido, reading, trawling the shops, or any one of a million preferable summer holiday activities. And just a little curious to see if there might be some seriously cool guys who'd spent their entire lives up to this point waiting to meet a girl precisely like me, Zoe Shaw . . . I had a bit of a project myself, you see. And it had started like this . . .

We'd had a sleepover at my friend Holly's the other night –

Holly, Josie, Alex and me. It was nice to see the others because I'd been in Italy with my family and I wanted to tell them about it. Holly had been away too, in Barbados (lucky thing) with the cricket team (doubly lucky) from the school where her dad teaches. Her family doesn't usually even go abroad, so it was a big deal for her. Josie had done some music course, and only Alex had been stuck at home the entire time. Now, I complain about my one twelve-year-old brother, but Alex has *twin* twelve-year-old brothers and two older ones as well! Tark is friends with the twins, and I suppose I have him to thank indirectly for introducing me to Alex – my great and hilarious mate.

When I first met her, Alex was a beanpole with short hair – she looked like a boy. We met up again when we both started at secondary school and I really liked her, because she was different from all the others and because she's such a laugh. We're both taller than average, I'm dark-skinned and she's fair (her hair's not quite so short now) – we probably make quite an odd pair. People tell me I should be a model, but that's just a Naomi Campbell thing – you know, if you're tallish and darkish-skinned you tend to get typecast. I can't quite see it, myself. Alex would be much better, but the fact that she isn't interested in clothes and never wears make-up could just be a drawback.

There are loads of things we don't have in common – Alex doesn't do particularly well at school (I do, I'm afraid, bit of a boffin, me) but she's brilliant at sports – well, tennis, anyway (and I'm not). I'm argumentative and question everything. She just turns everything into a joke. I like acting and debating: Alex doesn't like either. I've had boyfriends – usually older than me – and Alex can't stand boys (on account of all the brothers), or not in that way, anyhow.

Boyfriends were what the conversation turned to at the sleepover (now there's a surprise). Holly, who's incredibly pretty, had found herself a boyfriend in Barbados. An English boyfriend, dead posh and rich, and she's off to stay with him in his stately home this week. Holly was so thrilled by the boyfriend thing that she wanted the rest of us to get hitched up too! It's all very well for her, but I spent three weeks in Tuscany without a single gorgeous bloke falling at my feet. (I choose to think it was because our villa was two miles from the nearest village.) Alex wouldn't know what to do, I don't think, and Josie's just had train-tracks fitted on her teeth and doesn't fancy her chances.

We mumbled and grumbled but Holly wouldn't let it go, so we ended up all promising to have a holiday romance and report back on it. And if the others are going for it I suppose I'd better too.

And now I'm *here*, on a bus that has crawled through the morning rush-hour traffic but is just pulling up at the stop nearest the Centre, even though it's still a five-minute walk away. Tark skipped into the road to zigzag through the slow-moving stream of cars, leaving me standing, feeling all big-sisterish and wanting to make him hold hands for crossing the road like we had to when we were little. I'm nearly fifteen and Tark is twelve, but he still looks like a kid. Gingerly I stepped off the kerb and made my way across to where he stood laughing at me on the opposite side.

We walked past the tacky shops on the busy main road. The pavement was heaving with people, all head-down on their way to work. It was nine-twenty a.m. I couldn't believe I wasn't still in my nice warm bed in the basement of our house with at least an hour to go before waking up, any more than I could believe that I'd allowed Mum to talk me into sacrificing a whole week of my holidays.

We turned left into a bleak, treeless side street, where the front doors opened almost straight on to the litter-strewn pavements. All this was because Tark (Tarquin, I'm afraid, but the name does kind of suit him) was at a loose end and Mum, who's a psychologist as well as being American, decided that it would be good for him to have something positive to do before boredom forced him into bad company. Tark's excellent at sport, but the football and basketball courses all took place when we were in Italy, and Mum simply doesn't want him hanging around with some of his less desirable friends while she's at work. Actually I don't have a problem with any of his friends – they seem OK to me, all except for about one, but Mum thinks otherwise. Twelve-year-old boys are impressionable and easily led, she says. Normally Dad's at home a lot of the holidays because he's a university lecturer, but right now he's in Finland, of all places, at a conference.

Tark was beginning to lag behind. 'Do we really have to do this, Zo?'

'Might as well now we've got this far. Hang on—' I pulled him back dramatically against the wall on the corner. 'Look, there's all the other people going in. Let's watch them.'

The Centre was in a Victorian school building with high wire-netting round the brick walls of the playground and a high iron gate with spikes – just like our old primary school in fact. 'It's a bloomin' school!' said Tarquin, disgusted. 'I thought it might at least look like a theatre.'

'Maybe we'll see someone we know.' I tried to sound enthusiastic. A group of high-spirited kids about my age were bouncing in. They obviously knew each other.

A pair of boys, probably Tark's age, dribbled a ball between them as they went through the gate. They disappeared from view but we could hear the ball biffing against the walls as they kicked it inside the playground. Tark brightened. 'OK. Let's do it,' he said, sounding like a low-budget movie hero, but at least his curiosity had finally got the better of him.

As we headed for the entrance a group of studenty grown-ups came round the corner after us. I heard them laughing and turned to look at them. Two girls were in front, one skinny with spiky hair, dyed scarlet, the other Asian and very beautiful with short hair and huge eyes. Behind them came a Kenneth Branagh clone in trainers – and, running to catch up with them and panting – wowee! I caught a tantalising glimpse of Mr Gorgeous himself, the man of my dreams: tall, fit, black . . . Things were looking up. But the four of them turned off up an echoing concrete staircase while Tarquin and I followed the other kids through to the hall and joined the queue to register.

We were all given forms and everyone sat down on the floor around the hall to fill them in. Tark and I sat together, trying to concentrate, but glancing round whenever we heard giggles or an interesting snatch of conversation. (I was dying to get another look at that guy – or any other talent for that matter.) The form was quite encouraging. We had to fill in our name, address, age etc, but then they wanted to know about our experience, including dance and sport, and backstage stuff, like make-up or scenery design, mixing music, filming and recording. I saw Tarquin chewing his biro and frowning before ticking all sorts of boxes. Maybe I would be able to keep him here after all.

I still didn't have a clue what we were going to do, and it seemed as if it was going to be a while before we found out.

'Jackets off, everybody!' The spiky-scarlet-haired girl had appeared in the middle of the hall, and she had a surprisingly loud voice. 'Hand your questionnaires in if you haven't already. Strip down so you're comfortable and we'll do some warming up.' Sixty kids started milling about. If it had been school, someone would have shouted at us, but Minna, as she turned out to be called, just stood in the middle and smiled. She held the ball which the boys had been carrying earlier, and bounced it from time to time, as if to chivvy us along.

'Circle!' she yelled. 'Form a huge circle round me and quieten down, so I don't have to completely ruin my voice. Right.' She counted us off into five groups of twelve. 'Five circles!' she shouted, and found a ball for each group.

I'd been separated from Tark and found myself in a mixed group of a dozen kids who all looked about my age or older. They seemed to know what to do, but Minna reminded us anyway at the top of her voice – it was getting noisy in there. Then we started a sort of game. The first guy stood in the middle of our circle holding the ball. He had to say a few words about himself and then throw the ball to someone else. 'I'm Lee Ashton,' he said. 'I live near Albert Park, go to Albert Park School. Been here three times before. Chose to come. Into dance and drums.' He threw the ball to a beautiful but grumpy-looking girl and swapped his place in the centre for hers in the ring.

'Androulla Conios,' she said. 'I live on the other side of the park. You don't want to know where I go to school. Here because my mum made me – *again*. And I like . . .' She paused. 'Nothing really. I'm no good at anything. Dunno why I'm here.'

And so it went on, with kids from different schools and

all with different reasons for being on the Project, some enthusiastic, some not and lots in between.

A girl called Parminda threw the ball to me. I'd hardly heard what she said, I was so busy rehearsing my spiel. It's amazing how keyed up you get, waiting for your turn. The ball thudded against my chest as I caught it. I walked into the centre of the ring. I was aware of all eyes on me.

'Zoe Shaw,' I said. 'I live near Albert Park. Beechcroft School. First time here – because my mum made me' (this reason raised a laugh every time now because so many people gave it) 'and I'm into drama and – anything but singing. Can't sing to save my life!' I'd planned to say something more mature and impressive, but that's how it came out. Relieved that my turn was over, I chucked the ball to a guy I liked the look of – big nose, big smile, big personality, I guessed.

'I'm Stelios,' he began. 'Greetings, Minna!' he said, seeing the scarlet-haired student eavesdropping at the edge of our circle.

'Hi, Stelios,' she smiled. 'If you don't know Stelios already,' she said to the rest of us in the circle, 'you will by the end of today. You make it your business, don't you, Stel?' she said, with a laugh that was friendly, not patronising. 'Now carry on, don't let me stop you.'

'Albert Park,' he said. He spoke incredibly fast. 'Albert Park School. Fourth time here, because it's cool, and Lennie is a top guy. And Minna of course. And I'm into everything and I'm going to be a film director.' He mucked around with the ball for a bit before throwing it hard and fast at his mate and they exchanged places at a sprint.

The new guy in the middle was dark like Stelios but he was part Japanese and good-looking. Very good-looking. 'Simon,' he said. 'And I'm only here for the beer.' Which was great, because the circle game degenerated slightly after that and everyone began to loosen up. All intentional, I learnt later. And of course, it did the trick. Parminda, Stelios, Simon and I became an instant foursome.

We all sat on the floor again when we'd finished. I looked over to the last and noisiest group on their feet – Tark's. It consisted of the two footballers, Tark, another lad and an assorted bunch of girls, some large and stroppy, others obviously dance-trained and beginning to turn their toes out and look self-righteous. I was glad it wasn't my job to sort them out.

'What happens next?' I asked Parminda.

Stelios cut across us. 'Watch this space,' he said. 'Each time it starts as chaos – and ends as—'

'ART,' said Simon. 'We always end up quoting Lennie, you see.'

'And what's the catalyst?' quoted Parminda.

'ENERGY,' they all said together.

'OK,' I said. I was slightly taken aback. It was as if they'd got religion or something. 'You're claiming,' I said, somewhat loftily, 'that with a bit of energy the total chaos of sixty kids aged eleven to sixteen can be transformed into a work of dramatic art?'

But the three of them looked smug. 'Yup,' said Stelios. 'As I said, watch this space. Have a little faith.'

'None of us lot would come back if it wasn't quite so special,' said Parminda. 'Minna and Lennie know what they're doing.'

'I know that's Minna over there, but who's this Lennie guy you all keep going on about?'

'You'll meet him soon enough,' said Simon.

Tark's group had finished and Minna was calling for hush so she could explain the next warm-up exercise – another running around and shouting game, a bit like musical chairs. It was fun once you got into it: 'Anyone with a cat – run around . . . Anyone who had Sugar Puffs for breakfast.' And then it gets a little more risqué: 'Anyone who's wearing yesterday's underpants . . . Anyone who . . .' Stelios and Simon came up with some unrepeatable ones but we had a good laugh and got to know each other a bit better.

After the break we did still more of the same. This is all very well, I thought, as we trooped off for lunch. We were definitely warmed up, but what on earth were we going to perform in less than a week's time? I mean, I'm used to drama club at school, where at the first meeting we hear about the play, the second we do auditions and the third is a read-through.

This Lennie had better be good.

Two

The four of us sat round a table in the Turkish caff over the road. Tark was more than happy to stay in the Centre with his new-found mates.

'So have you three known each other for ages?' I asked, dipping pitta bread into hummus (it was great, this place), 'or did you just meet up at the Project?'

'Stel and I met on a film course a couple of years ago,' said Parminda. 'That's where I first met Lennie.'

'I'd already met Lennie here,' said Stel. 'It was him who suggested the film course. And Simon and I—'

'We're just good friends, aren't we?' said Simon putting his arm round Stel.

'Ah!' cooed Parminda. Together we regarded the two boys, Stel all big features and personality, Simon all good looks and charm. Quite a pair. I liked them both. They pretended to schmooze with each other, tipping back their chairs so far that they both fell over. The other customers looked a bit alarmed, but Simon, when he had dusted himself down, apologised to the owner while Stelios grinned sheepishly over at Lee and Androulla, the two in our group who'd been the first to introduce themselves.

'I thought Androulla wasn't very keen to be here,' I said, 'judging by what she said this morning.'

'Oh, I know Androulla,' said Stelios. 'She'll moan about anything. She always says she's useless and that she didn't want to come, but this is her third year, isn't it, Mindy?'

'Don't call me Mindy.'

'Isn't it, Parminda?'

'I think so. We did that dance routine together last year. She wasn't bad at that.' Parminda didn't sound hugely enthusiastic about Androulla.

Simon fixed me with his gaze. 'So what are you good at, Zoe?' He encouraged me with a lazy smile. Boy, he was good-looking! I was struck all over again and found it difficult to think straight.

'He's doing it!' said Stelios loudly. 'Look Mindy, he's at it again!'

'Don't call me Mindy! At what again?'

'Simon's doing that smile. Don't succumb to his oily wiles, Zoe!'

'I'm not oily!'

'All right – winsome wiles then.'

'Winsome's OK. Winsome, losesome,' said Simon, still with the indolent smile. 'Ignore them, Zoe. What are you good at?'

They were all waiting for me to answer. 'I don't know really. I do drama at school – usually get a speaking part in the play. Dance. Can't sing, though.'

'Lennie says everyone can sing,' said Parminda. 'It's one of his things.'

'Huh! I'd like to see him get me singing,' I said.

'Don't let him hear you say that. He'll take it as a challenge,' said Parminda. 'We get to sign up for workshops this afternoon.'

'Please, someone, tell me how this Project goes,' I said. 'Everyone's so vague and secretive. I don't want to "wait and see". I want to know how we progress.'

'Ooh,' said Stelios. 'I'm beginning to see the sort of person you are, Zoe. Bit of a control freak, huh? Don't like letting go, going with the flow?'

'How can you possibly say that! You don't even know me!' I felt quite angry. The trouble was, he was right. Ever since I was little, I've wanted to know what was going to happen next. I'd drive everyone nuts when we watched films, by asking 'What's going to happen now? Why are they doing that?' all the time.

'Don't be so mean, Stel.' Parminda leapt to my defence. 'It goes like this, Zoe. First morning – get to know each other, warm-up exercises, lose a few inhibitions. First afternoon – get to know each other a bit better with trust exercises and a bit of singing and dancing. Don't worry – we'll be told exactly what to do. Then, during tea, we get to choose our workshops, which might or might not have a bearing on the final performance, and THEN, only then, do we get the talk from Lennie about his vision of the Community Theatre Project, blah blah, and how we might go about choosing what we want to do. And that's only after we've sat through the Colonel's tedious welcoming speech.'

'The Colonel?'

'Lionel Saunders. You'll soon see why he's nicknamed the Colonel,' said Simon. 'Then on the morning of Day Two – tomorrow, after the warm-up, we start coming up with ideas.'

'Thank you,' I said. 'That was all I wanted. Just some idea of what we'll be doing. Otherwise I might have decided not to turn up tomorrow.'

'Course you'll turn up,' said Simon. 'You'll want to see me again.'

'And me,' said Stel.

Lee and Androulla came past our table on their way back. 'You'd better hurry up,' said Lee. 'We're quite late already.'

'OK, man,' said Stel, and we followed them out. I eyed up Lee's back view as we went. I hadn't quite taken him in before, because he was the first one to introduce himself. But he wasn't bad – in fact he looked a bit like Mr Gorgeous himself. Just younger. And not quite so gorgeously black. More like me, in fact. Still, he was into dancing and drumming. I didn't think we'd be spending much time together. And droopy 'Droulla was never far from his side.

We were back in the hall again. I wished it wasn't quite so like a school hall. 'We'll get into the Theatre soon,' said Parminda. 'I think we go there to sign up for workshops. I'll show you round if you like.'

Minna made us get into smaller groups for some trust exercises – you know, the sort where you have to let yourself be led around blindfold, and the one where you allow two people to push you backwards and forwards between them without dropping you. I ended up trusting Simon and Stelios, but I still didn't feel any closer to finding out what we were doing.

Minna's voice really was beginning to go, so she called on her friend Asha to take us through the dancing. Asha seemed tinier than ever when surrounded by sixty kids. She climbed up on to the stage at the end of the hall to direct us. 'This isn't going to be difficult!' she yelled. 'But I do want absolute quiet while I explain what to do.' And she stood there, hands on hips until there was silence. She had terrific presence. 'Now, we're going to start with a polka.'

Everyone turned to their neighbour to ask what the hell that was, but Asha just stood with her hands on her hips again until we were quiet. 'Watch me,' she said. 'This is how it goes.' She went to one side of the stage and stood with her hands clasped behind her back. 'Step-slide-step-hop, step-slide-step-hop, step-slide-step-hop!' she demonstrated, calling as she went.

'Now, go to the back of the hall and stand in a row with your big group, one row behind the other.' We obeyed. We stood in five rows of twelve. 'When I tell you to, I want you all to polka to the front. It won't be very good the first time, but by the fourth time it will be something like. OK? Here we go. Now! Step-slide-step-hop!'

We all polkaed to the front. It was a shambles. 'Back! Back! Try again.' It was still quite a shambles as we all talked ourselves through it. You could hear people muttering 'step-slide-step-hop' as they moved. Third time, it was a lot more coordinated. Fourth time – wow! We were really moving all together. We were all congratulating ourselves when Asha quietened us down again. 'Now we're going to do it to music,' she said, and flicked on a CD player. 'Watch me,' and she step-slide-step-hopped in time to the music. 'Think you can do that?' she said. 'Go back up the hall again, then.'

And we did it. It was an incredible feeling doing this all

together. The floor vibrated to our shuffling step-slide-step-hop rhythm. For the last try, she made us hold hands along our rows and swing them forwards on the beat. I found myself holding hands with Stelios and Simon. Stel's hands were cold and clammy. Simon's were warm and dry. 'Brilliant!' Asha called. 'Try it backwards now, and if you can do it I'll get the others in to watch.' Back we went. I looked over my shoulder to Tarquin's row, anxious that he might think this was embarrassingly awful, but there he was, tongue between teeth with concentration, getting on with it like everyone else.

Asha hopped down off the stage and we heard her calling Minna, Lennie and Algy (the Branagh clone I presumed) to come and watch. Minna and Algy soon joined her, but no Lennie. That was a disappointment. 'OK?' said Asha again. 'I'm going to start the music and you are going to move forwards and backwards twice in your very own version of the – let's call it the – People's Polka!'

When we'd done it and collapsed laughing on to the floor, Asha looked at her watch. 'You should have had a bit of a sing-song with Lennie now,' she said, 'but I'm afraid he's been called away. Go and have your tea and then make your way over to the Theatre. That's where the lists are posted and you can sign up for your workshops.'

'Must use that polka in a crowd scene sometime,' said Stel as we made our way over to the Theatre. 'Think how it would look with a cast of thousands, somewhere like Red Square!' Already I was beginning to appreciate how the Project might alter my way of looking at things. On the bus this morning I could never have imagined I might be discussing a cast of thousands polkaing their way across Red Square with a fifteen-year-old Greek kid.

Lee was right behind us. 'Cool, eh?' he said to Stel. 'Might develop that during the week. I'd no idea it would work so well.'

'Did you know we were going to do that, Lee?' asked Parminda.

'Yes. Well, I'll be doing the dance part of the performance with the younger ones, the boys anyway. Do any of you know who the dark kid in the red football shirt is?'

Tark was wearing a red football shirt. 'Might be my brother, Tark,' I said. 'Why?'

Lee smiled at me. His mouth went all pointy at the corners. Nice. 'Good dancer.'

'Tark? You must be joking!'

'We'll see.' He gave me another, appraising, smile. 'See you guys.'

'Does he teach?' I asked Parminda. 'I assumed he was one of us.'

'Lee's only a year older than me,' said Parminda, 'but they start young here! Last year they let him do the dance stuff with the smaller ones and it was one of the best parts of the show. So he's doing it again. He does Saturday mornings at some dance academy. Check out his muscles some time.' She nudged me conspiratorially, and we went into the canteen to queue up for tea and squash or hit the machines for something fizzy.

The Theatre was obviously a recent addition to the Centre and we approached it via a covered way across a courtyard. 'Lottery money,' said Stel. 'It wasn't built the first year I came. We had to be bused out to the youth theatre for the dress rehearsal and the show. The technical stuff here is amazing though. State-of-the-art. I really want them to let me do a video as a backdrop.'

'I still can't begin to imagine what it is we're going to

put on,' I grumbled. ' "Trust in Lennie," you all say, but Lennie's not even here, is he?'

'Stop yer moanin', woman,' said Stel. 'Come and look at the lists.'

The Theatre had a huge downstairs foyer, including a bar (with the shutters firmly closed). Tables had been lined up along the walls with information on the workshops posted above them. Parminda guided me through them – not easy with so many kids wandering about. As well as traditional theatre skills such as singing, dancing, mime, voice projection and so on, I had a fantastic choice of backstage things – make-up, set design, props, wardrobe, lighting. And on top of that there was music in theatre, film and video and writing for the stage. 'Impressive, isn't it?' said Parminda. 'Of course, all the eleven-year-olds go for singing and dancing and make-up. I reckon it's better to do one thing, myself. And I can't decide between writing for the stage and film and video. Maybe I've done enough film and video for a while.'

'No prizes for guessing what Stel will choose, I suppose,' I said.

'He's not joking when he says he's going to be a film director,' said Parminda. 'Stel has grand ideas. Lennie really rates him. He did this incredible little black-and-white movie on the film course. It was two years ago, so we were only thirteen, but because we were at the South Bank he just filmed all these people on stairs and escalators and kind of choreographed it. Really clever.'

'Well, I'd like to do the writing. I think that's what I'm best at. Who teaches it?'

'It'll say here. I think they've got someone in, unless it's Algy. Woh! It's Jim Wilde! Even I've heard of him!'

'It says he's got a play on at the National!'

'There's some link with the South Bank. They like youth projects. Anyway, I'll definitely do it with you.'

Simon was leaning across us to add his name to the list. There weren't many so far.

'I thought you were only here for the beer,' I said.

'Only kidding,' he replied. 'When Stel's a director, I'll be writing the scripts.'

Parminda and I added our names. 'If I do this with you, you have to do the singing with me,' she said.

'That's not fair. I didn't ask you to do the writing.'

'But you wouldn't want to be stuck on your own with sleazy Si, would you?'

'I might do,' I said. 'I might choose to be on my own with sleazy Si.'

'Oh no, you wouldn't! You'll need me to protect you. And I insist you do the singing. It's one sure way to get personal attention from Lennie.'

'What makes you think I want it? I've never set eyes on the guy.'

'I just think you'll love him. Because you're so – so sort of argumentative and . . . wordy.'

'Thanks a lot.'

'Are you political, though? Lennie's very political. Not in a Labour party and Tory party sort of way. Theatre as politics.'

'I like debating, if that's what you mean.'

'Dunno what I mean, really. Just do singing with me.'

'Oh, OK!'

She added my name to the long list of singers. 'You won't regret it.'

Tark came loping over. 'What you doin', Zo?'

'Singing—'

'You? Singing? You're tone deaf!'

'Thank you. I agree, but Parminda here says I must sing.'

'I can't really take the micky,' said Tark. 'I've gone and let myself be talked into dancing!'

'Who by?'

'Guy called Lee. Conned a whole bunch of us into it.' Tark laughed. 'Actually, man, I was quite getting into the dancing. Awesome. And Lee's into all that Stomp stuff. Could be cool.'

'Anything else?'

'I like the idea of something a bit technical, so I've signed up for lighting as well. Lighting suite's wicked. Have you seen it?'

'I haven't really looked around yet.'

'You ought to. I spent the morning thinking we were just going to be in school the entire time, but this place makes it OK. I've signed up for loads of other things, Zo. I can't even remember what they are.' He drifted back to his mates. It was great to see him with his eyes shining. I imagined that Tark, like Stel and Simon and Lee, would be turning up here for years to come. Shrewd old Mum.

We sat in the auditorium feeling very grand – a bit different from the floor of the old school hall. The seats were steeply raked and we looked down on the deep stage from quite a height. Algy, Asha and Minna came and sat on the edge of the stage, legs dangling over the front.

Lionel Saunders came on stage to address us first. He looked like a traditional actor – moustache and pointy beard, glasses, bow tie. (Ah! That's why he was known as the Colonel.) 'Hello, children,' he said. Not a promising start. 'I'm Lionel Saunders, the Project Director. Welcome to our Theatre Project and our excellent new Theatre which has all manner of facilities . . .' He droned on. No one had warned me *quite* how dull he was. I was glad I'd met the others first. I started listening again when he said, 'And now I'll hand you over to the Project Leaders . . .'

'(. . . while I go off sailing for a week),' Parminda whispered. 'He loathes Community Theatre apparently. He'd prefer us all to do Andrew Lloyd-Webber musicals.'

When the Colonel had gone, Algy stood up. 'I'm sorry Lennie's not here to do his bit today, but I'm assured he'll be back with us tomorrow for a second meeting like this when you've had a night to sleep on some of the ideas we're about to raise now.

'I'm going to start by going through some of the topics we've covered in Community Theatre in previous years. This doesn't mean you can't do them again – but it will help new people to see the sort of things we're after. Last year we discovered a local story about a Viking settlement here and based our whole drama around the idea of being invaded by foreigners and learning to accept the good with the bad. I don't need to tell you that the subject had its topical side.' Yawn.

'The year before that we did a dark Jekyll and Hyde sort of play based on the fact that a local man jailed for being a serial killer was very much in the news. We imagined what he was like as a child and a teenager as well as focusing on the murder mystery.' That sounded slightly more interesting.

'Other years we've taken a very different approach such as – what would this community do if great quantities of oil were discovered under this site? Would we knock it all down and disperse the community, albeit with quite a bit of money? (And how would we decide who had how much?) Or would we make the decision to stay as a community?'

'Batty one, that,' whispered Stelios to me. 'Everyone said

"take the money" but Lennie made us spin it out into "save the community". The parents liked it though.'

'OK, Stelios,' Algy called up to him. 'Not one of our best ideas, but it made a good play. This year we're going to try and be a bit realistic about the community. More honest.'

'It's not as if we're all part of this community though, is it?' a guy near the front piped up. 'I mean we don't live here precisely. Half of us are from the other side of the borough.'

'Oh, I think you'll find you're a community,' said Algy. 'A, you belong to the larger community of the borough, and B, you're already a little community doing this Project. Same issues, same concerns – in the broader sense.'

'Anyway,' said Algy, sensing that the younger kids were getting fidgety. 'You've pre-empted me. Our idea this year is to come up with a genuine expression of your generation's feelings about this area – whether they're good or bad, hostile, lukewarm – even a desire to get out as soon as possible. I want you to go home and think about positive and negative aspects. I don't mind if they're negative – plenty of good drama can be made from the negative. And then tomorrow you'll get to shape something out of it all with Lennie.'

We filed out of the Theatre. No one was exactly leaping about with enthusiasm for Algy's ideas. I certainly couldn't see how we were going to make a play out of them.

'The serial killer one was cool,' said Stelios.

'Bit gruesome,' said Parminda.

'It didn't really matter what it was about, though, did it?' said Simon. 'We had amazing actors that year, and some of the dance numbers were brilliant.'

'We're tired now, Zoe,' said Parminda. 'You'll just have to take it on trust that Lennie will lick us into shape. I have to rush off. See you all tomorrow!'

By the time I'd tracked down Tarquin, the Centre was nearly empty. Which was a shame because I reckoned Stelios and Simon didn't live far from us and we might have been able to travel home with them. In fact there was another brother and sister on our bus. The boy was Jake, the serious guy who'd raised the point about the local community, with his younger sister Lily, a tall, cool girl from Tark's group. We acknowledged them as we made our way down the bus, but they got off before us. Maybe we'd talk to them tomorrow.

THREE

The house was empty when we got home. Tark made himself toast and instant soup and flaked out in front of the television. I wanted to be on my own so I fixed myself a peanut butter and jam sandwich (Mum's answer to everything) and went downstairs to my room.

We used to let out the basement of our house to a succession of language students and divorcees. Not so long ago my parents decided the low rent they charged wasn't worth the stringent conditions that had to be met for the Letting Agency, which was great for me because they said I could move in. The basement consists of a bedroom and a bathroom and a pathetic kitchen the size of a cupboard, containing a tiny fridge and a gas ring, just off the utility room with the washing machine and tumble drier. I'm glad I'm not a student living here – I can imagine getting mightily hacked off with our family's laundry – but for me on my own it's bliss.

I like to get away from Tark and his mates and their

computer games and the Sports channel on the TV. Tark and I both have our own computers, but the TV in the living room is best for his PlayStation, so it was always a battle after school before Mum and Dad came home. Now I can take my friends down to my room, or just shut myself away there to do homework or watch the programmes I choose on my own ancient TV.

I helped Dad decorate it in really trendy colours and they let me have the futon so my friends can stay the night. I know I'm lucky. Dad and I put up loads of shelves for my books, too – I'm really proud of my 'library'. I've got a good atlas, a set of history part works, Dad's old encyclopedias, a complete Shakespeare, and now I'm building up a collection of all the plays I've been in – as well as various reference books I've bought at school fairs. I've still got all my old picture books, of course, and the world's largest selection of teenage fiction, which all my friends come and borrow. In fact I use the Internet more than my books for preparing a debate these days, but I like to have the books – they're my security!

I slumped on to the futon in front of *Neighbours*. It had felt like a long day and I wanted to clear my head of all the impressions and thoughts that were whizzing round. I often feel a bit hyped up when I've met a whole bunch of new people, and I found that I really cared what this lot thought of me, even the 'teachers', Minna, Asha and Algy. Probably Lennie too, if he ever put in an appearance. I'd met a nice girl – Parminda – and three really nice guys. The great thing about Parminda was that I felt we were quite alike. She didn't feel the need to hide the fact that she was clever and thoughtful and ambitious – which is what I find myself doing quite a bit at school, especially with Alex (don't get me wrong, I adore Alex for all sorts of other reasons). Of course I don't know anything about Parminda, but like me, she probably finds it quite a relief to be in a situation where nobody asks 'but where did your family come from *originally*?' As if they cared anyway.

Ideas about our 'play' kept surfacing, even though I was trying to veg out. I thought about where we live. Well, London is where we live – the metropolis. The melting pot. I wouldn't want to live anywhere else. Well, that's positive for a start! On the other hand, the streets round the Centre are grim. High crime rate, drugs, murder. A policeman was murdered there quite recently. A certain amount of racial tension. Poverty. Some of London's last tower blocks. If I lived there I'd want to escape. Escape. There's no reason why that shouldn't be a theme. Maybe I'd mention it tomorrow.

It wasn't frightening during the day though – and the Turkish caff and the Asian shops and the Greek shops and the Caribbean shops were all brilliant. There was a mosque next door to the Seventh Day Adventist Church. A Chinese take-away and a pub that served Thai food. I loved all that. That was positive.

Neighbours drained all thoughts from my brain at that point. Stel and Si and Lee and even Jake were floating around waiting to be dealt with, but Ramsay Street would keep them at bay for the best part of half an hour.

As the credits rolled I heard Mum coming in the front door. (Another good reason not to have students in the basement – they must have heard everything that went on upstairs.) 'Hi you two! So how was it?'

'Brilliant!' Tark was uncharacteristically polysyllabic. I leapt up the stairs to tell Mum all about it.

Tark was making her a cup of tea. We had both learnt to handle a kettle and make tea from a very young age as we vied for Mum's affections when she came home from work. You'd love Mum. She's tall with incredibly soft dark skin and smiley eyes and dimples. She wears her hair very short, and dresses smartly, which I really like. I don't even hear her American accent any more, but I'd know her laugh anywhere.

Mum and I sat at the kitchen table and Tark poured tea for us all. 'Tell me, then!' she said, and Tark was off, all about the footballing guys and the tall girl called Lily who was such a laugh (I hadn't heard that) and how this guy told him he was a good dancer after he'd seen him doing the polka.

'Er – excuse me?' said Mum, 'The polka? Community Theatre involves dancing the *polka*? My friend who told me about it said you'd be doing "Dance" with a capital D, but – good grief, you'll be learning how to foxtrot next.'

'It was so cool,' said Tark. He'd obviously got as much of a buzz out of us all moving *en masse* as I had.

'Did you have a good time, too, sweetheart?' Mum looked at me anxiously. She knew I hadn't really wanted to go.

'Actually, it wasn't bad,' I said. 'I met some quite nice people, surprisingly.' I stirred my tea, pensively. 'Though I don't see how we're going to put on a play at the end of the week. It's very different from drama group at school. Not like being given a great long script and told to go away and learn it!'

'What's our play about again, Zo?' Tark asked. 'I didn't really get what the Algy bloke was going on about.'

'I don't think he was that sure, himself.'

'I wish we were doing the thing about the serial killer again.'

'Tarquin!' said Mum.

'It's what they did one year,' I told her. 'Based on that guy

– you know, he lived round here in the sixties. All good local history.'

'Not quite what I had in mind for Tark,' said Mum, shuddering.

'Anyway, this year it's all to do with how young people feel about the area or something.'

'That's more what I was hoping for,' she said. 'Something positive about the city at the beginning of a new century.'

'It won't all be positive,' I said. 'How can it be? The area round the Centre is a dump. Nobody would choose to live there.'

'Oh well,' she said. 'I'm looking forward to seeing what you come up with.' She stood up and stretched. 'Now, I just want to watch the News and then I might start thinking about fixing us some supper. Talking of news – have a look in the local paper. There's something about the Project there. Just a few lines and a picture of the people running it. Nothing about the importance of the polka in Community Theatre . . .'

'Where is this newspaper?' I asked.

'On the coffee table – here.' Mum handed me the local *Post* before switching over to the News on TV. 'Oh – and something else. I bought you this.' She rifled through her briefcase and handed me a Ryman's bag. (Mum's a stationery nut.) 'Just a nice notebook. I couldn't resist the shiny cover. Thought you might like it for the course.'

'Thanks, Mum!' I'm a stationery nut too – I love folders and exercise books and sharp pencils and metallic rollerballs. Don't get me started! I took it down to my room along with the local paper and hunted for the article amongst all the muggings and stabbings. It was headed MAKING A DRAMA OUT OF IT, and the photo showed Minna, Algy, Asha and, presumably, Lennie in ridiculous theatrical poses outside the new Theatre – Algy bowing and flourishing a baseball cap, Minna curtseying, and Lennie on bended knee as if proposing to Asha, who had her hand up to her forehead as if she was about to faint. The text didn't really say much, except that Lennie and Asha had won recognition for some recent work in Manchester and to mention the South Bank connection and Jim Wilde (the playwright) coming to tutor us.

I looked more closely at the photo. OK, I'll be honest – I looked more closely at the famous Lennie in the photo, grainy as it was. Even in the ridiculous pose he looked pretty cool. Lean and loose-limbed. I couldn't wait to see him in the flesh. I do slightly go for that type.

I lay back on my bed and indulged in a little daydreaming about 'that type'. I went out with a guy, Errol, who looked a bit like Lennie. It was over a year ago now, but he was sixteen and I thought he was ever so grown up. Mum and Dad must have thought so too, because they were quite worried about our relationship! The trouble was – he was so thick! Like – *so* thick! He looked great, which was why I was so flattered when he wanted to go out with me, and wore all these expensive clothes, but that was all he cared about. At first he teased me about being a boffin and even seemed to think it was quite cute, but then he started having a go at me for using long words and reading books. He couldn't understand why anyone should *choose* to read a book! In the end we just sat in silence. I can't remember now which one of us dumped the other. I see him every now and then – we still say hello. He looks amazing, but I *don't* regret not going out with him any more. No way!

Then there was Iain, in the football team. He looked similar to Errol, but he wasn't stupid. I got quite keen on football for a bit (Tark kept me up to date). I didn't really go out with Iain, though I spent a lot of time watching him play football! I had the excuse of waiting after school to go home with Tark, who was practising on a pitch nearby. Iain did ask me to go out with him once, but I bottled out. I don't think he realised I was only fourteen. I don't know what he's up to these days.

I haven't had a boyfriend for a while now. Aagh! But I've just promised to have a holiday romance, haven't I? I'd forgotten that. Oh dear, now I'll have to eye everyone up for their romantic potential! It would be so cool if I could get a *real* man like Lennie to notice me, but I suppose I'll be stuck with the boys . . . Stel and Si and Lee are all quite nice in their different ways. And Jake's the sort of quiet, thoughtful guy who's cute-looking and doesn't know it yet. Ah well, we'll just have to wait and see what happens.

Loud thumps on my ceiling signalled that supper was ready as Mum banged the broom handle on the kitchen floor above my head. I'd been musing for longer than I thought.

I didn't quite know what to do with myself after supper. I felt in need of a girlie chat, but who with? Alex was all involved with tennis now – I didn't feel like ringing and getting hold of one of her brothers. Anyway – Alex doesn't really like talking about boys. Holly and Josie were both away. I wished I knew Parminda well enough just to phone for a chat – but I didn't even know her number. I paced round my room for a bit, switching the TV on and off, pulling books off my shelves and putting them back again.

I caught sight of the new notebook sitting invitingly on my desk. I sat down, picked up a pink metallic pen and inscribed *Community Theatre Youth Project* on the front page. Then I thought long and hard. It would be good to impress

Lennie in the morning with some brilliant ideas. I went into debate preparation mode and headed two columns – under a general title of THIS PLACE – *Positive and Negative*. I listed the points I'd been thinking about earlier, but then, under *Negative*, I kept coming back to two main points: one – poverty and two – violence. If I was preparing a debate I'd no doubt be questioning whether the first led to the second, and pestering Dad about economics and the poverty trap (one of the subjects he lectures in). But it wasn't a debate. It was a drama. Poverty and Violence. We couldn't be the first to deal with these themes. I jotted down a few plays and playwrights that came to mind . . . and films . . . and TV dramas . . .

TUESDAY: Day Two of the Project

I woke up bleary after falling asleep over my notes and going to bed far too late. Mum had already left for work and Tark was jumping about being irritating because he was so anxious not to miss a minute.

I grumbled at him. 'Honestly, Tark. This time yesterday you weren't half so enthusiastic. You wanted to bunk off, remember?'

'So? I was wrong. Now I reckon it's cool and I don't want to be late. I've got a drumming workshop – so COME ON!'

I stuffed my notebook in my bag and a bagel in my mouth and left the house with Tark. A bus came into view just as we turned on to the main road, so we had to run. Luckily we made it, and found two seats upstairs, but I was not a happy bunny. My hair was a mess, I'd put on some jeans that were too tight and my eyes felt gritty. The bagel was dry and I dropped some crumbs inside my shirt.

'Hi there, Tarquin!' It was Lily, Tark's new friend.

'Hi.' Jake looked as early-morningish as I felt. I grunted in response as Lily grabbed the seat in front of Tark. Jake sat further up the bus but I was quite grateful to Lily for twisting around to chat to Tark and providing an ear for all his enthusiasm. I decided I'd feel better once I'd had a drink and sorted my face out at the Centre. I shut my eyes against the jolting bus and its passengers for the next twenty minutes.

It was quite different at the Centre this morning, with everyone purposeful and cheerful rather than apprehensive. People knew one another's names and talked to each other in the queues at the canteen. Parminda stood beside me as I waited for coffee. I told her I felt a mess, so she offered to get the coffee while I went to the cloakroom to brush my hair and put on some make-up. 'You'll need to look ravishing for Lennie,' she joked.

I felt much more presentable when I returned and we took our drinks into the main hall where everyone was waiting for the first warm-up sessions. It wasn't long before we were joined by Stelios and Simon. 'Hi Zoe. Hi Mindy.'

'Don't call me Mindy.'

'OK everybody!' It was Minna, shouting at the top of her voice again. 'Jackets off. Spread out. A bit of music and movement for you now.' Pandemonium ensued for a couple of minutes, but no longer.

'Right!' Minna hollered. 'I'm going to put a CD on and there are three movements that I am going to call out for you to do, and this is what they are. Up!' She stretched her arms right up until she was standing on tiptoe. 'Down!' She crouched down with her knees bent. 'And spin!' She held her arms out sideways and proceeded to spin around the room. 'No bumping into each other, and I'll be varying the order. Here goes!' It was quite a clever exercise because it got us moving and concentrating – as well as making idiots of ourselves. Stelios spinning was quite a sight, I can tell you. I won't tell Tarquin, because he'll get big-headed, but he actually accomplished his pirouettes without looking like a prat. Quite graceful in fact.

After the warm-up Minna sat us down on the floor. 'Well done, everyone. Now normally we would reckon to have our "creative session" right now to discuss the performance and our progress with it. Then workshops followed by lunch and group work. Lennie is unfortunately still detained, BUT he will be with us in an hour or so, so we're proposing to reverse this morning's timetable. You can go off to your workshops now and we'll meet again here for the creative session at twelve noon!' She had to raise her voice still further against the kerfuffle that started as soon as she mentioned workshops. 'Quiet!' she yelled. 'I have the lists here, so shut up and listen while I read them out!'

There was relative silence while she read out our names. Parminda, Simon, Jake and I peeled off to meet the playwright. There were several sixth-form types and a tiny (though he had to be at least eleven) black kid, called Yodo. He wore bottle-glass specs and his English wasn't brilliant, so no one quite knew why he'd chosen this workshop, but we were all interested to find out. Jim Wilde was waiting for us in one of the seminar rooms (a classroom with carpets). Jim – as he asked us to call him – was a square, stocky guy, grey hair in a fringe and heavy-rimmed glasses. He spoke with a north-country accent, but, more importantly, he spoke to us as equals.

'It seems to me,' he said, 'that you have a harder task ahead of you than I have ever had to tackle. I gather that you – *as a group*,' he read, '*will attempt to weave a narrative around a number of different individual items to make a satisfying play* – which you will perform in under a week's time. You've certainly got your work cut out!'

He went on to make us introduce ourselves (again). The sixth-formers were two boys and two girls who tended to stick together, and then there was Yodo, looking frightened when anyone spoke to him. Jim went over and knelt down by his chair, as you would with a really little kid. He spoke very gently. 'So, Yodo. I'm very pleased you've chosen to come to my writing workshop. Erm – what made you go for this one, rather than, say, drumming – or—' He obviously wanted to make sure that Yodo hadn't got on to the wrong workshop by mistake.

'Want to write,' said Yodo, haltingly.

'Excellent,' said Jim, still slightly puzzled.

'Want to *write*,' said Yodo again.

'Good, then you're in the right place,' said Jim, laughing, and standing up again. 'Right – write! Haha! What a strange language we speak. Still, that's the beauty of words.'

But Yodo was still going. He reached up and caught Jim's hand, moving his finger over his palm like a pen. 'Learn to *write*,' he said again. 'My sister say I learn *writing*.'

Ohmygod. It dawned on all of us simultaneously. It was tempting to laugh, but Yodo looked so earnest. Jim was brilliant. 'And so you shall, Yodo. We'll all help you to write.'

He turned to the rest of us. 'I don't want to turn this kid away. I'll try and find out a bit more about him – he can't have been in this country long. I think we should make teaching him to write part of our workshop. After all, Yodo wants to be able to communicate his thoughts in writing, just as we do.' He quickly found some paper and copied

Yodo's full name from his list in big letters. 'Here, Yodo. Copy your name while I talk to the others. We'll find you some more to do later.' Yodo settled to his task apparently quite happily.

Then Jim talked to us about creating drama, with and without language. 'Much of your drama will be in the form of dance and song. But your part, the words, will have to be extra specially carefully expressed.'

It was a pity we were doing the sessions in reverse order. We all needed something to work on. Meanwhile, Jim did a few exercises with us – the sort where you get into pairs and tell each other things, such as an episode from your childhood, and then you have to tell it to the others. He said it would help us focus ideas and shape them for dramatic effect. The childhood incidents were interesting, too. Simon's was about his grandma's funeral in Japan. Parminda's and mine were more mundane – mine was getting lost in a supermarket and Parminda's was a hysterical account of wetting her knickers as an angel (aged five or so) in the school Nativity, and 'getting her own back on the Christians'. Jim was generous in his praise of everyone – he said he was already aware of our 'burgeoning talent'. He also held up Yodo's best rendering of his name for us to admire, and said he'd have more for him to do tomorrow.

The time for our 'creative session' had come at last, and with it my chance to get a proper look at the divine Lennie.

FOUR

There should have been a drum-roll. I played one in my head. We were sitting waiting in the hall, making a racket. Then Minna, Algy and Asha came in, in that order, and everyone quietened down. They were followed, with perfect timing, by Lennie Grant.

I nearly fainted. Seriously. He was that gorgeous. I glanced around to see if anyone else was as affected as I was and caught sight of Lily and a friend quietly giggling together and flapping their hands in front of their faces. And they were only twelve!

'OK folks,' he said. 'Cut to the chase. This is the first of our daily creative sessions where *you* get to write the play. I'm Lennie and I'm going to work you hard but, boy, will you be grateful! And if you're not, then see me afterwards.' He wiggled his eyebrows suggestively.

Then he started to pace about as he spoke. 'OK. Some thoughts. This area of London. We can't call a play "This Area", can we? Suggestions, please?'

There was a silence. 'Don't all shout at once!'

'This Place?' I ventured, but it came out all squeaky.

'Sorry – did somebody speak?'

I coughed to clear my throat. 'This Place?' I tried again.

'Good. "This Place"? Any advance on "This Place"? I quite like "This Place" actually.' I glowed. 'But come on, there must be some other ideas out there!'

'Gotta Get Out of This Place?' It was Simon.

'I know! I know!' One of our writing sixth-formers. 'How about just "Out of This Place", because then it's like – the good that comes out of this place as well as the need to escape from it!'

Stelios was jumping now. 'Outta Here!' he yelled.

Lennie smiled. 'Cool. What does everyone else think of "Outta Here"?' I thought it was brilliant. My head was beginning to buzz with excitement. 'All those in favour of "Outta Here" as the title of our play?' I don't think a single person objected.

'Wow,' said Lennie. 'You're like pussycats this morning! What else can I get past you?' He paced again, looking at us all. 'We haven't started yet, have we?' He stood by a flip chart. 'OK. Good and bad things about "Here".' He headed two lists, 'good' and 'bad'.

'I've got some!' I said, opening my shiny notebook, anxious for him to see how keen I was.

'Let's have it, then—?'

'Zoe.'

'Let's have it then, Zoe.'

It came out all of a rush. 'Er, good: London is a great place to live. All the different cultures and shops and religions and things. And . . .' I turned my page. 'Bad: crime, drugs, violence, no trees, racial tension, tower blocks . . .' I faltered, suddenly feeling schoolgirly and stupid with my lists.

But Lennie smiled warmly. 'That's great, Zoe. Now let's think a bit more in terms of our play and the items in it.'

'Oh—' I added, 'and – the need to escape. I – I thought "Escape" might be a good theme.'

Lennie had written my suggestions on his chart. He looked over to where Tark and co. were sitting. 'I can think of something truly excellent about this part of London,' he said. 'Come on, you guys.' He made encouraging gestures with his hands.

They looked at him blankly. He ran around as if dribbling a ball. 'Football!' they all shouted.

'Not one but two premier league football teams!' Lennie added football to his 'good' list.

'Nowhere green,' piped up one of the little dancers.

'Too much fighting,' said another, as Lennie scribbled away.

'I can see some set pieces here already,' he said, 'and I need your help.' He looked over to the little girl who'd said 'Nowhere' – Marsha. 'Does anyone else feel a song coming on –' he started to sing softly – 'We got white – we got black – you know, cos you've seen – we got pink – we got brown – we got plenty in between – but what we want now – and what we ain't got – is GREEN!'

'I know, I know,' said Marsha's friend. 'We can do it with coloured squares! You know! Like in the ads. We can turn it green! We can sing and we can turn it green!'

Lennie shrugged and held out his hands to us. 'I see I'm redundant. Brilliant, that girl! We have a number already.'

The hall was humming. I saw Tark put up his hand. 'Lennie Lennie!' he called. 'I've got an idea for a dance. A football dance!' And he got up – my little brother got up – and in front of us all he performed this amazing sort of stomp dance to a football chant, each stomp ending on a stylised football move. I couldn't believe it! Then two of his mates – and Lily – spontaneously jumped up and joined in.

'Amazing!' Lennie's laugh was a bit like my mum's. He called out to Lee. 'Lee – I think you've got a big dance number there, too!' He turned back to his flip chart. 'Keep thinking, keep thinking, but here are some topics I person-ally reckon might translate quite well into something for the stage. "Escape" is a good one. So is "Violence". Maybe we could get a good fight scene going. And have some thoughts about that old cliché, "The Melting Pot". What goes in, eh? And what comes out? And no one's mentioned "Transport" or "Journeys", always lots of material there.' He smiled at us. 'OK! Lunch!' And everyone got up and rushed off to eat.

'Well?' said Parminda in the Turkish caff. 'What do you think of our Lennie then?'

'What is it about Lennie?' Stelios asked Simon. 'Why does he always have this effect on women?'

'Charisma, innit?' said Simon. 'Lennie has it in shed-loads.'

'Could it be something to do with the fact that he is incredibly good-looking and sexy?' said Parminda, smiling with mock innocence.

'But it isn't just that, is it?' said Stel.

'Energy has something to do with it,' said Simon. 'I mean – I'm incredibly sexy and good-looking, but I don't have you two eating out of my hand, do I?'

'Considering the mess you've made of your doner kebab, it's a good job you don't,' said Parminda.

'It's a certain sort of energy,' I said.

'Sexual energy,' said Parminda. 'I told you so. Anyway Stel, what did you do this morning while we were with Jim Wilde? And did anyone tell you about our little kid – Yodo?'

'Yeah, poor little kid,' said Stel. 'All you lot laughing at him because he can't speak English.'

'It wasn't like that at all,' I said. 'The only funny thing was that he thought writing meant – you know – writing!'

Stel looked at me squarely. 'How's your French, Zoe?' he said. 'Or your German, or whatever other language you've been learning for the last three years? Could you distinguish between two identical words with different meanings? Because I tell you, at eleven years old, straight off the boat, it ain't easy, man.'

'Oh I'm crying I really am,' said Simon. 'No need to make Zoe feel bad, just because you were rubbish at English after speaking Greek all your life.' He grinned at me and threw out his arms in front of Stel and Parminda. 'Cos we're bilingual now! There! Do you think that would make a song?' He started to imitate Lennie. 'Good, good! I think we've got a number here – "Cos We're Bilingual Now". Hmm, not a brilliant title though – any ideas anyone?'

'Eh! Don't knock it!' said Parminda. 'You know he's inspiring. You're just jealous because we all fancy him.'

'Sorry Mindy.'

'Don't call me Mindy.'

'ANYWAY!' said Stel. 'Someone was kindly inquiring after my morning, which was spent, with a state-of-the-art video camera, following round the dancers. Lee's doing a workshop with all these pre-pubescent girls. Right little prima donnas they are too. Their dancing's hilarious. Lee was trying to get them to loosen up and all they wanted to do was Britney routines. No wonder he wants to get his hands on the boys.'

'I hope that doesn't mean what it sounded like,' said Parminda.

'I'll rephrase it. No wonder Lee wants to get his hands on some decent dancers.'

'Like my brother. Wasn't he amazing?'

'Do you mean you didn't know he could do it?' asked Parminda.

'Not a sausage.'

'That,' said Stelios, 'is the Lennie effect. Standard. I've

seen it happen again and again. It's almost like religion, man!'

We were back to the Lennie effect. I shan't go into detail about the effect Lennie had on me apart from the fact that I wanted him to smile on me, on me alone, and for ever.

We ambled back to the Centre. Stel was apologetic. 'Sorry, Zoe. Didn't mean to put you down. Just know a bit how the kid felt. Which one is he?'

Yodo, the sun glinting off his glasses, was in the playground with, I presumed, his sister, a girl I hadn't noticed before. They were both overdressed even for the British summer. Their faces were closed. I pointed them out. 'Oh man,' said Stel. 'They really are just off the boat. Refugees. God knows what they've left behind. My Mum's a social worker round here and she's dealing with them all the time. Can't think whose bright idea it was to send them on a Theatre Project. I might try and get them to talk to camera at some point.' He smiled in their direction and turned back to me. 'I think our group's got Lennie again this afternoon. D'you think you and Mindy can cope?'

'Don't call her Mindy.'

'I like this group. I like this group.' Lennie was making us feel at home and allowing us girls time to get over our hot blushes, even if he did probably say the same thing to all the groups.

'Somebody mentioned fighting and violence.' (Squeak, me!) 'Several people mentioned fighting and violence as features of this area. So let's talk about fighting. Hey! You!' He pointed at a boy whose name I'd already forgotten, a rather ratty-faced individual. 'What's your name?'

'Stephen.'

'OK Stephen. Come and fight me.'

Stephen stood up, bewildered. 'Now?'

'Yeah. Come on.' Lennie bounced around, shadow boxing.

Stephen approached him, poking his fist out every now and then.

'See? You don't know what to do. Now –' Lennie moved into a judo pose – 'anyone do judo here?'

'I do,' said Parminda.

'OK,' said Lennie. 'Come and fight me.'

Parminda went up to him and immediately they went into some judo moves – which was great, because Parminda landed him on the floor and everyone laughed. Parminda went back to her seat and Lennie brushed himself down. 'So that was stylised fighting,' said Lennie, 'and both Parminda and I knew the moves. For any *other* fighting—' he paused, 'you have to be angry. Don't you?'

I was really interested, because of all the reading I'd done last night. 'You have to look at causes of violence,' I said, speaking quickly. 'Inequality is a great cause of violence,' I said, 'and injustice. And jealousy, like in *Othello*.' I so wanted Lennie to praise me.

'Let's get a bit more basic than that,' said Lennie. I felt crushed. But he smiled at me. 'Zoe's right – there does have to be a cause, a spark. Anger, hatred. *Aggression*. Answer me this – do you think it is human nature to be aggressive, to fight? Think of it in terms of the natural world.'

'We have to be able to defend ourselves,' said Lee.

'And fight for what is ours,' said Stelios, who'd been thinking.

'To show who's strongest?' said Simon, flashing a grin at Stel.

'Good,' said Lennie. 'All those. Now, a little exercise. I want you to divide into two groups, one either end of the room, and approach each other as if you were about to have a fight. Try not to be self-conscious.'

That was hard (trying not to be self-conscious). I found myself lowering my head, bending forward, making my hands like claws and baring my teeth – which is what most people were doing. Lennie watched us approaching each other and stopped us just before we met. 'There. That was interesting. You all did the same thing, and it wasn't because you were taking cues from each other. I don't know, but I think there must be some fighting chip in the human make-up, however unaggressive a person is. Tonight I'd like you to think of the things that make you mad, personally, things you might just be prepared to fight over. I have some sort of fight scene in mind for our play, but I want it to come from you. Watch telly. Watch kids in the playground. Watch *toddlers* in action!'

When Parminda and I went for singing after tea – Lennie again (I wasn't complaining) – he was lying on the floor being tickled by a bunch of younger kids. 'Save me, you two!' he said. 'Save me from these fiends. And why are you all girls? I want some boys. Wait here while I go and steal some from drumming.'

He returned with half a dozen disgruntled boys of various ages. 'Can't sing,' said one of them, and 'Neither can I,' said some of the others.

'Neither can I,' I said, looking daggers at Parminda.

'Hush!' said Lennie. 'Everyone can sing, and you can certainly all chant, which is what we're going to do today.'

It was a bit like the polka thing yesterday. Lennie made us follow him round the room in a sort of stomping dance, shouting things like 'ya-da-da' and 'yu-du-du' at different pitches, working it into something quite like singing. Then he split us up into pairs and got us all doing different shouts at the same time. It wore us out! We were begging to be allowed to stop at the end.

'There,' he said to the boys. 'It wasn't so bad, was it?'

'No, it was cool.'

'Zoe thought so too, didn't you, Zo?' said Parminda to Lennie.

'Oh, hi Parminda,' said Lennie, recognising her. 'How's it going?'

'Great,' she said. 'This is Zoe, Lennie.' And she gave me a wicked little smile.

Lennie shook my hand. 'Pleased to meet you, Zoe,' he said, 'though actually we've encountered one another several times today haven't we? By the way, I'm sorry I raced over your examples from various plays. It's just that most of the kids aren't interested in the intellectual angle. Not knocking them – or you! We'll have a chat about it some time, yeah?' He was still holding my hand from shaking it, and now he gazed into my eyes – and I very nearly buckled. 'See you both tomorrow.' And he left us to speak to other kids who were waiting.

'Ooh, you've got it bad,' said Parminda, laughing and leading me to a seat. 'I've got to rush off in a minute.'

'Where do you live, Parminda?' (It's amazing how tempting it is to call her Mindy!) She told me. It wasn't that close to me. Shame. 'Give me your phone number then. I was dying to talk to someone last night about the course, and all my school friends are off doing things or away.'

'Good idea!' We exchanged phone numbers and then she shot off. I went to find Tark and came across Simon and Stelios on the prowl. 'Give me your phone numbers, boys,' I said.

'She's hot!' said Simon.

'She wants our babies!' said Stel.

'I might want to phone you, that's all. Do you go home on the 132 bus?'

'We go on the Tube.'

'Never mind. I have to find that little dancing brother of mine. See you tomorrow!'

'I'll come on the bus with you!' said Si gallantly.

'So will I,' said Stel.

'Forget it! See you tomorrow!' I spotted Tark and Lily talking to Lee. Lee looked up and smiled as I approached. He was nice, though the Lee effect wasn't a patch on the Lennie effect! 'Can I drag my little brother away?' I asked.

Tark went up on his toes and tried to look down on me. 'OK, big sis,' he said, patting me on the head. 'Lily and her brother are coming too.'

FIVE

Tark and I let ourselves in. Tark had been chattering nineteen to the dozen with Lily on the way home. I think she's the first girl he's ever liked. But he was all talked-out now. He raided the fridge and slumped in front of the TV with barely another word.

I went downstairs to my room and lay on my bed. Mum would be home soon and I could talk to her. My head was just bursting with all the ideas we'd chucked around. How were we ever going to turn them into a play? Everyone said that Lennie would make it happen. Actually, I agreed with them now. Lennie could make anything happen. I shut my eyes and thought of Lennie. What a guy. That first glimpse yesterday had shown me how handsome he was. Today's impressions were more of his incredible personality. He was so much more than just a pretty face! He'd had me *singing* for heaven's sake! I thought about his eyes searching mine as he held my hand. His grasp was warm and firm and – phew. I sat up and flapped my hands in front of my face, just as Lily and her friend had done.

The newspaper photo of the Theatre Project team lay on my table. I reached over and looked at it. It was too small, but I could do something about that. I took it upstairs to Dad's study. He has a scanner with his computer, which I use sometimes. I felt furtive. I didn't want Mum or Tark to see what I was doing. I scanned in the whole photo and then enlarged it on screen. Cool. It was grainier than ever, but I cropped it so that it was just Lennie (I didn't want to include the fainting Asha, even if I did know how she was feeling). Great. I printed it out. The printer seemed to take for ever, especially as I could hear Mum coming up the path. The front door slammed and I heard her calling 'Hi kids!'

I poked my head out of the study door. 'With you in a minute, Mum. Just printing something. Put the kettle on and I'll make you a cup of tea!' The picture finally emerged. I took the original out of the scanner and skipped down to my room to put my printout somewhere safe. But now I had a life-sized Lennie, I could look into his eyes whenever I wanted to.

Tark was already regaling Mum with tales from the Project when I joined them in the kitchen. Mum handed me a cup of tea. 'I can't believe this is turning out so well. Are you having a good time, Zodo?'

Her pet name for me reminded me of Yodo. 'We've got this little kid in our writing group who thought he was actually going to be taught how to write – you know, write his name and stuff.'

'So I guess a Jim Wilde workshop's a bit over his head?'

'Jim didn't turn a hair once he realised what was going on. He says we're all going to help Yodo to write – sort of part of writing the play. Honestly Mum, I don't know how we're going to get a performance out of all this. I'm quite worried about it.'

'That's because you're a worrier,' said Mum. 'Anyway, if the Project itself is this good, I don't think anyone's going to fret too much about the quality of the performance. It'll all be over by then.'

'Well, I'm a worrier, and I'll worry about the play until I can see it taking shape!'

'It is taking shape,' said Tark. 'There's our football stomp. There's the green song. Stelios is doing some video on escape, or flight or something. And aren't you lot doing a battle scene? That's four things already, and it's still only Tuesday.'

'You've just witnessed a perfect example of the Lennie effect at work,' I told Mum. 'This guy – Lennie – has a way of enthusing people and making them feel that anything's possible.'

'That's the kind of guy the world needs more of!' said Mum. 'What sort of age is he, this Lennie?'

'Dunno.' I didn't.

'Nearly twenty,' said Tark.

'How do you know?' (How come Tarquin knew more about him that I did?)

'Someone said so. Lee, I think. He hero-worships Lennie.'

'Well, he is amazing,' I said.

'And all the girls get their knickers in a twist when he's around.'

'Tarquin! I'm sure Zoe doesn't!'

Little did she know! Still, I didn't *quite* like Lennie being such common property. I was about to change the subject when the phone rang. I was glad to have an excuse to pick up the phone and take it down into my room.

It was Alex. She'd been invited to a swimming party and she was all worried in case the curse chose that moment to strike. I soon sorted her out and asked how she was getting on in the search for romance . . . Needless to say, she'd practically forgotten about it, and she had to dash off, so I couldn't even tell her how I was doing. I can't really imagine Alex with a boyfriend, but stranger things have happened . . . It wasn't as if I'd got anywhere myself. At least I'd met some nice guys. Stel was good fun, but I couldn't say I fancied him. Simon – well, yes, he was pretty good-looking. Lee, too – as a sort of poor man's Lennie. And then there was the man himself. Nearly twenty, though! That was a bit ancient! Still, only five years older than me, maybe less. I think (white) Grandpa is something like eight years older than Granny. So it's not *completely* mad.

I was about to return the phone to the kitchen when it rang again. 'Hello?'

'Hi.' It was a male voice. 'Zoe? Is that you?'

'Yes. Who is it?' The voice sounded familiar. It wasn't Lennie, was it?

'It's Lee. You OK?'

'Yes.' (As OK as I was when I last saw him less than two hours ago.)

'Tarquin OK?'

'Yes.' (Ditto.) I wished he'd get to the point.

'I just wanted to say—'

'Yes? Do you want to talk to Tark?'

'No – I just wanted to tell you that – that we always have a sort of party on the Friday night. For the older ones. In case you hadn't heard. I mean, we don't have a last-night party because most kids go home with their parents. Anyway, just thought I'd let you know.'

'Thanks, Lee. That's – very kind of you.'

'Right. Bye then. See you tomorrow.'

'Bye.' Weird, or what? I dug out my notebook with Parminda's number and dialled it. 'Parminda?'

'Yes? You were lucky – my dad usually gets to the phone first! Hang on. I'll take this in another room.' She put the phone down and picked it up again somewhere quieter. 'Hi. What can I do for you?'

'Lee just rang.'

'And?'

'Well, I don't know why he rang.'

'Didn't he say?'

'Well, he just told me about a party you always have on the Friday night.'

'We do, yes.'

'And that was it.'

'Weird. Perhaps he fancies you. That wouldn't be weird. I can see that all the guys do. Bit sickening really.'

'What makes you think that?'

'Oh, I know these things. I expect Jake does, too, but you're not having him because I like him.'

'Hey!'

'Just staking my claim before it's too late.'

'Fine. I don't have any particular preference for anyone.'

'Except you've been bitten by the Lennie bug.'

'Parminda!'

'As I said, I know these things. Ah well, far be it from me to try and put you off. You'll have to work out that one for yourself.'

'I never even mentioned Lennie.'

'I saw you blushing back there.'

'Oh God! Does that mean Lennie did too?'

'He's used to it. But Lennie's heart is with the Project, not with any of us – in case you hadn't noticed.'

Change of subject. 'Have you had any more ideas for the play, Parminda?'

'Ooh, one or two. I'll tell you in the morning, though. I'm in the middle of preparing a meal with Auntie.'

Mmm. I could practically smell the delicious food down the phone. 'You've just reminded me that I'm hungry.' I turned off the phone, opened the drawer with the Lennie printout – just to make sure he was safe – shut it again and went back up into the kitchen. Mum had moved from tea to a glass of wine and was leafing through the papers. I checked in the freezer. Great. 'Indian food tonight, Mum. I'll stick it in the microwave.'

So Stelios was doing a video on 'Escape' – or 'Flight' – was he? That would impress Lennie. I wasn't used to being outdone. After supper I went back down to my room and got out my notebook. Lennie had liked some of my ideas, hadn't he? How could we weave the various parts into a whole? We needed something extra. Another angle. I reckoned we really needed all the items decided tomorrow so that we could write our script and still have time to rehearse. If only I could come up with a good one on my own.

I went through my list of fight scenes and came to *Romeo and Juliet*. Of course! There was no romance in our play, no love interest, was there? We needed a pair of star-crossed lovers from hostile families? A Hindu and a Christian – or – hey! Need I look further?

I was back on the phone to Parminda in a flash. 'Parminda! It's me!'

'This is Parminda's father speaking. Parminda is busy right now. Who shall I tell her rang?'

'Oh. I'm sorry. Could you tell her Zoe rang? Thank you.'

Wouldn't happen like that in my house. Dad would've yelled for me to come to the phone no matter what I was doing. Still. Parminda's household was obviously different. But what a cool idea! I could script something for Parminda and Jake! That would throw them together! And impress Lennie. I slid him out of his drawer and smiled at him before shutting him back in again and making some notes.

I pulled my complete Shakespeare off the shelf and turned to *Romeo and Juliet*. I love that play! I loved the film too. But it's so sad! My lovers would overcome their family differences. They weren't going to die! I couldn't help lingering over some of the passages: 'Did my heart love till now?' Or how about 'But passion lends them power'? It made me think of Lennie. Nothing like a bit of Shakespeare to convince you that you are in love – as if you were in love all along, you just needed someone to find the words for it. Well, Parminda *had* found the words for it – 'You've been bitten by the Lennie bug.' It was true. I'd fallen under Lennie's spell.

WEDNESDAY: Day Three of the Project

Tark and I arrived a bit late on the Wednesday morning because Mum dropped us off on her way to work and the traffic was appalling. Anxious for Lennie to notice me, I'd put on more make-up than usual (a new lip gloss) and a tighter top (coral pink to show off my skin). That's how transparent I am! My notebook was full of ideas and I couldn't wait for the Creative Session.

The others had started on the warm-up exercises. Tark

and I waited until they had finished doing a chain 'dance'. It looked fun. I felt quite wistful as I watched Parminda, Stel, Simon, Lee and Jake dancing their reel. I joined in for the next warm-up, a stretching exercise, and held a whispered conversation with Parminda.

'Sorry about my dad on the phone last night,' she said. 'If I'm cooking, he likes me to cook.'

'That's OK. Its just that I had a brilliant idea, and I wanted to tell you.'

'Very keen on family time, my dad.'

'I thought we should include a love scene in the play.'

'What, you and all the boys?'

'No. You and Jake actually.'

'WHAT?' she shouted out loud.

'Everything OK, you two?' Asha called.

'Fine,' Parminda and I said back, and concentrated on the exercises for the next five minutes.

Parminda demanded an explanation as we sat waiting for Lennie to start the Creative Session. 'Well of course I'm not actually going to suggest you and Jake,' I said. 'I just thought we could manoeuvre that one. But I thought it would be a good cultural thing, you know?'

'What makes you think—'

'When you told us about your school Nativity?'

Parminda grinned. 'Yeah, well. My parents would certainly want me to marry a nice boy from a good family, but they're not too traditional. They wouldn't stop me marrying for love.'

'This is a play, Parminda! Don't take it personally. I just thought you'd like the opportunity to get together with Jake.'

She looked over to where Jake sat, and then back to me. 'That's not such a bad idea. In fact – nice one! Suggest a love scene to Lennie, I dare you! Bet you can't do it without blushing!'

I started blushing as soon as Lennie came into the hall. Really. He had such a powerful physical presence. I was aware of his muscles and his shoulders and his teeth and his hands . . . It almost took my breath away.

He started right in. 'OK! "Outta Here!" How are we doing? We have a dance – right, Lee? That's our big positive factor about the area – football. "More Green" – our first song. Positive from negative. What else? Our battle, of course. That's a negative. Stelios has started working on a video – maybe a backdrop on "Flight". That's a Stelios solo of course. Negative or positive, Stel?'

'Wait and see!' Stel called back.

'OK, boss. Any more ideas on "The Melting Pot" theme? Any more ideas at all? I'm confident the various working groups and workshops are going to come up with things – aren't you, drummers? – and that our writing team will weave it all together. I reckon we need ten to twelve items in all, depending on the link material. I'd like to have most of those established by this evening. Zoe? What is it?'

Not only was I blushing – I was shaking. Parminda had her elbow lodged in my ribs. 'I thought – a love scene?'

There were catcalls and wolf-whistles, but Lennie shushed them. 'Go on, Zoe.' His eyes were boring into me. My hands were clammy and cold.

'I thought – maybe – a Romeo and Juliet situation – where the families are enemies for some reason – like different cultures or religions. Except that the – lovers – unite them, type of thing.' My voice petered out.

'Not a bad idea, Zoe. Perhaps the writing team would like to get going on that? Go off to your workshops now and do some more thinking.'

'Of course, it could have been like that for my parents,' I said to Parminda, 'except that my grandparents were fine about it. I think some of the other relations weren't too keen.'

Stel was suddenly in front of me. 'I'll do it with you, Zoe,' he said. 'I could pretend I was from Iran, or somewhere.' He blinked his black eyes at me.

'Maybe . . . though I wasn't planning on being the girl, necessarily.'

'I'd be much more authentic!' said Simon, popping up at my side. 'Imagine putting my Japanese rellies in with your black ones.'

'Oy!' I said. 'They'd get on fine! Except mine live in the States. Anyway, I was thinking Parminda might be the heroine . . .'

'Whatever. Off you go now, Stel.' Simon got between Stelios and me and shunted him off towards his video workshop. 'I'll help Zoe with her love scene, don't you worry!' He linked his arm in mine and we went off to the theatre, followed by Parminda and Jake.

Jim was already sitting at a table working with Yodo. When we were all assembled he set Yodo up with some workbooks and left him to get on by himself. 'Morning all!' he said. 'So let's hope we've now got lots of ideas to work on.'

We told him what we had so far and he split us up into pairs. Parminda was with Jake and I was with Simon, working on – guess what – my love scene. We found ourselves a table in the far corner.

'I'm sorry about what I said earlier,' said Simon. 'I hope you didn't think I was being insensitive – about your black relations and stuff.'

'Of course not! I'm proud of them! I like having both. It's

like – I've got more of everything than most people. Plus I've got the American bit as well . . . So what about this love scene?' I tried to get him back on course.

'What? Oh, yes. OK. Let's start.'

'It doesn't matter what the different backgrounds are yet. We've just got to have them meeting and falling in love.'

'OK,' said Simon. 'Falling in love. OK.' He doodled on his notepad. And then – 'Can't they just fancy each other? I mean, isn't falling in love a bit naff?'

'No,' I said. 'They've got to fall in love. The real thing.' (The way I feel about Lennie, I thought to myself.)

'So the dialogue can't be slick and funny? Slick and funny is what I do.'

'Slick and funny with feeling would be good.'

'With song and dance?'

'I don't know. What do you think? Maybe we ought just to get them meeting and falling in love for the moment. Where should they meet?'

'This is like playing consequences, isn't it? Erm—' he thought. 'Dahn at the dogs?'

'I don't think so. Not if they're kids with protective parents. In fact – couldn't it just be at a disco? A school disco even?'

'School discos suck. I can't think of anywhere less sexy.'

'How about ice-skating or something? Tell you what –' I was warming to this – 'We could have them on roller skates. I wonder if Parminda and Jake can skate?'

'Parminda and Jake? What are you up to here, Zoe?'

'Nothing, nothing. Forget I said that. But what do you think of the skating idea?'

'As long as it allows me to write some slick and funny dialogue I don't mind.' Suddenly he put his hand on my wrist. 'Sorry, Zoe. Sorry – I keep apologising, don't I? I just find this quite hard – you being a girl and me being a bloke an' that . . .'

I hadn't foreseen this. 'So what's the problem, Si? I thought it would be a laugh.'

'OK, you're right. I'm being a prat. Let's get going. Don't want Jim disappointed. Girl meets boy at skating rink.'

'Their eyes meet—'

'They bump into each other and fall on their arses more like—' Si said.

'OK. And he helps her up—'

'More likely she helps him up—' Simon definitely wasn't going to get too carried away.

'Whatever.'

'No, but it's better that they bump into each other because then he knows she's got a sexy body and she knows how fit he is—'

'SIMON!' I yelled into a moment of silence in the class.

'I'm only being realistic!' he whispered, looking at me pleadingly.

'Haven't you EVER just looked at someone and thought they were completely terrific?'

He looked at me searchingly. 'Oh yes.'

'SIMON!'

Jim came over. 'Everything all right over here, or is the romance proving a little taxing? Have you got anything down yet?'

Simon sniggered.

'Sorry. Unfortunate turn of phrase,' said Jim, laughing. 'I'll leave you to battle on – but remember we have a deadline. Sometimes it's better to write something you're not happy with than nothing at all. It gives you a starting point.'

'Maybe I'd be better working with Parminda,' I suggested.

'Maybe,' said Jim looking over to where Parminda and Jake sat deep in discussion. 'But I think they've got a good partnership going there. Keep trying, you two. Have you decided where they're going to meet yet?'

'Skating,' I said.

'Lovely,' said Jim. 'Lennie will love a scene on roller skates. (I cheered, mentally.) Actually there is an ice rink near here, isn't there? Excellent. You can have some "bumping into each other" jokes, Simon.'

We ground on. Gradually a scene began to take shape. Only the thought of Lennie being pleased kept me going. Si was embarrassed and laddish by turns. I didn't know what to make of it. I was quite relieved when lunch time came around. Simon looked at his watch. 'Quick – we need to hurry if we want to sit down!' he said, and grabbed my hand. I'd noticed on that first day that his hands were warm and dry – nice. 'Sorry—' he said, embarrassed again at realising what he'd done. He dropped my hand, but smiled his sexy smile and laughed into my eyes. 'Stel would kill me,' he said. And we ran the rest of the way to the Turkish caff, Parminda and Jake following behind at a more leisurely pace.

SIX

Stel was pointing the camera at us as we walked in the door of the caff. He did the same when Jake and Parminda came in. 'Now look at this,' he said. Lee and Androulla were there too and we all crowded round the camera which had a tiny viewing screen. Stel fiddled with a few buttons and then played it backwards, showing all three pairs of us backing out of the caff at great speed. It was funny but it was also very clever. 'Couples fleeing the caff!' he said.

'We're not a couple!' said Lee quickly.

'Nor are we,' I added.

'Not the point,' said Stel before Jake and Parminda joined the protest. 'I have to use whatever I can get – whoever I can get!'

I was impressed again. 'Show me again, Stel,' I said. 'Oh – chips and hummus in pitta for me Si – ta.' Simon joined the queue and Stel ran the little sequence through again. 'Now do us coming forwards.' Each couple had a 'language'. Lee was most definitely not 'with' Androulla. But Si and I were obviously in tune – he was looking at me and I smiled back at him as we came in through the door. Jake and Parminda – now that was interesting. Lots of hesitant smiles and downcast eyes. That was more the language of love. (Writing love scenes gets you thinking like that.) 'Tell me again how you're going to use this?'

'I'm trying to get images of groups of people on the move. Not just people. I'm going to the park later this afternoon to try and get the geese flying over. I'll do planes too. And traffic. Might get the dancers to do something for me as well. Are you a dancer, Zoe?'

'I like dancing – but I'm not really a "dance" person.'

'Pity. I'd have liked to shoot you spinning off across the hall on your own.'

'No chance.'

'Never mind. My fit pal Simon is going to do some running for me, aren't you Si?'

Simon dumped our food on the table. 'You what?'

'You'll do some running for me, won't you? I thought

maybe tonight when it's nearly dark. Running and panting is what I'm after.'

'Wednesday. Not much on telly. OK. Want to come with us, Zoe? You live near the park don't you?'

'Other side from you. I don't mind meeting you up there, but one of you might have to see me home if it's dark.'

'I will.'

'I will.'

They both spoke at once.

'What's this?' Parminda looked up for the first time. She and Jake had queued together and were sitting at the next table.

'Filming in the park tonight,' said Stelios.

'Can I come?' Lee was on the case.

'Anyone can come. It's a public park. But I want to shoot some people running. "Escape". Remember?' Stelios knew what he wanted. He took it very seriously. He turned his wide smile on me. 'Wear trainers, Zoe. You might have to run away from Lee as well as Simon now.'

We had Algy for our group session and he thought the battle scene idea was wonderful. He made us think about pain (great) and we had to form Guernica-style tableaux (after Picasso's Spanish Civil War painting). Then he made us repeat the work we'd done with Lennie of two sides approaching each other, stopping to form tableaux whenever he clapped his hands. 'The lighting group could do something good with this. And the drummers. Come over here and we'll talk about it.' It was good. The fight scene was going to be good. It would need a lead from the script though.

'The older kids are writing something,' Parminda told

me. 'But I can't help feeling the whole play will need something amazing to pull it all together. That's what Lennie's expecting from us. Other years someone has always managed to have that brilliant idea. I suppose there's no reason why it shouldn't happen this year.'

Lee, Stel and Si were on the other 'team' in the battle. Jake was in a different group. Parminda was more than ready to gossip. 'How are you and Simon getting on with my love scene, then?'

'You bump into each other at a skating rink. We've got that far.'

'Oh great.'

'It's quite hard working with Simon. He gets all embarrassed and won't concentrate.'

'It's not quite his thing. He's good on the slick, funny stuff.'

'So he tells me. I'm sure we can make some of it slick and funny. You're right – it's the romance part. He said he found it difficult working with a girl. I suggested I worked with you, but then again . . . You and Jake seemed to be doing just fine . . .'

'I'll tell you about it on the way to Lennie's class. I expect you can't wait! – for Lennie's class, I mean.'

'I just wish it wasn't singing. I wish it was something I was good at. It was a good laugh yesterday, but I'd much rather be acting.'

'What's all this? What's all this?' Lennie had come up behind us.

'Oh, hi Lennie!' I warbled. 'I just wished I was better at singing, that's all.'

'You'll be asking for private tuition next,' he said with a laugh.

'Oh no – I didn't mean—' I felt faint.

'Don't worry! Neither did I! Don't believe in it. I'd like you two to come to the late session tomorrow night, though. I need good brains at that stage for tying up all the ends.'

'Fine,' I said. (Wow. Lennie thought I had a good brain.)

'Oh.' Parminda sounded disappointed. 'I can't do the late session I'm afraid – well, not if I want to be late on Friday night.'

'Pass any ideas on to Zoe, then.' We'd reached the singing room and soon Lennie had us immersed in African chanting – not that chanting comes easily when your voice has deserted you.

'I have to dash – as usual,' said Parminda. 'If you see Jake on the bus, er – just say – no, don't say anything. I'll see you tomorrow. Byee!'

We'd finished relatively late. I was exhausted after all that time trying to stay upright in Lennie's presence. Tark was waiting for me with Lily. It occurred to me that he was getting further with his romance than I was! Jake appeared and the four of us set off for the bus home, now very relaxed with one another. 'Do you have Parminda's phone number?' Jake asked me. 'I seem to remember you getting it off her the other day.'

'Yes, it's here,' I said, and wrote it down for him, smirking quietly to myself. So he was keen, too! 'It's quite hard to get hold of her. Her dad usually answers and says she's busy.'

'I'll persevere,' he said solemnly.

'Are you going up to the park tonight for Stel's video?' I asked him.

'I'm going to write tonight,' he said. 'That's why I need Parminda's phone number.'

*

I went up to the park after supper. Mum wasn't quite happy about me going on my own, but honestly, it's only five minutes away and the dog walkers were always out in force at that time in the evening. I was a bit later than I'd intended because Alex had rung – chiefly because she wanted to back out of the romance deal. I told her no way, but it reminded me yet again that I wasn't doing at all well in the lurve stakes myself. Basically – as I'd told Lennie's photograph earlier – it was because I was in love with him. How could any of these boys measure up?

I strode up the hill, mobile phone in pocket. Mum had insisted on that. It was strange how reluctant she'd been to let me go. 'Be back by ten o'clock,' she'd said. 'Any later and I'll worry. Make sure you leave your phone switched on.'

'Any later and I'll ring.'

'OK.'

I did actually run all the way to the park. We were meeting at the top of the hill and I was out of breath by the time I got up there. And there was Stel pointing his camera at me.

'Good panting!' he said.

'Where are the others?'

'On their way I trust. You're still panting. Can I film you?'

'If you must.' He pointed the camera at me again.

'You look very sexy like that.'

'Stoppit. You're making me self-conscious. I'll go home again.'

He took the camera down. 'Sorry.' Suddenly a flock of starlings was overhead and Stel was pointing it at them instead. 'Fly, little birds, fly!' he said. 'Wicked! Come and look at this, Zoe.'

I looked on the tiny screen and saw it filled with birds on the wing. He'd turned up the volume so I could hear their wings beating. It must be so amazing to have a mind – and eyes – like Stel's. I reminded him about his idea for a shot of massive crowds polkaing down Red Square. 'You wait,' he said. 'The playground at the Centre is quite big. And so, of course, is this park. I don't let go of grand ideas that easily.' He broke off to film an aeroplane flying overhead. Simon was walking up the other side of the hill. Just as he reached us someone grabbed me by the waist from behind and startled me.

It was Lee. 'Well, hi!' he said. I spun round. As before, I'd thought for a split second that it was Lennie. Stel and Simon both turned on him.

'Hands off!' said Stel.

'Leave the poor girl alone!' said Si.

'You don't mind, do you, Zoe?' said Lee. He flashed me a smile.

'Lee's OK,' I said.

'I want you all down on that path through the trees at the bottom,' said Stel. We went down the hill again. The light was beginning to fade, which was just what Stelios wanted. Si went on with Stelios and Lee stuck by me. He was being terribly friendly.

'It's really nice of you to do this for Stelios,' he said.

'No nicer than you doing it!' I said.

'Well, I'm glad you're here,' he said. 'It's nice to see people outside the walls of the Centre.'

'You make it sound like a prison.'

'OK!' called Stel. 'You three! I want you to run along the path, Zoe first with Si and Lee alternately overtaking each other and dropping back, as if you're both chasing her and both want to be the first to catch her. See what I mean? And

I want you to really run. Sprint! I'll be running alongside you on the other side of the trees.'

What a weird half hour! We were all so knackered afterwards. 'Come and have a look!' said Stelios. We sat on a bench and he ran through what he'd done. It was so clever. There we were, pounding through the 'wood', breathing heavily, dusk falling. He caught the whites of our eyes, Si's and Lee's determination to be the first to catch me, sweat on Lee's face. It looked incredible on a tiny screen – it would look fantastic blown up. Stel was well pleased. 'Thanks, guys,' he said, beaming broadly. 'I think I've got almost everything I need now. Unless – Lee? Do you fancy doing some spinning for me?' Si and I looked at one another. 'I've got the torches,' Stel added.

'Fine, yeah,' said Lee and the two of them set off for the tarmac ball courts. Simon and I followed them. It was nearly dark now – heavy twilight. Si and I squatted in a corner. I didn't know what was going to happen – Lee and Stel had obviously discussed it before. I'd never even seen Lee dancing properly. Stel and he stood at some distance from us and then Lee took off to the far corner. It was chilly and I found myself shivering.

'Hey,' said Simon. 'Have my jacket.'

'It's OK.'

'No have it – and shut up. They're starting.'

Lee, a torch in either hand, was crouching. He rose up a little, and then proceeded to spin, half-crouched on one leg, the other pointed out, left and right by turns, towards us. It was beautiful. He was so controlled, and the lights in his hands made patterns in the darkness. There was nothing effeminate about the dance – it was purely athletic. And still I was struck as he came closer how like Lennie he looked from some angles (and believe me, I saw him from all angles as he spun towards us!)

'My calf muscles hurt just watching you, Lee!' Simon called.

'Amazing!' said Stelios. 'Don't worry, I won't ask you to do it again, Lee. Come and look!' We crowded round the little viewer again. How had Stel known it would be so effective? I put my arms round him.

'Stel, you're a genius. I'm impressed.'

'Well, thanks Zoe! Praise indeed from a highbrow like you.'

I looked at my watch. Oops! It was ten past ten! And I'd switched the phone off while Lee was dancing. 'I have to go. Who's on walking-Zoe-home duty?'

'Me!' said Lee, possibly before the other two even had a chance.

'Thanks,' I said, and quickly dialled Mum.

'I'm not at all happy about this,' she said. 'But we'll talk later.'

'I have to hurry, Lee,' I told him. 'Bye, you two. Oh – Simon! Your jacket!'

'You can have mine if you're cold,' said Lee.

'I'm fine,' I said ungraciously, hurriedly taking off Simon's jacket. 'We'll just have to run. My mother's none too pleased with me.'

So there we were, running again.

'I knew you must be a good dancer, Lee,' I said, between puffs, 'but I've never seen you before. That spinning stuff was brilliant.'

'Stel's idea. Your brother's a good dancer, too, you know. Talented family, eh?'

'Oh, I'm not much good at any of this stuff.'

'Lennie seems to think you're great with ideas.'

'Does he?' I stopped short.

'Yeah. He said so. And you're very – beautiful, Zoe.'

(Had Lennie said that, or was this Lee talking? I went from sheer excitement to anxiety in a split second, as I realised it must be Lee.) I set off running again, Lee in pursuit. We were soon outside my front door, and Lee was looming over me. I shrank from any advances he might make, not least because Mum was on the other side of the door. 'ThanksLeeseeyoutomorrow,' I gabbled, leaning on the doorbell.

'So there you are!' said Mum as I fell in the doorway, and Lee was off like a scared rabbit.

'Please don't be cross, Mum. Wait till you see what we were doing. It's so brilliant – you'll see why I didn't notice the time. I had to switch the phone off so as not to interrupt the filming.'

'Hmmmph.'

I gave her a hug. 'I'm sorry, Mum. I really didn't want to upset you. Honestly – Stel's a complete genius. You'll be dead impressed by his video.'

'I'll make you some hot chocolate.' Mum had calmed down, thank goodness. The phone rang. 'That's a bit late, isn't it?' she said. 'It can't be Dad – they're an hour ahead. Hope nothing's wrong.'

I picked up the phone. 'Zoe, it's Stel. I just wanted to thank you again for tonight. Two blokes running is one thing, but two blokes and a beautiful girl is quite another. I – just – wanted you to know.'

'My pleasure,' I said, sounding corny.

'Night, gorgeous,' he said.

'Night, gorgeous,' I said back.

'Who was that,' Mum asked rather sharply. She realised it wasn't Dad.

'Stelios,' I said. 'D'you know, Mum – two guys have called me beautiful tonight?'

'And so you are, sweetheart,' she said, and I felt forgiven.

I took my hot chocolate down to my room and got ready for bed. I pulled out the drawer with Lennie in it. 'Do you think I'm beautiful?' I asked him. I shut the drawer before he could answer.

I looked up in the mirror. I'm OK – I know that, but all I want is to be beautiful for Lennie. I don't really care about Lee or Stel – or Simon. Not really. Though I was hugely impressed by both Stel and Lee, their *energy*. (I know what Parminda would say to that.) They'd both gained in stature for me after tonight. I got into bed. Simon was nice, too. He'd been very cute with the jacket, very gentlemanly.

I lay down. So who was the romance to be with? I certainly had a choice. Well, Lennie was number one choice, naturally, but who would number two be? Stelios, Simon or Lee? Physically, Simon and Lee were more attractive, but Stelios had this brain, this vision. Stelios was going places.

I snuggled down. This was daft. They probably said things like that to all the girls. Anyway, what did I care? We were already half way through the week. Lennie was all I wanted, and tomorrow I would do everything in my power to make him want me in return.

SEVEN

THURSDAY: Day Four of the Project

Mum woke me on her way out on Thursday morning. 'Bye darling. Got an early assessment meeting. See you later. Tark's raring to go, by the way.'

I rolled over and looked at my watch. It was eight o'clock. Three-quarters of an hour until we had to leave. Ten more minutes under the duvet, thinking about Lennie. He'd liked my love scene idea, hadn't he? He thought I was an 'ideas' person. But I felt I had to do more to please him. If only I could be the one with the big idea, the final piece of the jigsaw that would pull the whole play together. Perhaps tonight – at the late session . . . Bother. I'd meant to tell Mum. Never mind, Tark could tell her. That's what little brothers are for.

There was a knock on my door and Tarquin came in with a cup of tea spilling into the saucer. 'Please get up soon, Zo,' he said, setting the tea down next to me. 'I want to be on the same bus as Lily this morning. Hey, guess what – I think I might have a girlfriend!' He smiled sheepishly.

'Congratulations, Tarquin Shaw.'

'I did only say "might".'

'Whatever. Clear off, if you want me to get up.' He disappeared immediately and I felt obliged to haul myself out of bed and into the shower. I wanted a bit of time to choose my clothes. I peered up out of my basement window. It was a clear sky – no wonder yesterday evening had been chilly. So, something summery plus a jacket for later. I've got a sexy top that laces up. That would do. Trousers? Skirt? No choice, Zoe! Loose trousers for moving about. Anything else would be uncomfortable and daft.

Tarquin had laid out my breakfast for me and cleared away his own. This was unheard of. That Lily must be some girl! 'Do you think we'll have enough items for the show?' Tark asked, as I ate my way through cereal and toast. 'Your fight scene's going to be good with our lighting. And there are quite a few more dance numbers. Lee's unstoppable. I can't believe I'm dancing, Zo! Promise me you won't tell my friends.'

'Oh yeah! Like I'm going to ring them up and announce it. Talking of Lee – he did this cool dance last night for Stel's video. Spinning – a bit like a Russian dance.'

'Like this?' Tark got down and did the same steps Lee had done in the park.

'That's right.'

'He's got us all at it. It's agony after a while. Come on, Zoe. I want to leave now.'

Dear old Tark. He's been at the grunt stage since he started secondary school – I can't get used to him talking and being enthusiastic. Thank you Lee and Lily, is all I can say. Dad will be utterly amazed when he comes home. 'Two minutes and we're *outta here*!'

Tark and Lily were dead sweet on the bus. They sat up at the front together laughing at each other's jokes. Jake sat with me. 'Hi. How's it going?' he asked.

'Fine. Did you get hold of Parminda last night?'

'I got hold of her dad several times. But no, it was rather frustrating. We're trying to find a way to link the scenes and I'd had a couple of ideas.'

'Try them out on me.'

'Oh, OK. Well, it was quite basic really. Just that we could be showing a newcomer round, and pointing out what was good and bad. Oh dear! That seemed really exciting when I thought of it last night. It sounds so lame now!'

'No it doesn't. It needs a bit more to it – but you have to start somewhere. Once you and Parminda start pooling ideas I'm sure you'll crack it.' No harm in pushing him in Parminda's direction – if he needed any help.

The warm-up session was just stretching exercises this morning. Lennie wanted to get our Creative Session out of the way quickly, apparently. He had another meeting to rush off to. I was worried that might mean we weren't going to have the evening session, but he soon put our minds at rest, by reading out a list of names that included mine and reminding us to meet in the Theatre at five p.m. Stel and Simon were on the list. Jake and Parminda weren't. There were about eight of us in all, including the sixth-formers.

We were just about there! The dance team and the drummers, with some scripting from the older ones, had taken care of the 'Melting Pot' idea. The African singing was to be included, though we weren't quite sure where it would fit in. There was the love scene and a few others which Jim was helping with. People were coming up with ideas all the time. I just wished I could come up with that crucial link. Every time I caught Lennie's eye, and he smiled at me, I just wished . . .

Yodo and Jim Wilde were hard at work when we went in to start the writing session. Yodo was drawing all these grisly pictures and Jim was writing words under them for him to copy. There seemed to be a lot of blood and guns involved – typical little boy's drawing! I remember Tark going through that stage. Jim got us all started as quickly as possible, and said he'd come round to us in turn.

Simon was on good form this morning. He looked even cooler than usual in a singlet and his hair was still a bit wet from the shower. His skin is a gorgeous golden colour – looks kind of good next to mine (I couldn't help noticing as we sat together at the computer). He was businesslike about the writing and we sorted out the scene surprisingly quickly.

'We're going to have to suggest who does this, you know,' said Simon. 'Are you sure you don't want to do it with me? I'll behave myself. It can be just a little kiss, you know. Not too sloppy.' He gave me his winsome smile.

'In case you hadn't noticed,' I said, 'there is a fine quiet little romance going on right under our noses between Parminda and Jake, only Jake is too shy to do too much about it. A gentle nudge from us in the form of this scene would just set them up nicely, and make two people very happy!'

'I thought you were cooking something up!' said Simon. 'Oh well, that's my little chance down the toilet!' He looked over at Jake and Parminda and laughed. 'No, you're right. They're half way there already.'

'Thanks.'

'Anything to please you,' he laughed. 'Lee get you home all right last night? No funny business?'

'Nah! I was fine.'

'On with the love scene, then.'

We did quite well. Simon wrote fantastic one-liners for the lovers that made them seem quite real, and harder when it seemed that fate would tear them apart. 'Do you think we need to be specific about why their families can't stand each other?' I asked.

'I think we can be quite funny – and have them quoting their parents saying exactly the same things about each other. Bit like me saying it would be funny to put my Japanese lot with your black lot. You know – in fact it's the same for both sides only they don't realise it.'

We managed to get it all down. We had to, since it was already Thursday and our players would need to learn their lines. Jim called us all together and we went round the group explaining what we'd done. Jake and Parminda were before us. 'We've written ours for one person guiding another round here,' said Jake.

'And we've written them for Simon and Zoe,' said Parminda, winking at me.

'Well, that's neat,' I said, 'since we were kind of hoping that Jake and Parminda would act our scene for us . . .'

'Let's get these scenes handed out, shall we? I've had a look at all your work in progress and I think you've done very well,' said Jim. 'You can look over them together and tomorrow we'll prepare them for the performance. You might have to read them on stage if there's no time to learn lines, but no one will mind.'

Everyone went round handing out sheets of paper, including Yodo, who, smiling for the first time ever, presented Simon and me with a sheaf of his drawings. We thanked him and took them with us to lunch, along with the script that Parminda and Jake had written for us. They followed behind us as usual, laughing at Simon's one-liners.

'This is really good,' said Jake, 'if embarrassing.'

'Not that embarrassing,' said Parminda. 'There's only one real clinch.'

'But what a clinch, eh?' said Simon, suddenly stopping to put an arm round me in preparation for a clinch of our own. I flashed him a shocked look. 'Only joking!' he added.

'Worth it though, to see the looks on all your faces!' We'd walked in through the door of the caff and Stel was looking as shocked as I was.

'Watch it,' he growled at Simon, and then, 'Make mine a kebab and Coke.'

'I'll get them today,' I said, and joined Parminda in the queue.

'Thanks,' she said. 'I'm glad you've made it funny and not too soppy. I'd've had a problem acting it in front of my parents.'

'That was Si,' I said. 'He made it funny.'

'Told you he was serious about scriptwriting.'

'I feel useless, Parminda. The only thing I'm any good at is ideas.'

'Well, Jake wrote most of ours, if it makes you feel any better. I can't concentrate when I'm sitting next to him!' She turned her back on where the boys were sitting and giggled. 'Isn't he cute, though? He's all shy. I love it! He's got to whizz off early today – some family outing.'

I had to order at that point, so I didn't take in what she'd said. Which was a pity, as it turned out . . .

Jake, Simon and Stelios were looking at Yodo's drawings. 'I used to draw like that when I was a kid,' said Simon.

'Yeah, me too,' said Jake. 'Loads of guns and knives and people spouting blood.'

'I used to like doing tanks,' said Simon, 'and soldiers being gruesomely killed.'

Parminda and I unloaded our trays of food. Stelios held Yodo's drawings up out of harm's way. 'Thanks, Stel,' said Parminda. 'Put them away, now. All those morbid kid's drawings don't go very well with food.'

'But Yodo isn't a kid,' said Stelios. 'He's twelve. And these are not "kid's drawings". There's nothing *imagined* about them. They simply show what he saw when the soldiers came to his village. I told you – he's a recent refugee. My mum works with them.'

We were all silenced.

'I feel awful,' said Parminda bleakly. 'I don't know what to say.'

'Me neither.'

'Well, he's safely with us now,' said Simon. 'I know this sounds really callous, but can we eat lunch before it gets cold?'

After lunch Simon and I sat on a wall in the playground looking at our script, and I could sense that Stelios didn't like it. He kept sticking his video camera up our noses. 'Stel,' said Simon, 'is this because you don't have any lines to learn yourself?'

'Just wait till you see this video, guys,' Stelios said. 'Lennie's going to run it in our group workshop. I spent half last night and all this morning editing it and it is so cool. Man, are you going to be proud to have known me one day.'

'All the more reason to get on with our lines now,' said Simon firmly. 'It's good this – sort of all-purpose link – but there's still something missing.'

'We'll sort that out at the late session,' said Stelios. 'We always do. Someone manages to come up with the very thing at the last minute. It's how Lennie operates.'

'Go and bother Lee or someone, Stel,' said Simon, good-naturedly. 'We've only got ten minutes until we start up again.'

'OK, OK,' said Stel. 'I'll leave you two little – alone together then.' (He didn't say what we were, just a sort of 'e-e-er' sound came out!) He wheeled round and pointed his camera at someone else. As we leafed through the script, Yodo's drawings kept surfacing. I shoved them under the pile each time – they were too distressing. And yet, and yet – the germ of an idea was just beginning to take hold . . .

Lennie was pacing backwards and forwards on the Theatre stage in front of a large screen as he waited for everyone to come in. Have you ever seen someone *in that much detail*? This has to be love. From the front row I saw every muscle in his chest under his T-shirt. I saw the exact colour of the flecks in his eyes and every single variation in his smile as he welcomed us. I could feel his breath as he spoke to people and laughed. I could see how his whole body slotted together as he moved. And all this as I sat squeezed between Stel and Simon, who seemed to be vying with each other for who could sit closest to me. I felt faint enough without being crushed to death.

'Our video backdrop,' said Lennie, with no other introduction. 'Courtesy of Stelios.' Asha dimmed the lights and we all waited expectantly. Stel had got someone to animate the letters F L I G H T so they fluttered across the screen and away into the distance to the noise of the birds' wings beating, closely followed by flock upon flock of birds which were soon heard to be panting as the picture dissolved into us as runners in the woods. It was almost too good to be a backdrop. Stel was tense next to me, rubbing his palms together nervously. Si, on the other side, was languid and relaxed, leaning on me whenever he or I appeared on screen. When it came to an end, the theatre erupted in cheers.

'Good, wasn't it?' said Lennie as the lights went on and the screen went up. 'On to the stage, everyone. I just want to run through your fight.'

*

It was another of those Lennie afternoons. I had permanent butterflies in my stomach, clammy hands, a croaky voice and legs that felt all trembly. And yet Parminda and I hung on for the African singing sessions.

Yodo and his sister were with us. I couldn't be sure whether they'd been with us the other two days or not. Parminda couldn't say, either. They both had this talent for merging into the background. Yodo seemed more at ease than I'd seen him so far, as if unloading his pictures and being given words for them had freed him of some of his burden for an hour or so. His sister still had this heavily veiled look. I dreaded to think what drawings by her might depict. Yodo actually joined in the singing, along with the stamping and clapping that accompanied it. I saw his sister standing on one side as if she really wanted to join in. Lennie approached her very gently – she flinched at first, but he managed to be so unthreatening that in a while she briefly lost herself in a little swaying. Watching her made me want to cry.

Our so-called song was fine. With another couple of days' rehearsal we'd have no worries. A thrill of excitement ran through me as I realised the time for the late session had arrived. Lennie came over to Parminda and me and put an arm round our shoulders. (Does he *know* the effect he has on girls like me? It oughtn't to be allowed.) 'So you're staying on, I hope?'

'Not me, remember,' said Parminda. 'I wish I could. But Zoe's the one with the ideas this year – and she's staying.' She looked at her watch. I didn't know how she could do anything with Lennie's hand dangling over her shoulder – I could barely manage breathing. Surely he must feel the heat radiating off my skin?

He gave our shoulders a squeeze (which nearly pole-axed

me) and sauntered off. 'We'll be in the seminar room, Zoe. See you tomorrow, Parminda.'

'You OK?' Parminda asked, looking at my flushed face.

'You bet!' I said. 'Only I have to find Tark and make sure he tells Mum I'm going to be late home. I didn't get a chance to tell her this morning. I'll come out with you.'

Tark was talking to Lee by the gate. I'd hardly seen either of them all day. Lee welcomed me with his pointy-cornered smile. He hadn't been at the group session when Stel's video was screened. 'You missed a good 'un,' I told him.

'He's been too busy teaching us,' said Tark. 'I'd better go, Lee – we don't want to miss the bus.'

'Hang on, Tark. I'm not coming with you,' I called as he went spinning, literally, out of the gate. 'Tell Mum I'll be back by ten!'

'OK!' he said, and headed for the main road, the bus stop, and another bus-top rendezvous with Lily. Oh well, Jake would just have to play gooseberry. At least Tark would only have to go one stop on his own. Any twelve-year-old could manage that.

'Are you coming to the late session, Lee? I can't remember if you were on Lennie's list.'

'Lennie's favoured few?' I couldn't interpret the look Lee was giving me. 'No, I can't tonight, I'm afraid. I've got a performance with the dance company. Only chorus stuff, but classy, you know? Shame to miss the session, but there it is. Lennie's had a lot of input from me this week.'

'What do you mean, Lennie's favoured few?'

'Don't listen to me. I don't really know what I'm saying. I think Lennie's totally amazing, a complete one-off. I'm sure one day we'll be able to tell our grandchildren we knew the great Lennie Grant. But he lets people get only so close, Zoe.' I knew he was warning me off, but I didn't want to be warned. I wanted to tell my grandchildren – dammit – I wanted to tell my grandchildren how I'd met their grandfather at a Theatre Project when I was nearly fifteen . . . Lee went off with a wave, leaving me on my own in an empty playground.

I called in on the canteen for a cup of tea and a biscuit before it closed. A couple of the older kids were there. I joined them and we made our way over to the seminar room in the Theatre where Simon, Stelios and three other kids were in conversation with Asha, Minna and Algy, waiting for Lennie to arrive. I sat behind them and took the time to leaf through Yodo's drawings again.

EIGHT

'Lennie's chosen few.' I don't think Lee was implying anything sinister, but there had been an edge to that comment – disappointment almost. In this case the chosen few were Simon, Stelios, me and five older kids. Well, Stelios was certainly going places and Simon's writing was, when I thought about it, totally amazing for his age (and for a boy!). I felt a little adrenaline surge at the idea of being part of this elite, but I don't think that's quite what Lee was referring to.

Seen in the sinister new light Stelios had thrown on them, Yodo's drawings were extraordinary. The words were written in faltering, newly learnt letters on the backs. I hadn't really taken them in before. There was 'My House on Fire' and 'Running Away', 'The Soldiers Kill my Uncle' and one that just had the word 'Shooting' on it. They were all about his past life – grey old London didn't feature.

Lennie came in. I sensed the ripple that preceded his arrival before I saw him, and sat up attentively. He made us pull two tables together like a conference table, so that we could all sit around it. He looked at his watch. Then he nodded at us and smiled. 'Good of you to come. Good of you to come,' he said, his nods and smiles encompassing us all. 'So. We've got two hours to pull our play into shape. I'm sure you can do it.' He pulled out copies of the list of items so far, and passed them round. 'Here's what we have. The running order is completely arbitrary right now.' He tipped his chair back and stroked his chin as he perused the list. This is what was on it:

OUTTA HERE!
1 Football Stomp
2 Green Song
3 F L I G H T video
4 African Singing
5 Loving Enemies *(Si's title)*
6 Melting Pot – dance and drum
7 The Fight
8 Wheels *(in fact a sound and lighting number)*
9 My House *(younger kids came up with this piece)*
10 Poverty Trap
11 Give the People a Voice
12 Link material *(Jake and Parminda's stuff)*

'I hope you're all as impressed as I am,' Lennie said. He turned to the other leaders. 'Can you guys just take us through the pieces? We haven't all seen all of them, obviously.'

I personally didn't know anything about Wheels, My House, Poverty Trap or Give the People a Voice, and of course the others didn't know about Loving Enemies being on roller skates and stuff like that. It was exciting. But one of the titles on that list had had an extraordinary effect on me. My heart started to thump, my stomach churned, my legs felt weak. My House: the idea that had taken hold a while back was now growing inside me at such a rate, putting out shoots and bursting into blossom . . . It was the IDEA! The link!

I hardly took in what everyone else was saying. They were trying to impose an order on the items, quietly coming up with suggestions which Lennie and the others discussed with them. I found myself making little coughing sounds and scraping my chair backwards and forwards. Stel and Si were on the other side of the table, but I realised they were looking at me, quizzically. Suddenly there was silence.

'Zoe,' said Lennie. 'We haven't heard from you yet. Any ideas to throw in?'

'Yes!' I squeaked. 'I've got it. I've got our link!'

'Uhuh,' said Lennie, waiting.

I scrabbled through my sheets of paper and slapped Yodo's drawings on the table. 'Here!' I said. 'My House on Fire!'

Everyone looked at me. Apart from Simon and Stel, they hadn't got a clue what I was talking about.

'Brilliant!' said Simon.

'Of course!' said Stel.

'Would you like to explain this flash of genius to the rest of us, Zoe?' Lennie asked. He directed one of his sexy smiles at me (which didn't help). Deep breath.

'OK. Yodo. Kid just here from a war zone. He ended up in our writing class because he wanted to learn to write – you know, abc and stuff. Jim has been giving him words to copy, but today Yodo was drawing pictures and Jim wrote down what they were of, for Yodo to copy. OK? The younger kids do a piece on My House, as a place of safety and security, within this community. Yodo does this picture – "My House on Fire".' I held it up. 'Yodo's story ties up with ours. There's what he's escaped from and what he's come to. You know, we have fights, and rubbish and poverty – but it's nothing compared to what he's seen! I think we should use that story as our link. Jake and Parminda wrote their piece for an old-timer showing a newcomer round, but if the newcomer is someone like Yodo it takes on a whole different meaning . . .' I was starting to gabble.

'Zoe,' said Lennie, 'I think you've cracked it.' And he smiled. His smile went on and on for ever and this time I knew it was for me. I felt as if we were the only two people in the room. I smiled back.

'D'you agree, guys?' Lennie's voice brought me back to planet Earth. Gratifyingly everyone nodded.

Suddenly I remembered where I was and the important stuff I wanted to say. 'We could use Yodo's pictures as backdrops sometimes,' I said, 'in contrast – or complementing Stel's video.'

'Better and better,' said Lennie.

'Yeah – this is what we needed,' said Algy. 'Well done, Zoe.'

'Amazing how it always happens,' said Stelios. 'Shall the rest of us just go home now, Lennie?' he added with a laugh.

'Plenty more work to be done,' said Lennie, 'even though Zoe's come up with the master stroke. Before we go I want the whole programme comprehensively mapped out – not least so I can get it printed off in time for Saturday.'

We slogged on. Up until this evening everything had

seemed totally relaxed and laid-back. 'Don't worry, it will happen,' everyone had said. And, of course, it had. But now nothing was to be left to chance. Lennie was tackling it like a military operation. He and the other leaders were drawing up a rehearsal schedule as we went along. The great flood of ideas and plans swept us along. Two hours later Lennie decided to wrap it up. The chorus of grumbling stomachs was getting too loud.

It all happened very quickly. Stelios and Simon never lost sight of one another as they said goodbye to me and set off for their tube. The others went their separate ways and there we were. I was left alone with Lennie. 'I'll be off then,' I said, heading for the bus stop.

'Want a lift?' said Lennie. All sorts of things went through my mind, but I came back to the fact that Lennie was a responsible adult running a youth programme. I would be completely safe with him. Safer than I wanted to be, really.

'I don't want you to go out of your way,' I lied. 'The bus is fine.'

'Up to you,' he said. 'I think I'd marginally prefer to deliver you to your door than have you go on the bus alone.'

'Nothing wrong with the bus!' I said. Crikey! Why was I defending the bus at this point? When all I wanted to say was yesyesyes!

'Look,' said Lennie. 'I don't want to coerce you, but I'm leaving now and I go near the park on my way home. I know most of you lot live round there somewhere. Follow me if you'd like a lift.'

'Oh, *OK!*' I said, though I don't think my reluctance was very convincing. 'Thanks.'

Lennie drove a VW camper van, old. It was like a little

house in there. It smelt of coffee. 'Travelling players' transport,' he said, as I looked it over. 'Nothing like a brew on the way to Cardiff or Truro.'

'Or a kip,' I said, and immediately wished I hadn't, as an image of a BED filled my mind.

'Can you manage that seat belt?' he asked, and I prayed that I could because I didn't think I'd be able to survive him leaning over to buckle me in!

'Sure,' I said, and concentrated very hard so that I didn't mess up.

He started the engine. Music from the Buena Vista Social Club filled the van. Wow, even the way he drove was sexy. How wonderful to be able just to take off, anywhere, at whim.

'And where to, your Ladyship?' Lennie asked, as if in answer.

'What do you mean?' I stuttered, thinking Land's End or John o'Groats at least, please.

'Which side of the park?'

'The far side I'm afraid.'

'No problem.' We were waiting to get on a roundabout at the top of a hill. On our right was Pizza Express. We both watched as a family went in at the door. Lennie was looking so longingly at them that he missed a gap in the traffic and the car behind us hooted rudely. 'Mmm, pizza!' said Lennie, sounding like Homer Simpson. 'I'm starving.'

'So am I,' I said. 'I've got enough money on me, Lennie. Can we buy one to take away?'

'You're on,' he said, and shot round the roundabout to a parking place right near the entrance. We'd hit the early evening rush when people take children out for pizzas. With friends I go at eight or nine, when the kiddies are home in bed and it's not so noisy. But the smell of fresh pizza was irresistible. 'We could sit down,' he said. 'If you're not in a hurry, and don't mind being seen with an old man.'

I wondered just how people would see us. I mean he was obviously too young to be my father. Older brother, perhaps? Or even – as boyfriend and girlfriend? 'Fine,' I said as nonchalantly as I could.

'OK, grab a table when they offer you one. I left my mobile on the charger in the van. I can't afford to miss too many calls at the moment.'

I stood in the queue, a little nervous lest someone I knew turned up. I reasoned with myself that that was stupid – I'd just tell them the truth, wouldn't I? We'd stopped off for a pizza after a hard day on the Theatre Project. Meet Lennie, the *old* guy who is one of the Project leaders. Hmmm. I was at the front of the queue and a waiter with an exaggerated Italian accent asked me if madam wanted a table for two. Smoking or non-smoking? I tried to remember if I'd ever seen Lennie smoking. I wavered, but luckily Lennie came back in at that point. The waiter turned his attentions to him, instead. 'Smokking orr non-smokking, sir?' he asked.

'Non, please,' said Lennie and we were shown to our seats like a couple on a date. Did I think that? I mentally slapped my wrist. We were just two hungry – er – people. I couldn't quite make it sound right in my head. We sat facing one another across a vase with two flowers in it. The waiter handed us menus and offered us a drink. 'I'll have a beer, please,' he said. 'Zoe? Drink?'

I had enough money for a Pizza Margherita, just. I couldn't run to a drink. 'Tap water, please,' I said.

'Cancel the beer,' said Lennie. 'I'm driving. Make it a Coke. Go on, Zoe, have a Coke.'

I didn't want to go on about the money, so I just said that

I really, really liked tap water. And that I wanted a Margherita – before Lennie could persuade me to go for something more expensive. Lennie ordered an American Hot and we sat back and waited. Lennie fiddled with his mobile. 'One missed call,' he said. 'Caller withheld their number. That's not much use. No message either. Oh well.' He smiled at me. 'I'll switch it off while we're in here. Nothing worse than tedious people who make you listen to their boring phone conversations in public places. We won't be long.'

I was still having trouble believing that I was out having a pizza with Lennie. I mean, I could imagine our grandchildren – but this! I surreptitiously pulled on a single hair to prove to myself that I was awake and fully sensitised.

'So, Zoe.' Lennie had his elbows on the table and wove his fingers in and out. 'You pulled the big one out of the bag. I kind of thought it might be you.'

'I've been worrying about it,' I said.

'Hey,' he said. 'You weren't meant to *worry*! I bet the other guys told you that Lennie would take care of it.'

'They did, actually.'

'I do take care of it, because I set it up. I'm never disappointed. With a good group – like you are – someone always comes up with the good idea.'

I wanted to tell him how inspiring he was, but I knew it would sound naff. I wanted him to praise me some more, because it made me feel so good, but it would sound as though I was fishing for compliments. I decided to talk about Stel instead. 'Stelios's video is brilliant, isn't it?' I said. 'He was filming us in the park last night.'

'Stelios is exceptional. In fact, being able to shunt someone with Stel's talents in the right direction is what makes my job worthwhile. There's just so much untapped talent out there. It never ceases to amaze me. And how much more there must be that never sees the light of day.' I nodded and smiled, hanging on to every word he spoke, but I was quite relieved when our pizzas arrived, because hunger and passion combined were making me lose the plot somewhat.

We tucked in. 'What about you, Zoe? Tell me all about Zoe Shaw.'

I told him between mouthfuls. 'Well, my mum's American. She's a psychologist. And my dad's a university lecturer . . .' I had the feeling he found my middle-class background a bit boring. I tried to think of ways to spice it up a little, but I couldn't think of any. 'And that's it, really. Mum's parents live in New York. Grandpop used to be a teacher.'

'New York? So have you been there?'

'Oh yes, lots of times.'

'I never have, you see. Never even been to the States.'

'Oh, you ought to. You'd love it.'

'Funny you should say that.'

'Why? Everybody loves it. Everybody young, anyway.'

'No, it's just that—' He stopped and chewed on a bit of pizza for a while. 'Never mind. There's something I can't quite talk about yet.'

'Oh, all right.' That was a shame. The conversation had been flowing so well, too.

'How about a pud?'

'No – I can't.'

'Not on a diet, surely. Beautiful figure like yours?' I blushed. Teachers aren't meant to say things like that. But Lennie had said it to me. He thought I had a beautiful figure. I looked up at him. 'No – I—'

'Go on! Have a tiramisu or something.'

'Lennie, I can't afford one.'

'Well, why didn't you just say so? Pud's on me. Prize for coming up with the best idea of the whole week. Chocolate fudge cake's good. Go on! You know you want it!'

Good job I don't try and read things into what people say. He was right of course. Yeah, I wanted chocolate fudge cake, but I wanted him far more. I wanted him to lean across the table and pick up my hands in his, and lift them to his lips and kiss them . . .

'OK. Thanks.'

He looked at his watch. 'Are you still OK for time? No curfew?'

'I told Tarquin to tell Mum I'd be home by ten at the latest.'

'Goodness – what were you planning on doing?'

'I just didn't want her worrying from seven o'clock onwards.'

'Fair enough.' He ordered the puddings.

The families with young children were leaving. The waiters were busy with bills. Not knowing what to say, I found myself looking round at them, working out the situations that brought them to Pizza Express on a Thursday evening. A lot of fathers only – access night, I suppose. A tenth birthday (I could tell from the writing on the balloons). A bunch of eleven-year-olds eating out on their own and having trouble divvying up the bill. The queue in the doorway consisted more of couples now. I had a horrible fantasy of one of my old boyfriends – Errol or Iain – turning up. I'd have to introduce them to Lennie, and I wouldn't know how to do it, because, of course, I'd dearly love them to think I was going out with him. I was gazing at the people queuing but I sneaked a look at Lennie. He was so relaxed in one way, but humming with energy in another. I saw women giving him a second look – not least because Lennie looks like someone famous, someone you ought to recognise. Perhaps they thought we were *both* famous! Holly always said I looked very glamorous in my lace-up top. I surreptitiously loosened it at the neck. At the same time Lennie rearranged his incredibly long legs under the small table and started to get them entangled with mine. My whole body fizzled with electricity and he tried to fold them back so quickly under his chair that he knocked the table and sent the flowers flying over me. The cold water was a second shock. I leapt to my feet, trying to wipe myself down with my paper napkin.

Everyone was looking at us. 'Really sorry,' said Lennie. 'Are you soaked?'

'No, I'm fine, honestly.'

A waiter came rushing over and moved us to another table with dry chairs. A second waiter brought our puddings. I couldn't speak, partly because I was grossing out on chocolate fudge cake but mostly because there was so much I wanted to say and couldn't. Had Lennie felt that same jolt when our legs collided? Was he in fact taking me out for a meal? Did he like me? Did he think I was special, even? 'You've gone very quiet,' he said, and gave my arm a little rub with his knuckle. He was trying to make me look into his eyes, I know he was.

I did. They were so deep brown and warm. I lost myself in them. 'Zoe—' he started, but then the waiter appeared and they sorted out the bill. I offered Lennie my five-pound note but he waved it away. 'We'll talk outside,' he said.

He guided me by the elbow past the queue at the door and held it until we reached the van. I couldn't believe what was happening. My legs felt like pieces of string. I had to tell him how I felt. I collapsed against the side of the van. He leant his arm on it above my head and looked down at me. 'Lennie,' I croaked. 'What were you going to say in there?

'I was going to say that you are a very beautiful, talented and special girl. I couldn't make these Theatre Projects work without stars like you – and since Community Theatre means everything to me, that counts for a lot. And though I didn't plan it – thank you for having dinner with me.'

I was practically sliding to the pavement by the time he opened the door for me and went round to the driver's side. Once in, he switched his phone on. There was a message this time. He put the phone to his ear, but I couldn't fail to hear Minna's anguished voice. 'For God's sake Lennie, answer your bloody phone. I'm ringing from the hospital. Tarquin Shaw was mugged on the way home from the Project and his mother's distraught because the daughter's gone missing as well. Come straight over as soon as you pick up this message.'

NINE

Lennie dumped the A–Z on my lap and said, 'Get me there.' Map reading isn't my strong point, but I knew the hospital was signposted once you got on to the Ring Road and I could navigate that far. While we were waiting at traffic lights Lennie rang Minna to say we were coming as fast as we could. A little later I tried phoning home, but Mum was obviously already on her way to the hospital, so I just left a message. I tried not to think too hard about what we'd find when we got there. I just had this little image of Tark dancing out of the gate at the Centre to catch up with Lily, the love of his life.

At one point Lennie patted my knee and said, 'Don't worry, I'm sure he'll be OK.'

'I kind of feel it's my fault.'

'How d'you work that one out?'

'Because I wasn't with him.'

'Rubbish. Kids travel on buses every day without being beaten up. He was unlucky.' We'd reached the hospital and had to negotiate the barriers and car park. They don't make it easy for you. It seemed to take an age.

We finally parked and paid and displayed and found ourselves running up to the main entrance. Of course the main entrance wasn't the entrance for the Accident and Emergency department, so we had to run half way round the building to find the right one. We fell panting on to the Reception desk where a pathologically unhelpful nurse waved us in the general direction of the waiting area. Fortunately Minna's hair makes her easy to spot. We picked our way over the crutches and buggies and stray toddlers to where she sat on her own. She and Lennie hugged one another. She hugged me too.

'Where is he? How is he? Will he be all right?' The questions tumbled out.

'He's being X-rayed. Your mum's with him. He's got a right shiner and they've had to stitch his forehead and there's a possibility he suffered a broken rib when they punched him in the stomach.'

'So he's OK then?' I said, relieved that Tark was still alive, and both Lennie and Minna roared with laughter.

'Apart from a black eye, a cut forehead, a punch in the stomach and a possible broken rib – yes,' said Minna.

'It's not funny—' I knew I was going to cry.

Lennie put an arm round me and stroked my hair. 'It's OK, Zoe. We know it's not funny really. Just a release of tension I suppose.' Minna also put an arm round me – so it didn't look too bad when Mum came back into the waiting area. I didn't spot her at first. She'd thrown on a fleece of Dad's and her shoulders were hunched with worry – not the smart Mum I'm used to.

'Mum!' I leapt out of my seat and ran to her. 'Where's Tarquin? What are they doing to him?'

'He'll be OK, darling. They're finishing cleaning him up while they wait for the results of the X-rays. He's amazingly cheerful, considering.'

'*Cheerful?*'

We sat down with Lennie and Minna. 'I think he feels a bit of a hero now he's survived a mugging. I've been trying to piece together what happened, but it's not altogether clear yet.'

'The bus company rang me,' Minna said. 'They'd rung your home and found you weren't there, but Tarquin had a Project leaflet on him, with a phone number.'

'Bus company?' I was confused.

'He was actually mugged on the bus,' Mum said.

'Oh dear. That makes it even worse that I wasn't with him.'

'We'll discuss that later,' said Mum. 'But an elderly gent found Tark and told the driver. He'd seen the muggers running off when he'd got on – but he said he was used to that sort of behaviour and didn't think anything of it. Until he went upstairs and saw poor old Tark. Lucky he went upstairs. Lucky they got hold of Minna to come and be with him. I didn't get home until six.'

'Did they take anything?'

'Just the money he had on him – a fiver.' (Our emergency money – like the fiver Lennie had waved away.) Mum sank her hands into the pockets of Dad's fleece and subconsciously sniffed at the collar.

'Wish Dad was here,' I said.

'At least we've found you, Zoe love,' she said. 'You see, Minna told me about Tarquin, but of course she didn't know where you were. And I didn't want to ask Tarquin because I didn't want to worry him. They've both told me since that you were at the late session – but why didn't you go straight home, darling? I was worried sick when I kept phoning and getting no reply. I thought you'd been mugged too.'

While Mum was talking I couldn't help catching snatches of the conversation going on between Lennie and Minna. 'Where were you?' she hissed. 'I thought you had your phone permanently switched on at the moment, in case you got the call from the States.'

'I was in a restaurant,' he said, 'and I had it switched off, OK?'

'Who with?' she demanded.

Lennie stood up. 'Will you two be all right now?' he asked us. 'We'll stay if you need us.'

'Thanks so much,' said Mum. 'No, I've got the car – we'll be fine.'

'See you tomorrow, Zoe,' said Minna. Lennie waved too, and they were gone.

Mum started talking again, but I wasn't listening. The call from the States? What was that? Lennie had been mysterious about New York earlier, hadn't he? Oh well. None of my business. I was wrung out. All that quality time alone with Lennie and then this Tark crisis. Any minute now, Mum was going to turn on me.

'Zoe? Zoe? You're not listening to me, I want to know

why you weren't with Tark. You know how I feel about you going around by yourselves.'

'He wasn't on his own, Mum. He was with Lily and—' A little bell went ping in my head. Parminda had told me in the caff. Jake had to leave early for a family outing – which would no doubt have included Lily. Tark had danced off to a rendezvous with no one, unless you counted his muggers.

'So what happened to Lily and Jake?'

'They left early today. I didn't take it in when Parminda mentioned it, Mum. I was thinking about something else. But Tarquin is twelve. It was broad daylight. You don't expect kids to get mugged on the bus.'

'You do round here.'

'We're meant to be saying how great this area is, not knocking it!'

'I still don't understand why you decided to stay on without him.'

'There was a later session for some of us older kids – I'd asked Tark to tell you. It wasn't a big deal. I just forgot to mention it this morning because you left before I was properly awake.'

'So where were you at eight o'clock this evening?'

I was spared from answering this direct question by the appearance of Tark, his head swathed in bandages. He had a fat lip but he was smiling. 'Nothing broken!' said the nurse who accompanied him. 'Antibiotics.' She shook the bottle of pills. 'And nothing too energetic for a bit.' She propelled Tark towards us by the shoulders and grinned down at him. 'And you'll be right as rain, Tarquin.' She looked at Mum. 'Good name. Tarquin. Off you go then.'

'I like nurses,' was the first thing Tarquin said. 'Perhaps I'll be a doctor when I grow up.'

'Perhaps you'll be a *nurse*,' I said.

'Come on, you two. Let's get home – and perhaps ring Dad. I expect you're both starving as well. I am.'

Tark filled us in on the way home. 'It's because I came out of the Centre dancing like a prat,' he said. 'Two kids follow-ed me all the way to the bus stop, calling me a pouftah and a lady-boy. I ignored them and started running for the bus – I wanted to catch the same one as Lily and Jake. But the boys followed me. I went upstairs – no sign of Lily or Jake – and these two jokers sat behind me and carried on calling me names and laughing. The other passengers probably thought we were all together. I told them to eff off, but that just made it worse. I realised that the top deck was emptying and I was going to be left alone with them up there, so I started to make my way to the stairs. Then one of them punched me in the stomach. I lashed out, but then the other one hit me in the face. The bus was slowing down, so they smacked me around for a bit, frisked me and skipped off at the next stop. I couldn't do anything. I just sat down. Then this old guy came upstairs and got someone to call an ambulance. I must have looked quite a mess. I couldn't really talk either, because of this lip. The nurse said mouths heal very quickly.'

'I think you're really brave, Tark,' I said.

'Huh – didn't feel brave when they were beating me up. I couldn't believe they were hurting me for no reason.'

'Did you get a good look at them?' Mum asked.

'Oh yeah.'

'What were they like?'

'The police came to the hospital and I described them, but no one will catch them. They were just – kids. Zoe's age. Fourteen or fifteen. One was black and one was white – so it wasn't racial. They were just – hard. Harder than me.'

'Ironic, isn't it?' Mum snorted as she parked the car. We went indoors. Home felt a very good place to be. Safe.

'I'll make some tea,' I said.

'Tea?' said Mum. 'A stiff gin and tonic, at least.' She took off Dad's fleece. 'Perhaps you could get those pizzas out of the freezer, though. I'm going to fix myself a drink and ring Dad.'

I made cups of tea anyway for Tark and me. A little bit of normality. Maybe it was the wrong thing to do, because once Tark was drinking tea, he started to shake and then to cry. 'S'OK Tarky,' I said, cuddling him like the nice big sister I am.

'It's getting to me now, Zo. I wasn't so scared back there. But no one's ever knocked me about for no reason before.'

'You'll never see them again.'

'Unless they hang around the Centre. I'm not sure I want to go back there.'

'We'll look after you.'

'I'd forgotten Lily wasn't going to be on the bus. She did tell me earlier, but I forgot.'

'I'd been told about Jake, too, but I forgot.'

'I'm glad they didn't follow me home. At least I feel safe here.'

Mum came back into the kitchen with the phone. 'Dad sends his love.'

'Oh,' said Tark, disappointed. 'Have you said goodbye? I wanted to talk to him.'

'He was in a noisy hotel bar – they had to find him. He'll call in the morning – they're two hours ahead of us. How are those pizzas getting on?'

'I – haven't put them in yet. Are you sure that's what you want? I'm not really hungry. I've – sort of – eaten.'

'I definitely want one. What about you, Tarquin?'

'I think eating might be a bit of a problem.' We both looked at his bandaged head and his fat lip.

'The lip's slightly less swollen already,' I commented. 'We could cut the pizza up into bite-sized pieces, like when you were a baby.'

'Good idea. Go on, Tark. You need something inside you.'

'What I really feel like is a bowl of cereal,' he said.

'Sorted,' I said, and put a pizza in the oven for Mum and poured cereal in a bowl for Tarquin. I wanted to stay in Mum's good books for as long as possible, because I had this nasty feeling that she wouldn't approve of me eating out with a much older boy, and it couldn't be long now before she wrested a confession out of me. I'm a hopeless liar.

Tark started flagging pretty soon after that and Mum put him to bed herself for the first time in about five years. I decided to quit while the going was good, and skipped down to my basement with a hastily yelled 'Goodnight'. I wanted to be on my own anyway – to savour in peace the time I'd had with Lennie. If Tark hadn't been beaten up I'd be so happy right now.

How had it gone? First of all Lennie had liked my Yodo idea – my 'master stroke'. And that was all I'd dared hope for! But then he'd offered me a lift and I'd been in the van. That van was so *him*! His little pad that smelt of coffee and marvellous long journeys to the highlands of Scotland and the rocky Cornish coast. I couldn't believe I'd been in there. It was so – *personal*, somehow. Music from Cuba. I'd think of him whenever I heard it now. And then the pizza. Just the two of us – I don't think I've *ever* eaten out with just one other person. We always go in a group. I never ate out with

Errol or Iain. And he'd told me all that stuff about creative expression and I'd told him about my family . . . Phew! Surely this would be a fine romance to report back on to the others! I hadn't even reached the bit where our knees had touched or when he'd said . . .

I pulled Lennie's picture out of the drawer and clutched it to me. He'd said, 'You are a very beautiful, talented and special girl.' I held the picture at arm's length: 'a very beautiful, talented and special girl'. I couldn't ask for more. Well, not much more. Yet. After all, he'd stroked my hair in the hospital. Actually, it had been a bit weird in the hospital, with Minna there. Why hadn't he wanted to tell her he'd been out with me? And there was something funny going on about America, too. I didn't want to dwell on that part.

Mum knocked on my door at some point, but I'm afraid I pretended to be asleep. I didn't want to be reminded of the horrible things that had happened to my little brother. I wanted to dream about my future with Lennie.

FRIDAY: Day Five of the Project

I was woken by the phone ringing upstairs. I heard Mum clomping across my bedroom ceiling to pick it up. Yesterday evening came rushing back to me. I burrowed back under the duvet for a while. But even while I was cushioned against the world by fluffy duckfeathers the realisation that today was the last day before the performance bore down on me. Everyone still had to learn their parts. Jake and Parminda had to practise on roller skates. Yodo's drawings had to be tried out on the overhead projector. Aargh! I threw off the bedclothes and propelled myself straight into the shower.

Tark was up. His lip had gone right down and his bandages had slipped to reveal some dangly bits of thread from the stitches and a stupendously impressive black eye. He said his chest was a bit sore, but he could still stomp. 'So I'm going in, Mum. I can't let everyone down.'

'No way!' said Mum. 'You heard what they said at the hospital. Take it easy today!'

'Come in this afternoon,' I told him. 'You won't miss much this morning. And you'll be a bit more rested. Can't he do that, Mum?'

'What – and go in on the bus alone again? I don't think so.'

'So are you going to work as usual, Mum? Or did you want me to stay behind with Tark?'

Mum sat down, heavily. Usually we get on so well, but it was as if we both knew that there was something uncomfortable still to be discussed.

'You're right, love. I'll have to take today off. Stuff my patients. It would be the same if I was ill. I'm not letting Dad go away in the holidays again, though, I can tell you.' She looked at Tarquin. 'Let's see how you go, Tark. I'll drive you in later if I reckon it'll do you more harm to stay away from all the action than join in.'

'Way to go!' said Tark.

I helped myself to breakfast. 'As for your antics last night, Ms Shaw . . .' Mum said. 'I haven't quizzed you yet, but Dad wants chapter and verse on where you were, so it'll have to come out sometime.'

'OK,' I said, swallowing hard. 'It's no big deal.' I was just going to tell her straight. It was the only way. The fact that I was in love with Lennie was my secret, nothing to do with her at all. 'Lennie gave me a lift home, because I was the last one left, and – ironically – he thought I'd be safer with him than alone on the bus.' Mum started to interrupt, but I carried on. 'We drove past Pizza Express and decided to get a takeaway, but then we decided to stay and eat there. And then he was about to drop me off and we got the message about Tarquin.' (Phew. Did that sound convincingly matter-of-fact?)

'Wow!' said Tarquin helpfully. 'Did sexy Lennie take you out for a meal then?' (Thanks, Tark.)

'It wasn't like that,' I said.

'I sincerely hope it wasn't,' said Mum, 'or that young man would be seriously in breach of his duties. Taking advantage of impressionable young girls. I'll have to talk to Dad about it.'

'Mum! That's ridiculous. Lennie means nothing to me.'

'Ooh! I've seen him looking at you!'

'*Have you*, Tark?' (Hey, that was so cool!)

'I like the sound of this less and less,' said Mum, bringing me down to earth again, 'and I'm sure Dad will be even more concerned. He knows all about how scrupulous you have to be with female students – and at least his students are over eighteen. Not fourteen, like you!'

'Mum, don't listen to Tark. I told you, I don't think of Lennie like that.' (I was lying, of course.) 'I'd better go. What shall I tell Lily, Tark?'

'That I'm coming in as soon as possible.'

'We'll see,' said Mum. 'I'm afraid I'll have to talk to Dad again, Zoe. This Lennie person shouldn't be allowed to get away with inappropriate behaviour in his position. I might need to have a word with him when I bring Tarquin in. Just to clarify the situation.'

'Stop fretting, Mum. It was all perfectly natural. It's not as if I fancy him or anything.' My fingers were tightly crossed.

'Hmm,' said Mum. 'Lots of things are perfectly natural –

that doesn't make them OK. I hope I can trust you on this one. Anyway, off you go. See you later, darling.'

TEN

Lily and Jake were appalled when they heard what had happened to Tarquin. Like me, they couldn't help blaming themselves for not being with him. Lily was desperate to see him, but I said he wasn't a pretty sight, with stitches hanging out of his forehead.

'Lily had her head stitched up when she was tiny,' said Jake. 'I can still remember how horrendous she looked. Not that she minded at the time.'

'Tark's surprisingly cheerful. He wanted to come in this morning, but Mum wouldn't let him. He was in shock last night though – shaky and crying.'

'Oh, poor Tark,' said Lily. 'I'll try not to act too horrified when I see him. But we need him for the Stomp, we really do. Lee will be devastated if Tark can't do it.'

Minna told everyone about Tark at the warm-up. Lee was over like a shot, full of concern about me as well as my brother. He remembered Mum's anxiety about me being mugged. When I said that Tark would probably be back in the afternoon he practically hugged me.

I didn't know whether to be embarrassed or flattered in the Creative Session. Lennie went on and on about the missing piece of the show for which Zoe Shaw was to be thanked. He was so bright and cheerful and full of compliments, but it felt strange: I'd wanted to please him so much – now his praise seemed slightly impersonal. Still, no time to dwell on things today! Lennie handed round copies of the running order and the rehearsal schedule (he must have stayed up half the night preparing it) and sent us off for a coffee break before the real hard work began.

Jim Wilde was also excited by the Yodo idea. So was Yodo! He was going to be a star. Jim offered to work it in to Jake and Parminda's linking script, which left them free to start rehearsing 'Loving Enemies'. Jim had also been incredibly busy printing out legible scripts from what we'd all written. I couldn't imagine either Mum or Dad being quite so dedicated to their jobs and students. Community Theatre obviously got people like that – as Lennie had been trying to tell me.

Si had brought skates – rollerblades – for both Parminda and Jake. Luckily he'd hung on to an outgrown pair that was fine for Parminda. They had both done a bit of ice-skating at the local rink, but they needed practice on wheels. Jim sent the four of us out into the playground. I sat next to Parminda on a bench as she laced up the boots.

'You OK about this?'

'Of course. I tried ringing you last night, but you were out.'

'At the hospital probably. Why didn't you leave a message?'

'It wasn't very late – eightish – and I was going to ring again, but I got caught up in something else.'

'I was out with Lennie then—'

'You WHAT?'

'OK guys!' Simon was in director-mode.

'Tell me after this,' Parminda said. 'I want to know EVERYTHING.' She got up and tottered over to Simon and Jake. 'Whooo-er!' And fell on her butt, just as predicted.

Si and I sat on the bench in the sun while Jake and Parminda went through their paces. Once they'd found their feet they glided around pretty well. Parminda was beautifully graceful from the start – after her initial fall – and Jake soon got into synch with her. I could already visualise this scene on stage. Looking at the freshly printed script I couldn't believe that Si and I had put it together in cold blood in a classroom. There was some passionate stuff in there. I must have been thinking of Lennie. But Si's one-liners were heartfelt too.

'What do you think, Zoe?' Simon's voice brought me back into realtime. 'Should they keep the skates on the whole time? It's effective. Like lovers being in a slightly different world from the rest of us.'

I watched Parminda and Jake gliding towards each other, crossing over, turning and returning. It was stunning. Her long dark hair streamed out behind her. Jake's floppy T-shirt flapped around his body, defining it.

'Hardly need words, do they?' Simon said. 'I feel kinda proud. Do you?'

'Yeah,' I said. 'We done good.'

'Maybe we should have given the parts to ourselves,' he said, leaning forward to fiddle with his trainer lace.

I had to squint into the sun to talk to him. 'But we don't fancy each other like Jake and Parminda do.'

Simon sat up. His face was shaded. 'No. Of course we don't.' He looked straight ahead at the skaters. 'So what do you think of them staying on skates all the time?'

'It saves taking them off! No I think it's good.' I looked at the script. The six short episodes had handwritten headings. *1 Bumping into each other. 2 Meeting for the second time and falling in love. 3 Meeting in secret because their parents disapproved. 4 Being kept apart (on opposite sides of the stage, having one-sided conversations with invisible parents). 5 Meeting in secret – the clinch. 6 The final scene (where they persuade their families that this is where the future lies).* Sounds corny, but it lasted less than ten minutes and it worked. I looked up at Jake and Parminda too. They had reached the clinch, and they were taking their time.

'Can't linger too long!' Simon called, a bit tetchily. 'Or we'll overrun.'

Parminda and I finally caught up with each other on the way to the loo. 'More!' she said. 'You can't just casually drop "I was out with Lennie" into the conversation and expect me not to be curious. Was this before or after you came up with the Yodo idea? Cool idea by the way.'

'Thank you. After.' I looked around to make sure no one was listening. 'It was nothing really, Parminda. Well, it was to me. But I mean it wasn't like you and Jake snogging away back there.'

Parminda's eyes were still shining. 'I should hope not! So where did you go?'

'He gave me a lift home – so I wouldn't get mugged on the bus. I'd told Tark to tell Mum I'd be back at ten, just to stop her worrying if I was late, and we got held up in traffic outside Pizza Express. The temptation to eat pizza overcame us both so we went in and had one. End of story. Because then Minna rang Lennie about Tarquin, and we shot off to the hospital.'

'But you must have chatted while you ate. What does Lennie talk about – if he's not talking about the Project?'

'He did talk about the Project. He's passionate about it. It was fascinating.'

'Are you sure?'

'Well, *he* was fascinating. I just like watching his mouth move when he talks.'

'That's lucky.'

'My mum's not too happy about it. She thinks he was taking advantage of his position working with young girls.'

'I expect she was just cross because you weren't with Tarquin. Anyway, Lennie takes his job far too seriously to be caught messing about with kids on the Project.'

'She threatened to "have a word with him" when she brings Tark in after lunch.'

'Poor you. It's much simpler if you pick on someone your own size, you know. Mind you, I could have problems with my family about Jake. Except I won't tell them.' We were washing our hands and checking our faces in the mirror. 'Sexy Si was looking lovesick this morning.'

'He's always like that. He and Stel are forever coming on to me. I don't notice any more.'

'Oh. I like Simon.'

'So do I. I like Stelios too. I even like Lee. But they aren't you-know-who.'

'I probably shouldn't tell you this, but both Stelios and Simon think you're going to get off with them at the party tonight.'

'You're joking!'

'No. Jake overheard them.' Parminda imitated both their voices – 'Shefancies*me*man' (Stel's high-speed talk). 'I think you'll find that she prefers me' (Simon's sleazy-Si voice).

'Oh well,' I said brightly. 'It's nice to be popular, isn't it?'

We were running through the fight scene with Lennie before lunch. The drummers and lighting kids were waiting to do their bit, but first we had to rehearse on our own. Lennie was hard to please. 'Come on!' he yelled. 'More aggression! You hate each other, remember? ACT!' That was the trouble – we'd all grown too fond of one another.

Lennie stopped us. 'Can someone dim the lights, please?

I've got a picture to show you on the overhead projector.' It was one of Yodo's. His handwriting saying MEN FIGHT-ING was shown below a hideous scene of men fighting with knives and guns. Loads of blood and tears spurting. Lennie paced around as he spoke to us. 'We're showing that this still happens all over the world. It's something bad. We don't know how to prevent it. Think of Tarquin Shaw's attackers. Think of *real* violence. It's shocking. It's *bad*. OK? Be bad!'

He put us with the drummers and then added the lighting. Tark should have been doing that. I found myself thinking of Tark's attackers and what I'd like to do to them. Suddenly the scene became powerful, unsettling. I realised how much violence scares me.

All through lunch I was dreading Mum coming in. What would she say to Lennie? I mean, she's a psychologist – she wouldn't just rush straight in with an accusation. But she can be pretty scary, my mum. And it wouldn't exactly help my cause with Lennie's heart. He'd steer well clear of me for the rest of the week.

I felt fragile but Stelios was being particularly raucous. He kept telling Androulla things in Greek and making her laugh. Just to be annoying. 'OK guys,' he said. 'So what about this party tonight?'

'I don't even know where it is,' I said. 'Is it a proper party with booze and music and dim lights?'

'So that's your idea of a proper party, is it, Zoe?' said Stel. 'That's my kind of woman!'

'It's not that I drink, really,' I said. 'I just wondered if it was that, or a sandwiches and juice in the hall affair.'

'I wasn't allowed to go last year,' said Parminda, 'so I don't really know what it's like.'

'You have to be over fourteen because we use a room in that pub down the road,' said Simon. 'It's not even a proper room, just an annexe. And they're a bit fussy about who they serve alcohol to. But it's darkish and crowded with loud music. That's party enough for me.'

'Sounds cool,' I said.

'Last year the older guys went wild and had terrible hangovers the next day. Lennie wasn't too pleased.'

'Lennie's not really a party animal, is he?' said Lee, joining us with a tray of food.

'Isn't he?' I was surprised.

'Doesn't like things getting out of control,' said Stelios. (Hmm, a fellow control freak, then.) 'So you're all coming? Zoe, Jake, Parminda, Lee, Androulla? I know you are, Si, you sleazy so-and-so.'

'More sleazy than usual?' I asked.

'I'd say so,' said Stel, grinning. Si smacked him one, a little harder than necessary, I thought.

I looked out for Mum and Tark all the way back to the Centre, but I didn't see them. I prayed that Mum hadn't already spoken to Lennie. We waited in the hall for him to start the afternoon rehearsal, which was a run-through of everything, just to see what needed most work. Lennie had already started the session when Tark came in and nudged me to go out and talk to Mum. I crept outside.

'Obviously I can't talk to your Lennie now,' said Mum, 'but I'm picking Tark up this afternoon and I'll have a word with him then. Dad thinks I should.'

'What can I say, Mum? It was perfectly innocent.'

'Next thing.' Mum was being efficient. (I couldn't wait for Dad to come home so she would loosen up and laugh again.) 'What's this about a party tonight?'

'Rehearsals go on until six. Then the older ones go on to

the pub. Which closes at eleven. Don't worry. I won't drink.'

'Have you thought how you're going to get home?'

'Oops.'

'Here's a twenty-pound note. I expect change. Here's the card for the cab firm we always use. Here's the mobile. You can take other people if you want. And you are to be home by eleven-thirty. OK?'

'Thanks, Mum.'

'I do trust you really, darling. Have a lovely time. I probably won't see you when I pick Tark up. Bye now.'

I rejoined Lennie's briefing. Everyone was about to head off to the Theatre, clutching their sheets of running orders. It was quite an exciting moment, waiting to see if it held together as a play, wondering how OUTTA HERE! would all fit together.

The excitement soon wore off as one ragged offering followed another. Everything that could possibly go wrong, went wrong. The video backdrop had the technicians screaming at each other and the overhead projector blew a fuse. It was a nightmare. Simon and I limped through our links with Yodo. Two hours later Lennie called us all together and we anxiously awaited his disappointed verdict.

'OK guys,' he said. 'That was terrible. But I expected it to be terrible. How could it be anything else? Having said that, there were some great moments, weren't there? The Stomp was terrific and so were the skaters. And lots of parts of other numbers, even if they didn't work in total. I want you to go and get yourselves some tea while I sort out my notes with Minna and Asha and Algy and then we'll get started on fixing it. Don't worry. You'll be great tomorrow. Believe me.'

*

'Is it always this bad?' I asked the others.

'Oh yes,' they said in unison.

'Worse, actually,' said Simon. 'A couple of years ago it didn't hold together at all at this point. At least the Yodo link gives it a point.'

'Doesn't really matter anyway,' said Stel. 'Does it? I mean, we want to get it as good as possible, but nothing hangs on it. We've had a good week. I've got a video I can use to show people what I can do.'

'Lucky old you, then, Stel,' said Parminda. 'The rest of us just have the prospect of making prats of ourselves tomorrow to look forward to.'

'Your thing with Jake was really good,' said Stelios.

'Well written,' said Simon.

'Well skated, I was going to say,' said Stel.

'Shame the video didn't work,' said Simon, sharply.

'Give it a rest, you two,' said Parminda.

'Sorry. Sorry,' said Simon. 'Just feeling a bit depressed, that's all.'

'Don't worry, Si,' said Stel, also conciliatory. 'You said yourself that it's always rubbish at this point. It's certainly been bad each of the three times I've been.'

'Has Lennie run it all that time?' I asked.

'He wasn't actually running it the first year, but he was so good, he might just as well have been. He was sixteen then.'

Lee joined us. 'Great that Tark's recovered enough to come back,' said Lee. 'I've told him not to overdo it. Good job he's too young to come to the party. You're coming though, aren't you, Zoe?'

'Yeah, yeah,' I said. I was feeling distracted at the thought of Mum picking Tark up and cornering Lennie. I needed to talk to my brother. I found him at a table with Lily – of course. 'Tark, can I talk to you a minute?'

'Go on. Lily doesn't mind.'

'I'm worried about Mum having a go at Lennie. He didn't do anything out of order last night. He was just being helpful.'

'Then he'll say so to Mum and she'll stop fretting.' I hadn't thought of that. 'Anyway, you know Lennie. He'll have Mum eating out of his hand in no time. She'll probably fancy him as well.'

'As well?' I said icily.

'As well as Lily,' he replied cheekily.

On with the show. The tutors worked us incredibly hard. Lennie took us through the African chant four times before saying, 'That'll have to do. I have to go. I'll see the older ones later on and the rest of you tomorrow. Try and get a good night's sleep!' We drifted back for our next briefing. Where was Lennie off to?

We were running through our link scenes – without Yodo this time. 'Where do you think Lennie's gone off to?' I asked Parminda.

'Dunno,' she said. 'Come on, you two. You're flagging. You can't let me and Jake down. We worked hard this morning on the stuff you wrote.'

I mumbled words to the effect that there was something in it for them, but Simon grabbed me by the hand (reminding me again that he has nice hands) and we set off on our tour of a grotty area of north London once again.

I earwigged the tutors' conversations. There was something mysterious about Lennie disappearing so often. Perhaps it had something to do with America? Then it occurred to me that he was well out of the way. Mum wouldn't be able to buttonhole him! Great! The future (i.e. the party) was bright.

ELEVEN

Thank goodness they'd laid on sandwiches and crisps for us in the pub. We were starving as well as exhausted – relatively speaking of course. (Yodo's story put everything in perspective.) I don't go into pubs much, so I'm not a connoisseur, but this was one of those huge Victorian, red-and-gold sort of places, and we had a whole L-shaped section to ourselves. We even had our own door on to the garden. I saw the landlord checking us out as we piled past.

Lennie wasn't with us. I'd reached the point where I felt more relaxed in his absence than in his presence – even though I missed him. It was very complicated. I was listening out for him all the time – waiting for the ripple that always preceded his entrance. But I was having fun with our guys, and Parminda and even droopy 'Droulla, though she didn't say much. Whenever either Simon or Stelios edged up to me, Parminda seemed to catch my eye. In fact Lee was the one who stuck closest. I didn't really mind. Lee reminded me of Lennie. You could say I was leading him on, but I was only flirting mildly. Honest.

The food kept us indoors. Once it was eaten, people moved into the pub garden which caught a corner of the evening sunshine. It was scrappy and the grass hadn't been cut, but sitting at one of the rusty tables with my new friends I felt as happy as I've ever been. What a week! And it was nearly over. This time tomorrow night we'd be acting our socks off and then that was it.

'We'll all stay in touch, won't we?' Parminda must have read my thoughts.

'Can't help it, can we?' said Stel. 'I see you at school.'

'I see *you* lot,' said Parminda, 'but not Zoe or Jake.'

Jake had his arm round her. 'You know you'll see me, Mindy,' he said.

We all waited for the retort, but none came. 'Boy, you *are* honoured,' said Simon.

Parminda grinned. 'Jake's different,' she said.

'Clearly,' said Stelios.

'I can't believe we won't meet up,' I said. 'Perhaps we should start organising a reunion, now.'

'Lennie did that for us last year, didn't he?' said Lee. 'But of course he won't be able to this year.'

'Why not?' asked Parminda.

'He's going to America, isn't he?' said Lee.

'I didn't know that,' said Stel, obviously not liking not knowing.

'I'd heard a rumour,' said Simon, taking the opportunity to show off his superior knowledge.

'He keeps having to go off for interviews and sort out references. That's where he is now,' said Lee. He looked at his watch. 'He should be here any minute.'

I felt short of breath. So that was the funny business about America. Lennie was going away. I might never see him again. I took a sip of my Coke but it went down the wrong way and I started to cough.

'Hey, are you OK?'

'Zoe, you all right?'

'D'you want a pat on the back?'

All of a sudden, Lee, Stelios and Simon were very attentive. And I didn't want their attention. I wanted Lennie more than I could bear. I got up and headed indoors.

Perhaps I should just get my taxi and go home now. What was the point in hanging around for Lennie? He was about to walk out of my life for ever. And even if something did happen, my parents would be on my back. It seemed so unfair. All I wanted was a sign that he felt something for me. A kiss, a touch, a loving word to remember him by.

I went in search of a loo while I decided whether or not to stay. Minna, Algy and Asha were propping up the bar. 'Hi Zoe! Not going, are you?' Minna asked.

'Party hasn't got started yet!' said Algy.

'You don't want to miss the dancing, surely?' said Asha.

'I'm just looking for the Ladies,' I told them.

'That's OK then,' said Minna. 'See you in a bit. Lennie should be here soon.'

As I left them I heard Asha saying, 'Ooh, I wonder how he got on. He wants this job so badly.'

'It's not fair to hope he doesn't get it so we can keep him, is it?' said Minna.

'Perfectly fair!' Algy said just before I went down the stairs and out of earshot.

When I came back upstairs, the party had moved into a different gear. Very few people were left in the garden, which was now in shade. People had crowded indoors and turned the music up, so they had to shout to make themselves heard above it. It felt like a real party.

Simon grabbed hold of me as I pushed my way into the room. 'I thought for a horrible moment that you'd gone home,' he said, 'or choked to death. Come and share this can of drink with me. Stel's found a bottle of wine, but we're saving that till later.'

We found ourselves a space with a little bit of wall to lean against. It was funny, because although we'd spent a lot of time working together, I'd never felt quite so – close – to Simon as I did now. Suddenly we were at a party and he was chatting me up. I was aware of the difference in our heights, his smooth, bare arms and his nice hands. 'It's been good this week,' he said.

'As good as usual?' I asked.

'I meant – it's been good working with you. I've enjoyed it.'

'It's not over yet.'

'I don't want it to be over.' He reached out his hand and touched my arm. I looked up at him. 'I don't want it to be over, Zoe. I – can we carry on seeing each other?'

'Of course,' I said, shouted in fact, as someone had just turned the volume up even higher. Stelios, I suspect, because he came bounding over and demanded to dance with me.

Stel's a flailing-around kind of dancer, whereas I tend to stay in the same place. He gambolled around me in circles, yelling at the top of his voice. 'One day, Zoe Shaw, when I'm a famous film director and you're a famous beautiful actress, will you star in my major film, and be up there on stage with me when we receive our Oscars?'

'Sounds a good idea,' I shouted back. The music changed abruptly to a smoochy number. Some people cheered, some jeered, but Stel pulled me in to his slightly sticky grasp. He still jogged about a bit, but now he spoke hotly into my ear. 'You're gorgeous, Zoe,' he said, and dropped his head on to my shoulder. I didn't quite like the way this was turning out, so as soon as the song ended I made my excuses and set off for the loos again. I remembered what Parminda had told me about Stelios's and Simon's expectations of this evening. I didn't want to join in their games.

I passed Lee, dancing alone. No sign of Androulla. Wow,

he was a wonderful dancer. I looked on in admiration despite myself. A wonderful dancer with a wonderful body – you couldn't help noticing. I caught myself lingering, but walked on before Lee got the wrong impression. He'd already seen me. 'Come on, Zoe, you promised me a dance,' he called.

'I'll be back in a minute,' I said, not wanting to offend him, but hoping that he might have found someone else by then. I did like Lee, and I fancied him too, but I suspected we didn't really have much in common. I knew that what I liked best about him was his similarity to Lennie.

Androulla was putting on lipstick. I looked at her face in the mirror. It was puffy and she looked droopier than usual, and she seemed slightly drunk. 'What do I have to do to make Lee fancy me, Zoe? I mean, what's the matter with the guy? Isn't he attracted to women?'

It had never occurred to me that Androulla might be interested in Lee. She's so negative about everything. 'Oh, I think he is,' I said cautiously.

'You know – Stel chats me up, Si chats me up, but Lee – who I want to chat me up – doesn't seem to find me the least bit attractive any more. Grrrr,' she growled at her reflection and dashed the lipstick against her lips. 'I'll make one last attempt.' She bared her teeth at me and snapped her make-up bag shut. 'Here goes. Just you try and resist me, Lee Ashton. Just you try . . .' I mentally wished her good luck as I leant towards the mirror to touch up my eyelash-defining mascara.

I checked my watch as I went back upstairs. It was nearly nine. Nearly half way through the evening and still Lennie hadn't shown. Looking purposeful, so I didn't have to dance with anyone, I went in search of Parminda and Jake to sort out taxi arrangements. They were in the garden, cuddled up on the seat with Parminda's leather jacket round both of them, talking to – Lennie!

My jaw dropped. 'Do the others know you're here?' I asked him.

'I doubt it,' he said, smiling. 'I've only just arrived. But I wanted to talk to you, Zoe.'

'Me?'

Parminda hauled Jake to his feet in a flash, and dragged him indoors before he had time to ask why.

Ohmygod. Had Mum said something? It was chilly outside, and I shivered. Or did he simply want to talk to me? To carry on where we'd left off last night when we got the news about Tark?

I sat quickly on the bench, hoping to pick up some of Parminda's warmth. Lennie sat down beside me. 'I heard your Mum was looking for me. Is everything all right?'

'Oh yes,' I said quickly. 'Fine. Absolutely fine.' I nodded vigorously to make my point.

'You don't know what it was about?'

I was still nodding. 'Oh, probably about Tark. That's probably it. Probably to thank you for going to the hospital or something.'

'Good,' said Lennie. 'Hey, guess what?' he said, grinning like a kid.

'What?'

'New York. I couldn't talk about it before, but I think I'm going there!'

'Wow!' I feigned innocence.

'I'm so nearly there, I think it's safe to tell people. They want me to run a Community Theatre Project in New York. Just one more little reference to pick up, and I'm there, man. I can't wait!'

'That sounds very exciting,' I said stiffly.

'I'll miss all this. Minna and Asha and Algy are like my family. I'll miss all you bright kids.'

'I was kind of hoping you'd be here next year,' I ventured.

'You'll do it again, though, won't you?' said Lennie. 'You're hooked, aren't you? There's nothing like it, I tell you. Maybe I'll do straight theatre again some day, but I can't imagine I'd ever get the same buzz as I do from drawing things out of ordinary people.'

'Thanks,' I said.

'Oh not you, Zoe. You're not ordinary.' I felt myself blushing. 'Well, no one's ordinary, but I meant kids like Yodo – kids who otherwise don't get any chances. It can change their lives. People like us can change lives!'

'What's this last reference you've got to pick up before you get the New York job?'

'I was offered the job half an hour ago. This reference is just a formality. It should be a cinch. It's only the Colonel. When he gets back from his sailing trip tomorrow. He has to confirm that I'm an upright citizen, safe to work with kids, that sort of thing. I don't have a lot of respect for the guy actually – he'd prefer it if we simply put on a play with talented drama students from your side of the borough. But he can't deny what we achieve. He'd like to, but he can't fly in the face of what we do for the kids or the quality of what we produce.'

'What will you be doing in New York exactly?' Little niggly thoughts of Mum making a complaint were worrying me. I wanted to push them aside.

'It's such a cool job. It's only two years, but it's everything I've ever wanted, with the Big Apple thrown in.'

'Two years.' I felt forlorn. I mean, it was fantastic to be out here alone in the dark with Lennie. He was talking to me like another adult. I was flattered. But it was hopeless.

'Are you all right, Zoe?'

'Everyone's been asking me that, this evening.'

'Why's that?'

Dammit, I had nothing to lose. 'I'll really miss you, Lennie.'

'Hey.' He tilted my head so that I was looking at him. And then he smiled – that special smile. I couldn't bear it. 'How old will you be when I come back?'

I tried to return the smile, but I couldn't. 'Sixteen,' I wailed. 'Nearly seventeen. That's so long.'

'I wish I could kiss you,' he said tenderly, 'to show you that I care, Zoe. But I can't, and you know I can't. There aren't many girls who could make me even consider putting my reputation on the line. It'll seem patronising however I say it – but you've come pretty close. You're a sweet kid – and now I must go in before I do anything I regret.' He almost sounded angry. 'Right now, my job comes first. I have to be squeaky clean. You do understand that, don't you? I would never, ever lay a finger on a fourteen-year-old student.' And he went in.

I stayed put. I was shivering now, and the tears were rolling down my cheeks. He did care. But he was a good guy. No one could ever accuse him of exploiting his position with his young students. My virtue was safe with him. Huh.

But he was coming back. He was running back. I could hardly see him through the blurry dark, but I staggered towards him and he caught me up in his arms. 'I knew I'd get you in the end,' he said, and finally I had the kiss I'd been waiting for.

'Wow,' he said, coming up for air. 'I didn't realise you felt the same . . .' I pushed my hair out of my eyes and gazed at him.

I was gazing at Lee. I screamed. 'Aaagh! Aaagh!' I backed away, but I couldn't stop screaming.

'Zoe! What have I done? I'm sorry. What have I done wrong?' Poor Lee was almost as distraught as I was.

'Just leave me alone! Leave me alone!'

I turned and ran into the darkest corner of the garden. Lee didn't follow me. I was shivering so much I thought my teeth would drop out. And then I was so sick into the bushes that I thought my guts would turn inside out. My sense of self-preservation told me that I couldn't stay out there getting any more chilled. I rubbed my arms and walked briskly through the garden to the front of the pub. Surely someone would lend me a jumper. I was thinking more clearly again. I felt in my bag. The mobile was there, and the money and the cab firm's card. I could ring for a cab now. I'd be home and in my own warm bed in twenty minutes.

I was about to dial when I saw that something was going on in the pub car park. A small crowd of onlookers – Project kids and members of the public – was gathered in a huddle. Even above the sound of my rasping breath and the blood beating in my ears I could hear strange noises emanating from the centre of it. Muffled thumps and yelps. A voice was saying, 'Somebody break them up.' It was Parminda. 'Get Algy or Lennie, Jake. Quick, before they beat the hell out of each other.'

I was drawn to the action, afraid of what was happening in the middle of it. Algy and Minna came rushing out and the crowd parted to let them through. On the ground, bleeding, sat Simon and Stelios. I retreated into the shadows. Parminda ran towards them and let fly a hail of invective that her father would have been deeply shocked to hear. Lennie came out and raced to his van, returning a couple of minutes later with a first aid box. He, Minna and Algy proceeded to clean up the boys and patch their wounds.

I heard Lennie say, 'The party's over. I'm going to drive you two idiots home, now. Come on, into the van – one in the front and one in the back with Minna.' They led Stel and Si off. 'See you all at eleven a.m. sharp tomorrow morning,' said Lennie to the rest of us as he slid his door shut.

'Well, where is Zoe?' Parminda said to Jake.

'How should I know?'

'I'm just worried. I want to see her before Dad comes to pick me up. What if something happened to her too?'

Androulla joined them. 'Something will happen to her if I get my hands on her.'

Parminda was startled. 'Excuse me?'

'Stel and Si both thought they'd seen her snogging the other one. That's why they were fighting. I tried to tell them I'd seen her too – but she was with Lee. Just shows what a jealous mind will do.'

'Lee?' said Parminda. 'Sure that's not *your* jealous mind at work, 'Droull?'

'I wish.' She went back indoors.

'Pssst!' Jake and Parminda looked about them.

'Pssst! Parminda!' Parminda realised that my voice was coming from the bushes. She tiptoed in my direction.

'Zoe! Come out of there, you looney. How long have you been hiding in the bushes? Stand up, stupid. Aren't you freezing? What's got into everyone tonight?' She hauled me out and wrapped her leather jacket round me. 'Come indoors. My dad's due any minute. He'll give you a lift home.' Gesturing at Jake, she wheeled me back round through the pub garden to our door and into the warm.

'Don't take this badly, Zoe, but I think I'll have my jacket back now. You stink. Have you been throwing up?'

'Yes. It's OK, I'll get a cab. Would Jake come with me?'

'You stay here, I'll get him.'

Our room was half empty. I didn't look very hard, but I couldn't see either Lee or Androulla. I'd have to face them tomorrow, but tomorrow was definitely another day. Parminda came back with Jake. She kissed him goodbye and said she was going to wait for her father out at the front. I gave Jake the cab firm card and the mobile and he ordered one for us. 'Five minutes. You look terrible, Zoe. Can I do anything?'

'Could you just borrow a sweatshirt or jumper off someone for me? I can't face anyone right now. Tell them I'll wash it and give it back tomorrow.'

Jake came back with Asha. She pulled a cardigan from her big woven bag and wrapped it round me. 'Get her home, Jake. Every year I tell Lennie we shouldn't do this the night *before* the play, but he insists it's part of the deal.' She sighed. 'Ah well, he probably won't be here next year, so perhaps I'll get my own way at last!'

Jake's a love. He made the cab driver drop me off first, and waited until I'd gone in my front door before driving off.

What he wasn't to know was that Mum was right there in the hall waiting for me, with a face like thunder and Lennie's blown-up photo in her hands.

TWELVE

Mum's angry expression turned to one of concern as soon as she saw me properly. 'Good grief, Zoe, don't tell me you've been mugged, too!'

I was about to start telling her some of what had happened but sobs came out before the words could emerge. Mum hugged me and soothed me. 'There, there, sweetheart. Just tell me nothing's badly wrong – no one's hurt you?'

'I got cold. And I was sick. But no one's hurt me. Not physically. Oh Mum!' I clung on to her and cried afresh.

Mum drew away a little. 'You're a bit whiffy, darling. I'm going to run you a nice bubbly bath and fix you a hot drink. D'you want a hot water bottle in your bed too?' I sniffed a yes. My mum's the kindest person in the world when you most need her to be. I followed her downstairs to my bathroom and sat wanly on the side of the bath while she ran it in and frothed up the bubbles. 'In you get, missy,' she said, 'and don't lock the door. I don't want you drowning in there, or doing anything stupid.'

I managed a smile. 'It's not that bad,' I said.

'I'm glad to hear it,' she said, heading back upstairs. I'd obviously had her worried.

I lay back in the bubbles, letting my hair float out round my shoulders. The hot water was bliss. My brain emptied. All the weird strands of the evening slipped back from my mental grasp into a tightly tangled ball of emotions that I'd have to unravel later. Mum came downstairs with my drink and hot water bottle. 'Into bed!' she called. 'Sleep well. I don't think there's anything wrong with you that warmth and sleep won't cure. I'll wake you at nine. We'll talk then.'

I stood up in the bath. My hair was full of bubbles. The bath was lovely but what I really needed was a shower. I let the bath water out and stood under the shower. I washed my hair vigorously. The words 'squeaky clean', 'squeaky clean', drummed a rhythm on my head. I wanted to wash it all away. Down the drain. I sat on my bed with my hot drink and dried my hair. I wanted to pull Lennie out of his drawer and talk to him, but of course he wasn't there any more. Mum had him. What was she doing, looking in that drawer?

I slipped into bed and warmed my feet on the hot water bottle. The chill I'd felt for the past few hours was finally dispelled. I'd meant to work it all out in my head before I fell asleep, but my body didn't give me a chance. I slept.

SATURDAY: Final Day of the Project

I woke at eight. I looked at my clock blearily, without taking in what eight o'clock on this particular Saturday morning meant. My duvet was too cosy. Keep the day at bay. Whatever it held in store, I didn't want it.

Gradually the fragments of last night came back to me. I checked the clock again. Thank goodness I had nearly an hour to myself before Mum was due to wake me. Lennie. Lennie had said wonderful things to me. All I'd wanted was a few words to show he cared – and I'd got them. Maybe he shouldn't have said anything, but he's human – still only nineteen. He knew I was in love with him and he was trying to deal with me gently. And he's honest too. He wasn't going to deny that he felt something. He knows he's going away anyway. That was the worst part. But Mum had found my photo of him. It would be obvious now that all my protestations about him meaning nothing to me were false. No. I'd face Mum later. Maybe I could hold out until Lennie had left the country.

But last night had been far more than just Lennie. There was Lee! I'd kissed him! And people had seen me. Eeugh! Poor Lee. He must be very confused. How could I ever tell him I'd thought he was Lennie? And then Androulla – she'd just informed me that she really fancied Lee, and the next thing she knew, there I was, snogging him passionately. How could I tell *her* I'd thought he was Lennie? What must they both think of me?

As for Simon and Stelios . . . were they really having a fight over *me*? That was quite cool. I slapped my hand. No. It was not cool, it was stupid. (Well, quite cool.) I thought back to the earlier part of the evening. If I'd flirted with anyone, I'd flirted with Lee. (I really owed that guy an apology.) Simon had said that thing about 'carrying on seeing each other' and Stel had asked me to fetch his Oscar with him. Nothing more. I hadn't made any serious promises. Offered my body. Well, really! Silly asses. Today was going to be horrendous, though. We all had to rehearse together. Put on a show! If anyone was in a fit state. What if they'd really damaged each other?

I could hear Mum and Tark overhead. Tark was thundering about. It didn't *sound* as if his injuries were slowing him down. I got up. Today had to be faced.

Upstairs Tark said hi, cheerily, and then made himself scarce. Mum said, 'Pour yourself some cereal, Zoe, and then we have to talk. There are some very serious questions to be asked before you go into the Project today.'

Eek. I poured milk on to some Sugar Puffs and started munching slowly. Waiting.

'Dad and I talked about this for hours on the phone last night.'

'What, exactly? I can't see that anyone has done anything wrong.'

'OK.' Mum reached out for my precious picture of Lennie. 'Why did you blow up a picture of Lennie, Zoe, and keep it hidden in your bedside drawer?'

'What is this, Mum? Some sort of inquisition? You had no right to look in that drawer. It's private!'

'Zoe, I was looking for the mouth-ulcer gel which I remembered giving to you, and which, incidentally, I found, in that drawer. Listen, if your teenage daughter swears there is nothing between her and a guy and then you come across a great big photo of that same guy, you start to ask yourself some questions. I want you to be truthful with me if you don't want him to get into trouble.'

'What do you mean, Mum? What sort of trouble?'

'He overstepped the boundaries. Young men in positions of authority where teenage girls are involved have to be trustworthy. Squeaky clean.'

'He's still only a teenager himself, Mum. Who cares?'

'Lots of people. His employer for a start.'

The Colonel! How awful if the one barrier to Lennie going to America was a complaint from *my* mother!

'Mum. Sit down. Look, let me explain. I promise I'll tell the truth. And you've got to be on my side, OK? Try and remember when you were my age – please?'

'Shoot.'

'You've seen the photo, Mum. He's gorgeous. And he's not only gorgeous, he's really inspiring. A really good guy. And he's very professional, and – he told me himself – he'd never, ever lay a finger on one of the kids he was working with.'

'So what happened the night Tarquin got mugged?'

'He gave me a lift home. We were going to pick up take-away pizzas but decided to sit down and have them there instead.'

'Did he know how you felt about him?'

'I'm not sure. I was probably being a bit obvious about it.'

'Has he made any advances to you, or given you any idea that your feelings might be reciprocated?'

'No, Mum. I mean – yes. I mean – no.'

'Make up your mind.'

'Promise you won't twist my words if I tell you?'

'Promise.'

'Last night I told him how I felt. Now you probably think he should have laughed it off, or been cross with me – or maybe never allowed himself to be alone with me. But he dealt with it. He was very kind, but he said it was more than his job was worth to act on his own feelings. And he went away. And he's going to the States any day now – for ever.' I started crying.

Mum patted me absent-mindedly, but she was frowning and chewing on a nail. 'I think you've probably convinced me, love, but Dad might not be such a pushover. The Tark business put the wind up him.'

'What was he planning on doing?'

'You know what Dad's like. He's very protective of his family. But he's spent years working with pretty girls and having to remain detached.'

'Mum, that's disgusting. Dad's really *old*, and he's married to you!'

'Same principle. Students are out of bounds.'

'Lennie doesn't treat us as students. He treats us as friends.'

'Dad wouldn't quite approve of that. Anyway – you ask what he's planning on doing. All he wants to do is to write to Lennie's boss and suggest that Lennie is "cautioned" if you like – and reminded that what he did with the best of intentions might not actually be the most appropriate way to behave with a fourteen-year-old. Nothing more. Just like a little tap on the wrist. Dad wouldn't want him to lose his job or anything like that. He's written something already.'

'Dad's written already – from Finland?'

'I mean he's just done a letter. He'll probably drop it in when he's home later today.'

I let this sink in. It really could happen. A little letter from my parents to a man he doesn't really get on with could ruin Lennie's whole future career. I couldn't let it happen. 'Mum, you've got to trust my judgement on this one. And you've got to convince Dad that it's not fair to complain. Girls are quite safe with Lennie. But the thing is, he won't be doing the Project again anyway. He's been offered a fantastic job in New York. And Mum – listen to this – this job is in the bag for Lennie apart from one tiny character reference – from his boss, the guy Dad wants to write to. Remember, you're meant to be on my side, Mum.'

'I'm trying to but . . .' Mum was still frowning when Tarquin came into the kitchen to get a drink of water. 'What do you think of Lennie, Tark?' Mum asked.

'Cool. Ace. Top bloke. Diamond geezer. Wicked.'

'OK, OK. I'll try and ward Dad off.' She seemed decided at last. Phew! Then she looked up to check that Tark had gone again. 'So does that mean you're nursing a bit of a broken heart, my love?'

I nodded, my eyes filling up. 'Just wait till you see him in action tonight, Mum. You'll see why he's so fantastic. And why I'm going to miss him.' I sighed. But then I decided I had to pull myself together. I poured myself another bowl of Sugar Puffs and ate them while they were still crisp.

It was only nine o'clock. I decided to veg out in front of the living room telly with Tark. He'd taken off the bandages and his eye-patch to reveal a very impressive black eye. 'Does it hurt?' I asked him.

'Sometimes. It's not too bad.'

'What about where they punched you?'

'I'm OK.'

'Unless Lily's already spoken to you on the hotline, I don't suppose you know that Si and Stel had a fight last night, do you?'

'You're joking? What was it about?'

'I'm not too sure about discussing these things with my little brother, but – apparently – they each thought the other had got off with me.'

'Wow! I'd heard the Friday party was always interesting. And, er – tell me, big sis – had either of them? Got off with you?'

'NO! Anyway, I can't tell you any more because it's far too complicated for your tiny little brain. Believe me when I say I didn't get off with anyone. Not really. Not knowingly.'

'I know when not to ask questions. Anyway, Jake will tell Lily and Lily will tell me.'

'You can wait then. I wonder what state Si and Stel will be in?'

'They'd better be fit enough. I know I had to recover. Though actually, Stel's done his video, and you could do the link scenes without Si couldn't you?'

'Everything will get sorted. After today I don't need to see any of them ever again. Let's just watch telly until it's time to go.'

Every cartoon, every video clip we watched seemed to have characters fighting each other. The 'thuds' and 'biffs' and 'oofs' were just like Si and Stel last night. But they'd been real then. They were hurting each other in earnest. It must have been painful.

I watched Tark – with his black eye and his bruises – watching the violence on TV. He didn't flinch. 'Has being beaten up for real made you think differently – when you see it happening on TV, Tark?'

'Nah. Cos they're only acting. It's *not* real. That's the difference.'

'I keep thinking about Stel and Si hurting each other.'

'Bet they feel stupid today. D'you think either of them will have a black eye?'

'I didn't get a good look at them. Parminda did. I suppose Jake might have had a close up, too, but he didn't mention it in the taxi.'

'He might have told his sister, though. Shall I ring Lily?'

'Go on, then.'

Tark brought the phone in from the kitchen. 'Lil? Hi, it's me, Tark . . .' (Bless him.) He wandered around with the phone, uttering lots of 'wow!'s and 'no kidding!'s and 'you're joking!'s. He went on so long in this vein that I started watching TV again, but eventually he rang off and sat down beside me again.

'Well?'

'Well,' he said, making me wait. 'Split lips, bleeding faces and ripped knuckles apparently. Standard fight damage.'

'So you would know?'

'Yup.'

'Any black eyes?'

'You can't tell straight away, can you?'

'And no stitching up, I suppose?'

'I don't think they had to go to hospital. Not like me.'

'That's pretty horrible actually.'

'Proud of yourself for being the cause of it?'

'Not any more. God, it really is horrible. I hate violence.' The image I actually had right then was of Si's beautiful face, damaged. I sat back on the sofa and drew up a mental list of people I didn't want to see today: Stelios, Simon, Lee, Androulla. Lennie was in a category of his own. I both dreaded and longed to see him. The person I really *did* want to see was Parminda.

'Pass me the phone, Tark.' I dialled Parminda's number. Joy! She answered herself. 'I need to talk,' I said.

'Fine,' she said. 'There's a whole hour until I leave. I'll talk for as long as you like if it's your phone bill.'

'Great. Hang on while I take the phone downstairs to my room.'

I made myself comfortable. I can quite happily talk on the phone all day. It's one of my talents.

'Are you OK this morning?' Parminda asked. 'I don't know what happened last night. It was mad. Were you really snogging Lee, like Androulla said, or was she just fantasising?'

'Here goes. Yes, I was – but not on purpose.'

'Say again?'

'I thought he was someone else.'

'Who, for goodness sake?'

'Lennie, if you must know.' (I thought of telling Parminda everything, but I stopped myself. My actual conversation with Lennie was going to have to stay a secret.) 'He'd just told me about going to New York. He said a few nice things and then went indoors. Lee came out—'

'You're not going to tell me all black guys look the same in the dark . . .'

'*I'm* hardly likely to say that, am I – to *you*?'

'OK, I'll let you off.'

'Lee and Lennie have the same build, but it's their voices that are alike.'

'I suppose they are.'

'So. Gaffe number one. I kissed Lee rather enthusiastically.'

'Was it nice?'

'Not bad, actually, but then I realised what I'd done and screamed and screamed. Poor old Lee.'

'Poor old Lee indeed.' Parminda laughed.

'I'd just been talking to Androulla in the loo about him. She told me she was out to pull him, you see. I'd no idea she even fancied him.'

'She's stuck pretty close, if you think about it.'

'What am I going to do, Parminda? She'll kill me.'

'Keep out of her way! You don't do much together in the play, do you?'

'What about Lee? I don't want anyone to know I was expecting it to be Lennie.'

'No, you don't, for Lennie's sake. Perhaps a little note for Lee, just saying sorry, can you still be friends, sort of thing?'

'Good idea. I'll write it now.'

'Hang on!' Parminda was enjoying herself too much to want our conversation to end. 'What are you going to do about Si and Stel? According to Androulla, they saw you kissing Lee too – from separate vantage points.'

'Simon must have been a long way away if he thought Lee was Stelios. And vice-versa. Lee could be confused with

Lennie, but not with either of them,' I said. It was bizarre. 'What were they all wearing last night?'

'Stel had on a pale T-shirt and jeans. So did Lee.'

'I remember Si was wearing a light-coloured, short-sleeved top – because it showed off his arms.'

'Did you, indeed? Shock horror – three blokes in light-coloured tops and jeans mix-up. Well, Zoe, I've said all along they all fancied you. I think they just assumed it was the other one – they've both been bragging about how they're going to go out with you. I suppose they've put each other straight now – about how it was *someone else* messing about with you in the garden.' She giggled at the thought of me and Lee.

'Don't! So how do you suggest I deal with them?'

'Apart from banging their heads together? You could always pretend you didn't know about the fight. After all, they never saw you lurking in the bushes, did they?'

'Good idea. I'll assume they both walked into a lamp post.'

'I feel a bit sorry for them,' said Parminda.

'Oh?'

'Well – they both had reason to think they were in with a chance.'

'Come off it!'

'You were so infatuated with Lennie, you didn't notice.'

'Now you're saying it's my fault!'

'Forget it!' she said. 'They're stupid. Hey, it's nearly time to leave. See you in a bit. Break a leg, and all that!'

THIRTEEN

I did a little note for Lee. It said:

> *'Lee – I'm really sorry about last night.*
> *The real explanation's too complicated –*
> *just believe me when I say I'm one confused girl.*
> *Don't stop being friends – please? Zoe xxx.'*

Next. 'Mum?'

'Uhuh?'

'Please don't let Dad write to the Colonel. It's bad enough for me that Lennie is *forbidden* to get too friendly. Like it's the dark ages! But I couldn't bear it if he didn't get this job because of me. He'd hate me for ever.'

'I'll try and talk Dad out of it.'

'Let him see the play tonight before he complains?'

'I'll do my best.'

Tark and I bumped along in the bus for the last time. It took even longer than usual because of all the Saturday morning traffic. Tark was hyper. I was in a terrible state – because of last night, because of performing, because of what Dad might do . . . I would so willingly have gone back to bed, and stayed there for a couple of days. Years. (Until Lennie came back from America.)

I stuck close to Parminda and Jake for the warm-up exercises with Minna, and for the Creative Session with Lennie. He bounced in and told us to work hard and have fun. I tried to glean something personal from what he said, but it wasn't there. Looking at him I couldn't believe that last night had happened.

The first bogeyman I had to face was Si. His hand was bandaged, and he had a few grazes on his cheekbones. One of his eyes looked a bit closed up and his top lip was slightly swollen. 'My, my,' I said. 'That was one vicious lamp post.' I didn't expect to raise much of a laugh. 'Are you OK?'

He looked at me warily. 'I can get through today,' he said. He certainly disguised the fact that he was in pain – to most people, but I could see him wincing sometimes. He had courage. I was impressed.

The first time I saw Stelios was, ironically, in the fight scene. Androulla and Lee were in there somewhere, but I managed to avoid them. Stel looked terrible. Simon must have had the upper hand last night. Stel was stooped and had one arm in a home-made sling, like a war casualty. He had a big dressing on his forehead as well. It looked dramatic. I was worried that the two of them wouldn't be speaking to each other, but they grinned wryly. 'Hey, Si,' said Stel. 'Remind me how to do this, would you? Right hook – feint – under and up?' His speech was a bit slurred.

'Watch it!' Si warned with a fat-lipped smile, shadow-boxing.

I felt enormously relieved. All right, they were putting on a brave front, but at least they were leaving me out of it. We only had half an hour for lunch so everyone stayed in the Centre instead of going to the caff. Lee was keeping out of my way as much as I was keeping out of his, so I'd have to seek him out to give him my note. I was still scared of running into Androulla on my own, so in the end Parminda offered to deliver my note to him.

I should have taken it myself. I was left alone at a table in the canteen, cuddling a cup of tea. Si and Stel hadn't been quite their rumbustious selves, but they'd sat with me and behaved relatively normally, still competitive about everything. They'd just gone to check out projectors for the video and Yodo's drawings. Jake and Parminda had wandered off to find Lee. As I sat there, Lennie came in to the canteen and ordered a coffee. He smiled in my direction as he waited for it to arrive, a smile that sent the world spinning. Just then, Androulla stormed up to me. 'Bitch!' she yelled. 'Who do you think you are?'

I recoiled. I thought she was going to punch me. 'Why did you hit on Lee, just when I'd told you I fancied him? Uh?'

'I didn't mean—'

'How could you not *mean* to snog him? Ooh dear – was it a case of mistaken identity then?'

She was leaning closer and closer across the table. I was tipping my chair further and further back. 'It was – sort of—'

'There's only one guy round here who looks at all like Lee—' She stood up, folded her arms, and sneered. 'Don't tell me you've got the hots for Lennie! You have, haven't you? Too good for our boys, then? Have to go for someone older?'

'I didn't say—'

'It's obvious. Ha! Wait till I tell Lee!'

Lennie was suddenly right beside her. 'If you start bad-mouthing *anyone*, Androulla – you'll regret it, is all I can say.' Androulla shrank, visibly. She practically spat at me, but she backed away and left the canteen.

Lennie sat down. I went all wobbly. I felt shy, as if I really had kissed him rather than Lee. Not that he knew anything about that. I half-wondered whether to warn him about Dad, but I couldn't do it.

'This time next week—' he said. He looked at his watch. 'This time next week I should be on a plane to Noo York!'

'Don't rub it in!' I found I could say that, and still smile. Something in me had shifted, just a little.

'But there's a long way to go before that fat lady sings!' he said. 'Time to go back to the fray.' He said it as if it was a chore, but there was still such a sparkle in his eyes and a spring in his step that he couldn't fool anyone. He *loved* this Project.

The first technical run-through was another disaster. Lennie, Minna, Asha and Algy took it in turns to yell at us, but they didn't seem too fazed. The projectors were working but now the screen was misbehaving. I caught up with Parminda while they were fiddling with it. 'Thanks for taking my note. Was Lee OK?'

'Did you want him to be heartbroken?'

'Of course not?'

'He was fine. Said he'd come and find you. Something about Androulla.'

'I've seen *her*.'

'Oh yeah?'

'But I'll tell you some other time. Stuff I don't understand.'

We were ready for the dress rehearsal. Costume and Make-up had had a rather lean time of it compared with the technicians, but they'd had fun with the little 'Green Song' kids and the 'Melting Pot' dancers – that was the spinning dance. This was the first time the rest of us would see it done properly. In fact, it felt like the first time most of us had seen anything. Suddenly it was coming together.

They'd sorted out the technical problems and it was beginning to feel exciting again.

The whole play began in darkness with Stel's opening sequence of flapping birds, now with the letters of OUTTA HERE! flying off. Then the drummers started up quietly and the first sequence of Yodo's pictures came up, one after the other, starkly. It made my spine tingle. Our link scenes were all done in flickering light, like firelight. It felt dark and tense.

The second half was far jollier, but whenever it got too jolly – the younger kids doing their 'My House' number, for example – one of Yodo's pictures went up on the screen. I felt the message hitting home – as if it hadn't already: violence is so close to the surface.

Jake and Parminda on skates came quite close to the end. They were brilliant – light and breezy, and funny. My words sounded a bit turgid to me, but Si's one-liners brought the house down. I glanced up at him as we watched from the wings. I nudged him in the ribs. 'You're funny, you are,' I said.

'I know.'

I was looking forward to 'The Melting Pot'. The dancers, including Tark and Lee, appeared in the wings wearing what could only be described as grass skirts round their waists (over their trousers), drums slung across their bodies. The paper strips of 'grass' were plain matt colours on top and shiny silver underneath, so they'd flash silver as the dancers twirled. Again, the number began with Stel's silent video, this time with Lee spinning round the dark ball court in the park with his torches. The dancers (with their drums) came spinning on in a line that whirled into a spiral as they all went into the melting pot, turning and turning. There came a point of meltdown (lots of drumming as they spun around) and then they shot out from the centre in pairs and threes. The drumming was part of the dance. I watched Tark concentrating and remembered the kid who had wanted to bunk off before we'd even reached the Centre. Lee had been a real friend to him.

They all spun off into the wings just before we took a break. Lee tapped me on the shoulder. He was sweating with exertion. 'Can I talk to you for a moment, Zoe?' he asked rather formally. I followed him to the back of the stage. He flung a sweatshirt round his shoulders and we went outside.

'Thanks for your note,' he said.

'I'm really sorry, Lee.'

'The explanation isn't too complicated, you know. I guessed the mistake you made. You thought I was Lennie, didn't you?'

I didn't want to say anything incriminating.

'You see, I've been there before, sort of. Last year I was quite keen on Androulla, but she had a thing about Lennie. Not like you. I mean she followed him everywhere, she wouldn't leave him alone. She was like a stalker, man! And then, when she couldn't get any response from him, she went on the attack, and she said she was going to accuse him of hassling her, make trouble for him. Know what I mean? She told me, and I cared enough to listen. 'Droull was only fourteen, but he was only eighteen, you know? It was hard for him. He talks to me sometimes. He likes you, Zoe, but I'm telling you, he wouldn't lay a finger on you, not while you're under sixteen and he wants to work in Youth Theatre.'

'I don't know what to say.'

'You don't have to say anything, Zoe.'

'Thanks, Lee.' I tipped forwards and pecked him on the cheek.

'I preferred it last night,' he said, and ruffled my hair. 'Only joking! Let's go in.'

I was beginning to relax. I was dying to go up to Androulla and say that I knew her little secret, and no wonder Lee wasn't so keen on her this year, but there wasn't any point. Anyway, Lee was too good for her. He was such a gentle guy.

The performance was scheduled for six. The idea was that we would all be home in time for supper. By five we were all hungry and tetchy. The course leaders decided to call it a wrap. 'Great stuff, guys,' said Minna. 'The audience is going to love it. No point in worrying any more now. Some things will work better than others. Just go out there and have FUN!'

We headed back to the hall for a ten-minute relaxation session before descending on the canteen for sweet drinks and biscuits. I found Si and Stel and Tark all comparing cuts and bruises. I had a fleeting moment of feeling responsible for all of them, but it didn't last. I felt too nervous about the performance. I was all jittery. So was Parminda. The parents were starting to arrive. 'Ooh,' she said. 'Why did I ever agree to do a love scene?'

'Because you wanted to get off with Jake,' I reminded her.

'So I did.'

'And because your parents sent you on a drama course, so presumably they expect something of the sort.'

'You're right. I'm just scared, OK?'

We went off to the girls' changing rooms together. 'I talked to Lee. He's a nice guy and I feel guilty. Did he ever tell you about Androulla trying to set Lennie up last year?'

'Now you mention it, I remember rumours. She's not so bad, Androulla. Unlucky in love! And screwed up!'

'Oh, that's all!'

'Hey – I never told you. Mystery solved! Stel said Androulla told him Si was with you. And Si told Jake Androulla had told him Stel was with you!'

'Just a little screwed up. My heart really bleeds for Androulla.'

'She was jealous of you. Could have been me if you hadn't let me have Jake!' I hit her. 'Oi! No violence!' We sat down next to each other ready to be made up.

I knew my parents were out there somewhere, and it was more than likely Dad had a letter in his pocket that could ruin Lennie's future. It was another reason for praying the performance would be brilliant. As the cast waited patiently backstage I looked around and marvelled at what a difference a week could make. I'd learnt so much.

Five minutes. Lennie did the rounds. 'Good luck, guys. This will be the best we've ever done. Mr Saunders is out there. Prove to him how brilliant the Project is, or next year you'll be doing *She Stoops to Conquer*!' He left us to it, and I wondered if I'd ever see him again after tonight.

Curtain up. We could hear the flapping birds' wings, and then the drums started . . .

We had to stay backstage during the interval. I was desperate to see Mum and Dad. Desperate to make sure Dad wasn't going to send the letter, but Minna said the younger kids got over-excited if they started mingling. The play was going really well – naturally. Si was with me. 'We said Lennie would make it happen, didn't we? Do you believe us now?'

'Lennie could make most things happen.'

'You reckon?'

'What do you mean, Si?'

'Are you as infatuated with the guy as ever?'

I looked at Si's beautiful face. 'Maybe not as much as I was.'

We romped through the second half. It seemed to go so quickly. I loved this half – there was one good number after another. Jake and Parminda were superb – the audience wouldn't stop clapping. Si and I were about to go on with a link scene. He squeezed my hand. 'We write a good romance, don't we?'

I squeezed back. 'Stop being so corny.'

I spotted my parents during the curtain call. It was great to see Dad again. I felt almost certain he wouldn't want to complain to anyone after what he'd just seen.

The Colonel gave a speech. Honestly, he made it sound as if he'd directed the whole thing himself, instead of spending the week sailing. He took all the credit. The leaders came on to bow immediately afterwards. Lennie winked at us all, and we gave them the biggest, noisiest, longest, stompiest ovation ever. Lee rushed into the wings and came back with four bouquets. He thrust one into my hands – 'Lennie!' he hissed; one into Parminda's – 'Algy!'; Tark's – 'Asha!' and took Minna's himself.

So I got my kiss. In front of my parents. Just as Tark got one from Asha. *It's the way luvvies behave, Dad*, I thought. But then I went back into line for the final curtain call, and all I could think was, *It's over*.

'Dad!' I ran and gave him a huge hug. 'We missed you, didn't we Mum?' I gave her a questioning look.

While Dad and Tark were punching each other's shoulders in a manly sort of way, Mum said, 'I don't think there's any way after that performance Dad would want to spoil Lennie's chances. You were all so good! I'd no idea that's what you were doing. Or that you'd written it all yourselves. Amazing!'

You could hear all the parents saying the same thing. And you could hear the same name cropping up in all the kids' replies: 'Lennie.'

Dad turned to me. 'No complaints, darling!' was what he said, and he gave me an extra hug. He looked around at the milling parents of this incredibly multiracial community. 'This is what I like to see. This is how it should be. This is your Lennie's vision, isn't it?'

'Not *my* Lennie, Dad.'

We were practically out of the door when Tark suddenly said, 'But I haven't said goodbye to anyone!'

'Me neither! Wait there, parents!' Tark and I dived back inside. We found Lee, then Lily, Jake, Parminda, Stelios and Simon. No Androulla, thank goodness.

We were all hugging and kissing each other goodbye when Lennie came by waving a piece of paper. 'This is it, kids! My passport to New York. The Colonel has given me his blessing! Promise me you'll all come back next year and keep the Project alive? Then I can leave with a clear conscience.'

He looked round at our group. His eyes were a bit misty. 'I'll miss you guys a lot. Take good care of all that talent won't you? Anyway, I'm leaving next week and I won't see you before I go, so it's goodbye. And if anyone wants a bed in New York, you're all welcome. Only perhaps don't tell your parents I said that! OK?' He waved back at us as he moved on through the crowd of kids.

'Come on, Tark,' I said. 'Everyone's leaving.'

'See you tomorrow, Lil?' he said, before following me. So

he was sorted. I'd said my goodbyes and we'd all exchanged phone numbers. There was nothing more to be said and Mum and Dad were waiting. I saw them standing there, my beautiful black Mum and my tall, fair-haired Dad. What a couple! I was so proud of them. They'd struck up a conversation with some other parents who were waiting – a Japanese woman with long, soft, black hair and an English dad with film-star good looks. 'We're Simon's parents,' said the woman to me. 'We've heard all about you!'

'Oh,' I said. 'Yeah, well, Si and I did a lot of scriptwriting together.'

It was time to go.

FOURTEEN

You think I didn't have a holiday romance, don't you? That I fell in love with someone who was basically out of bounds, and blew it? I might have pulled – once – but it was all a horrible mistake? Well, I'm sorry, but you're wrong. Josie was in Cornwall for two weeks. Holly came home and did family stuff for the last week, and Alex – I won't say how Alex spent the last week of the holidays, but not much of it was spent with me. So I had another whole week in which to fulfil my promise to the other three.

That night I crossed Lennie off my list. I mean, what a guy, but hey, he was off to the States for two years. I lay in bed and tried to figure out what had altered my feelings. It boiled down to two things, two equally compelling reasons for not spending a large part of my life hankering after a guy in New York who was five years older than me:

Androulla had actually done me a favour, in a twisted

kind of a way. The fact that she'd had a crush on Lennie last year made mine seem more – commonplace. It didn't make *him* any less special. And he had liked me . . . No! I was putting the Lennie episode behind me. Anyway, I hadn't enjoyed my run-ins with Mum. It would be a terrible hassle going out with someone they disapproved of for one reason or another. So. Droopy 'Droulls was reason number one.

Reason number two was less formed. Something was just beginning. A little embryonic glimmer of something. It stemmed from how I felt when I saw Si's face all cut about. First, I was reminded how beautiful it was, and then, I thought – he got that fighting for me. Huh! Another reason to thank Androulla! I'd brushed away the remark at the time, but I was touched when I heard that Simon had been talking about me at home. So I started to think about him. Differently.

By Monday I was hovering over the phone in a fever of indecision. Should I phone him? Would he phone me? Had I given him any reason at all to think it was worth phoning me? The phone rang, and I leapt a mile into the air. Tark grabbed it almost before I landed. It was Lily, of course.

I was still in my dressing gown. I was dithering that badly – I didn't even know whether to get dressed or not. I managed to have a shower. I put my dressing gown on again because choosing clothes was beyond my powers that morning. I phoned Alex. One of her six million brothers told me that she was at the tennis club. What a surprise! For the first time in my life I wanted *her* advice, and she wasn't there to give it to me.

I phoned Parminda. Her dad answered. 'Parminda is not at home,' he told me. 'Who shall I say rang?'

Damn! I needed female help here.

The doorbell rang. My heart started to thud. Perhaps it was Simon? This was ridiculous. How could it possibly be Si? He wouldn't just turn up out of the blue, would he? Tark let someone in. I heard Lily's voice. No, I wasn't going to stoop to asking my little brother's girlfriend for advice.

'Is your sister in? My brother's outside with Parminda.'

I rushed to the door. 'Hey, you two! Come in! This is brilliant!' I brought them in, took them to my basement, made them a drink. I felt a bit embarrassed in front of Jake in my dressing gown, but he was too wrapped up in Parminda to notice.

'Wow,' said Parminda. 'So this is your own space. It's cool.' She sat down on my sofa. 'It's funny seeing someone at home when you've got to know them somewhere else.'

'Are you two off somewhere?'

'Oh, yes. That's why we called in. We're going up to the café in the park. To meet a mate. Want to come?'

'Now?'

'Yes.'

'How long will you give me to dress?'

'No more than five minutes. Come on, Jake, let's leave the lady to it. We'll wait upstairs.'

I peered up through my basement window at the sky. It was a clear late-summer blue. I decided to wear a summer dress, for a change. I tied back my hair. Smidgen of make-up. Purse. And I was ready.

We walked up the hill to the park. The café was by the boating lake. It had been taken over at the beginning of the summer and served fantastic Italian ice-creams and nice coffee and muffins, home-made soup – that sort of thing. Last time I'd been in the park was with Stel and Si and Lee.

It seemed so long ago. 'Is this a mate of yours, Parminda? Or yours, Jake?'

'Sort of both of ours, really,' said Parminda. 'A guy.'

'Does he know he's got a blind date with your friend?'

'Possibly not,' said Jake.

'Is he good-looking?' I asked Parminda.

'Oh yes,' she said. 'Undeniably good-looking.'

The lake was rocking with families in pedaloes and rowing boats. The café was making the most of the last week of the summer holidays. Nearly all the tables were taken. We scanned the crowds for a few empty seats. Then a group suddenly vacated a table with a parasol under the trees. 'Grab it!' said Jake, and we installed ourselves, smugly.

'So where's the date?' I asked Parminda. 'Or is this a wind-up?'

'Coming towards us right now,' said Jake.

I turned round. Si was walking in our direction, peering through the hordes, jumping out of the way of splashing kids and ducks and trikes. He had a slow, easy stride. He wore shorts and a shirt. He looked – sexy.

'Whoa!' he said when he reached us. 'Oh no! You can't do this! You didn't tell me it was her!'

'You've set us up!' I said. 'What's going on?'

Parminda was giggling. 'You don't mind, do you?'

'Here, have a seat, mate,' said Jake. 'What does everybody want? I recommend the cookie-dough ice-cream.'

'Whatever,' said Si, dismissively. 'Honestly, Zoe, I had nothing to do with this. They just said they were meeting a mate.'

'Same here,' I said.

'I'll go and help Jake,' said Parminda, still sniggering. 'Give me your money, guys.'

We both handed her our money, but carried on staring at each other. 'I suppose I don't really mind,' said Si.

'I just wish they hadn't made a secret out of it,' I said.

'Would you still have come?' he asked.

'Oh, I expect so.'

'Yeah, so would I. I don't like people playing games with me, though.'

'Me neither.'

'You look very pretty in that dress. I've only ever seen you in trousers.'

'Thanks. You don't look so bad yourself.' Phew. Well, we'd definitely reached the end of that little exchange. We sat in silence for a while.

'D'you fancy going out in a boat after this?' he asked.

'OK.'

We both looked down at our hands. I sneaked a glance at his face. I couldn't resist reaching out to touch the newly mended skin above his cheekbone. 'Hey – it's almost healed. That was quick!'

He grabbed my hand before I had a chance to retract it. He held it briefly in both of his. 'You know what Stel and I were fighting over, don't you? Or rather – who?'

'I've been told, yes.'

'Good. Just wanted to make sure you did.' He let go of my hand. Jake and Parminda bustled up with a tray full of ice-creams, cappuccinos, soup, rolls.

'I like a big breakfast,' said Jake.

All of a sudden I wasn't very hungry. I toyed with my ice-cream. I noticed Si was doing the same.

'We – thought we might go for a boat ride,' I said. 'Didn't we, Si?'

'Go!' said Parminda. 'Don't mind us.' She was giggling again. 'See you soon!'

Simon and I got up. Si put his hand on my back to steer me through the crowds towards the boat-hire kiosk. I've lived here for ages, but I've never actually been on the boating lake. It seems to be the sort of thing visitors do at the weekends, and then it's more like the dodgems.

'Pedalo or rowboat?' asked the boat-hire guy.

'Rowing,' said Simon.

'I can't row,' I told him.

'I can,' he said. So it was settled. We climbed into the wet wooden boat. The skirt of my dress was instantly soaked through. 'Sorry about that,' said Si when I told him. 'I just prefer these because they're wooden. And I can show off my rowing skills.'

Si, rowing, was quite a sight, I can tell you. They put rowing machines in gyms with good reason. Six-pack, broad shoulders and good biceps, that was Si. I'd always thought he was good-looking, but what with one thing and another, I was seriously beginning to fancy him. He negotiated the other boats and rowed us round the back of the little island in the lake and tied us to a post there under a weeping willow. 'Come and sit by me, Zoe. We can take an oar each. I'll teach you.'

I stood up, making the boat tip violently, and tottered the two steps to his side. I stumbled on to him as the boat listed and he caught me. 'Whoa! Not so fast!' He kept his arm round me. 'Hang on a tick,' he said. 'I'll just ship the oars.' He pulled them on board and the boat rocked some more. By now I was kind of enjoying the way our bodies kept knocking against each other. 'Now,' he said. 'Before your rowing lesson,' and pulled me towards him. I just saw his bruised skin again before I closed my eyes and we kissed. It felt so easy and right kissing him. The boat bobbed about gently under the weeping willow, and we carried on kissing, minutes at a time, almost until our half hour was up. A few people wolf-whistled, but mostly they left us in peace.

I saw Si glancing at his watch. 'Better go,' he said, straightening up. 'You're lovely, Zoe.'

I stroked his beautiful, sinewy arm. 'So are you, Si.' I really meant it.

'Not sleazy?'

'Oh that, yes! But I'm not complaining.'

We rowed back together. It was one of the sexiest things I've ever done.

Jake and Parminda were waiting for us when we got out. Si and I walked arm in arm. 'Mission accomplished, I'd say, Jake, wouldn't you?' said Parminda. 'Anyone want to come swimming tomorrow?'

The last few days of the holiday were magical. I saw Si every day, sometimes with the other two, sometimes not. Stelios rang one day while I was out. Mum had answered. 'You didn't tell him who I was with, did you?' I asked, panicking.

'Of course not. I don't want any more fighting.'

Stel was someone Si and I never mentioned, but I thought I probably ought to raise the subject. After all, Si would be back at school with him any day.

'We'll be able to forget that fight when all the bruises have gone,' Si said. 'We were fighting over you, Zoe, but there were other things too. He's quite ruthless, old Stel. All that "sleazy Si" stuff is just to put me down. He has to be the winner. He always has to compete. Some blokes are like that. Maybe he's had to be a fighter. I dunno. We're mates, but sometimes we need time to cool off.'

'Do you reckon we'll ever do things all together?'

'Not yet.'

'Do you think he knows about us?'

'He'll have suspected it.'

I loved being with Si. We'd really got to understand each other when we were scriptwriting together. There was something to build a relationship on. It wasn't *simply* that he was good-looking and sexy. Honest. And right now, I can't imagine us ever breaking up. We've agreed to take it slowly. It's going to be harder to get together in term time.

There was a point, sometime around lunch time on Saturday, when a big plane was flying noisily overhead, that I thought of Lennie on his way to New York. I felt a moment's sadness, almost grief, for the intense feelings I'd had for him and for what was over. But then I got on the phone to Si and we started planning the evening ahead.

EPILOGUE

I couldn't wait for the sleepover. Alex wanted it at her house to start off with. Astonishing! No one ever goes to Alex's. She's always tried to keep us away before. Something must have changed. We agreed to have it at my house in the end – there's more room in my basement, and food is never a problem. Mum just points us in the direction of the freezer.

It was great to see everyone again. It felt like so much more than a fortnight since we'd met at Holly's. Alex was extraordinary. She'd scraped her hair up and she had new trousers and a top that showed off a suntanned stomach. I gave her a great big hug – it was just so nice to have her around. I hoped she hadn't changed too much. Holly seemed a bit sombre, and Josie seemed older. I think there's quite a lot about Josie that we don't know. She gives the impression of being silly, but there could be hidden depths there.

Alex was desperate to start, so we let her. (Useful having an A and a Z.) She mucked about, Alex-style, doing silly voices and stuff, so much that we had to scream at her to get on with it. She's never been that interested in girly things before, least of all boys, but hey! Alex got herself a boyfriend and sorted out a few other problems on the way. I hoped he wouldn't take her away from me, but she assured me it wouldn't be like that.

Holly's week with the rich people sounded the complete reverse of mine! They'd made her feel like a poor little waif at times. My God. When I think of Yodo and his sister. Still, she said she'd seen one of my debating topics at first hand – people who hunt – and had all sorts of opinions of her own about it now. (I suppose the Project had been like one long debate!)

Josie had got into trouble in Cornwall. I don't think she'd behaved that badly. We all make mistakes, don't we? She tried to explain to us about a concert she performed in and how special it was. Perhaps I wasn't as sympathetic as I should have been – after all, I knew precisely what she was on about.

And then it was my turn. I started to tell them all about the Project and how fantastic it was, and how it brought all those people together and what it had done for me. I found myself sounding like Lennie, wanting to inspire everyone to express themselves and be creative for a purpose. Funnily enough, I didn't say much about Si. Looking back, the Project had been the big thing. And so had Lennie – at the time.

Right now it was brilliant to be with my friends. Anyway, Si wasn't just a holiday romance. I reckoned he'd be around for quite a while.

Josie

ONE

Cat's always got one over me. She sent this e-mail saying she was dying to see me, signing off with – 'PS I got my nose pierced. It's wicked.' What she meant was that she was dying to show off her nose stud to me so that I could be envious. Which I will be.

Cat is my friend in Cornwall. She stays in the cottage behind us and we're the same age (fourteen). I've seen her every summer since I was one year old, though we don't see each other the rest of the year. I live in London and she lives miles away.

What made the nose stud information harder to bear was the fact that I've also had some metal inserted into my face recently – that must-have fashion item: train tracks on my teeth. I've had a sort of miniature metal coat hanger affair that I wear at night for some time, but this was the big one, a whole year of agony and ugliness to look forward to.

As a list sort of person I had to try and sort out this sorry state of affairs:

Things you can't do with a fixed brace
Eat
Smile
Play the clarinet
Kiss

I thought that ruled out most of my life's essential activities, but then I had to try and squeeze out another list for things you *can* do.

Things you can still do with a fixed brace, maybe
Drink
Dress up
Swim
Sunbathe
Dance
Cuddle
(I won't go on)

So maybe it's not *too* bad. Mind you, several of the above recreations do depend on you being at least half way attractive.

I'm sort of looking forward to seeing Cat down in Cornwall – we have a lot of laughs together. And there are loads of other people that I can't wait to see. But before we go on holiday there's a sleepover here at my friend Holly's house. Holly rang me when I'd just had the brace fitted and it was total agony. I haven't seen her since she got back from a free trip to Barbados with her dad's school, so no doubt I'll feel envious of her too. She has some secret plan she wants to share with me and, unlike Cat, these are friends I feel safe with. (Sounds funny, I know, but Cat's someone who keeps you on your toes. You can't drop your guard.) And I adore sleepovers, especially when we talk for hours and hours about everything.

We had the video and we had the food. Then Holly made us shut up and listen. Alex never shuts up and listens – she's the tomboy, always telling jokes. But Zoe was curious and so was I. As I said, Holly spent the first half of the summer holidays in Barbados. So she's come home with a deep tan – and a boyfriend! So I am envious, twice over. Holly's never had a real boyfriend before, but she's madly in love with this guy, Jonty. She met a whole crowd of people on the beach who were rich enough to stay in a really posh hotel. Jonty's practically a member of the royal family, and Oliver O'Neill (you know, famous film director?) was there with his two kids, so Holly got to meet them all. But the weird part is, there was another girl at the hotel, called Maddy, and *she's* a friend of a girl I know. Small world!

And that brought us on to the thing Holly wanted to tell us. Maddy and three friends (including Hannah, the one I know) had made a pact that they would all have a holiday romance and then report back afterwards. Apparently Maddy got together with the film director's son in Barbados, and Hannah, who was on a music course with me, certainly had a thing with one of the guys (one of the few decent ones) there. Of course, I'd no idea she was doing it for a dare, it all seemed pretty real to me.

Holly wanted the four of us to do the same thing. All very well for her – she's already snared her man. Zoe won't have any trouble, but Alex hasn't shown much interest in the opposite sex to date, and as for me – well I don't exactly fancy my chances with this thing in my mouth! But Holly was so enthusiastic that I had to say I'd do my best. In fact there are quite a few guys I like in Cornwall, and it's a really romantic place, so perhaps it won't be too impossible a task.

There are only two more weeks left of the summer holidays, so the pressure's on. Holly's going to visit Jonty in his stately home but the other two are staying in London. Alex plays a tennis tournament every year, which could be interesting, and Zoe's doing a theatre project, so that could be a rich hunting ground as well. Hmm. Not such a bad idea after all. In fact, I was warming to it – it would be a laugh to hear what the others got up to!

*

When I got home next morning the car was packed for our trip to Cornwall. My brother Tim was already jammed amongst the beach towels and wetsuits with his headphones on, nose in a magazine, his hand dipping automatically into a packet of crisps, as if we were already driving down the motorway at eighty miles an hour.

'In you get, Jo-jo,' said my dad, 'and I'll pack the last things around you. I want to be on the road by midday. The thought of that first cool beer by the barbecue at the cottage is what's keeping me going.' Dad shares the cottage with his two sailing-mad brothers and their families. Sometimes we overlap with them, but it's better when we don't because my cousins are small and noisy and can be annoying. My brother Tim is fairly annoying too, but he's only a year and a bit younger than me (and almost taller). He has his own friends in Cornwall and I have Cat, so our paths don't cross that much.

Some people moan about going on holiday with their families, but I don't mind being with mine. Mum seems to enjoy me being a teenager and we go shopping together – I get most things I want in the way of clothes and make-up. Dad thinks he's dead funny and witty. He shows off to my friends – he likes them to think he's still pretty cool (as *if*) – but he's OK.

My parents are a bit over-protective, I suppose – they took me away from the comprehensive I went to with the others because they thought it was too big and impersonal. It wasn't bad, but I did feel intimidated sometimes, and I do prefer the school I'm at, so perhaps they did the right thing. I've never quite got over not fitting in at the first school. I tried to be like the others. Holly and I both got on fine at first, but somehow Holly made new friends more quickly. She never left me out – we're still really close – I just wasn't as confident as her. Before, it had always been Alex who was the odd one out, being so tall and boyish, but once she and Zoe got together they were cool in their own eccentric way. So Holly didn't miss me when I left – she's very pretty and she'll be popular wherever she is. I got on better at a girls' school – though even there I'm still conscious of the fact that everyone knew each other before I arrived and that I've got a lot of catching up to do. I've got some good friends now, and I've been invited to a few parties, so I shouldn't really worry. Luckily I get to meet people, especially boys, because of other things I do – like playing the clarinet, and going to Cornwall – surfers' paradise.

I think about boys all the time these days. It's terrible! I might be waiting for the bus or walking to my music lesson or just looking out of the car window, and if I see a boy I start to fantasise about him straight away. When I went on this music course earlier in the holidays, I spent half the time wondering which boys might fancy me. I had a big thing about one guy – a drummer. I kept thinking he was looking at me. He even spoke to me once or twice. But in the end he started going out with a really pretty girl who was older than us, so I suppose he hadn't been interested in me at all. I was quite depressed when that happened. I get crushes on guys in films and soaps – I think about them all the time and have little daydreams about meeting them and me being the only girl they really care about. That's partly why having this brace is such a downer – it makes it so much harder to fantasise about being kissed!

Dad threw in the last few bits and pieces. 'Strange to be leaving your clarinet behind,' he said. The brace means I can't play for a year at least, though I'm sure I'll pick it up again. I've already done Grade Seven. I can still play a guitar if there's one to hand.

'Dad? Do we need to bring a guitar or is there one already at the cottage?'

'There's usually a crummy one there,' he said. 'Anyway, there isn't an inch of room left in the car. And it's twelve o'clock, I want to go.'

Dad behaves like a team leader over the journey. He never lets Mum take a turn at driving. We set off with military punctuality. Two and a half hours. Stop at Gordano services. Another two and a half hours and we're there. Lots of travelling time for thinking and wondering how it's going to be. Will I fit in this year? Will people like me? Have I brought the right clothes? Do I *own* the right clothes? Cornwall holiday fashions are always slightly different from the ones at home – like a darker tan, they set apart the people who've been there for weeks. Surfie stuff – you'd expect that – plus little hippie touches, like bracelets or henna tattoos or hair wraps, and you can't tell exactly what they're going to be until you get down there. In London terms Cat isn't as fashionable as my friends, but in Cornwall she's always got it just right. I wondered what it would be this year. Well, the nose stud for starters. And I'd never be allowed one of those! No, I always have to go for the instant fashions – the ones that can be bought in beach shops.

I thought about the boys I know in Cornwall, surprise, surprise. If I'm honest, it's not many. I made a mental list. It went like this:

The boy at the bike hire place who I used to think was cool.
A couple of guys Cat and I used to see on the beach most
*   days.*

*The kids I see every year, of course – Archie and Harry,
whose dad sails with my uncle.*

Tanya-down-the-lane's older brother, Ivan.

*Seth who lives at the top and isn't happy unless he's
standing on a board of some kind.*

*All the boys who camp in the garden of Liza's house. They're
friends of Liza's older sister Ellie, and a bit too old for us.
(Ellie's boyfriend last year was gorgeous.)*

And each year there's an older kids' scene that starts in the
pub, but I wasn't part of it last summer. *This year it will be
different*, I thought. I will simply make it my business to get
to know people. And have a holiday romance, of course.

'Fifty pence to the first one to see the sea!' my dad said.

Already! And there it was. 'I can see it!' Tim and I both
yelled, as we always do.

'You'll have to have fifty pence each, then,' said my dad,
as he always does. Twenty minutes of winding, high-sided
lanes with leaning, windswept trees later we were there.
'Tredunnet,' it said on the gate, and we piled out of the car
and made our way up the long front path to the low doorway where my Uncle Alan and Aunt Pat and two small
cousins – plus their big white labrador – were waiting for us,
blue smoke already curling up from the barbecue, cold beer
for Dad and Mum at the ready.

Two

The cottage is brilliant. I absolutely love it. I knew which
room I wanted and I was desperate to bag it. 'Which rooms
are ours?' I asked my uncle. My parents were already

ensconced by the barbecue. They said the unloading could wait.

'We're in the yellow room and the boys are in the bunk beds next door. We thought Tim might like to join them.'

'Please can I have the blue room?' I asked, trying not to make it sound too desirable. If I was Tim, I'd definitely want it.

'Go ahead,' said the adults, wanting to get back to their conversation.

'Tim?'

'I don't care,' he said, miraculously. 'I'll go in the bunks – or downstairs if I don't like it.'

Great! I hauled my bag upstairs and made myself at home. The blue room is the smallest room in the cottage. It's over the front door and it has a deep window-seat where you can sit and watch over the front garden and the lane beyond. The cushion in the window-seat is covered with the same blue-striped material that the curtains are made of. There's a little hanging wardrobe in the corner, also blue-striped, and a pretty chair and chest of drawers. It's perfect. I always used to have to go in the bunks with my brother and cousins. The blue room was usually set aside for an elderly relation, but we didn't have any with us this time.

I unpacked my clothes and put them away in the drawers and the hanging wardrobe. It made me feel as though I was staying. I pulled out my mini speakers (birthday present) and my favourite CDs and set them up on the bedside table. My make-up went on top of the chest of drawers. Then my drawing things – I always have a sketchpad with me – in the window-seat. And then Monk. Down the bed. Monk, I'm afraid, is my oldest soft toy, a monkey (you guessed). He's been quite a comfort to me recently, with my mouth hurting so much. Anyway, no excuses. I'm sentimental about him and he comes everywhere with me. It was odd not to be unpacking my clarinet for a quick toot. It might seem a bit tragic practising a musical instrument on holiday, but I just say it's not tragic if you enjoy it. I must remember to dig out the crummy guitar, though Dad's bound to find it if I don't.

I opened the window and waved to the others down in the garden.

'Do you want a burger?' my aunt called up.

'You might as well,' said my mum, 'because I'm not cooking again later.'

I looked back at my little room, heard the seagulls calling and the sheep bleating in the field at the back. It would keep. 'OK! I'm coming down.'

It was so great to be here again. Tim was rolling around on the grass with the two cousins and the dog. As soon as I'd eaten my burger I joined in.

'Hi! Hi there, Josie!' It was Cat. She appeared at the side gate. It was nearest to their cottage which is behind ours. I stopped mid-roll and sat up, squinting into the sun. I already had grass stains on my trousers.

Cat looks like a cat. She has dark hair, short at the moment and still wet from swimming, though I detected some coloured streaks in there. Her green eyes slant upwards at the sides, accentuated by her good cheekbones. And of course there was the nose stud, twinkling. Cat wore a bikini top with shorts and flip-flops. I took in the extras, logged them so that I could replicate them as quickly as possible: a henna tattoo round the top of her arm; a leather thong with a square of tiny beads on it round her neck; a plaited leather bracelet; amazing nail varnish on her finger-nails and toenails.

'Hi, Cat.'

She came over. 'Wow, Josie, you've got train tracks!'

As if I hadn't noticed them myself. 'The nose stud is cool,' I said.

'There's a shop in Newquay where you can get it done,' she said.

I looked over to Dad, but he was making throat-slitting gestures. 'My parents might take some persuading,' I said. Cat and I usually settle in for a long gossip as soon as we meet up. I wanted to know exactly what was what and who was who. 'Have you got time to talk?' I asked.

'Of course,' said Cat, 'but I'm going down to the pub later. Do you want to come?'

'I don't know,' I said. 'Don't know if I'll be allowed.'

'But you're on holiday,' said Cat. 'Surely you'll be allowed? That's where everybody goes.'

I could practically see my dad's ears flapping. He was listening in disapprovingly. 'Let's go to your house,' I said. 'I want you to do my nails.'

'So when will we see you?' asked Dad, still wanting to keep tabs on me.

'I don't know,' I said, wishing he'd back off.

'Well, I'm going out in an hour,' said Cat.

'In an hour!' I said, and followed her.

Cat's cottage is almost directly behind ours in the jumble of buildings that make up the old part of the village. New and quite ugly houses line the road to the sea, but back here it's surrounded by fields and still pretty. I wouldn't want to be anywhere else, though I suppose the best place would be right down by the beach and the sailing club, so you could walk everywhere. That's where the pub is.

I followed Cat into her kitchen. Her parents were out the back, sipping gin and tonic and reading the papers. They're older than mine and seem vaguely amused by their only daughter. Cat gets away with murder. They probably think the nose stud is a hoot. Cat helped herself to a couple of cans of Coke from the fridge and offered one of them to me. We sat down. 'I want you to come to the pub because I want you to meet my boyfriend,' she said, watching my face for a reaction.

'Cat!' I squealed. 'Why didn't you say?' This would change things a bit. 'Come on, who is he? Tell me all about him.'

'He's one of the crowd down the pub. A windsurfer. There's a whole group of them. Gorgeous hunky blokes.'

'What's he called? What does he look like?'

'Big. Hunky. Windsurfery.'

'Was he here last year? Might I have seen him?'

'I don't think he was. I'd never seen him before. He's called Matt.'

'More! Tell me more! What colour's his hair? Is he cute or is he hard? Was it love at first sight?'

'Josie! It's not that big a deal.'

'But it is! My friend Holly's just started going out with a guy and she's madly in love with him and it's just so exciting! She can't stop talking about him.'

'OK. Well, he looks kind of cute but he acts hard. He's got dark hair and a good body.'

'Is he sexy? Is he a good kisser?'

'Oh come on, Josie. Give me a break. I'm not going to tell you everything.'

I was stung. 'You always have until now.'

'Well. This is different. More grown-up.'

'Oh. All right.' I felt hurt. This was meant to be the fun part, wasn't it? Talking about boys with your friends? But I tried to swallow my disappointment. I didn't want Cat to think I was some silly little innocent. 'Huh, say no more, Cat. I get your meaning. Now tell me about everyone else while you do my nails.'

We went up to her room – a beautiful attic that ran across the top of their cottage. You could see the sea from here. She sat me on her bed and brought over loads of little bottles. She shook them vigorously one by one. 'Feet first.'

'Harry and Archie? Tanya and Ivan? Seth? Liza and Ellie?'

'Harry, Archie and Ivan are all juvenile and I don't see them.' (So that was half my entire list of boys ruled out.) 'Tanya's broken her ankle and her leg's in a plaster cast, so she hasn't been much fun. Liza goes around with her. But it's worth staying in with Liza because of all Ellie's friends camping in their garden. D'you know there are about fifteen of them – mostly guys?'

'What about Seth? You forgot him.'

'Never knowingly not on a board. He goes all the way down to the beach on his skateboard. Ever so dangerous when there's traffic around. Then he spends all day on a surfboard and hitches a ride back!'

'Good old Seth. Does he look the same?'

'Got dreads this year. Oh, and train tracks like you, poor guy!' Cat had finished my toenails. They were a work of art. 'Hands,' she commanded, and set to painting my fingernails.

'What are you wearing to the pub?' If I could persuade my parents to let me go I wanted to turn up looking right.

'Nothing special. You know, trousers, top.'

Cat's hair had dried. 'Hey Cat, you've got colours in your hair.'

'Good, aren't they? D'you want me to do yours?'

I thought about it. Dad's protective of his darling daughter but he's learning to be indulgent. He's used to make-up and nail varnish but he hated it when I had my ears pierced. He might react badly to coloured streaks in my fair hair. Mum wouldn't mind at all, but I wanted them to let me go down to the pub, so I thought I'd better go easy. 'Tomorrow. Tonight I'm pleading for a late pass and I don't want to frighten my dad.'

'Make him say yes. I really want to know what you think of Matt. I'm cycling down in about ten minutes. See you there!'

'Oh there you are,' said Mum. 'We were about to set off for our traditional first night walk along the dunes to say hello to the sea. You're just in time.'

'I was about to change, Mum. Cat wants me to go to the pub near the sailing club.'

'The pub? I'm not having my fourteen-year-old daughter going to the pub!' thundered Dad, coming down the stairs.

In fact my uncle came to my rescue. 'Oh all the kids go there, Jim. They stand outside in a great heaving mass with their Cokes. Josie'll be perfectly safe.'

'And how do you intend getting there?' asked my dad, determined not to be mollified too easily.

I hadn't thought of that. 'I suppose I hoped you'd give me a lift. I'd like to hire a bike at some point, and then I wouldn't be so dependent on you.'

'And get yourself killed by some idiot coming too fast round a bend? Not likely.'

'We'll wait for you to change, love,' said Mum, the pacifier. 'Come down with us and we'll drop you off.'

'But I thought we were all going for a walk,' said Dad. 'I wanted Josie to be with us.' He wasn't going to make it easy.

'I'll come for the walk,' I said, sensing that I was going to have to work at this, but that it would be worth it in the end. 'And then, perhaps, I could go to the pub with Cat for a bit, and then ring you and you could come and fetch me.'

'Oh, taxi service is it now?' said Dad, but he was coming round.

'I just thought you'd prefer me not to be home too late,' I said sweetly, and knew I'd won.

I changed into my Kookaï trousers and top and slapped on a bit of make-up, though nothing seems to detract from the metal on my teeth. Sometimes I can hardly bear even to see myself in the mirror. I bunged a sweatshirt and my purse into a bag. I didn't know if I was wearing the right things or not. I swapped my sandals for my new trainers, a label no one can quarrel with, and went out to join my family.

We passed the pub on the drive down to the car park by the dunes. People were already spilling out across the road. None of them looked very old. I couldn't see Cat amongst them, but it didn't matter until I got back from our walk.

The dunes are lovely. When you've climbed up above the beach you can just let go and sprint with the wind in your hair along tiny sandy footpaths up and down the tussocky little hills. Mum and Dad walked along arm in arm while Tim and I chased each other all over the place. It was a beautiful evening – plenty of people were still in the water, paddling, rockpooling, windsurfing, sailing. Idyllic. It was great to be back.

I said I'd walk from the car park. I'd be fine as long as I had the mobile. But Dad insisted on coming with me. In the end it was go with him or don't go at all. He even put his arm round my shoulders, and I didn't dare shake him off – partly because I didn't want him to change his mind and partly because I didn't want to hurt him.

And there was Cat. She was cuddled up to a guy who I assumed must be Matt and she had a drink in one hand and a cigarette in the other – as did all the people around her. They were sitting on a low wall on the opposite side of the road from the pub. I spotted Tanya with her plaster not far away and Liza and Ellie. I couldn't wait to join them. 'OK, Dad? I've got the mobile.' I wanted to lose him before he took in what my friends were up to and changed his mind.

'Not so fast young lady.' Aagh. 'I want to find someone sensible to leave you with.' He peered into the gloomy interior of the pub. 'Good, I thought so, there's David.' (David is Archie and Harry's dad.) 'David? David!' he called, and David came blinking out into the road. 'I'm leaving Josie here for a while. Could you keep an eye on her? Thanks so much.' He turned to me. 'There, you'll be fine,' he said, and set off in the direction of the car park.

I wanted to die, but it wasn't over yet. 'Hello, Josie,' said David jovially. He has a loud booming voice, good for yelling instructions to his crew. 'Can I get you a squash or something?'

'I – I'm with some friends, thank you David,' I said. 'Over there.'

'Oh, jolly good, jolly good,' said David. 'Over there, did you say? Just so I can do my duty by your old dad. Fine.'

I crawled over to Cat and her group. 'Oh great,' said Cat. 'That's all I need, Harry and Archie's dad watching my every move.'

'Sorry,' I said. 'I don't really think he'll be looking in this direction, though, not if he's drinking inside.'

Liza and Tanya were more sympathetic. 'Parents!' said Tanya. 'Mine expect me to do everything with Ivan. It would be easier if Ivan had a few bad habits!'

'Mine have given up,' said Liza, laughing. 'With a houseful of Ellie's friends you have to! The lads are shameless. They're nice though. Mum adores them – twelve boys as well as three of Ellie's friends from school.'

Cat had calmed down. 'Hey, Josie,' she said. 'This is Matt.' Matt nodded in my direction but carried on talking to his group of boys. He was so-o-o good-looking. It was obvious that he was very popular. I felt envious of Cat all over again. I was going to have to work extra hard with this brace blighting my features.

'Does anyone want a drink?' I said, thinking that I couldn't start soon enough, as well as needing one for myself. I had twenty pounds of assorted savings and holiday money in my purse. That got Matt's attention all right!

'I'll go to the bar for you if you like,' he said kindly, holding his hand out for the money. 'They know me there. They think I'm eighteen. What are you having – Josie, is it?'

He knew my name! 'Ooh . . .' I remembered not to smile too broadly in case I put him off and tried to think sophisticated. 'I'll have an Archers please. Thank you.' And he was off into the crowd.

'That was really nice of you,' said Cat, and I glowed, feeling forgiven.

Matt came back with a huge tray of pint glasses. He handed me my little glass and bottle of Archers. Cat was having the same. 'No change I'm afraid,' he said. 'In fact, you owe me thirty pence.'

'I'm sorry,' I said, and delved into my purse. I probably had thirty pence in coppers. I put my drink on the wall and started counting out my change, though Matt seemed to have forgotten as he handed round the beers. I offered it to Cat. 'Here, you give it to him.' Cat took it and I sipped at my drink. Liza and Tanya had moved away to join a swirling group of slightly older kids – Ellie and the campers. They had a raucous game going that looked fun, but I felt pretty cool being with Matt and his friends.

I looked around. Leaning against the front of the pub near the door, slightly separate from any other group, were two more guys, who seemed to be gazing out over our heads towards the boats on the estuary. I don't know why I hadn't noticed them straight away, because if I'd been listing people in order of charisma (might try that later on) I could have been tempted to put them above even Matt and the rest of our lot. I watched them when no one was talking to me. They both had sunbleached hair and tanned faces and limbs, wore long shorts and T-shirts like all the other boys. They looked very easy in themselves, as if they were very old friends, maybe related. Everyone stopped to say something to them on their way in and out of the pub. I decided to go to the loo so I could get a closer look.

One of them was probably about eighteen, the other more like fifteen. They weren't saying anything when I went past, just two pairs of sea-grey eyes looking out to sea. They were both wearing leather bracelets, each with a tiny carved dolphin knotted in. I determined to find out more about the dolphin boys (as I'd already christened them), but when I came out of the pub again David was right in the doorway beside them and booming, 'Gracious, Josie. I'd almost forgotten you. How terrible of me! Would you like a lift up now or is your father coming to fetch you?' The younger boy caught my eye. I thought he looked sympathetic at first, but then I realised he must despise someone so pathetically controlled by their parents.

I kept my eyes on David. 'I'm fine, thank you, David. I've got the mobile to ring Dad when I'm ready.'

'Oh very sensible. I'll call in at Tredunnet to tell him I'm back but you're still at large. Don't want to neglect my duty. See you soon, dear. Harry and Archie are looking forward to seeing you too.'

I dived out and went back to my group, who somehow all seemed to have another drink. Cat was handing round cigarettes. 'Go on, Josie,' she said. 'You've got to have some vices.'

I saw David driving off, so although I don't smoke really I thought this would be a good chance to up my reputation. 'Don't mind if I do,' I said, and took one.

'There,' said Cat. 'This is just so cool, don't you think? Everyone's here. It's like a big party every night. So who do you fancy?' She nudged me. 'I think Paul over there is cute – not as cute as Matt, but I know he hasn't got a girlfriend.' I looked at Paul. I could see straight away why he hadn't got a girlfriend, but I didn't say that to Cat. The nicotine was going to my head and my knees. Matt was starting to grope Cat and I was beginning to feel like a gooseberry, too tired to chat up anyone, let alone hunky guys.

It was nearly dark. A pair of headlights drilled into the crowd, who were pressed against the edges of the road as a car pushed its way through. 'Oy!' shouted Matt, thumping the roof as the car edged past. Everyone laughed.

Except me. The window slid down and my dad stuck his head out. 'Anyone seen Josie Liddell?' he asked the world in general. I stamped out my cigarette and jumped in, if only to put an end to my embarrassment. I knew of course that the road was a dead end because of the sea, and the only way back was through the crowd again.

'Did you have a nice time, dear?' said my mother from the sofa as Dad and I ducked in through the low front door. No sign of Tim or my young cousins.

I said, 'Fine thanks. I'm off to bed,' and shot upstairs to the haven of the little blue room. I wasn't going to mention a round of drinks costing twenty pounds. I just hoped it had bought me a bit of popularity. I sat up in bed with my sketchbook and did a drawing of the dolphin boys – I just had to – along with a few frames of dolphins morphing into humans. Then a list of the people I'd seen already:

Have seen

Cat

Matt – Cat's gorgeous boyfriend. Everyone seems to look up to him.

The dolphin boys: two cool guys, v brown, blond, sort of Viking looks. Don't know who they are, but everyone seems to know them.

Matt's friends: Luke, Paul and Sebastian. I just about got them sorted out. Paul was one of the ones on his own.

Tanya (leg in plaster), Liza, Ellie.

Ellie's friends – recognised some of the boys vaguely.

Haven't seen

Harry and Archie, Ivan or Seth. Looking forward to seeing Seth with dreads and a BRACE like mine!

THREE

I slept in quite late. Surprising considering how bright the sunlight was and the noise my cousins were making. I lay there dozing awhile, listening to the seagulls, savouring the fact that I was in Cornwall in the blue room and that it was a sunny day. And that I'd slept right through the night without being woken by the pain of the train tracks.

I heard a strange gushing sound going down the side of the house and continuing down the lane towards the sea. It took me a few moments to work out that it must be Seth on his skateboard. I leapt over to my window, but I was too late. Seth with dreads and brace, carrying a surfboard and riding a skateboard would have been quite a sight! 'Outta sight,' he would have said.

I was up now, so I shambled downstairs in my pyjamas. Tim was eating breakfast on his own. I could hear the rest of the family dispersed around the house. Tim grunted at me. 'What was the pub like?'

'Cool,' I said, putting aside the hideous memory of the twenty pounds.

'Waste of money,' said Tim, as if he'd read my mind. 'Stick around with Mum and Dad – they'll buy you a drink.'

'Not the point, Tim. It's the company you go for. I only had one drink.'

'Bet it was that nasty sticky stuff.'

'None of your business.'

He sniffed my hair. 'Bet you were smoking.'

'All pubs smell of smoke Tim. Anyway, what's got into you?'

'Dunno. I just haven't met up with any of my friends yet.'

'You will, as soon as you get down to the beach. You always do.' Tim does all the Cornwall things, like sailing and windsurfing and proper stand-up surfing. Dad often says he should have been one of my uncles' sons. Dad was the least sporty one in the family, more into music than watersports. He'll go out in a boat, but he doesn't own one. One of the reasons we come to the cottage when we do is to coincide with a music festival in a little church a few miles away. It's one of those bizarre tiny festivals that attracts really big names. Some years they run a scratch orchestra and choir for kids. You have to be good, but you get to sing or play under a famous conductor. I don't talk about it to Cat and the others – people have funny ideas about classical music. Anyway, this year I can't play because of my brace, so perhaps that's better all round.

Mum and my aunt came into the kitchen together. 'Beach picnic at the bay today,' said Mum. 'Is that OK with you two?'

'Of course it is,' I said. 'It wouldn't be our Cornwall holiday without at least three picnics down there.'

'When's Uncle Alan going down to the beach?' Tim asked my aunt.

'I'm sure he'd take you and the boys down this morning,' she said. 'It would give me a break.'

'Can we go shopping this morning, Mum?' I asked. 'Just one of the beach shops.'

'Is that OK, Pat?' Mum asked my aunt.

'That'll make it a real break!'

'You're on, Josie. Get dressed quickly.'

I called in on Cat before we left, but there was no one about. Mum drove me to the beach shop. We parked and walked over the beach we call the surfing beach. The shop sells and hires out surf gear, but it has a whole floor of other stuff. Mum enjoys it as much as I do. 'It doesn't change much from year to year, does it?' she said. 'Look, here's the little dress we bought you last year. And they've still got these trousers.' Surfing fashion labels have really silly names, like Kangaroo Poo and Rip Curl and Sex Wax.

'Oooh, this is gorgeous. Can I try it on Mum?' I'd fallen for a little top. It was just the right size and Mum agreed to buy it for me.

As we were waiting to pay I rummaged around in the baskets on the counter. They were full of small things – hats, sunglasses, bracelets. One of them had the knotted leather jewellery Cat was wearing. I found some with tiny bead squares, just like hers, but I didn't want to get something identical. And then I found a single bracelet with a tiny carved wooden dolphin knotted into it. I knew exactly where I'd seen it before. It was beautiful. 'Last one, that is,' said the shopkeeper in her Cornish accent. 'I tried to order more, but they said they were turning out too costly to produce.'

'Could I have it, Mum?'

'Well, I'm paying for the clothes – don't you have your own money for that, darling?'

'I've left my purse behind,' I mumbled.

'Oh well, I haven't handed over my plastic yet,' she said. 'Can you add the bracelet on? And then you can pay me back, love. It's only one pound fifty.'

As we left the shop I could have sworn I caught sight of one of my dolphin boys amongst the hanging wetsuits, but I suspect it was an illusion.

Cat was home when we got back. She asked me if I wanted

to come over after our picnic so she could put the colours in my hair. Great!

We always go to the bay for picnics. It doesn't change. It's a great curve of beach with rocky coves all round. The waves are very gentle because the sea here is still part of the estuary. You get a few windsurfers, but mostly it's little kids paddling and building sandcastles. Alan arrived a bit after us with Tim and the boys. They'd been sailing with Archie and Harry, who came along too. It was the first time I'd seen them this holiday. We've grown up with them. Archie's a bit younger than me and Harry's a bit older. They're kind of dorky, but nice.

'Heard about Cat and Matt?' said Harry, as we chucked pebbles into the sea. He hadn't said a word about my brace.

'I met him last night in the pub,' I said.

'Oh yeah, Dad said you were down there. I know those guys from windsurfing. I think Matt's a bit of a show-off, myself.'

(Dear old Harry.) 'Cat seems to like him.'

'I suppose girls would find him quite good-looking.'

'And he probably finds Cat quite good-looking!'

'Yeah.' Harry's always been a bit in love with Cat.

Two windsurfers were sailing across the bay. They were very close to the shore. Harry and I stopped hurling pebbles to watch them.

'They're good,' said Harry.

I recognised them! 'Hey, Harry! Do you know who they are?'

'Don't think so!' said Harry. He peered after my dolphin boys, but they'd vanished behind the rocks.

Mum was calling. 'Josie, do you want to go and get ice-creams for everyone? The shop at the top's open.'

'I'll come with you,' said Harry, when Mum had given me the money.

I took everyone's orders. There were twelve of us. Harry and I would have to make two journeys. As we did the last shift Harry said, 'Why didn't you have one yourself, Josie?'

'I'd rather have the money,' I told him. 'Don't tell anyone, please. I've eaten it, OK?'

Liza and Tanya were already in Cat's bedroom when I arrived. 'This is going to be wicked,' said Cat. 'Colours look great in fair hair.'

'It didn't work on me,' said Liza. She's got very thick, bushy hair, mid-brown.

'It would probably work on me,' said Tanya, 'but I'm not letting you near it!' Her hair's about the same colour as mine. 'I feel distinctive enough hobbling along with this thing on my leg.'

'I feel *distinctive*,' I said, 'with these horrendous train tracks. I just want to divert people's attention from them.'

'I think they're quite attractive,' said Liza.

'Huh!'

'No, really. They're sort of twinkly. And you've got a nice mouth. They draw attention to that. You ought to wear lots of lip gloss.'

'Thanks, Liza. That makes me feet a bit less awful about them.'

'And you get them on the National Health,' Liza went on. 'Cheaper than a nose stud, eh, Cat?'

Cat laughed. 'But not so cool.'

'No, you're right,' said Liza. 'I want to get my eyebrow pierced but my parents won't let me.'

'Just do it,' said Cat. 'Then it's too late to stop you.'

'My mum would hit the roof if I got my nose pierced,' said Tanya. 'She did when Ivan got an earring. About the only cool thing Ivan's ever done.'

'I haven't seen him this year,' I said. 'Where is he?'

'Where every sensible person goes when they come to the seaside – in a church, playing his violin!' said Tanya, and the others all screeched with laughter. I didn't say anything. As I said, I keep quiet about my musical activities with this lot. I'd forgotten Ivan was a musician. He probably hadn't been a high enough standard before.

'Come on,' said Cat. 'Strip off, Josie. Let's do your hair.'

'Keep it subtle,' I said.

'Trust me,' said Cat.

Half an hour later I regarded myself in the mirror.

'What do you think?' said Liza. 'I think it looks great. Really pretty.'

'Not bad,' said Tanya. 'It makes you look interesting.'

'Thanks!'

'No! An interesting person. A bit hippie-ish.'

'Exactly,' said Cat. 'It'll go down a storm in the pub. Matt has this thing about girls who colour their hair. He thinks it's dead sexy.'

'I'm not out to get Matt, am I?' I said, secretly pleased to know I might get his attention. 'He's bagged.'

'I'm supposed to like Luke,' said Liza, 'but I'm not sure yet.'

'And I quite like Sebastian,' said Tanya. 'Though I don't expect he likes me.'

'Oh don't be so Eeyoreish, Tanya,' said Cat. 'I'm sure he does, and he's better looking than Paul.'

The one she'd reserved for me. I didn't remind her of it. 'Are you all coming tonight?' she asked.

'I don't have a lot of money,' was my answer. 'I might have enough by tomorrow night though.'

'Depends,' said Liza. 'If I just stick with Ellie I might. But her friends are so noisy, it's embarrassing. They were playing these silly pub games last night. I really wanted to disown them.'

'They just looked as if they were having fun, to me,' I said.

'I'd have been embarrassed if it had been my sister,' said Tanya.

'But you went over to join in last night, didn't you?' I said.

'Sort of,' said Liza. 'I had to find someone to drive me back. I had to be home by half past ten.'

So I wasn't the only one with a curfew.

'What about you, Tanya?'

'I need a lift too.'

'If getting there is the only problem,' said Cat, 'I'll get one of my parents to drive us all down. Please come, Josie.'

'I haven't got the money, Cat.' I thought she'd realise why, but she obviously didn't.

'Can I make you all up, now?' said Cat. 'And I can do nails, too. Show them yours, Josie.'

We had such a cool afternoon, mucking about with clothes and make-up. I nipped back to the cottage to get my new things to show everybody. I do like being just girls together. I was glad Cat wasn't spending all her time with Matt.

'What were you lot doing this morning?' I asked. 'I called round here, Cat, but you weren't in.'

'We were on the beach,' said Tanya, 'weren't we, Liza? Where were you, Cat?'

'Oh – I – got home pretty late. I was probably still asleep.'

*

I went back to our cottage for supper. I thought about going to the pub and buying an orange squash or something with the 90p I'd saved on the ice-cream, but I couldn't really face having to persuade my parents all over again. Although Mum really liked my hair, Dad wasn't so sure. I told him it washed out (I didn't tell him how many washes it would take) and he said he might get used to it. Then Seth called in on his way home from the beach. We were all sitting in the garden still, digesting treacle tart and clotted cream, one of our holiday specials from the local delicatessen.

'Yo, dudes!' he called. You have to see Seth, he's a complete one-off. He has gingerish hair which he wears in dreadlocks with extensions, all tied back in a ponytail. He's my age, but about ten feet tall. With a mouth full of metal. He goes everywhere on a skateboard. Right now he was carrying both a surfboard and a skateboard. Needless to say, he's a great snowboarding person in winter. He's a bit of a dude, really.

My mum has a soft spot for Seth. 'Yo, Seth!' she called, embarrassingly. 'There's some treacle tart going begging if you fancy a bit.'

'I always fancy a bit, Mrs L,' said Seth, loping up the path. 'Hey, Jo-jo – like the stripy hair, and the metalwork.'

'Yours isn't so bad, either,' I said.

'Bummer, isn't it?' he said.

'Yup. But temporary. Think how beautiful we're going to be.'

'You, yes. Me – I don't think so.'

'Well I think you're both quite beautiful as it is,' said Mum. *Do shut up, Mum, ple-hease*. (She'd been at the wine.)

Seth simply beamed at Mum and redirected his charm at Tim. 'Yo, Tim. How's it going?'

'All the better for seeing you, mate,' said Tim. Seth has this effect on people.

Seth turned back to me. 'Fancy a little twang later on?' he asked. 'I've done a couple of songs. Just waiting for you.' Seth writes grungy songs. Every now and then he persuades me to sing along with him.

'Do we know where the crummy guitar is yet, Dad?'

'I've put it in your room,' he said.

'OK, Seth. When?'

'Come over eightish?'

So that's what I did while the others went to the pub, and I couldn't help feeling I was missing out. Seth's cottage is right at the top. His family is totally laid back and happy. They spend all summer here – I don't know what they do the rest of the year. Actually I think his dad teaches art somewhere, or CDT or something. His mum bakes bread, does crystal readings and raises a whole tribe of little Seths. Their cottage is full of patchwork and barefoot toddlers and nappies and the garden is full of strange herbs.

Seth's songs weren't bad – they were all about waiting for some girl to come home and longing to see her face again. Etc, etc. Fairly standard words, but the music was pretty interesting.

'You're getting better, Seth.'

'Hey!'

'No, I mean it. I quite enjoy singing this one, and the chords make sense for a change.'

'That's because I've been practising.'

'Good man.'

Seth made some drinks and we took them outside. I tried

to sound him out about the guys Cat had met. I told him I thought Matt was really cool.

'Yeah, he's cool,' said Seth. 'They're pretty cool. Top surfers too. Matt's been in Portugal most of the summer. Bit keen on himself.'

'So what do you think of him and Cat?'

'What's to think?'

'Cat's my best friend. Is he nice enough for her?'

'Don't ask me questions like that, Jo-jo. And don't ask Harry! He's gutted.'

'Poor old Harry.'

Cat's car drew up as I made my way home at about eleven. She didn't see me. They dropped Tanya off, and as she was hobbling down her garden path I heard Cat's dad having a go. 'I don't care, Catherine. We were worried sick about you last night, and I'm not having it happen again.' And then a door slammed. Perhaps Cat's parents don't always find her amusing.

In bed I drew some pictures of my leather bracelet with the little dolphin and wrote down some of the words from Seth's song:

Hey, Mama, where you bin?
So long and I ain't seen
you-hoo-hoo.
And I missed your smile
And I missed your guile
And I missed your sweet, soft
eye-heye-heyes.

And so on. Cute, hey?

Things I want to do while I'm here
Find out about the two mystery boys.
Get in with Cat's crowd – on the beach if I can't make it to the pub.
    (Matt's so gorgeous and I think he quite liked me.)
Not spend too much time with Seth, Harry etc. As Cat said, they're a
    bit juvenile.
Water ski-ing.
Body-boarding.
Try standing again – Seth started teaching me last year. Maybe one
    of Matt's crowd would teach me, or perhaps I should even get
    proper surfing lessons.
Get a tan.
Go for a bike ride.

FOUR

Cat came bounding into my bedroom. 'Wakey, wakey! We're going to the surfing beach. You're coming in our car with me and Liza and Tanya and your family are coming down later. Get up!'

'Thanks for asking me what *I* want to do.'

'You want to come to the beach with us, you know you do. It's a lovely day.'

'I suppose so. Now go away and let me get up in private. I'm not at my best in the mornings.' I could see Cat heading for my sketchbook on the windowsill and I didn't want her to look inside. 'Go on, out!'

Cat laughed and went downstairs. 'You'll make sure she comes, won't you?' she asked my dad.

'Of course,' said Dad. 'Can't have anyone wasting a day like this. See you later on the beach, Cat.'

I hadn't realised quite how late it was. Mum had gone shopping with the others, leaving Dad behind. I grabbed a bit of toast and packed a beach bag. 'Should I take one of our boards, Dad?'

'Leave them for us to bring later. You can hire one if you're desperate.' He dug into his pocket. 'Here's a fiver for a board and an ice-cream or whatever. Go on, off you go. I know Cat's waiting – she's acting as though she has some secret assignation down there.'

'Bound to have. See you, Dad!' A whole fiver. Great. I could pay Mum back for the bracelet and still have money for the pub.

Cat's father dropped us off at the surfing beach and we followed her to a place by the rocks where Matt and Sebastian were dug in. Luke and Paul were making their way down to the water. The boys were wearing boardies – none of your fancy stuff. Matt and Sebastian had baseball caps and shades. We laid out our towels beside them and stripped off to our bikinis. I wondered if Matt would notice the colours in my hair. I thought I caught him registering me in my bikini as I put on the suntan lotion, but he and Sebastian were deep in conversation. I lay on my front to read my book and slipped my straps down. I thought I caught him looking at me then, too. It made me feel kind of sexy.

Cat and Liza finally got the boys talking. Soon they were mucking about, chasing each other round. Tanya grumbled to me, 'Liza's supposed to like Luke, but Sebastian likes her better than me. It's not fair. I can hardly walk, let alone run.'

'How was it at the pub last night?' I asked her, hoping for a bit of background to Cat's row with her parents.

'The pub was fine. Packed. Everyone was there. Just that

Cat had gone back to Matt's tent with him the night before, and didn't get home till really late – small hours – and her parents were worried, so they came and got her. Matt's dead sexy, isn't he? And now I suppose Liza will get off with Sebastian and I won't have anyone to be with. I knew this leg would ruin my holiday.'

'I'll be with you, Tanya.'

'You'll probably get off with Luke and I'll be left with the dreaded Paul.'

The others came racing back. Matt and Sebastian were laughing and gasping for breath. Liza was kicking sand at Sebastian. 'Who's coming in the water?' Cat asked. 'The sea's a bit flat, but it's OK for body-boarding.'

'Sebastian said he'd give me a bit of coaching,' said Liza.

'What did I tell you?' Tanya said to me.

'What about you two?' said Cat. 'Are you going to hire boards?'

'I'm not going anywhere,' said Tanya.

I was dying to go in the sea. I thought about hiring a board and then I thought about the money I could save if I didn't. I thought about being a good friend to Tanya last of all.

'I'll stay with Tanya,' I said nobly. Perhaps Matt and Sebastian would be impressed by my sympathetic nature. Anything, *anything* to make them notice me and like me.

'OK,' said Cat, lightly, and the four of them ran down to the waves.

'Now Sebastian will think I'm just someone who people are kind to,' said Tanya gloomily.

Honestly, some people are never satisfied.

Cat and Liza came back first. Liza went off with Tanya to

find a loo and I was left with Cat. 'Oh wow, that was so brilliant,' she said.

'Could I have a quick go with your board?' I asked.

'Oh, I suppose so,' she said, smiling up at Matt who was sitting down beside her. They were both glistening with oil and water. They looked very sexy together.

'Damn,' said Matt, feeling in the pocket of his shirt. He held up a lighter and looked mournful.

'What's the matter?' asked Cat.

'I've run out of cigarettes and I haven't got enough money to get any more. I'll have to go to a bank later on.'

'Oh, I need cigarettes,' I said airily. 'I'll nip over and get some. What do you smoke?'

Matt and Cat touched foreheads, sharing a secret giggle. 'Marlboro would be fine.'

I went over to the shop and bought twenty Marlboro. I tried to speak without opening my mouth too wide and no one asked me if I was over sixteen. I didn't get much change from my fiver.

'Hey, cool,' said Matt when I got back. 'Thanks, Josie.' I loved the way he said my name. He lit a cigarette and hung on to the pack.

I picked up Cat's board and went to find some waves. I needed the sea. I suppose it had been worth buying the cigarettes. I wanted Matt to like me, didn't I? I thought of the way his mouth had looked when he said the 'o' in 'Josie'. I wished I could kiss him like Cat did. I wondered what else they did together and then wished I hadn't. The very thought made me feel weak. I ran into the water. Soon I'd have a boyfriend of my own. It couldn't be long – I was making new friends fast.

*

'That was really sweet of you,' said Cat a bit later, when we were on our own for a while. 'Matt thinks you're great.'

'No problem,' I said.

'I'm so lucky,' she said with a sigh, and rolled over on to her stomach on the towel next to me. 'Matt wants me to go back to his tent with him again tonight. You'll come down to the pub this time, won't you? Please say you will – my parents won't let me go on my own any more. They think the boys are a bad influence.'

'So you'll go off with Matt and be back by eleven?'

'That's right.'

'What do you do?'

'Josie! Well, we go to his tent, and—' she looked at me slyly. 'Hey! I'm not telling you! Use your imagination!' She sat up to avoid more questions. Not that she'd given me any answers. It was lunchtime and there was a general movement of people leaving to find food and arriving with picnics. Loads of kids seemed to know Cat this year. They said Hi as they went past, or asked where Matt was. It must be brilliant going out with someone so popular.

I saw a large group of people coming in our direction. I heard David's booming voice before I realised that it was our Tredunnet lot and Harry and Archie and their dad. (Their mum stays behind usually. She obviously appreciates having a bit of peace and quiet.) 'Here comes my lunch,' I said.

Tanya and Liza appeared behind us, and Tanya said, 'There's mine, too.' I looked at our group now hammering in a windbreak and saw that along with Tim, Archie and Harry there was a fourth boy – Ivan, Tanya's boring brother.

'Do you want to come?' I said to Cat.

'No, I'm fine,' she said. 'I'll wait for Matt and the others. He can buy me some lunch. He's loaded.' (I refrained from pointing out that he didn't have enough money to buy his own cigarettes.)

'I think it's disgusting. It looks like a large, pus-filled white-head.' Ivan was waxing lyrical about Cat's nose stud.

'And you would know, of course,' said Tanya scathingly to her older brother. 'Personally I think it's cool.'

'I think it looks quite pretty.' Dear old lovesick Harry. If only he knew how far removed from his orbit Cat was these days.

'I read a magazine article all about piercing,' said Archie. 'People do it for the most bizarre reasons—'

My brother joined in. 'And people get the most bizarre parts of their bodies pierced—'

'That's enough, Tim,' said my mother. 'Have a chipolata and be quiet.' Needless to say, all six of us teenagers fell about laughing. I wished Cat was with us, though. I sort of missed her. In the old days she would have joined in our picnic and regaled us all with her fantastic tales that no one ever quite believed – except for Harry of course. Cat's parents aren't really beach people. They've always been happy for her to spend the day with us while they explored the local towns and gardens, or went on cliff walks. I sat with my sandwich and a packet of crisps and observed the others. I almost wished I had my sketchbook with me, except that I don't like people looking at it. Tanya sat leaning against a rock. She's on the solid side, with fairish hair, liquid brown eyes and, despite her gloomy nature, a mouth that curls readily into a smile. Ivan's hair is cut very short, but he's got the same eyes, magnified behind glasses, and the curly-lipped smile too. And of course he sports the famous earring. Sadly it would take more than an earring to make Ivan look cool.

Harry and Archie are sailing types like their father. You see them everywhere from Norfolk to Cornwall, and they come in all ages and sizes. Dark wavy hair, blue eyes and usually navy-blue jerseys and jeans. The boys will be nice-looking when they're older but at the moment they're both *so* painfully straight. Now an earring could make a difference to the way Harry looks. Perhaps I should suggest it. It might make Cat look on him more kindly.

'How's the music going, Ivan?' asked my dad as he came round offering more sandwiches.

'Oh don't get him started,' said Tanya.

'Good, thanks,' said Ivan. 'They're starting the scratch choir on Friday for a concert on Sunday. Anyone interested?'

'Don't be daft!' said Tanya. 'Who wants to sing hymns in a cold old church when they could be on the beach?'

'My sentiments precisely,' I said with a warning glance at Dad. He knows I don't like to talk about music in front of my friends.

'Well, all I can say is, plenty of people,' said Dad. 'And it's not hymns, Tanya, it's choral works, Handel and so on.'

'Same difference,' said Tanya contemptuously. She looked wistfully over to where Cat was sitting with Matt and the other three. 'Bet they're not discussing classical music,' she said.

I peered in their direction. I could just make out Cat and Matt snuggled up together on a towel. Liza and Sebastian were still at the chasing each other around stage. Paul and Luke arrived from somewhere with some cans. They sat down and handed them round. Matt sat up and I could see him offering round a pack of cigarettes.

'Did you hire a board this morning?' Dad asked.

'Yes,' I said quickly.

'No you didn't,' said Tanya. 'I never saw you go off and hire a board.'

'You weren't there all the time, Tanya. It was when you'd gone off with Liza somewhere.'

'Oh yeah. We went to the loo didn't we?' (When I'd bought the cigarettes.) 'And the surf shop to look at swimsuits.' (When I'd borrowed Cat's board.) 'I'd forgotten that.' (Phew.)

'And I expect you spent the rest on drinks and ice-creams, didn't you?' said Dad, indulgent as ever.

'You spoil our daughter,' said Mum. 'Don't forget you still owe me for that bracelet.'

'I won't forget, Mum.' Cat didn't have to put up with this sort of stuff. 'Shall we go back and join the others, Tanya?'

'I'll come too,' said Ivan.

'No you won't,' said Tanya.

We spent the rest of the afternoon lazing around on the beach. I was still borrowing Cat's board, so we alternated our turns in the sea and I didn't see much of her or Matt. 'Are you going back home before going out again?' I asked her.

'Yeah,' she said. 'Expect one of my parents to ask yours if you can be at the pub with me. I expect we'll get a lift. You know the score, don't you?'

'It's cool,' I said, smiling at Matt in an understanding way.

'That's the point, Dad. Everyone's there. We can all keep an eye on each other. We're only sitting outside drinking Coke.' (A small lie to spare the parents.) 'The good thing about Cat's parents being worried is that they'll come and get us. Except they won't try and drive past – we'll meet them in the top car park at eleven.'

'I want you home by eleven-fifteen.'

'Yes, Dad.'

'And that doesn't mean you can come in that late every night.'

'Da-ad!'

I ran out to where Cat was leaning on the horn. It was just her and me for now. There was a slim chance that Tanya and Liza would come later with Ellie and friends.

'One thing, Cat,' I said, as we scanned the crowds for Matt.

'Mmm?'

'You have to pay for my drink. I haven't got any money left.'

'Oh OK,' she said, in that offhand way she has sometimes. 'Matt will pay, I'm sure.'

The crowd parted. Matt, Luke, Sebastian and Paul had arrived. This was just so cool. 'Hi guys,' I said with my new smile that showed off my lips but not my teeth.

'Matt, give me some money,' said Cat. 'I'm going to buy the drinks.'

'Just don't get caught,' said Matt.

'You and Josie bag that bit of wall,' said Cat. 'I won't be a sec.'

I was left sitting on the wall with Matt. The other three were standing up, talking amongst themselves. It was chillier than before. I pulled my jacket round me. Matt offered me one of my cigarettes. I took one and let him light it for me. I tried to smoke it without coughing.

'I know you want to be with Cat tonight,' I said. 'I don't mind covering for her.' Ms Nice Guy, me. Matt didn't respond. 'Sometimes,' I said, 'two people just have to be alone together. I appreciate that. I mean, I just love being on my own with a guy. The freedom to do what you want. Be uninhibited.'

'You're a nice kid, you know?' said Matt, but he wasn't able to say any more because Cat arrived with the drinks. Mine was a Coke. I was going to have to make it last quite a long time, three hours to be precise. Cat and Matt knocked back theirs and disappeared. I was left sitting in the middle of a circle of standing guys.

'Why don't you sit down?' I said.

'Oh, OK,' said Paul, and sat. 'Go and get some more drinks, Luke. What do you want Josie? Still on the Archers like last time?' He didn't give me a chance to say no. I was enjoying myself. It was great being with this popular group. Other girls cast envious glances, I could tell. At last. Despite my brace, I was surrounded by three amazingly cool surfers. I wished my friends from home could see me. And for once I wasn't stuck with Ivan and Harry, or Seth. Luke brought me two Archers, to save time! How thoughtful! And then they all talked to me – about Cat, about me, about themselves. They asked me all about the boyfriends I'd had in the past. I had to improvise a bit. I pretended something had really happened with the drummer on the music course, and I invented a longterm boyfriend (I called him Tim, after my brother – the first name that came to mind!).

'Quite a girl, eh?' said Luke to Sebastian, when I'd finished.

'Of course, Tim was very passionate about me,' I said. 'He was devastated when we finished. We'd had such an – intense – relationship, for as long as I can remember.' (That was true. I have had an intense relationship with my wretched little brother as long as I can remember.) Two more Archers later, and a lot of cigarettes, I can't remember what I was telling them.

At ten to eleven Cat and Matt came back. I was very relieved to see her. I'd been worried about what to do if she didn't turn up. She had bright red spots on her cheeks and she looked quite upset. 'You OK, Cat?'

'Why shouldn't I be?' she said sharply. 'Just going to the loo, Josie, and then we'll go and meet the beloved parent.'

My head was spinning a bit. I tried to organise my brain, ready for Cat's dad. I heard the boys talking, but I didn't really grasp the implications of what they were saying.

'Well?' Sebastian was asking Matt.

In reply, Matt just gave a thumbs down sign. He looked rather sad. I felt quite sorry for him. Cat came back, more her old self.

'Bye, gorgeous,' she said over her shoulder to Matt, and linked her arm in mine. She hauled me up the hill to the car park where the car was already waiting for us. I found it a great effort putting one foot in front of the other. 'Now remember,' she hissed, 'I was there all the flaming time.' I rehearsed my line as we climbed.

'Cat was there *all* the flaming time,' I said slowly and carefully to her dad, and promptly threw up in the hedge.

FIVE

I was in trouble, big trouble. Not with Cat – I'd covered for her, and even taken the heat off her for the time being. But my parents – wo-oh!

Next morning: 'Josephine, you have completely abused our trust in you. I am very disappointed,' said my dad.

'Drinking *and* smoking!' said my mum.

'You are aware,' said Dad severely, 'that under-age drinking is illegal? That you could be putting the landlord's licence at risk? His livelihood?'

'And how come you were so ill and Cat wasn't?' asked Mum. 'Good friends look after each other. I don't think these boys are very good friends either.'

Actually it was Tim who came to my rescue – a bit. 'Lighten up, you two,' he said. 'Don't you think you're overreacting? She only went to the pub, for God's sake! Everyone else does. At least she's not getting stoned out of her brain down at the campsite.'

'Well, she's not going again, is all I can say,' said Dad, and went off, grumbling, to make some coffee.

'I'm sorry,' I said feebly. 'The boys bought me drinks and they just kept on coming. I started off with a Coke, honest.'

Mum relaxed a bit with Dad out of the room. 'Let's hope you've learnt your lesson, darling. At least you've come out of it safely. You'll probably never want that particular drink again. But don't smoke, sweetheart. It'll ruin your voice.'

'It was only one or two, Mum. I can't believe you didn't try things out when you were my age.'

'That doesn't mean I can stand by and watch when you're being silly.'

'All right, Mum. I really am sorry. Have we got anything for headaches?'

'Go back to bed. I'll bring you something. But it will take a while for your father to calm down. It's probably better if you're out of the way.'

I cuddled Monk for comfort and slept half the morning, so I felt normal by the time I was properly awake. I sat up and reached for my sketchbook. I drew the view through my low window. A thrush had been sitting amongst the roses that stretched across the sill, so I drew that too. I fingered my dolphin bracelet and stayed in bed, enjoying the solitude. I felt a list coming on, a private, personal list:

Reasons why Matt might be attracted to me
My hair
My figure (I'm slim, look OK in a bikini)
I'm generous
I'm sympathetic
I'm experienced (he thinks)
I'm popular (i.e. Cat likes me)

Reasons why Matt might not be attracted to me
BRACE
Young
No good at surfing
(No good at anything much!)
Actually, not that popular

As you might conclude, I fancy Matt. I admit it. I know he's Cat's boyfriend and everything, but he's dead nice to me, and he didn't look that happy about her last night. Perhaps she'd dumped him or something. She said goodnight to him, but she didn't kiss him or anything. I'd have to ask her what was going on, very tactfully of course. I shut the sketchbook. Then I panicked in case anyone picked it up and frantically scribbled out the name Matt and put a question mark there instead, so it read *Reasons why ~~Matt~~ might be attracted to me.* After all, Cat is quite capable of walking in here any time. I pushed Monk under the duvet for the same reason.

I couldn't remember that much about last night after about the second drink. I know the boys were interested in me, trying to find out about me. I'm not used to being the centre of attention! I remember vaguely looking out for the dolphin boys. They were there some of the time. I was aware of the respectful way people seemed to treat them, as they stood outside the door gazing out to sea. Very romantic!

Cat was running up the stairs, calling 'Josie! Time to move your arse!' I shoved the sketchbook (lucky I'd scratched out Matt's name!) down the bed with Monk, and slid back under the duvet.

'I'm surprised they let you in,' I said.

'What do you mean?'

'Might you just be considered something of a bad influence round here?'

'Nah. Not any more. I saw your dad, said I was sorry I hadn't looked after you better. You hadn't really had much to drink, perhaps you had a stomach bug or something.'

'And he bought it?'

'He didn't stop me coming in.'

'Good. That means he's calmed down. I'm not allowed to go tonight though.'

'I'll have to ask Liza or Tanya then.' (Gee, thanks, Cat.) 'But we're planning a beach party tomorrow night! You'll have to come to that. Surely your mum and dad wouldn't say no?'

'I'll have to work on them. I'm on best behaviour now.'

'Get up then. Come down to the beach.'

'The surfing beach?'

'No. This one. We can sunbathe.'

'Is Matt going to be there?'

'Oh yes. We'll all be there.' She got up from my bed. 'You

can ride pillion on my bike if no one gives us a lift. Come and get me when you're ready.'

As soon as I went downstairs I gave my dad a hug. I don't like upsetting him. 'Sorry, Daddy.' He said something gruff and unintelligible but I knew I was basically forgiven. 'Where is everyone?'

'They've taken the little ones to the bay.'

Easy does it. 'Can I go to the beach with Cat?'

'I suppose she can't lead you into any trouble down there. Mum left us some sandwiches, so make yourself a picnic. And I want you back by six. Mum's got the mobile, so just make sure you're not late, or I'll have to think seriously about letting you do things with your friends.'

'Thanks, Dad.' I think he must have assumed Cat's parents would drive us – he really doesn't realise how independent she is. I gathered up my stuff and went over to Cat's. We went round the side way so Dad wouldn't see me riding pillion on Cat's bike. We caught up with Seth on his skateboard half way down. I reminded myself that Cat thought he was a bit weird and prepared myself not to take any notice of him, but Cat seemed to have forgotten herself.

'So-o-o dangerous!' squealed Cat as we overtook him.

'I kno-o-ow!' he shrieked back, laughing.

We found everyone else in the dunes. There was a huge bunch of kids, including Liza and Tanya and even Ivan.

'Hi guys!' said Cat. 'It's me!' (You have to be very self-assured to say that sort of thing.)

'We all heard what you got up to last night!' said Ivan. Cat gave me an anxious glance before she realised it was my notoriety up for discussion, not hers. She went over to Matt. The others all said hi, but he barely acknowledged her. What had she done to upset him?

Seth turned up and sat beside me. I tried to act aloof. 'Heard about last night!' he said. Cat glanced over and looked relieved when she realised Seth was also referring to me and not her. It made me wonder again – what had she been up to? I felt slightly wistful for other summers when we'd told each other everything, even if it had only been about Seth and Harry and Ivan (well, not really Ivan), and the bike hire boy.

'What I want to know, Seth, is *how* everyone heard about last night,' I said. 'Cat?' I called over to her. 'What have you been saying about me?'

'I certainly didn't say anything to Seth or Ivan,' she said, as if she wouldn't have bothered speaking to them.

I suppose I didn't altogether want Matt to think I was comfortable consorting with a ten-foot ginger rastafarian either, so I got up and went to join Cat and the lads. I mean, Seth's OK in private, but it was different being seen with him in public. 'So who did you tell?' I asked, trying to make a joke of it.

'I might have mentioned it to Tanya,' she said. 'She and Liza couldn't make it last night, so they wanted to know.' Liza was schmoozing with Sebastian, I noticed. Tanya was looking resigned with Paul. That left Luke. I was glad I'd moved over here. Seth and Ivan were really pretty sad. They looked like weirdos.

Luke was quite friendly. People came and went, but our little group stayed put. It was cool, really. Cat and Matt, Liza and Sebastian, Tanya and Paul, me and Luke (except that I fancied Matt and Tanya didn't think much of Paul).

'So, Josie,' said Luke, 'how do you know Cat?'

'Her cottage is just behind ours,' I said.

'You're quite a pair, I gather. You and Cat.'

'Oh yes,' I said, though I didn't quite know what he was

talking about. 'Anyway. How about you? How do you four know each other?'

'From school,' he said. 'We've been planning this holiday for ages. My parents are staying further down the coast, but we persuaded them to let us camp and surf here.' That was the first time any of them had mentioned parents. They seemed so grown-up. 'Matt said it would be a brilliant way to – er – meet girls. He was right!'

'Have you all got girlfriends at home?'

'Only Matt—' he said, and then stopped. 'Of course we have. Though not right now.' He laughed nervously when I looked at him. Actually, he had a nice smile. When I first met the boys it was, like, Matt – the best-looking by far – and three others, with Paul and his big ears definitely the least attractive. Matt has classic gorgeous features, short dark hair, chiselled cheekbones, green eyes. Sebastian and Luke just look like hunky surfers, with longish, light-coloured hair. Sebastian is the fairer of the two, with blond eyebrows and stubble. Luke looks slightly younger with a more girlish skin – and the nice smile. That's why it was Sebastian who got to buy the drinks. Actually Paul's not that bad. It's just that he has these rather thin features and short hair, which make his ears look worse. He and Tanya seemed to be getting on fine now. He was writing something on her plaster cast. Something witty – it made her laugh.

I didn't want Matt to think I was being too friendly with Luke. Cat was lying on her front and he was leaning back against a dune, one hand stroking her back (I noticed with envy) and the other holding a cigarette. But they weren't talking to each other. In fact, I reckoned he was watching me quite a lot.

'Anyone coming for a swim?' I said brightly. There was

no reply. Cat seemed to be asleep and Tanya and Liza were anointing one another with suntan lotion.

'OK, we'll come, won't we?' said Matt to the other boys, and they went ahead of me down into the water. I swam around to keep warm but they floated about chatting to each other. I couldn't help earwigging their conversation.

'How are you getting on with yours?' Sebastian asked Paul.

'Better, now you've let me switch!' said Paul. 'And I don't have to ask you – it's obvious!'

'That's because you let me switch, too!' said Sebastian.

'Matt messed up, didn't he? He thought he would be miles in the lead by now.'

'Don't let him hear you say that!'

I quickly swam in the opposite direction. What were they on about? Amazing how they respected Matt – 'don't let him hear you say that'. I was nearest to him now. I nearly drowned just gazing at his muscles. Wow. I'd give anything to swap places with Cat.

Then Matt said something that really surprised me. 'Let's go surfing. I'm not going to get those points with her, am I?' Was he talking about Cat? I was forced to duck and swim underwater to get further away so they wouldn't think I was listening. I popped up where I couldn't hear them at all. Actually I'd heard enough (though I wasn't sure I liked what I'd heard), and I'd swum enough too – I was quite cold. So I went back to our place in the dunes alone, wondering if the four boys would stay after their swim or do something different.

Tanya, Liza and Cat were all lying on their fronts either sleeping or reading. Seth and Ivan were playing a game of football with a beer can. Ivan said hi, but Seth seemed intent on ignoring me, which hurt. I flopped down by Cat.

Had Matt been talking about her? I had to get to the bottom of it. I nudged her. 'Cat? You look as though you're burning. I'll put lotion on your back if you'll do mine.' I started on her back anyway – it was looking rather pink. 'Is – everything OK with Matt?'

'Yes,' she said lightly, too lightly.

'Cat? What's the matter?'

'Nothing. It's fine really. We're cool.' She rubbed lotion into my back vigorously.

The boys returned and said they were going back to the campsite and then surfing. Cat said she'd follow them on her bike. Seth said he'd join them too and I was left with Tanya, Ivan and Liza and a long walk back to Tredunnet. In fact it was a long walk back with Liza because Tanya and Ivan were meeting up with their parents and going somewhere else.

Liza was bubbling over. 'This holiday is turning out so brilliant!' she said. 'And I really thought I was going to be forced to spend it with my sister and her friends. There's nothing wrong with them – they're just older, but none of them are half as cool as Sebastian! I think I'm in love!'

'We're so lucky, aren't we?' I said. 'And Tanya seems quite keen on Paul, too.'

'He's nice, despite the way he looks. And Tanya's hardly the most beautiful girl in the world, is she?'

'Liza!'

'Well, it's true. She'd be the first to acknowledge it. What's Luke like?'

I didn't want to talk about Luke. He was nice but I didn't have any feelings for him – not like I did about Matt. Just then two boys came down the hill on bicycles. It was the dolphin boys! There was something so special about them.

'Who are those boys, Liza? Do you know anything about them?'

'No, but everyone else seems to. Everyone goes up and talks to them at the pub. I've seen them surfing too. I'll try and find out. Sebastian's bound to know.'

'Matt will, I expect.' There, I'd said his name. 'Liza – is everything all right with Cat and Matt?'

Liza giggled. 'Everything except their names! Cat sat on the Matt!'

'Has she said anything about last night? I know I was out of it, but she didn't look at all happy when she came back to the pub.'

'What do you mean?'

Oops. Blown it. But it would be nice to share this particular problem. 'Last night. I was covering for her while she went off to Matt's tent with him. Then she could tell her dad she'd been with me at the pub all along.'

Liza stopped in her tracks. 'Blimey. I didn't realise that's what she was up to. I *suppose* she knows what she's doing. I'm not sure that I would have wanted to be her alibi.'

'I'm her best friend. I had to.'

'Hmmm.'

'She wouldn't tell me what they did.'

'Honestly Josie, would you expect her to? I assume it was either sex or drugs, or both.'

'Do you think so? I just thought she and Matt wanted some time alone together. It didn't seem too much to ask.'

'Well, let's hope you're right.'

'What would you do if Sebastian asked you back to his tent?'

'I'd think hard about it first. I might be a bit scared actually.'

'You know Cat. She doesn't scare easily. Think how brave she must have been to have the nose stud. I screamed when I had my ears pierced. Mind you, nothing could be as bad as these train tracks.'

'I kind of wish you hadn't told me about Cat. I said I'd keep her company at the pub tonight, but then I'm dying to be with Sebastian again. You should get together with Luke. He's nice. Four of us and four of them – sorted! How about the beach barbecue tomorrow? Go on, go for it! You know you want to!'

We'd reached the point where we went our separate ways. I felt funny after my conversation with Liza. Had I been wrong to cover for Cat? And why did I have to fancy Matt when it would have been so much better all round to go for Luke?

That evening I felt bad about Seth too. I heard him scooting uphill on his skateboard at one point and thought how nice it might have been to go round to his cottage tonight and carry on with his songs. In fact I was experiencing something of a remorse-fest. I didn't like myself very much. How could I even be slightly interested in my best friend's boyfriend? But then I'd heard him say weird things about her. What sort of 'points' were they talking about? I went up to my room after supper and drew pictures of dolphins, which calmed me down a bit. I'd so love to talk to the dolphin boys – pity they're way out of my league.

My parents were off to a concert with my uncle and aunt and David. Harry and Archie came over to help us babysit my little cousins. Tim produced a pack of cards and a box of Smarties. 'We play for Smarties, OK?' and a daft game got under way. Archie got hiccups and had to be bashed very thoroughly. We made so much noise that my cousins came downstairs to join in. We ended up playing charades. 'Jaw-ass-sick-Park' was my cousins' favourite, though they just romped around pretending to be dinosaurs. Tim made me act 'sick'. Harry got it straight away. News travels fast.

'Tell me again why you and Cat were both sick in the pub last night?' said Harry. Anything to talk about Cat.

'Only *I* was sick! And we'd left the pub. Cat wasn't even there. She wasn't at the pub!' Oops. Done it again.

'So where was Cat? I heard her parents telling Dad she was fine because she was with you.'

'Ah. Well. Yes, she was sort of with me.'

'Get your story straight, Josie,' said my brother. 'People keep asking me, too.'

'OK. Promise you won't tell anyone? I was Cat's alibi, so I stayed at the pub while she went off with Matt, her boy-friend.'

'Don't say any more,' said Harry. 'I don't want to know. I've never spoken to this Matt person and I'm not sure that I want to. I suppose he's really cool.'

'He's got an earring,' I said, thinking it was never too early to plant the seeds.

'So's Ivan,' said Archie. 'But that doesn't make him cool.'

'Nothing would make Ivan cool,' said Tim. 'You'd look good with an earring Harry. Maybe you and I should go together. There's a place in Newquay. Gideon was telling me.'

'Who's Gideon?' the rest of us asked together.

'Gideon and Caleb – surely you've seen them?'

We all looked blank.

'They're brothers. They go around together. Fair hair.'

The dolphin boys! Gideon and Caleb. Such romantic names. But already my heart was set only on Matt.

Later I drew a three-quarter portrait from memory of

Matt's head and shoulders, with slick wet hair and goose-bumps on the skin of his biceps. I was so jealous of Cat. I tried not to think about the two of them together.

SIX

At breakfast Tim was full of it. He'd already heard it from Seth who'd heard it from Ivan who'd got it first-hand from Tanya. I don't know, these sad boys who get up early and gossip! Cat had been caught out. I couldn't wait to go over and hear all the details.

Dad was full of something, too. The concert in the little church had been wonderful. And there was the art exhibition next door. They always set aside an area for 'children's work'. Dad thought I ought to do something for it.

'Probably not, Dad. I don't really want to sit and paint on this holiday.'

'Think how proud you'd be to have your work displayed for all to see during the interval of the concert.'

'I'm not going to be in the concert either this year.'

'Oh Jo-jo. I was hoping we could still persuade you to sing.'

'No. No way.'

I ran over to Cat's. She was just getting into their car. 'See you at the barbecue, Josie!' she said cheerfully. 'Half-past seven! Bring a potato or something!' Her dad shut her door for her and directed a grim nod of greeting at me before driving off. I went on to Tanya's, half hoping I could meet Seth and make up with him on the way. But there was no sign of him.

Tanya's parents were delivering Ivan to the church, and picking up some shopping, so she was on her own. She was perched on a stool in her dressing-gown, eating toast and vaguely watching breakfast television. 'Hey, Josie! You missed a whole lot of drama last night.'

'And you're dying to tell me about it.' I pulled up another stool and waited expectantly.

'OK. Well, we were down at the pub last night, sitting on the wall outside like good little girls and boys. Liza and I had our nice soft drinks.' (I felt envious already. That was all I had wanted the other night. Just fun and good company.) 'I'm really beginning to like Paul, and Liza and Sebastian are pretty much an item. Luke was a bit lonely! But Cat and Matt were going to do their disappearing trick. Liza actually tried to talk her out of it, but Cat said she knew what she was doing. Matt seemed pretty grumpy to me, actually, but he cheered up a bit and waved to all his friends as Cat dragged him off.'

Tanya clomped over in her cast to pour some tea and carried on. 'So it was all fine. My brother and Seth even stopped off for a bit. Luke told them about the barbecue tomorrow, which hacked me off – I *so* don't want my brother there, but what can you do? They were chatting with some other lads and then disappeared. But THEN, at about ten o'clock—' Tanya got up and poured yet another cup of tea. She was really laying on the suspense – 'Cat's dad appeared. He marched past us and went into the pub. When he came out again, he said, "Has anyone seen Catherine? She led me to believe she would be here." Panic stations. We all faffed about, didn't know what to say. Then Luke said, all innocent, "I think Matthew had left his wallet behind and they popped back to fetch it. They'll be here in a minute I'm sure." "Popped where?" said Cat's dad. He was ever so suspicious. "To the campsite," said Sebastian, who hadn't quite sized up the situation. "Well, she'd better be on her way back," said her dad, "because I'm driving over to meet her right now!" Exit Cat's dad.'

'So what did you all do?'

'Quick as a flash, Luke sent Matt a text telling him to leg it back here with Cat – the story was that he'd left his wallet behind.'

'So did Cat get away with it?'

'We didn't see her, because her dad drove her straight home. Matt said it had been a close thing, though he wouldn't exactly tell us why. The guys all sniggered a lot. But he said Cat play-acted like mad with her dad – "Oh Daddy, we'd only just nipped out to get Matt's wallet, etcetera, etcetera." My lift appeared soon after, so that's all I know. Liza stayed on awhile – she might know more. Let's go over to her house. I'll just put some clothes on. I had a wash earlier – can't even have a shower with this flaming thing on my leg.'

We went down the road to Liza's. It's quite a shock when you go in the door of an ordinary-sized holiday house to see all these millions of boys milling round in their boxer shorts. I felt quite embarrassed, but none of them seemed to mind.

'We want you to tell us what happened after I left the pub last night,' said Tanya, leading Liza out on to a patio at the side that was off the boys' beaten track between tents and kitchen.

Liza had a dreamy expression on her face. 'Sebastian kissed me,' she said. She was obviously still on Cloud Nine. 'He said he was crazy about me. He even likes my hair!' She ran her hands through her thick, tangled mop. (He must be keen.) 'I can't wait for the barbecue this evening. We can't see each other before then because of some surfing competition they're all doing first.'

'Seth's doing that too,' said Tanya. 'But tell us about Matt. What did he say about Cat's dad and everything?'

'He said Cat's dad wasn't too pleased. More or less accused him of leading Cat on, pushing drugs, blah blah.'

I pictured Matt's beautiful troubled face as he was so unjustly picked on and my heart bled for him. But then I suddenly felt naive. 'Is that what they were doing? Smoking dope?'

'Quite likely,' said Liza matter-of-factly. 'People do, you know.'

'Do *you*?' I asked, wide-eyed. My cosy world was cracking slightly.

'No, as it happens, but I can't vouch for anyone else in this madhouse.' Liza always seems so sorted. It must come from having an older sister and understanding parents.

'Anyway, Cat's coming to the barbecue tonight,' I said. 'I saw her going off this morning and she told me.'

'OK guys. So how shall we pass the time until then?' said Tanya.

'Not so fast, Tanya,' said Liza. 'I want to hear more about you and Paul. How's it going?'

'So-so. He wouldn't have much luck dragging me and my peg leg off to his tent for an evening of passion – it would take us all evening to get there!'

'I wouldn't go anyway,' said Liza. 'I bet their tent's disgusting. You should see inside some of the ones in our garden! Their sleeping bags stink. They wear the same underpants for days before leaving them lying around. Plus damp socks. Beer cans. Cigarette stubs. Nasty.'

I kept quiet. There's obviously so much I don't know.

Secretly I felt pretty sure I'd go anywhere with Matt if it made him happy.

'Now I've given you the lowdown on Paul,' said Tanya. 'What's it to be for us? Girly morning?'

It's funny – although I've always known these two, this is the first summer I've felt part of the crowd. It's been me and Cat some of the time, and me and my old playmates – Harry, Archie and Seth – the rest. But the whole thing of the four of us girls is just so brilliant, and it's all because of Matt and his friends. They've made the holiday so much more fun. I thought for a moment about the 'holiday romance' that I'd promised to have. That was a tricky one. As far as I was concerned, there was only one candidate, and he was taken.

'We could go shopping,' Liza suggested.

'I need to buy some postcards and presents for my friends,' said Tanya. 'Let's do that.'

'How are we going to get you there?' asked Liza.

'Wait for my parents to get back and then make them drive us to the ferry. I can walk around the shops if you lot don't mind going slowly.'

'I'll have to ask my parents first,' I said. 'Don't go without me will you?'

'See you back at my house,' said Tanya. 'Don't be too long.'

Once in a while I wish someone here would say: 'Please come with us, Josie. It won't be any fun without you. We'll wait for you – for as long as it takes.' That sort of thing. Holly, my friend at home, would. Perhaps it's my brace. Perhaps it makes me look young and they don't want to be seen with me. That's the downside of being in with a popular group. You're always having to keep up. It feels like hard work sometimes. And now three of us have got boyfriends. And the fourth – me – hasn't.

'Good idea, darling,' said my mother. 'Good opportunity to spend some of your holiday money. By the way, you still owe me £1.50. How about giving it to me now, so we're square?'

I could just about scrape that amount together, with some odds and ends of change I found in a pocket, but it left me completely and utterly stony broke again. I gave Mum the money. It was worth it to stop her going on about it. 'Would you pay for my ferry fare?' I asked tentatively.

'I suppose that comes under expenses,' she said. 'Here it is exactly. Remember to hang on to the return fare too.' Huh. I'd have to, because I didn't have any other money.

'Did Dad tell you about the art exhibition?' Mum asked. 'Do one of your clever paintings and you might even make some money!'

I hadn't thought of that aspect. 'I'll think about it. Mum, I have to go – I'm worried the others won't wait. But please, *pleasepleaseplease*, can I go to a barbecue down on the beach tonight? Everyone's going.'

'I expect so,' she said. 'We'll ask Dad when you get back. Convince him that you'll stay out of the way of temptation. I think he reckons it's time to give you another chance.'

I raced over to Tanya's. I needn't have hurried. Her dad was having a cup of coffee before he turned round and went out again. Tanya and Liza were comparing how much money they had to spend. Before they could ask me, I said I was only going to buy something if I really really wanted it. I was mulling over the idea of doing a painting and selling it. If I could sell it over the weekend it would solve my money problems for the rest of the holiday.

The ferry is a lovely little boat that leaves from the beach here and drops you in the middle of girly shoppers' paradise on the other side. We cruised round jewellery shops, shell shops, card shops, gift shops. The other two bought loads. I tried to focus on what I might be able to buy next week. I even saw the perfect present for Holly, but I would just have to be patient. It was hot, and what I wanted most was an ice-cream. I didn't want to tell them I'd come shopping with no money, so I just had to grin and bear it when they assumed I didn't want one, and bought gorgeous, mouth-watering ice-creams for themselves.

We were on the return ferry when Liza started nudging and giggling. 'Hey,' she whispered. 'Don't look round straight away, but at some point turn your heads and have a look at two really fit guys. They even put my lovely Sebastian in the shade.'

'Wouldn't take much to put Paul in the shade,' said Tanya, but we both turned our heads simultaneously and saw – the dolphin boys. 'I've seen them at the pub,' she said. 'I think Paul knows them. They're surfers. Dead cool. What do you think, Josie?'

I wanted to show off my inside knowledge and say that I knew their names, but I couldn't because I'd caught the younger one's sea-grey gaze and it had rendered me speech-less. We'd anyway arrived on the home side and the skipper was helping us off the boat and Tanya was phoning for a lift.

'Did you buy anything?' called my mum as I went upstairs.

'Not today,' I called back. I'd had the idea that Dad might be more inclined to let me go to the barbecue if I was more amenable about the painting. I turned to a fresh page of my sketchbook and stared at it. Then I looked at my drawing of a boy morphing into a dolphin. Maybe I could do something with that if I used colour. Sea colours. All sea colours. I sat and sketched for half an hour. Suddenly I was ravenous. The others had bought pasties, but I'd had to decline again. I went downstairs and started making a sandwich.

'Didn't you have any lunch?' asked Mum. A bit of quick thinking. 'Yes, I had a pasty. Had to pay for it myself.'

'I'll pay you back for that. I should've thought.' So now I had £1.75. And I'd paid Mum back for the bracelet. Things were looking up.

'Did you say anything to Dad about me going to the barbecue?'

'I haven't had a chance – he's been out with your uncle's lot and Tim all morning. He's getting over your antics the other night but he's still quite upset about you not doing a picture *or* singing in the concert.'

'I've changed my mind about the picture. In fact, I've already started sketching.'

'But that's marvellous. Dad will be thrilled. He's so proud of you, you know!'

'No need to go over the top, Mum. Just say I can go to the barbecue.'

'I'll certainly make a very strong case for you.'

'Thanks. You've got four hours.' Which meant I had four hours too. To decide what to wear, shower, change, make up, etc. I nipped over to Cat's but she wasn't back yet. Tanya was round at Liza's. I called in there. The two of them were still at the deciding-what-to-wear-stage, so I joined in. 'Anyone can borrow my stuff if they want,' I offered.

'Your clothes wouldn't fit me,' said Tanya, blunt as always.

'I don't even know what *sort* of clothes to wear,' said Liza.

It was a beautiful clear, sunny afternoon. It looked set fair for a beautiful summer evening too.

'Trousers, nice top, plus shirt or something,' I said. 'We are on the beach, after all.'

'I'd thought maybe bikini and sarong,' said Liza.

'Midges,' I said. 'Better to be covered up a bit.'

'I agree,' said Tanya. 'Though I don't think Paul would give a stuff what I wore.'

'Ooo-ooh, I wish I knew what Sebastian expected!'

'As few clothes as possible I imagine,' said Tanya, 'but you don't have to dress to please him. Be comfortable, that's far more important!'

'Exactly,' I said. But I was worried now. I knew I'd dress to please Matt if I only knew how, Cat or no Cat. Perhaps 'as little as possible' was the answer.

'I wish Cat was back,' said Liza. 'She's brilliant on make-up. And she'd know exactly what to wear. I've got this cool dress I'd put on if I knew other people were dressing up.'

'Short or long?' said Tanya.

'Short. Show off a bit of thigh.'

I had a short skirt, kind of silvery, and a bit inappropriate for the beach – but if Liza was wearing a short dress . . .

'I think you should go for the nearly naked look, Liza,' said Tanya. 'That's what blokes like, isn't it? I wish Cat was back too. She's got the most experience with boys. I'd ask Ivan straight out, but we all know his opinion would be worse than useless. It's bad enough that he's coming.'

'What about Seth?' I asked. 'He might know.'

'You must be joking,' said Tanya. 'He's almost as bad as Ivan.'

'Oh, I don't know,' said Liza. 'Seth has a certain style, in a new age, surfie kind of way. He's been here for months. He might have been to other beach barbies.'

'I'll go and ask him,' I volunteered. I was anxious to be friends with Seth before tonight. And I needed to go back home and reassess my wardrobe for the naked look. 'I'll call in on Cat, too. How are you two getting down to the beach?'

'Lift, I expect,' said Tanya. 'Sometimes it's good to have your leg in plaster!'

'I'll go down with Cat,' I said. 'If she's in, we'll come over.'

Cat wasn't in. That was strange. I thought she'd have *forced* her parents, at gunpoint if necessary, to get her back in time to change for the barbecue. I slogged on up the hill to Seth's, praying he'd be up from the beach. I stood in the porch and knocked on the kitchen door of the crowded little cottage. Wind-chimes jingled in the breeze off the sea. I peered in to a tumbling litter of small children. Then I saw Seth stepping over them. He opened the door, and looked down on me from his great gangly height. 'So what brings you here?' he asked, guardedly.

'Seth, I'm sorry I was a bit offhand yesterday. Don't know what came over me.'

'The presence of better-looking guys, I suspect,' said Seth.

'I shouldn't have been like that. It's just that I – I really like one of them.'

'Oh yeah?' said Seth. 'I won't ask which one. I dare say all will be revealed down on the beach tonight.' He coughed. 'Anyway, gotta go, man. I'm helping to build the bonfire, gather driftwood and stuff.'

'You've done this before?'

'Yeah, man. Lots of times.'

'I know it's a silly question, Seth, but what did people wear?'

Seth hooted with laughter. 'Not a lot!' he said. He ducked

back into the cottage for his guitar and slung it on his back. Then he came into the porch again and picked up his skateboard. 'Check out my beach gear,' he said holding out his arms, 'style guru that I am! Don't ask me about clothes, Jo-jo. I don't even care about the right labels. Ask one of your cool guys. Bye! See you later!' I watched him glide down the hill, still not quite sure if we were friends.

I tried Cat again before going home. Still no one there. Home. My lot were all back. 'So what's this about a party on the beach tonight?' said Dad.

'Just a barbecue, Dad. Everyone else is going. Good clean fun, don't you know?'

'I know. Mum told me. Well, it just means all the more supper for us up here! You can go, Jo-jo, but I don't want you staying out until all hours.'

'What's your problem, Dad? Surely you can't object to a barbecue on the beach with all my friends? Or aren't I supposed to have any fun on holiday? It's practically Sunday-school-outing stuff.' I was beginning to get exercised, but luckily Dad was in a benign mood.

'It's OK, darling. Alan and Pat are going to the pub down there later on. Alan's said he'll run you home – and any of your friends who need a lift.' I thought better of objecting, and went upstairs to rethink my clothes for the evening.

On the bed I'd laid out my Jeffrey Rogers trousers and the new top from the surf shop, with a shirt to put on if it got colder. But now I wasn't so sure. Perhaps I needed to dress up a bit. Deep down, I knew I wanted to make Matt fancy me rather than Cat, but I was hardly admitting it even to myself. I certainly wanted to look nice for him. There wasn't anyone else. So what did I have that was sexy? There was the bikini top and short shiny skirt option. It wasn't quite my style, but it was as near naked as I could get. What if it got cold? I packed a sweatshirt in a backpack, along with a towel, just in case we swam. I wasn't sparing with the make-up. Foundation to hide a couple of spots, a bit of lipstick and a lot of eye-liner. I put my hair in plaits to look trendy and I was all ready bar the shoes. Nothing looked right. The high-heeled strappy sandals looked the best. I tottered downstairs, chucked a couple of cans of Coke, a potato and the last frozen veggie-burger in its box into the backpack, along with the sweatshirt and towel, and set off for Cat's, hoping I could ride pillion in these shoes. But Cat's house was still all dark. No one there. I went back home and rang her mobile number. No reply. I went down to Tanya's. She and Liza had already gone. So I had to go down with my uncle and aunt. I sat in the back of their car and had to endure Uncle Alan's comments on my outfit until Aunt Pat took pity on me and made him be quiet.

Once they'd dropped me I saw Tanya and Liza walking over to the dunes in front of me and took off my shoes to run and catch them up. They were both wearing cargo shorts with sleeveless tops, and flip-flops. They turned as they heard me panting after them.

'Blimey!' said Tanya. 'You look like a townie off to the disco on Friday night.'

'Oh, she doesn't look that bad,' said Liza. 'I like your skirt, Josie. I decided against mine in the end. I thought it maybe made me look a bit tarty. You've got better legs than me, though. I'm sure the boys will be impressed. Just make sure you don't try anything on with my Sebastian.' She peered along the path behind me. 'So what have you done with Cat?'

'She wasn't there. I'm sure she'll be down here soon.' I was determined not to be put off by anything this evening.

I knew I looked sexy. The other two didn't understand about fashion. Cat would probably be dressed just like me – we often did the same things without even knowing. 'Hey, look, they've got the bonfire going! Tonight is just going to be *so* fab!'

SEVEN

We came down from the dunes on to the beach. The bonfire builders had made an area theirs, although there were still plenty of families and dog-walkers around. Everyone was good natured. Somehow you got the feeling that the adults remembered doing this when they were younger and the parents knew their children would do it when they were older – no one seemed to resent the intrusion of a large group of teenagers.

I stood on the edge of the dunes while the other two went ahead. I wanted to assess the situation. I hadn't expected to be here without Cat. I missed her, even though she would have gone off with Matt soon enough.

Seth was hard at work on the bonfire with a couple of other boys. They had amassed a huge pile of driftwood. Blue smoke spiralled up into the sky. The scent of woodsmoke wafted over to where I stood. With the gleaming sea, the wash of waves and the sun slowly dropping, it was all too romantic for words. I looked for our boys. Tanya and Liza had already claimed Paul and Sebastian. They were standing talking in an excited group, though Liza and Sebastian never stay still for long – I saw Liza darting off along the shallows for Sebastian to chase her. Luke and Matt were smoking and chatting to each other, drinking from cans. There were plenty of kids I knew only by sight, including a stunningly beautiful new-agey girl called Bathsheba. She was circling round our group in a predatory way. I thought I'd better keep an eye on Matt, if Cat didn't turn up!

Not wanting to appear as the sad loser who always hovers on the fringes of popular groups, I decided it was time to go and join in. Now, did I want to be with Seth and his hippie friends – it might help to re-establish our relationship (platonic, naturally) – or with Tanya, Liza and the boys? No contest, really. Shoes still in hand, I was drawn as if by a magnet to Matt and the group that surrounded him.

'Hi guys,' I said. In fact, Bathsheba was the only one who answered.

'Hi,' she said. 'Can you introduce me to these people? I've seen you at the pub. You lot always seem to be having a good time. I'm Bathsheba, by the way.'

I was flattered to be considered part of the elite. 'Well—' I started.

'I'm Luke,' said Luke, before I had a chance to introduce her.

'And I'm Matt. Good to meet you, Bathsheba.'

'And I'm Josie,' I added in rather a small voice.

Suddenly Tanya was bellowing in my ear – 'Seth! Hey, Seth! Is that fire hot enough for barbecuing, yet? I'm starving!'

'Thanks for deafening me,' I said.

'Sorry,' she said, 'but I'm so hungry. Fancy coming over to the bonfire with me to find out?'

'OK.' If I stuck with Tanya at least I'd have a good reason to go back to the group. 'Do you want an excuse to get away from Paul or something?'

'No, I'm just hungry, that's all. Come on, let's go and ask

Seth.' (Tanya doesn't have problems with Seth.) The bonfire was well under way. 'How's it doing, Seth?' Tanya
asked.

'Cool,' said Seth, '– I mean hot. We're ready to roll. You
could go and tell people to bring their food.'

'I'll go,' said Tanya. 'You stay with Seth, Josie.' Was she
trying to keep me away from Matt? Seth smiled at me,
which was a relief after our stand-off.

'You look cool,' he said. '*Très* sexy.'

'Oh, thanks,' I blushed. I definitely hadn't dressed like
this for Seth's benefit, but it was nice to be complimented.

'Got a burger or something?' he asked.

I delved into my backpack for the potato and the burger.
He put the burger on the barbecue they'd set up and pulled
off a bit of tinfoil to wrap my potato in. Very efficient. 'How
will I know which potato is mine?'

'I'll know,' Seth said. 'Trust me.' He gave me a glittery
grin. 'Do us a favour, Jo-jo?'

'Depends what it is.'

'Sing my song with me? I told a couple of people about it.
Said I'd play it later on. And a few of our others? There's
another guitar you can play.'

I really did want to be friends with Seth again. 'OK.
When?'

'About half an hour, when people are eating?'

'If you think it won't ruin their digestion.'

Seth flipped my burger over. A queue was already forming
and he was busy. 'Paper plates over there. Salads over on
that rock. Ivan and Tanya's mum did them.' I grabbed a
plate and he put the burger on it. 'See you later, then, where
the guitars are.' He pointed to another large rock where
several guitars and a radio rested on a groundsheet. I carried
my food back to the others.

Tanya looked up from where she was sitting with Paul (on his lap, virtually). 'Seth let you go, then?' she said.

'Yes. Why shouldn't he?' I didn't want Matt and co. to think there was anything going on between me and Seth. I say Matt and co. – in fact Paul and Tanya were now being all misty-eyed with one another, Liza and Sebastian had come to rest, literally, and were lying down together – I didn't like to look too hard at what they were up to – and Luke was deep in conversation with Bathsheba. So Matt was the only person likely to benefit from this information anyway. And he didn't look that interested. In fact I almost felt sorry for him without Cat.

I decided to suppress my own feelings for him and go and commiserate. I sat down beside him. 'Want a bit of burger, Matt?'

He actually smiled at me. 'OK, don't mind if I have a nibble. I forgot to bring any food. Thought Cat was going to sort that out.'

'I – I thought she'd be back for this. She was really looking forward to it.'

'So did I. Seems like Daddy from the Dark Ages has won the day.'

'What do you mean?'

'He's managed to keep her away from Evil Matt.'

'You're not evil, Matt. That is so unfair.'

'Isn't it, just.'

I handed over the burger, dripping with ketchup. He took a bite and passed it back, but a bit dropped off and fell down my bikini top. It was still quite hot, and I leapt up, but Matt said, wickedly, 'Sit down. That bit was mine, and I want it.' So I sat down and he hooked out the bit of burger with his finger from where it was lodged and put it in his mouth. 'Mmmm,' he said, licking his finger, and smiled at me, long and slow. I nearly keeled over. 'You should wear more clothes,' he said, and gave my bare shoulder a sly stroke. 'Then accidents wouldn't happen.'

I looked around nervously to see if anyone else had heard this little exchange, but they were all engrossed in each other. Someone waving caught my eye and I was suddenly terrified that it might be Cat, but it wasn't, it was Seth.

'I promised Seth I'd sing,' I said to Matt, forgetting that he didn't know that this was quite a normal occurrence.

'Suit yourself,' he said. 'Perhaps I'll catch you later if Cat doesn't show.'

'OK,' I said, running off, and it was a while before I registered his words. Matt was going to 'catch' me – if Cat didn't turn up! Perversely I prayed that Cat was all right. I couldn't bear the thought that the power of my wishes had somehow put her out of action. It was all too scary.

Seth handed me a guitar. He'd spread a blanket on the sand near the fire for us and people were sitting round expectantly. I raised my eyes to where I'd been, and saw that even my lot were waiting for something to happen. I tried not to focus on where Matt was sitting. His lazy smile and deft touch were still with me.

Seth and I should have practised more, but we managed to play for nearly half an hour. Our voices worked really well together, and I concentrated on playing the guitar to take my mind off Matt. Even Seth's latest composition, the 'sweet soft smile' one, sounded good in that setting. I sang it on my own, and caught Seth's eye as we were finishing. He motioned for us to do a repeat, so we sang it again and he put in some really excellent harmonies. Everyone clapped when it came to an end.

'Thanks, Jo-jo,' said Seth, punching my arm as I put the guitar down. 'Thanks mate, that was cool.' He quickly turned on the radio which was tuned to Latino FM and everyone came down to join in the dirty dancing. Seth retired to talk to some friends. *Some friends?* It was the dolphin boys! I hadn't seen them earlier, but they seemed to be congratulating Seth. I'd forgotten he knew them. But then everything went from my mind because someone had their hands on my behind and was dancing with me – Matt!

'Yeah, well,' he said, when I glanced at him questioningly, and went into a pretty fair version of the salsa. I can salsa – Holly and I went to classes – but it's hard, and most boys I know can't get into the rhythm of it at all. They waggle their shoulders and not their hips. Not Matt.

WOW! Was I happy! Gloriously happy. I was on the beach, with *my* crowd, dancing with Matt. I hooked my arms around his neck and he slid his hands round to my hips. I felt very naked indeed as his warm breath lapped my ear. 'You can certainly dance,' he murmured, and moved my hips in time with his.

The dancing was getting pretty riotous. I let Matt guide me away from the crowd. 'Perhaps we should find a bit of privacy,' he said, and edged me further round the beach. We climbed up a little and found a patch of soft sand and tussocky grass. I could hear the waves, but not see them. The music was just a distant beat. I lay back next to Matt. As the sun set over the dunes I closed my eyes and waited for the inevitable kiss.

But Matt wasn't so hasty. He kissed my eyelids and stroked my face. He ran his thumb over my lips and teeth tantalisingly (except I died a thousand times thinking it was because he couldn't bring himself to kiss my train tracks) until I tried to bite it, and only then did he bring his mouth down on mine. With passion. Crikey. This was serious stuff and it was wonderful. Matt and me – I couldn't believe my dreams had come true as he pressed the full weight of his warm flesh against me.

'Josie! Josie?' Two girls were calling out my name as they descended on our hiding place. Tanya and Liza. 'I thought I saw her go off in this direction.'

'So did I. I saw her shiny skirt.'

'Was she with a bloke?'

'I think so, but I didn't see who.' She called again. 'Josie?'

Matt swore quietly. 'Do yourself up,' he whispered. 'And here, have my T-shirt.'

'It's OK,' I whispered back. 'I've got a sweatshirt in my bag here.' I put it on.

'I think we'd better pretend this didn't happen, don't you?' Matt said, as the voices got closer.

'OK,' I said, feeling hurt, but knowing it was for the best. I stood up and waved. 'Hi you two!' I called. 'I'm up here. With Matt. We went for a walk. We were talking about Cat,' I added, for authenticity.

'Well, your dad's looking for you,' said Tanya.

'Oh no, not another dad on the warpath,' groaned Matt quietly.

'I thought my uncle was fetching me. Oh well. Better go back then,' I said, determined to stay cool. I climbed down. Matt ran down the slope behind me, digging his heels into the sand.

'So what have you done with my mates?' he said to the girls. 'I thought they were going to take you back to the campsite?'

'No way!' said Tanya and Liza sanctimoniously, and I didn't know whether to feel smug or terrible. As it was, I was far too worried about Dad's reaction to me going missing.

As we came back round the beach I heard music again. Not the radio, but someone playing rock and roll. It was pretty dark, but I could make out figures hunched over guitars by the bonfire. One or two people were listening, but most had drifted off. We went up closer. Someone was singing 'Hey Jude' – badly, but with feeling. The other guitarist had something glinting in his ear. No wonder everyone had disappeared. The artistes in question were my dad and Ivan. I could have died.

'Oh God,' said Tanya. 'My brother. How embarrassing.' Then she looked at me pityingly. 'But not half as bad as your dad!' she said as Paul and Sebastian turned up to stare at the awful spectacle.

Matt was right behind me. I so much wanted to reach back and take his hand, but I didn't dare. As we both stood, mesmerised by this terrible performance, Dad put on a pair of swimming goggles that he'd found and started on the Na na na nana na na's in a falsetto voice, before grabbing Ivan and waltzing him round the bonfire. I stepped back. 'I'm really sorry you had to see that,' I said to Matt, mortified.

I had to stop Dad and the only way to stop him was to make my presence known and offer myself up for the lift home. 'Bye Matt,' I said, and gave him a peck on the cheek. He caught me and kissed me on the mouth, in front of everyone. 'You're sweet,' he said. 'But this is all it was, OK?' and he turned to the others and led their retreat.

I gulped and stepped towards the fire. 'Dad! I'm here!' I thought I might as well lay it on thick. 'Good guitar playing!'

He removed the goggles and tossed them back to where he'd found them. 'Thank you. I enjoyed that. Now, got your gear? And where's Seth? Alan and Pat are waiting in the bar to take us all home.'

Seth stepped from the shadows. He spoke to the dolphin boys who were staying by the fire. (I still couldn't get used to the idea that dear old Seth was on speaking terms with such cool guys. Everyone else I knew was rather in awe of them.) He picked up his guitar and his skateboard but he didn't speak to me. People were threading their way through the sand dunes along the little paths. It was dark now. As the paths converged I overheard little snippets of conversation. I was pretty disgusted by what I heard. 'I'm glad my dad doesn't make a tit of himself in front of my friends . . .' 'Matt, you jammy so-and-so – you didn't, did you? That'll up your score.' 'Not as such. But no one's to tell the other one . . .' 'Luke's bird's a goer – I reckon he'll get more points than me.'

I hurried on, sticking close behind Dad. Seth followed. He was still silent. My uncle and aunt were waiting outside the pub for us. 'Well, that seemed to be a jolly little do,' said Dad. 'I reckon we'd have had a wilder time in our day, Alan!' (Hypocrite.) 'But you enjoyed yourselves, didn't you, kids?'

'Josie obviously did,' said Seth, glowering at me.

I climbed into the back of the car with him. Aunty Pat was leaning forward to talk to my dad. 'What's the matter, Seth?' I asked. 'We were great!'

'Exactly,' said Seth. 'And then you had to go and spoil it.'

I looked at him. This wasn't fair. 'What did I spoil?'

Seth didn't reply. But after a while he said petulantly, 'And you never came back for your potato. I was guarding it for you.'

This had to be so ridiculous. I was about to round on him for being babyish but from the way Seth was humming and jigging his legs I judged I'd better keep quiet. When we got home he grabbed his things and took off up the hill without saying goodbye.

I went straight up to bed too. I needed to be on my own. A quick glance in the mirror reminded me how messed up my make-up was – thank goodness it had been dusk on the beach. But I didn't want to look too hard in the mirror right now. I wanted to forget Seth, forget what I'd overheard. I just wanted to dive into bed and relive my time with Matt.

I lay there in the dark for a while, clutching Monk. Matt had been really sexy. We hadn't – you know – or anything, but he'd been pretty passionate. And he'd kissed my eyelids! That was so gentle and so sweet! But there was no one I could share it with. That was the irony. I'd just got off with the most popular boy in Cornwall and I couldn't tell anyone. If only Cat hadn't got there first. It seemed so unfair. Everyone would have liked me so much more if they'd seen how attractive Matt found me.

I sat up and switched on the light. Part of my brain was singing 'I got off with Matt. I got off with Matt,' but another part was asking, 'What about Cat? What about Cat?' I could sort of justify it. After all, I really did fancy Matt, and he must have fancied me at least a little bit. And Cat had been funny about him lately.

And then I did one of those awful, horrified intakes of breath. 'Oh no!' What if Cat found out somehow? What if anyone found out? I mean, everyone would know about the very public kiss on the beach because Matt had done that intentionally, so that he could say, yes, I gave her a quick kiss, but everyone saw it and there was nothing to it. Quite cunning really. I suppose he could even say it was because I was Cat's friend. But what if they found out that we'd gone a bit further than that? Cat would kill me. But no one knew, did they? Would Matt tell anyone? *'Matt, you jammy so-and-so, you didn't, did you?'* Matt already *had* told someone.

I wrote a quick and very private list that included quite a few things you *can* do with a fixed brace. Then I put out the light and tried to dream about Matt and not think about tomorrow. I was just dropping off when I heard a car pulling up outside Cat's cottage, followed by the voices of Cat and her parents as they made their way indoors, though I couldn't make out what they were saying.

What had I done?

EIGHT

I didn't sleep brilliantly. I woke up at some unearthly hour – the rooster down the road was making a racket – and wrote another list to try and sort things out:

Best case scenario
Matt to finish with Cat and her not to mind.
Matt to start going out with me.
Cat to go out with one of the others, perhaps Luke.
Cat only to hear about the public kiss and not mind.
For us to be a cool eightsome.
Seth to just be friends again.

Worst case scenario
Cat to hear about me getting off with Matt.
Cat to mind terribly.
Cat to hate me.
Cat to make everyone else hate me, including Matt.
Seth to hate me.

The best case scenario was slightly overoptimistic. I did another more realistic one:

Most likely best case scenario
Cat hears about public kiss and doesn't mind much.
Cat carries on going out with Matt.
Matt blanks me and pretends nothing happened.
Seth goes back to being my friend.

Hmm. Since the first best scenario was pretty unlikely, the future looked bleak. It all depended on who knew what, and I needed to find that out as soon as possible. I finally fell asleep again and woke to hear small cousins thundering up and down the stairs, probably with the express purpose of torturing me. I threw on some clothes and tottered down to breakfast.

'Good _morning_, big sister!' said Tim, looking far too bright for the early hour. Oh God, what did _he_ know?

'Harrumph.' I tipped Coco Pops into my bowl.

'Gather you and Dad and Ivan entertained the troops last night.'

'Shut up. I thought you might come. Where were you?'

'Sailing with Harry and Archie. Much more fun. Hey, guess what?'

'I don't know. What?'

Tim moved closer. 'Harry and I are going to Newquay today.'

'Oh yeah?' I failed to see the significance of that. Dad came in, still in his dressing-gown. I think he'd overdone it somewhat in the pub. Time to get my own back. 'Oh God, it's the rock and roll star. Morning, Dad.'

'What about this singing then, Jo-jo?'

'You were embarrassing, Dad. I can say that in the cold light of day.'

'I didn't mean last night. The DIY oratorio. It starts this evening. We'll have Nicholas Elliott conducting us!'

Now that was pretty amazing. For those not in the know, Nicholas Elliott conducts the last night of the proms sometimes. It would definitely be something to hit my muso friends with. Even my favourite drummer would be impressed. But no. Singing in a choir on holiday was too deeply sad and tragic.

'Sorry, Dad. No go. I'm doing a painting, for heaven's sake. Some people are never satisfied.'

'Oh well,' Dad sighed. 'How about clocking up some brownie points by popping down to the shop for some milk and a paper. Your cousins seem to have had a cereal feast judging by the state of the table. They've all gone off to the beach. I told Mum we'd join them later.'

I was going to tell him to ask Tim, if he was that desperate, but then I reconsidered. If I went out I could call on Tanya or Liza and test the water a bit. 'OK, Dad. Give me some money then.'

I glanced up at Cat's cottage, and Seth's beyond that. The sound of children's voices drifted down from Seth's, but in Cat's the curtains were still drawn. The car was there though. I carried on down the hill. I thought I'd go to the shop first – it would take a bit of courage to call in on Tanya or Liza. Such a shame when in other circumstances my friends would have rallied round to congratulate me. I wished I could talk to Holly, but she wasn't at home. She was staying with her new boyfriend in the country. I wondered how she was getting on. Holly wouldn't get off with her best friend's boyfriend, would she? We just wouldn't do that to each other. So was Cat a different sort of best friend?

I pushed open the shop door. As it clanged to, that lovely village shop smell washed over me – sweets and newspapers and an undertone of talcum powder. I gathered up a big plastic bottle of milk and queued to collect our paper. The door clanged again, and Tanya and Liza came in. 'Hi!' I called, waving.

I waited while they went round the shelf unit that ran down the centre of the shop. They reappeared with baskets of shopping and stood behind me in the queue. 'Hi, you two,' I said again.

At first they didn't reply.

Then Tanya came up to me and hissed, 'We don't associate with people like you.'

I stared at them both, at a loss for words.

'And I wouldn't like to be in your shoes when Cat gets to hear about it.'

I tried to summon some sense of righteousness. 'It was only a friendly kiss,' I said, making light of it.

'Oh yeah,' said Tanya. 'We're not stupid, Josie. Matt doesn't exactly drag girls off into the dunes for a *chat*, now, does he?'

I paid for my paper and milk. I wanted to go. But Tanya had more to say. 'Just because Luke preferred Bathsheba, you thought you'd go for Matt instead, didn't you? As soon as Cat's back was turned! Never mind that he's already spoken for.'

I'd had enough. 'Oh shut up, Tanya. You don't know anything!' Suddenly all those snippets of the boys' conversation added up – about points and scores and winners. They were having a competition! And we were their willing victims! I wanted Tanya and Liza to feel as bad as I did. 'I never fancied Luke anyway. All four of those boys are only in it for a competition – a bet! They're notching us up. And Matt's winning – in one department. But in fact, Luke's winning because Bathsheba is a bit easier than you two are. So there!'

I marched off. I'd scored a few points, but I can't say I was happy. Liza hadn't said a word. And I was dreading meeting Cat.

I dumped the stuff on the kitchen table. 'I'm going to work on my picture, Dad. And I'm having more positive thoughts about the singing. Try me again this afternoon. The Nicholas Elliott factor might just win me over.'

Dad smiled. 'That's my girl,' he said. I went over and gave him a hug. At least in Dad's eyes I could be perfect.

I set myself up in the window of my bedroom, kneeling on the floor with the paper on the broad window-seat. I had a board to rest on and a good selection of materials to work with. I pulled out my sketches. I'd gone off the idea of a boy morphing into a dolphin. Better just to have a boy with the dolphins, almost indistinguishable from them. I did some sketches of a boy with his arms pointed over his head as if diving, and flippers on his feet. It was possible to make him into a dolphin shape. I drew loads of them. I imagined the scene from just below the water's surface. The sky would be pearly with dawn or sunset, perhaps some smoke up there too, from a bonfire on the beach. And this boy, he was joining in the playing and leaping. He didn't want to be human any more – he wanted to lose his human form – he simply wanted the freedom to *be*.

I worked away for ages. There was a diminishing pattern of dolphins, like an underwater dance, and then there were three bursting out of the water, with the water breaking up in the light. And if you looked really hard you would see that in fact one of the three was a boy. It was hard to make out his features, but in my head it was the younger dolphin boy, the one who'd caught my eye on the ferry. (I mean, it was sort of me, too – you probably gathered that – but right then I wasn't quite sure precisely *what* I was expressing, I just knew I needed to express it.)

The hours slipped by. Tim put his head round the door to say he was off to Newquay with Harry. They'd worked it all out and Harry was dead excited. He plucked at his earlobe. 'Watch this space,' he said.

'Tim! They'll murder you!'

'Why should they? You had yours done.'

'Suppose so.'

Tim saw what I was doing and came over to look. 'Honestly, Jo-jo,' he said, and I braced myself for the insults. 'You spend ninety per cent of the time acting like a total bimbo and then you go and produce stuff like this. It's going to be brilliant. I'll never understand women, not even my own sister.'

He went off to Newquay. It had been a backhanded compliment of a sort.

Then Dad came up. 'Do you want to come to the beach with me?'

'No thanks, Dad. I'm doing this.'

'And what's "this"?' He came over to the window. 'You're a clever little thing, Jo-jo, you really are. You must show Grandma this some time. She'll be thrilled.' (My grandad who died last year was quite a well-known artist. I used to paint with him when I was little.) 'Well, you stay here and work on it by all means. I can see quite a big price sticker going on this.'

I'd forgotten that. Dad went off, and I wondered just how

much I might get for it. Ten quid would come in very handy right now. I made myself a sandwich and started colouring. I laid down a mauvey watercolour wash to start with. I'd collected a few shells during the week and I crushed them into the colour I was using for a bit of sparkle. It was coming along nicely. As I painted I thought of me and Matt in the dunes once or twice, but I put the memories away and concentrated on working. It was the best cure, it really was. If Cat had come by on her bike or Seth on his skateboard, I hadn't heard them.

At six o'clock Tim came back with Harry. They came upstairs to find me. They were extremely pleased with themselves. 'Look!' they cried, both displaying rather red ears with a little gold hoop in.

'Tim squealed,' said Harry proudly. 'But I didn't.'

'Harry wants a haircut, now, Josie,' said Tim. 'I said you'd do it for him.'

'What, now? Can't you see I'm busy?'

'Well, you're not going to finish that tonight if you go off singing. Go on, Josie!'

'I want to give my parents the fright of their lives,' said Harry, beaming.

'But—' I looked at dear straight old Harry. I wasn't sure *I* wanted him different. 'Couldn't you just style it differently? Lose the parting? You could do that for him, Tim. I've got to finish this for Sunday whatever happens.'

'Oh, OK,' said Tim. 'Come into the bathroom Harry. I might snip a bit off for you. I think I know what to do.'

'Cool!' said Harry, and they left me in peace.

But not for long. I think it was deliberate. A few minutes later, Tim pushed Harry in at the door. 'Josie! Oh look what I've done!' And there was Harry with great chunks chopped out of his hair. It was long on one side and short on the other.

I heaved a sigh and followed them back to the bathroom. 'One thing,' I said severely. 'I didn't do this, OK? You had it done at the hairdresser's. I'm in enough trouble already and I don't want your parents blaming me for ruining their precious little Harry.'

'Were you caught down the pub again, Josie?' asked Harry as I tucked a towel round him.

'Far worse than that!' said Tim. 'She was caught *in flagrante* with Cat's boyfriend!'

I spun round, scissors in hand, and nearly took his eye out. 'What? Is that the story that's going round?'

'It's true, isn't it?'

I started snipping Harry's hair. 'Only sort of,' I said. 'Matt started it. He came up and danced with me and then – led me away.'

'Led you astray by the sound of it,' said Tim.

'That,' I said, 'is none of your business. He – kissed me, that's all.'

'So what were you up to when Tanya found you both? Ivan says you were—'

'No one knows what we were doing because no one was there. I told Tanya we were talking about Cat. Anything else is the result of her fevered imagination.' It was true. No one had seen us, I knew that. And it gave me a bit of hope. I could simply deny that anything had happened. We had been alone. It had been between Matt and me. He started it. I fancied him, so I went along with it. Anyone would have. It was hard enough for me that it wasn't going to carry on, without everyone giving me grief.

'Ow!' I'd snipped Harry's other ear, the non-pierced one. It was time to concentrate.

'Pass me Dad's electric razor, Tim.'

By the time I'd finished, Harry really was transformed. The short hair suited him. Showed off his navy-blue eyes as well as the earring and the sore ears. 'Cool!' he said, over and over again, when he looked at himself in the mirror.

'My pleasure,' I said. 'You two clear up, and mind you make a good job of it. The parents will be back any minute now.'

The church is tiny and ancient and beautiful. At this time of year it's like a little boat sailing on a golden sea of cornfields. Nicholas Elliott was already there organising people into voices. Dad and Ivan are tenors. I'm an alto. He organised us so the tenors stood behind the sopranos and the basses stood behind the altos. As I picked up my music and went to my place, Nicholas said, 'Good, you must be the lass. I'd like a word with you later.'

I didn't have time to wonder why because we started straight into the Haydn, sight-reading it. Then we had a short break and whizzed through the Handel. Nicholas knew exactly what he wanted out of us, but this was just a taster. By the end of the weekend we'd sound professional. There were a few songs included in the programme. One had apparently been written especially for us, something Cornish and evocative, Nicholas said.

We were just gathering up the music at the end when two boys came down the aisle towards us. Gideon and Caleb! 'Well, thank you very much for deigning to turn up, boys,' said Nicholas.

'Sorry Dad,' said the older dolphin boy. 'Big drama on the beach. One of the surfers we know had an accident. Did something stupid over on Breakneck Rock. Nearly drowned.'

'But he's OK,' said the younger one. 'Just staying overnight in hospital. Didn't you hear the helicopter?'

I saw Ivan prick up his ears. He went over to the boys. 'Who was it? Who was it?' he asked. 'Was it anyone I know?'

'Guy called Matt,' said the older dolphin boy. 'You know him, don't you?' He was looking at me.

My heart was in my knees somewhere. 'But he's OK, isn't he?'

'Yeah, fine,' said the younger one, looking at me with his sea-grey eyes. 'Now have you talked to Dad about the song?'

'Not yet she hasn't,' said Nicholas to him. 'Can you give me five minutes, dear, just while I sort this music out?'

'Of course,' I said.

I nipped outside to one of my favourite places in the world – the part of the graveyard with a view over the fields to the sea – and leant against a headstone. It was all a bit too much to take in. Vying for space in my brain were the major items of news:

1 *Matt was in hospital.*
2 *The dolphin boys were Nicholas Elliott's sons – and they knew who I was!*

All this quite apart from the traumas of last night (Matt) and today (Tanya and Liza, not to mention the rest of the world).

I stood there, letting the tranquil evening wash over me. My life was far too complicated for me even to attempt to untangle it. Matt wasn't dead or anything. But I was about to have an interview with a very famous conductor.

I took a few deep breaths and went back into the church.

Dad was in the porch with Ivan. 'Oh, there you are,' Dad said. 'Thought we'd lost you.'

'Worried about Matt, are you?' said Ivan, a touch sneakily.

I ignored him. 'Nicholas Elliott wants to talk to me, Dad. Don't know why. I'll be out again in five minutes. See you in the car?'

Nicholas was down at the front of the church. I suddenly felt dreadfully in awe of him. 'Ah, Jo – is it? Giddy wasn't altogether sure that that was your name.'

'Yes,' I said, brain still reeling. 'Jo is fine.'

He carried on sifting through piles of music as he spoke. 'We need the voice of a very young woman for this Max Barnes song. Raw and inexperienced. Innocent. It's about the Annunciation, you see. He wants us to imagine Mary, terrified and overawed. But she's pierced to the heart by love, you see – for God, for the angel, for her unborn child.' (Nicholas Elliott talked like that.) 'I was going to do auditions, but there aren't many teenage girls here, and Giddy's heard you sing. Says you'd be perfect. How would you feel?'

'Is – is it very exposed?'

'No. That's the thing. It's accompanied by woodwind and cello. They weave in and out. The voice is mostly another instrument. It's a lovely piece. Quite folky and haunting. Have you ever sung or played in an ensemble?'

'Yes. I'm a clarinettist – or was until this thing.' I pointed at my brace. 'But I sing and play the guitar.'

'Talented girl.'

'Not really.'

'Well, it's late and I have to be getting home. Unfortunately I've forgotten the music. Stupid of me.' He tapped his forehead while he thought. 'Did you come here in a car?'

'Yes. With my dad.'

'Then perhaps you could drop me off at my house and I'll hand it over. We're only a few hundred yards down the lane.'

We went out into the car park, past the church hall where the art exhibition was to be held. Dad was standing on tiptoe trying to peer in the window. He heard me approaching, and spoke without turning his head. 'So what did the great man want with my little Josie?'

'To sing one of our songs,' said Nicholas to his back. 'And she's kindly offered me a lift home so she can pick up the music. I hope that's all right by you.'

Poor Dad did a wonderful double-take. 'Good grief! Yes, of course.' He opened the car door. 'Into the back, Ivan. I think we'll let Nicholas Elliott sit in the front seat, don't you?'

When we reached the Elliotts' house I got out with the conductor. The younger son opened their front door to us. 'Whatcha, Gids,' his father said, thus answering my question as to which brother was Caleb and which was Gideon. Nicholas turned to me. 'Come in, young lady, come in.' He called to his wife in the kitchen. 'Eileen, I think we've found our Virgin at last! Can you lay your hands on the music?' I stood there nervously, not daring to catch Gideon's eye. Did his father have to put it like that?

Caleb bounced down the stairs. 'Is Gideon's Virgin here?' he called. I nearly died. Then he ducked round the corner and saw me. 'Of course. I hadn't made the connection. You're the one that was with the guy who had the accident! And you're Gideon's Virgin! One and the same. Well, well.'

I took the pages of music, thanked Nicholas, and ran out of the door. Today had been altogether too much.

NINE

I found solace in my painting.

It was half past ten by the time Dad and I got in. Tim was in trouble about the ear-piercing, particularly because Harry's parents had been really upset. Tim had already gone to bed, but Mum wanted to discuss the whole business with Dad. So I made my excuses and left. I put my head round Tim's door but he didn't wake up. If he'd spent the evening rowing with Mum, it was quite likely he hadn't picked up any gossip about the accident anyway. What I really wanted to do was pop round to Cat's, but that seemed so impossible now.

The paintings had to be on display for the interval of the concert on Sunday evening, so people could look at them while they had a glass of wine or whatever. They were numbered but not named, and people wrote down what they were prepared to pay. Then the exhibition stayed up for a few days and the pictures went to the highest bidders and the money went to the artists, with ten per cent for the church roof fund. The children's art was sold in the same way – usually parents buy their own children's pictures – but it's quite a good way of fund-raising.

So. It was now late on Friday night. Tomorrow the rehearsal would run from eleven until one; break for lunch; and then from two until four plus a bit of time for extras, like Barnes's 'Annunciation'. I had tomorrow morning and evening (great way to spend Saturday night) and Sunday morning to finish the picture. I set it up and worked on sketching in the leaping dolphins for a bit. I still wasn't quite sure which one was going to be the boy. And then, with a slip of the pencil it was as if I'd given one of them bigger eyes, and hair. It was a sign. I made that one the boy, roughed in the rest of the face. And suddenly – it looked like Gideon. Weird. Somehow I'd made it look like Gideon. It would have made more sense if it had turned out like Matt.

Definitely time for bed!

I spent a long time in front of the mirror taking off my make-up. I wasn't sure who I was any more. I was lots of people:

1 *Sisterly sort of person to Tim, Harry – maybe Ivan and Seth, too.*
2 *Scarlet woman to Tanya and Liza.*
3 *One-time friend to Cat.*
4 *Silly girl with brace, not much good at anything, e.g. surfing.*
5 *Muso.*
6 *Daughter not to be trusted, but OK at painting.*
7 *Gideon's Virgin.*

OK. I know everyone pretends they're not (a virgin, that is), but most of my friends are waiting for someone really, really special to come along. Anyway, that had nothing to do with how I felt about my latest persona as 'Gideon's Virgin'. Hideous embarrassment aside, I was excited by the realisation that Caleb and Gideon and Nicholas Elliott had referred to me like that before they knew my name. And it was because they thought I was good at something. And, compared to all the other Josies, 'Gideon's Virgin' was a clean slate, full of potential. 'Jo' in fact. And I'd hardly even spoken to Gideon! Just seen him from a distance, gazing out to sea. Why did he and Caleb do that gazing thing? What were they looking for?

I snuggled down to sleep. All the stuff with Matt seemed a long time ago. (Certainly not like just last night!) I hated the thought of him having an accident, but the way he'd cut me off had hardened me somewhat, not to mention their points system, and I wasn't as worried for him as I might have been. I couldn't quite see him welcoming me with open arms at his hospital bedside.

As for Cat – I decided that honesty was going to be the best policy with her. Perhaps I should just tell it how it was: yes, I had fancied Matt and he'd been very happy to take advantage of that fact while she was away. She had let him down by not turning up, hadn't she? They both had mobiles. She could have called him.

Tim burst into my room. 'Morning Big Sister! Hey, did your ear hurt the next day?'

'Yup. Went yukky, too. You'll need some surgical spirit.'

'My little pierced ear is nothing compared to what happened to your Matt. Ivan told me about it this morning.'

'Not *my* Matt, as you must have gathered. Cat's Matt.'

'His parents are taking him home today, so he's not anyone's Matt. But it was a big emergency. Helicopter and everything.'

'What happened?'

'Tanya found out that the four of them have some long-running competition.' (Bet she didn't say it was from me.) 'You know, points for girls pulled, daring feats, drinking, eating and stuff. Apparently they were level-pegging by yesterday afternoon, and the surf was up, so they decided to ride this really dodgy bit – Breakneck Rock.'

'That's what I heard from Caleb.'

'Matt was the last to go – and he lost it. Went under. As soon as he didn't surface, one of the others called the emergency services. They turned up almost straight away and managed to fish him out. He'd hit his head.'

'Yeah, Caleb said—'

'Hang on! How do you know Caleb? He's a surfer. So's his brother. Aren't they a bit out of your league?'

'Thanks very much. In fact, they're so far out of my league they're singing in the choir.'

'Get away!'

'Their dad is Nicholas Elliott, the conductor.'

'Just shows, doesn't it, how deceptive looks can be. I'd never've had those two down as musos.'

'All right, big head. Harry's parents are none too happy about the new-look Harry, a little bird told me.'

'They'll get used to it.' Tim twiddled the gold hoop in his ear. 'Ooh. Ouch. I wonder if he's suffering as much as I am.'

'I expect so. What are you doing today, while I sing my heart out?'

'The usual. Down to the beach. What's up with Liza and Tanya, by the way? They were dead snotty with me.'

'That'll be because you're my brother, and I committed an unforgivable sin.'

'Is this about you getting off with Matt?' He giggled.

'Yes. Stop laughing! Why are you laughing?'

'All those Cat sat on the Matt jokes. And—'

'And what?'

'Oh, I dunno. It's just that they think they're so cool, those guys. And Liza and Tanya and Cat think they're so cool to be going out with them.'

'They *are* cool, thank you very much. Anyway, what would you know? Red-ears!' I lunged at him and he scampered out of my room.

He made me feel a bit better, though. No one could deny that Cat is cool, but Tanya?

I had three hours until the rehearsal. I decided to devote two of them to the painting, even though part of me was desperate to get the Cat/Matt situation sorted. I worked on all the greys in the sea, remembering the colour of Gideon's eyes as I painted. Then I spent time on the sparkle as the dolphins broke through the waves. I used a bit of glittery make-up for that! It was all blocked in now, and nearly finished, but I needed to spend more time on the figures. I'd have to do that after the rehearsals tonight. Aagh! The Barnes 'Annunciation'! I shot downstairs to find Dad. 'Dad, could you just plunk this through with me on the guitar?'

'Of course. I sometimes wish, oh daughter of mine, that you realised what a little bundle of talent you are.'

'Oh Dad. All parents are programmed to think that. I'm useless at most things. Have you ever seen me try to stand up on a surf board? Come on. It's in C minor.'

We ran through the song. It was really beautiful. It starts off with a sort of splash – that's the angel arriving. But then the angel's words are all soothing – the cello actually plays them. Then the Virgin comes in, all breathless and frightened. First she's overawed by the responsibility but then finally she's overcome by love. Barnes lives in Cornwall and he'd seen paintings of Our Lady of the Sea in a local church – so it inspired him to think of the angel as the waves, or something. I guess I'll just have to bone up on the programme notes! The other thing was that he reckoned Mary was only fourteen or so, which is why he wanted a young voice. It's not a difficult piece, luckily. I'm quite looking forward to it, sad person that I am!

I looked at my watch. Ten-thirty a.m. I decided to bite the bullet and call in on Cat. I was going to say that whatever she'd heard was probably only partially true, but that I was sorry, and how was Matt? I ran up the path. Seth was coming down. 'Hi Seth!' I ventured. He simply carried on. Great.

I knocked on Cat's door. Her mother answered. She wasn't any use. 'Oh, I hear you're in the concert on Sunday dear. I do wish we could persuade Catherine to do something like that.' Not what I wanted to hear. 'Catherine?' she called up the stairs.

'Who is it?' came Cat's voice.

'Josephine.'

'Well you can tell her to bog off, for a start.'

'I'm so sorry dear,' said her mother.

Oh well. I turned and left. There were Tanya and Liza coming towards me. Liza was about to say something but Tanya stopped her and they both blanked me. I wanted to ask all sorts of questions about the boys and Matt's accident, but I decided to save my breath. I felt like crying, though.

And as soon as I got indoors I ran up to my room and burst into tears. I hauled Monk out from under my duvet and soon his fur was soaking wet. I knew I'd behaved badly with Matt, but – well, no excuses, it was bad. No wonder they didn't like me. Dad knocked on the door while I was putting on make-up to try and hide the fact that I'd been bawling. 'Coming, Dad.' I had to feel a bit glad I was doing the singing – I wasn't sure what I'd be doing otherwise right now.

The church was lovely and cheerful in the morning sun. There were pools of coloured light on the floor from the stained glass and it felt bright and airy. We started with the Handel this time. Caleb and Gideon are both basses, so they were standing in the row behind me. I could hear them booming away, Caleb particularly, as he's older and his voice is fuller. I felt shy of them, especially after what Tim had said about them being out of my league. I talked to Dad and Ivan in the coffee break. We spent the rest of the morning on the Handel – it was beginning to sound great. I love Handel anyway – it's always so sort of *jubilant*! You can't feel gloomy if you're singing Handel.

Dad and I whizzed home for lunch, dropping Ivan off on the way. Ivan was still being creepy, but he was up-to-date with the latest gossip from Tanya. He knew I was a social outcast, but I think he felt he had some sort of diplomatic immunity in our car. He told me that apparently Cat had missed the barbecue because they'd gone to visit relations and couldn't get away. (I still think she should have phoned Matt.) But she hadn't exactly hurried to see him yesterday, and that, Ivan informed me, was *before* Tanya and Liza had given her the news about Matt and me – or '*told her what you'd done*' was how he put it. Cat had been put in the picture around lunchtime and then all three girls had gone down to the surfing beach to meet up with the boys, Cat primed to forgive Matt and excommunicate me. Obviously Ivan couldn't tell me what had gone on between Cat and Matt, but anyway it wasn't long before the boys decided to go for the Breakneck Rock competition (to sort out those extra points, I guessed). Then Matt had had his accident.

We arrived outside Ivan and Tanya's cottage at this point and dropped him off for lunch. I was determined to catch up with any further developments on the way back.

Which were as follows: the girls had spent yesterday evening at Tanya's house slagging me off. (Thanks Ivan.) Then the six of them had gone to visit Matt in hospital this morning. He'd had an incredibly lucky escape, but his parents were definitely taking him home. Luke's parents were also pressing for the boys to spend the rest of their holiday with them. Matt's accident had put the wind up everybody. So now it seemed as if Tanya and Liza and Cat were all going to be without boyfriends, and apparently it was all my fault. Great.

I felt pretty wretched as we went back into the church for the afternoon rehearsal. Scared, too, about the Barnes 'Annunciation' later on. The Haydn was difficult and Nicholas Elliott was getting frustrated with us. I sensed his sons' discomfort from the row behind and wondered why on earth I was subjecting myself to this on my holiday. But towards the end of the afternoon, we got some of it right, and it was such a fabulous sound as the harmonies soared up to the roof that I remembered why I did it.

Then everybody left and it was time to rehearse the Barnes.

I say I was nervous, but the singing in itself doesn't actually bother me. I open my mouth and I know I can sing in tune, so it feels – well, natural. Nicholas didn't have the musicians there, so he had to accompany me himself on the church organ! I followed him up to the organ loft. It sounded gorgeous and echoey in the church – like singing in the bath. It was quite good, because I did start off a bit nervous and in awe (of Nicholas Elliott), but then I felt I could let rip because it sounded so nice. We went back over some of the harder bits, but I could tell he was pleased with me. 'Well done, Jo,' he said. 'Now, I've got the players coming over to my house this evening. Could you possibly spare the time to come along? No barbecues to miss tonight, eh?'

I had been going to finish my painting, but I supposed

there'd be time for both. 'I have got something else to do later. Might we be finished by half past nine?'

'Oh yes. My Gideon's playing the cello, and he'll want to be off and out by then too.'

We went down into the church. Gideon and Caleb sat sprawled in the pews. 'You're very good,' Caleb volunteered.

'Don't sound so surprised,' said Gideon. 'I *said* she was good.'

'OK, you two, don't embarrass the poor girl or she'll change her mind about rehearsing tonight,' said Nicholas.

Dad and Ivan appeared from the back of the church. Dad's eyes were glistening slightly. Oh God. He always cries when I perform. What d'you do? Ivan started telling me more about the girls hating me on the way back, but I'd suddenly had enough. 'Ivan, shut up. I don't need this. OK. I screwed up. End of story. Maybe Cat will have forgiven me by next year. Maybe she won't. Quite frankly I don't care if I never speak to your sister again. Maybe I'll just go somewhere else for my holidays. Meanwhile I've got a scary solo to worry about.'

Ivan did shut up. Then he said, 'By the way, you've got a great voice,' and got out.

'Might I ask what's going on?' asked Dad as we walked up the long front path.

'No,' I said. It was half past five. The Barnes rehearsal was at eight and it would take twenty minutes or so to get there. I had to get on with the painting. After tonight there would only be a couple of hours in the morning. Dad had bought one of those clip frames for it already.

The cottage was full of idiotic boys. Tim and the cousins were playing another mad card game with Harry and Archie and Seth. I saw Seth about to slip off, but I was still feeling bullish.

I went up to him. 'Seth – I want to talk to you.' He started to look away and ignore me, but I wasn't having it. 'Now,' I said. 'In my room.' Seth looked hunted but I made him go up the stairs in front of me so he couldn't escape. I sat him on the bed. 'OK. Now I know I wasn't too pleasant the other night, but since then we've made friends *and* I sang with you when you asked me, so what's the matter now? It's bad enough that Tanya and Liza are punishing me, but I'm not having you being so childish.' Seth wouldn't look me in the eye. 'Go on,' I said.

'Liza and Tanya don't like the fact that you went off with Cat's boyfriend, and neither do I.'

'What's it to you?'

'You – let yourself down.'

'I'll say! But that's my problem, not yours.'

He thought for a bit. 'No, OK. You're right. Why should I care what you do?'

'What's the latest on Matt by the way?' I asked.

'Gone home with his parents. Can't say I'm sorry.'

'What do you mean?'

'Well. He was a show-off. Tried to impress people. Didn't respect the sea. The Breakneck Rock stunt was crazy, man. The other three were just lucky.' Seth threw up his hands in disgust.

'I heard that they were in for a bit of parental guidance too.'

'Yeah, well. I'd got bored with them. Acting like they were so grown-up.'

'Unlike you lot downstairs! What were you playing?'

Seth sensed that the mood was lifting and his eyes lit up. 'Ooh! Can I go now, miss? I'm not going to explain the game – it would take too long and I have to go home to eat.'

'You can go,' I said, 'as long as you promise to stop giving me a hard time. Matt's not even here now.'

Seth grinned – properly, at last. 'Matt the prat has shot through.' He mimed standing on a surfboard (not hard for Seth) and intoned 'No fear!' at me. Then he set off out of the door and cracked his head on the lintel. I thought we were probably all right again.

Once he'd gone downstairs I couldn't resist a quick list:

Friends
Seth, Harry, Archie, Gideon?
Enemies
Tanya, Cat (though we haven't seen each other), Liza (though she hasn't actually said anything).
Neutral
Ivan
and Matt, Luke, Paul and Sebastian have all gone anyway.

Things would be looking up if only I could get things straight with Cat. Seth was right in a way – why did I have to go and spoil everything? Had Matt been worth it? Almost certainly not.

I set up my painting things and started to finalise the figures. I wasn't consciously making the boy look like Gideon, honest. Nor had I realised until now just how much the picture resembled a surfing poster. Oh dear. I'd have to live with that. And though I've been here for years and years I've somehow never managed to see dolphins leaping, so I've had to take them from a photo. Right now they looked as if they were made from rubber. I was going off this picture rapidly.

It was quite a relief to stop for supper, though Dad had to drop me off at the Elliotts' again as soon as we'd eaten.

The Elliotts' house is a beautiful old farmhouse with stone flags and nice faded carpets and lots of paintings on the walls. I hadn't quite taken in how lovely it was, first time round. They had a music room, of course, with a harpsichord as well as a grand piano and that's where I was taken. The woodwind players were all adults. Gideon was the only other teenager. He was still shy and inscrutable, but he gave me the old sea-grey gaze as he greeted me. It was strange, being caught in the same small space as one of my 'dolphin boys'.

Nicholas (as I was beginning to think of him) was more relaxed with the smaller group. He called everyone by their Christian names, so I didn't know who they were until I suddenly realised that James, the clarinettist with the Cornish accent, was James Trevarron – my hero! I was so glad I was singing and not playing the clarinet. I've had some singing lessons, but I knew that it was the folky quality of my voice that they were after, so I didn't have to try and do anything different from when I was singing with Seth.

It was all woodwind to start off with. The cellist as the angel came in later. Gideon and I sat and listened while the grown-ups went through the overture. They made a wonderful sound. I couldn't believe I was hearing a private performance by James Trevarron! Then it was Gideon's turn to be the angel arriving like a great rolling, splashing, sparkling wave (Nicholas explained it all before they began). I shut my eyes and listened. Nicholas swished a pair of cymbals along with the cello, and it worked – it did sound like pounding surf. Then the voice of the angel – the solo cello. Then Nicholas played my part on the piano along with the cello, to show how the voices and emotions interwove. I opened my eyes. I'd had a temporary memory lapse about Gideon playing the cello. He was brilliant, even better, maybe, than the amazing violinist on our music course. When he finished, everyone congratulated him, and I picked up from their mutterings about Rostropovich and the Paris Conservatoire that Gideon was something of a prodigy. 'How old are you, Gideon?' asked James Trevarron.

'He's still fifteen,' said Nicholas proudly. 'OK, Jo? Are you ready to begin?'

'I – I haven't got a highly trained voice,' I reminded him, humbled after hearing Gideon. 'You do know that, don't you?' I didn't want all these professional musicians being disappointed.

'You have a beautiful, *un*tutored voice,' said Nicholas. 'As specified by Max Barnes.' He turned to the musicians. 'She's perfect you know. You're in for a treat.' He did the cymbals with the cello for the wave again and Gideon and I were on our own before the woodwind joined in. I was enjoying myself.

'Excellent!' said Nicholas. 'What do you think, James?'

'Wonderful, my dear,' said James Trevarron. (I couldn't believe it!) 'You've got a lovely clear voice, with just the right amount of throatiness – if you don't mind me saying. Max will be so pleased.'

'OK everybody!' called Nicholas. 'Let's run through it again. Eileen will be appearing with coffee and biscuits in fifteen minutes precisely.'

By the end of the rehearsal the 'Annunciation' was up to performance standard. Nicholas said we might run through the piece once tomorrow, but he was more than happy with it. He also didn't want me to be over-rehearsed, or we'd lose the effect he'd been looking for. 'Now, I'm dropping this young reprobate' (Gideon) 'off at the pub – strictly for soft drinks and socialising, I'm told. Is that where you're bound, Jo?'

'Not tonight, no. I've got things to do at home.'

'Oh,' said Gideon. 'I thought you might be going there too.'

'I would,' I said, 'but not tonight, I'm afraid.'

'Of course, I'd forgotten,' said Gideon. 'Those guys – your friends – they've all gone, haven't they?'

'Yes, but that's not why I don't want to go. It's just that – I've got other things to do.' I didn't want to explain about the painting. It sounded so naff. Even though I would really have loved to go down to the pub with Gideon. But the painting had to be finished. So I was taken home and Gideon was driven on to the pub alone.

TEN

On Sunday morning I got up early and finished the picture. I was moderately pleased with it. I'd made the dolphins look less rubbery and the boy/dolphin idea worked quite well. Once Dad put it in the frame it looked more promising. Anyway, it was done.

'You're looking peaky, Josie,' Mum told me at breakfast time.

'I've been busy, Mum. This is worse than term-time – finishing off bits of art and rehearsing till all hours!'

'Then I'm going to take you down to the beach for a blow in the wind. I've hardly seen you this holiday.'

'Do I have to, Mum?'

'Yes. I insist. It's probably going to rain later, so it might be the only time I get down there too. Come along.'

I followed her meekly to the car. As we drove down the hill we had to squeeze past a group of girls – Cat, Tanya and Liza. They were up early. Mum tooted and waved at them in her usual friendly way. They turned away and ignored us.

'What's up with them?' Mum asked. 'They'd usually have jumped at the chance of a lift down to the beach, especially Tanya with that leg.'

'They don't like me any more.'

'What?'

'I did something stupid, and they don't like me any more.'

'Silly girls. What sort of stupid?'

'No, they're not silly, Mum. I deserved it.'

'How could you possibly deserve that sort of rudeness?'

'I'm ashamed to say I, er, got off with Cat's boyfriend when she wasn't there.'

'It takes two to tango,' Mum said drily. 'Do they hate Cat's boyfriend as well?'

'He's not here to hate. He's the one who had the accident. All that crowd of boys has moved on now, and they sort of blame me for that, too, I think.'

We'd arrived at the beach. It was windy and spitting with rain. I wondered if the sun would ever shine in Cornwall again. We walked into the wind, heads bent. 'Have you apologised to Cat?'

'She won't let me.'

'Dear me. It seems to me that you were silly, but they're not behaving much better. Do you want me to talk to their parents about it?'

I was horrified. 'ABSOLUTELY NO WAY!' I yelled. 'Please, no, Mum. I've got to sort this one out myself. Tomorrow. When all the singing's out of the way.'

'Suit yourself. I just don't want them being mean to you and making you unhappy.'

'It was my fault, Mum. And the guy's.'

'Ooh, I'm glad I'm not a teenager any more.'

The sea always has a calming effect on my brain. I listened to the noise of the waves breaking on the beach. 'Hear that noise, Mum?'

'The waves?'

'They manage to make that sound with a cello and cymbals in the Max Barnes piece. It's really effective.'

'I'm longing to hear it. Dad said that all sorts of famous musicians were playing in it.'

'James Trevarron for one! I'm the only non-professional there. Apart from Gideon Elliott. He plays the cello.'

'I can't believe how you can take it all in your stride.'

'It's not a difficult piece. It's like a Christmas carol or a hymn. And they want me for my "untutored" voice.'

'You wouldn't call it untutored if you'd seen your singing teacher's bills!'

'That was ages ago. And she taught me lots, but I'll never be an opera singer.'

'The main thing is that they chose you and like you.'

'Thanks to Gideon Elliott. He heard me singing with Seth at the barbecue and told his dad. Good job I decided to do the choir thing after all this year! It was only because the girls were being so nasty to me!'

Mum looked at her watch. 'We'd better get you back for your rehearsal. Dad wants to leave a bit early so he can take your picture in.'

'And I want a shower before we go.' I linked my arm in

hers and we walked quickly back to the car with the wind behind us.

I spent all day being very aware of Gideon and Caleb but not speaking to them. They were in the row behind me for choir, so they were singing down the back of my neck, and I heard them chatting too. Caleb needles Gideon constantly, but compared to some brothers I know they seem to be good mates. I picked up from someone else that Gideon was two years younger than Caleb, which made Caleb seventeen. They're both fairish with these grey eyes, but Caleb is built more squarely and his hair is crisper and curlier than Gideon's. Gideon is lankier, with longer, straighter hair that flops into his eyes. Shaking his hair off his face is one of Gideon's mannerisms, though when he plays the cello it almost hides his face completely.

They talked a lot about surfing. My ears pricked up when they were discussing some girls they'd met down at the pub, but they didn't mention any names. I was longing to go back down there, but I wasn't quite sure who I'd go with now. Seth maybe. At one point Caleb asked Gideon if he'd seem 'them' yet. That was intriguing, too, but they never said who 'they' were either.

I caught Gideon's eye once or twice during the day. He was looking at me, I know, but we never said anything. We had a run-through of the 'Annunciation' after lunch when the players had arrived for the afternoon rehearsal, and the two of us complimented one another, but I couldn't think what else to say to him. It was frustrating, because I was beginning to feel we might have quite a lot to say if only we knew where to begin.

Everyone in the choir was dressed for the concert in a

holiday version of white tops and black bottoms. I had on a short white top and some baggy black trousers. The younger men and boys were in white T-shirts and black shorts. We were doing scales and warming up exercises in the church hall where the art exhibition was still being mounted. I couldn't see my picture in the children's section anywhere. Then I spotted it on the wall in the main exhibition. I panicked at first because I felt it looked so amateurish in comparison with some of the paintings there, but then I had a moment of pride. It wasn't so bad! The light caught the glitter of the splashes very satisfactorily – it was going to be quite an evening for surf, what with the 'Annunciation' and everything!

We filed into the little church. The rain had stopped and the sky was clearing. It was still light outside, but there were candles waiting to be lit for the second half of the concert once the sun went down. We were starting with the Haydn and finishing with the Handel, with the three songs in between – two at the end of the first half and the 'Annunciation' before the Handel. I was excited rather than nervous – a healthy adrenalin rush pumped through me. The first half was lovely – Nicholas just brought the best out of everybody in the Haydn. Then the first two songs, which were also sea songs, one by Benjamin Britten and one by Vaughan Williams, both sung by professionals. I had a moment of sheer terror when I thought of myself standing up there, but then I remembered that I was merely another 'player' in the Barnes. I wouldn't be so exposed.

I felt a bit jittery in the interval. The crush in the church hall was incredible. Mum and Tim were there to support Dad and me, though neither of them is particularly musical. Tim came back with his hands full of plastic cups of orange squash and wine, and a couple of wrapped KitKats held between his teeth. When he'd unburdened himself he told us that he'd heard loads of people commenting on my picture. 'I reckon quite a lot of people are going to put in bids for it. I saw Cat's parents looking at it and they sounded quite keen to buy it.'

'Cat's not here, is she?' I don't think I could have coped with that.

'No, but Tanya's been dragged along to hear Ivan.'

'Don't you let those horrid girls put you off your singing, dear,' said Mum.

'It's only Tanya,' I said. 'I'm amazed they persuaded her to come to anything as dorky as a concert in a church.' I peered in the direction of my painting. 'And can you all keep quiet about my picture? I don't want people to know I did it just yet, especially as it's not in the children's section.'

'You never know,' said Dad. 'You might make some money!'

Nicholas Elliott was beckoning me. 'Wish me luck,' I said and made my way over to him, along with Gideon and the other musicians.

Gideon was chattering nervously. 'I don't know about you, but I'll be happier when this is over.'

'I'm not too bad,' I said. 'Anyway, you don't strike me as someone who gets nervous.'

'I suppose I'm fine once I get going. It's just this bit I don't like. The waiting.' It was a conversation, of a sort. I liked his resonant voice. I even quite liked the hair-tossing mannerism. It gave the gaze a better chance. We went into the church and set up our chairs and stands. The players tuned up. I didn't need to warm up – I'd been singing all day. We got into our positions. Unlike the other players I was standing, but not out at the front. Gideon and I were at the top of the semicircle facing Nicholas. Nicholas gave us a little pep talk before the audience came back in. 'You two,' he said to me and Gideon, 'is there any chance that you can look at one another in your duet? It is a dialogue. Give it a little try.' My part was simple – I didn't need the music, but Gideon knew his as well. We tried the first few lines. Nicholas was right – it gave the notes a kind of buzz.

'I can do it,' said Gideon, 'if you can.'

'It's not a problem for me,' I said. 'I've got the words fixed in my brain.'

'Think you can both do it?' said Nicholas.

'Yes,' we chorused, and the audience started coming back in and taking their seats. The candles had been lit. 'Typical Dad,' said Gideon to me as we waited to start. 'It's one of his trademarks. Get performers to do something just a little bit different at the last minute. He always says it "makes the music more exciting and immediate".'

'Help.'

'No, it works. Don't worry Jo – I'll look after you!' That's what he said. It was so lovely. He shook back his hair and smiled at me.

Nicholas gave a little spiel before we began about the *Madonna of the Waves* etc, and the fact that the piece had its roots in folk music. And we were off. Something about the candlelit church made the music quite magical. The woodwind sounded watery and the cymbal clash with the cello was perfect. I turned to face Gideon during the Angel words (which meant I didn't have to look at the audience) and then we managed to look at one another as he played and I sang. It was like a dance or a conversation – very intimate, as if we were communicating at an immensely profound level. I could see Gideon, and I was conscious of

Nicholas's baton, but I wasn't aware of anyone else beyond the barrier of candlelight. It was over almost too quickly. Nicholas hushed the audience's applause to make a further announcement. He wanted to thank the performers but he particularly wanted to thank Max Barnes for writing the piece and, wait for it, would Max himself like to come and take a bow . . .

A marvellous white-haired whiskery gentleman came up to the front. I was so glad I hadn't known beforehand that the composer was going to be listening. 'Did you know about this?' I mouthed at Gideon, and he nodded. They must have realised it would freak me out to tell me.

Max Barnes came and gave us each a hug. 'The future of music is obviously in safe hands,' he said. Then he made his way back into the audience and Gideon and I rejoined the choir for the Handel.

It was so strange when the concert was finished. All that work – and it was over. And the 'Annunciation' – my moment of glory – had passed! More to the point, for me, my time with Gideon had ended almost before it had begun. So weird to have experienced something so intense with him. I felt he was mine!

Mum and Dad took me home. Tim informed me that Ivan and Tanya were going down for a last half hour or so at the pub with Caleb and Gideon, but I was suddenly exhausted. I certainly didn't want to cope with Cat and co. 'You were impressive, big sister,' said Tim. 'Pity I couldn't see you.'

'Yes, that was a shame,' said Mum. 'That's the only problem with a concert in a church. It's hard to see over people's heads.'

'So you couldn't see that Gideon and I were meant to look as if we were having a conversation?'

'I could,' Dad said. 'It lifted the whole performance another few notches – if that was possible! The bigwig musos were thrilled. You're a clever little girl, Josie Liddell!'

'With such a modest dad,' said Mum. I let her make me some cocoa when we got in.

'When will I know how much I get for my painting?' I asked Dad.

'Ah, now. I did ask. The bidding goes on until Wednesday, but I was able to discover that you have five bids already, and the highest is £80!'

'Wow! Really?' I couldn't believe it. 'Any chance of a loan of £40 against that? I'm broke. Don't ask me why.'

'I expect so,' said Mum. 'Go on, go to bed, you look finished.'

I had loads of lists to write:

<u>Highs this holiday</u>
1 Doing the Annunciation with Gideon.
2 Getting off with Matt (despite the train tracks).
3 Hearing that I might have made £80 with my crappy old painting!

<u>Lows this holiday</u>
1 Spending all my money on one round of drinks.
2 Tanya and Liza being horrible to me.
3 Cat not speaking to me.
4 Hearing that Matt had had an accident.
5 Falling out with Seth.
6 Having to wear a brace this year of all years.

Hmm. The lows were still winning, but the highs were all good highs.

Things I like(d) about Matt
1 *Good-looking*
2 *Sexy*
3 *Sure I'll think of some more . . .*

Things I like about Gideon
1 *Eyes*
2 *Hair*
3 *Shyness*
4 *Voice*
5 *Body – surfer's body and quite tall.*
6 *Fantastic musician*
7 *Being 'Gideon's Virgin' and him thinking I can sing.*
8 *The way he called me Jo and said he'd look after me.*
9 *Doesn't appear to have a girlfriend.*

Hmm. Gideon's good points far outweighed Matt's. But though I really liked him, and felt that I already had a sort of relationship with him, I couldn't imagine getting off with him. Especially as I had a very clear memory of getting off with Matt. What a mess.

I went to sleep more determined than ever to make my peace with Cat. Apart from anything else, I was going to need some friends to do things with now the singing was over.

ELEVEN

There's nothing quite like the bliss of waking up in a seaside cottage with the sun forcing its way through the gaps in the curtains and the gulls calling outside. I must have slept for hours.

I lay there for a while feeling cosy. Great! No pressure. Painting completed. Performance over. Both satisfactory.

I thought about Matt and me in the dunes for a bit, but the memory had become like a film where the part of Josie was played by someone else. Then I thought about Gideon and me in the 'Annunciation'. That was definitely me. I had been through all those emotions – of fear, of awe and of love – in the space of six minutes. I say 'love'. I hadn't fallen in love with Gideon, or not in the way I was used to. It wasn't like chatting someone up and hoping they'd snog you at the end of the evening. But we'd definitely shared a pretty intense emotional experience.

I felt a new set of lists coming on but, all of a sudden, breakfast seemed a more appealing option. I wrapped my dressing-gown around me, leading-lady style, and swanned down the stairs.

Tim was dressed and ready to go. 'Surf's up!' he said. 'It's going to be a perfect day. Your mates would be kicking themselves if they could see what they're missing. You coming, Josie?'

'You must be kidding. Boogie boarding in gentle waves is all I can cope with. Your sort of surfing's far too scary.'

I helped myself to breakfast. Mum and my aunt were packing a picnic. Dad, my uncle and the kids had gone somewhere. 'Hi, love!' called Mum. 'I've just been telling Pat about your concert last night.'

'You don't half hide your light under a bushel,' said Pat. 'No one in my family can sing to save their lives. I suppose Alan's got a good voice. I used to be impressed when he belted out the hymns at our friends' weddings.'

'Just like Jim, probably,' said Mum. 'And Josie's inherited it. She certainly doesn't get it from me.'

'Did you have to audition?' said Pat. 'I wouldn't fancy an audition.'

'No,' I said. 'I wouldn't have liked that either. I didn't do anything – one of the conductor's sons heard me singing with Seth on the beach.'

'Talk of the devil,' said my mum. 'Seth's on his way down to the beach right now.' I peered round her, out of the kitchen window. Seth was gliding past on his skateboard, surfboard over his shoulder, followed by Cat on her bike, also carrying a surfboard. Damn. I'd been hoping to talk to Cat today. I had this feeling that if I got her on her own, I could make her realise that I was genuinely sorry. We go back such a long way, I really didn't want us to end up hating each other.

Tim was pacing up and down. 'Wish Dad would get back,' he said. 'He promised me a lift. I'm going to miss the good waves if I don't get there soon.'

'Shall I take him?' Pat asked Mum.

'Would you?' said Mum. 'It would take the pressure off the others. I'll let them know that's what's happening.' She started dialling Dad's mobile number.

'What about you, Josie?' asked my aunt.

'No, I'm going to slob around here for a bit longer, thanks.' Pat whisked Tim away.

Mum put the phone down. 'Hey, guess what? Dad called

in at the church hall to see how the bids on your painting were going. He said the £80 bid came from one of the Elliotts!'

'Wow. The Elliotts? Cool! No one's supposed to know that. Whose arm did Dad twist? Can they just stop the bidding and let the Elliotts have it? I'd be ecstatically happy with £72 or whatever.'

'No. They always close it on the Wednesday evening at the do. Don't you remember? Glass of plonk to make people up their bids still further (in case someone else has offered more) and then at a certain time they draw a line under the offers and stick the successful buyers' names on the paintings. I helped one year.'

'Do I get to go to the do?'

'Of course, if you want to. You always went when you were little.'

'But I just whizzed around outside, and you always bought my paintings.'

'Exactly. This will be much more exciting.'

'How long till you go down to the beach?'

'Dad won't be back now for an hour or so.'

'Great. I'm going to have a long bath.'

I was fretting about Cat. It was more than four days since we'd last spoken. We'd had tiffs before, but none had ever lasted this long. Cat's fun, Cat's my mate. She's a bit difficult at times, and she always has to be ahead of the game, but I've always known that. I so don't want us not to be friends. It's always been Josie and Cat, in Cornwall. Tanya and Liza are around, but it's always been me and my family that Cat has spent time with while her parents went in search of culture (as Dad said – so why come to Cornwall and not Venice?).

I couldn't quite believe what had come over me last week. I'd really wanted to impress Matt, that's for sure. I'd had this barmy idea that being in with Matt somehow meant being in with all the others. If only I could have plumped for Luke. And where was the beautiful Bathsheba now? I suppose it's quite likely that there's another whole group of people arrived this weekend. That was a cheering thought. Perhaps there would be new boys for all of us! I washed my hair and shaved my legs extra carefully.

I've got several bikinis. I tried on one I haven't worn so far, a silvery one, and regarded myself in the mirror. I looked OK. On the skinny side, especially my legs, but not embarrassingly so. My hair's a bit wispy, and the brace is horrendous – but from a distance I look fairly normal. My skin's going pink – it will go slightly brown eventually. I peered at my face in the mirror. And I've got some spots. Great. I whacked on some make-up to hide them, and put on a pair of shorts and a top. And then changed them for a sarong and a vest. And then I changed the vest for a chiffon top and tied the ends together to show off my midriff. Then I got involved in drawing a pretend tattoo with a biro just above my right hip bone. Then Mum called me and it was time to go down to the beach.

'You look very swish,' said Uncle Alan.

'He means "nice",' said my dad, laughing. 'And don't make her self-conscious, Alan. It's hell being a teenage girl, isn't it Josie?'

'Huh. Yes,' I said, thinking about the mess I was in with Cat and co.

As soon as we got down to the beach I could see exactly where my family were going to position themselves. Practically next to the rocks where Tanya, her plaster-cast leg sticking out, and Liza were sitting. My one-time friends ignored me, so I ignored them. I laid out my towel, stripped down to my bikini, slapped on some suntan lotion, put on my sunglasses and settled down to read. The one thing I'd forgotten was my CD player. So I couldn't completely block out what Tanya was saying to Liza.

'. . . dragged along to this *awful* concert in a church, just because my dorky brother and all these other tragic people were singing classical music . . .'

Oh well, I suppose I might have complained in the same way myself if I hadn't been part of it.

'. . . a bit *amateur*. I mean, if someone's singing a solo you do expect them to have a really strong voice . . .'

I began to realise Tanya was intent on winding me up. The only thing was to get out of earshot. I tied on my sarong and drifted down to the sea. The breeze whipped the soft material about my legs and swept my hair off my face. I felt a solitary soul as I stepped through the shallows. I walked almost as far as I could and then had to turn round and come back. My little cousins were running towards me to tell me that they were starting the picnic, so I had to return.

'. . . tattoos are incredibly affected, don't you?'

'I wonder when she got that done?' That was Liza speaking – and it wasn't meant for my ears! They really thought I had a tattoo! And I knew they were dead jealous, because we'd been talking about it last week. Cat was thinking up something new to shock her parents with.

I helped myself to some sandwiches and crisps, which were noisy to eat, so I didn't hear what they were saying for a while, whether or not I was intended to. Then I offered to build sandcastles with my cousins further down the beach, which they were thrilled about. 'I can't imagine why anyone would want to plaster themselves with make-up to come to the beach,' was the only other Tanya comment I heard – she must have gauged the exact speed and direction of the wind.

We built a brilliant sandcastle with moats and flags. And then I moulded a car out of the sand for them to sit in. And all the time I managed to stay just far enough away from Tanya and Liza, though it hadn't escaped my notice that Liza wasn't the one dishing out the dirt. It was funny though, because Tanya isn't really that catty. It was almost as if it she was playing a game. But if the desired result was to make me feel unhappy, then they'd definitely succeeded.

'How about a swim, Josie?' Mum had got up and was walking around in a hideous swimsuit. I wanted to protect her from the critical gaze of the two girls, but I felt pretty embarrassed to be seen with her myself.

'OK, Mum, but please put a towel round you!'

As we went down to the water, Mum said, 'I hope it's not Liza and Tanya's opinion that you're worried about. Because I tell you, if they carry on making bitchy comments just within earshot I am going to go over and – and – I don't know, kick sand in their faces or something!'

'I didn't realise you could hear them.'

'Well, I can, and I don't like it.'

'If I could only make it up with Cat, it would be a lot better, but I just can't catch her. She's avoiding me.'

'You could do a note, perhaps?'

'Good idea, Mum. Maybe I'll do that tonight if I don't manage to speak to her.'

Tim needed fetching and it was time to go back up to the cottage. Tim was full of his day's surfing. 'It was wicked today! Caleb and Gideon were with us. And Seth. And Cat. She's pretty good – for a girl!'

'Do you mean to say she spoke to you?'

'Not as such. I was with Seth, anyway. She was more interested in the other two.'

'But did she blank you?'

'Not really. Dad gave Seth and her a lift home, too.'

I couldn't believe it. 'Dad? Did you really give Cat a lift? You know she's not speaking to me?'

'Oh, isn't she?' Dad said vaguely. 'Well, she's speaking to me.'

'That's because you didn't get off with her boyfriend, Dad!' said Tim.

'Enough!' I said, and glared at Tim. I felt wretched. Tanya and Liza were one thing, but Cat being chummy with all my friends and family but not me was another.

'Has Dad told you about this evening?' Tim asked me, changing the subject.

'No. What about this evening?'

Dad filled me in. 'Half-price water-ski lessons. I booked you and Tim in. I know you've always wanted to try it, and two for the price of one seemed like a good deal.'

That cheered me up a bit. 'Excellent. What time are we going?'

'After supper. Half past seven. Is that OK?'

'You bet!' I went up to my room. The thought of Cat being friendly with Gideon and Caleb didn't exactly thrill me either. Or the fact that she could surf with the boys. It meant that she could be with them when I couldn't. Even Seth. And as for new boys – I couldn't go down to the pub on my own, so I wasn't going to meet any, was I? And it all came back to the same thing. I'd got off with Matt, my best friend's boyfriend. What an idiot.

*

Tim and I waited down by the water for our lesson. It was a stunning evening. The wind had dropped and we were quite sheltered. Dad had taken off over the dunes with the labrador. It's weird because I've been past the water-skiing school so many times but never come down below the road here. It's spitting distance from the pub but you can't see one from the other.

Tim went water-skiing first and came back in a high old state of excitement. 'We saw dolphins!' he said. 'Only one or two. Unfortunately we scared them away, but that's the first time I've seen them!'

I asked the instructor to take me out to the same place, which he did, but either I was concentrating so hard on holding on and staying upright, or the dolphins had disappeared, because I never saw them. The water-skiing was great though. Whizzing over the water like a surfer, but without having to do all the work yourself!

Dad and Taffy (the labrador) were sitting on the wall with Tim when I got back. 'Thanks, Dad, that was brilliant.'

'Did you see the dolphins, too?' Tim asked. 'Dad did.'

'No. You'd frightened them all away.'

'Shame,' said Dad. 'They were a splendid sight.'

'Crazy, isn't it?' I said. 'I've sold a painting of them for loads of money, but I've still never actually seen one.'

We were walking towards the car. 'You will,' said Dad, 'when things are going a bit better for you. Your grandfather had some little rhyme about "see dolphins play when the world goes your way". Dolphins are kind of magic. We all know that.'

'Things are certainly going my way,' said Tim to me in the car. 'I met this girl today, called Cleopatra! She's got a sister called Bathsheba. And she thinks I'm great.'

'How do you know?' I asked him.

'Because she said so!'

Of course I'd forgotten that we'd have to inch our way through the crowd outside the pub. Luckily I was in the back seat, so I couldn't really be seen. I could *see*, though. And what I saw was this: three boys and three girls – Seth, Caleb and Gideon with Cat, Tanya and Liza. Cat was doing an impression of someone surfing – she must have been telling them about something that had happened today. And they were obviously all having a brilliant time, Seth included. No wonder I hadn't spotted any dolphins.

Dear Cat,
I know you'll never forgive me for kissing Matt when you weren't there,

(I thought I'd stick to this story until I had to say more)

but I'm really VERY, VERY SORRY, and I didn't set out to do it – it just happened.

(Actually that wasn't strictly true, but I hadn't expected Cat not to turn up. I never dreamt it would actually happen.)

I know you must hate me, but please talk to me and let me apologise properly. I really want us to be friends again.
Love from Josie   XXXXXX

I stuck some shiny stickers on the envelope, went up the lane and posted it through her door.

TWELVE

By midday I'd given up hope of Cat rushing round in response to my note and went shopping in one of the nearby towns with my parents. They advanced me some of my painting money, so I was able to buy a few bits of make-up and some presents for my friends, though I'd have to wait to get Holly's. We bought pasties for lunch and took them home.

After yesterday's winds it was still and grey, and the sea was flat. Tim was mooching round disconsolately. He wanted an excuse to be in the same place as the girl he'd met, Cleo, and surfing was the only one he could think of, but today just wasn't a day for it. I decided to call on Seth, since he'd probably be in the same mood as Tim, and in need of company.

I went up to his cottage after lunch. He was there, taking refuge from his family by reading in his room. His mum pointed me up the stairs. 'Seth?' I called.

'Hi!' He didn't look too fed up that it was me.

'I know it's flat today – thought you might like some company.'

'Where've you been, Josie? I haven't seen you around.'

'You know where I've been. Singing all Sunday. And then yesterday you were off surfing, so you wouldn't have seen me anyway.'

'Thought you might have come down to the pub.'

'No one to go with, have I?'

'Oh, I think the girls have simmered down.'

'Tanya hasn't. She was near us on the beach yesterday,

making bitchy comments just within earshot. Even my mum heard them.'

'Well, you know Tanya. Anyway, she's missing that guy – the first ever guy to kiss her, according to Cat – how's that? So she's kind of taking it out on everyone.'

'She looked OK at the pub last night,' I said.

'How do you know that?' Seth was puzzled.

'We drove past after a water-ski lesson. I saw you all.'

'Oh, poor little Miss Nobody-loves-me! Come on, Josie,' said Seth, rubbing my wrist sympathetically. 'Listen – come down to the pub with me tonight. You can have a ride on my skateboard. I think it's time you all made friends. Especially now those cretinous guys have gone away. You can see how desperate the girls are, they're even talking to me!'

'Thanks, Seth. It's Cat I care about. We've always been friends. Like you and me have always been friends.'

'We-ll,' said Seth. 'You do have to treat friends like friends . . . Anyway. Let's play some music. I gather our little gig on the beach got you some more work. Wish I'd heard it now. Even Caleb said it was good.'

'Tanya thought it was rubbish.'

'Pah! What does Tanya know? Stop talking! Sing!'

Gideon and Caleb were not at the pub. Cat, Tanya and Liza were. 'Come on, girls,' said Seth. 'Make up!'

'I'll buy everyone a drink,' I said, 'because I want to say I'm sorry. I've made some money, so I can afford it.'

'Ooh, what on?' said Cat, intrigued. But none of this lot knew my painting was in an exhibition. I thought I'd better wait until I knew it had been sold.

'Sold her body, probably,' said Tanya, refusing to be mollified.

'Not quite,' I said. 'But I have sold something. I'll tell you on Thursday.'

'Cokes all round, then,' said Seth. 'Give me your money, Josie. I'll get them.'

'Did you get my note?' I asked Cat, anxiously.

'Yup,' said Cat, and then, quickly, 'Liza said you've got a tattoo. When did you do that?'

'Shall I show you my tattoo?' I said.

'Go on, then,' said Cat. Liza turned away from her conversation with Tanya to have a look, as I pulled the waistband of my jeans down over my hip. The biro had faded somewhat.

'Hey! It's a fake!' said Tanya.

'Of course it is,' I said.

'I thought you might have gone to Newquay with your little brother,' said Tanya.

'It's quite realistic,' said Liza. 'Would you do one for me?'

'And me,' said Cat.

'What are you all looking at?' said Seth, coming back with five Cokes.

'Josie's tattoo,' said Liza.

'I didn't know you had a tattoo?' said Seth. 'Let's see.' I rolled down my waistband again. He peered at it. 'It's not real, is it? Good dolphins though.'

'Uhuh,' I said non-committally. I wondered where Gideon and Caleb were, but I didn't want to be the one that asked.

Cat was tapping her fingers and looking bored. She'd spoken to me. That was good, but I can't say I felt forgiven. I sipped my drink. Liza talked about Sebastian. She and Tanya were hatching a plan to visit the boys further down the coast before they left Cornwall altogether. I was itching to know how Matt was, but that was a name I certainly had no intention of introducing.

'How's Matt, Cat?' said Seth.

'How should I know?' said Cat, her eyes raking the pub crowd for someone or other.

'What's on for tomorrow, then?' said Seth.

No one answered.

'Anyone fancy the bike ride?' I ventured.

'OK,' said Cat, surprisingly. 'If there's no surf.'

'I don't know why you're so keen on surfing all of a sudden,' said Tanya crabbily. 'You know I can't do any of these things with my leg.'

'It's those boys, isn't it, Cat?' said Liza. 'I fancy the bike ride, though. Can't not do any of the usual things, Tanya, just because of you.'

'We're doing something anyway,' said Tanya. 'Some garden in a clay pit. Ivan's been going on about it.'

'Ellie's boys went there. It's amazing, apparently.'

'Bike ride, Seth?'

'Not really. I expect I'll go over and see what the waves are like anyway.'

Seth seemed disappointed about something. 'Tim will come with you,' I said.

'I'm going to get another drink,' said Cat. 'But you lot will have to give me the money if you want one.'

'Have your parents still stopped your allowance then, Cat?' asked Liza.

'Yes. Ironic, isn't it?' said Cat as we all counted out coins for her.

'They stopped it after they caught her with Matt,' said Tanya pointedly to me.

'As Cat said,' I replied, 'it's ironic.' We followed her with our eyes. She stopped to chat to a group of lads on the way in to the pub.

'Who are they?' asked Liza.

'Some surfers we met yesterday,' said Seth, waving at them.

'Hope Cat brings them over,' said Liza.

'She's hardly likely to, with *her* here, is she?' said Tanya.

'Excuse me,' said Seth, 'I'm just going to go and have a word with them.'

'Daft hippie,' said Tanya, as soon as he'd left us.

'Seth's OK!' I said.

'Oh! Standing up for our friends are we now?' said Tanya.

'Shut up, Tanya,' said Liza. 'I'm fed up with you going on and on.' Tanya slumped back in a sulk. 'She's missing Paul, aren't you, Tanya? And her cast's getting her down, isn't it, Tanya? I miss Sebastian, but it doesn't mean I'm not interested in new talent. That guy Seth's talking to looks pretty yummy.' Cat arrived. 'Are you keeping those lads to yourself, Cat?' said Liza.

'Oh, I was only asking them something,' said Cat. 'Drink up, everyone. My dad will be here to take me away any minute now. And anyone else who wants a lift.'

When the others went, I joined Seth and the new boys. They were OK in a surfing sort of way. They all talked surfspeak. I'd thought Matt and the others were cool when they talked like that, but I wasn't so impressed this time. Seth and I walked home together, about a mile and a half in the dark (could have been romantic with someone else). It was restful, though, to be with a friend. 'Did you meet those guys with Cat?' I asked him.

'Yeah,' he said. 'And Caleb and Gideon. That's who Cat was asking after. They weren't here tonight.'

'Does she know I know them?'

'I doubt it. Don't muscle in on those two, Josie, please. I wouldn't be able to rescue you a second time.'

'I wouldn't dare,' I said, reeling. (Gideon was *mine*!) 'Thanks for tonight, Seth. It's great that Cat's talking to me again. And the bike ride will be good. Sure you don't want to come?'

'Look at me, Josie. In case you'd forgotten, I'm not built for cycling.' I stopped and looked at him. He stopped too, and then flinched. His brace shone in his querulous half smile, just like mine must have been. 'On the other hand, don't look at me like that. I'm not sure I can cope.' And he loped on ahead, leaving me to scamper along after him.

Mum drove us to the bike hire place. Liza nudged me. 'Hey, it's the guy we all fancied last year!'

'Hello, girls. What can I do for you?' He was gorgeous.

I dug Cat in the ribs while Liza stammered her request for a mountain bike, but she didn't really respond. 'That one please,' Cat said when it was her turn. Not a flicker of a giggle or a blush. It took me several minutes to choose mine. We set off on the trail, a cycle path that follows an old railway track to the fishing port where I'd seen Holly's present.

Cat cycled on ahead. 'I might even dump Sebastian if *that* guy asked me out,' said Liza as we rode side by side behind Cat.

'Cat didn't seem very interested.'

'That's because she's interested in someone else.'

'You mean Matt?'

'No. Well, he's not around, is he?'

'Who then?'

'Dunno. She won't say. Someone she met surfing the

other day I think. I don't think she'd be talking to you now if Matt was the only guy in her life!'

'I suppose not.'

We struggled uphill, and neither of us spoke for a while. Cat was some way in front. 'Liza?'

'What?'

'I know I did a terrible thing, but it was Matt as well, you know.'

'Hardly the point, Josie. Imagine how you'd feel if someone did that to you – especially a friend.'

That was the trouble. I couldn't really imagine it. People at school have treated me badly in all sorts of ways – I'm used to it, but no one's ever nicked a boyfriend. I've never really had a real boyfriend anyway. It's either been admiring from afar or a quick grope at a party. I was upset when the drummer on the music course started going out with someone else, but that just seemed inevitable at the time. No, I couldn't imagine how Cat felt.

Cat had stopped and was sitting on the bank at the side of the track swigging from a bottle of water. 'You guys are so unfit!' she laughed. 'You wouldn't last five minutes surfing!'

'Don't expect I would,' I said meekly, getting off my bike.

'Neither would you if you'd spent the week chaperoning Tanya,' said Liza. She threw her bike down. 'Ooh, my bum is sore already!'

'This bike's more comfortable than my own,' said Cat. 'I don't mind being with Tanya if I'm not surfing, Liza. You can do things with Josie.'

I don't know how Liza felt, but I found that statement quite hurtful. I busied myself with my rucksack and found a drink and packet of biscuits. 'Biscuit, anyone?' Liza took one. Cat declined. Cat usually eats more than anyone.

We set off again. It's a great ride, sore backsides apart,

with loads of people on the trail on tandems, tricycles, little trailers with babies in. It would be impossible to spend the whole time worrying, and as time went by Cat was whooping and cheering with us as we went over bumps and dips, over the old railway bridge, skirted the sea and finally arrived at the fishing port and padlocked our bikes together.

We bought ourselves chips and sat by the harbour watching the world go by.

'Hey-eh!' said Liza. 'Look over there!' It was Luke and Paul. No Matt, obviously, but no Sebastian either. The two of them looked unremarkable on their own amongst the other tourists – just a couple of teenage boys, one of them fairly unprepossessing. I didn't want to talk to them. Memories of their wretched competition and where it had landed me made me want to forget them altogether. But Liza ran over to greet them while Cat and I sat and watched from a distance.

'Don't you want to go and say hello?' I asked her.

'Nah,' she said, and turned to face the sea.

'No, neither do I. I hope Liza doesn't bring them over.'

Liza didn't bring them over. While she was with them Bathsheba came and claimed Luke and a strange girl (who looked like the back of a bus, Liza said) linked arms with Paul, so it was embarrassment all round. Sebastian had already gone home, but Liza knew that – they were still in contact.

'We don't tell Tanya, OK?' said Liza when she came back to report and Cat and I nodded in agreement. 'Gosh! Last week seems so long ago,' she said wistfully. And then realised that last week wasn't a tactful subject for discussion with Cat and me, so she leapt to her feet and dragged us off to the shops. I'd seen some of those beads you thread your hair through for Holly – they had tiny shells on them and I thought they'd look lovely in her dark hair, like a mermaid. I have to admit I bought some for myself too. We bought fudge as well before setting off on the return journey.

There were fewer people on the trail going back. Liza started singing a song that was in the charts and Cat and I joined in. It was almost like old times. Almost.

Dad was picking us up at five so that I could be ready in time for the art do. I didn't particularly want to talk about it to Cat or Liza, but I couldn't stop Dad blathering on as we drove home.

'Oh, that,' said Cat. 'I think my parents are going. They said they'd already put a bid in for something I'd like. I suppose your picture's in the kiddie section, is it, Josie?'

Fortunately, Dad was concentrating on the traffic at that moment, so I just mumbled something in reply. I really wasn't going to say, 'no, it's in the adult section actually' to Cat in her current unpredictable mood.

'How was your cycle ride?' Mum asked when I came in. 'Are the other girls being nicer to you now, darling?'

'It was good,' I said. Sometimes Mum's over-protectiveness really gets to me. Sometimes I think it's why I get picked on in the first place. I went straight up to have a shower and change. I put on some clean jeans and my new top. I looked closely at my face. The spots had gone and my skin had a bit of colour in it. I decided to wear a bit of eyeliner and nothing more. Quite radical for me!

'Hurry up Jo-jo,' Dad was calling. 'The suspense is killing me. I can't wait to find out who's bought your painting and how much they've paid for it!' Tim was out with my uncle and aunt and cousins, so it was just me and my parents heading for the church hall.

The art auction was quite a feature of some people's

holidays. It was advertised in all the local papers and, because one or two well-known Cornish artists submitted paintings anonymously along with complete novices, it was possible to pick up a bargain. The church hall was buzzing. I felt nervous – more nervous in some ways than when I had been about to perform the Barnes. The drinks were on long trestle tables covered in white cloths at one end of the hall. The business part went on at the other end. Each picture had a number sticker. When the bidding was closed, the names of the final buyers were called out. Buyers didn't discover the artist until they paid up.

I stood with Mum while Dad fetched us drinks. I recognised quite a few faces from the concert. I spotted Gideon looking at my painting and my heart missed a beat. The only time I'd seen him since the concert was when we'd driven past the pub and he'd been with my friends. I remembered seeing him and Caleb for the first time – my dolphin boys, gazing out to sea. They'd seemed mysterious then – they still were in some ways. And somewhere along the line I'd had this 'relationship' with Gideon, this exchange. *He was mine.* That was the phrase that always popped into my head. I watched him from a distance. He stood in front of the painting for some time before going back to Caleb and pointing it out to him. Of course – the Elliotts were paying £80 for it! Weird (but wonderful) to think of my dolphins on a wall of their house with all the other paintings. Flattering!

I saw Cat's parents, and Tanya's too. I followed Gideon round the room with my eyes. He looked good today in a faded blue T-eshirt and pale shorts. I noticed his legs for the first time – surfer's legs (now they are nice!) I wanted to go and talk to him, but I felt terribly shy. I didn't know where I'd begin.

But then he must have felt me looking at him, because he suddenly glanced up and caught my eye. He smiled at me with his eyes – I could tell, even across that space, and started to walk towards me. 'Hi Jo,' he said. 'What are you doing here?'

'Oh, just looking,' I said.

'My little brother's got a painting in the children's section. My mum and dad will buy it.'

'That's what my parents used to do with my pictures. I didn't know you had a *little* brother.'

'Oh yes – Ebbie. Ebenezer. Another good old Cornish name, I'm afraid. But since he's going to be a conductor when he grows up he won't mind.'

'Where is he?'

'Over there.' He pointed. And there was a miniature Gideon, floppy hair and all, about six years old. 'Mistake, according to Dad, but we don't tell him that. He's a gas. Ebbie!' he called. 'Ebz – come over here and meet my friend Jo.'

Ebbie came over. 'I know her,' he said. 'She's your Virgin, isn't she? I saw her singing with you.'

Gideon was embarrassed. 'Not funny any more, Ebz,' he said. 'Ignore him, Jo,' he added, and then switched into distant gaze mode. 'Oh, there's my new friend! See you in a bit—' and dashed off. I tried to see who this new friend was, but Ebbie was pulling on my arm to get my attention. 'See that picture over there?' he said. 'My mum and dad are buying it for my brother. At least, they want to.'

'Which picture?' I asked him.

'That one,' he said. Dad had been right. Ebbie was pointing at my picture.

Ebbie drifted off and I went back to my parents. Then I saw who Gideon's new friend was. It was Cat.

Someone banged a gavel. 'Ladies and gentlemen, you have five minutes to make your final bids. There are twelve people here waiting to add them to their lists. Ladies and gentlemen, the bidding will cease in five minutes and we will announce the buyers' names after that.'

I looked over at my painting. Cat was standing in front of it with her parents. Gideon was conferring with them and then Cat and Gideon shot over to his parents, who then rushed over to the desk. 'Well,' said Cat's mum, seeing us as she walked away, 'I just hope no one else is in the running for that picture. I wanted it for Cat but she wants her new boyfriend to have it, so they might just have to up their bid. I've already offered £150.'

Dad winked at me. 'We are talking about the dolphin painting, aren't we?'

'Oh yes,' said Cat's mum.

'Perhaps you ought to warn them then,' said my dad, wickedly, 'that I've just bid £200.'

'Oh gracious!' said Cat's mum, and ran after Cat and Gideon.

'Tee hee,' said dad. 'That's put the cat amongst the pigeons!'

'Dad!'

Cat's new boyfriend? Please, not Gideon. Please don't let Cat want my picture for *my* Gideon.

I went outside. I sat on the raised tombstone and looked at the sea, the dusky grey sea. Gideon. Gideon. My Gideon. My dolphin boy. And I was Gideon's Virgin. Please God, not Cat and Gideon, I couldn't bear it. I felt tears rising. She didn't even know. She didn't even know I knew him, let alone – loved – him.

Was that it? Was I in love with him? Surely it didn't have

anything to do with the fact that he was 'Cat's boyfriend'? I'd loved him all along, hadn't I?

'Couldn't you stand the suspense?' Dad sat down next to me. 'Come on, they've nearly reached yours.' We went back in.

'. . . and picture number 166 goes to Nicholas Elliott for – £250!'

I didn't speak to Gideon after that. I'd receive a cheque in the post and Cat and Gideon would get a shock to discover the artist, but it wouldn't hurt them half as much as the sight of her skipping over to him and throwing her arms round him hurt me.

THIRTEEN

'Pub?' said Seth, poking his head round the front door. I was sitting listlessly turning the pages of a magazine.

'No thanks,' I said. 'But thanks for asking.'

'Oh, go on! Cat's in a very good mood this evening. I hear the bike ride was a success. She went to the art thing, too, didn't she?'

'Yes.'

'She's already down at the pub with Gideon and his brother. They're celebrating, apparently. You never know, someone might buy you a drink!'

'No thanks.'

'For me?' he looked at me pleadingly, not a look I recognised. Anyway, it didn't work.

'No, really. I'm knackered after that bike ride, and stiff! I need a hot bath more than a trip to the pub.'

'OK. Suit yourself.' He looked disappointed again. 'See ya.'

I kept thinking, oh no, not Cat and Gideon, but it was too late. There was nothing I could do about it. And it had been literally at the very moment I realised I'd fallen in love with him that I'd heard he was her boyfriend. The situation was too hideous.

I lay in the bath and thought about Gideon. It was as if he had suddenly shifted into sharp focus. I loved his wet-sand-coloured hair and his grey eyes and his mysterious bearing. I loved his lanky form and his surfer's legs. Each one of the few things he'd said came back like stabs to my heart – 'I *said* she was good', 'Don't worry, Jo, I'll look after you.' Even 'Hi Jo,' and 'Don't mind him,' took on a new significance. But mostly it was our unspoken exchanges – the looks, catching his eye, not to mention the 'Annunciation'. He'd chosen *me*.

I washed my hair and dried it and then tried threading some of the little beads with shells on into it. It was bedlam in the cottage – my little cousins were over-excited and Tim was winding them up still further. I shut myself into my room. I don't normally go to bed at nine, but there was nowhere else I wanted to be.

I thought of sorting myself out with a list, but the facts of this matter didn't fit into lists. Cat had fallen for Gideon, the one guy in the whole of Cornwall that I had feelings for. She had no idea that I knew him personally, let alone that he meant anything to me.

I re-ran the images of her flinging her arms round him. I imagined the way her body and her energy would have felt to him. 'My new friend.' Oh yeah.

I day-dreamed for a bit that it wasn't true. If only he'd

never met Cat. If only I'd taken him up on his offer of going to the pub with him on Saturday night. Maybe we would just have walked over the dunes instead, or along by the sea. Maybe he would have told me again why he chose me to sing with him. Maybe he'd have held me. Maybe we'd have kissed. Oh why'd I spent time on that silly painting! At least it was going to be in his house. I wondered if he knew yet that I was the artist. I didn't know how Dad had entered it. Josie Liddell? Josephine Liddell? J. Liddell?

I imagined them all in the pub right now. (I tried *not* to imagine Cat and Gideon walking along by the sea.) What would they be saying about me? Would Tanya be there, slagging me off? Would Cat be dismissive? Would Seth or Ivan make the connection for her – that I knew Gideon and had sung with him?

And then, the worst images of all. I imagined Cat and Gideon together. I imagined them in the dunes. Like me and Matt. And sleep overtook me cruelly at that point, so that the world of my imagination became the world of my nightmares. Again and again I was forced to watch Cat and Gideon together and it was just like my memories of me and Matt where someone else seemed to be playing the part of Josie.

When I woke up it was morning, but there was no sun shining through my curtains. I looked at my watch. It was five a.m. I tried to get back to sleep, but I was wide awake. The images of Cat and Gideon slipped back into my mind. I knew I had to get up and do something, something that would chase the images away.

I tiptoed downstairs to fetch myself a drink. Taffy the white labrador was delighted to see me. She slid towards me, wagging her tail. She made little excited barking noises and then ran over to where her lead was hanging and jumped up at it. 'No, Taffy, it's too early,' I said. She frowned at me in that doggy way, and whimpered.

I tried to ignore her, and opened the fridge. I sat down with some orange juice, still ignoring her. But then she gave a little yap and I made the mistake of looking at her, and she got all enthusiastic again.

'Wait, Taffy,' I whispered. 'Wait until I put some clothes on. Lie down! Good girl!' and I crept upstairs to dress.

I unplugged the mobile from the charger, put it into my pocket and wrote a note. Then Taffy and I went out into the early morning. The washed sky was still pink from the sunrise, with pearly clouds. I walked down the long road to the sea. It was nice having the dog for company. She was well behaved on the road, not that there was any traffic, because she knew that soon she could hurtle over the dunes and along the beach. She knows me – she'll come back if I call her.

As we plodded along, the thoughts in my brain jogged about, trying to fall into some sort of pattern. I felt remorse about Matt, anxious about Cat, in love with Gideon, sick about Cat and Gideon – but there was no shape to these feelings, just jagged edges.

It took me nearly half an hour to get right down to the sea. I walked along the road past the pub, into the car park and up and over the dunes, where I let Taffy off the lead. It was absolutely gorgeous up there, a beautiful new day – no footprints in the sand below. I dropped down to the beach. Taffy had scrambled down ahead. The tide was a long way out. I kept on walking.

At low tide you can walk right round the headland to the bay. The tide was so far out I knew there was no danger of being cut off, and I could probably have climbed up into the dunes if necessary. I walked on, the prints left by my trainers in the sand looped and cut through again by small doggy ones. Usually the beach in the bay is full of families and small children, digging sandcastles, flying kites. Sometimes there are a few novice windsurfers, who spend more time in the water than skimming over it. On this fresh morning there was no one. I couldn't resist collecting the shells that were washed up on the sand – pearly razor shells, opalescent coils from tiny snails, mussel shells. Taffy ran wild on the empty beach. I would see her miles away and then she'd come racing back and off and away again.

By the time I reached the end of the bay where the car park is I must have walked for over an hour. But it was still early and glorious. There is a cliff path that runs from the car park over the top to the surfing beach. I felt fine with Taffy there, and though it was years since my mum and dad had been able to persuade me to do a cliff walk, I still remembered the exhilaration of the sky above and the sea below with only you and the white gulls and yellow gorse in between. I sat on a bench looking out to sea for a few minutes. Taffy came and panted beside me. 'What d'you think, Taffs? Over the top?' It was seven a.m. I thought the café on the surfing beach would probably be open at seven thirty for a drink, and I had a bit of money in my pocket. Taffy ran round in little circles enthusiastically, so I took that as a 'yes' and we carried on along the cliff path.

Plod, plod, Gideon. Plod, plod, Cat. Plod, plod, Matt. Plod, plod, Cat and Gideon. Plod, plod, so unfair. Plod, plod, I can't bear it. Plod, plod, but Gideon's mine. Plod, plod, I can't bear the thought that the boy I love might be kissing my friend. Plod, plod, I can't bear the thought that my friend might be kissing the boy I love . . . BINGO!

I hurt so much, and yet I had it. This was how Cat must

have felt. Because of me, Cat had felt like this. Only worse. Matt was already her boyfriend. And I'd known it.

The realisation was so terrible that I had to sit down. I cried real tears of shame and remorse. No *wonder* Cat hadn't wanted to speak to me Not if she'd felt like this. In Seth's words, I hadn't treated her as friends should treat one another.

Part of me wanted to run all the way home and throw myself on Cat and beg forgiveness. Maybe she had been going off Matt. Maybe it had all been a competition and maybe Matt was as much to blame as I was. Except that I was Cat's friend and I had betrayed that friendship.

I was a terrible person. There were no two ways about it.

Taffy came over and snuffled at me sympathetically. I hugged her and cried some more, and then I got up and walked on. The breeze off the sea blew my hair and I realised it was still beaded with shells. I must have looked a fright – no make-up, big hooded sweatshirt. The occasional dog-walker greeted me, but there was hardly anyone around.

I resolved to make it up with Cat. I so much didn't want to be that person any more – the girl who stole her best friend's boyfriend. I felt better for my resolve. But then, almost punching the wind out of me with the enormity of it – the thought of Cat and Gideon! Maybe I could just get on a train and go home. Forget Cornwall.

Cat and Gideon. The thought niggled me. How could I be sure that I was in love with Gideon for himself, and that it had nothing to do with him being Cat's boyfriend and therefore unavailable? It was no good. I needed to write a list. I felt in my pockets for a pencil or a biro and a receipt or something to write on. Nothing. There was no way down to the beach here. I was high up on the cliff path. I'd just have to speak it.

I half sung, half spoke my lists as I walked:

Reasons why I thought I was in love with Matt:
1) He was good looking.
2) He was popular.
3) He was quite nice to me.
4) Because, because, he made a move on me.

Oh, face it, Josie – you weren't in love with him at all. You just wanted to be accepted by the in-crowd. OK, OK, enough of this self-loathing.

Reasons why I think I'm in love with Gideon:
1) I can't bear the thought of losing him to anyone, not just Cat.
2) He's so often been there and I've always noticed him and thought he was special.
3) Because he's good looking – well, I like his looks.
4) Because I feel he knows who I am.

I stopped short. That was it! I felt that Gideon knew the real Josie, the real me.

And I was, I was in love with him. And he was going out with Cat.

I'd reached the top of the cliff. The early morning haze was lifting. The sea below was turquoise and the air smelt sweet and coconutty with gorse. I stood on the headland and stared out to sea, tears of remorse still trickling down my cheeks.

'Jo!'

I whipped round. It was Gideon.

'Jo? Are you OK?'

I didn't know what to say to that. But what was he doing here, right here, so early in the morning? 'What are you doing here?'

'I only live just over there.' He pointed inland, and I realised that, of course, that's where the Elliotts' house was. 'And I was on the look-out for dolphins. We're doing a sort of unscientific survey for my grandfather – you know – when, where, how many . . .'

'Have you seen any today?'

'No – I think evenings are better.' He looked at my tear-stained face. 'Hey, Jo, are you sure you're OK?'

I grunted something non-committal.

'Anyway, what are *you* doing out here at this time of the morning?'

Taffy came panting up to us. 'Walking the dog.'

'And that makes you unhappy?'

'No. I'm unhappy about something else.'

'OK,' he said cheerfully. 'None of my business. I won't ask.'

'Thanks.' I couldn't believe Gideon was here, beside me. My knees felt weak, my heart was thumping and my stomach was full of butterflies.

'Are you going to carry on walking round the cliff, or are you going back?' Gideon asked. A perfectly reasonable question.

'I – I don't know.'

He pushed back his hair and looked me in the eye. 'Well, I'm going back to my house for breakfast, and if you want to come with me I'm sure someone will give you a lift home.'

I thought about it. I'd been going to phone Dad at some point and ask for a lift. No one from my family had called the mobile, though actually the signal wasn't that good on the cliff. All I wanted to say to Gideon was, 'Forget Cat, go out with me.' The words were going round in my head so fiercely I was afraid I'd say them out loud by mistake. 'All right,' was what came out.

'You can have breakfast with us if you like.'

Taffy and I followed him home. When we arrived, Eileen put out a bowl of water for Taffy and she gulped it down. 'Hello, Jo,' she said. 'We're just about to hang the painting. Tell your father we're delighted, especially Caleb, of course.'

I sat down at the kitchen table. Ebbie was roaring round. 'Hello Virgin!' he said.

'Still not funny, Ebz,' said Gideon.

'That's enough, Ebbie,' said Eileen. 'You can watch the grand picture-hanging if you like, Jo, and then report back home. It's going on Caleb's landing, naturally.'

I looked at Gideon, confused.

'Caleb's the big surfer round here. I do it too, but he's almost a professional. And he fell in love with your dad's painting. And then Cat's parents were going to buy it, but Cat persuaded them that Caleb should have it – and saved them some money.'

'Worth it though,' said Eileen. 'I imagine your father's paintings normally fetch thousands, don't they?'

I drank the coffee and ate the croissant put in front of me without remembering that I don't much like coffee, apart from the smell, and I usually have butter and jam with croissants. Caleb appeared, looking chirpy.

'Spare us!' said Gideon, before Caleb could say anything.

'I was just going to comment on the fact that we have the daughter of the guy who painted my fabuloso surfing paint-ing, and—'

'I'm just going to phone home,' I said. 'I left a note, but they might be wondering where I've got to.'

'Fine, phone's in the hall,' said Gideon.

'No, it's OK, I'll just take the mobile outside.' I stood outside the kitchen door. 'Dad? Hi, it's me. I bumped into Gideon Elliott and they've given me breakfast. Any chance of a lift?' Dad said he'd be over in twenty minutes.

Gideon had been listening. 'I said we'd give you a lift. I thought you might stay a bit.'

I looked at him. 'Gideon? There's a lot of confusion going around. Do you think we could talk?'

'Sure,' he said. 'What sort of confusion?'

We sat down on the bench outside the kitchen. 'OK, one: you, Cat and the painting. Who was it for, precisely?'

'Caleb.'

'Cat wanted it for Caleb?'

'Well, I think it's cool, too, but it's Caleb's sort of thing, pictures of surfers.'

'Two: have you looked closely at the painting, and seen what it's actually of?'

'It's not up yet.'

'It's a picture of dolphins. There's only one human in it.'

'Ha! Don't tell Caleb, then.'

'Three: what makes you think the painting is by my dad?'

'Mum said it was by J. Liddell, tenor in the choir. She even checked the concert programme.'

'Have you still got the programme?'

'Yeah. I think I've even got one scrumpled up in the pocket of this jacket.' He pulled it out. 'Here!'

'Just point out J. Liddell to me, would you?'

'What's all this about, Jo?'

I didn't quite know why I was spinning all this out, either, but it seemed important to get everything, all the mix-ups, absolutely straight, because I was beginning to think that the biggest mix-up of all was going to change everything. I pointed to my name under *Alto* in the Barnes 'Annunciation': Josephine Liddell.

Gideon looked at it and then looked at me. 'You mean—'

'It's my painting. And it's dolphins, with one boy. Have a look at him when it's up. And don't tell the others yet, they might think they've been fleeced if it's a kid's painting.'

'*Your* painting?' His eyes were gratifyingly wide.

'Four: what's going on between—' I hardly dared ask the question in case the answer wasn't what I wanted to hear – 'Caleb and Cat?'

'Well – they – seemed to click. And they've only got four days left so they're making the most of it. Any more confusions?'

The smile I turned on him almost cracked my face. I couldn't manage the tight-lipped, hide-the-brace one. 'No,' I said. 'None whatsoever. Thank you.' I heard my dad's car arriving. I didn't want the Elliotts to buttonhole him about the painting, so I put Taffy on her lead and asked Gideon to say thanks to his mum for breakfast.

'Hey!' he shouted after me. 'Round about eight this evening there might be dolphins!'

Dad drove off. 'Perhaps you'd like to tell me what all this is about?' he said.

'Guess what, Dad?'

'Can't.'

'The Elliotts think my painting was done by you. Mrs Elliott thinks she's got a bargain and that your paintings must normally fetch thousands!'

'Great!' Dad laughed. 'Well, they won't be able to hound me today because we're having a family outing to Heligan. A treat for Mum. Bring your sketchbook!'

'But that's a garden. Dad. How did you manage to persuade Tim to come?'

'Partly by reminding him that another family is doing the same outing today – a family of girls with long names.'

'Oh, Cleopatra and Bathsheba?'

'And Tallulah, apparently.'

'Nearly as bad as the Elliotts. Perhaps Tallulah and Ebenezer will get together some day.' I felt ridiculously happy. 'Tim must be smitten if he'll go to a garden for Cleo.'

'It's quite a place. You and Tim will both be pleasantly surprised I think.'

'When will we be back?'

'Oh, don't worry. Long before eight p.m.' He winked at me.

'There's something important I have to do before that, Dad. I'll come if we can be home by six.'

'Done.'

FOURTEEN

True to his word, Dad got us back at five to six. I'd spent most of my time at Heligan sitting in the jungle bit working up a tendrilly design of flowers. As soon as we got in I dug out one of the little frames Dad had bought along with the big one for my painting and put the picture into it. I took it up the hill with me to Cat's. Her mum told me I'd find her in her bedroom.

'Cat?'

'Hi, Josie.' She was gazing dreamily out of the window.

'I've come to say sorry, properly.'

'Oh?'

'It's taken me this long to realise how I must have made you feel.'

'Completely ghastly, humiliated, suicidal, you mean?'

'All those. I can't believe I – I mean, being friends with you is more important than – and I – Matt was your boyfriend, you know? – and I—'

'Yeah, well. I was pretty hacked off with you. Just the thought of my friend and my boyfriend—'

'I know, I know. I'm sorry. Look, this is a sort of peace offering.' I handed her the picture.

'Ooh, cool. It looks like a tattoo!'

I hadn't thought of that. 'I'll draw one on you if you like. Got a biro?'

'Brilliant. I want it just above my left boob, so Caleb gets a tantalising glimpse of it . . .'

'So it's cool with Caleb?'

'Totally. And don't you dare . . .'

'Never again, Cat.'

The tattoo looked great. 'Are you seeing Caleb tonight?'

'Of course. He's meeting me down the pub at seven thirty, though I dare say we won't stay there all evening.'

'And your parents don't mind?'

'They're terribly impressed by the Elliotts – famous conductor, all that art. By the way, did you see Caleb's painting? My mum and dad nearly bought it for me, but it was perfect for him. I don't usually like that sort of thing, but I did like that one.'

'Yes,' I said. 'I saw it.'

'I really wanted him to have it.' She gave me one of her sly Cat looks. 'Hey, Josie. I like him much better than Matt. There were times when Matt didn't seem really interested in me as a person, just what he could make me do with him. That's what we quarrelled about. It was almost as if he was trying to score points. I suggested that and he got really angry.'

'Perish the thought.'

'D'you want to come down to the pub with us?' Cat asked. 'I can't wait to see Caleb's face when he sees this. I bet he thinks it's real.'

'I might come along later, but there's something I want to see at eight.'

'I wouldn't know what's on TV – we haven't got one here.'

I didn't fill her in. 'Maybe see you later, then. If not – beach tomorrow?'

'Whatever. I'll call for you.'

'So I suppose you'll be wanting a lift to the Elliotts'?'

'How did you know? Actually, the bit of the cliff path nearest their house.'

'And how are you going to get home?'

'I'll take the mobile, if that's OK.'

'Come on, then.'

Dad dropped me off. It was perfectly light and there were people around, though he took some persuading that I'd be all right even if I didn't meet up with Gideon.

I climbed up the steps that led to this bit of cliff path. It was a gorgeous evening – the colours were fabulous. I ran up, anxious at the point before the steps turned the corner that I'd got it all wrong and Gideon wouldn't be there.

I reached the top. There was the headland. And there was Gideon staring out to sea. I went up to him. 'Hi!' I said quietly.

He turned to me and took my hand as if he'd known I would come to him. We listened to the surf crashing below. 'I think I'm slightly afraid of you, Jo,' he said, not looking at me.

'Me? Why?'

'Because you're so – so. Well, that painting! It's brilliant. And I did look at the boy. And I—'

'Coming from someone who's already a prodigy—'

'Jo – I've never been crazy about anyone before. I'm crazy about you, and I've never felt like this. It's new. It's kind of awesome, scary.'

I suffered a moment of horror, thinking the scary part might be snogging a girl with a brace, but Gideon didn't flinch. 'Not with me it won't be,' I tried to soothe him. We were gazing into each other's eyes. We'd been here before.

Gideon took both my hands in his. 'The boy was me, wasn't it?'

'Of course.'

And then we kissed. We'd reached the love part.

I had my arm round Gideon's waist. He was stroking my hair. We were both watching the sea. Suddenly – 'Yay!' he yelled. And there they were, three of them, leaping.

I have never seen anything like it. The sight of dolphins playing simply fills your heart with joy, there is no other way to describe it.

'They're doing it for us,' said Gideon, rubbing my cheek with his. I felt his silky hair on my face, and neither of us knew whether to kiss again or watch the dolphins – a dilemma which could be a definition of happiness! We sort of managed to do both until we realised we were surrounded by quite a crowd of people all pointing at the dolphins.

'Shall we walk over the cliffs to the pub?' Gideon asked. 'Caleb will be there. With Cat,' he said, squeezing my shoulder.

'It depends on the tide at the bay doesn't it?'

'We can go over the top there, too.'

We set off, holding hands. I wanted to know when he'd first noticed me and he wanted to hear all about me worrying that he was the one Cat fancied. I told him how cool he'd seemed and he said he thought I was much more interesting than the rest of that crowd – 'though I like Seth,' he said.

'Seth's my mate,' I said.

'And mine,' said Gideon. 'He'll kill me.'

'Why?'

'Because – he's – kind of proprietary about you. But you must know that?'

'I don't want to think about it.' I didn't.

Gideon's fingers caught in my dolphin bracelet. He lifted my wrist. 'Hey, it's the same as mine!'

'I know. I saw yours when I first noticed you and Caleb outside the pub. I suppose you were looking for dolphins?' Gideon nodded. 'And when I found the last bracelet in the shop I had to have it. You see, I thought you were kind of magic from the first time I saw you.' He looked at me with the sea-grey gaze. 'And you always will be.'

The tide was out round the headland of the bay, and still going out, so we splashed our way across. It was almost dark and a moon was rising, but we made out two more people splashing and giggling further round.

'Oh great,' said Gideon. 'My brother. So they're not at the pub.'

Cat and Caleb were larking about. We'd both had the same idea, except we were going in opposite directions. I pulled Gideon back behind a rock. 'Actually, I'd rather just be with you tonight. We can all four be together tomorrow.'

'Actually,' he said, 'so would I.' We let them go past the way we'd arrived.

'Cat's a laugh,' said Gideon, 'but she's not my type.'

'That's lucky.'

At some point my phone rang – Dad checking up on me. In fact we were both cold and it was late, so I let Dad pick us up and run Gideon home. We arrived at the same time as Cat and Caleb, so we gave her a lift back too. It all felt so civilised and easy compared with last week. I got in the back with Cat. 'Sorry, chauffeur,' I said to Dad. 'Cat and I have a lot of catching up to do.'

The next day, Friday, was our last full day, Cat's too. We spent it on the surfing beach. Everyone was there, all the parents, Seth, Archie and Harry, Tim, everyone. Cat surfed with the boys. I stayed back with the girls. My relationship with Gideon was too new to be public and so was Cat's with Caleb, so Seth was spared and so was poor old Harry, though Liza and Tanya were taking quite an interest all of a sudden in this good-looking guy, earring and all. Ivan was as creepy as ever, but even he felt like someone we'd miss tomorrow.

Talking of which . . . The thought of leaving Gideon was ghastly. I spent quite a lot of our last evening together feeling weepy. He was pretty wobbly, too. We were on the bench on the cliff path. 'I'll nip up and look at your painting every day,' he said. 'And there's a recording of the Barnes. I'll listen to that. There'll be a copy for you, by the way.'

'Thanks,' I sniffed. 'Gideon?'

'Yes?'

'There's something I'll never understand.'

'What's that?'

'You don't seem to mind my brace.'

'Why should I? It's just another part of my beautiful Jo. If you haven't got it next year I'll quite miss it.'

'Do you think we'll survive until next year?'

'I'll be very upset if we don't.' And then we started kissing again. And we didn't stop until my phone rang and Dad said he was waiting in the car park for me with Cat.

Gideon gulped. 'So it's goodbye, then,' and we clutched at each other desperately, all tears and hair and final kisses, until I had to pull away and run to the car.

We were leaving pretty early. Cat's parents were packing up at the same time as mine, so Cat and I spent the last hour or so chatting together. We really were friends again. 'I still want to know,' she said, 'what made you finally realise how I'd felt when I heard about you and Matt. Go on, tell me – you owe me.'

'I wasn't going to, but I suppose it's only fair. You see, I started to get a thing about Gideon after the concert. I didn't know quite what I felt about him. Then I suddenly realised that I really, really wanted him, far more than I'd wanted Matt. And then almost straight away I found out that you were interested in one of the Elliott boys, and I assumed it was Gideon. I couldn't stop imagining the two of you together. I went to hell and back. And then I realised that you must have felt like that about me and Matt – only worse. So I – well, I reckon this holiday's taught me a lot.'

Cat cuffed me affectionately. 'Idiot!' was all she said.

'Do you think we'll still be going out with the Elliotts next year?' I asked, to dispel the slight awkwardness.

'Dunno,' said Cat. 'It partly depends who else I meet.' I couldn't agree. Gideon was there in my subconscious – he was there at every level. He'd be there, somewhere, all my life. 'Maybe, one year,' Cat said, 'Seth will get a chance.'

'Oh thanks Cat. And you'll give Harry a chance too?'

'Well, who knows?' she said. 'That's the great thing – there'll always be next year.'

'Are you *ever* going to stop gassing and help pack, Josie?' Mum called, exasperated.

'OK, Mum. So where's Tim?'

'We're picking him up from Cleo's. Last-minute farewell.'

Seth, Harry, Archie, Liza, Tanya – and even Ivan – managed to get out of bed and wave to Cat's family and mine as we drove off. I was kind of glad Gideon and I had said our goodbyes last night – it meant I could savour them in private.

On the way home I wrote a final Cornwall list. Just the good things:

Good things about Cornwall
The sea
The cliffs
The cottage
The music
My friends: Seth, Harry, Archie, Liza, Tanya, Ivan (just).
My best friend: Cat.
My boyfriend: Gideon.
Coming here every year.

And that just about said it all, really.

EPILOGUE

The journey home took for ever. Tim and Cleo had disappeared, so we had to wait, making polite conversation with Bathsheba and Tallulah and their parents until they returned. Then it took ages to get lunch at the motorway service station. And then, most frustrating of all, we had to stop off at Granny's and eat tea and tell her everything. We didn't walk in the front door until after eleven p.m. and we were all tired and crotchety.

'Bags the phone first!' I yelled, not that anyone else was going to use it at that time of night. I rang Holly and prayed that she hadn't gone to bed. She hadn't. 'Hey Holly, you'll never guess what—'

But she stopped me and said I should save it for tomorrow night. Quite a good thing, perhaps. It gave me more time to think about all the things that had happened. I thought I'd tell them about Matt as well as Gideon, almost to punish myself I suppose. Though when I think about the competition the boys themselves were having, I don't feel quite so bad. Nor, with a bit of distance between us, would I put Cat past doing the same thing to me in those circumstances.

Holly and I arrived at Zoe's house together, just after Alex. It was great being back with the other three. Zoe practically has her own flat in the basement and there's always masses of food – it's a bit like going to a self-service restaurant. We loaded up with food and then – da-dum! It was time for us all to report back. I wouldn't have minded kicking off, but Alex was absolutely bursting to tell us, so Zoe made us go in alphabetical order.

So, Alex. Alex the tomboy. Alex the tomboy no longer, it seemed! She even looked different. I have to admit I never thought Alex would have a romance to report on, but she certainly did. And she seemed to have grown up a lot in the process. I started to worry about how my story was going to sound.

595

Then Holly told us what had happened to her. I was quite shocked when I heard that she'd done the best-friend's boyfriend thing too, only the other way round! The stately home sounded brilliant though, and it's typical of Holly that if she goes off one guy, it's never long before she finds another one who fancies her.

Suddenly it was my turn. I'd already decided I would tell them about Matt, though the more I tried to explain the complicated situation, the worse it sounded! I even wondered if it was because we'd all promised to have romances that I'd behaved so badly, but I don't think anyone agreed with me! And then when it came to the music and Gideon – I couldn't quite find the words. It was all too recent. Still, I'm sure we'll all talk more later on, especially Holly and me.

And then it was Zoe's turn. Sometimes Zoe just seems so grown-up. The way she described what had happened to her, and the voyage of self-discovery she had been on, made my silly little episode with Matt seem so trivial! Like the others I listened to her wide-eyed. But then I thought about Gideon and me and remembered that our feelings for each other were incredibly profound. We had managed to express ourselves at a deeper level than words. And how many people could say that?

It was time to write some more lists, private ones.